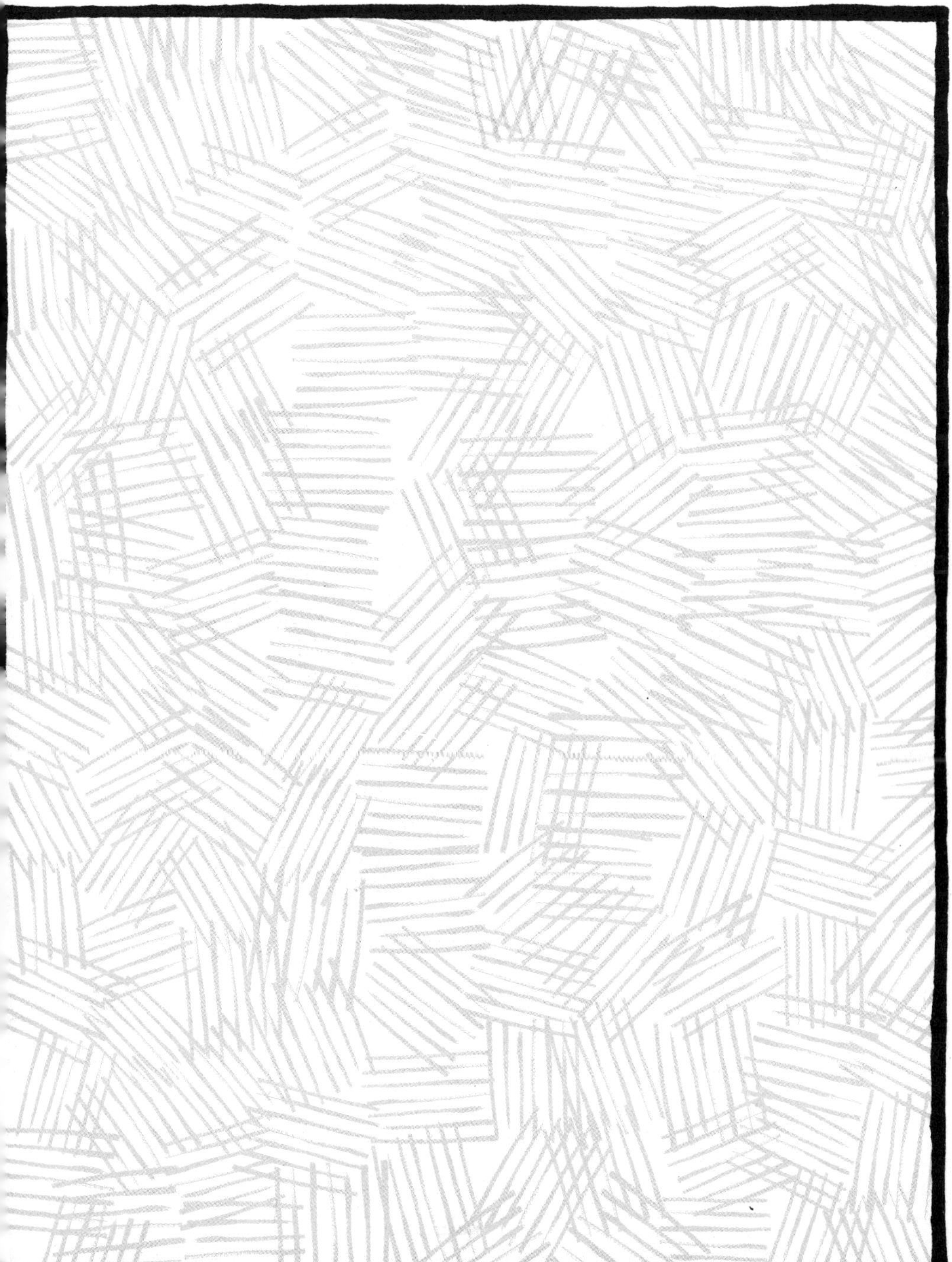

Published by Don Giovanni Records, Philadelphia, PA

First Edition 2024, Printed in the USA

Book Layout & Design by Patricia Ramos

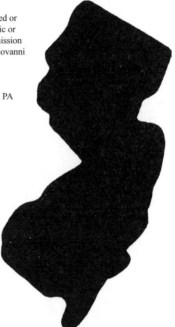

MERRIMENT

BY JOE STEINHARDT
AND MARISSA PATERNOSTER

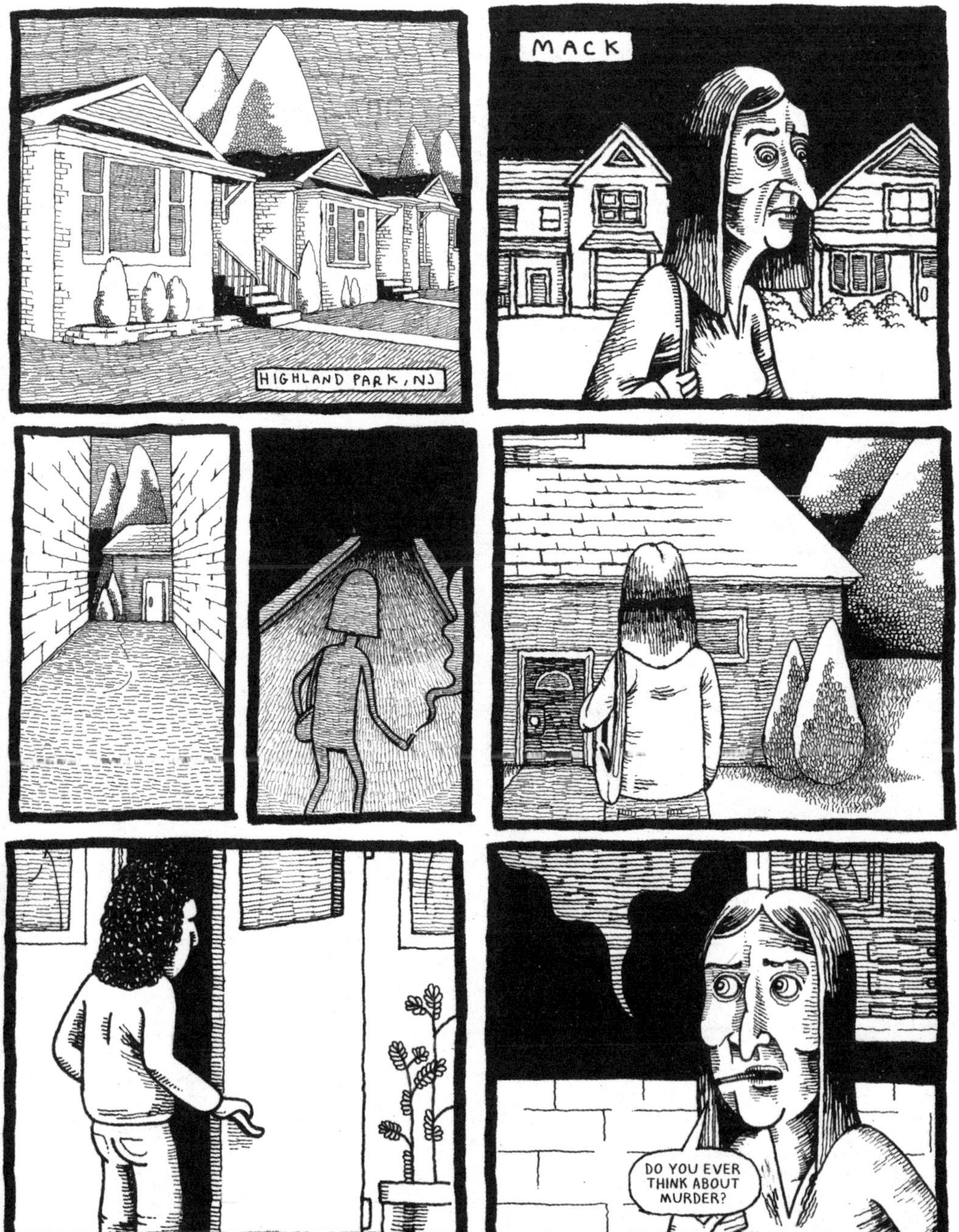
HIGHLAND PARK, NJ
MACK
DO YOU EVER THINK ABOUT MURDER?

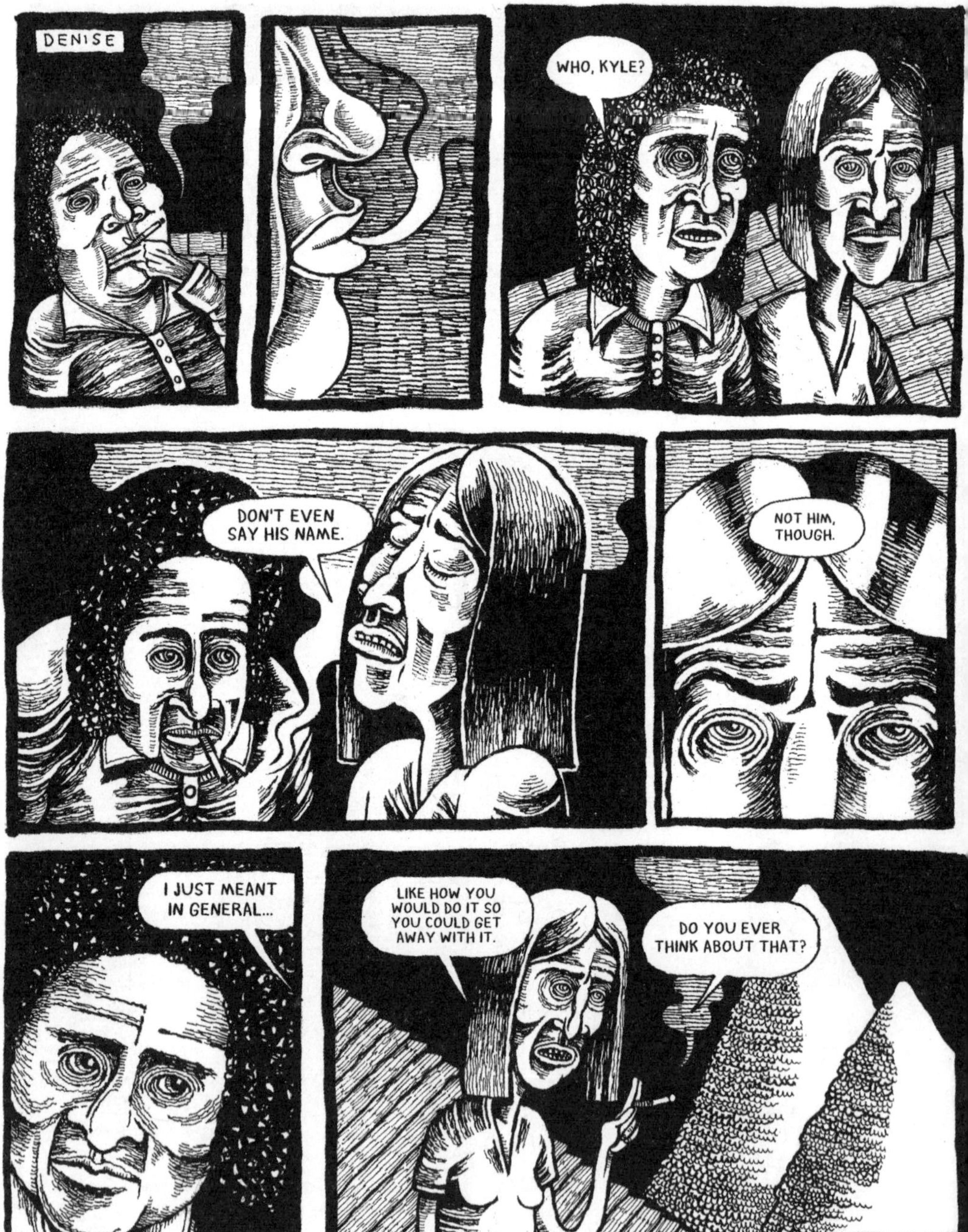
DENISE
WHO, KYLE?
DON'T EVEN SAY HIS NAME.
NOT HIM, THOUGH.
I JUST MEANT IN GENERAL...
LIKE HOW YOU WOULD DO IT SO YOU COULD GET AWAY WITH IT.
DO YOU EVER THINK ABOUT THAT?

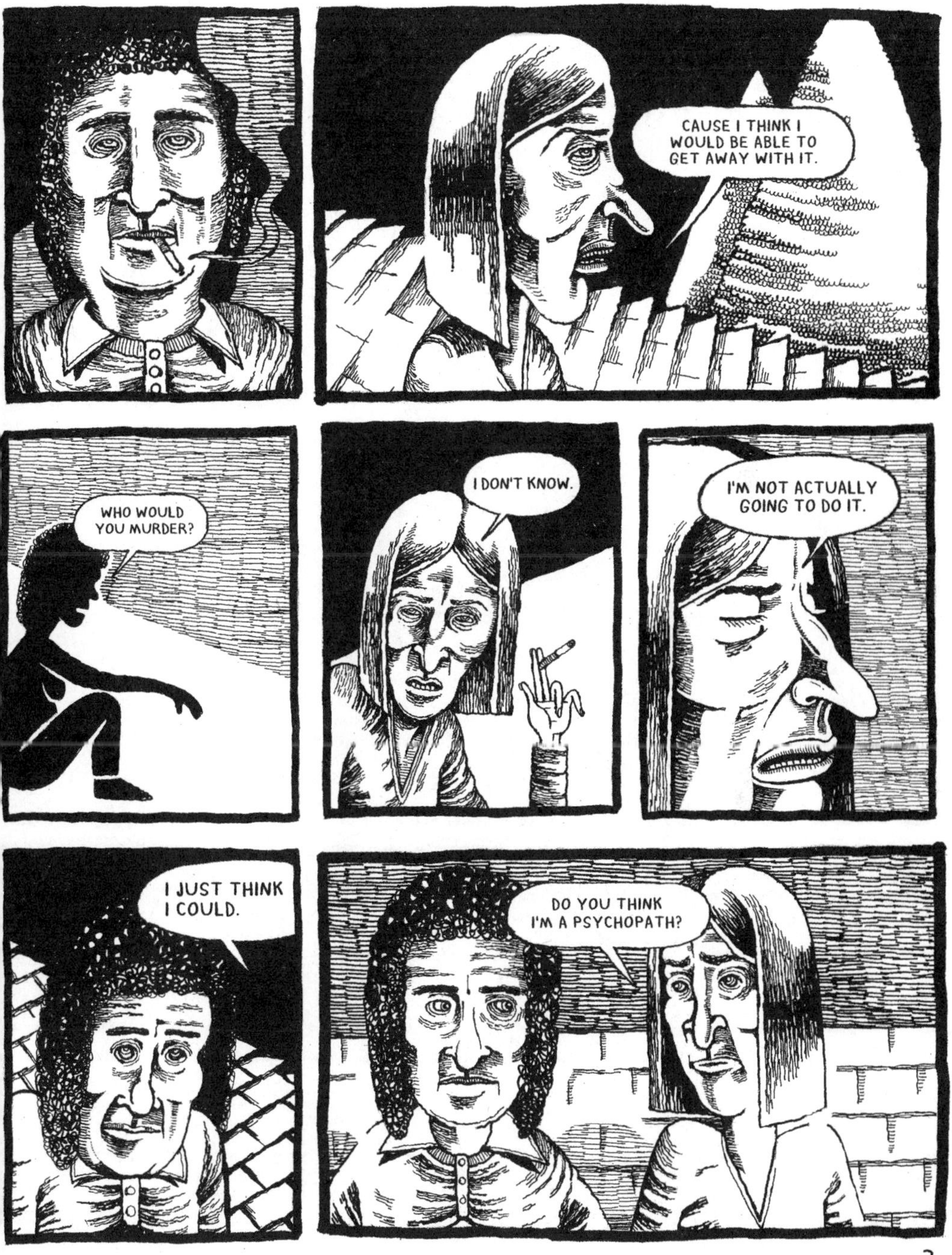
CAUSE I THINK I WOULD BE ABLE TO GET AWAY WITH IT.
WHO WOULD YOU MURDER?
I DON'T KNOW.
I'M NOT ACTUALLY GOING TO DO IT.
I JUST THINK I COULD.
DO YOU THINK I'M A PSYCHOPATH?

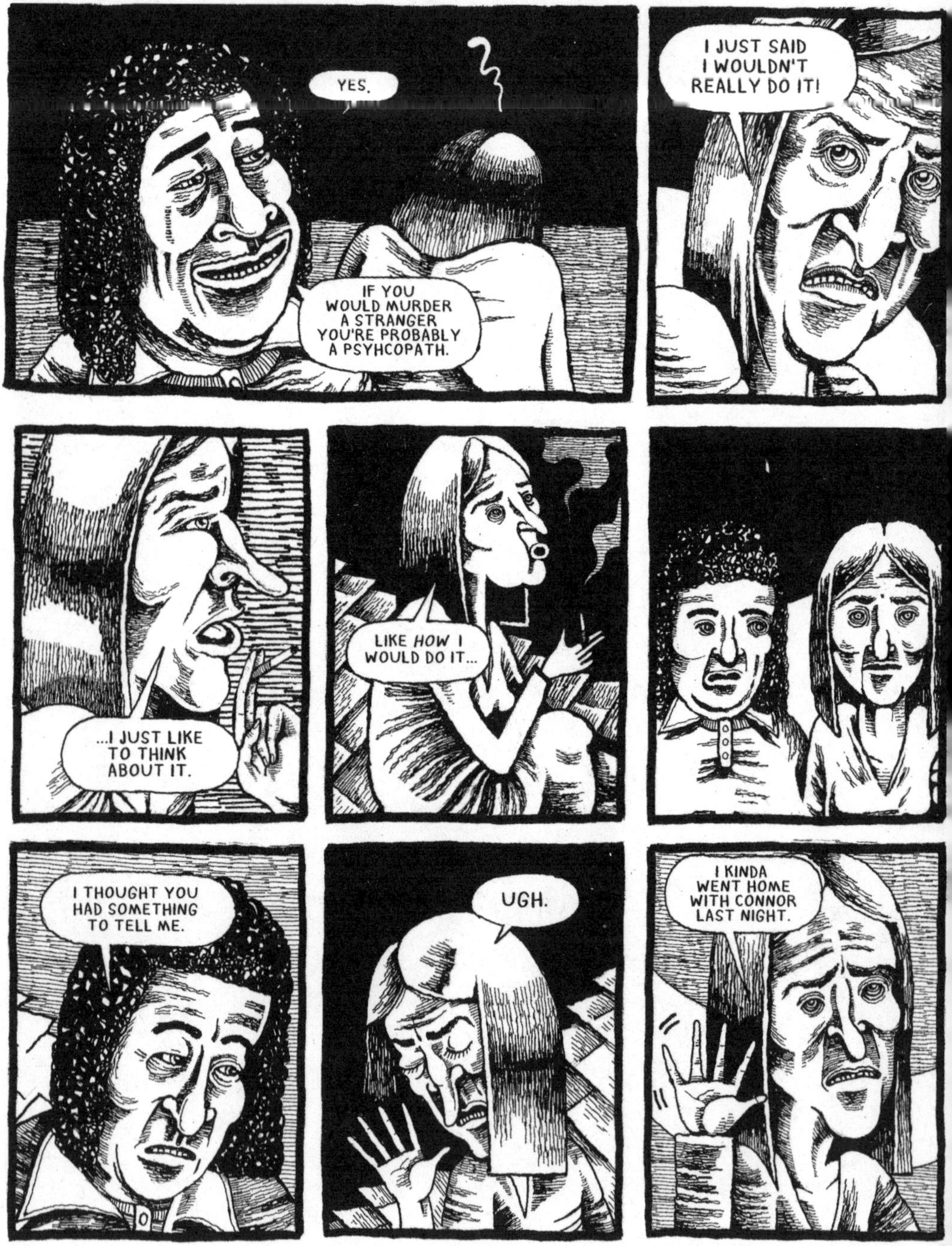
YES.
IF YOU WOULD MURDER A STRANGER YOU'RE PROBABLY A PSYHCOPATH.
I JUST SAID I WOULDN'T REALLY DO IT!
...I JUST LIKE TO THINK ABOUT IT.
LIKE HOW I WOULD DO IT...
I THOUGHT YOU HAD SOMETHING TO TELL ME.
UGH.
I KINDA WENT HOME WITH CONNOR LAST NIGHT.

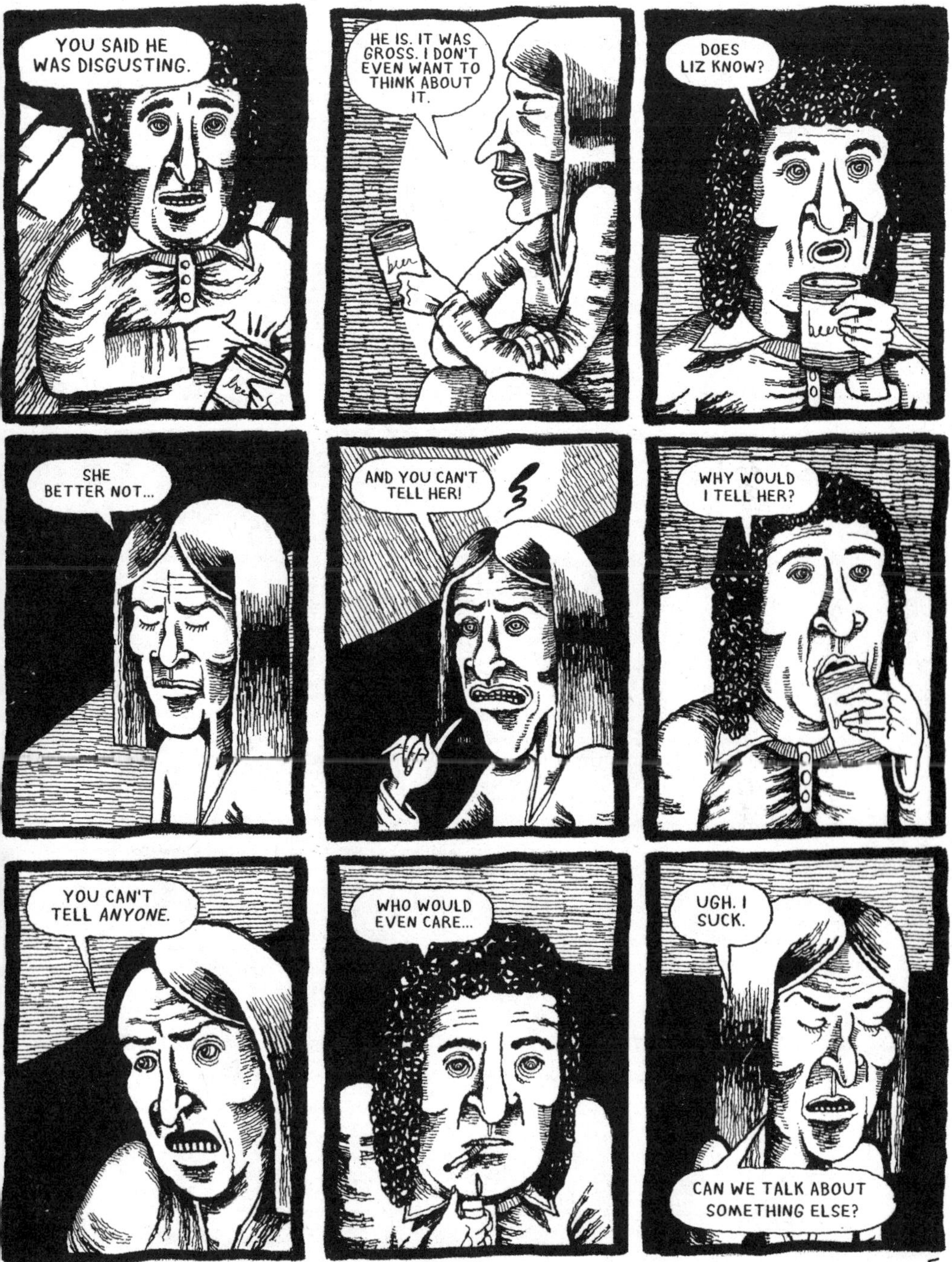
YOU SAID HE WAS DISGUSTING.
HE IS. IT WAS GROSS. I DON'T EVEN WANT TO THINK ABOUT IT.
beer
DOES LIZ KNOW?
SHE BETTER NOT...
AND YOU CAN'T TELL HER!
WHY WOULD I TELL HER?
YOU CAN'T TELL *ANYONE*.
WHO WOULD EVEN CARE...
UGH. I SUCK.
CAN WE TALK ABOUT SOMETHING ELSE?

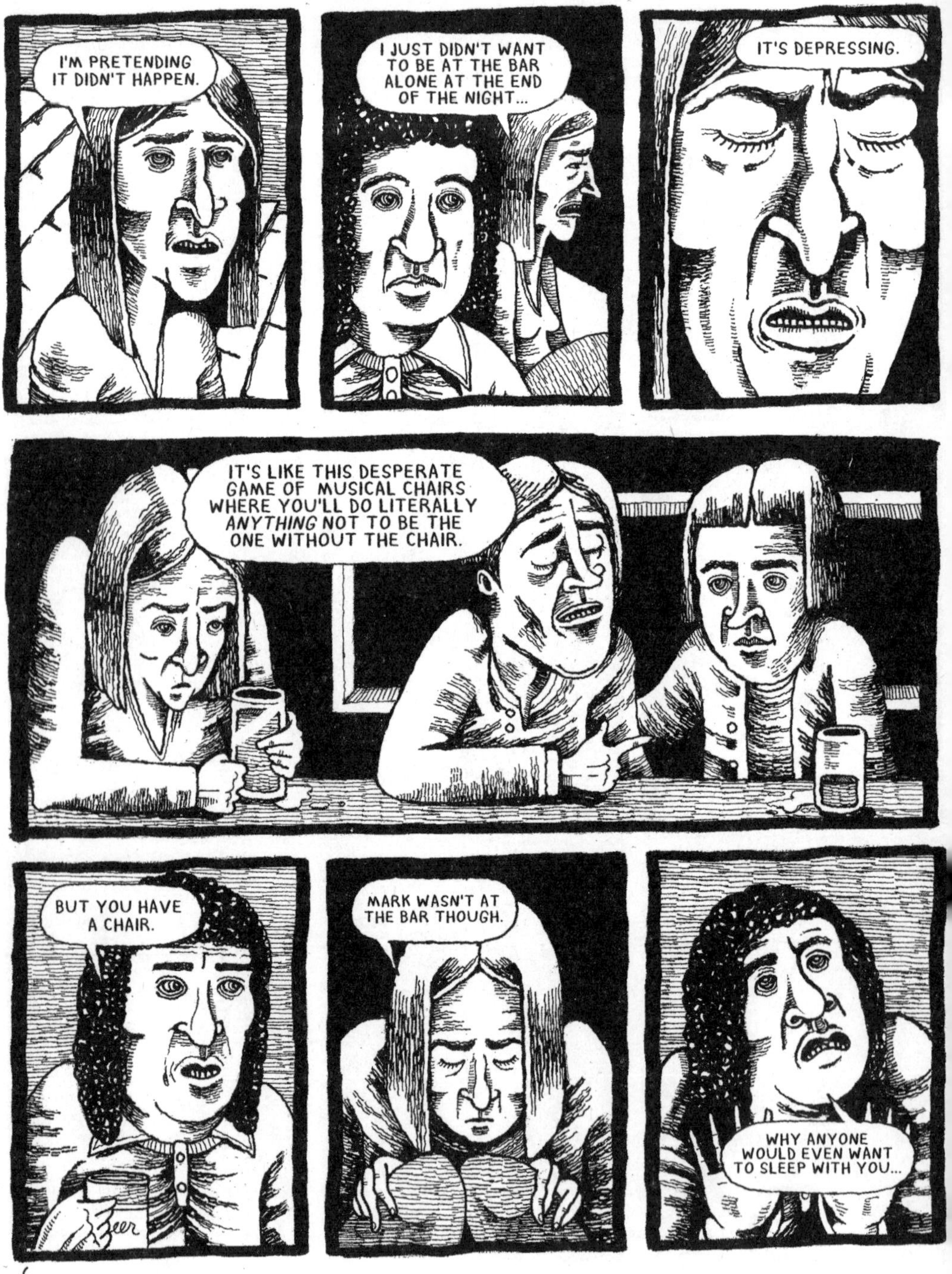
I'M PRETENDING IT DIDN'T HAPPEN.
I JUST DIDN'T WANT TO BE AT THE BAR ALONE AT THE END OF THE NIGHT...
IT'S DEPRESSING.
IT'S LIKE THIS DESPERATE GAME OF MUSICAL CHAIRS WHERE YOU'LL DO LITERALLY *ANYTHING* NOT TO BE THE ONE WITHOUT THE CHAIR.
BUT YOU HAVE A CHAIR.
Beer
MARK WASN'T AT THE BAR THOUGH.
WHY ANYONE WOULD EVEN WANT TO SLEEP WITH YOU...

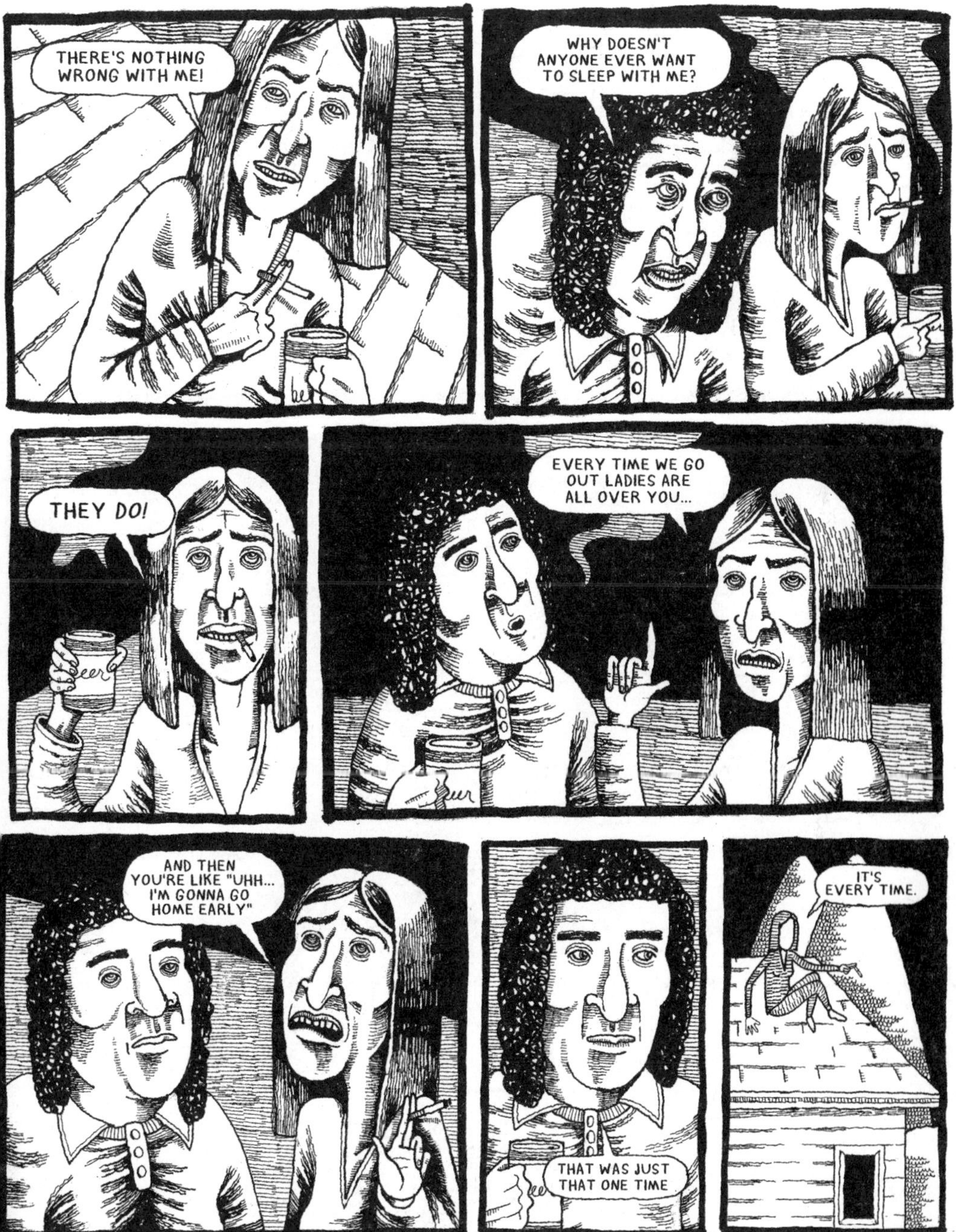
THERE'S NOTHING WRONG WITH ME!
WHY DOESN'T ANYONE EVER WANT TO SLEEP WITH ME?
THEY DO!
EVERY TIME WE GO OUT LADIES ARE ALL OVER YOU...
AND THEN YOU'RE LIKE "UHH... I'M GONNA GO HOME EARLY"
THAT WAS JUST THAT ONE TIME.
IT'S EVERY TIME.

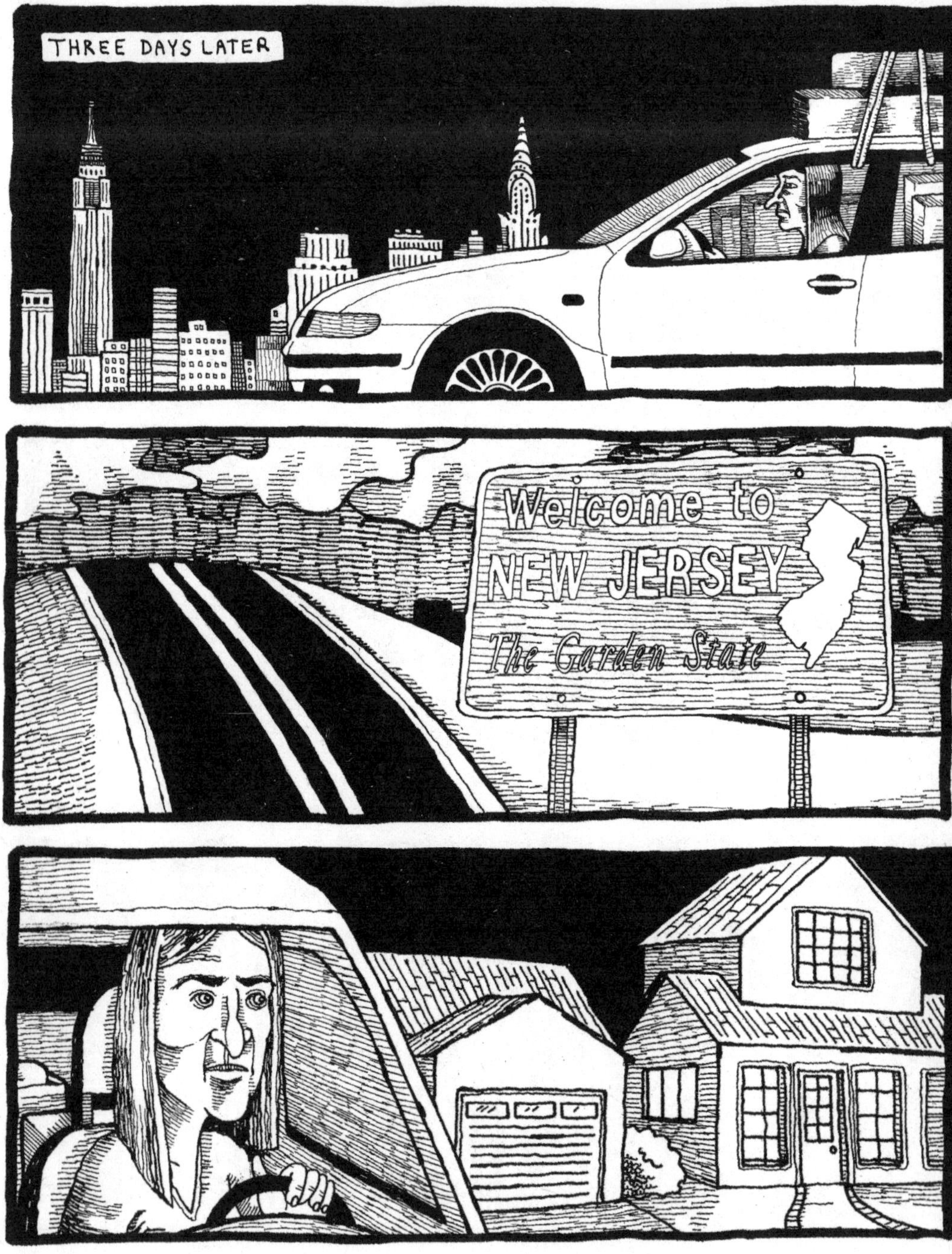
THREE DAYS LATER
Welcome to
NEW JERSEY
The Garden State

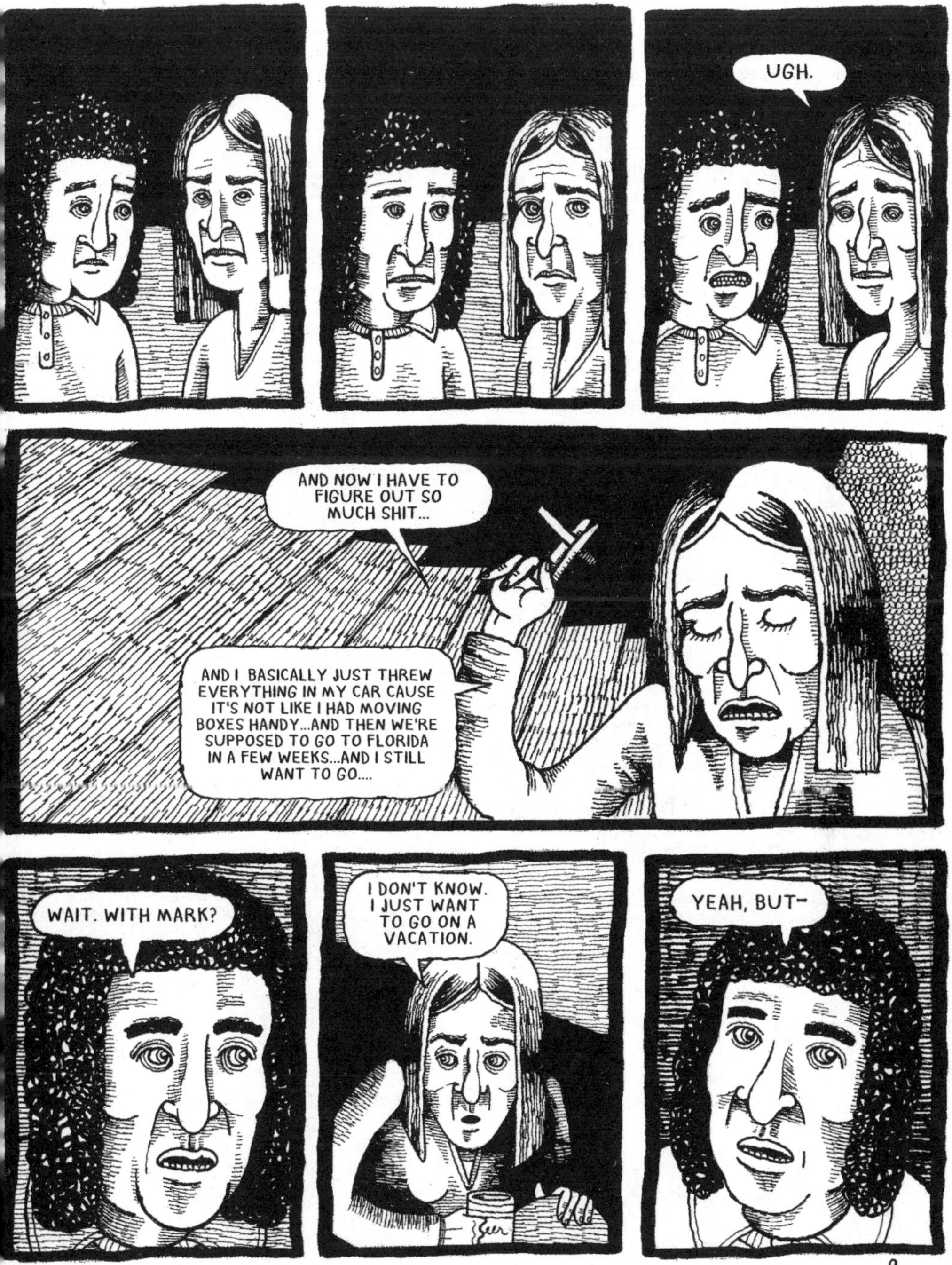
UGH.
AND NOW I HAVE TO FIGURE OUT SO MUCH SHIT...
AND I BASICALLY JUST THREW EVERYTHING IN MY CAR CAUSE IT'S NOT LIKE I HAD MOVING BOXES HANDY...AND THEN WE'RE SUPPOSED TO GO TO FLORIDA IN A FEW WEEKS...AND I STILL WANT TO GO....
WAIT. WITH MARK?
I DON'T KNOW. I JUST WANT TO GO ON A VACATION.
YEAH, BUT-

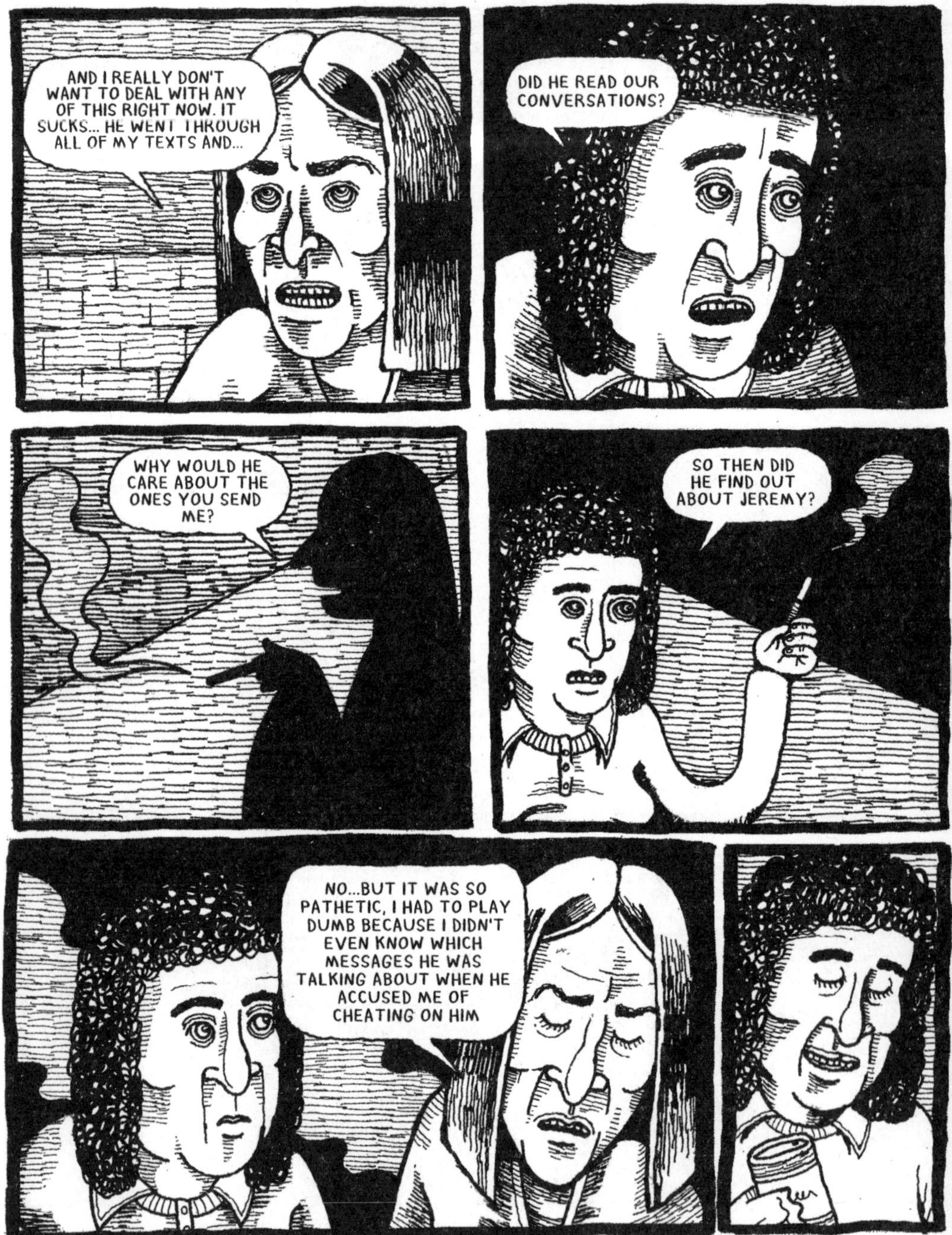
AND I REALLY DON'T WANT TO DEAL WITH ANY OF THIS RIGHT NOW. IT SUCKS... HE WENT THROUGH ALL OF MY TEXTS AND...
DID HE READ OUR CONVERSATIONS?
WHY WOULD HE CARE ABOUT THE ONES YOU SEND ME?
SO THEN DID HE FIND OUT ABOUT JEREMY?
NO...BUT IT WAS SO PATHETIC, I HAD TO PLAY DUMB BECAUSE I DIDN'T EVEN KNOW WHICH MESSAGES HE WAS TALKING ABOUT WHEN HE ACCUSED ME OF CHEATING ON HIM

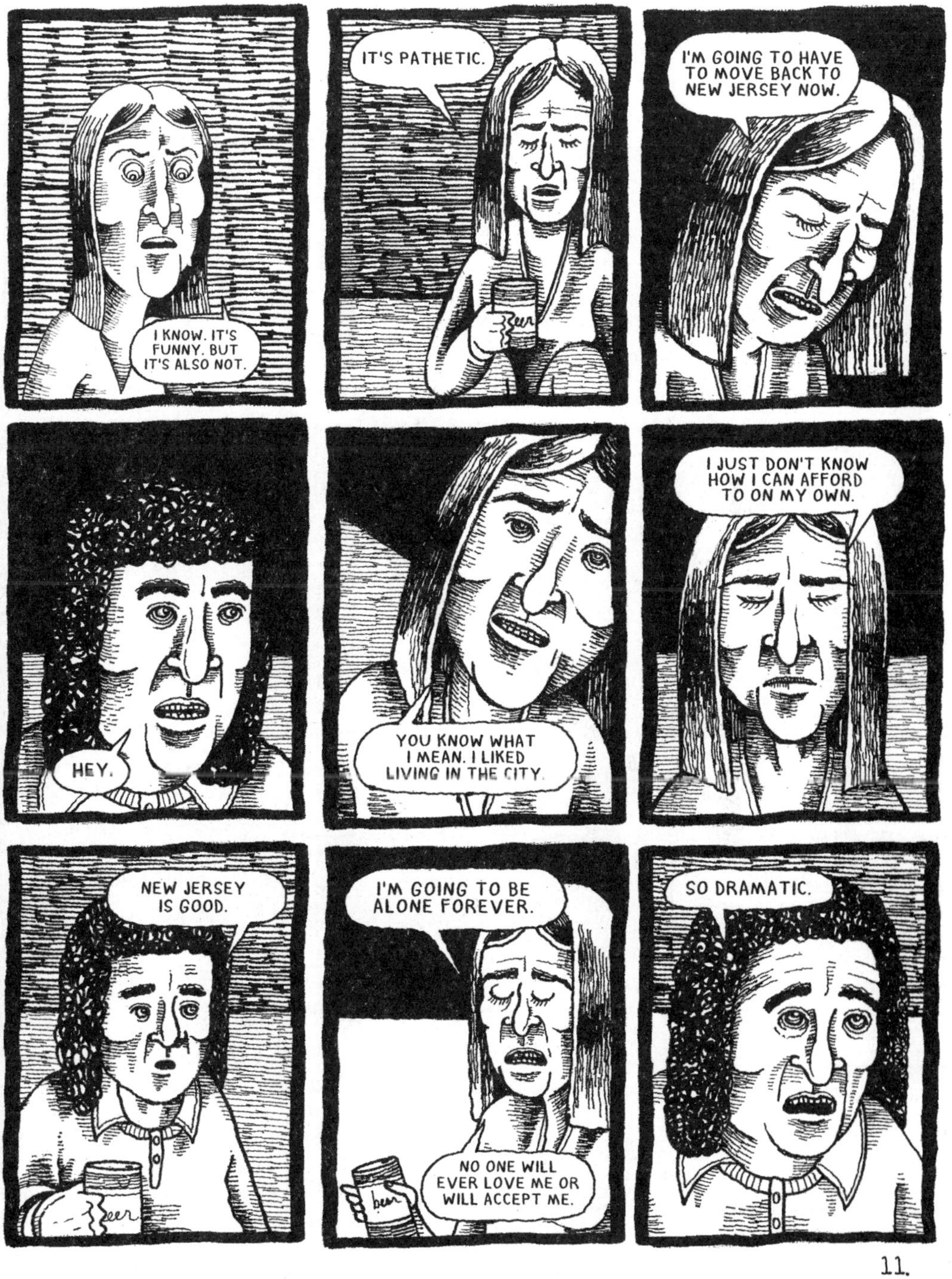
I KNOW. IT'S FUNNY. BUT IT'S ALSO NOT.
IT'S PATHETIC.
I'M GOING TO HAVE TO MOVE BACK TO NEW JERSEY NOW.
HEY.
YOU KNOW WHAT I MEAN. I LIKED LIVING IN THE CITY.
I JUST DON'T KNOW HOW I CAN AFFORD TO ON MY OWN.
NEW JERSEY IS GOOD.
I'M GOING TO BE ALONE FOREVER.
NO ONE WILL EVER LOVE ME OR WILL ACCEPT ME.
SO DRAMATIC.

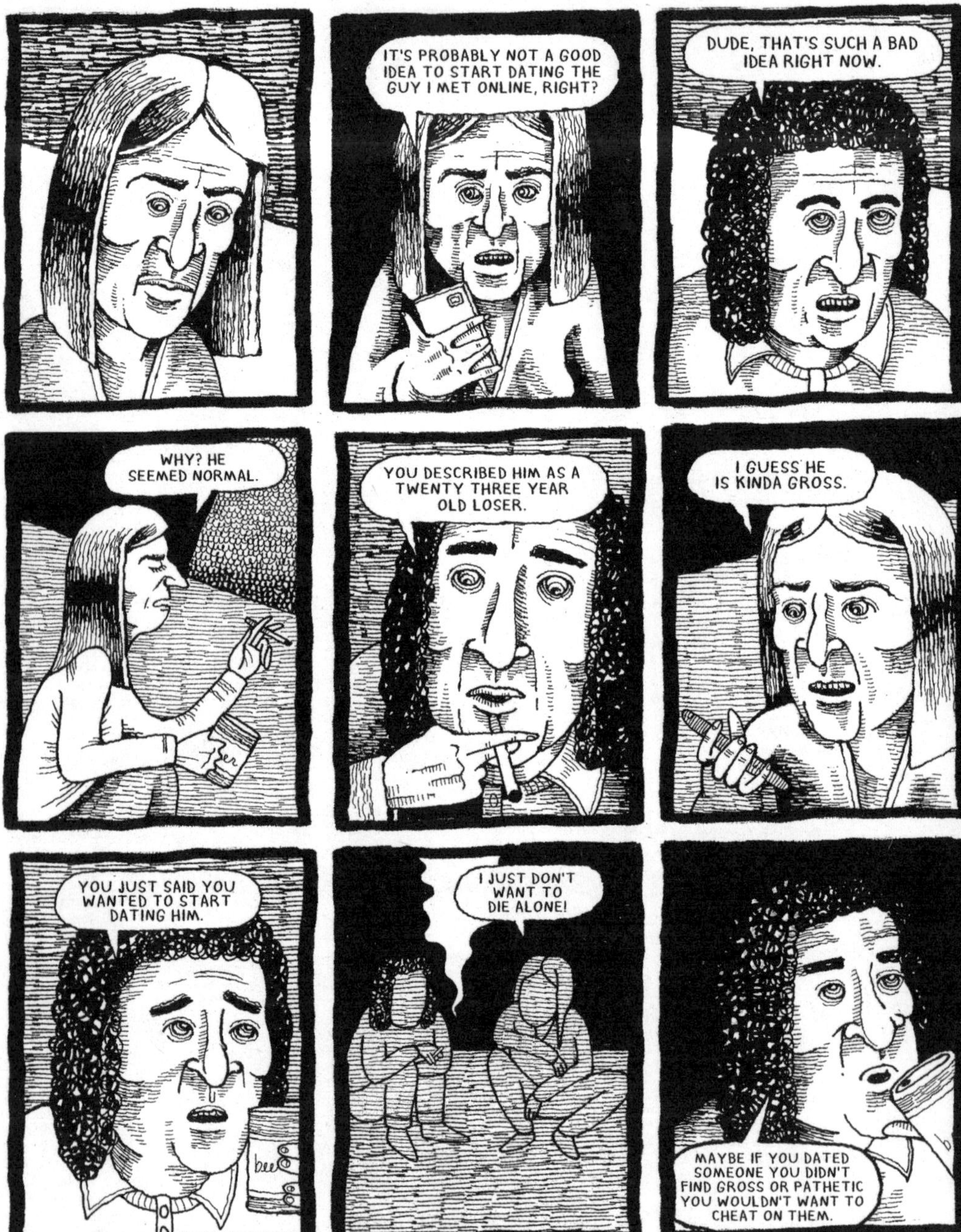
IT'S PROBABLY NOT A GOOD IDEA TO START DATING THE GUY I MET ONLINE, RIGHT?
DUDE, THAT'S SUCH A BAD IDEA RIGHT NOW.
WHY? HE SEEMED NORMAL.
YOU DESCRIBED HIM AS A TWENTY THREE YEAR OLD LOSER.
I GUESS HE IS KINDA GROSS.
YOU JUST SAID YOU WANTED TO START DATING HIM.
I JUST DON'T WANT TO DIE ALONE!
MAYBE IF YOU DATED SOMEONE YOU DIDN'T FIND GROSS OR PATHETIC YOU WOULDN'T WANT TO CHEAT ON THEM.

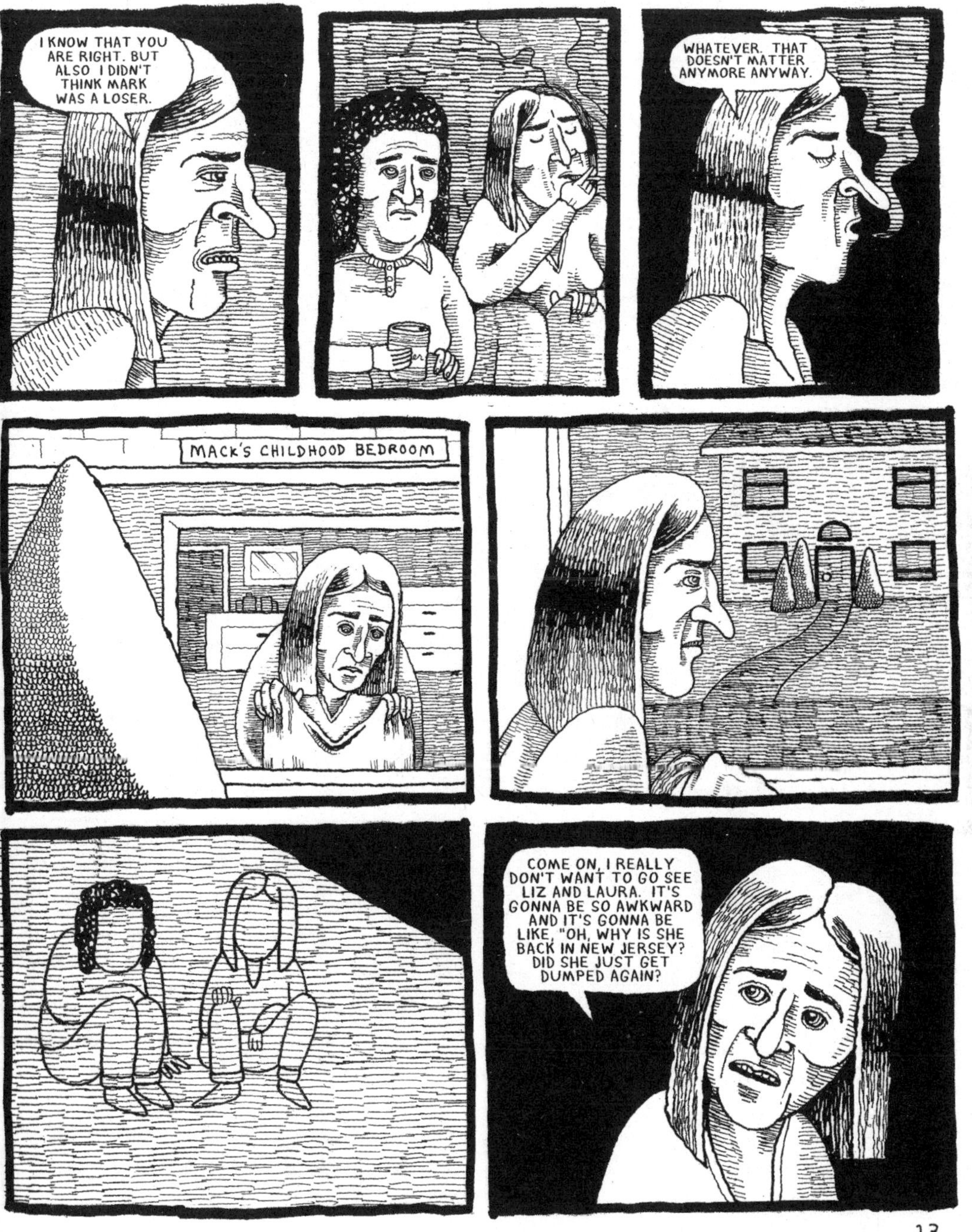
I KNOW THAT YOU ARE RIGHT. BUT ALSO I DIDN'T THINK MARK WAS A LOSER.
WHATEVER. THAT DOESN'T MATTER ANYMORE ANYWAY.
MACK'S CHILDHOOD BEDROOM
COME ON, I REALLY DON'T WANT TO GO SEE LIZ AND LAURA. IT'S GONNA BE SO AWKWARD AND IT'S GONNA BE LIKE, "OH, WHY IS SHE BACK IN NEW JERSEY? DID SHE JUST GET DUMPED AGAIN?

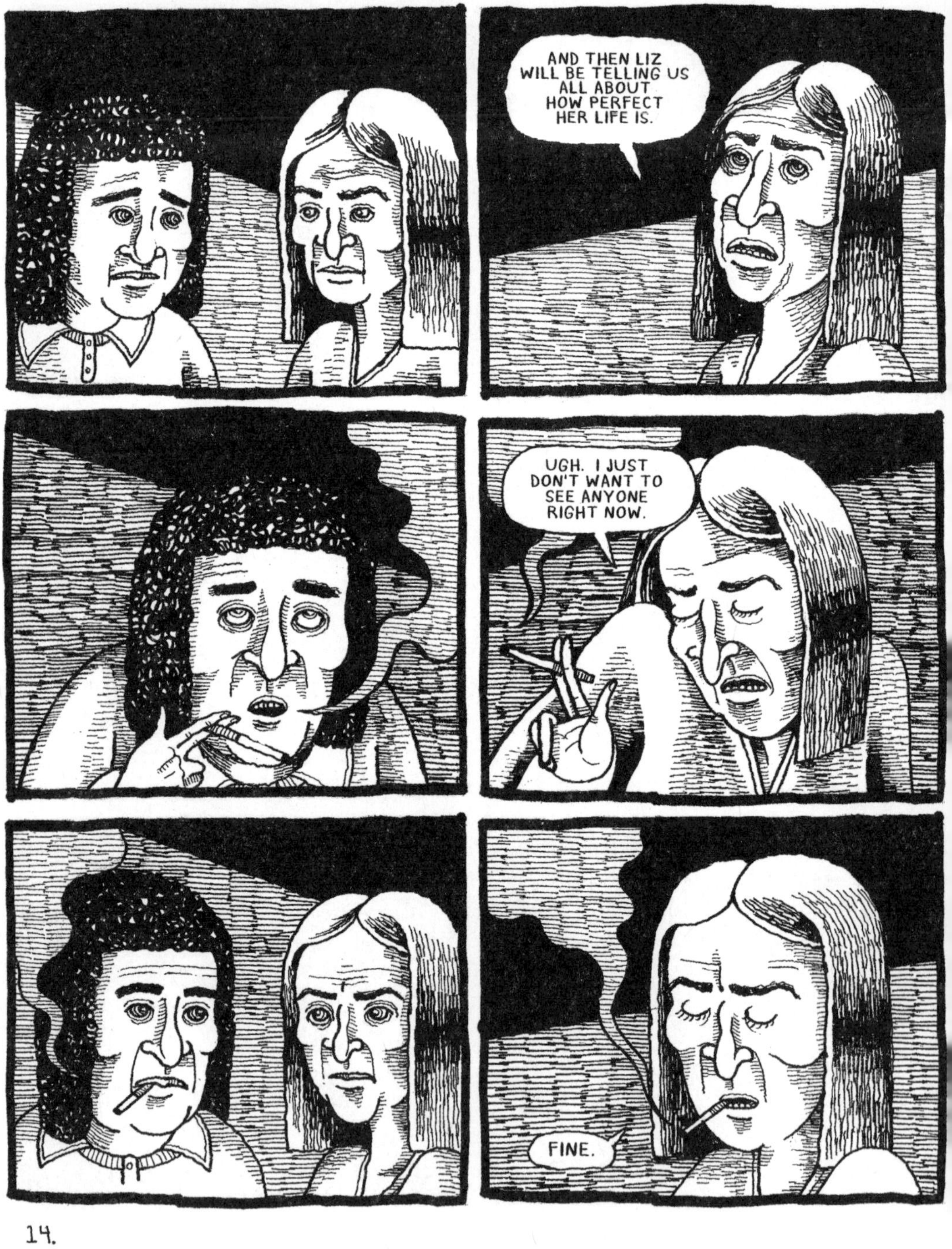
AND THEN LIZ WILL BE TELLING US ALL ABOUT HOW PERFECT HER LIFE IS.
UGH. I JUST DON'T WANT TO SEE ANYONE RIGHT NOW.
FINE.

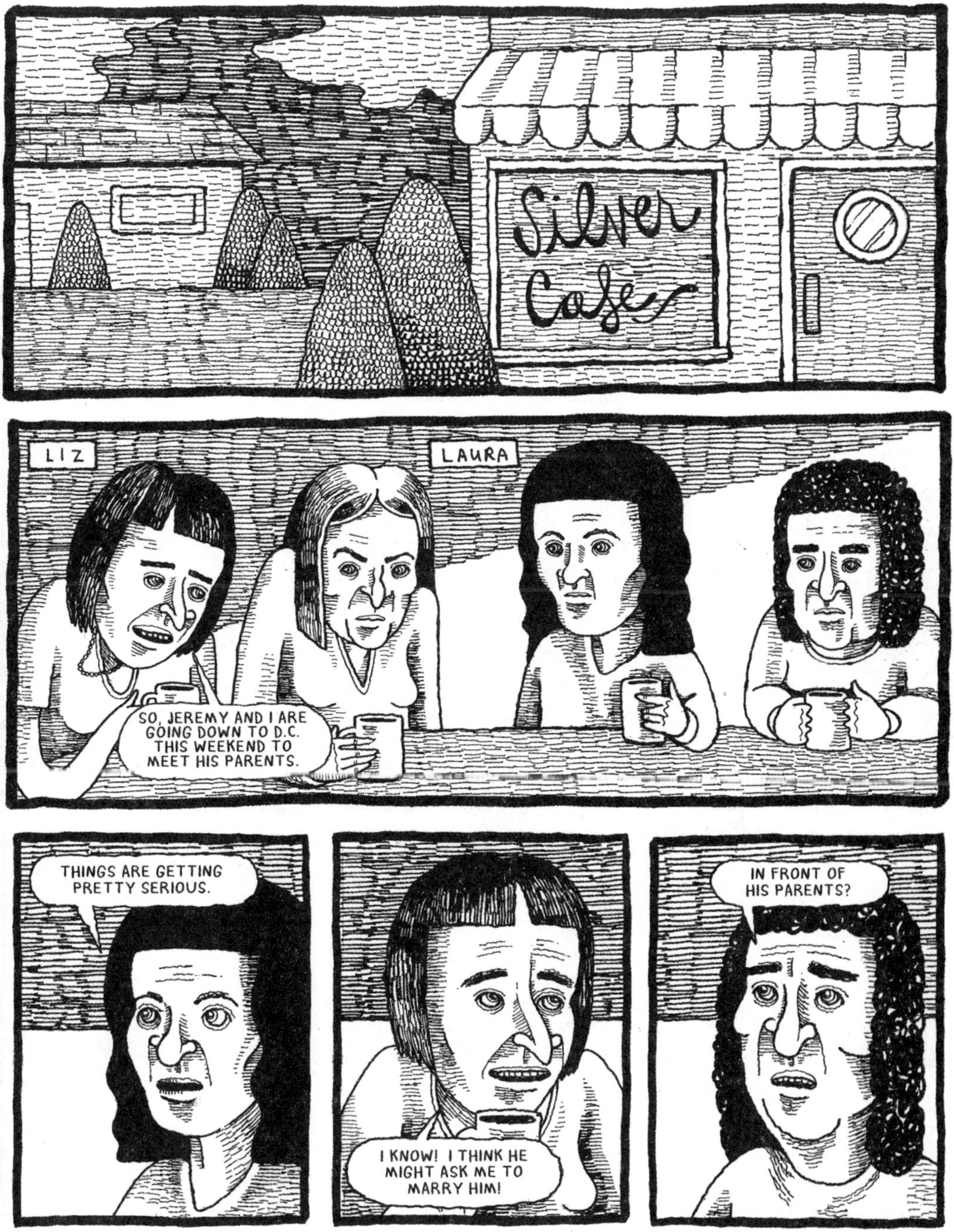
Silver Cafe
LIZ
LAURA
SO, JEREMY AND I ARE GOING DOWN TO D.C. THIS WEEKEND TO MEET HIS PARENTS.
THINGS ARE GETTING PRETTY SERIOUS.
I KNOW! I THINK HE MIGHT ASK ME TO MARRY HIM!
IN FRONT OF HIS PARENTS?

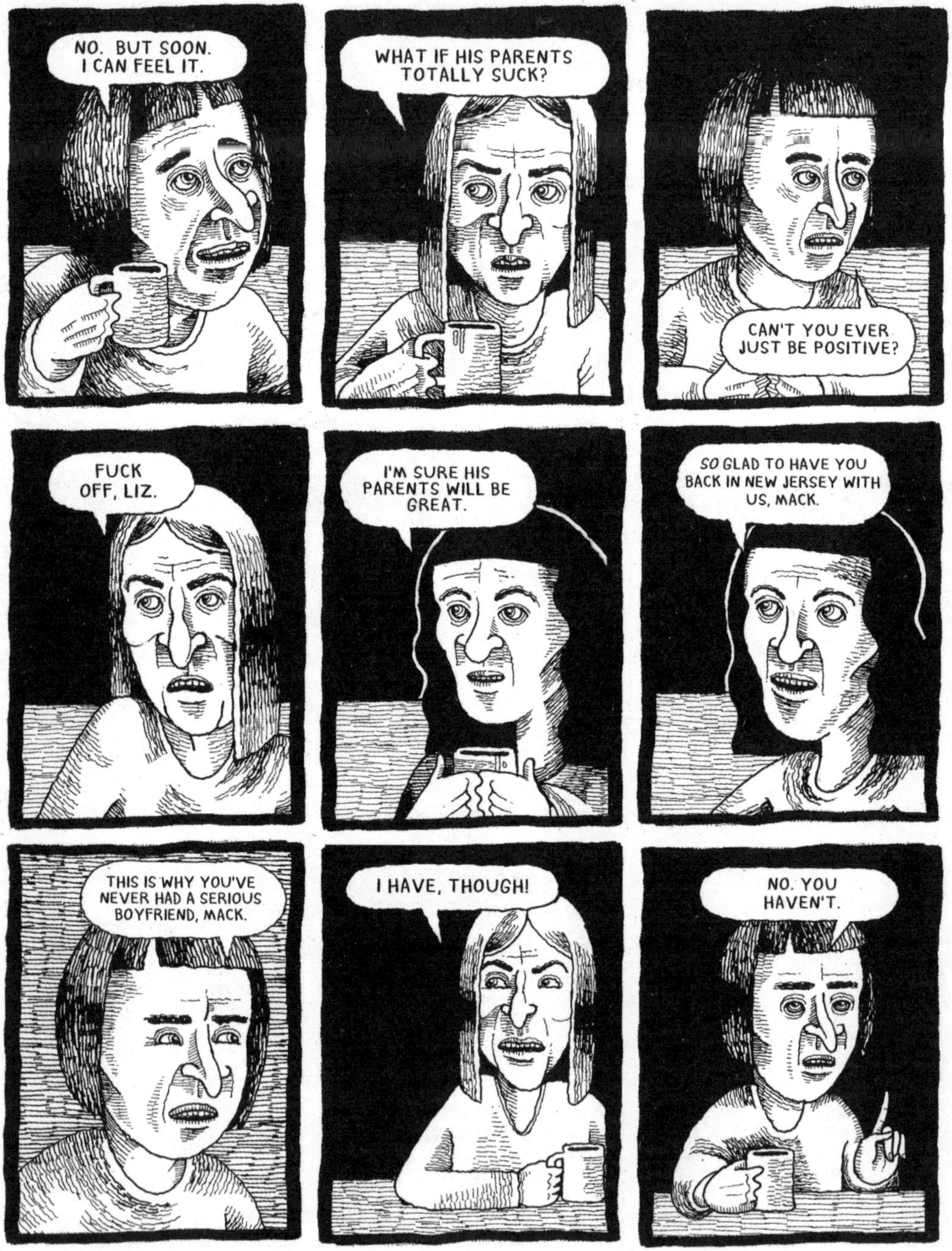
NO. BUT SOON. I CAN FEEL IT.
WHAT IF HIS PARENTS TOTALLY SUCK?
CAN'T YOU EVER JUST BE POSITIVE?
FUCK OFF, LIZ.
I'M SURE HIS PARENTS WILL BE GREAT.
SO GLAD TO HAVE YOU BACK IN NEW JERSEY WITH US, MACK.
THIS IS WHY YOU'VE NEVER HAD A SERIOUS BOYFRIEND, MACK.
I HAVE, THOUGH!
NO. YOU HAVEN'T.

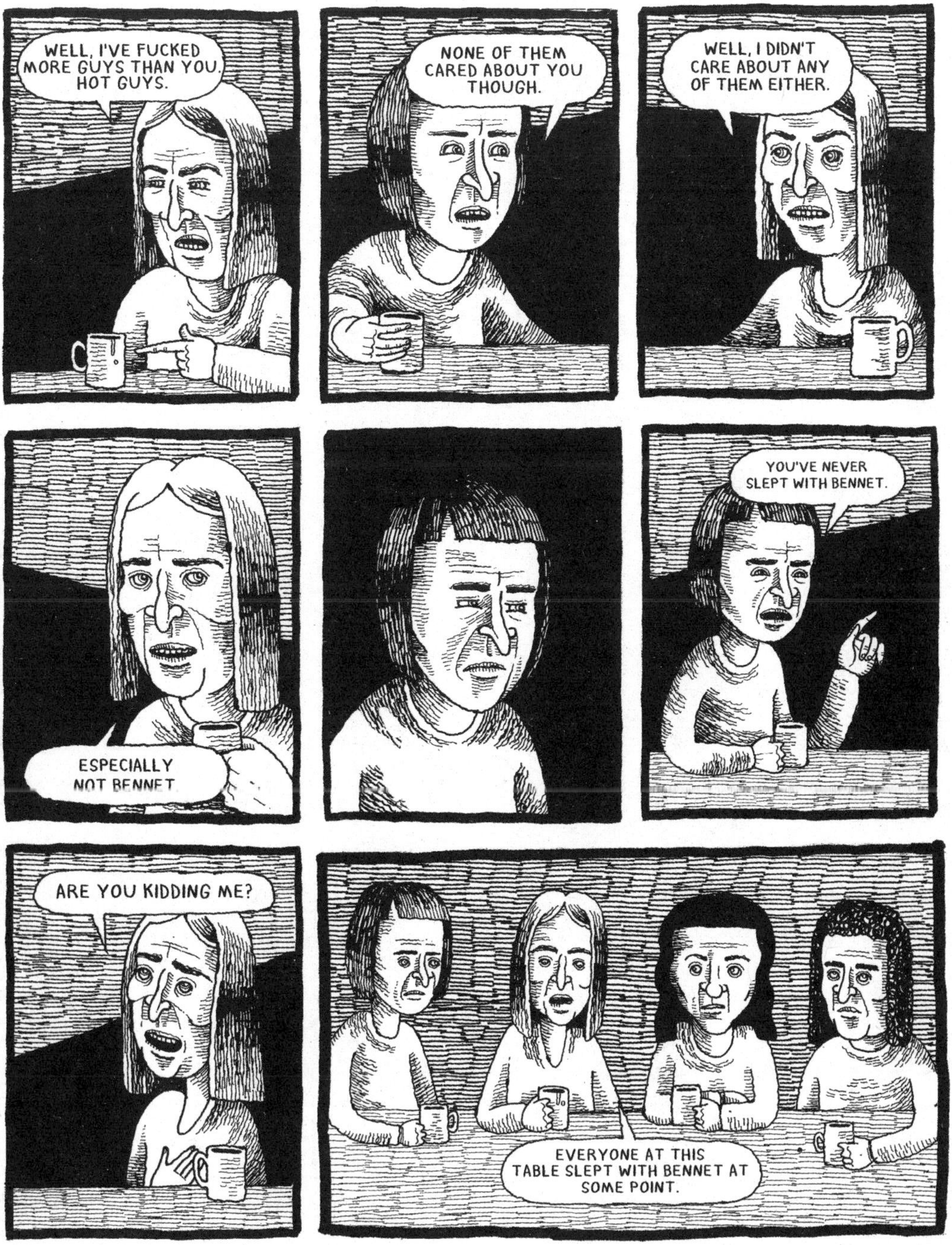
WELL, I'VE FUCKED MORE GUYS THAN YOU. HOT GUYS.
NONE OF THEM CARED ABOUT YOU THOUGH.
WELL, I DIDN'T CARE ABOUT ANY OF THEM EITHER.
ESPECIALLY NOT BENNET.
YOU'VE NEVER SLEPT WITH BENNET.
ARE YOU KIDDING ME?
EVERYONE AT THIS TABLE SLEPT WITH BENNET AT SOME POINT.

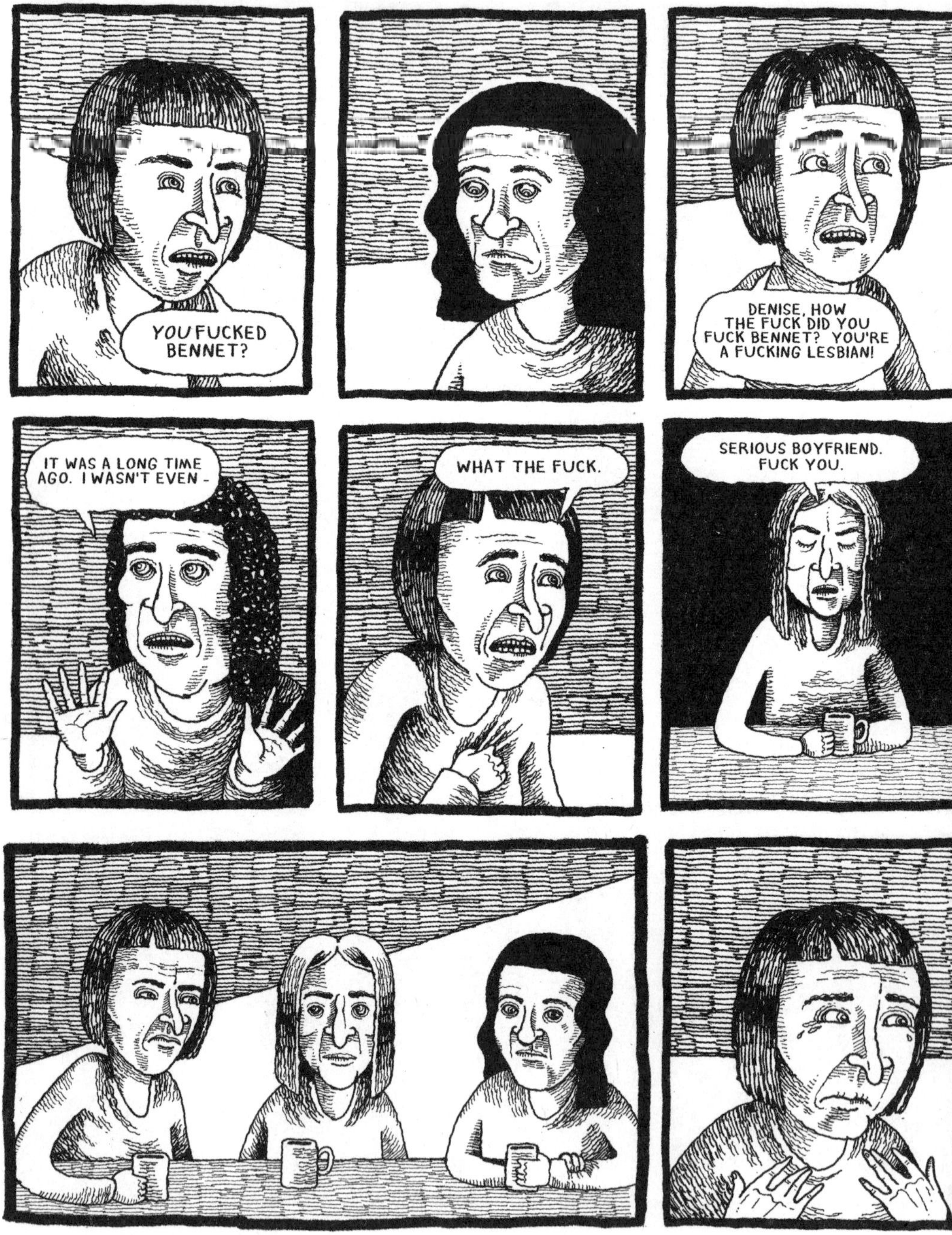
YOU FUCKED BENNET?
DENISE, HOW THE FUCK DID YOU FUCK BENNET? YOU'RE A FUCKING LESBIAN!
IT WAS A LONG TIME AGO. I WASN'T EVEN -
WHAT THE FUCK.
SERIOUS BOYFRIEND. FUCK YOU.

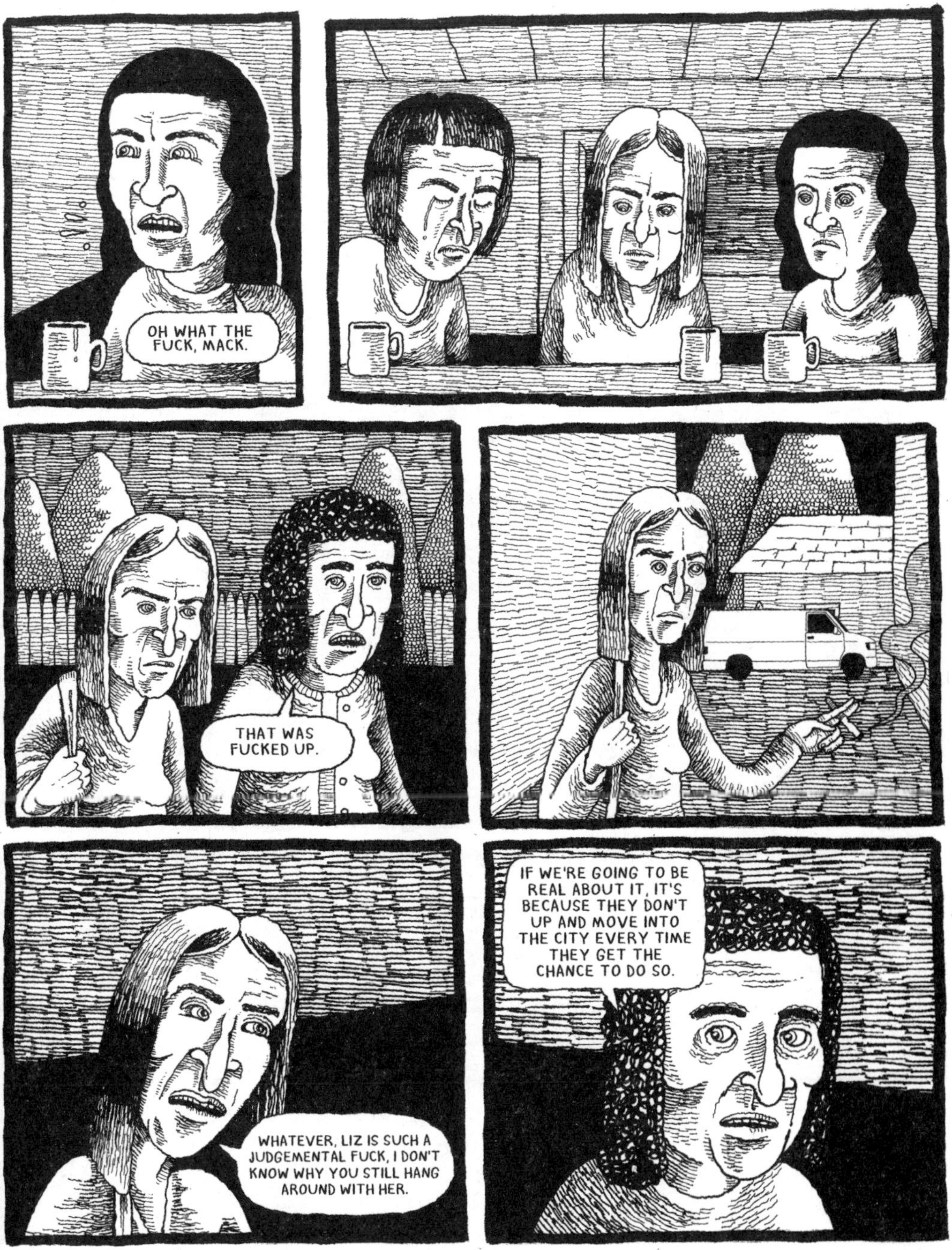
OH WHAT THE FUCK, MACK.
THAT WAS FUCKED UP.
WHATEVER, LIZ IS SUCH A JUDGEMENTAL FUCK, I DON'T KNOW WHY YOU STILL HANG AROUND WITH HER.
IF WE'RE GOING TO BE REAL ABOUT IT, IT'S BECAUSE THEY DON'T UP AND MOVE INTO THE CITY EVERY TIME THEY GET THE CHANCE TO DO SO.

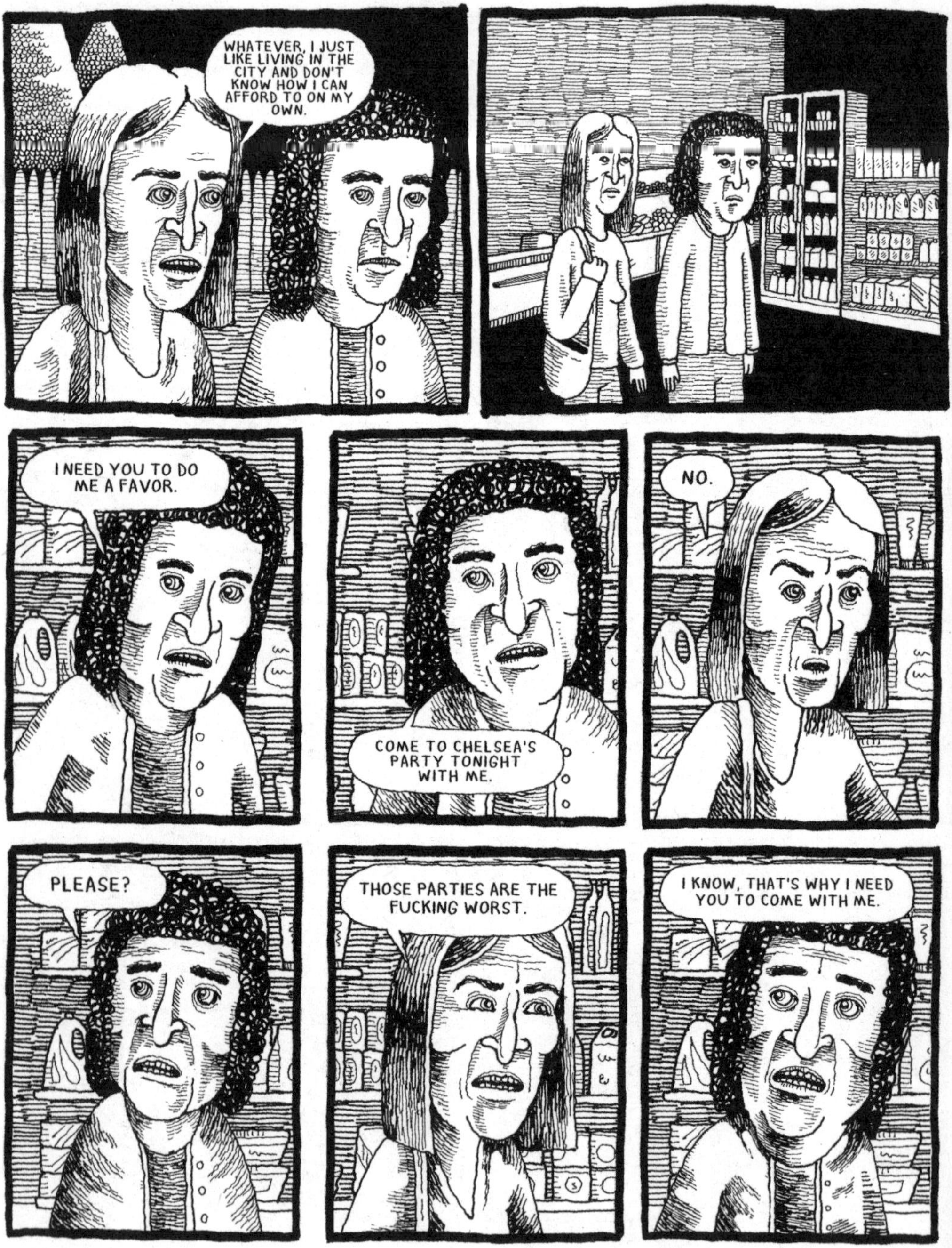
WHATEVER, I JUST LIKE LIVING IN THE CITY AND DON'T KNOW HOW I CAN AFFORD TO ON MY OWN.
I NEED YOU TO DO ME A FAVOR.
COME TO CHELSEA'S PARTY TONIGHT WITH ME.
NO.
PLEASE?
THOSE PARTIES ARE THE FUCKING WORST.
I KNOW, THAT'S WHY I NEED YOU TO COME WITH ME.

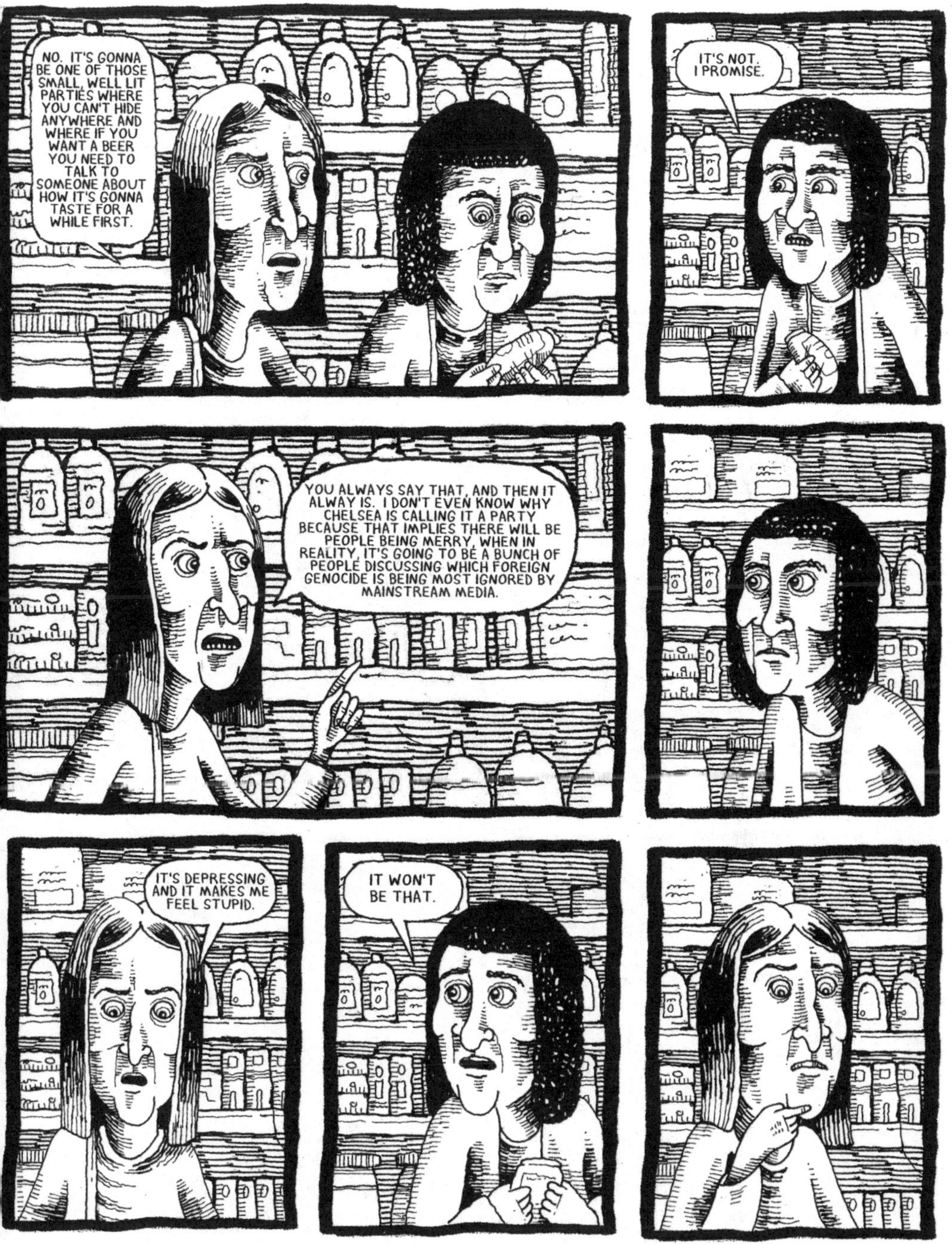
NO. IT'S GONNA BE ONE OF THOSE SMALL, WELL LIT PARTIES WHERE YOU CAN'T HIDE ANYWHERE AND WHERE IF YOU WANT A BEER YOU NEED TO TALK TO SOMEONE ABOUT HOW IT'S GONNA TASTE FOR A WHILE FIRST.
IT'S NOT. I PROMISE.
YOU ALWAYS SAY THAT, AND THEN IT ALWAY IS. I DON'T EVEN KNOW WHY CHELSEA IS CALLING IT A PARTY BECAUSE THAT IMPLIES THERE WILL BE PEOPLE BEING MERRY, WHEN IN REALITY, IT'S GOING TO BE A BUNCH OF PEOPLE DISCUSSING WHICH FOREIGN GENOCIDE IS BEING MOST IGNORED BY MAINSTREAM MEDIA.
IT'S DEPRESSING AND IT MAKES ME FEEL STUPID.
IT WON'T BE THAT.

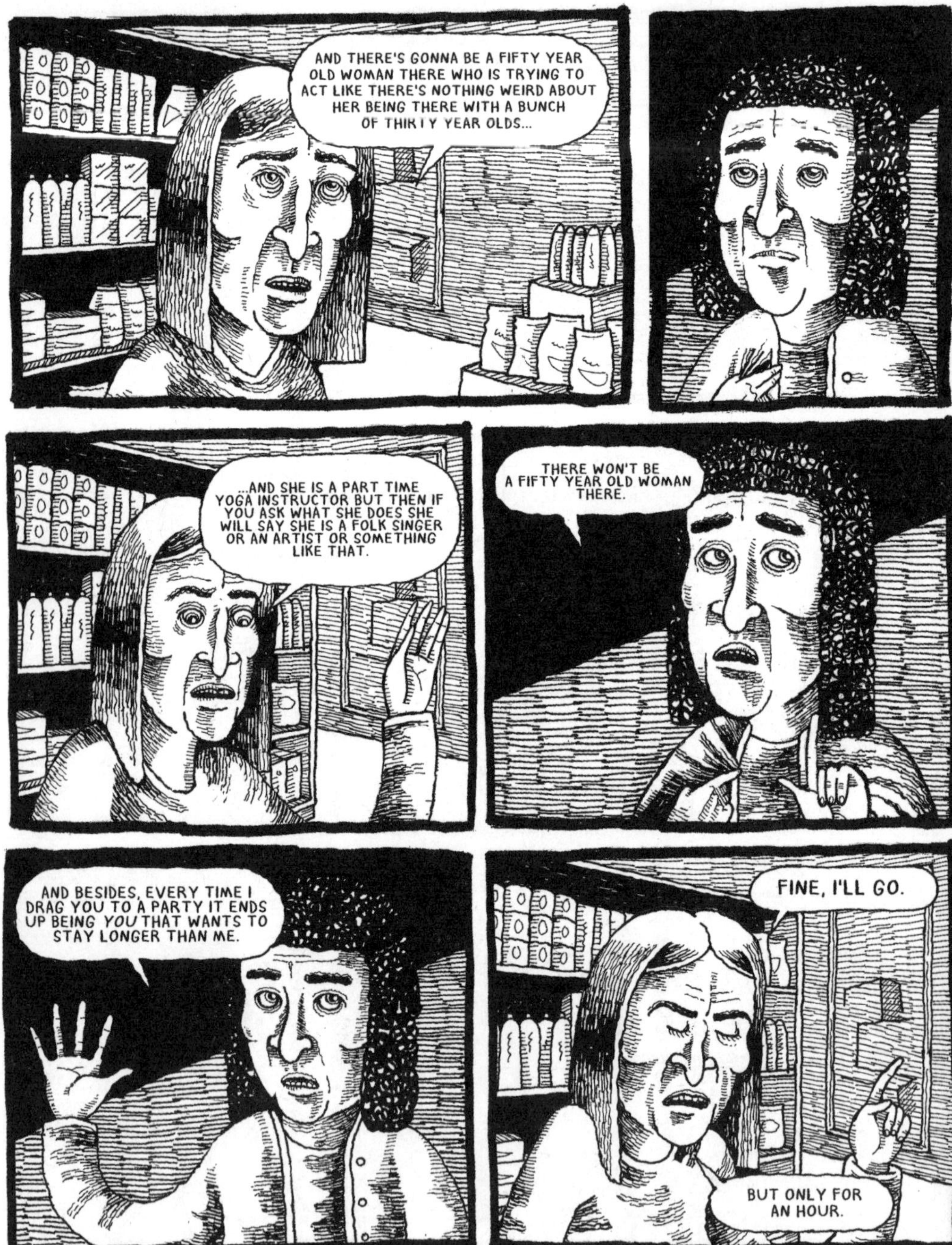
AND THERE'S GONNA BE A FIFTY YEAR OLD WOMAN THERE WHO IS TRYING TO ACT LIKE THERE'S NOTHING WEIRD ABOUT HER BEING THERE WITH A BUNCH OF THIRTY YEAR OLDS...
...AND SHE IS A PART TIME YOGA INSTRUCTOR BUT THEN IF YOU ASK WHAT SHE DOES SHE WILL SAY SHE IS A FOLK SINGER OR AN ARTIST OR SOMETHING LIKE THAT.
THERE WON'T BE A FIFTY YEAR OLD WOMAN THERE.
AND BESIDES, EVERY TIME I DRAG YOU TO A PARTY IT ENDS UP BEING *YOU* THAT WANTS TO STAY LONGER THAN ME.
FINE, I'LL GO.
BUT ONLY FOR AN HOUR.

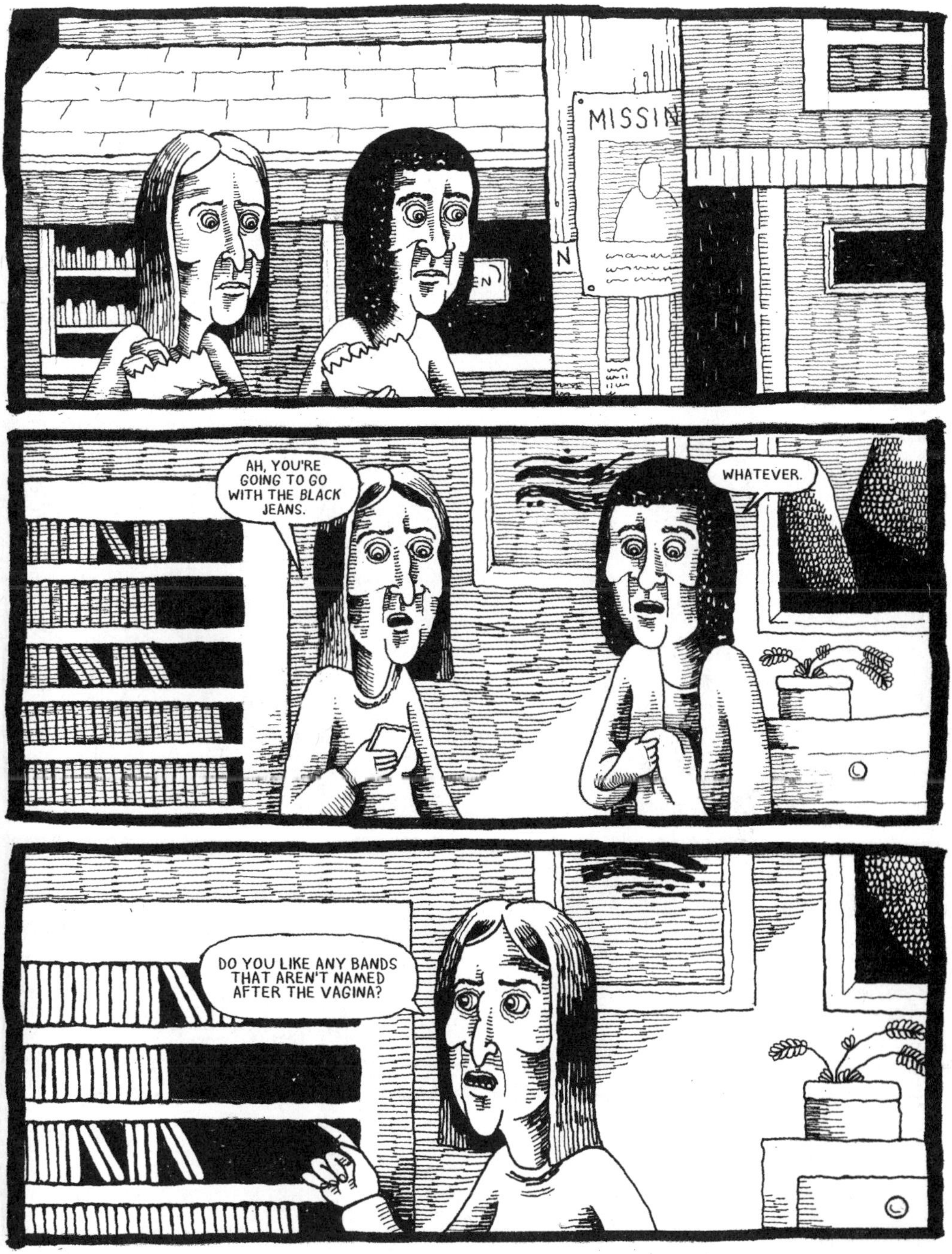
MISSIN
AH, YOU'RE GOING TO GO WITH THE *BLACK* JEANS.
WHATEVER.
DO YOU LIKE ANY BANDS THAT AREN'T NAMED AFTER THE VAGINA?

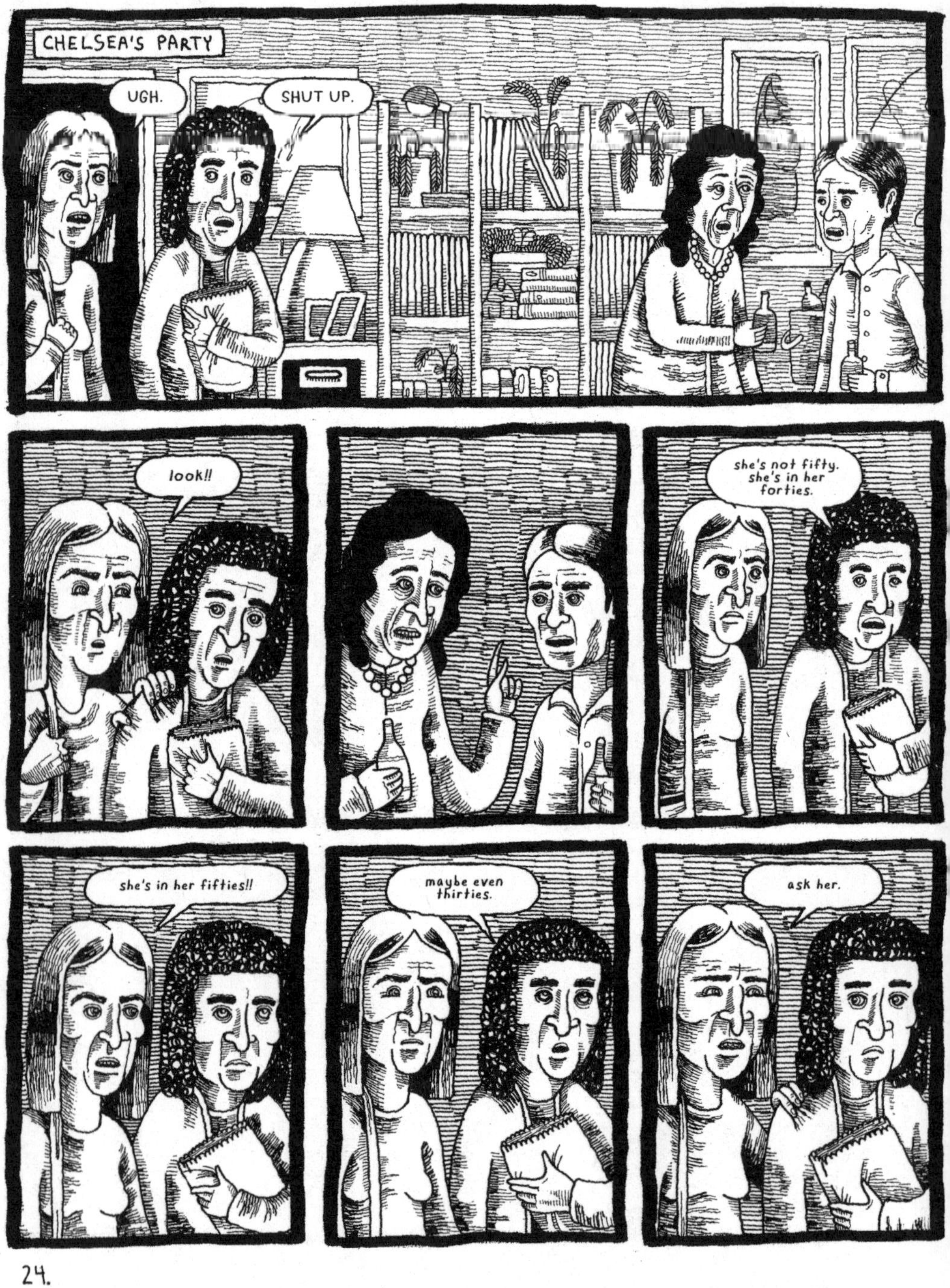
CHELSEA'S PARTY
UGH.
SHUT UP.
look!!
she's not fifty. she's in her forties.
she's in her fifties!!
maybe even thirties.
ask her.

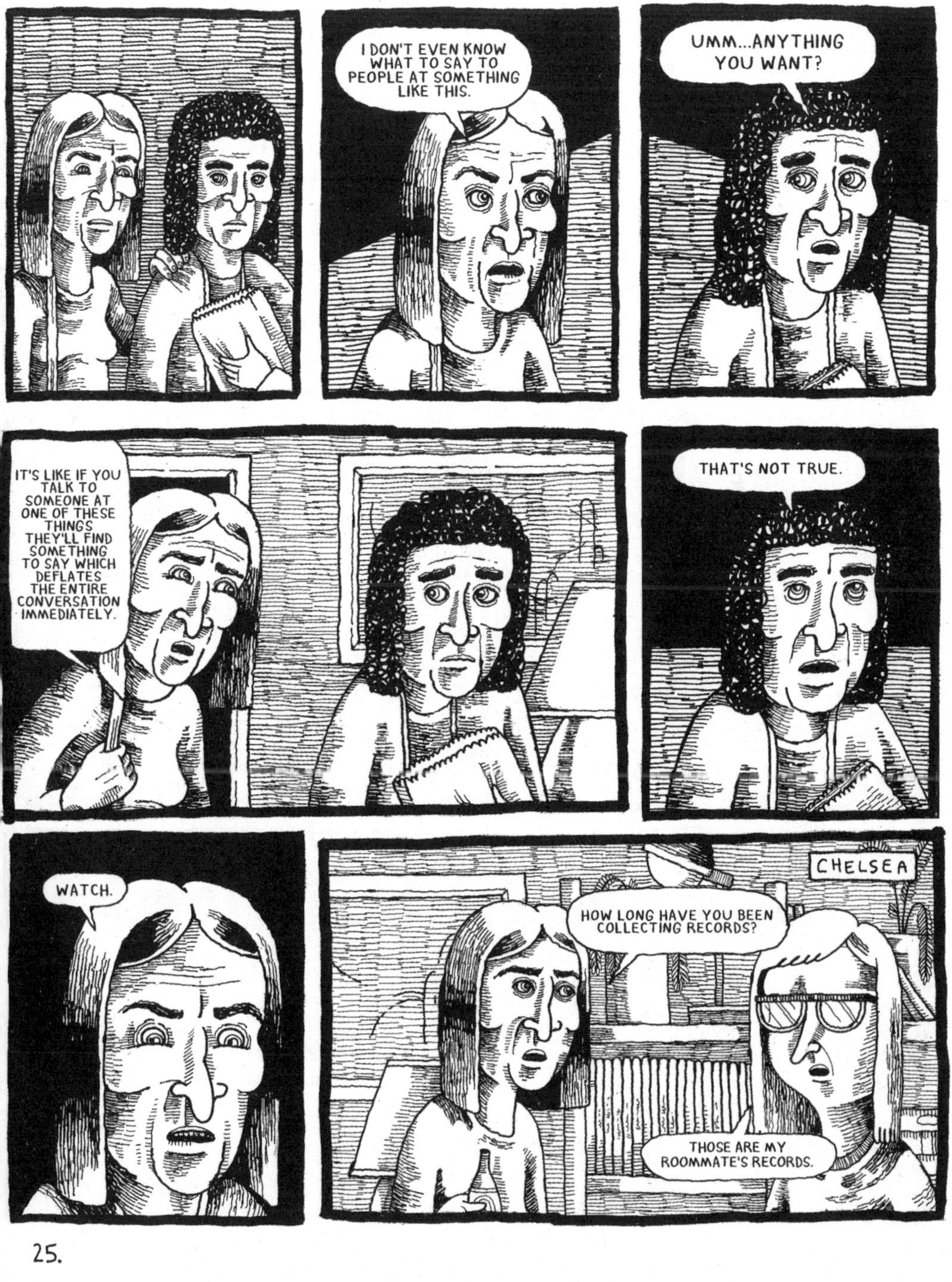

I DON'T EVEN KNOW WHAT TO SAY TO PEOPLE AT SOMETHING LIKE THIS.
UMM...ANYTHING YOU WANT?
IT'S LIKE IF YOU TALK TO SOMEONE AT ONE OF THESE THINGS THEY'LL FIND SOMETHING TO SAY WHICH DEFLATES THE ENTIRE CONVERSATION IMMEDIATELY.
THAT'S NOT TRUE.
WATCH.
CHELSEA
HOW LONG HAVE YOU BEEN COLLECTING RECORDS?
THOSE ARE MY ROOMMATE'S RECORDS.

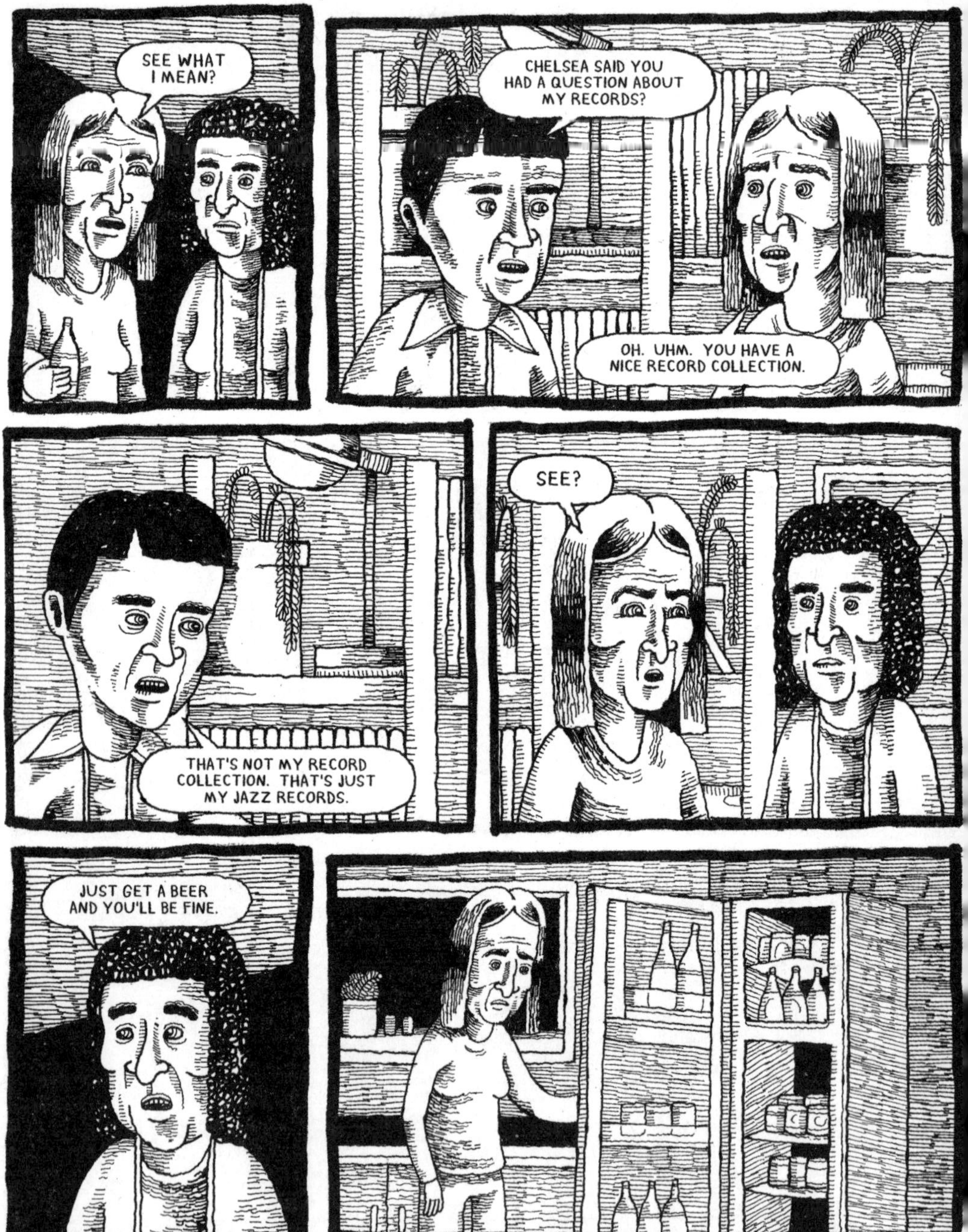
SEE WHAT I MEAN?
CHELSEA SAID YOU HAD A QUESTION ABOUT MY RECORDS?
OH. UHM. YOU HAVE A NICE RECORD COLLECTION.
THAT'S NOT MY RECORD COLLECTION. THAT'S JUST MY JAZZ RECORDS.
SEE?
JUST GET A BEER AND YOU'LL BE FINE.

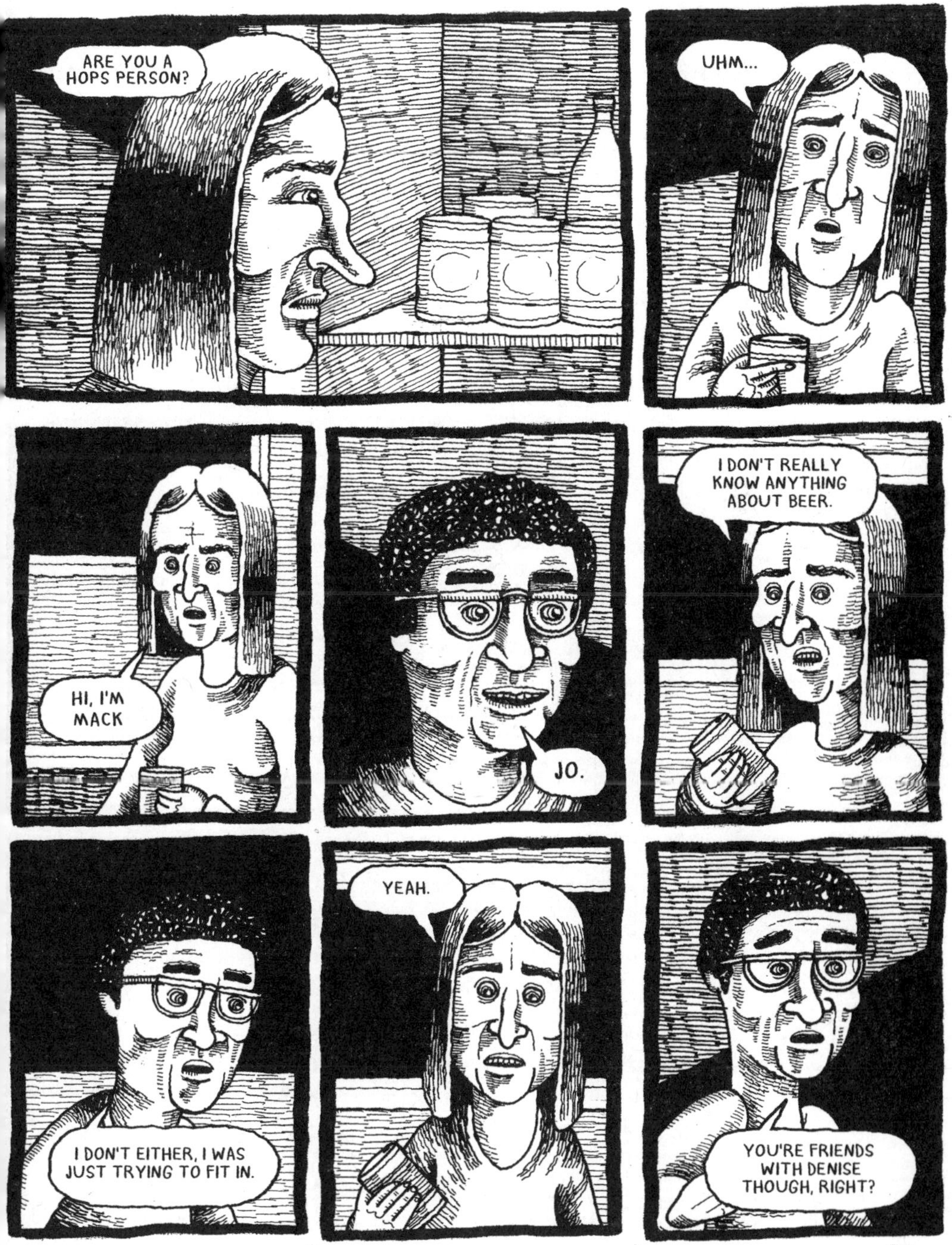
ARE YOU A HOPS PERSON?
UHM...
HI, I'M MACK
JO.
I DON'T REALLY KNOW ANYTHING ABOUT BEER.
I DON'T EITHER, I WAS JUST TRYING TO FIT IN.
YEAH.
YOU'RE FRIENDS WITH DENISE THOUGH, RIGHT?

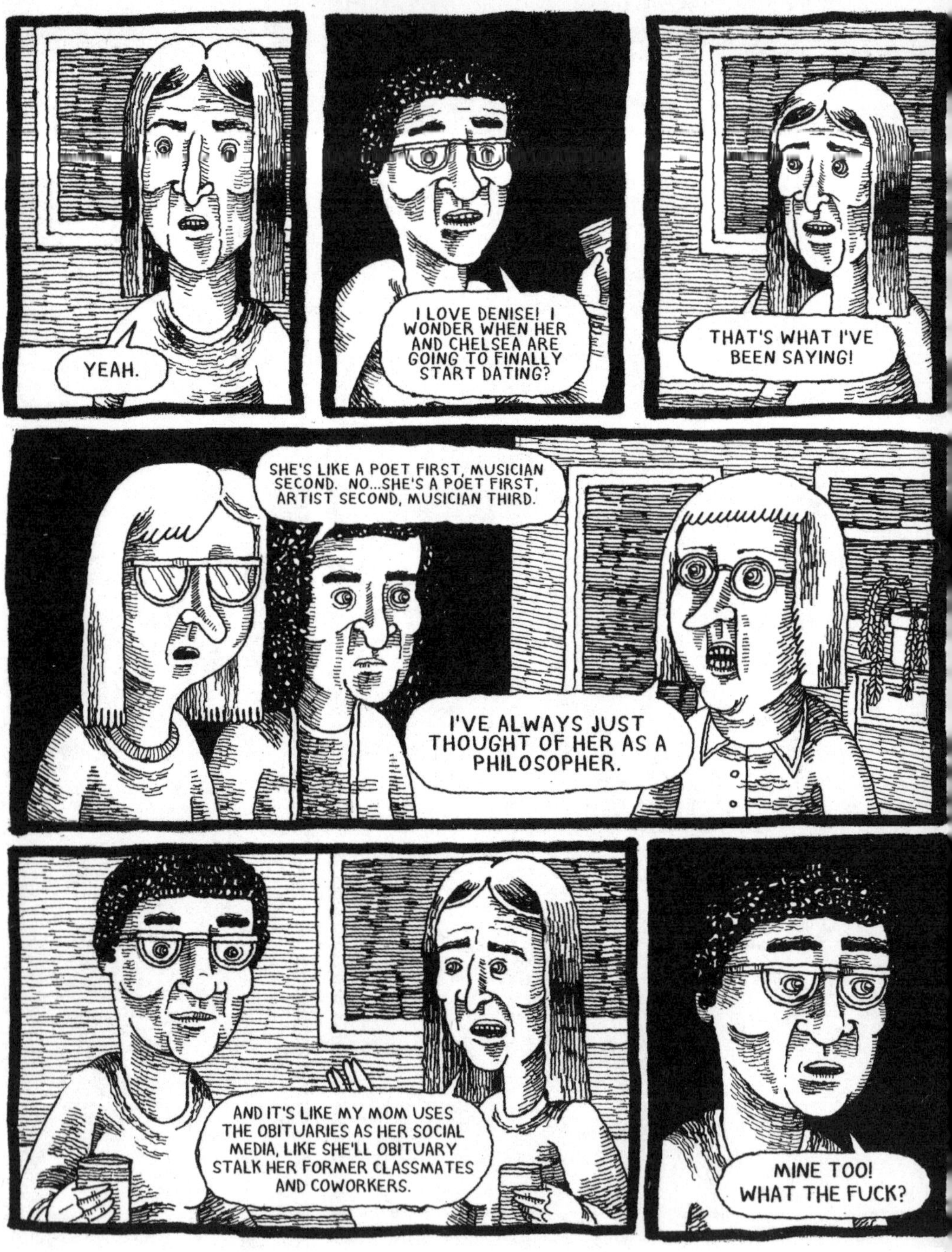
YEAH.
I LOVE DENISE! I WONDER WHEN HER AND CHELSEA ARE GOING TO FINALLY START DATING?
THAT'S WHAT I'VE BEEN SAYING!
SHE'S LIKE A POET FIRST, MUSICIAN SECOND. NO...SHE'S A POET FIRST, ARTIST SECOND, MUSICIAN THIRD.
I'VE ALWAYS JUST THOUGHT OF HER AS A PHILOSOPHER.
AND IT'S LIKE MY MOM USES THE OBITUARIES AS HER SOCIAL MEDIA, LIKE SHE'LL OBITUARY STALK HER FORMER CLASSMATES AND COWORKERS.
MINE TOO! WHAT THE FUCK?

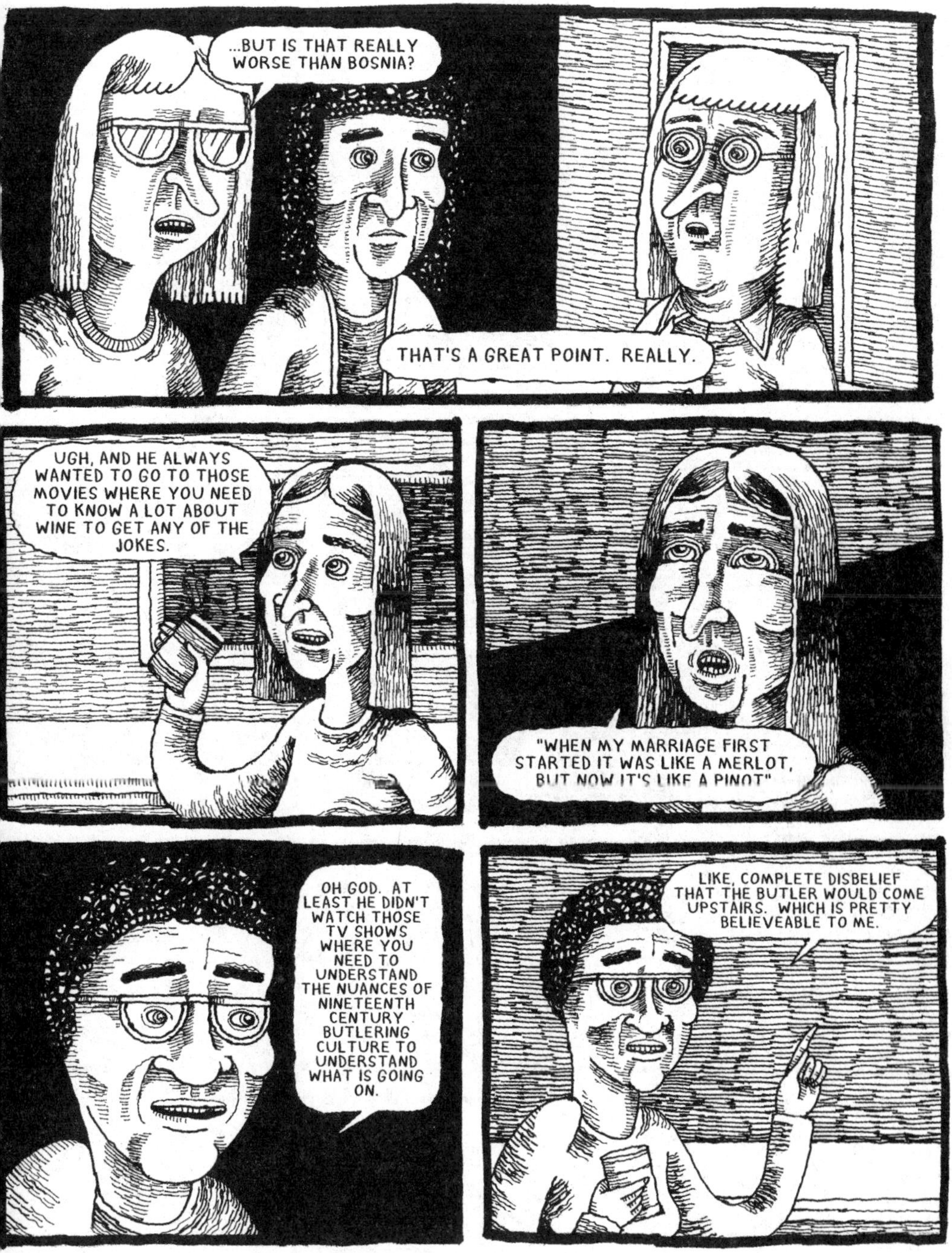
...BUT IS THAT REALLY WORSE THAN BOSNIA?
THAT'S A GREAT POINT. REALLY.
UGH, AND HE ALWAYS WANTED TO GO TO THOSE MOVIES WHERE YOU NEED TO KNOW A LOT ABOUT WINE TO GET ANY OF THE JOKES.
"WHEN MY MARRIAGE FIRST STARTED IT WAS LIKE A MERLOT, BUT NOW IT'S LIKE A PINOT"
OH GOD. AT LEAST HE DIDN'T WATCH THOSE TV SHOWS WHERE YOU NEED TO UNDERSTAND THE NUANCES OF NINETEENTH CENTURY BUTLERING CULTURE TO UNDERSTAND WHAT IS GOING ON.
LIKE, COMPLETE DISBELIEF THAT THE BUTLER WOULD COME UPSTAIRS. WHICH IS PRETTY BELIEVEABLE TO ME.

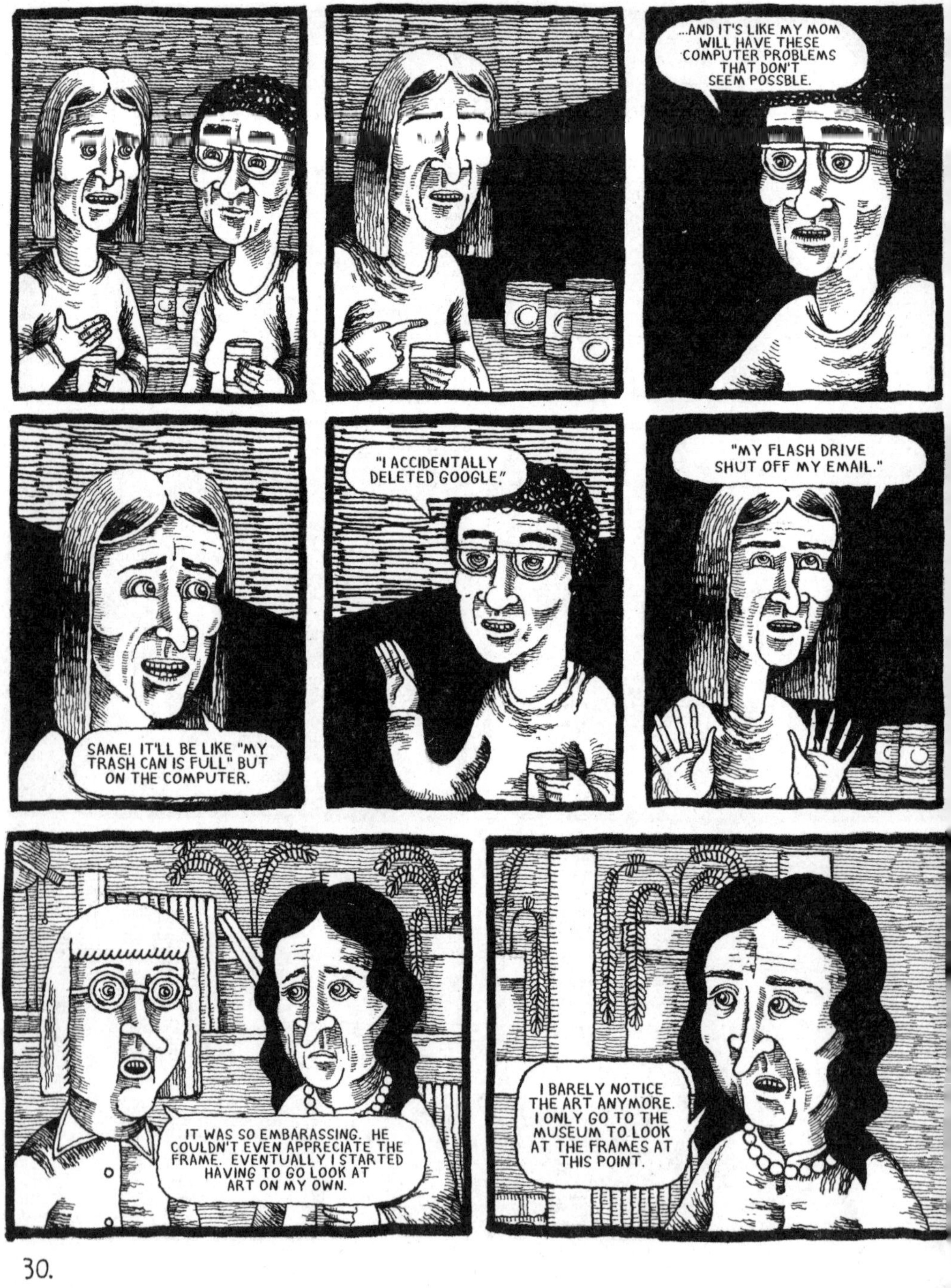
...AND IT'S LIKE MY MOM WILL HAVE THESE COMPUTER PROBLEMS THAT DON'T SEEM POSSBLE.
SAME! IT'LL BE LIKE "MY TRASH CAN IS FULL" BUT ON THE COMPUTER.
"I ACCIDENTALLY DELETED GOOGLE."
"MY FLASH DRIVE SHUT OFF MY EMAIL."
IT WAS SO EMBARASSING. HE COULDN'T EVEN APPRECIATE THE FRAME. EVENTUALLY I STARTED HAVING TO GO LOOK AT ART ON MY OWN.
I BARELY NOTICE THE ART ANYMORE. I ONLY GO TO THE MUSEUM TO LOOK AT THE FRAMES AT THIS POINT.

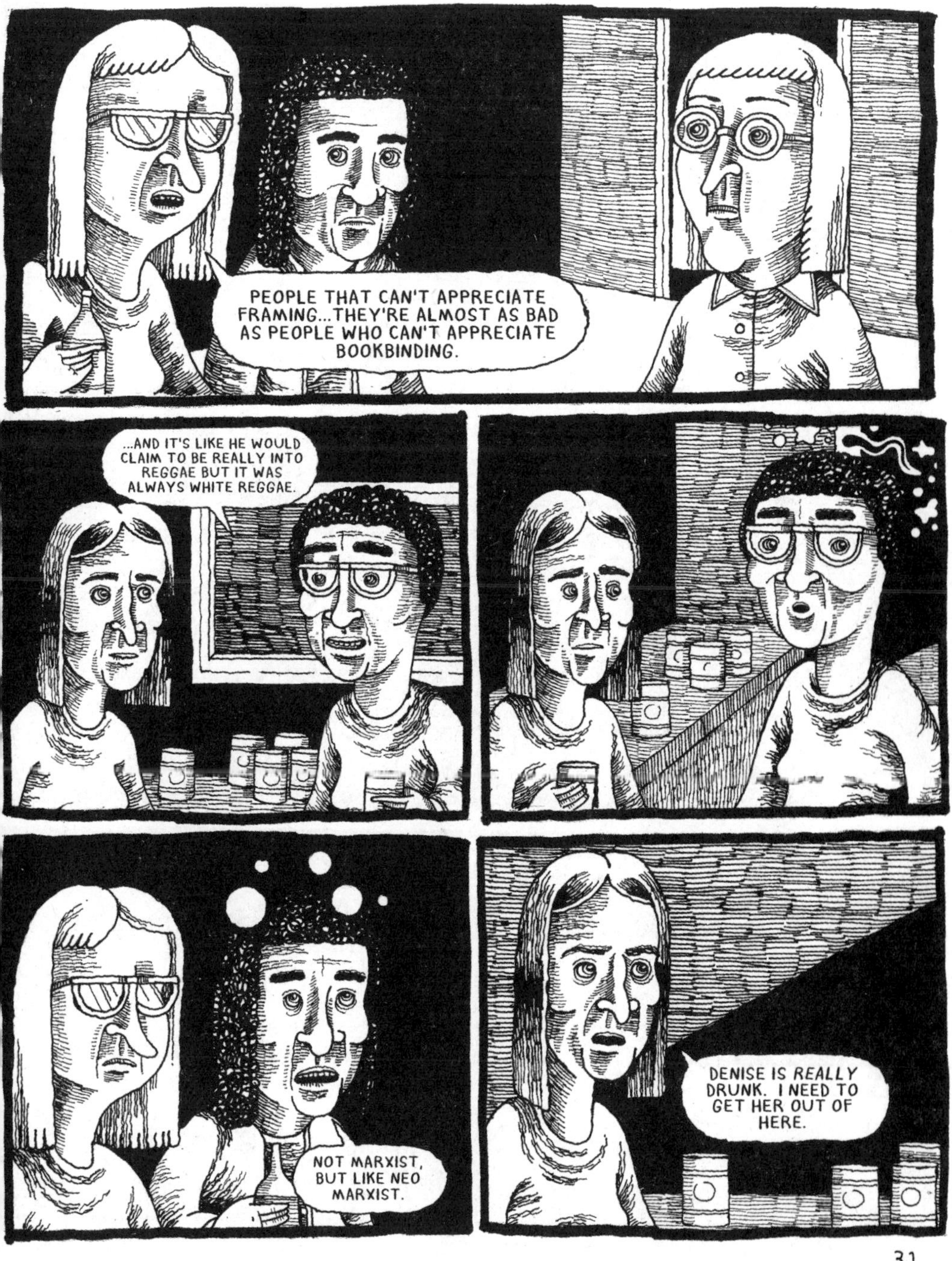
PEOPLE THAT CAN'T APPRECIATE FRAMING...THEY'RE ALMOST AS BAD AS PEOPLE WHO CAN'T APPRECIATE BOOKBINDING.
...AND IT'S LIKE HE WOULD CLAIM TO BE REALLY INTO REGGAE BUT IT WAS ALWAYS WHITE REGGAE.
NOT MARXIST, BUT LIKE NEO MARXIST.
DENISE IS *REALLY* DRUNK. I NEED TO GET HER OUT OF HERE.

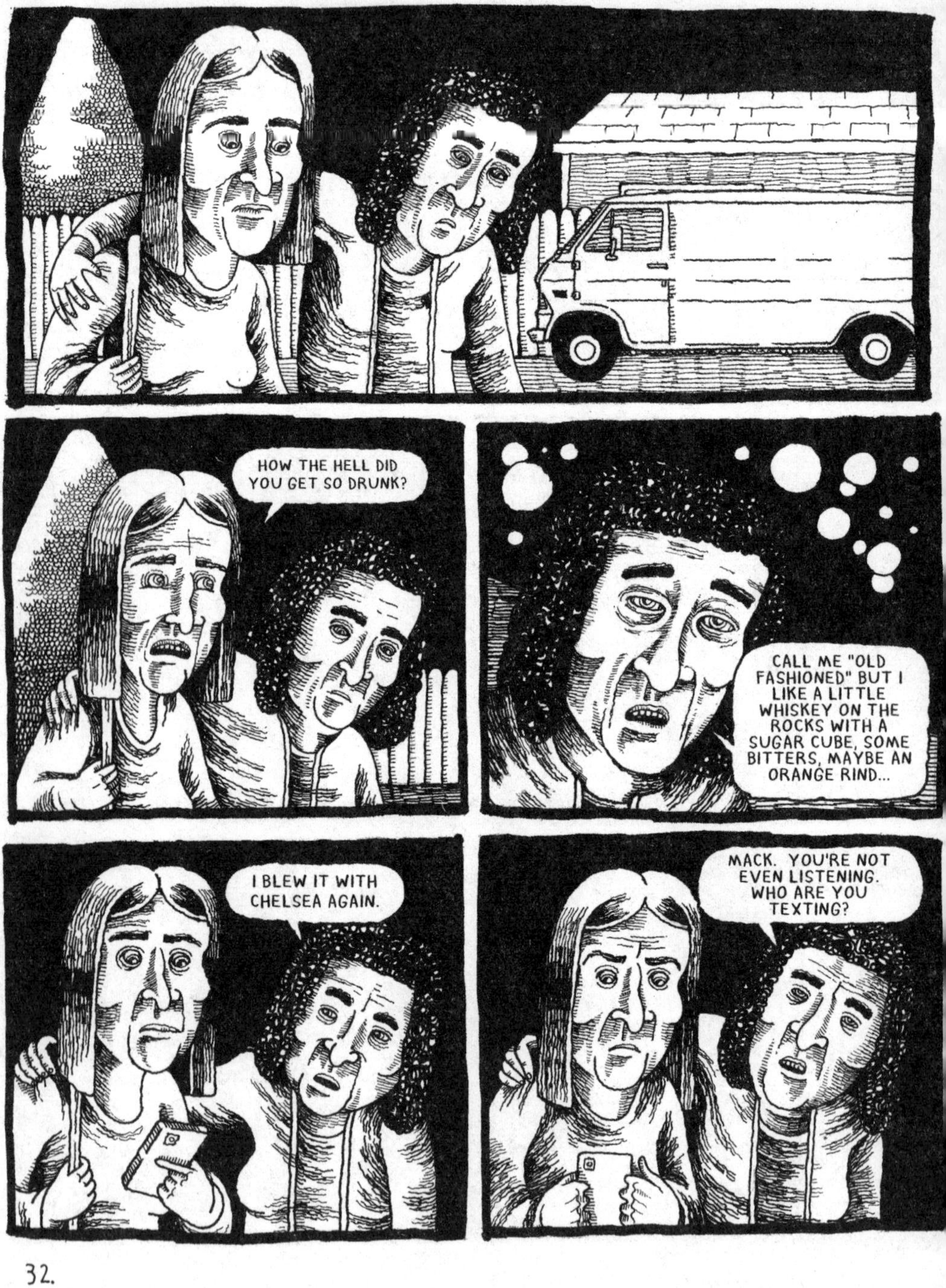
HOW THE HELL DID YOU GET SO DRUNK?
CALL ME "OLD FASHIONED" BUT I LIKE A LITTLE WHISKEY ON THE ROCKS WITH A SUGAR CUBE, SOME BITTERS, MAYBE AN ORANGE RIND...
I BLEW IT WITH CHELSEA AGAIN.
MACK. YOU'RE NOT EVEN LISTENING. WHO ARE YOU TEXTING?

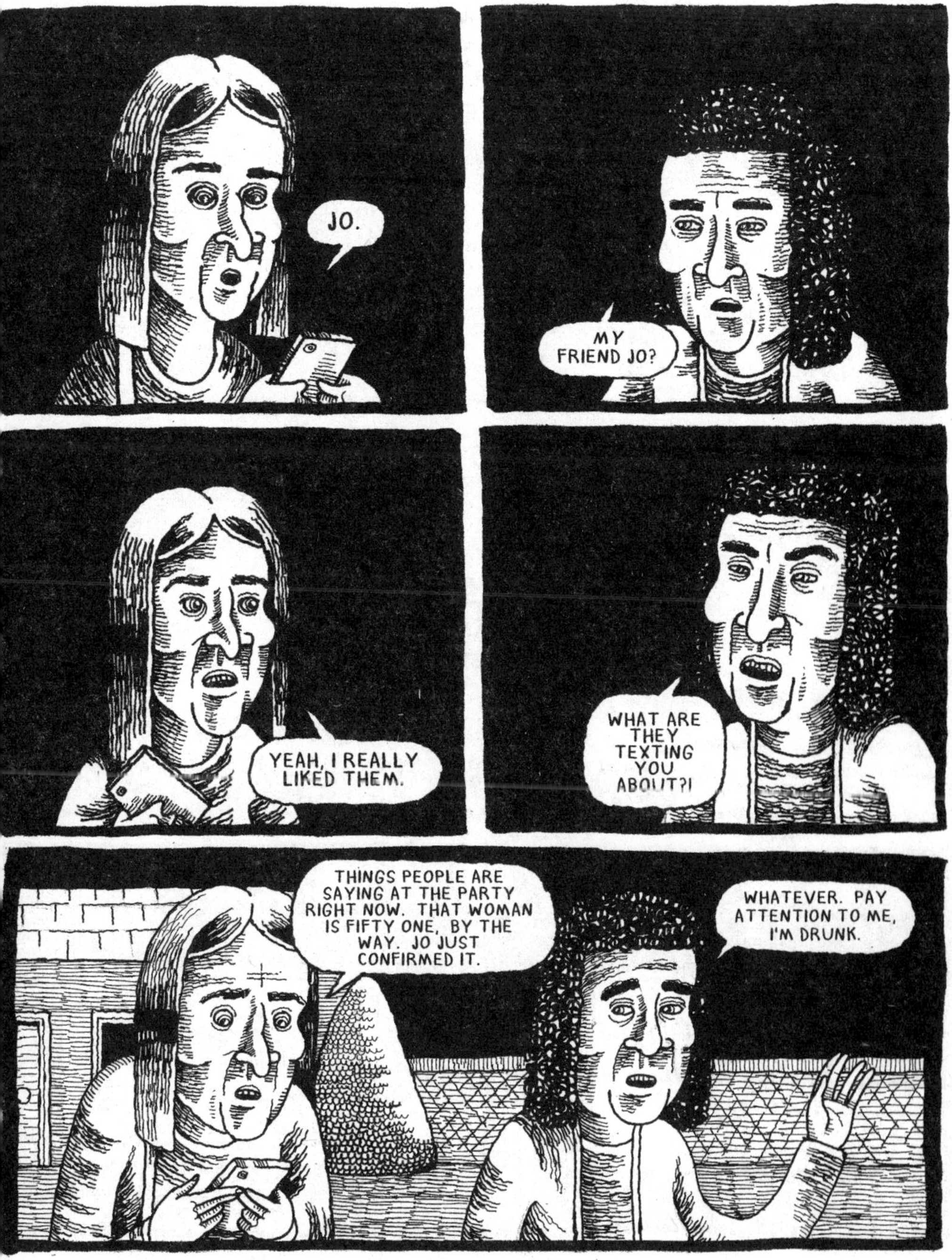
JO.
MY FRIEND JO?
YEAH, I REALLY LIKED THEM.
WHAT ARE THEY TEXTING YOU ABOUT?!
THINGS PEOPLE ARE SAYING AT THE PARTY RIGHT NOW. THAT WOMAN IS FIFTY ONE, BY THE WAY. JO JUST CONFIRMED IT.
WHATEVER. PAY ATTENTION TO ME, I'M DRUNK.

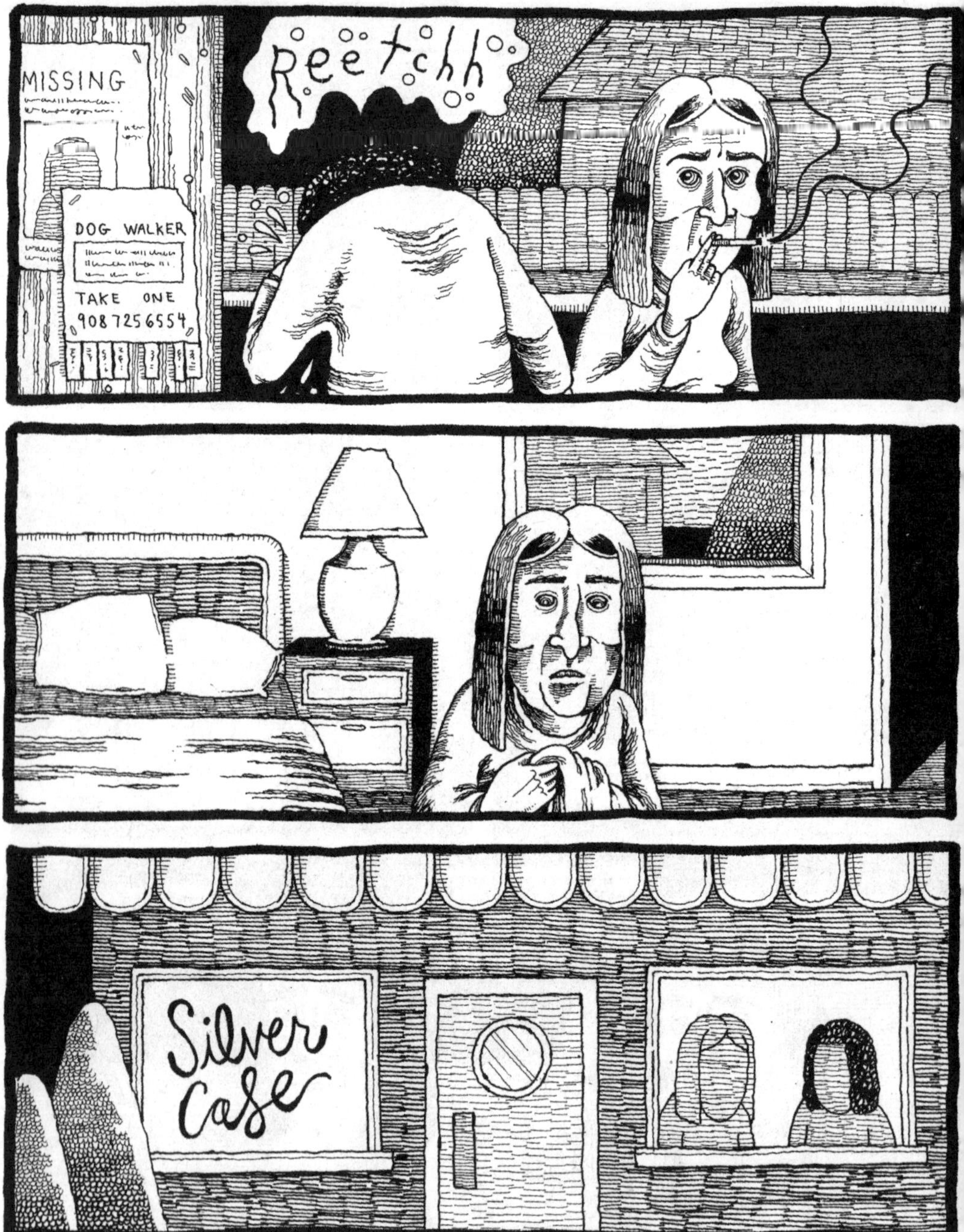
MISSING
DOG WALKER
TAKE ONE
908 725 6554
Reetchh
Silver Case

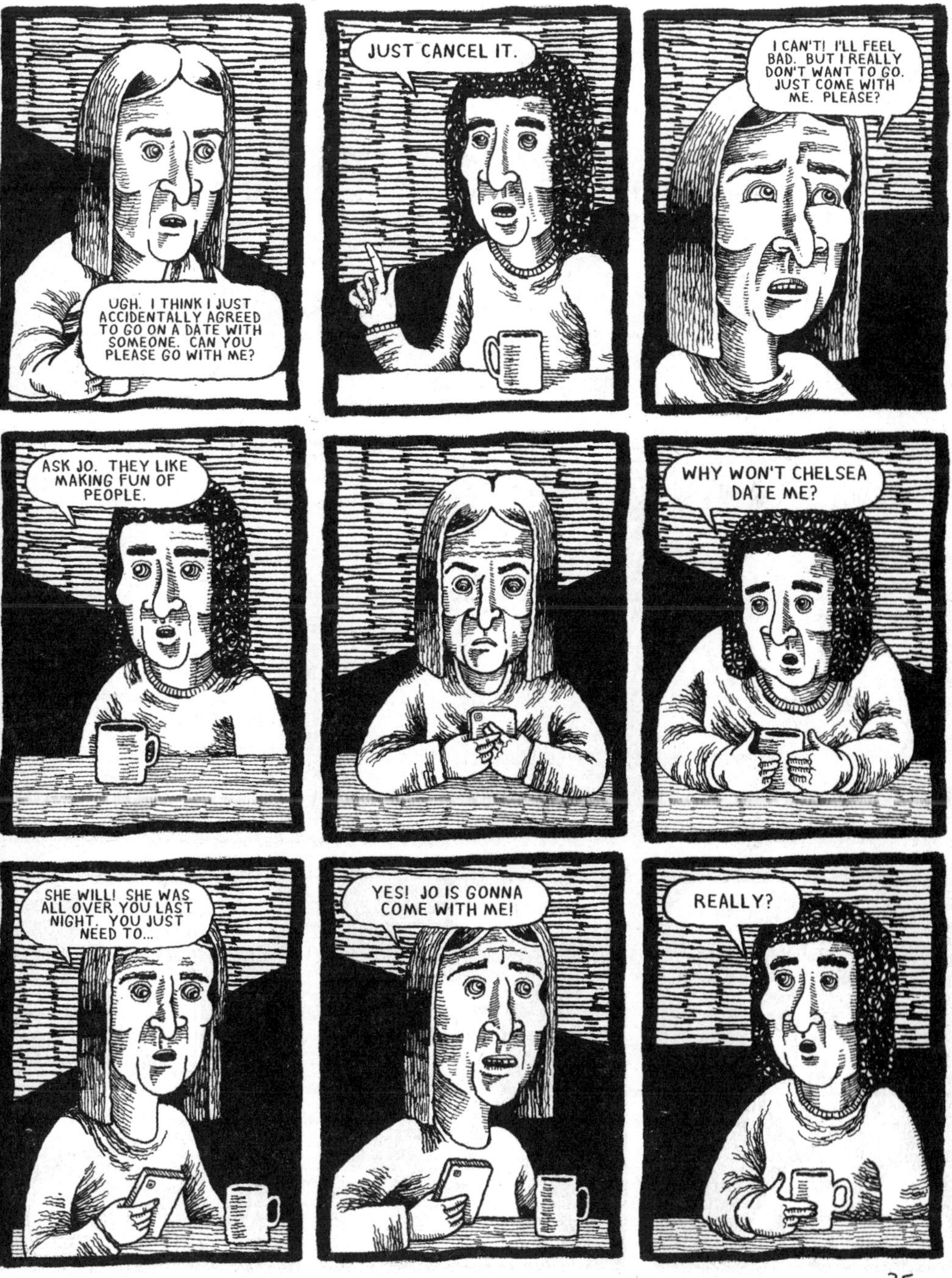
UGH. I THINK I JUST ACCIDENTALLY AGREED TO GO ON A DATE WITH SOMEONE. CAN YOU PLEASE GO WITH ME?
JUST CANCEL IT.
I CAN'T! I'LL FEEL BAD. BUT I REALLY DON'T WANT TO GO. JUST COME WITH ME. PLEASE?
ASK JO. THEY LIKE MAKING FUN OF PEOPLE.
WHY WON'T CHELSEA DATE ME?
SHE WILL! SHE WAS ALL OVER YOU LAST NIGHT. YOU JUST NEED TO...
YES! JO IS GONNA COME WITH ME!
REALLY?

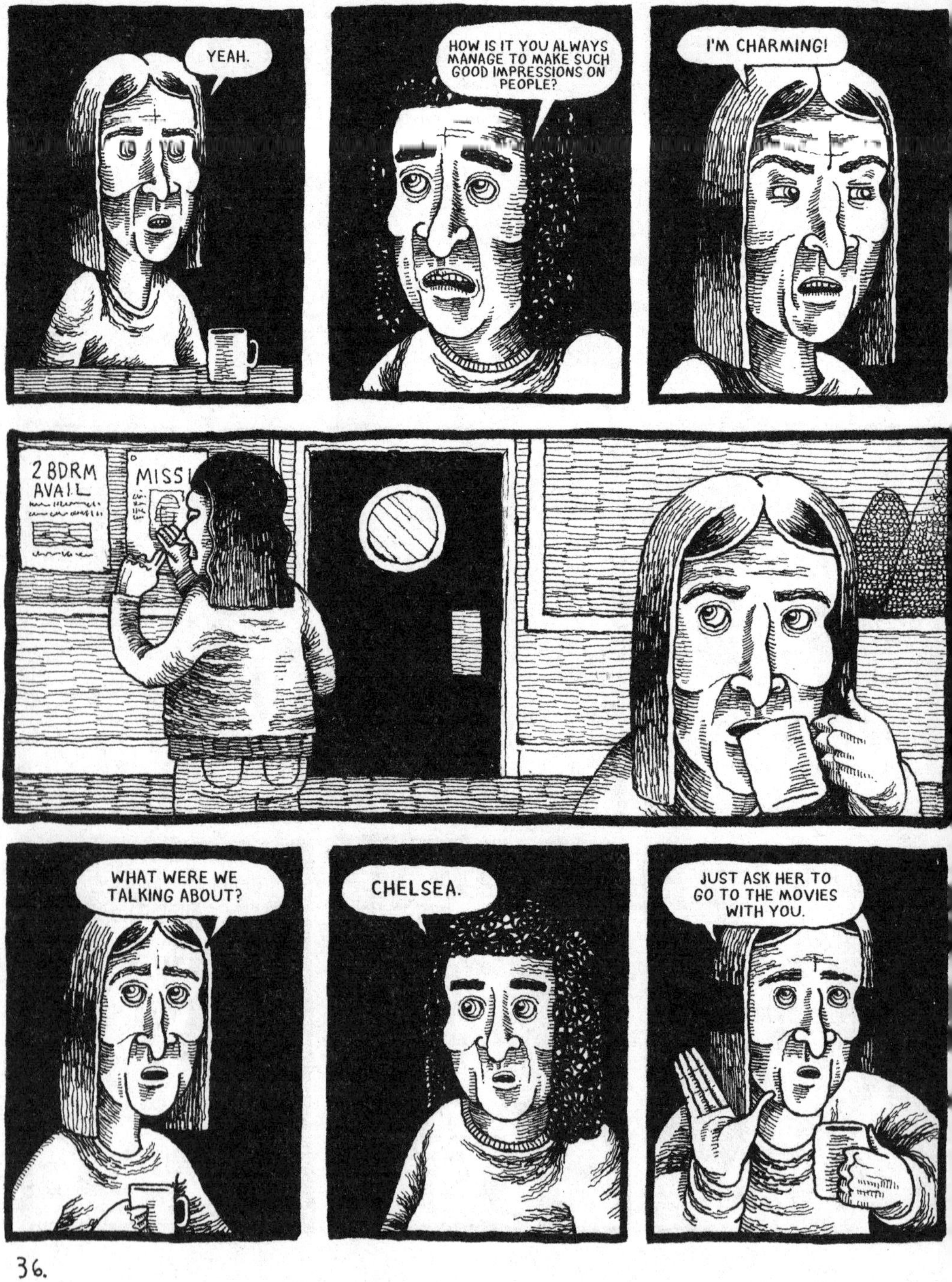
YEAH.
HOW IS IT YOU ALWAYS MANAGE TO MAKE SUCH GOOD IMPRESSIONS ON PEOPLE?
I'M CHARMING!
2 BDRM AVAIL
MISS
WHAT WERE WE TALKING ABOUT?
CHELSEA.
JUST ASK HER TO GO TO THE MOVIES WITH YOU.

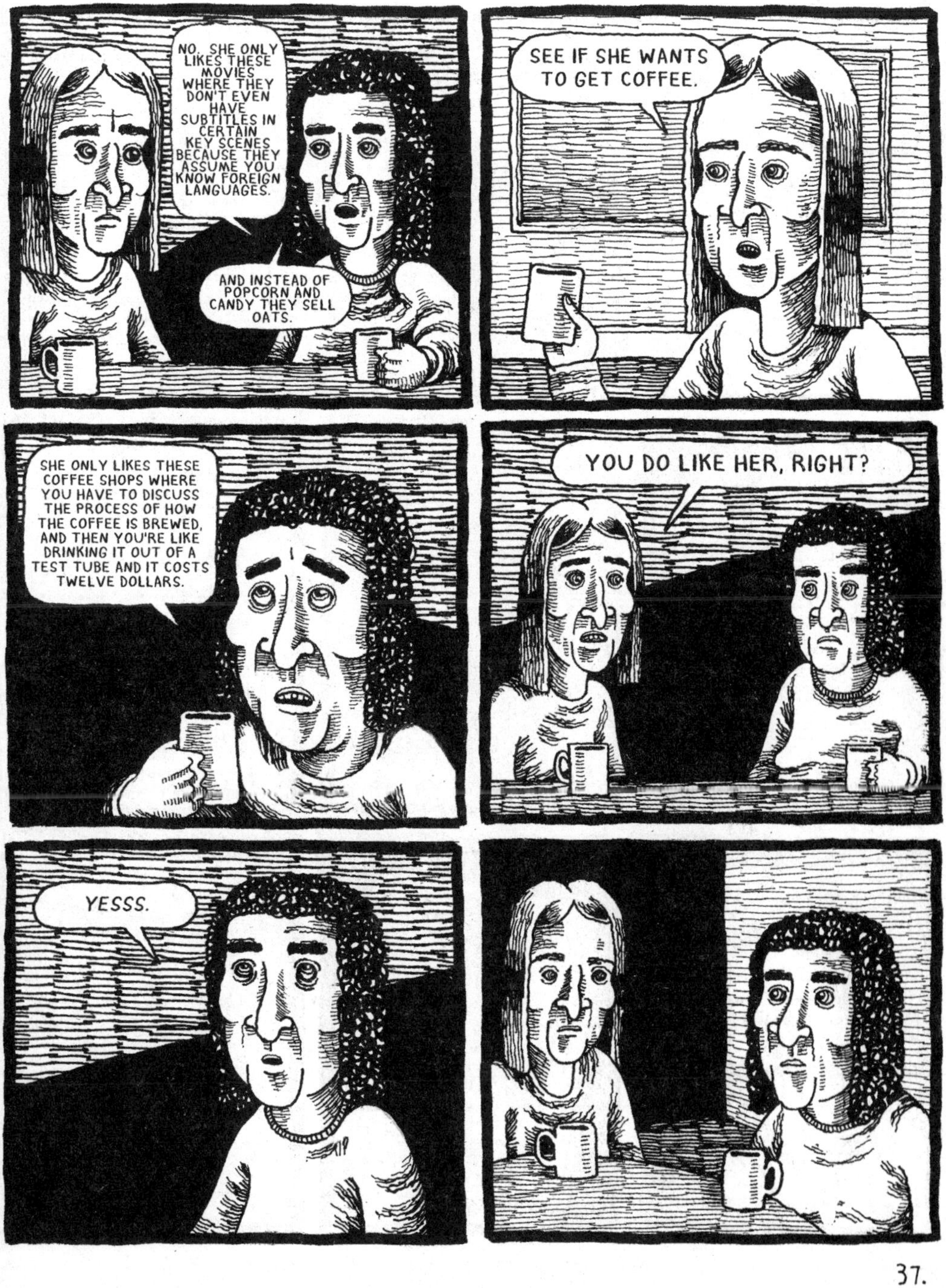
NO. SHE ONLY LIKES THESE MOVIES WHERE THEY DON'T EVEN HAVE SUBTITLES IN CERTAIN KEY SCENES BECAUSE THEY ASSUME YOU KNOW FOREIGN LANGUAGES.
AND INSTEAD OF POPCORN AND CANDY THEY SELL OATS.
SEE IF SHE WANTS TO GET COFFEE.
SHE ONLY LIKES THESE COFFEE SHOPS WHERE YOU HAVE TO DISCUSS THE PROCESS OF HOW THE COFFEE IS BREWED, AND THEN YOU'RE LIKE DRINKING IT OUT OF A TEST TUBE AND IT COSTS TWELVE DOLLARS.
YOU DO LIKE HER, RIGHT?
YESSS.

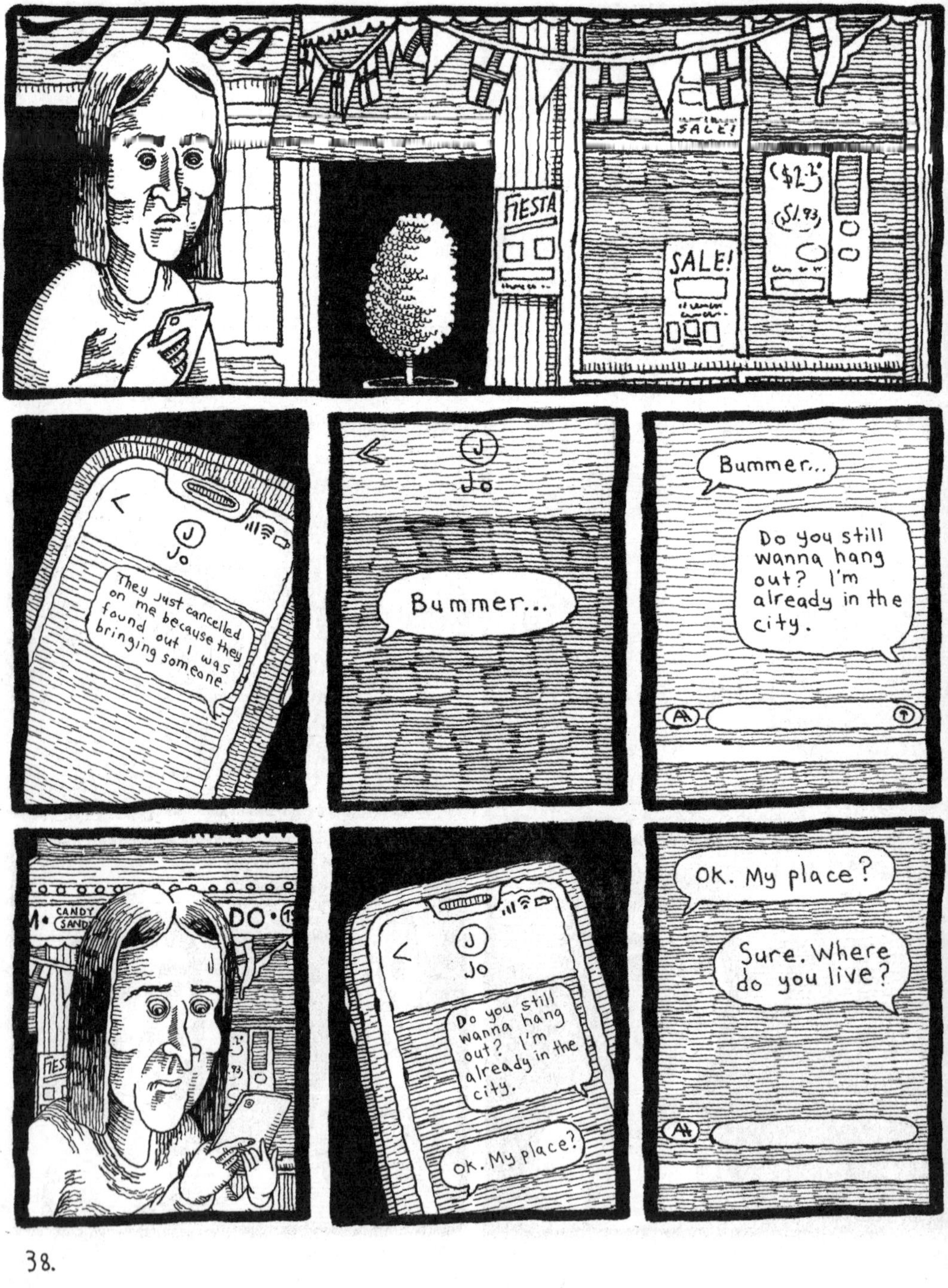
FIESTA
SALE!
SALE!
($2.2)
($1.93)
Jo
They just cancelled on me because they found out I was bringing someone.
Jo
Bummer...
Bummer...
Do you still wanna hang out? I'm already in the city.
CANDY
DO
FIES
Jo
Do you still wanna hang out? I'm already in the city.
OK. My place?
OK. My place?
Sure. Where do you live?

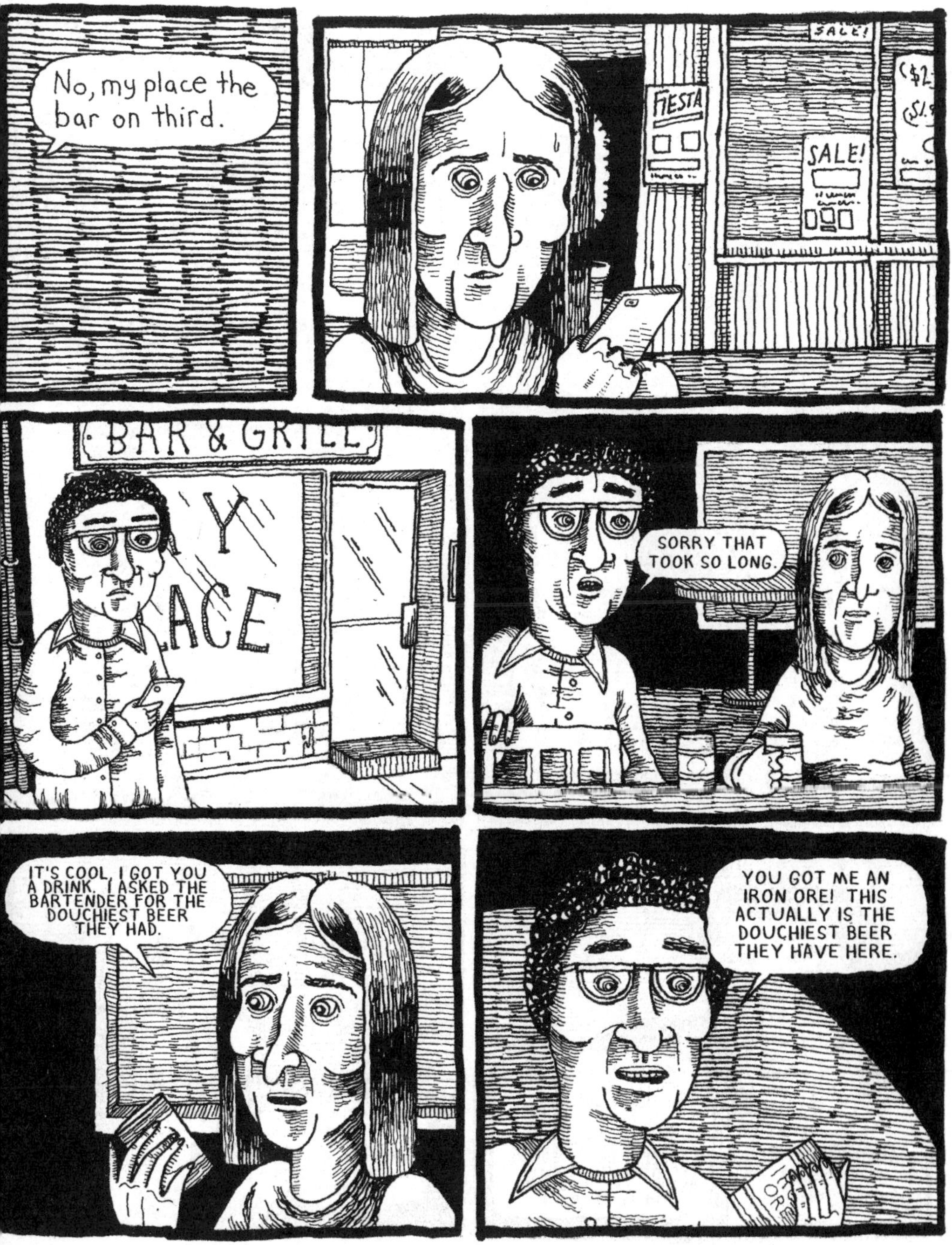
No, my place the bar on third.
FIESTA
SALE!
BAR & GRILL
SORRY THAT TOOK SO LONG.
IT'S COOL, I GOT YOU A DRINK. I ASKED THE BARTENDER FOR THE DOUCHIEST BEER THEY HAD.
YOU GOT ME AN IRON ORE! THIS ACTUALLY IS THE DOUCHIEST BEER THEY HAVE HERE.

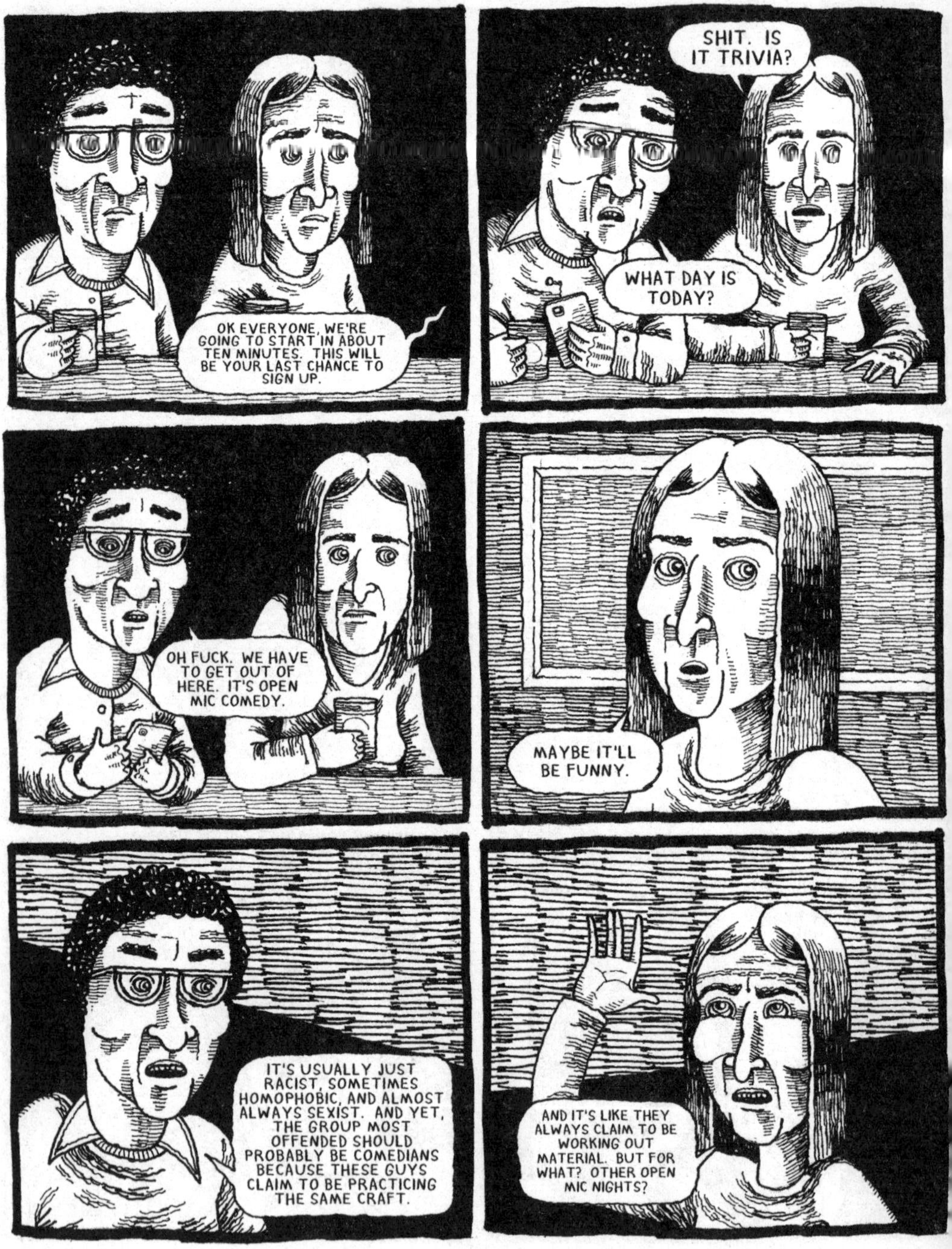
OK EVERYONE, WE'RE GOING TO START IN ABOUT TEN MINUTES. THIS WILL BE YOUR LAST CHANCE TO SIGN UP.
SHIT. IS IT TRIVIA?
WHAT DAY IS TODAY?
OH FUCK. WE HAVE TO GET OUT OF HERE. IT'S OPEN MIC COMEDY.
MAYBE IT'LL BE FUNNY.
IT'S USUALLY JUST RACIST, SOMETIMES HOMOPHOBIC, AND ALMOST ALWAYS SEXIST. AND YET, THE GROUP MOST OFFENDED SHOULD PROBABLY BE COMEDIANS BECAUSE THESE GUYS CLAIM TO BE PRACTICING THE SAME CRAFT.
AND IT'S LIKE THEY ALWAYS CLAIM TO BE WORKING OUT MATERIAL. BUT FOR WHAT? OTHER OPEN MIC NIGHTS?

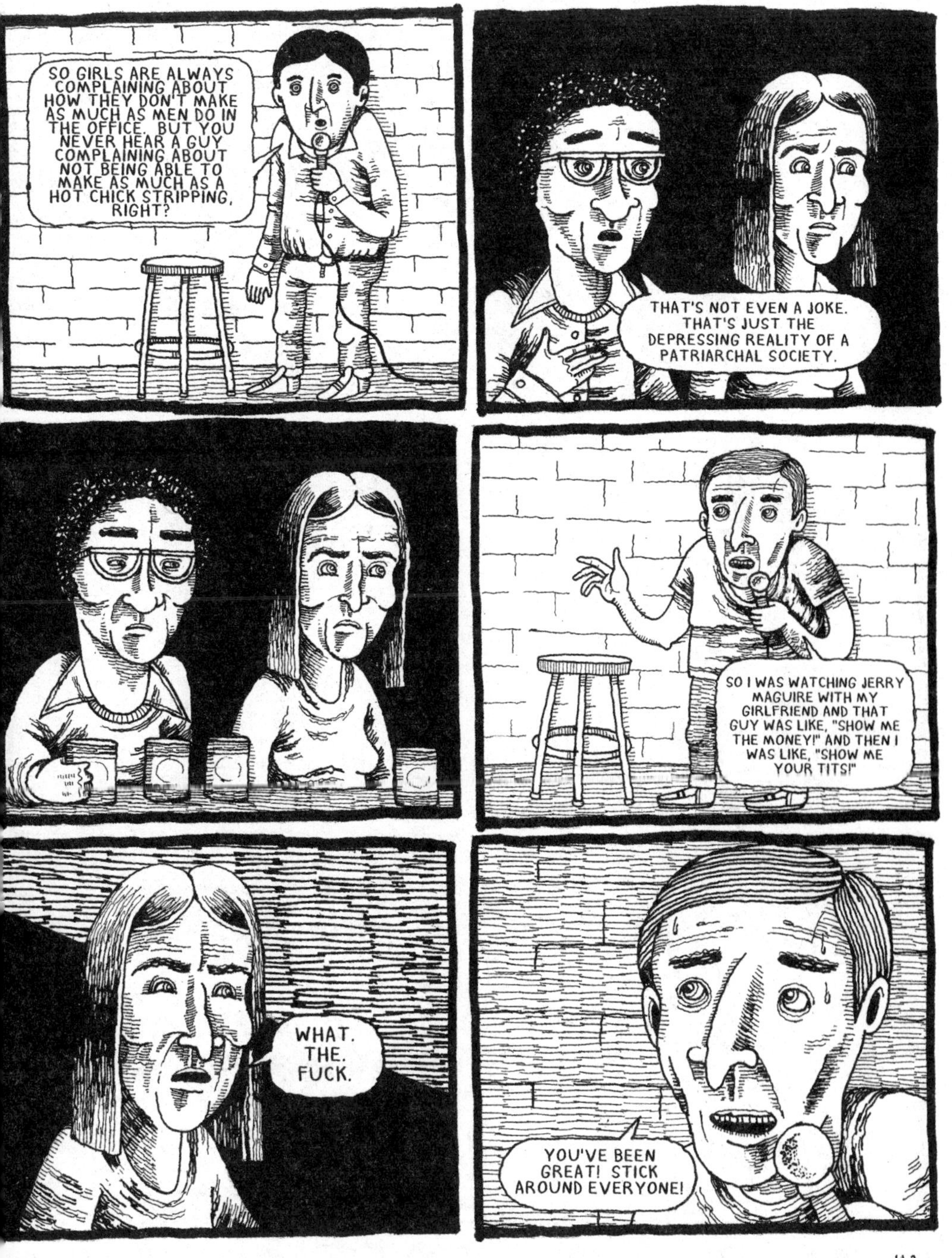
SO GIRLS ARE ALWAYS COMPLAINING ABOUT HOW THEY DON'T MAKE AS MUCH AS MEN DO IN THE OFFICE. BUT YOU NEVER HEAR A GUY COMPLAINING ABOUT NOT BEING ABLE TO MAKE AS MUCH AS A HOT CHICK STRIPPING, RIGHT?
THAT'S NOT EVEN A JOKE. THAT'S JUST THE DEPRESSING REALITY OF A PATRIARCHAL SOCIETY.
SO I WAS WATCHING JERRY MAGUIRE WITH MY GIRLFRIEND AND THAT GUY WAS LIKE, "SHOW ME THE MONEY!" AND THEN I WAS LIKE, "SHOW ME YOUR TITS!"
WHAT. THE. FUCK.
YOU'VE BEEN GREAT! STICK AROUND EVERYONE!

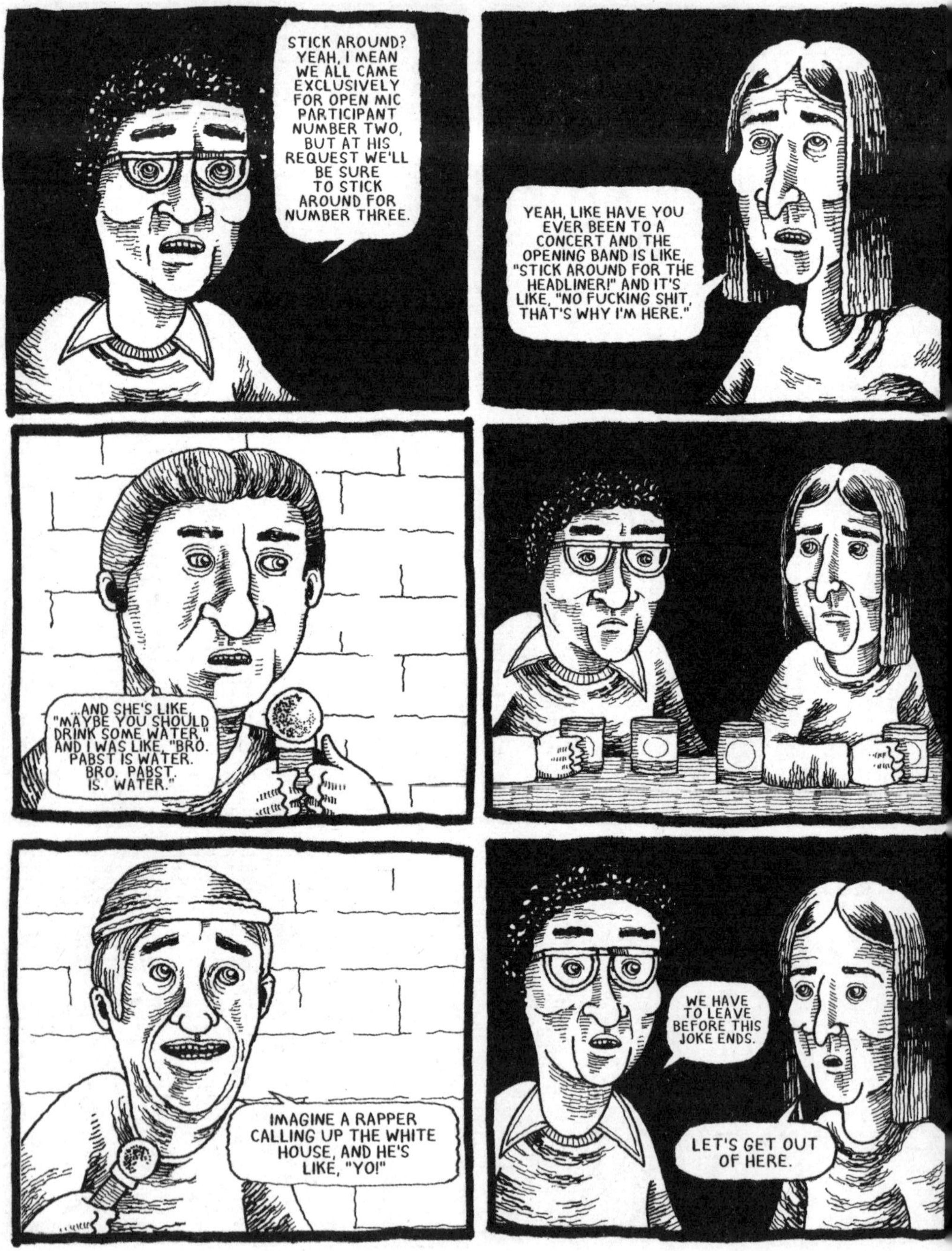
STICK AROUND? YEAH, I MEAN WE ALL CAME EXCLUSIVELY FOR OPEN MIC PARTICIPANT NUMBER TWO, BUT AT HIS REQUEST WE'LL BE SURE TO STICK AROUND FOR NUMBER THREE.
YEAH, LIKE HAVE YOU EVER BEEN TO A CONCERT AND THE OPENING BAND IS LIKE, "STICK AROUND FOR THE HEADLINER!" AND IT'S LIKE, "NO FUCKING SHIT, THAT'S WHY I'M HERE."
...AND SHE'S LIKE, "MAYBE YOU SHOULD DRINK SOME WATER," AND I WAS LIKE, "BRO. PABST IS WATER. BRO. PABST. IS. WATER."
IMAGINE A RAPPER CALLING UP THE WHITE HOUSE, AND HE'S LIKE, "YO!"
WE HAVE TO LEAVE BEFORE THIS JOKE ENDS.
LET'S GET OUT OF HERE.

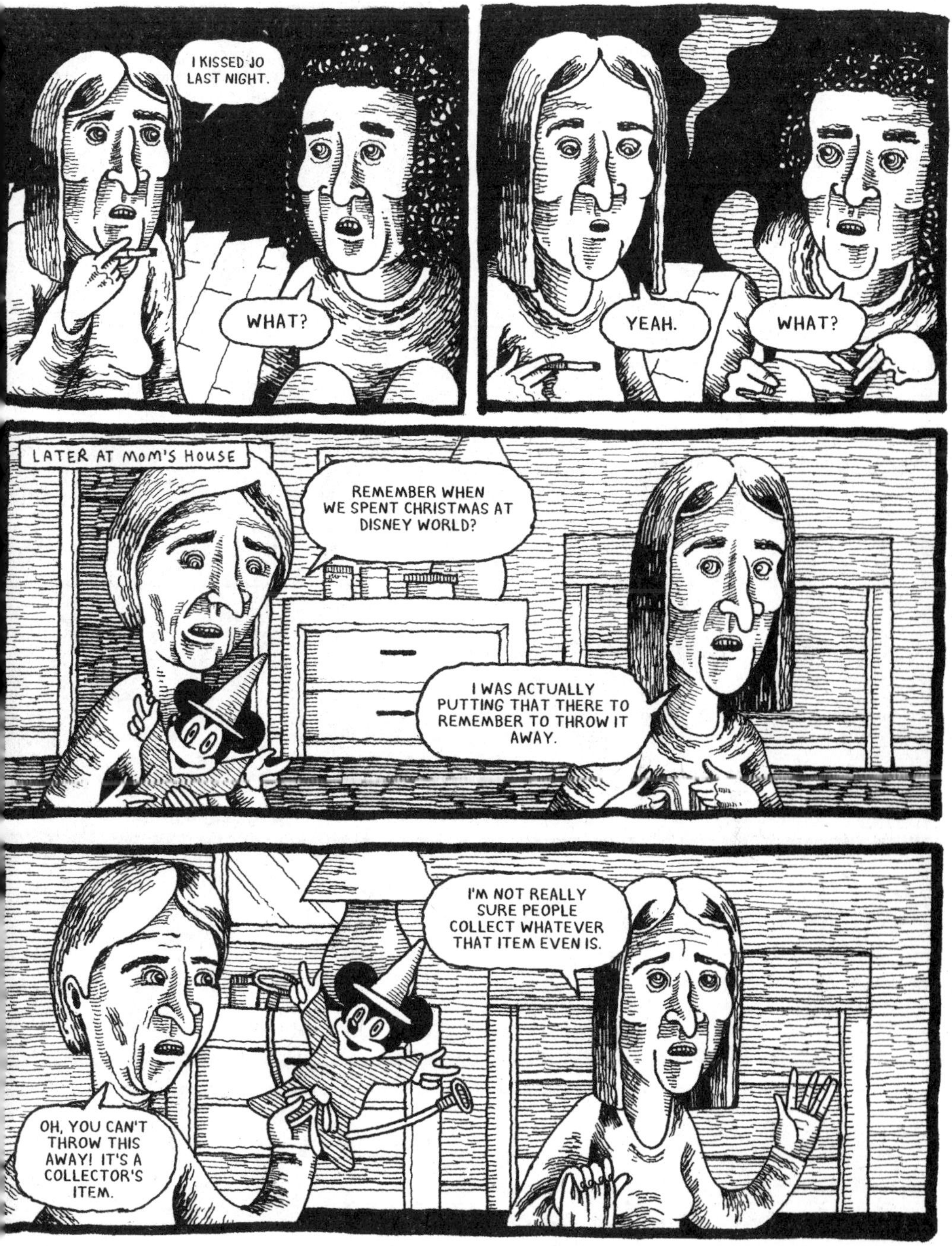
I KISSED JO LAST NIGHT.
WHAT?
YEAH.
WHAT?
LATER AT MOM'S HOUSE
REMEMBER WHEN WE SPENT CHRISTMAS AT DISNEY WORLD?
I WAS ACTUALLY PUTTING THAT THERE TO REMEMBER TO THROW IT AWAY.
I'M NOT REALLY SURE PEOPLE COLLECT WHATEVER THAT ITEM EVEN IS.
OH, YOU CAN'T THROW THIS AWAY! IT'S A COLLECTOR'S ITEM.

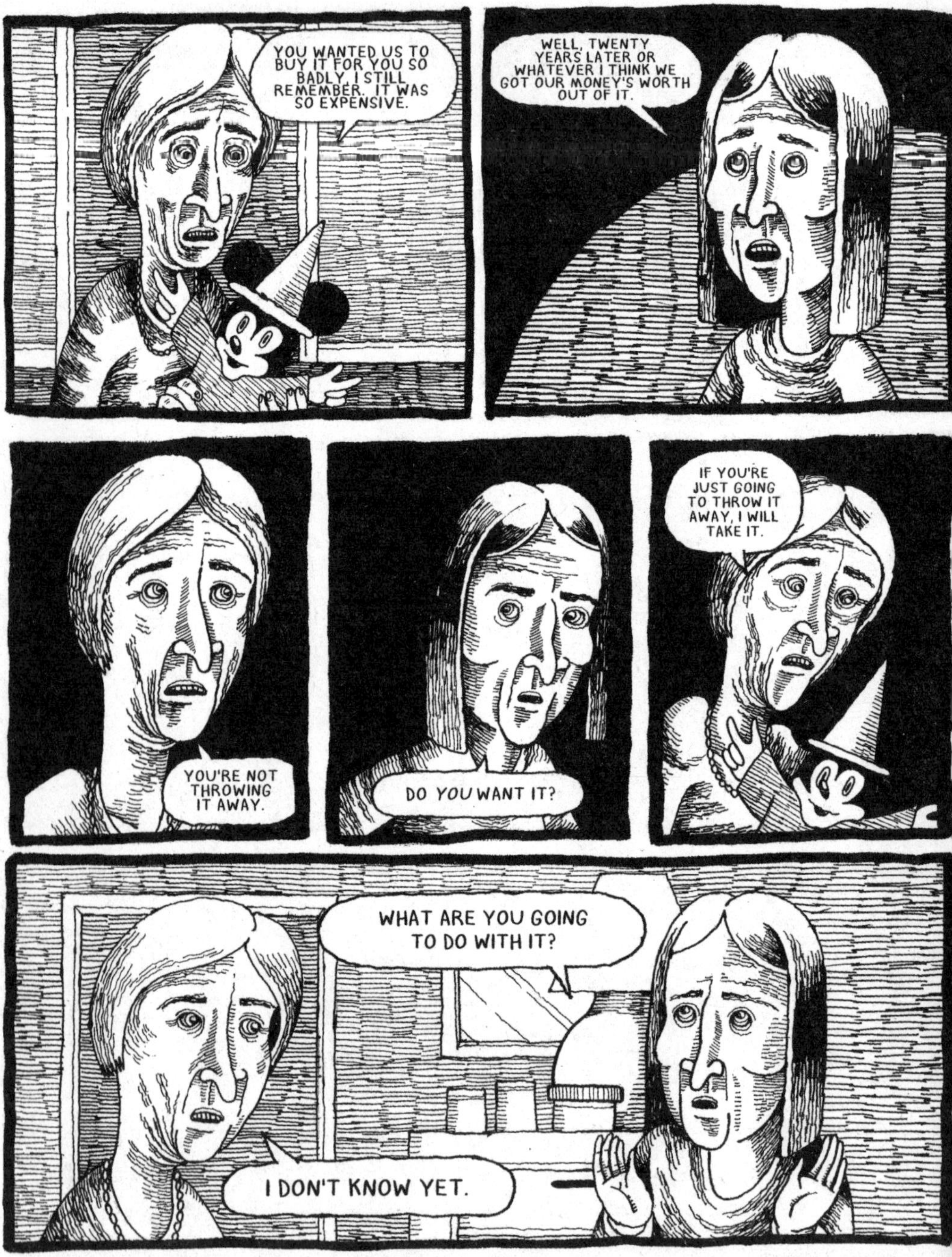
YOU WANTED US TO BUY IT FOR YOU SO BADLY, I STILL REMEMBER. IT WAS SO EXPENSIVE.
WELL, TWENTY YEARS LATER OR WHATEVER I THINK WE GOT OUR MONEY'S WORTH OUT OF IT.
YOU'RE NOT THROWING IT AWAY.
DO *YOU* WANT IT?
IF YOU'RE JUST *GOING* TO THROW IT AWAY, I WILL TAKE IT.
WHAT ARE YOU GOING TO DO WITH IT?
I DON'T KNOW YET.

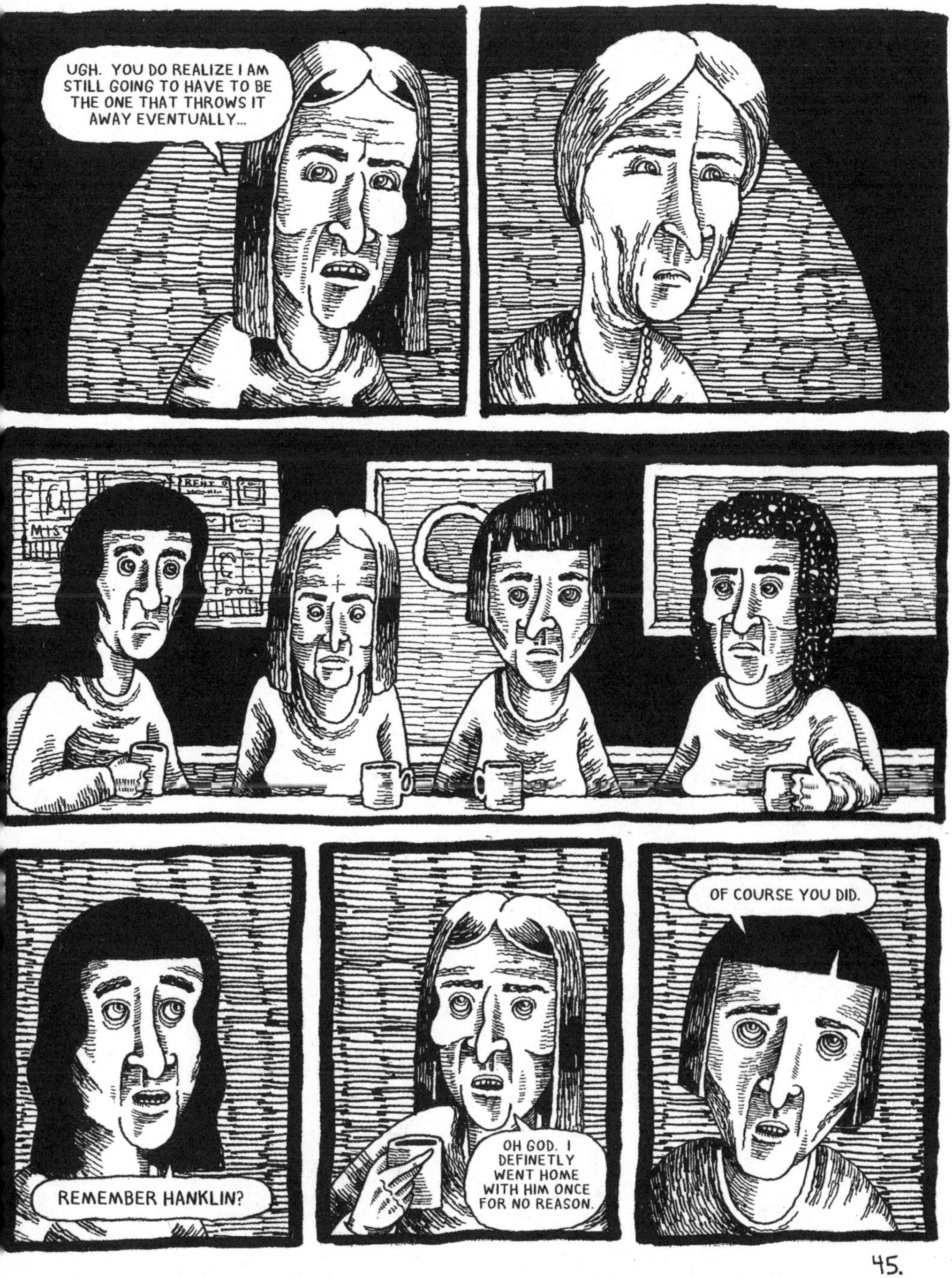
UGH. YOU DO REALIZE I AM STILL GOING TO HAVE TO BE THE ONE THAT THROWS IT AWAY EVENTUALLY...
REMEMBER HANKLIN?
OH GOD. I DEFINETLY WENT HOME WITH HIM ONCE FOR NO REASON.
OF COURSE YOU DID.

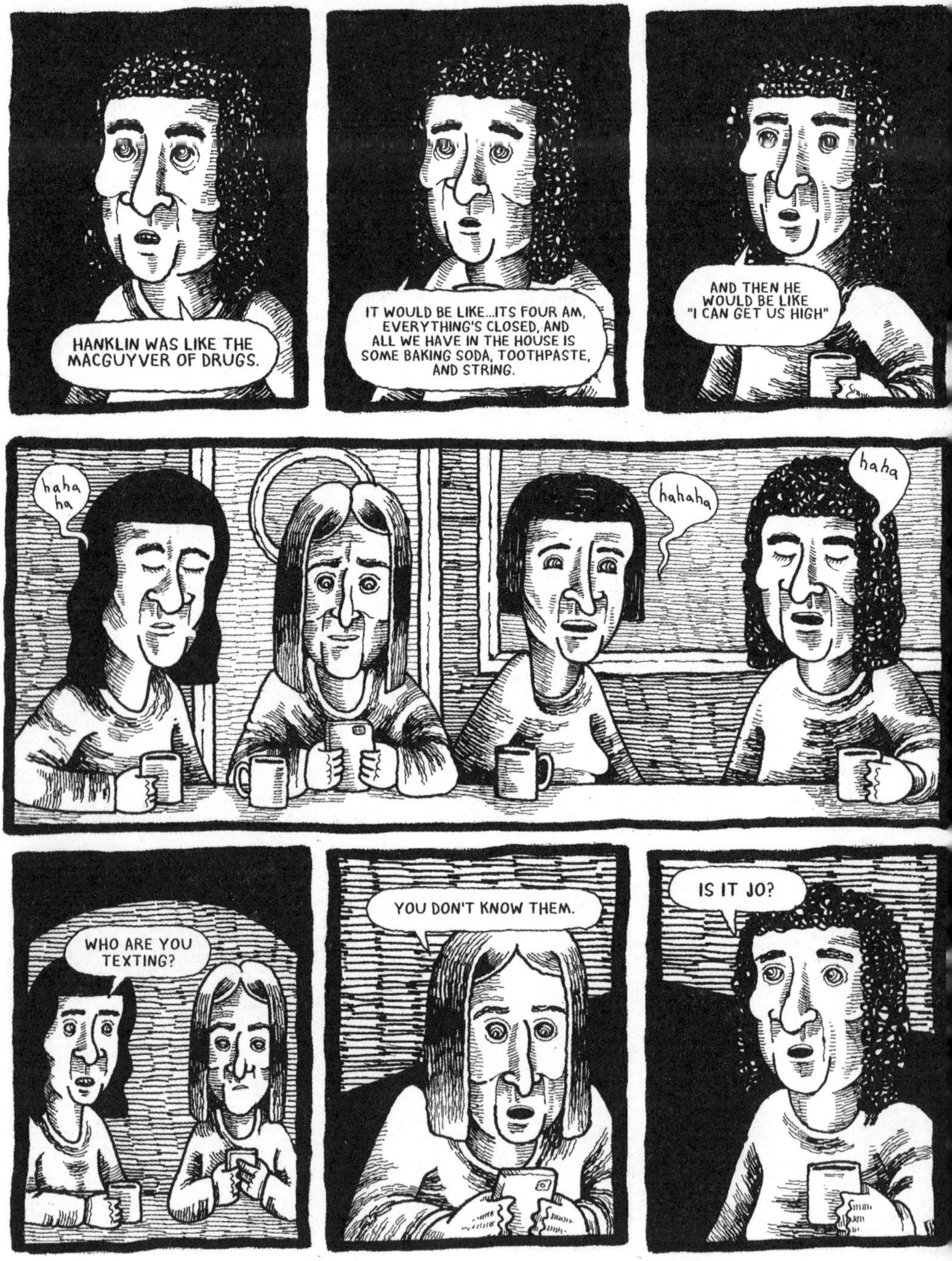
HANKLIN WAS LIKE THE MACGUYVER OF DRUGS.
IT WOULD BE LIKE...ITS FOUR AM, EVERYTHING'S CLOSED, AND ALL WE HAVE IN THE HOUSE IS SOME BAKING SODA, TOOTHPASTE, AND STRING.
AND THEN HE WOULD BE LIKE "I CAN GET US HIGH"
haha ha
hahaha
haha
WHO ARE YOU TEXTING?
YOU DON'T KNOW THEM.
IS IT JO?

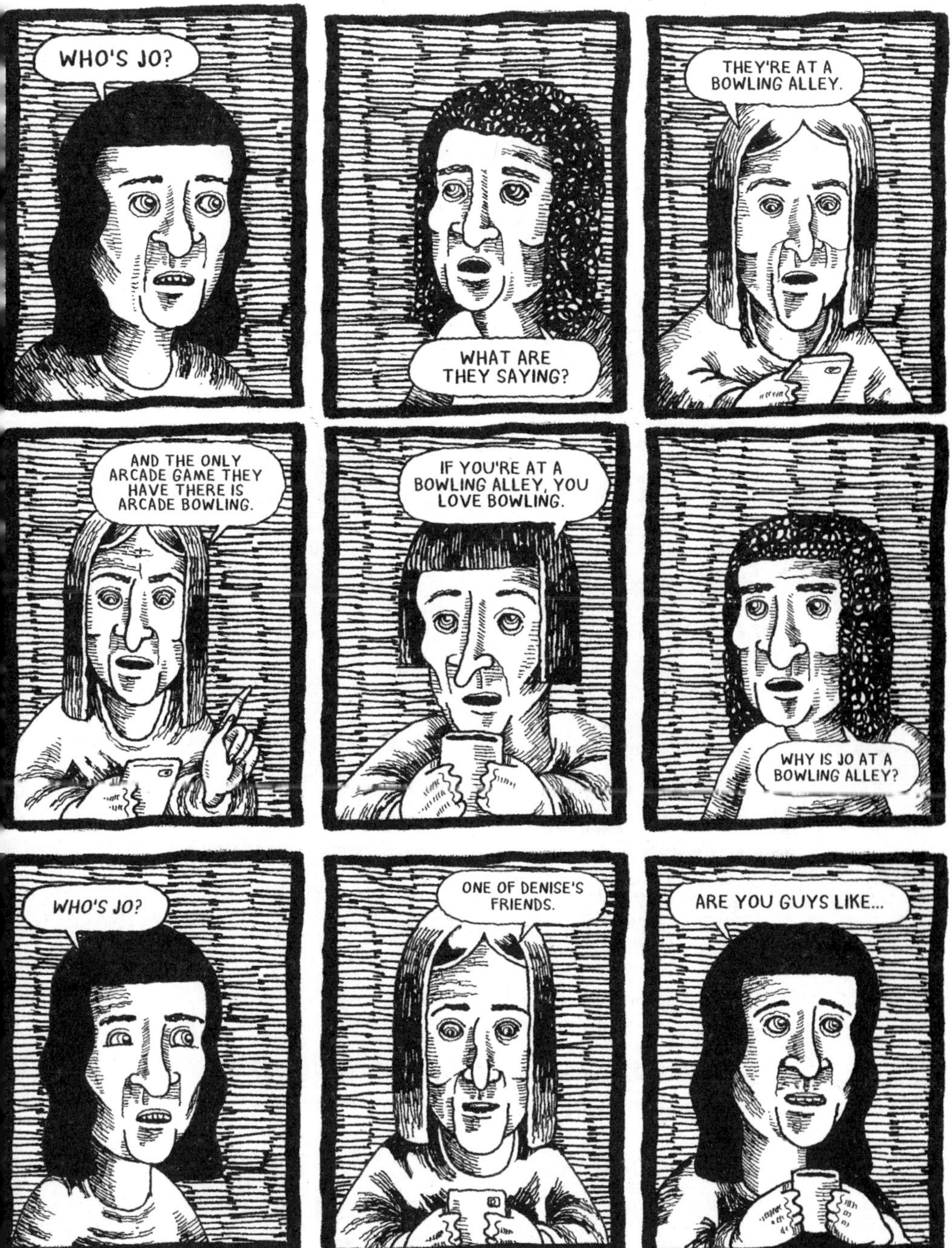
WHO'S JO?
WHAT ARE THEY SAYING?
THEY'RE AT A BOWLING ALLEY.
AND THE ONLY ARCADE GAME THEY HAVE THERE IS ARCADE BOWLING.
IF YOU'RE AT A BOWLING ALLEY, YOU LOVE BOWLING.
WHY IS JO AT A BOWLING ALLEY?
WHO'S JO?
ONE OF DENISE'S FRIENDS.
ARE YOU GUYS LIKE...

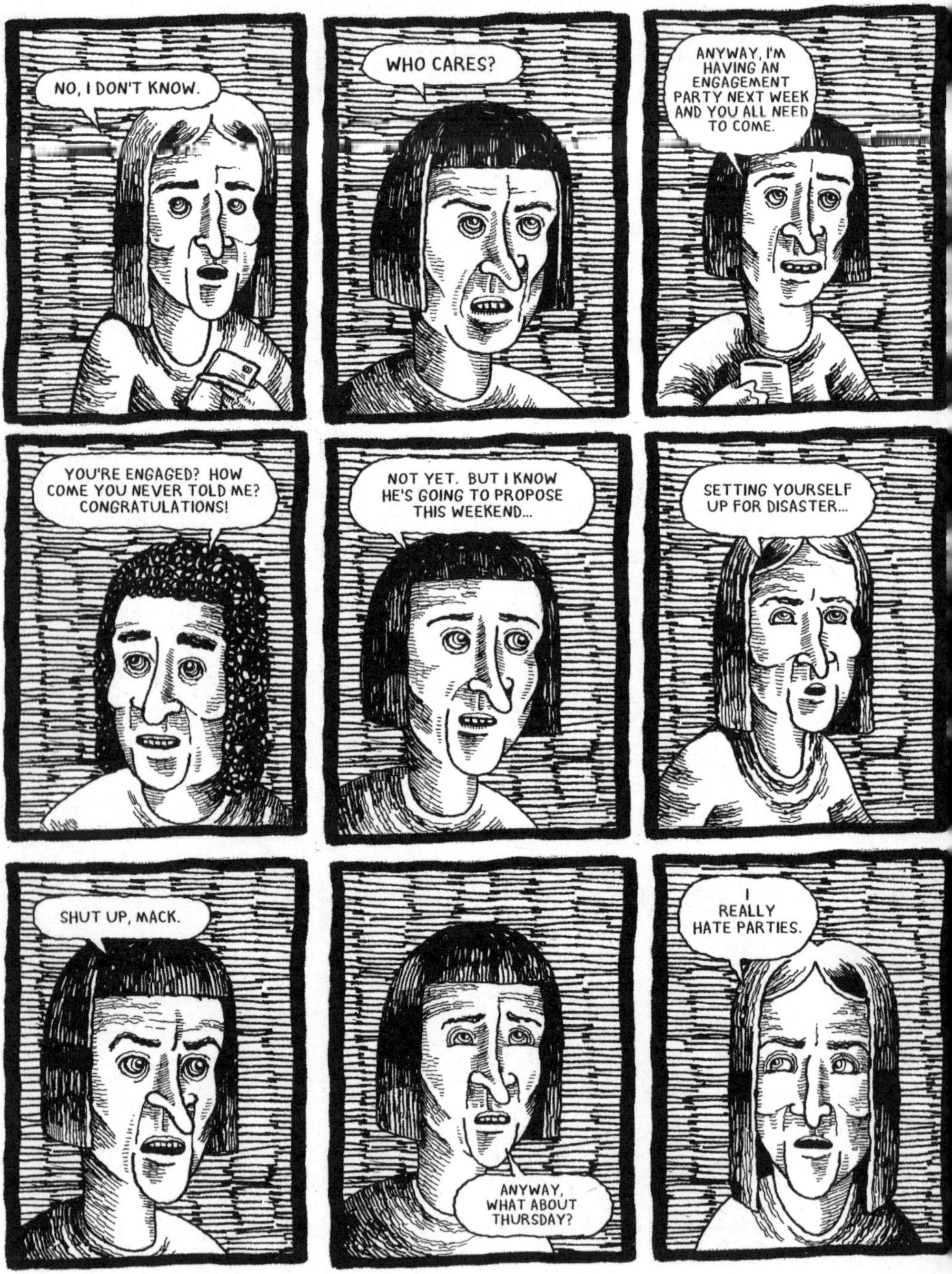
NO, I DON'T KNOW.
WHO CARES?
ANYWAY, I'M HAVING AN ENGAGEMENT PARTY NEXT WEEK AND YOU ALL NEED TO COME.
YOU'RE ENGAGED? HOW COME YOU NEVER TOLD ME? CONGRATULATIONS!
NOT YET. BUT I KNOW HE'S GOING TO PROPOSE THIS WEEKEND...
SETTING YOURSELF UP FOR DISASTER...
SHUT UP, MACK.
ANYWAY, WHAT ABOUT THURSDAY?
I REALLY HATE PARTIES.

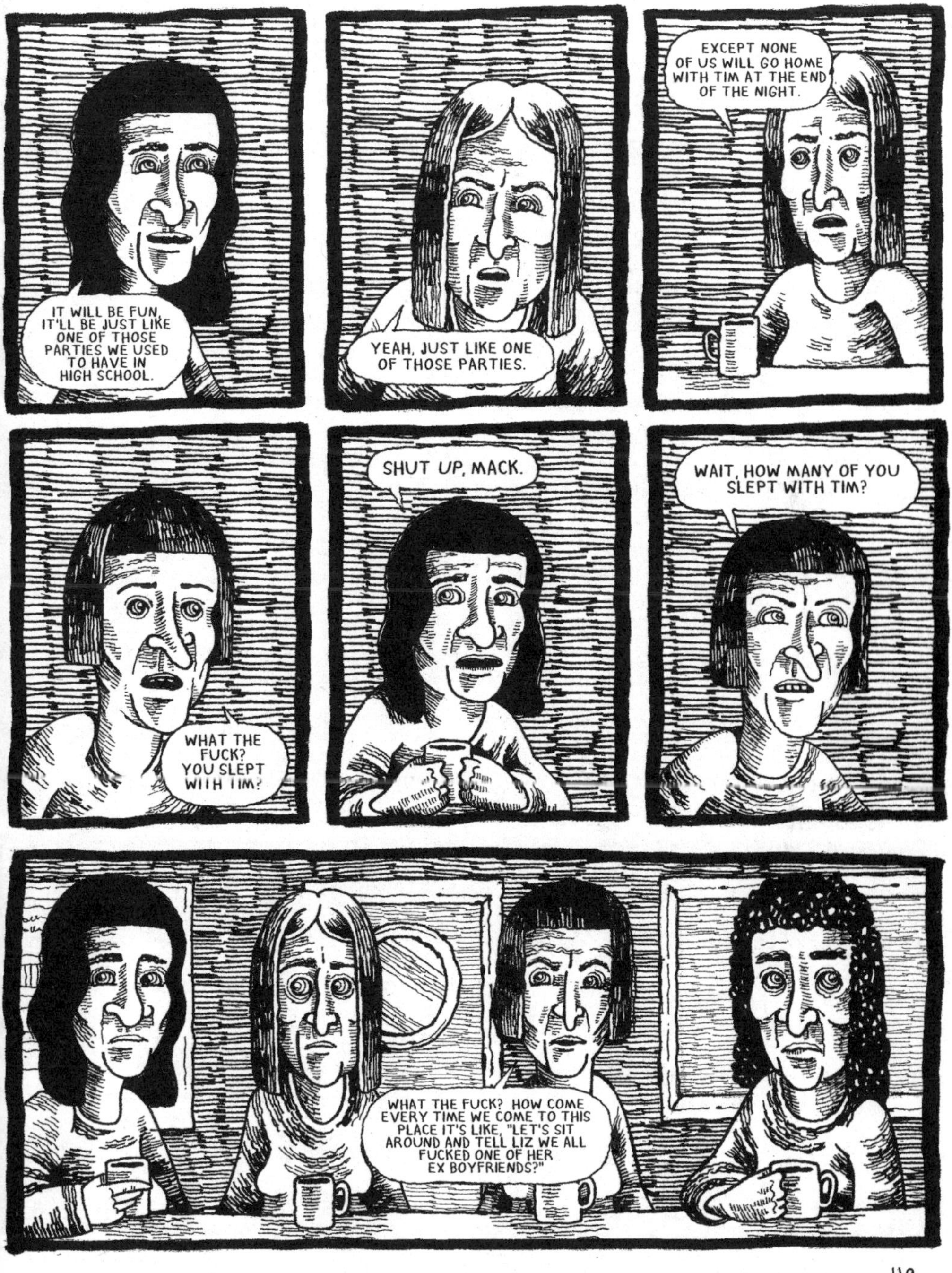
IT WILL BE FUN, IT'LL BE JUST LIKE ONE OF THOSE PARTIES WE USED TO HAVE IN HIGH SCHOOL.
YEAH, JUST LIKE ONE OF THOSE PARTIES.
EXCEPT NONE OF US WILL GO HOME WITH TIM AT THE END OF THE NIGHT.
WHAT THE FUCK? YOU SLEPT WITH TIM?
SHUT *UP*, MACK.
WAIT, HOW MANY OF YOU SLEPT WITH TIM?
WHAT THE FUCK? HOW COME EVERY TIME WE COME TO THIS PLACE IT'S LIKE, "LET'S SIT AROUND AND TELL LIZ WE ALL FUCKED ONE OF HER EX BOYFRIENDS?"

EVERYONE SLEPT WITH TIM IN HIGH SCHOOL FOR SOME REASON.
THAT'S GROSS. AND REALLY NOT HELPING. WHAT THE FUCK!
MIS
ENT
MISSING
NT
ING
...AND COULD BE IN DANGER. AFTER GOING MISSING IN MIDDLESEX COUNTY ON SATURDAY...

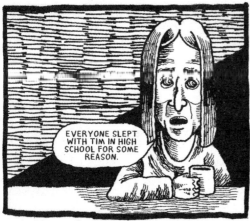

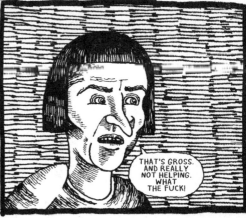

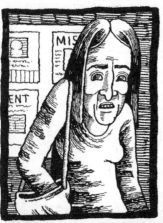

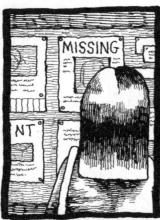

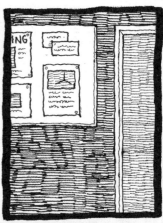

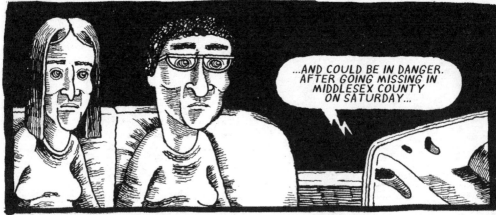

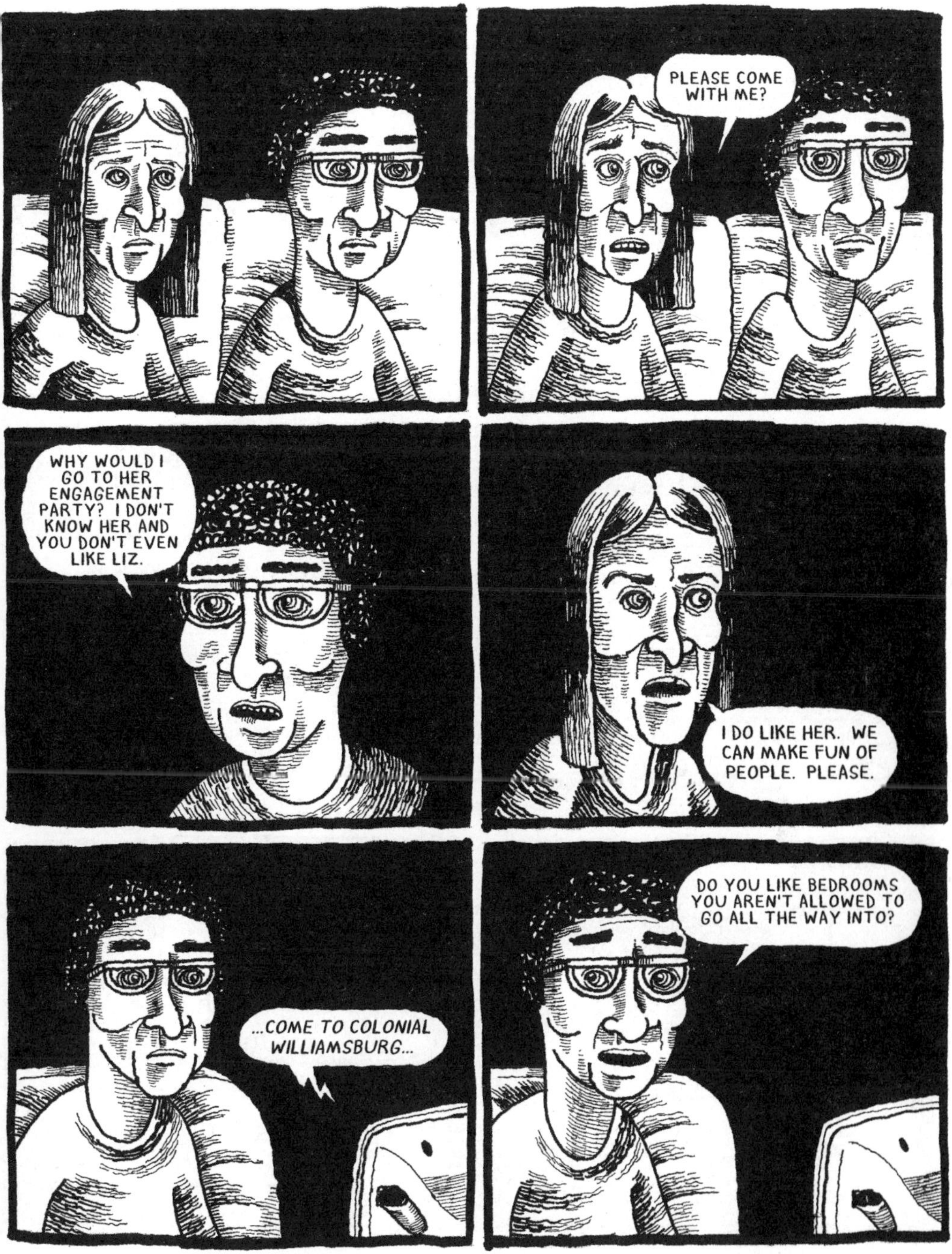
PLEASE COME WITH ME?
WHY WOULD I GO TO HER ENGAGEMENT PARTY? I DON'T KNOW HER AND YOU DON'T EVEN LIKE LIZ.
I DO LIKE HER. WE CAN MAKE FUN OF PEOPLE. PLEASE.
...COME TO COLONIAL WILLIAMSBURG...
DO YOU LIKE BEDROOMS YOU AREN'T ALLOWED TO GO ALL THE WAY INTO?

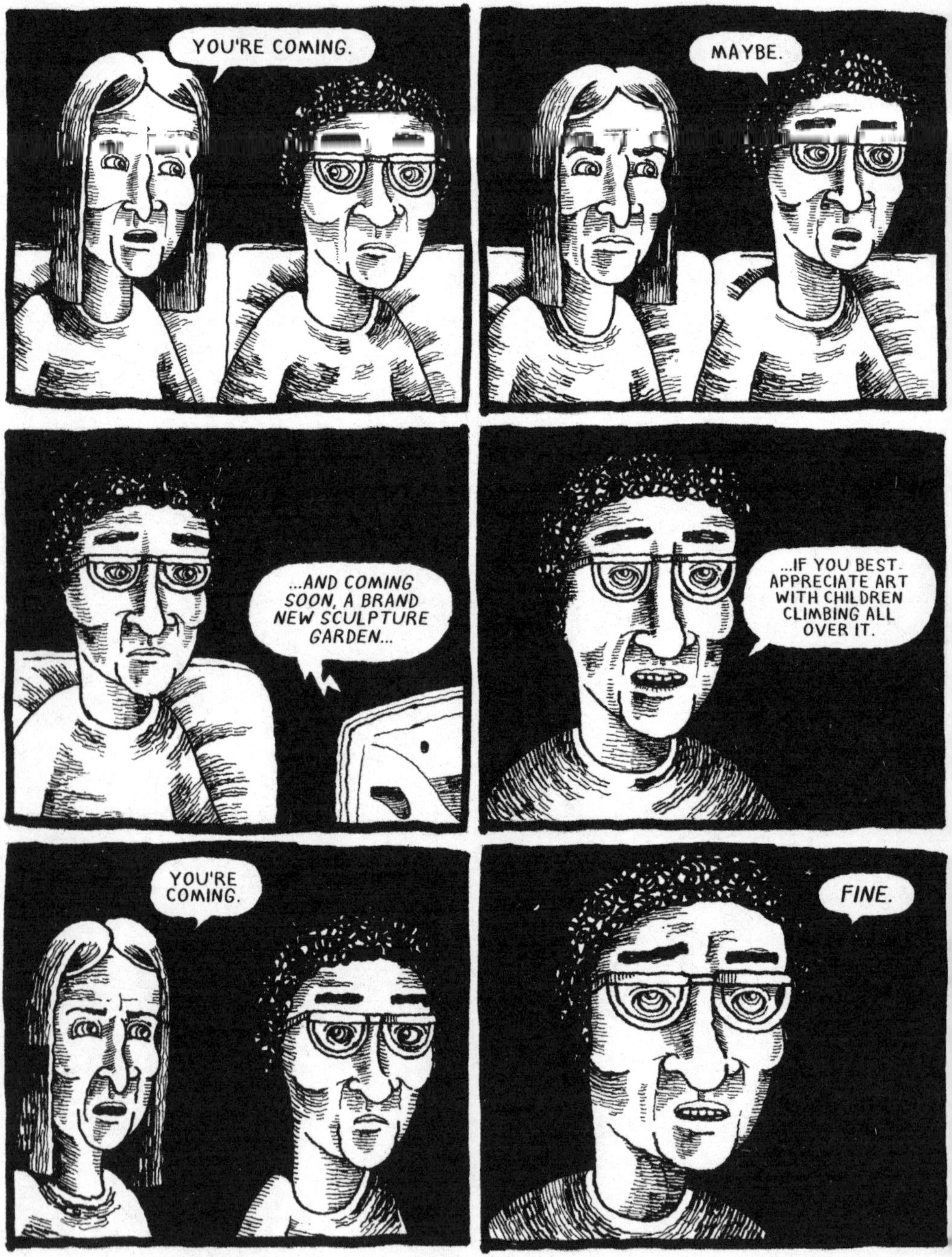
YOU'RE COMING.
MAYBE.
...AND COMING SOON, A BRAND NEW SCULPTURE GARDEN...
...IF YOU BEST APPRECIATE ART WITH CHILDREN CLIMBING ALL OVER IT.
YOU'RE COMING.
FINE.

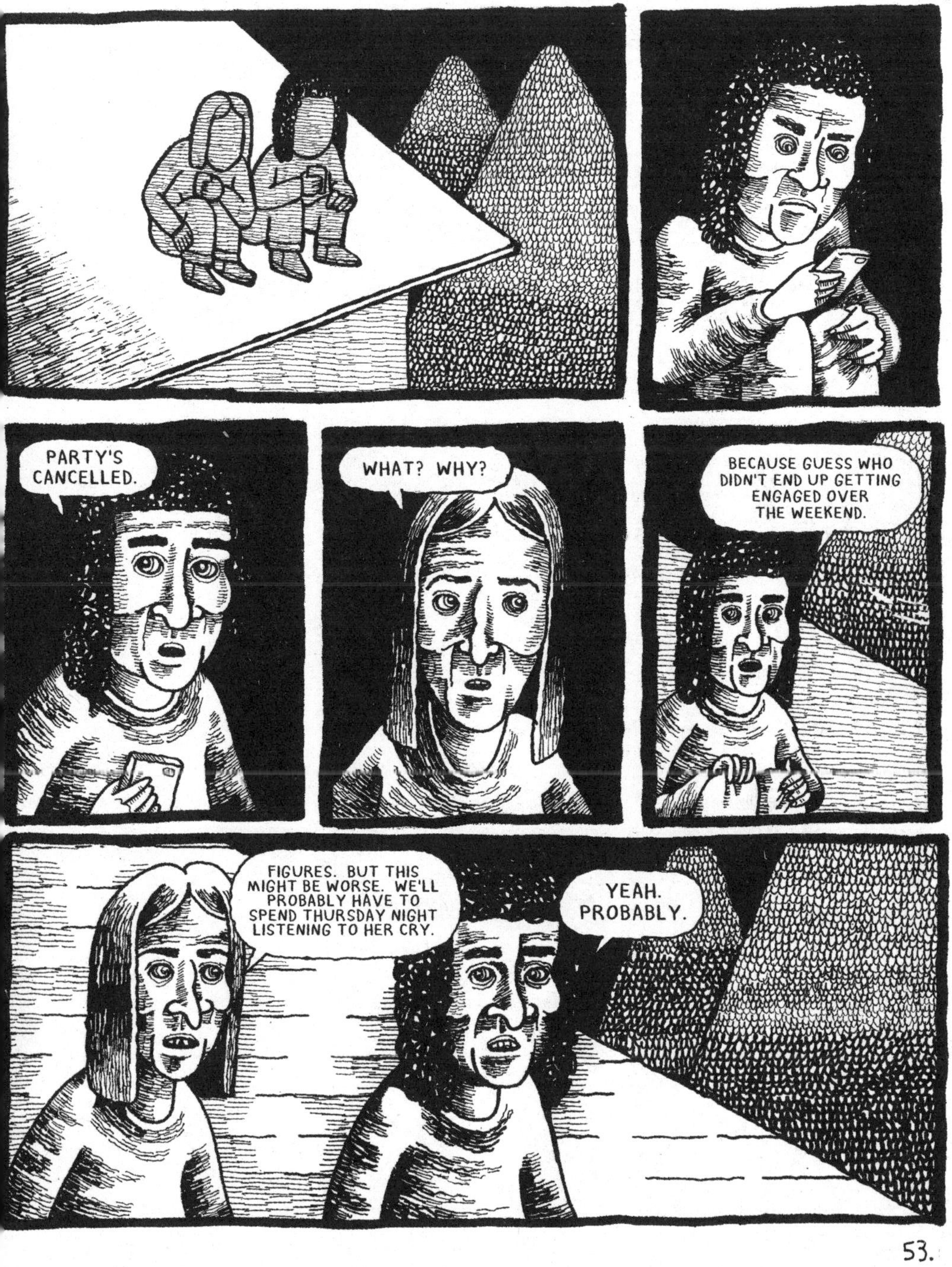
PARTY'S CANCELLED.
WHAT? WHY?
BECAUSE GUESS WHO DIDN'T END UP GETTING ENGAGED OVER THE WEEKEND.
FIGURES. BUT THIS MIGHT BE WORSE. WE'LL PROBABLY HAVE TO SPEND THURSDAY NIGHT LISTENING TO HER CRY.
YEAH. PROBABLY.

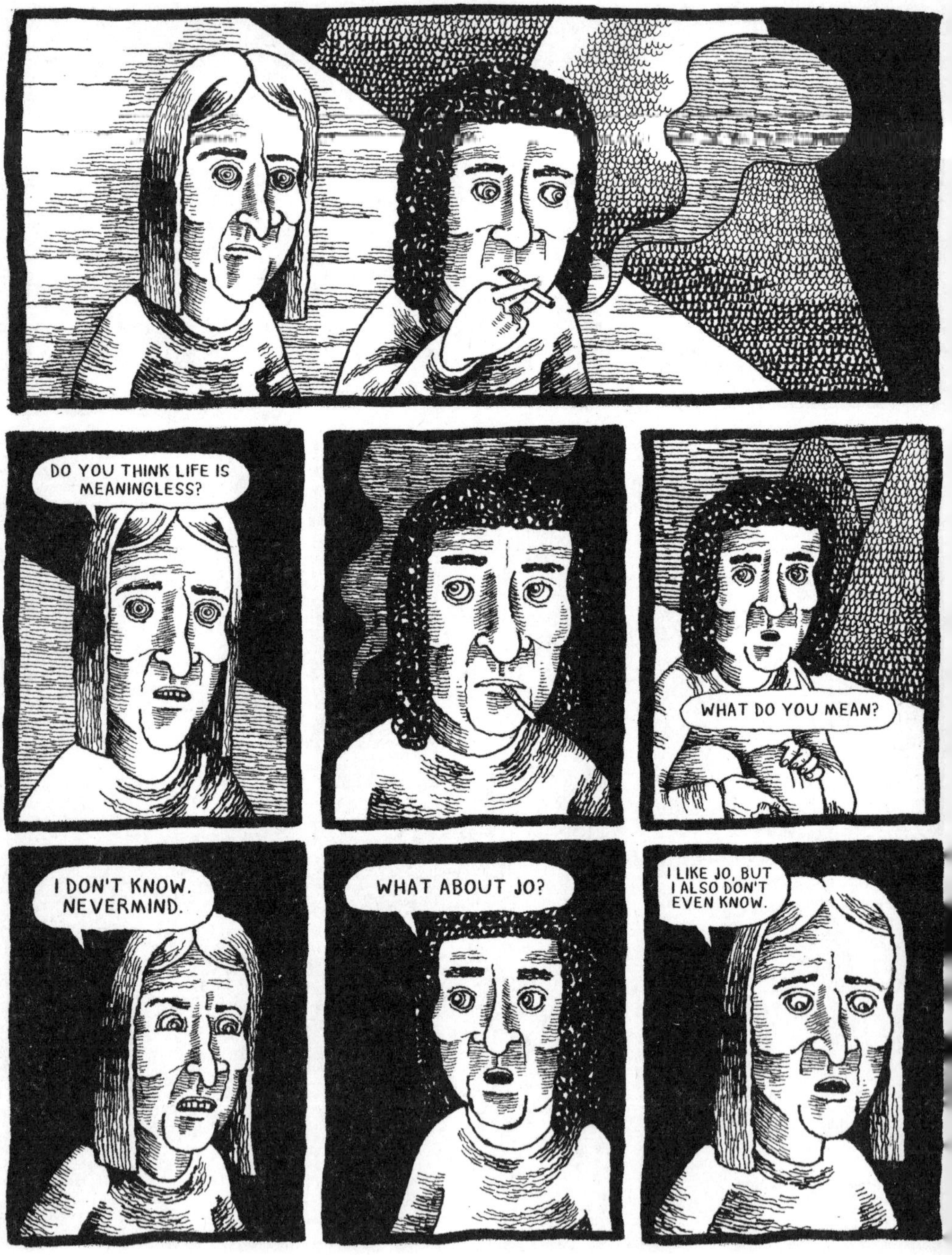
DO YOU THINK LIFE IS MEANINGLESS?
WHAT DO YOU MEAN?
I DON'T KNOW. NEVERMIND.
WHAT ABOUT JO?
I LIKE JO, BUT I ALSO DON'T EVEN KNOW.

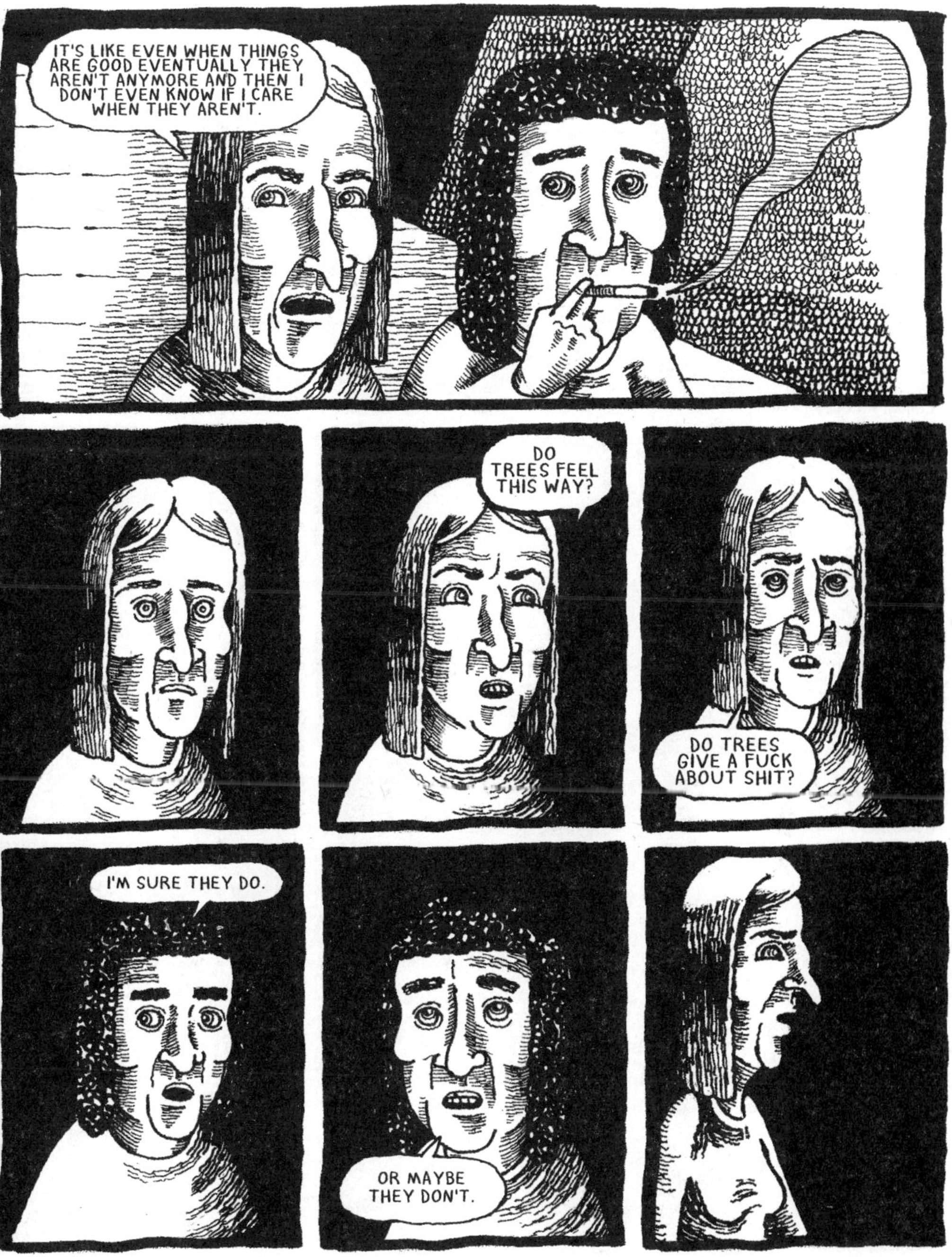
IT'S LIKE EVEN WHEN THINGS ARE GOOD EVENTUALLY THEY AREN'T ANYMORE AND THEN I DON'T EVEN KNOW IF I CARE WHEN THEY AREN'T.
DO TREES FEEL THIS WAY?
DO TREES GIVE A FUCK ABOUT SHIT?
I'M SURE THEY DO.
OR MAYBE THEY DON'T.

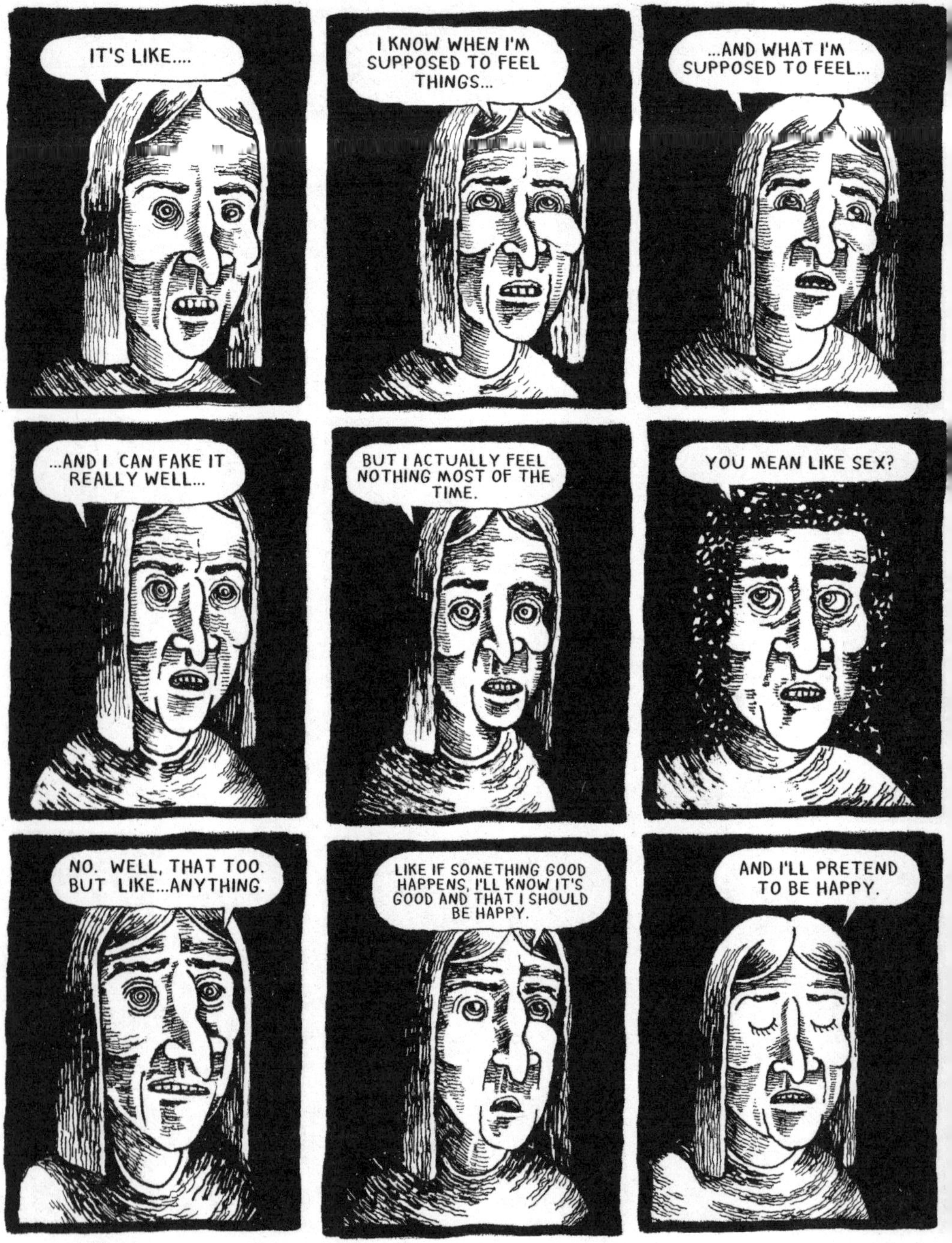
IT'S LIKE....
I KNOW WHEN I'M SUPPOSED TO FEEL THINGS...
...AND WHAT I'M SUPPOSED TO FEEL...
...AND I CAN FAKE IT REALLY WELL...
BUT I ACTUALLY FEEL NOTHING MOST OF THE TIME.
YOU MEAN LIKE SEX?
NO. WELL, THAT TOO. BUT LIKE...ANYTHING.
LIKE IF SOMETHING GOOD HAPPENS, I'LL KNOW IT'S GOOD AND THAT I SHOULD BE HAPPY.
AND I'LL PRETEND TO BE HAPPY.

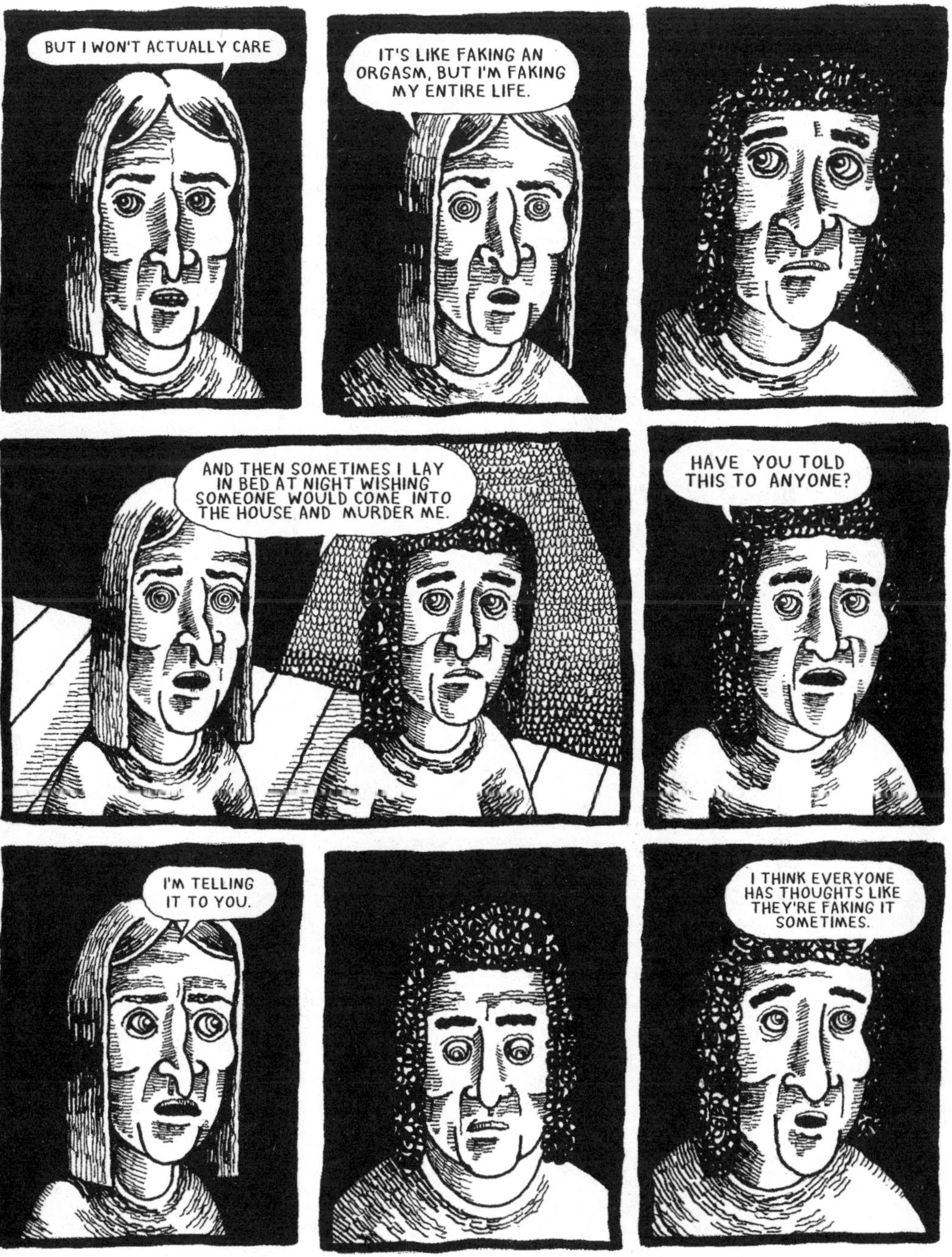
BUT I WON'T ACTUALLY CARE
IT'S LIKE FAKING AN ORGASM, BUT I'M FAKING MY ENTIRE LIFE.
AND THEN SOMETIMES I LAY IN BED AT NIGHT WISHING SOMEONE WOULD COME INTO THE HOUSE AND MURDER ME.
HAVE YOU TOLD THIS TO ANYONE?
I'M TELLING IT TO YOU.
I THINK EVERYONE HAS THOUGHTS LIKE THEY'RE FAKING IT SOMETIMES.

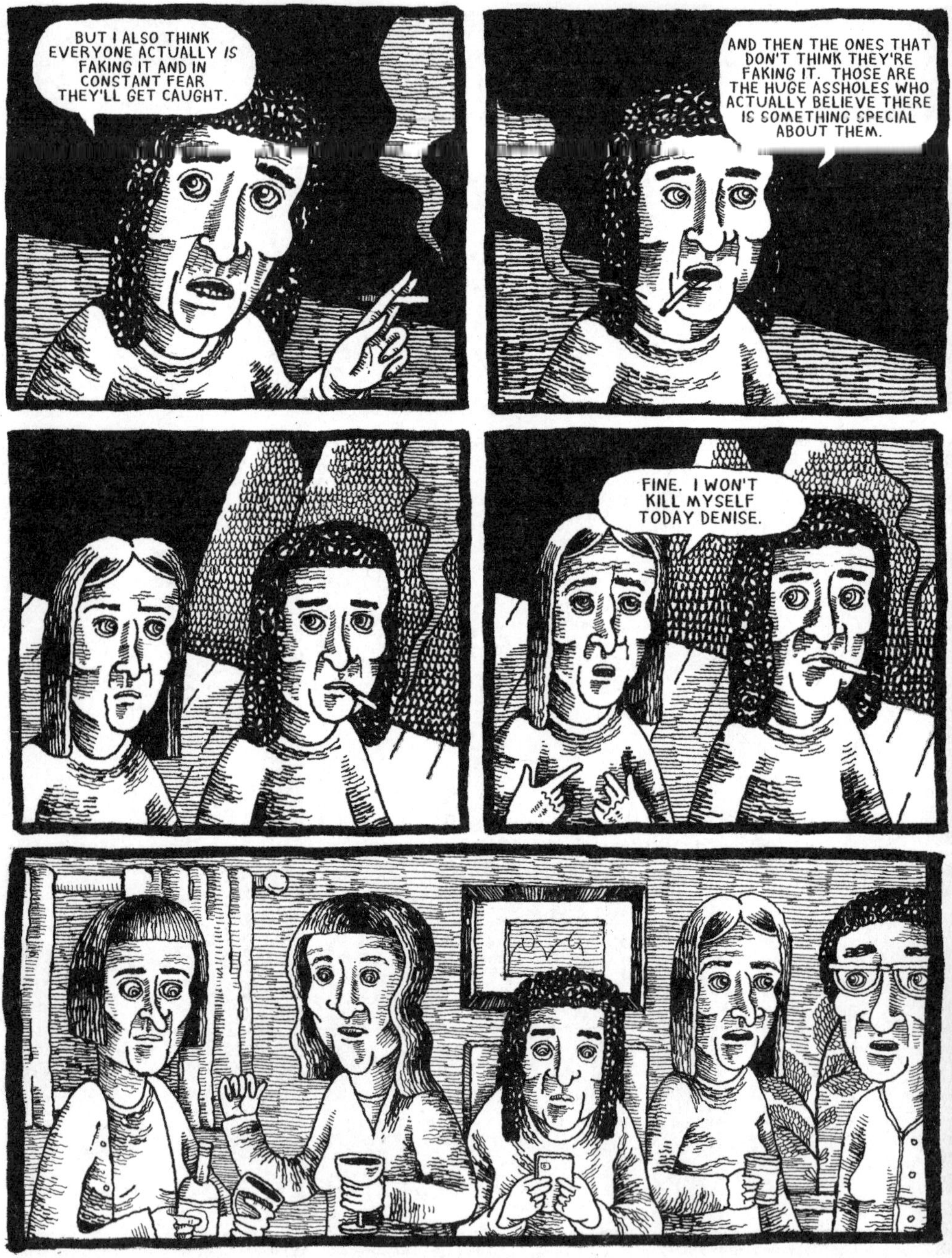
BUT I ALSO THINK EVERYONE ACTUALLY IS FAKING IT AND IN CONSTANT FEAR THEY'LL GET CAUGHT.
AND THEN THE ONES THAT DON'T THINK THEY'RE FAKING IT. THOSE ARE THE HUGE ASSHOLES WHO ACTUALLY BELIEVE THERE IS SOMETHING SPECIAL ABOUT THEM.
FINE. I WON'T KILL MYSELF TODAY DENISE.

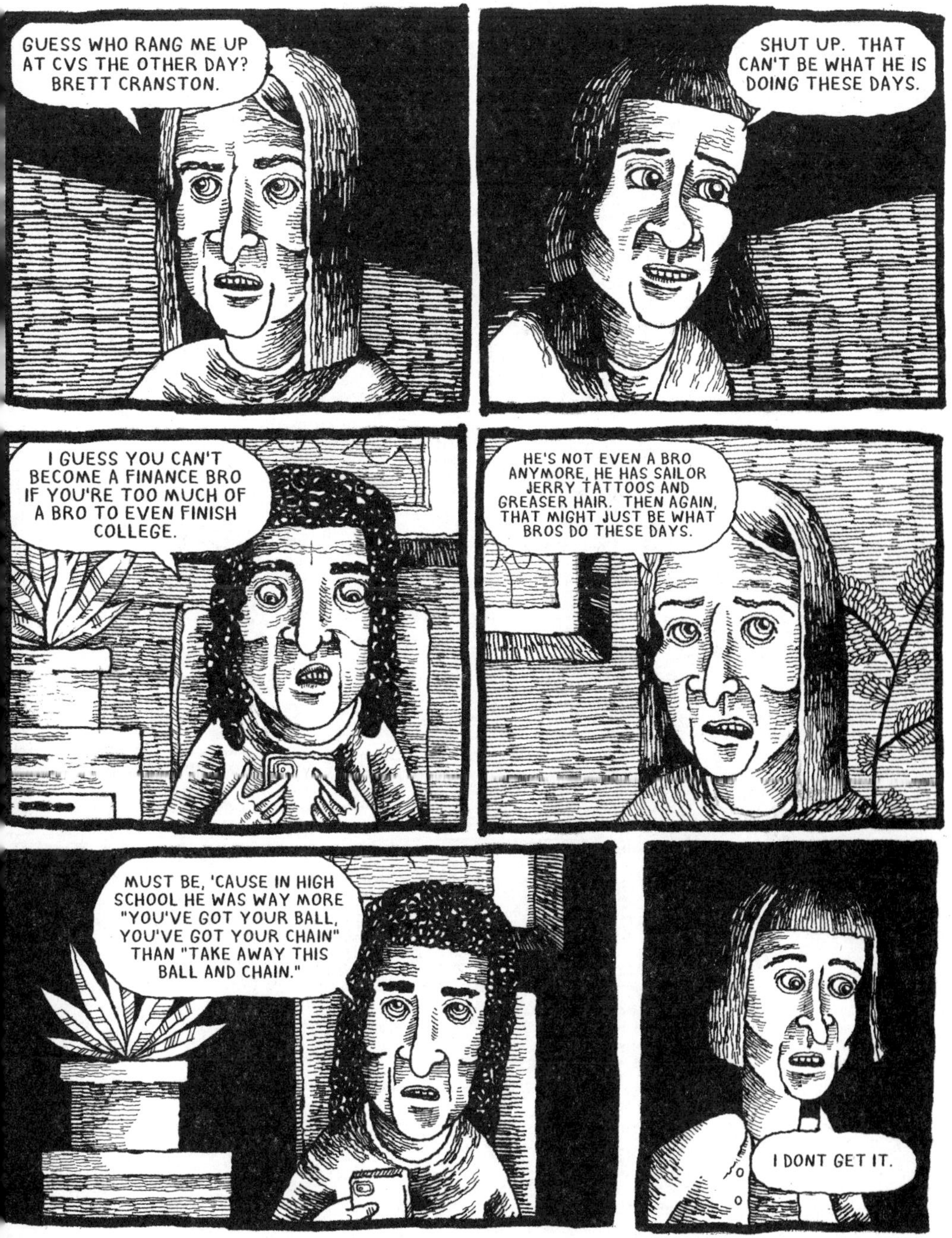
GUESS WHO RANG ME UP AT CVS THE OTHER DAY? BRETT CRANSTON.
SHUT UP. THAT CAN'T BE WHAT HE IS DOING THESE DAYS.
I GUESS YOU CAN'T BECOME A FINANCE BRO IF YOU'RE TOO MUCH OF A BRO TO EVEN FINISH COLLEGE.
HE'S NOT EVEN A BRO ANYMORE, HE HAS SAILOR JERRY TATTOOS AND GREASER HAIR. THEN AGAIN, THAT MIGHT JUST BE WHAT BROS DO THESE DAYS.
MUST BE, 'CAUSE IN HIGH SCHOOL HE WAS WAY MORE "YOU'VE GOT YOUR BALL, YOU'VE GOT YOUR CHAIN" THAN "TAKE AWAY THIS BALL AND CHAIN."
I DONT GET IT.

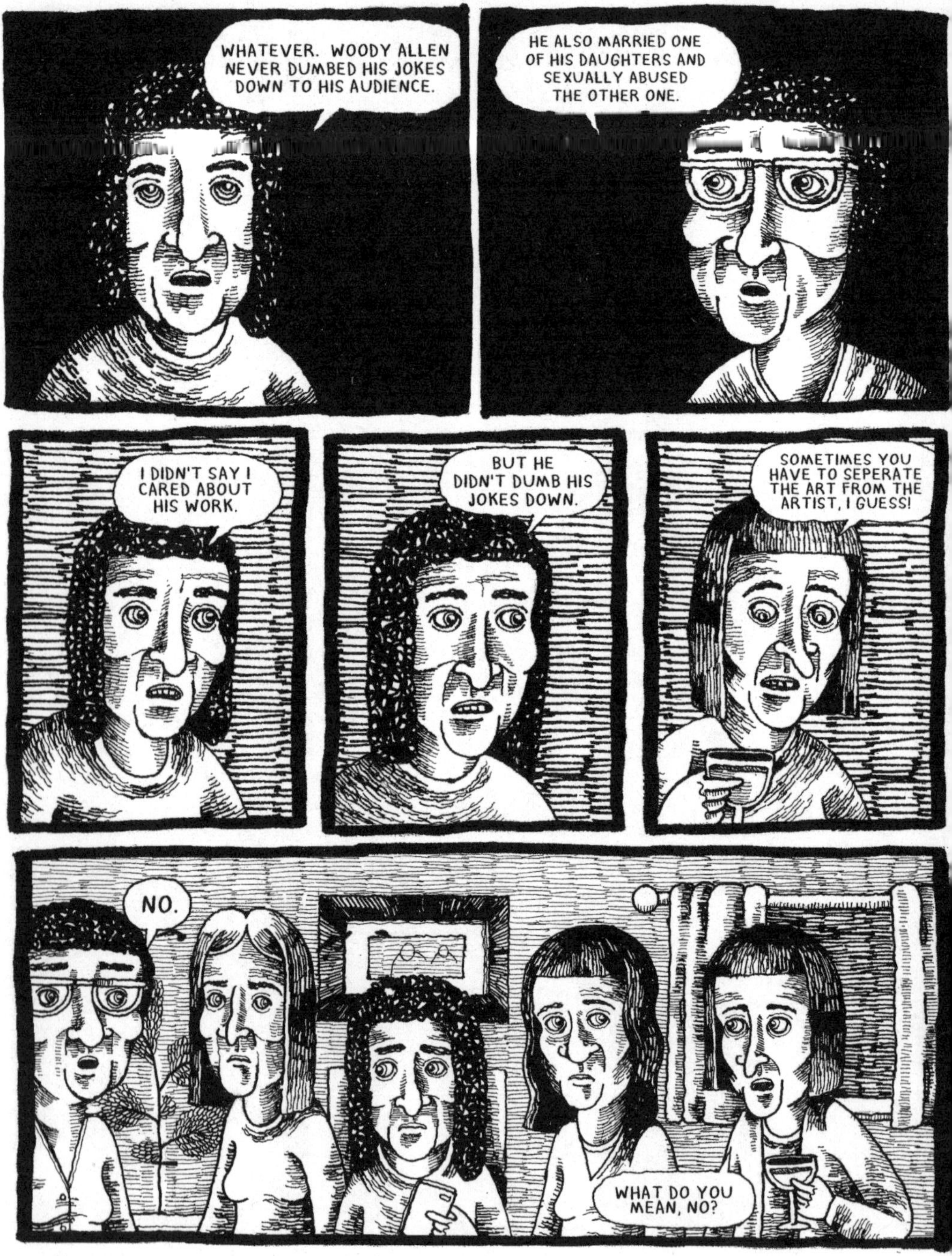
WHATEVER. WOODY ALLEN NEVER DUMBED HIS JOKES DOWN TO HIS AUDIENCE.
HE ALSO MARRIED ONE OF HIS DAUGHTERS AND SEXUALLY ABUSED THE OTHER ONE.
I DIDN'T SAY I CARED ABOUT HIS WORK.
BUT HE DIDN'T DUMB HIS JOKES DOWN.
SOMETIMES YOU HAVE TO SEPERATE THE ART FROM THE ARTIST, I GUESS!
NO.
WHAT DO YOU MEAN, NO?

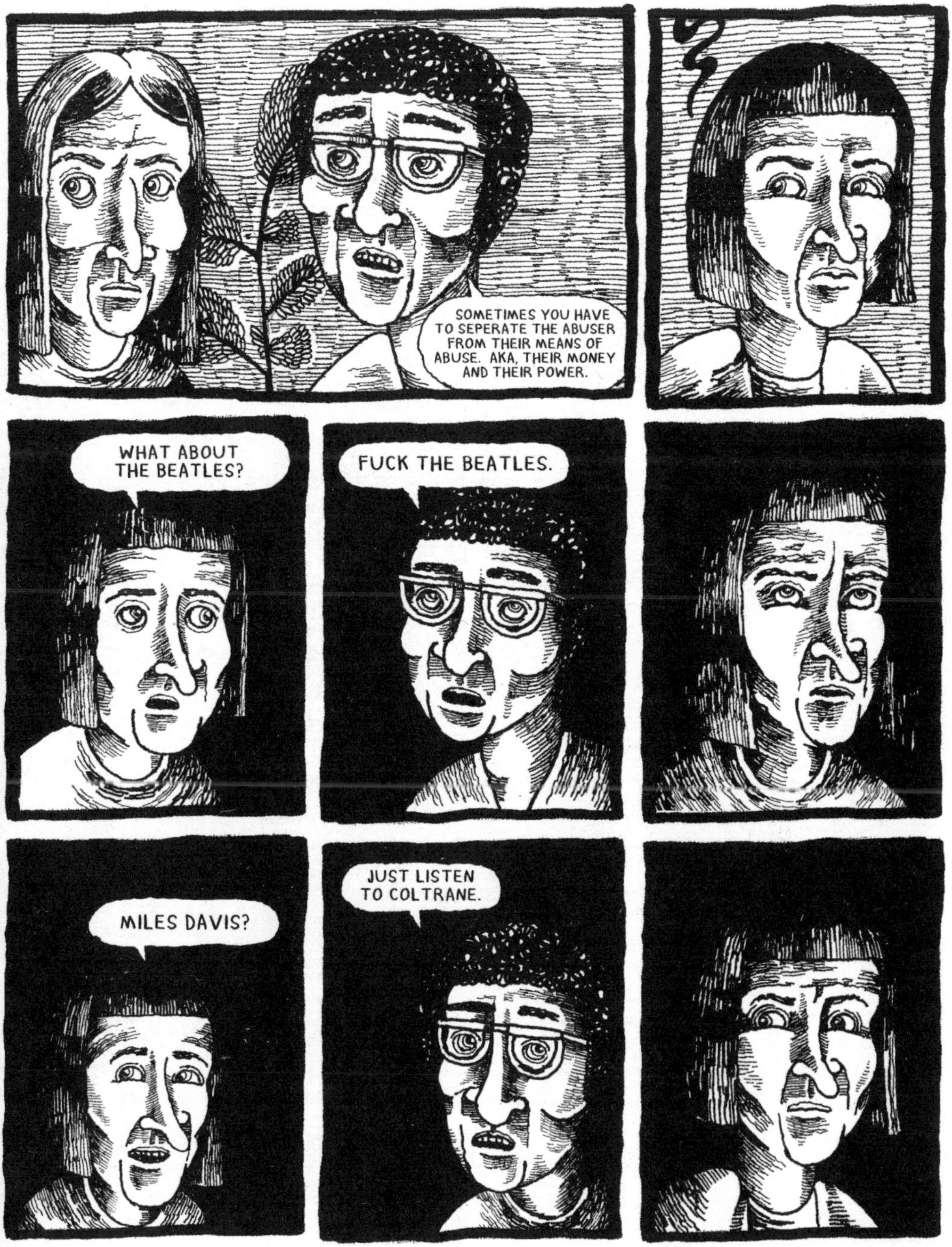
SOMETIMES YOU HAVE TO SEPERATE THE ABUSER FROM THEIR MEANS OF ABUSE. AKA, THEIR MONEY AND THEIR POWER.
WHAT ABOUT THE BEATLES?
FUCK THE BEATLES.
MILES DAVIS?
JUST LISTEN TO COLTRANE.

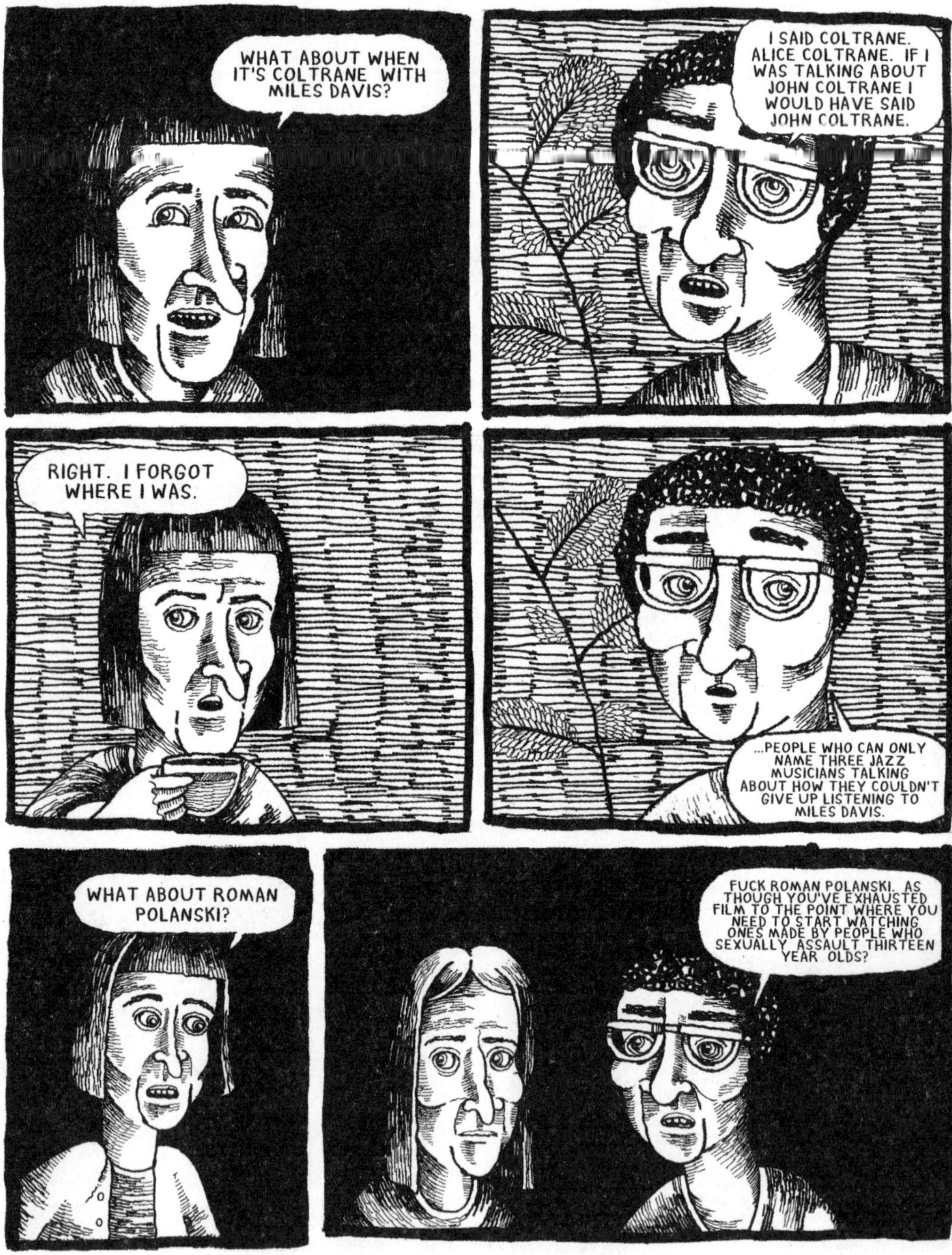
WHAT ABOUT WHEN IT'S COLTRANE WITH MILES DAVIS?
I SAID COLTRANE. ALICE COLTRANE. IF I WAS TALKING ABOUT JOHN COLTRANE I WOULD HAVE SAID JOHN COLTRANE.
RIGHT. I FORGOT WHERE I WAS.
...PEOPLE WHO CAN ONLY NAME THREE JAZZ MUSICIANS TALKING ABOUT HOW THEY COULDN'T GIVE UP LISTENING TO MILES DAVIS.
WHAT ABOUT ROMAN POLANSKI?
FUCK ROMAN POLANSKI. AS THOUGH YOU'VE EXHAUSTED FILM TO THE POINT WHERE YOU NEED TO START WATCHING ONES MADE BY PEOPLE WHO SEXUALLY ASSAULT THIRTEEN YEAR OLDS?

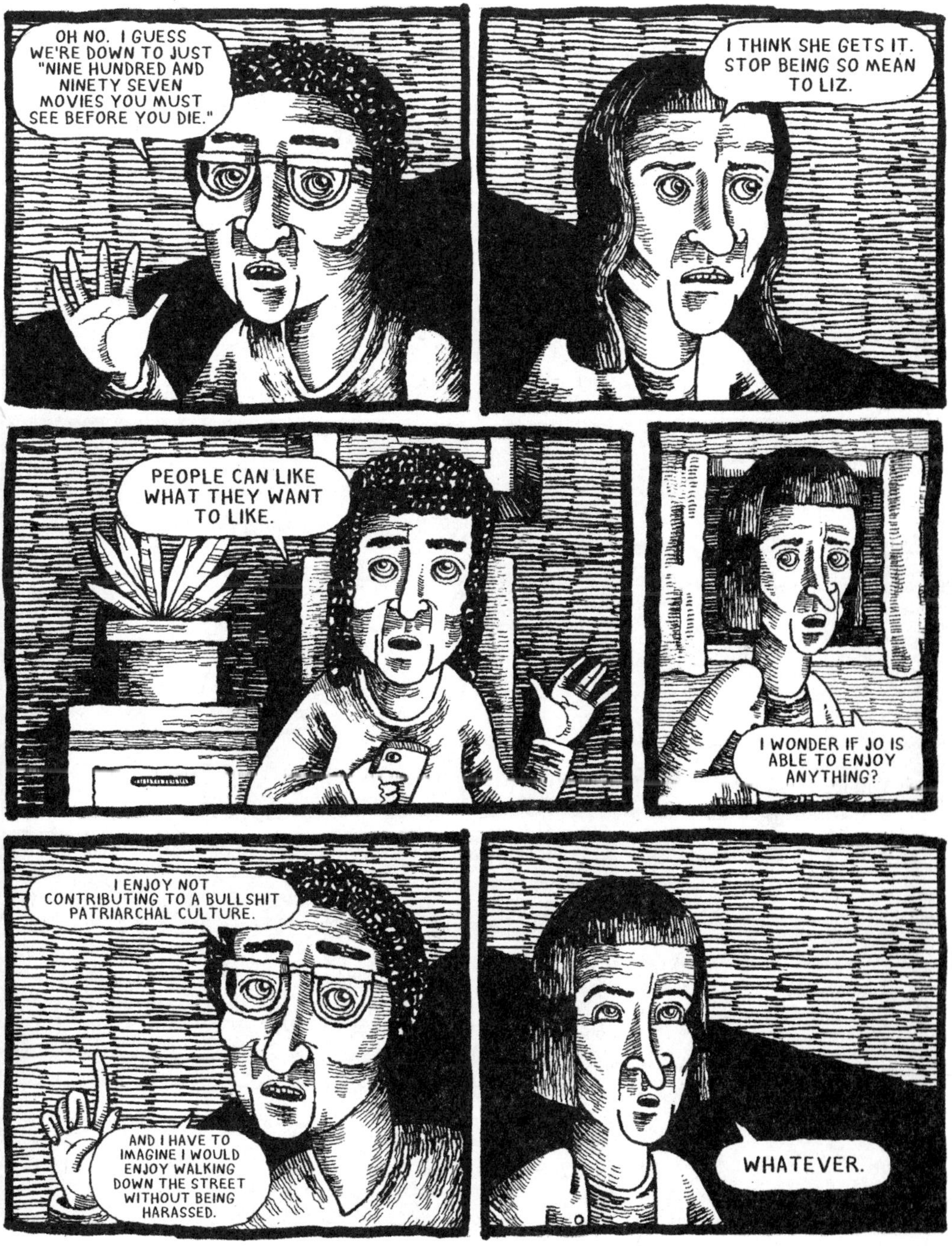
OH NO. I GUESS WE'RE DOWN TO JUST "NINE HUNDRED AND NINETY SEVEN MOVIES YOU MUST SEE BEFORE YOU DIE."
I THINK SHE GETS IT. STOP BEING SO MEAN TO LIZ.
PEOPLE CAN LIKE WHAT THEY WANT TO LIKE.
I WONDER IF JO IS ABLE TO ENJOY ANYTHING?
I ENJOY NOT CONTRIBUTING TO A BULLSHIT PATRIARCHAL CULTURE.
AND I HAVE TO IMAGINE I WOULD ENJOY WALKING DOWN THE STREET WITHOUT BEING HARASSED.
WHATEVER.

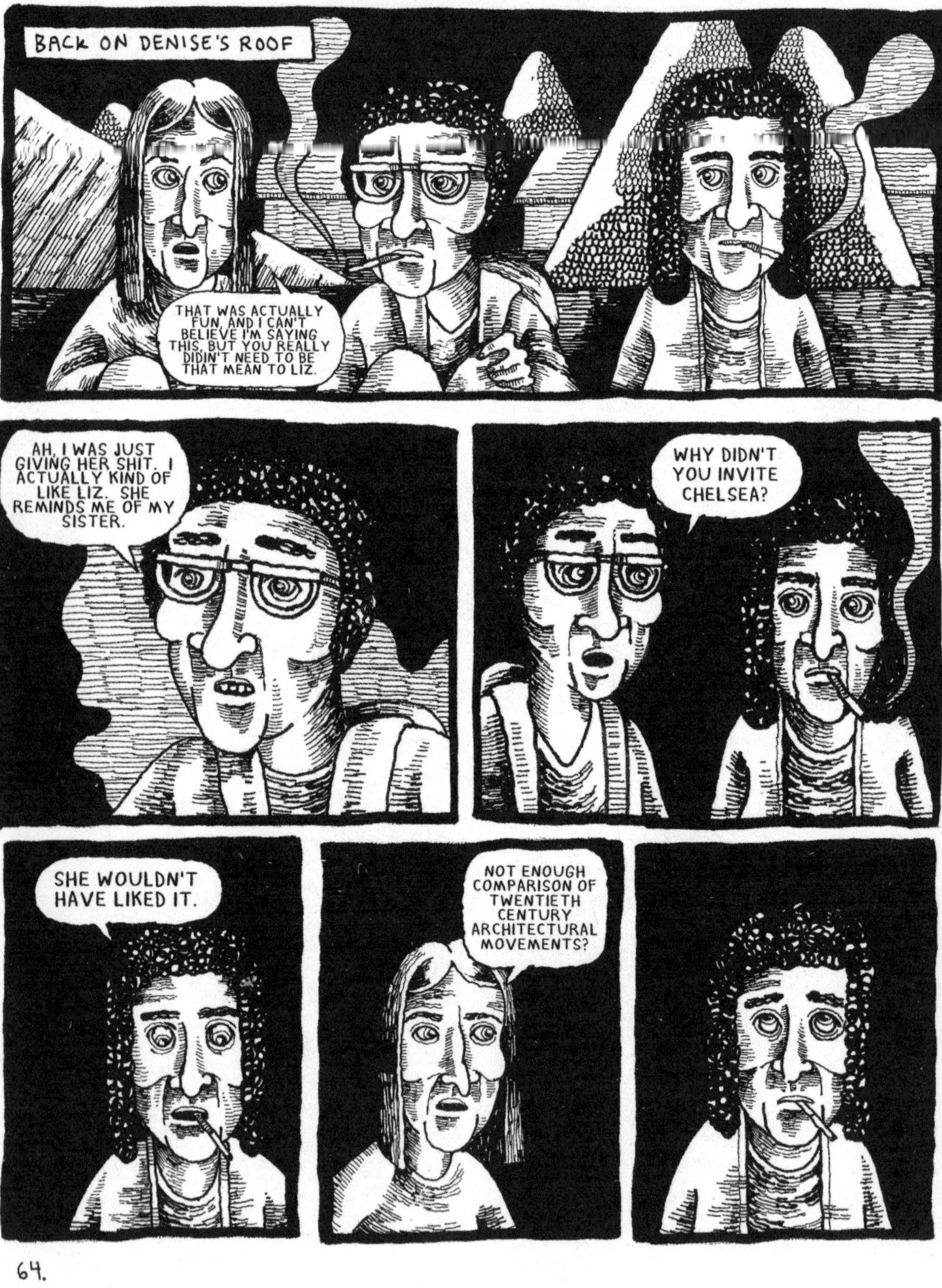
BACK ON DENISE'S ROOF
THAT WAS ACTUALLY FUN, AND I CAN'T BELIEVE I'M SAYING THIS, BUT YOU REALLY DIDIN'T NEED TO BE THAT MEAN TO LIZ.
AH, I WAS JUST GIVING HER SHIT. I ACTUALLY KIND OF LIKE LIZ. SHE REMINDS ME OF MY SISTER.
WHY DIDN'T YOU INVITE CHELSEA?
SHE WOULDN'T HAVE LIKED IT.
NOT ENOUGH COMPARISON OF TWENTIETH CENTURY ARCHITECTURAL MOVEMENTS?

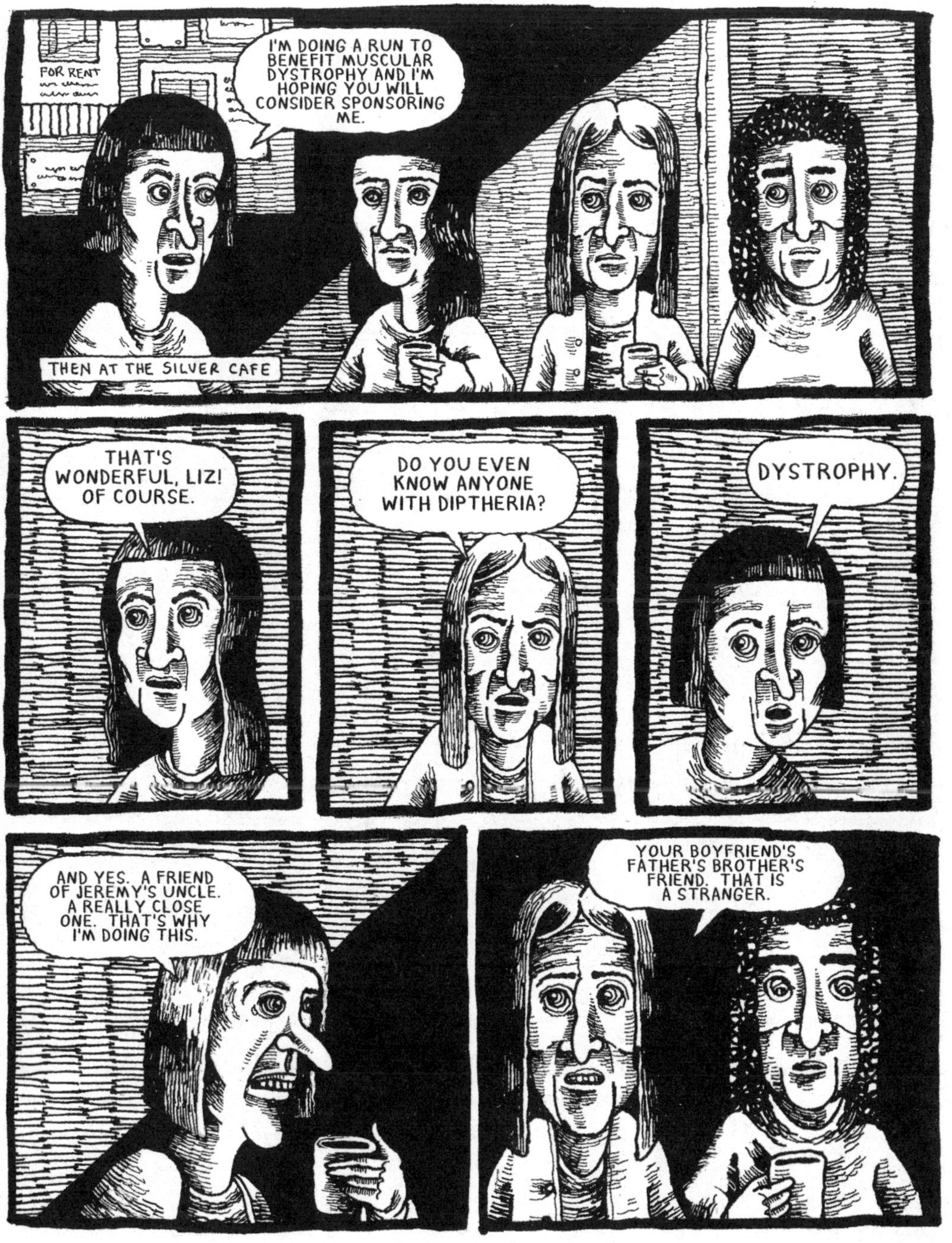

FOR RENT
I'M DOING A RUN TO BENEFIT MUSCULAR DYSTROPHY AND I'M HOPING YOU WILL CONSIDER SPONSORING ME.
THEN AT THE SILVER CAFE
THAT'S WONDERFUL, LIZ! OF COURSE.
DO YOU EVEN KNOW ANYONE WITH DIPTHERIA?
DYSTROPHY.
AND YES. A FRIEND OF JEREMY'S UNCLE. A REALLY CLOSE ONE. THAT'S WHY I'M DOING THIS.
YOUR BOYFRIEND'S FATHER'S BROTHER'S FRIEND. THAT IS A STRANGER.

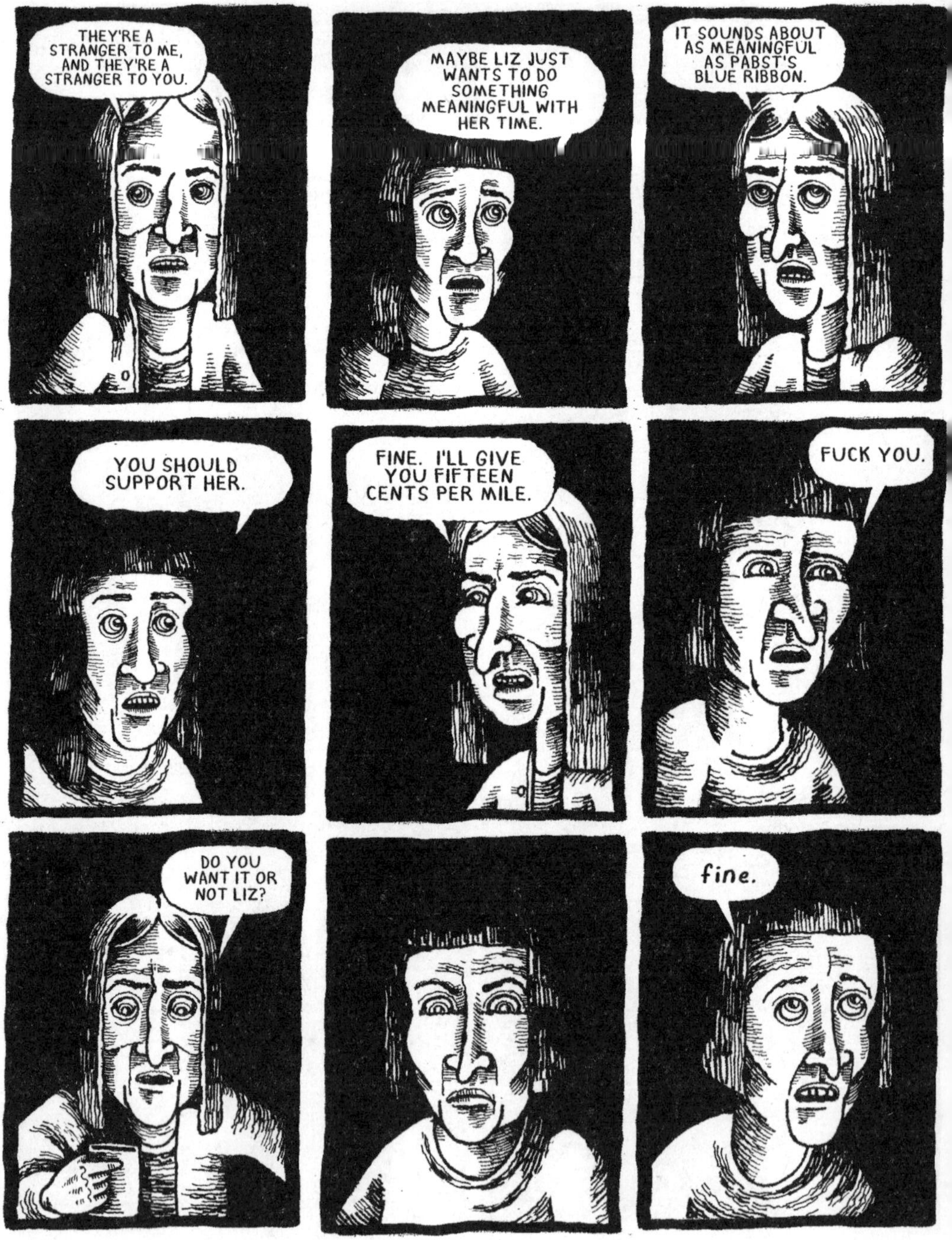
THEY'RE A STRANGER TO ME, AND THEY'RE A STRANGER TO YOU.
MAYBE LIZ JUST WANTS TO DO SOMETHING MEANINGFUL WITH HER TIME.
IT SOUNDS ABOUT AS MEANINGFUL AS PABST'S BLUE RIBBON.
YOU SHOULD SUPPORT HER.
FINE. I'LL GIVE YOU FIFTEEN CENTS PER MILE.
FUCK YOU.
DO YOU WANT IT OR NOT LIZ?
fine.

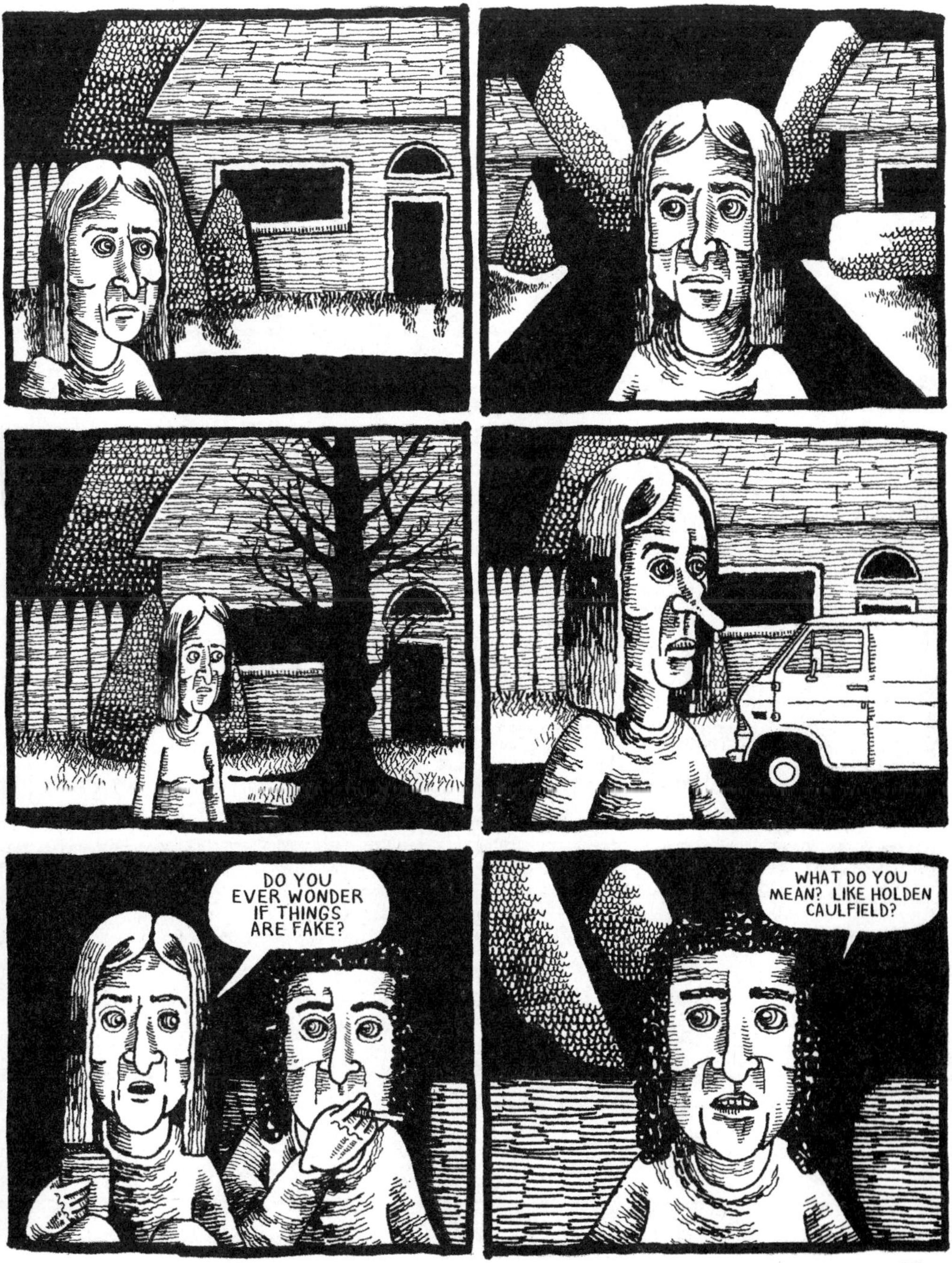
DO YOU EVER WONDER IF THINGS ARE FAKE?
WHAT DO YOU MEAN? LIKE HOLDEN CAULFIELD?

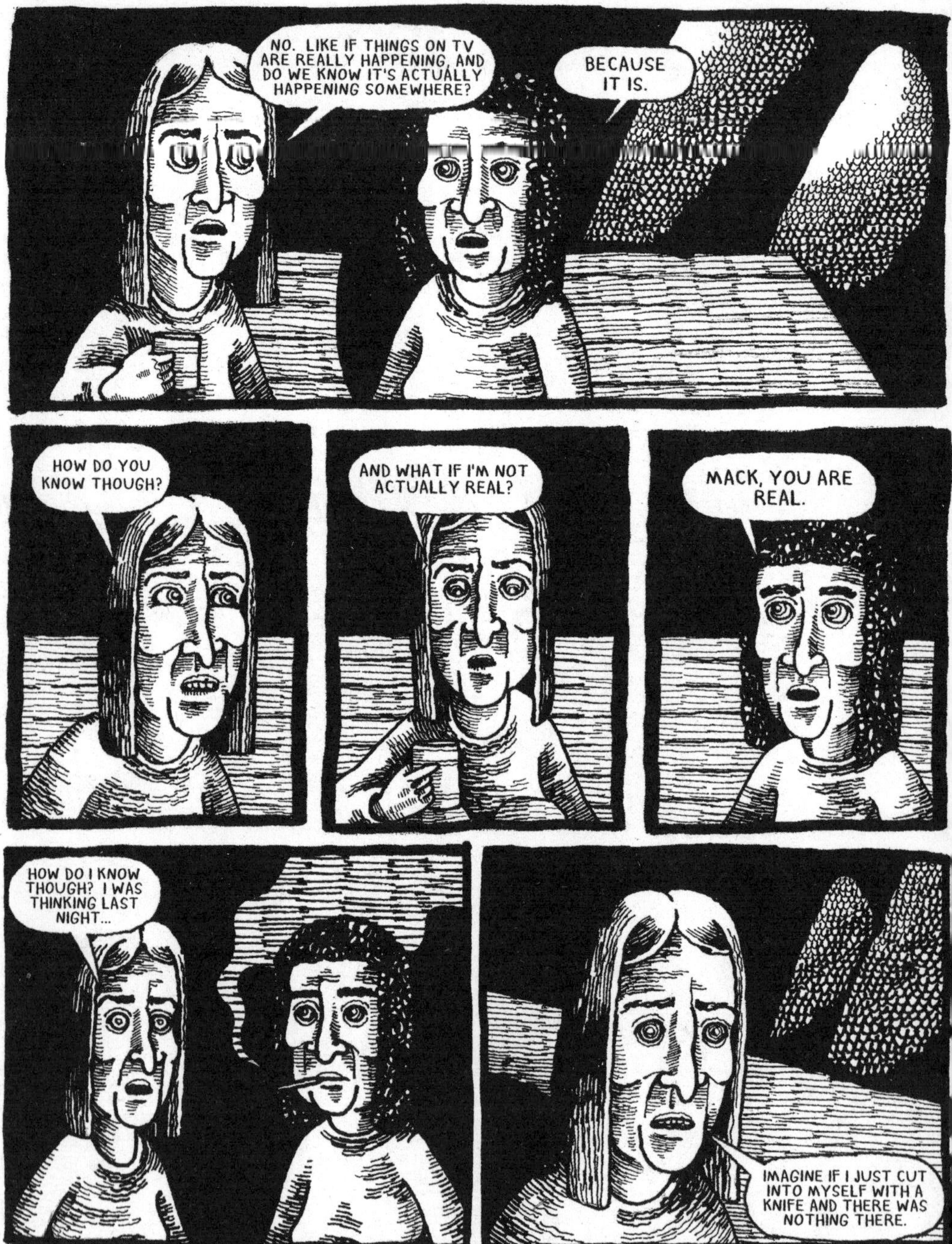
NO. LIKE IF THINGS ON TV ARE REALLY HAPPENING, AND DO WE KNOW IT'S ACTUALLY HAPPENING SOMEWHERE?
BECAUSE IT IS.
HOW DO YOU KNOW THOUGH?
AND WHAT IF I'M NOT ACTUALLY REAL?
MACK, YOU ARE REAL.
HOW DO I KNOW THOUGH? I WAS THINKING LAST NIGHT...
IMAGINE IF I JUST CUT INTO MYSELF WITH A KNIFE AND THERE WAS NOTHING THERE.

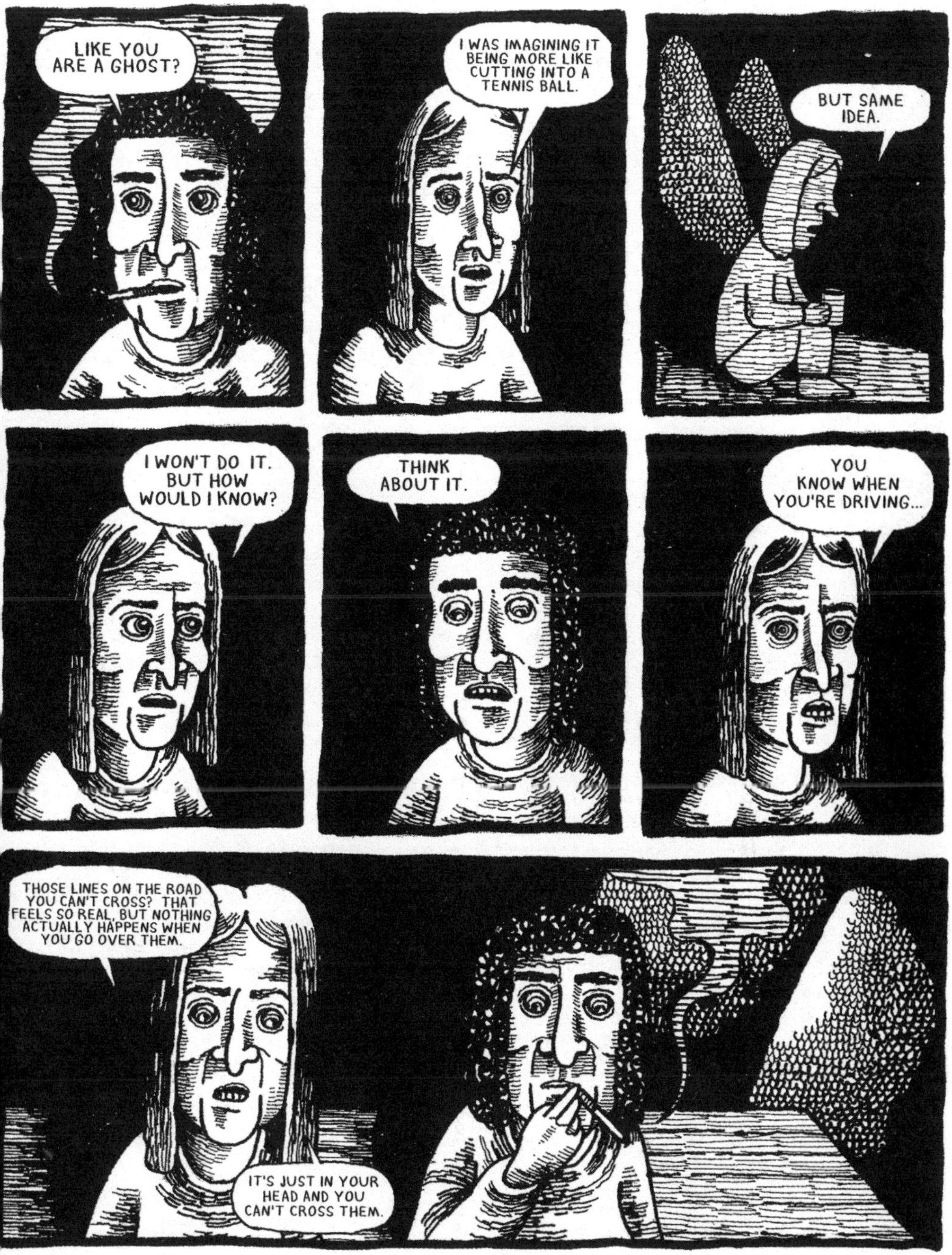
LIKE YOU ARE A GHOST?
I WAS IMAGINING IT BEING MORE LIKE CUTTING INTO A TENNIS BALL.
BUT SAME IDEA.
I WON'T DO IT. BUT HOW WOULD I KNOW?
THINK ABOUT IT.
YOU KNOW WHEN YOU'RE DRIVING...
THOSE LINES ON THE ROAD YOU CAN'T CROSS? THAT FEELS SO REAL, BUT NOTHING ACTUALLY HAPPENS WHEN YOU GO OVER THEM.
IT'S JUST IN YOUR HEAD AND YOU CAN'T CROSS THEM.

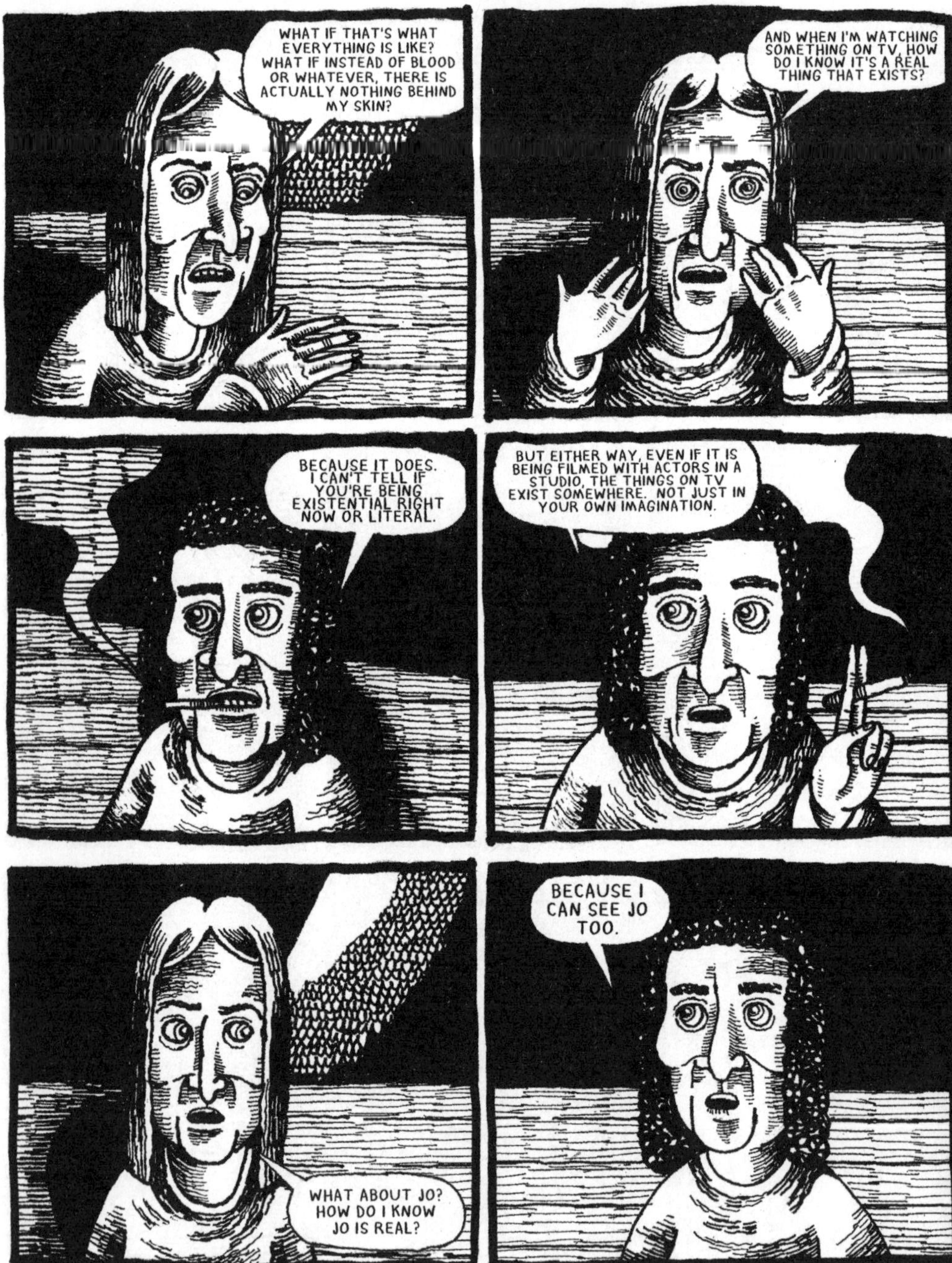
WHAT IF THAT'S WHAT EVERYTHING IS LIKE? WHAT IF INSTEAD OF BLOOD OR WHATEVER, THERE IS ACTUALLY NOTHING BEHIND MY SKIN?
AND WHEN I'M WATCHING SOMETHING ON TV, HOW DO I KNOW IT'S A REAL THING THAT EXISTS?
BECAUSE IT DOES. I CAN'T TELL IF YOU'RE BEING EXISTENTIAL RIGHT NOW OR LITERAL.
BUT EITHER WAY, EVEN IF IT IS BEING FILMED WITH ACTORS IN A STUDIO, THE THINGS ON TV EXIST SOMEWHERE. NOT JUST IN YOUR OWN IMAGINATION.
WHAT ABOUT JO? HOW DO I KNOW JO IS REAL?
BECAUSE I CAN SEE JO TOO.

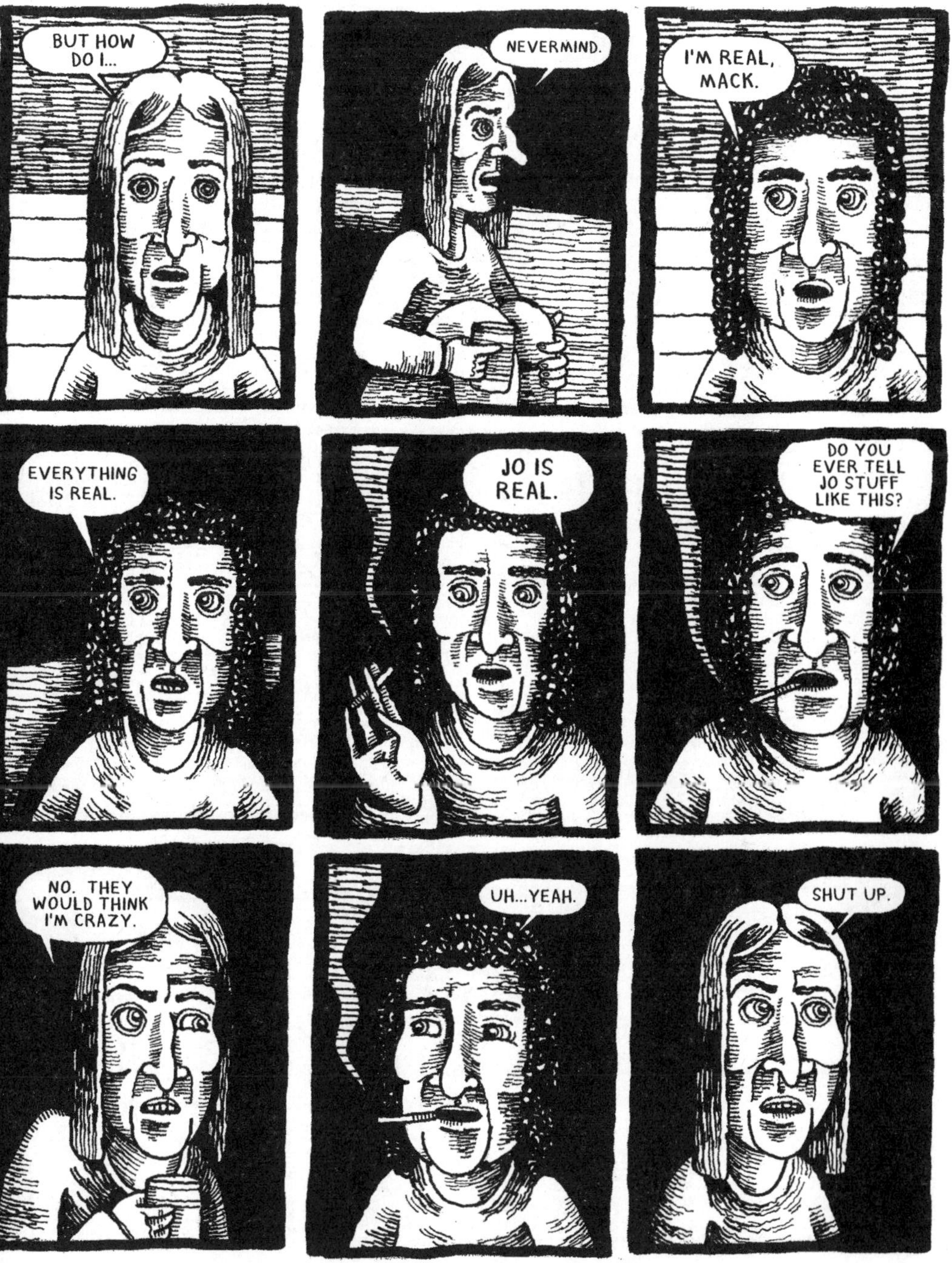
BUT HOW DO I...
NEVERMIND.
I'M REAL, MACK.
EVERYTHING IS REAL.
JO IS REAL.
DO YOU EVER TELL JO STUFF LIKE THIS?
NO. THEY WOULD THINK I'M CRAZY.
UH...YEAH.
SHUT UP.

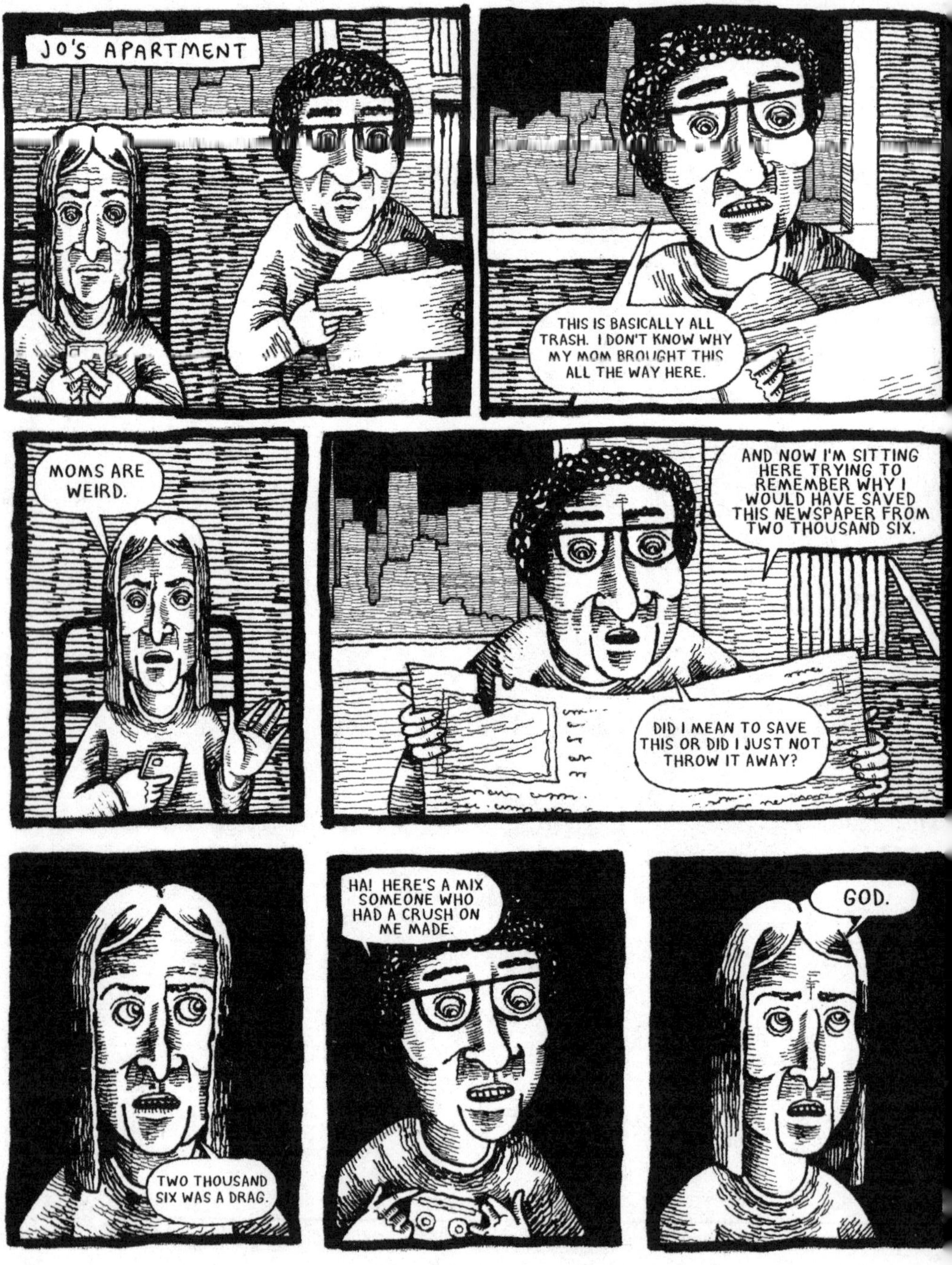
JO'S APARTMENT
THIS IS BASICALLY ALL TRASH. I DON'T KNOW WHY MY MOM BROUGHT THIS ALL THE WAY HERE.
MOMS ARE WEIRD.
AND NOW I'M SITTING HERE TRYING TO REMEMBER WHY I WOULD HAVE SAVED THIS NEWSPAPER FROM TWO THOUSAND SIX.
DID I MEAN TO SAVE THIS OR DID I JUST NOT THROW IT AWAY?
TWO THOUSAND SIX WAS A DRAG.
HA! HERE'S A MIX SOMEONE WHO HAD A CRUSH ON ME MADE.
GOD.

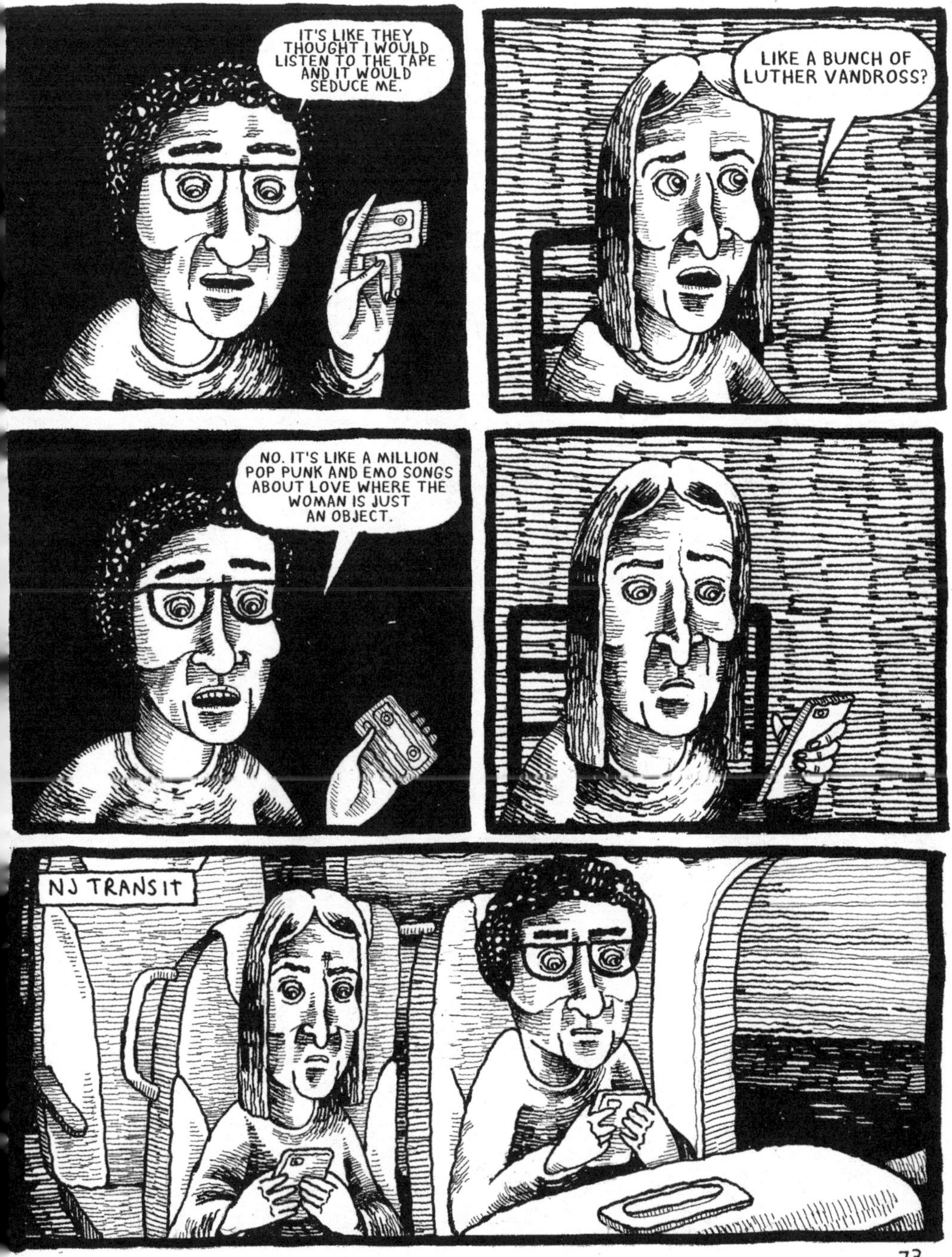
IT'S LIKE THEY THOUGHT I WOULD LISTEN TO THE TAPE AND IT WOULD SEDUCE ME.
LIKE A BUNCH OF LUTHER VANDROSS?
NO. IT'S LIKE A MILLION POP PUNK AND EMO SONGS ABOUT LOVE WHERE THE WOMAN IS JUST AN OBJECT.
NJ TRANSIT

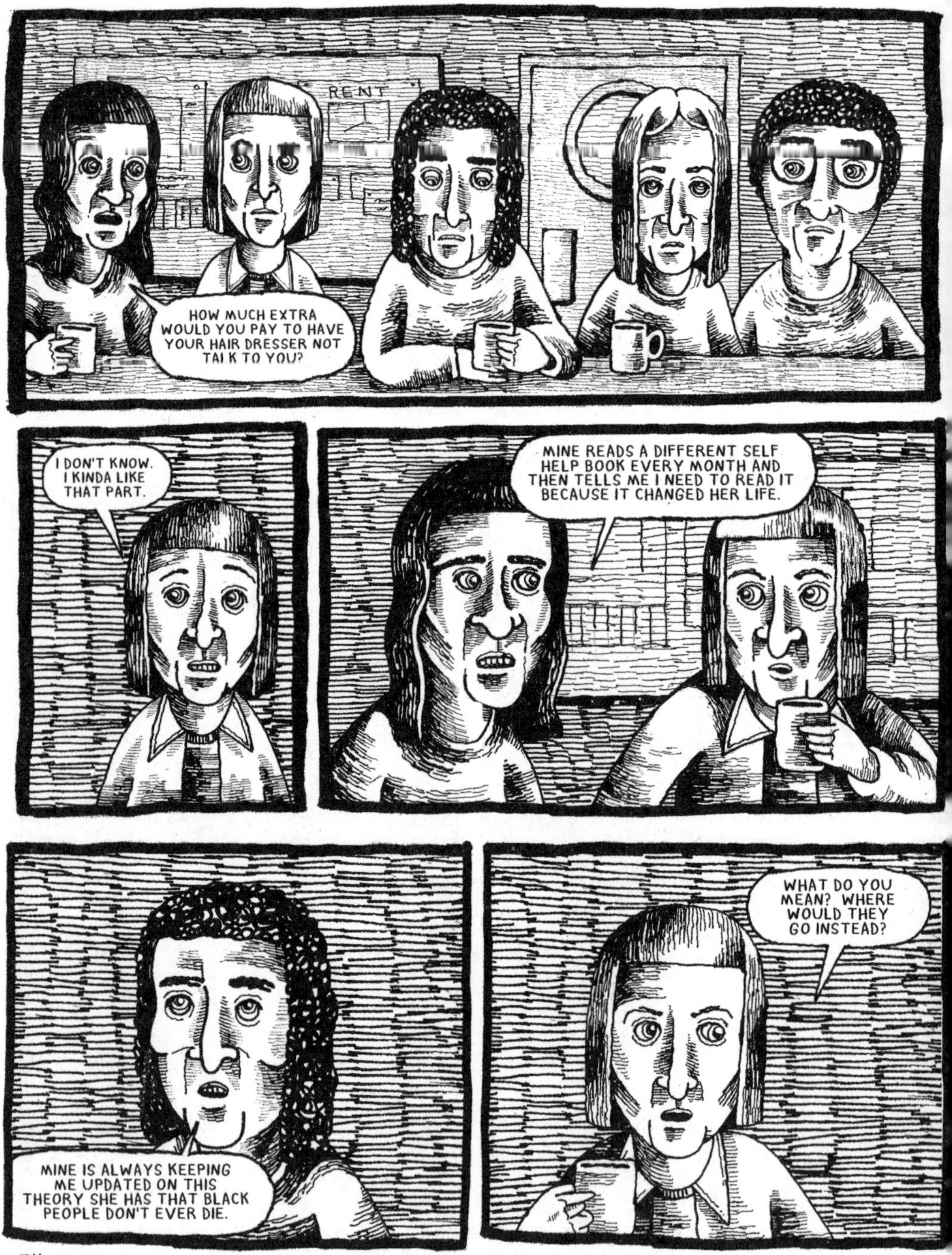
RENT
HOW MUCH EXTRA WOULD YOU PAY TO HAVE YOUR HAIR DRESSER NOT TALK TO YOU?
I DON'T KNOW. I KINDA LIKE THAT PART.
MINE READS A DIFFERENT SELF HELP BOOK EVERY MONTH AND THEN TELLS ME I NEED TO READ IT BECAUSE IT CHANGED HER LIFE.
MINE IS ALWAYS KEEPING ME UPDATED ON THIS THEORY SHE HAS THAT BLACK PEOPLE DON'T EVER DIE.
WHAT DO YOU MEAN? WHERE WOULD THEY GO INSTEAD?

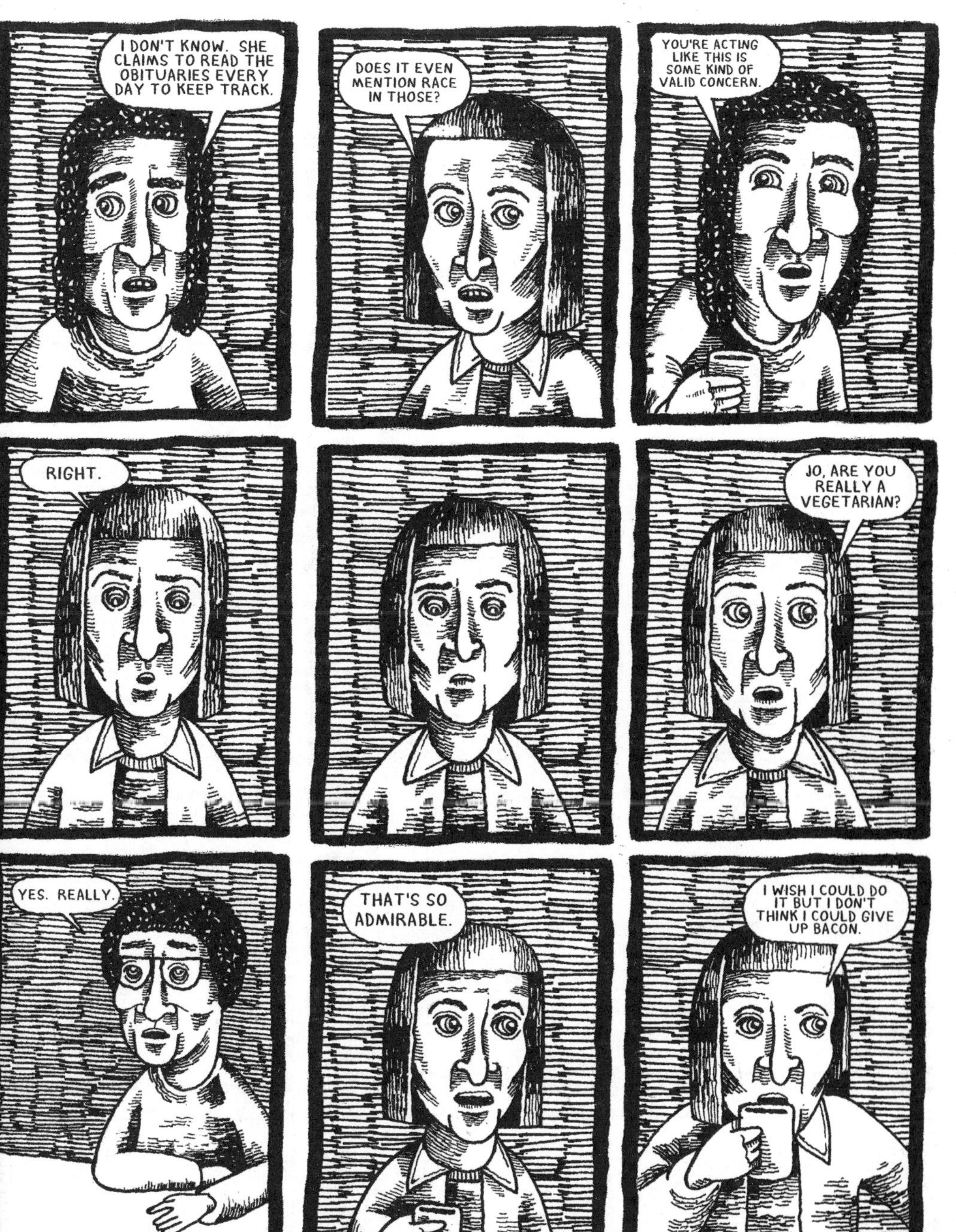
I DON'T KNOW. SHE CLAIMS TO READ THE OBITUARIES EVERY DAY TO KEEP TRACK.
DOES IT EVEN MENTION RACE IN THOSE?
YOU'RE ACTING LIKE THIS IS SOME KIND OF VALID CONCERN.
RIGHT.
JO, ARE YOU REALLY A VEGETARIAN?
YES. REALLY.
THAT'S SO ADMIRABLE.
I WISH I COULD DO IT BUT I DON'T THINK I COULD GIVE UP BACON.

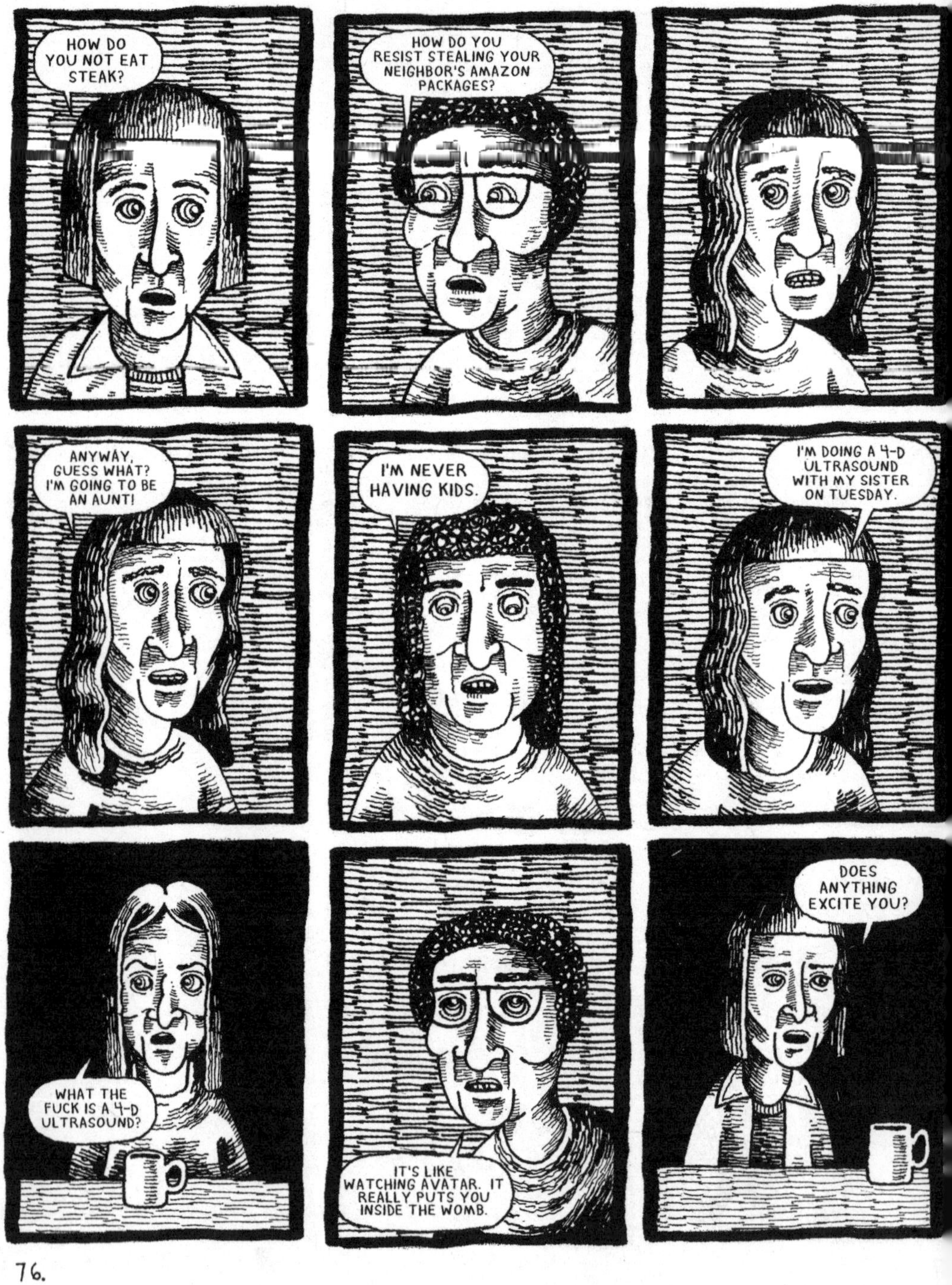
HOW DO YOU NOT EAT STEAK?
HOW DO YOU RESIST STEALING YOUR NEIGHBOR'S AMAZON PACKAGES?
ANYWAY, GUESS WHAT? I'M GOING TO BE AN AUNT!
I'M NEVER HAVING KIDS.
I'M DOING A 4-D ULTRASOUND WITH MY SISTER ON TUESDAY.
WHAT THE FUCK IS A 4-D ULTRASOUND?
IT'S LIKE WATCHING AVATAR. IT REALLY PUTS YOU INSIDE THE WOMB.
DOES ANYTHING EXCITE YOU?

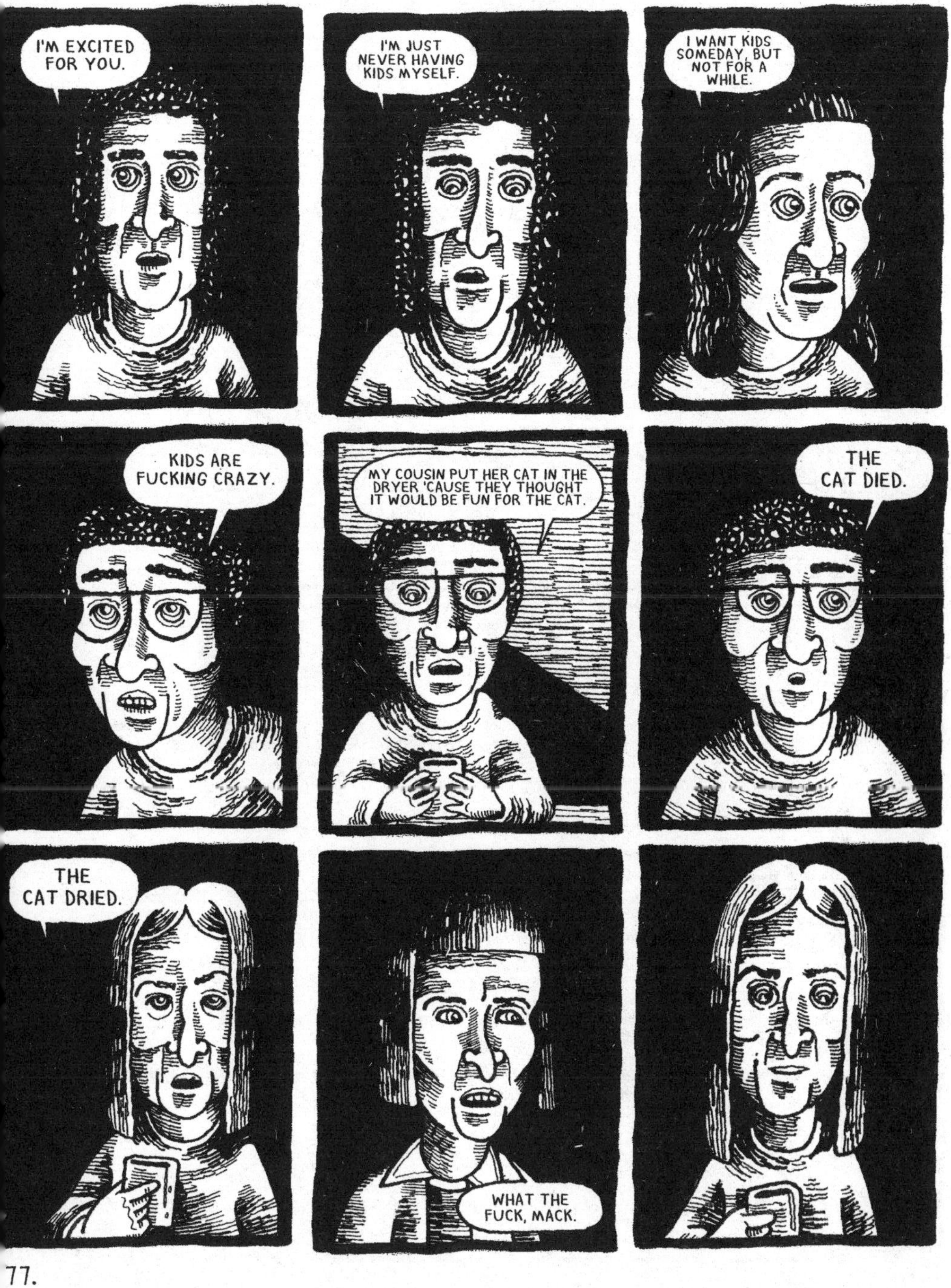
I'M EXCITED FOR YOU.
I'M JUST NEVER HAVING KIDS MYSELF.
I WANT KIDS SOMEDAY, BUT NOT FOR A WHILE.
KIDS ARE FUCKING CRAZY.
MY COUSIN PUT HER CAT IN THE DRYER 'CAUSE THEY THOUGHT IT WOULD BE FUN FOR THE CAT.
THE CAT DIED.
THE CAT DRIED.
WHAT THE FUCK, MACK.

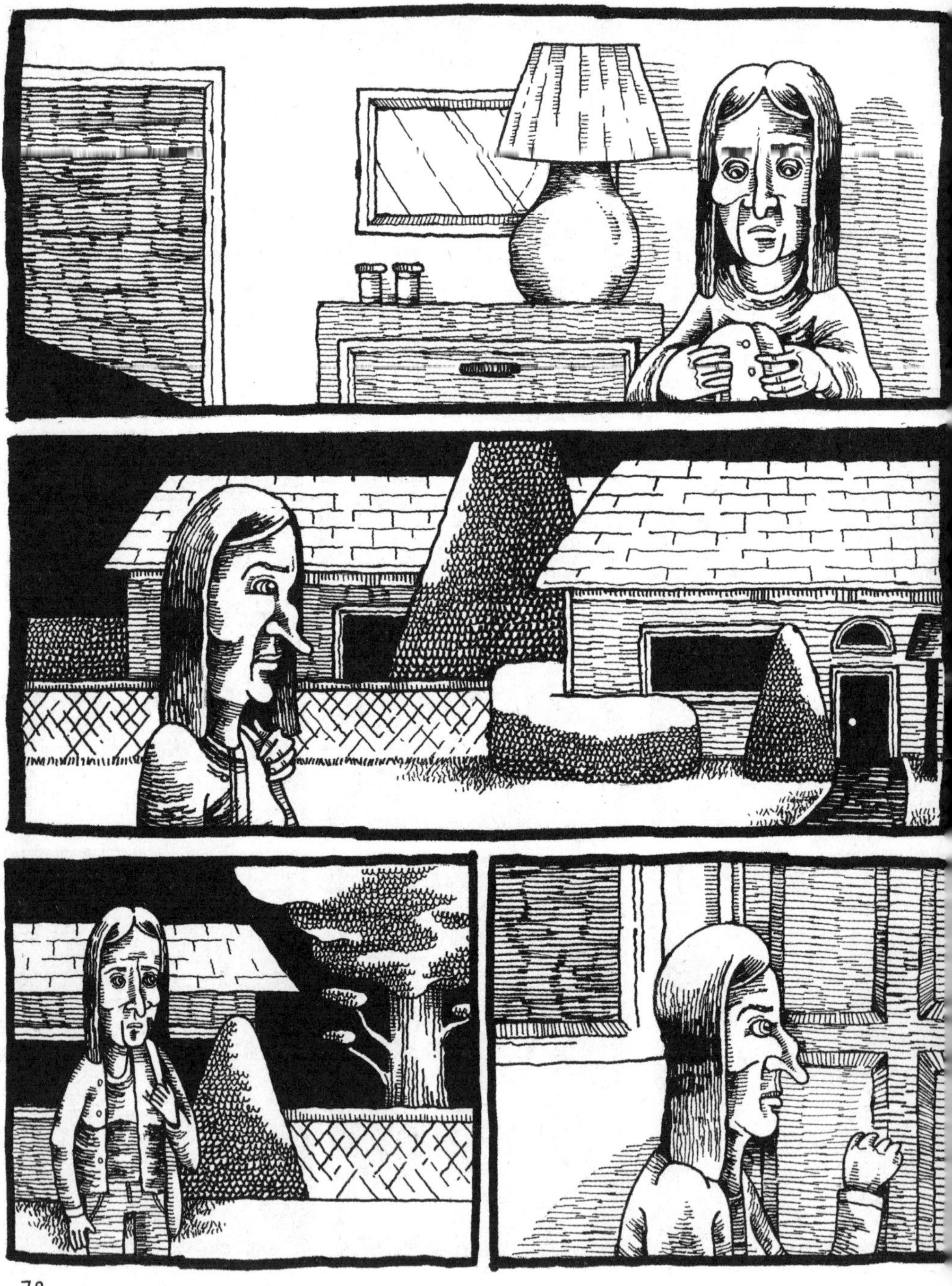

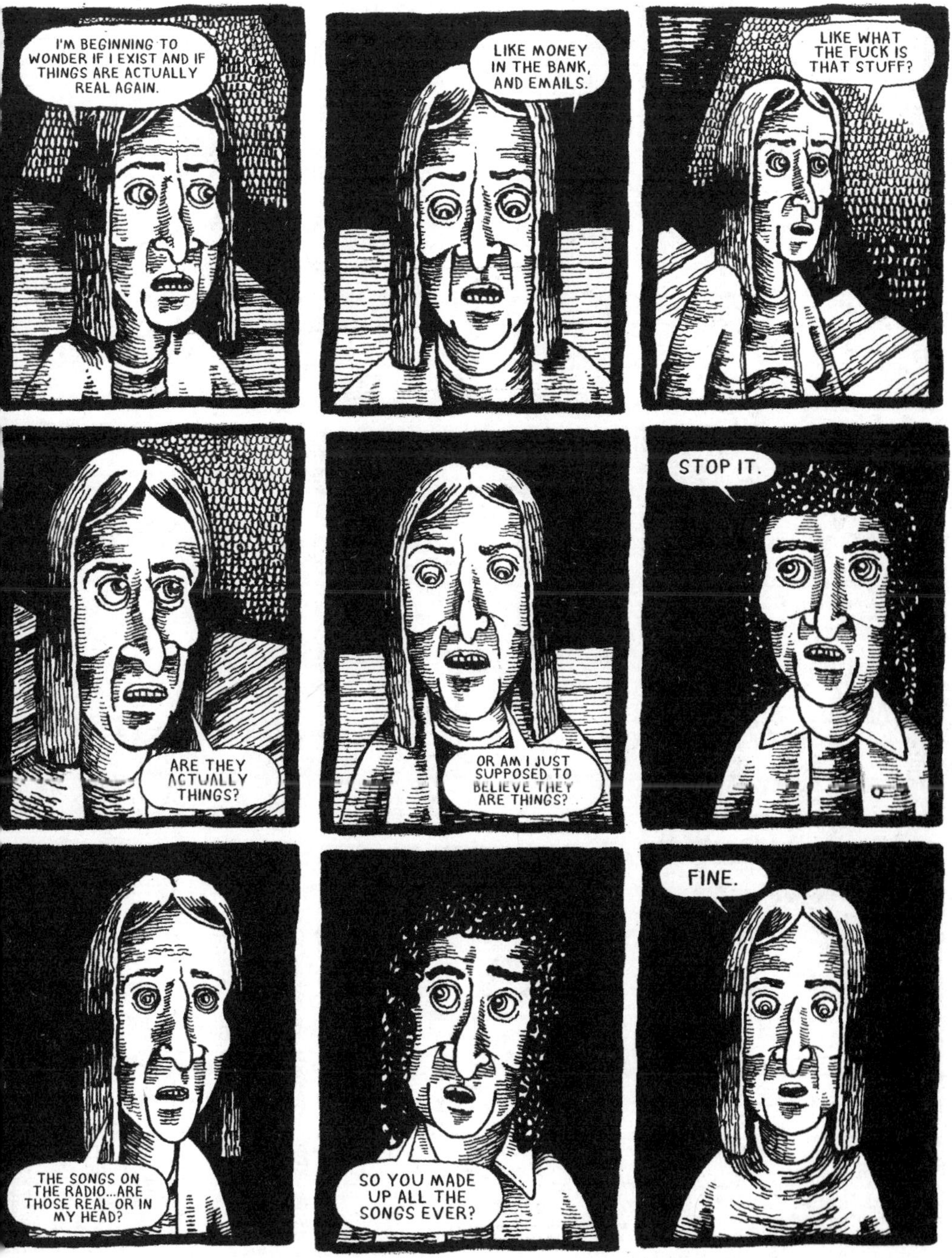
I'M BEGINNING TO WONDER IF I EXIST AND IF THINGS ARE ACTUALLY REAL AGAIN.
LIKE MONEY IN THE BANK, AND EMAILS.
LIKE WHAT THE FUCK IS THAT STUFF?
ARE THEY ACTUALLY THINGS?
OR AM I JUST SUPPOSED TO BELIEVE THEY ARE THINGS?
STOP IT.
THE SONGS ON THE RADIO...ARE THOSE REAL OR IN MY HEAD?
SO YOU MADE UP ALL THE SONGS EVER?
FINE.

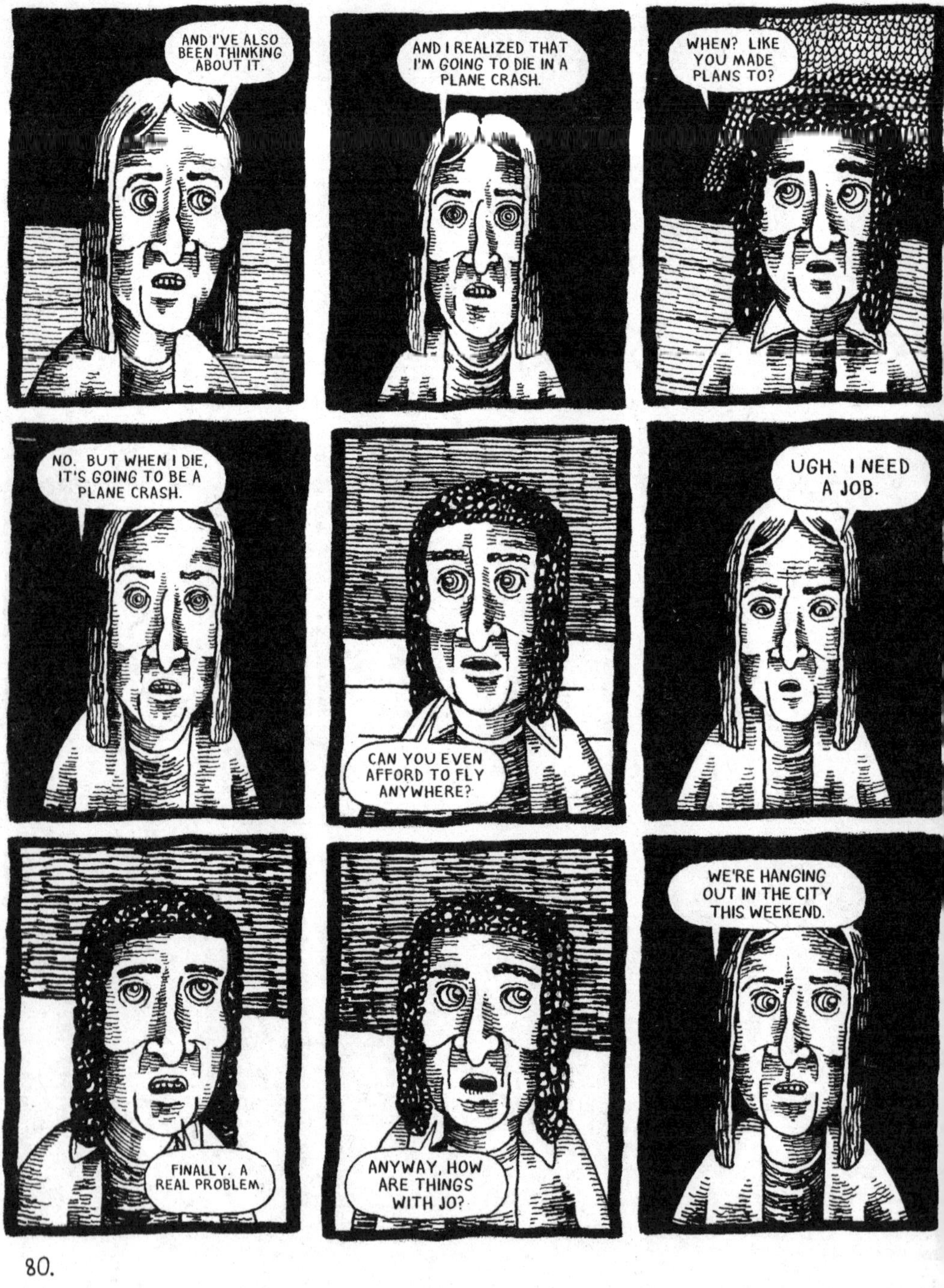
AND I'VE ALSO BEEN THINKING ABOUT IT.
AND I REALIZED THAT I'M GOING TO DIE IN A PLANE CRASH.
WHEN? LIKE YOU MADE PLANS TO?
NO. BUT WHEN I DIE, IT'S GOING TO BE A PLANE CRASH.
CAN YOU EVEN AFFORD TO FLY ANYWHERE?
UGH. I NEED A JOB.
FINALLY. A REAL PROBLEM.
ANYWAY, HOW ARE THINGS WITH JO?
WE'RE HANGING OUT IN THE CITY THIS WEEKEND.

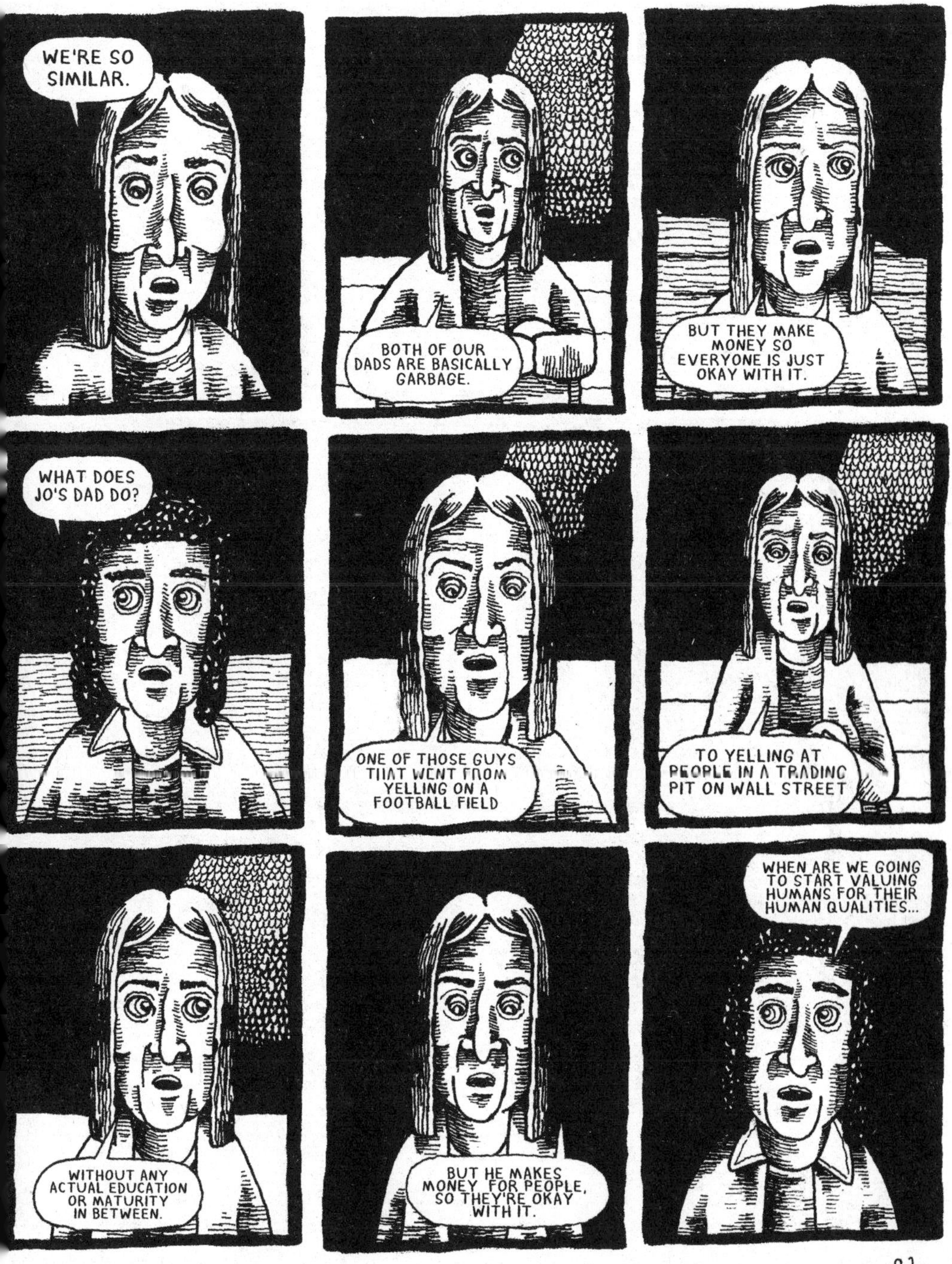
WE'RE SO SIMILAR.
BOTH OF OUR DADS ARE BASICALLY GARBAGE.
BUT THEY MAKE MONEY SO EVERYONE IS JUST OKAY WITH IT.
WHAT DOES JO'S DAD DO?
ONE OF THOSE GUYS THAT WENT FROM YELLING ON A FOOTBALL FIELD
TO YELLING AT PEOPLE IN A TRADING PIT ON WALL STREET
WITHOUT ANY ACTUAL EDUCATION OR MATURITY IN BETWEEN.
BUT HE MAKES MONEY FOR PEOPLE, SO THEY'RE OKAY WITH IT.
WHEN ARE WE GOING TO START VALUING HUMANS FOR THEIR HUMAN QUALITIES...

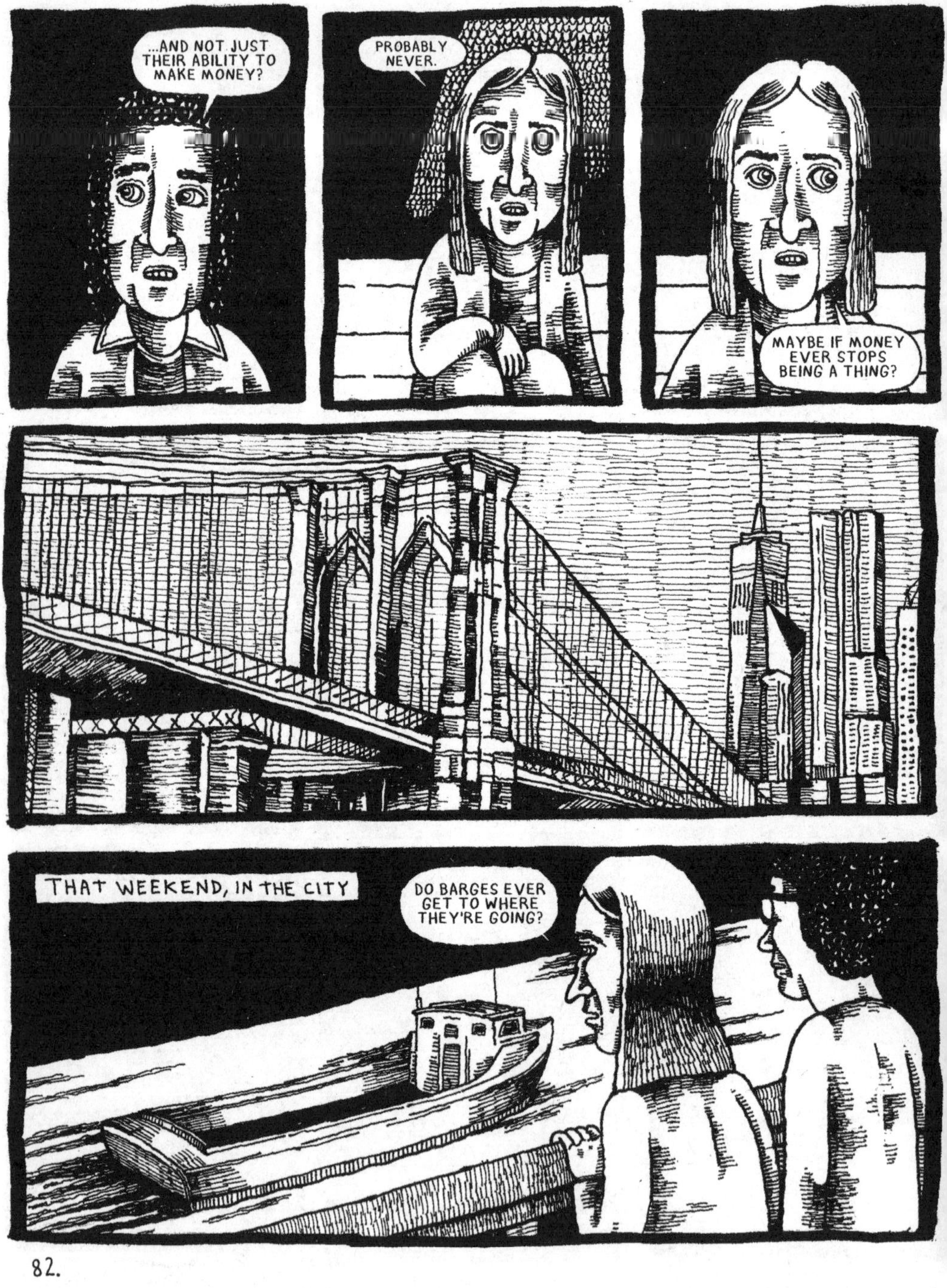
...AND NOT JUST THEIR ABILITY TO MAKE MONEY?
PROBABLY NEVER.
MAYBE IF MONEY EVER STOPS BEING A THING?
THAT WEEKEND, IN THE CITY
DO BARGES EVER GET TO WHERE THEY'RE GOING?

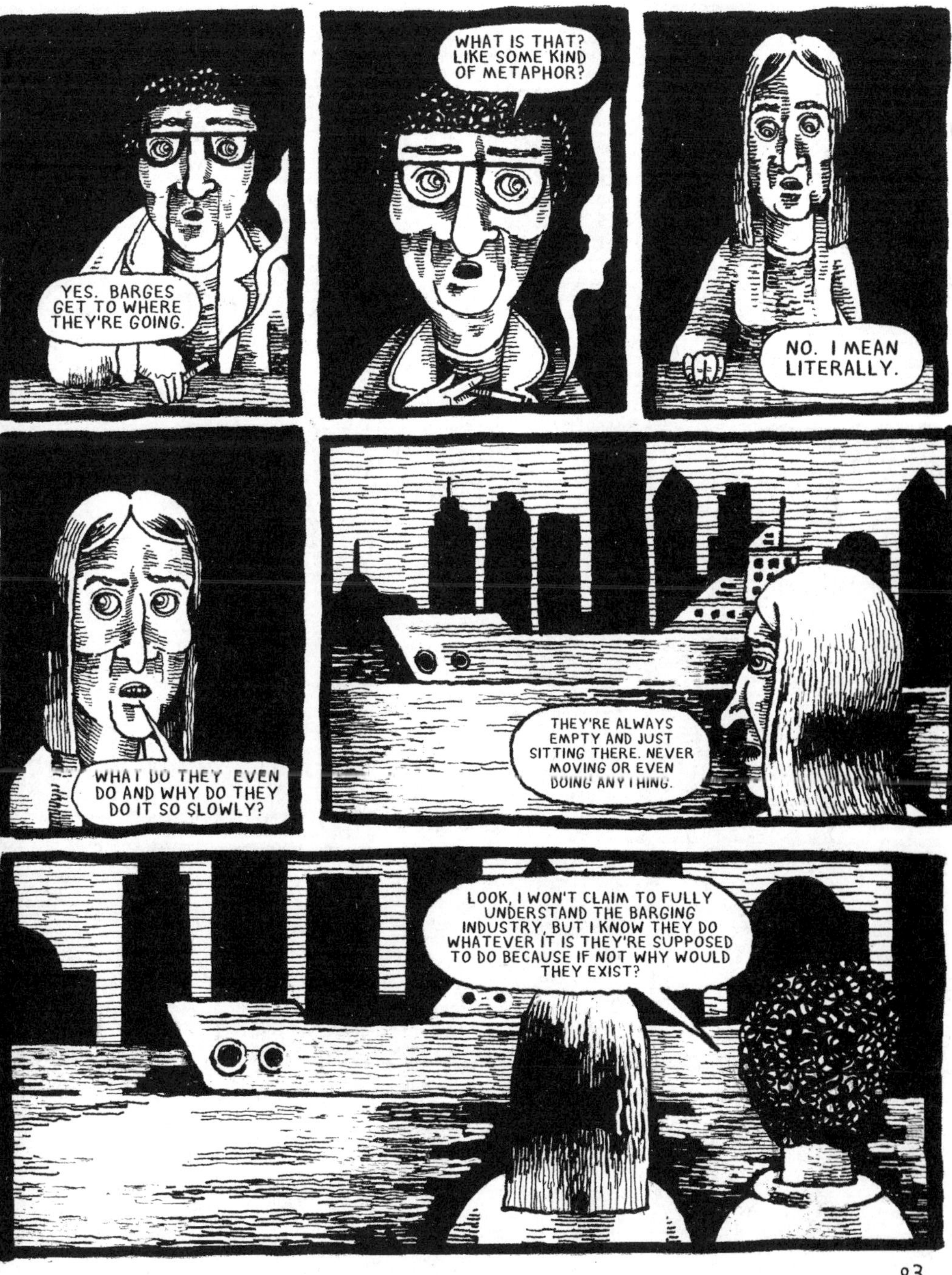
YES. BARGES GET TO WHERE THEY'RE GOING.
WHAT IS THAT? LIKE SOME KIND OF METAPHOR?
NO. I MEAN LITERALLY.
WHAT DO THEY EVEN DO AND WHY DO THEY DO IT SO SLOWLY?
THEY'RE ALWAYS EMPTY AND JUST SITTING THERE. NEVER MOVING OR EVEN DOING ANYTHING.
LOOK, I WON'T CLAIM TO FULLY UNDERSTAND THE BARGING INDUSTRY, BUT I KNOW THEY DO WHATEVER IT IS THEY'RE SUPPOSED TO DO BECAUSE IF NOT WHY WOULD THEY EXIST?

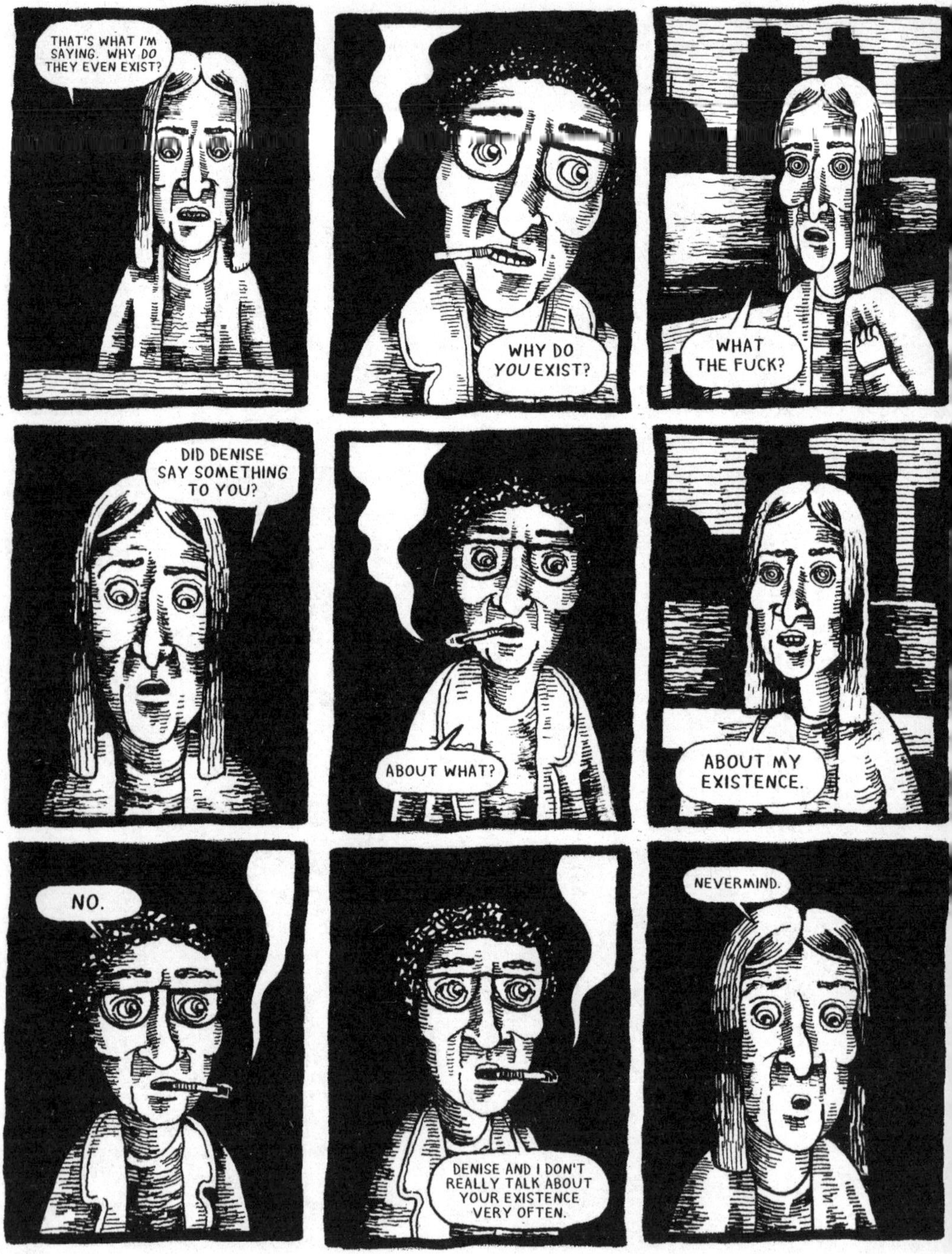
THAT'S WHAT I'M SAYING. WHY DO THEY EVEN EXIST?
WHY DO *YOU* EXIST?
WHAT THE FUCK?
DID DENISE SAY SOMETHING TO YOU?
ABOUT WHAT?
ABOUT MY EXISTENCE.
NO.
DENISE AND I DON'T REALLY TALK ABOUT YOUR EXISTENCE VERY OFTEN.
NEVERMIND.

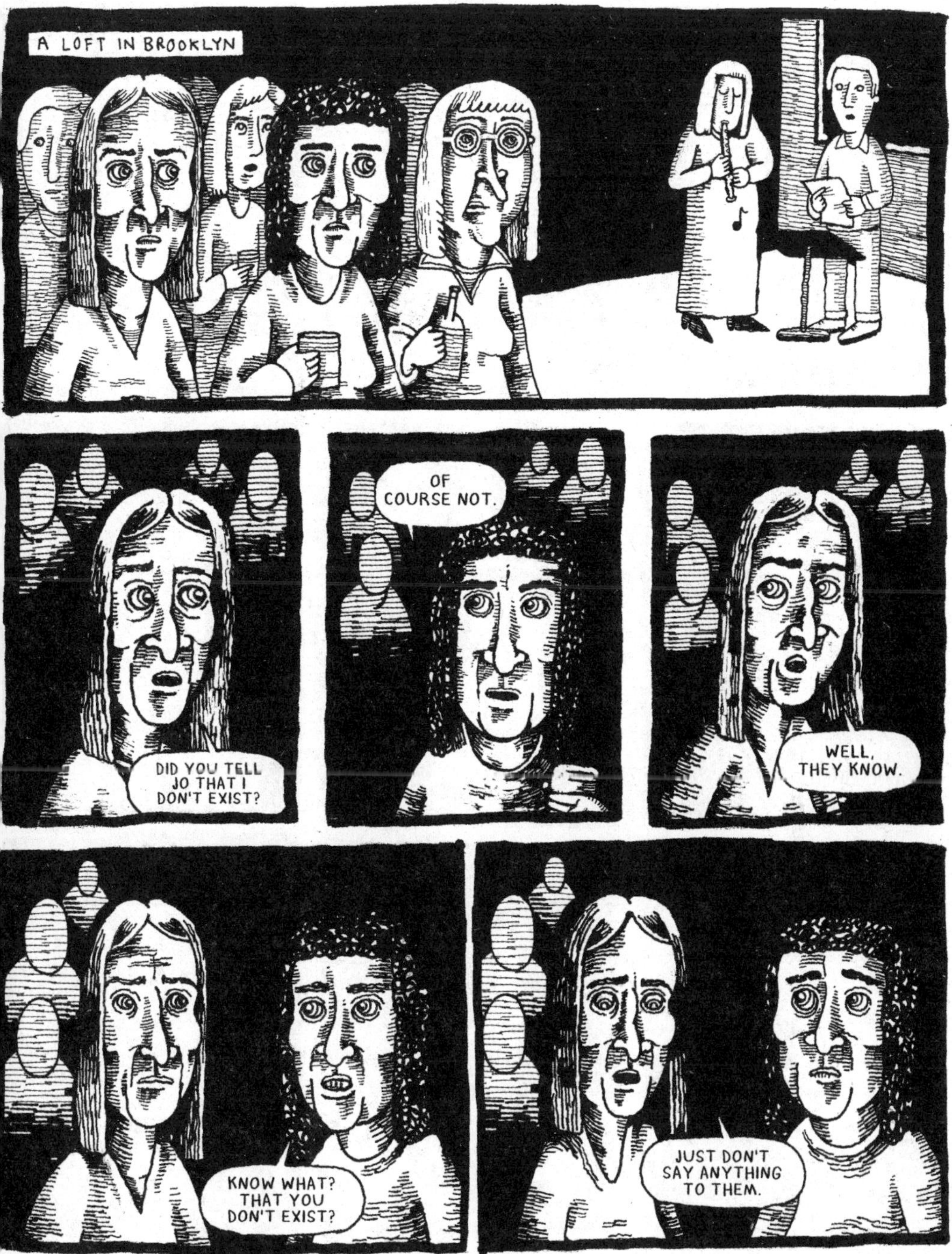
A LOFT IN BROOKLYN
DID YOU TELL JO THAT I DON'T EXIST?
OF COURSE NOT.
WELL, THEY KNOW.
KNOW WHAT? THAT YOU DON'T EXIST?
JUST DON'T SAY ANYTHING TO THEM.

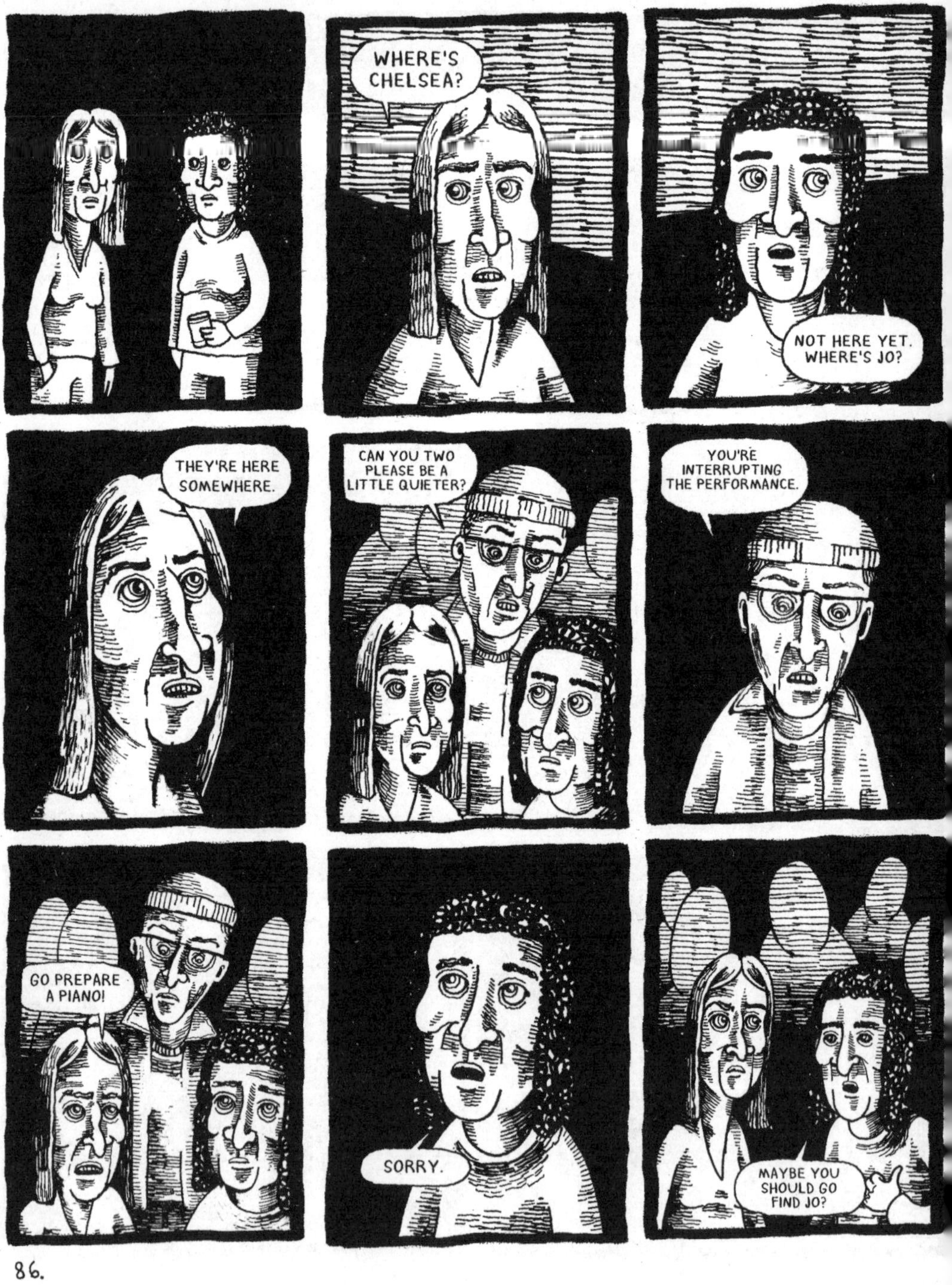
WHERE'S CHELSEA?
NOT HERE YET. WHERE'S JO?
THEY'RE HERE SOMEWHERE.
CAN YOU TWO PLEASE BE A LITTLE QUIETER?
YOU'RE INTERRUPTING THE PERFORMANCE.
GO PREPARE A PIANO!
SORRY.
MAYBE YOU SHOULD GO FIND JO?

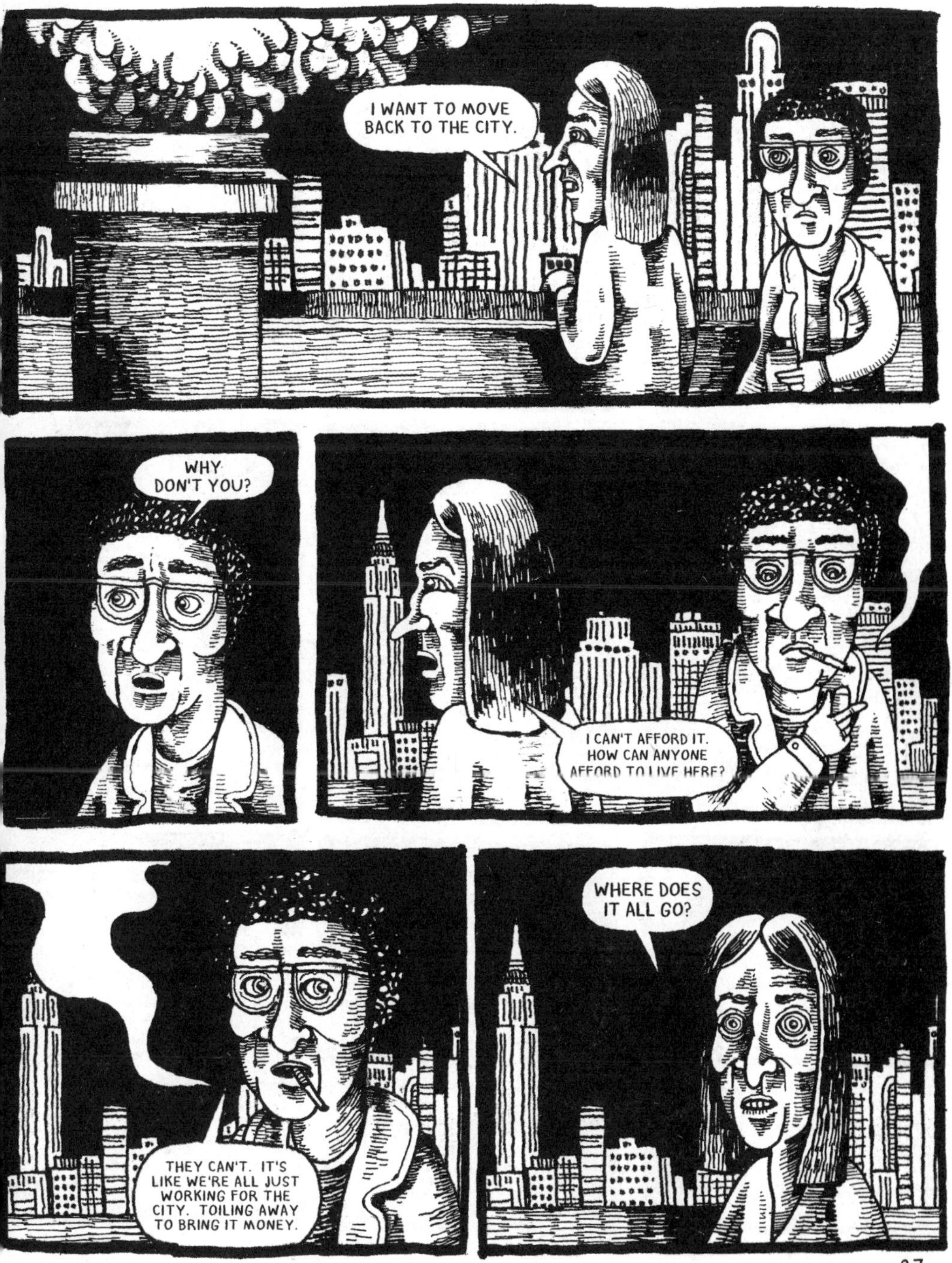
I WANT TO MOVE BACK TO THE CITY.
WHY DON'T YOU?
I CAN'T AFFORD IT. HOW CAN ANYONE AFFORD TO LIVE HERE?
THEY CAN'T. IT'S LIKE WE'RE ALL JUST WORKING FOR THE CITY. TOILING AWAY TO BRING IT MONEY.
WHERE DOES IT ALL GO?

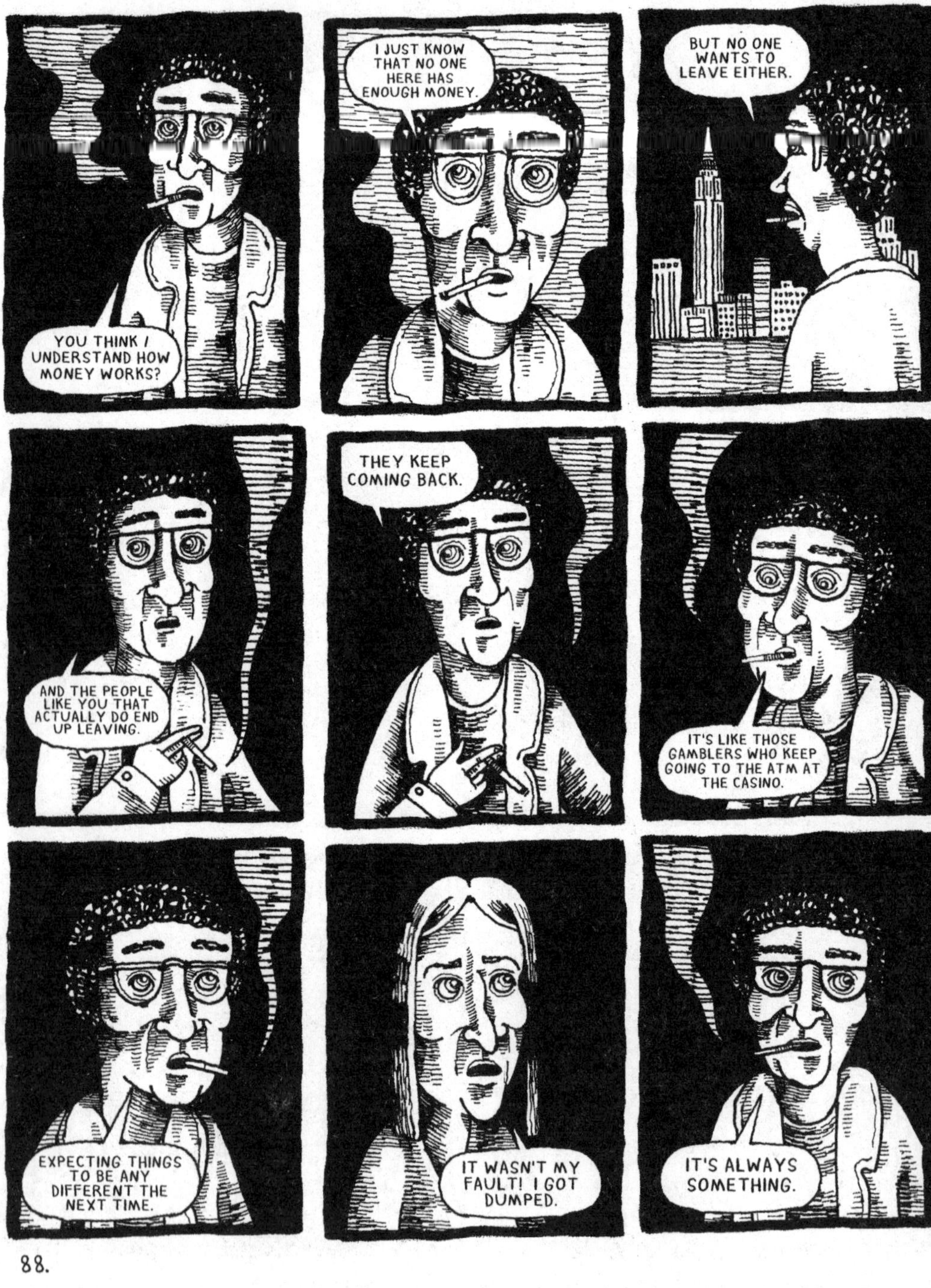
YOU THINK I UNDERSTAND HOW MONEY WORKS?
I JUST KNOW THAT NO ONE HERE HAS ENOUGH MONEY.
BUT NO ONE WANTS TO LEAVE EITHER.
AND THE PEOPLE LIKE YOU THAT ACTUALLY DO END UP LEAVING.
THEY KEEP COMING BACK.
IT'S LIKE THOSE GAMBLERS WHO KEEP GOING TO THE ATM AT THE CASINO.
EXPECTING THINGS TO BE ANY DIFFERENT THE NEXT TIME.
IT WASN'T MY FAULT! I GOT DUMPED.
IT'S ALWAYS SOMETHING.

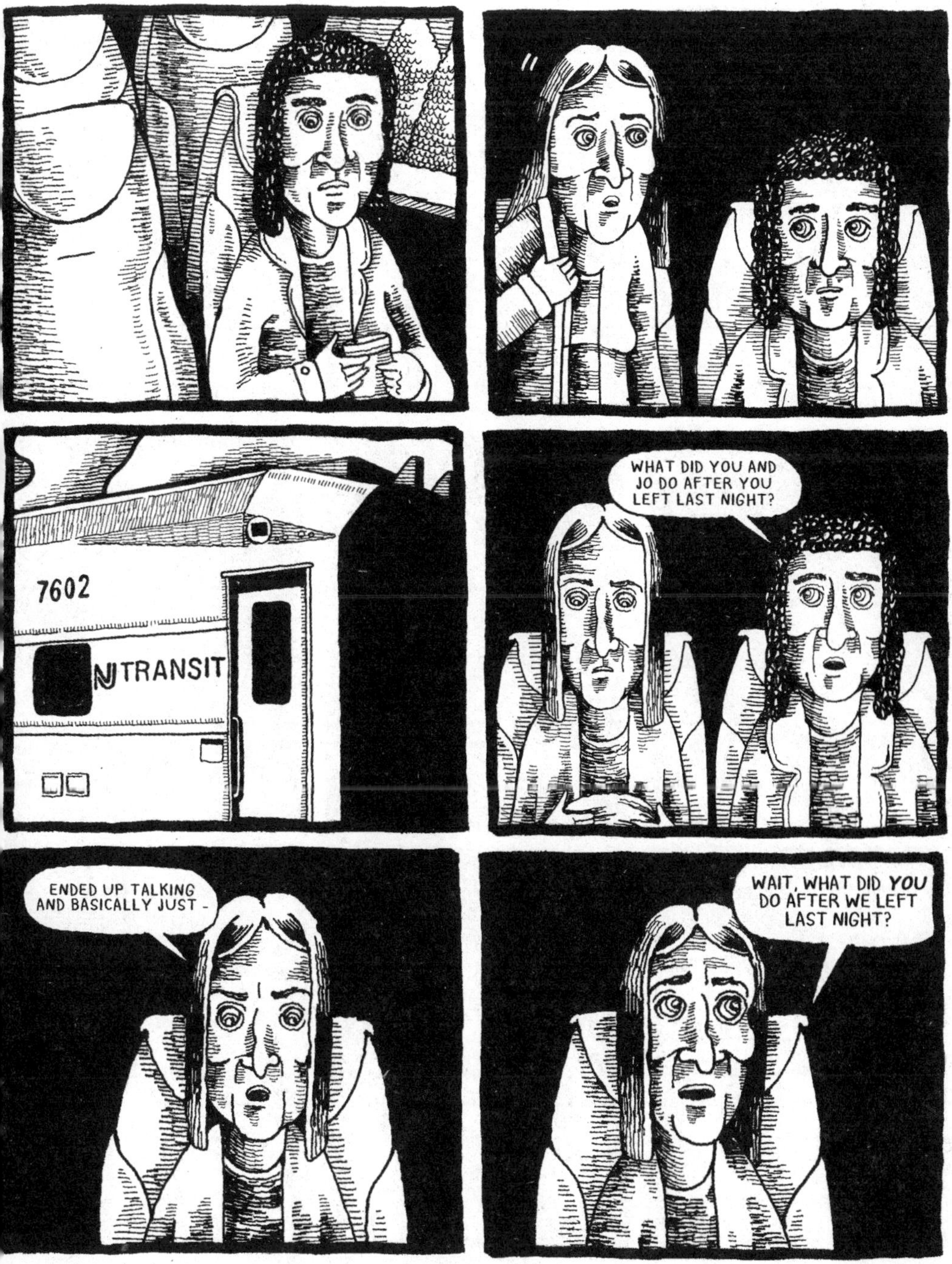

7602
NJ TRANSIT
WHAT DID YOU AND JO DO AFTER YOU LEFT LAST NIGHT?
ENDED UP TALKING AND BASICALLY JUST -
WAIT, WHAT DID *YOU* DO AFTER WE LEFT LAST NIGHT?

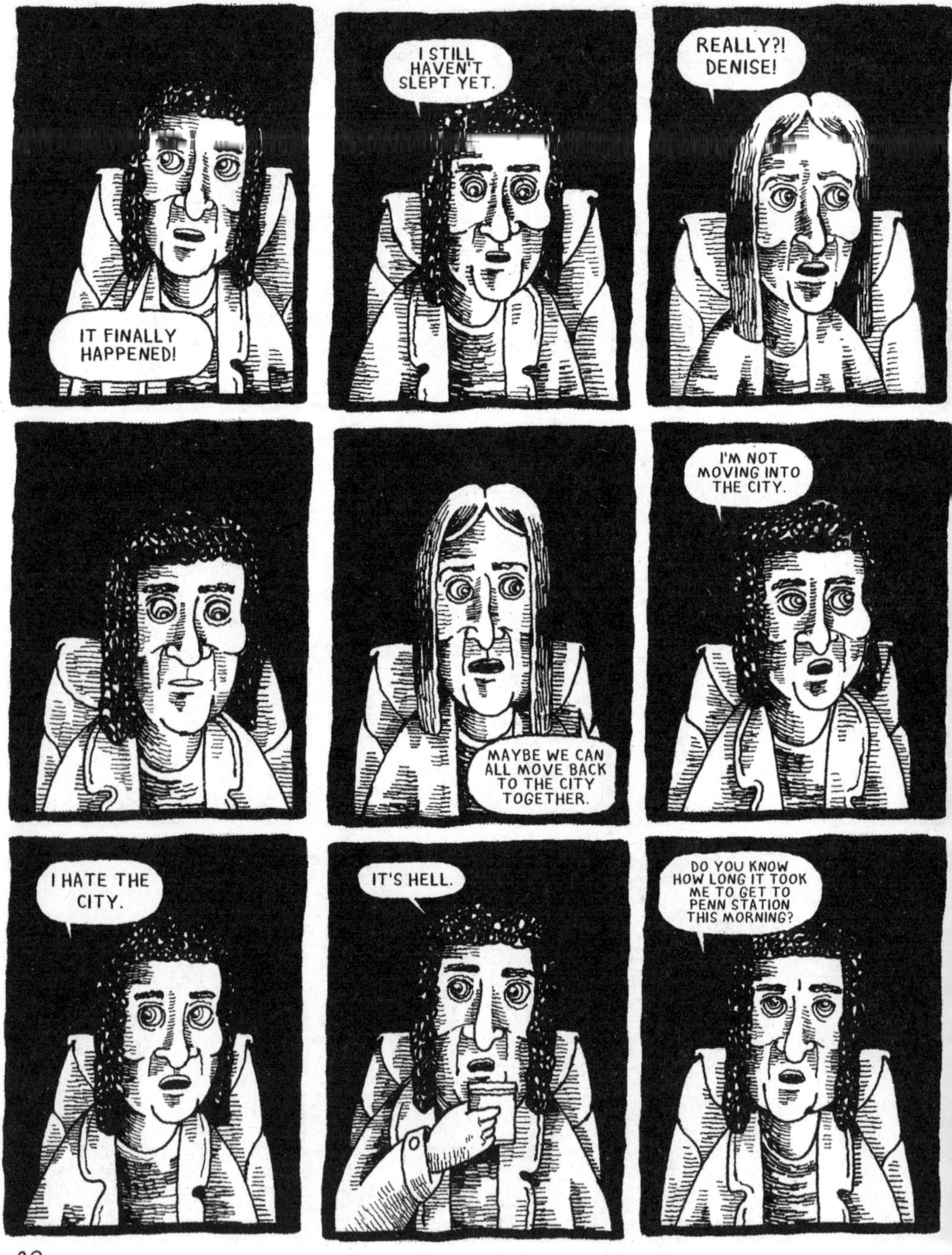
IT FINALLY HAPPENED!
I STILL HAVEN'T SLEPT YET.
REALLY?! DENISE!
MAYBE WE CAN ALL MOVE BACK TO THE CITY TOGETHER.
I'M NOT MOVING INTO THE CITY.
I HATE THE CITY.
IT'S HELL.
DO YOU KNOW HOW LONG IT TOOK ME TO GET TO PENN STATION THIS MORNING?

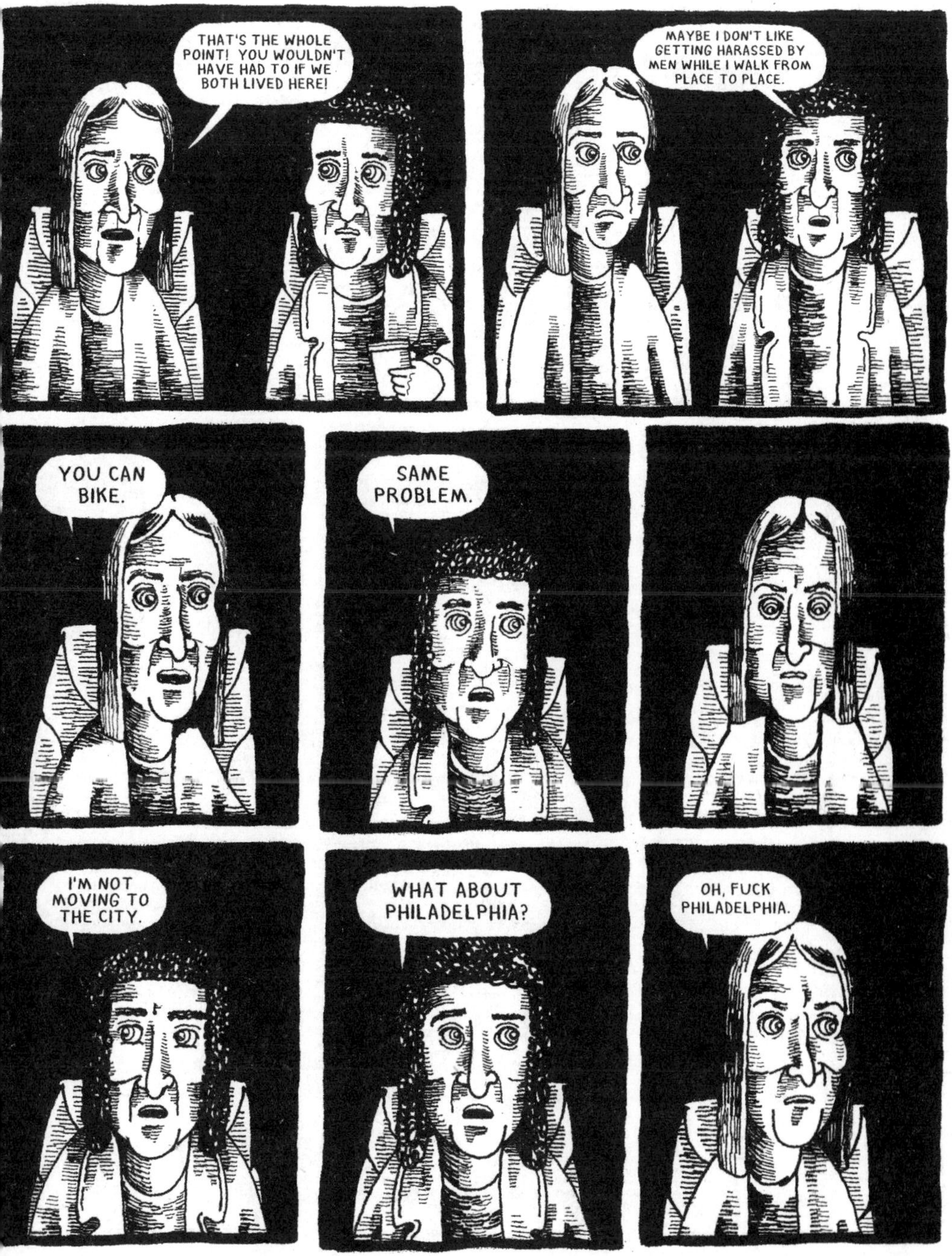
THAT'S THE WHOLE POINT! YOU WOULDN'T HAVE HAD TO IF WE BOTH LIVED HERE!
MAYBE I DON'T LIKE GETTING HARASSED BY MEN WHILE I WALK FROM PLACE TO PLACE.
YOU CAN BIKE.
SAME PROBLEM.
I'M NOT MOVING TO THE CITY.
WHAT ABOUT PHILADELPHIA?
OH, FUCK PHILADELPHIA.

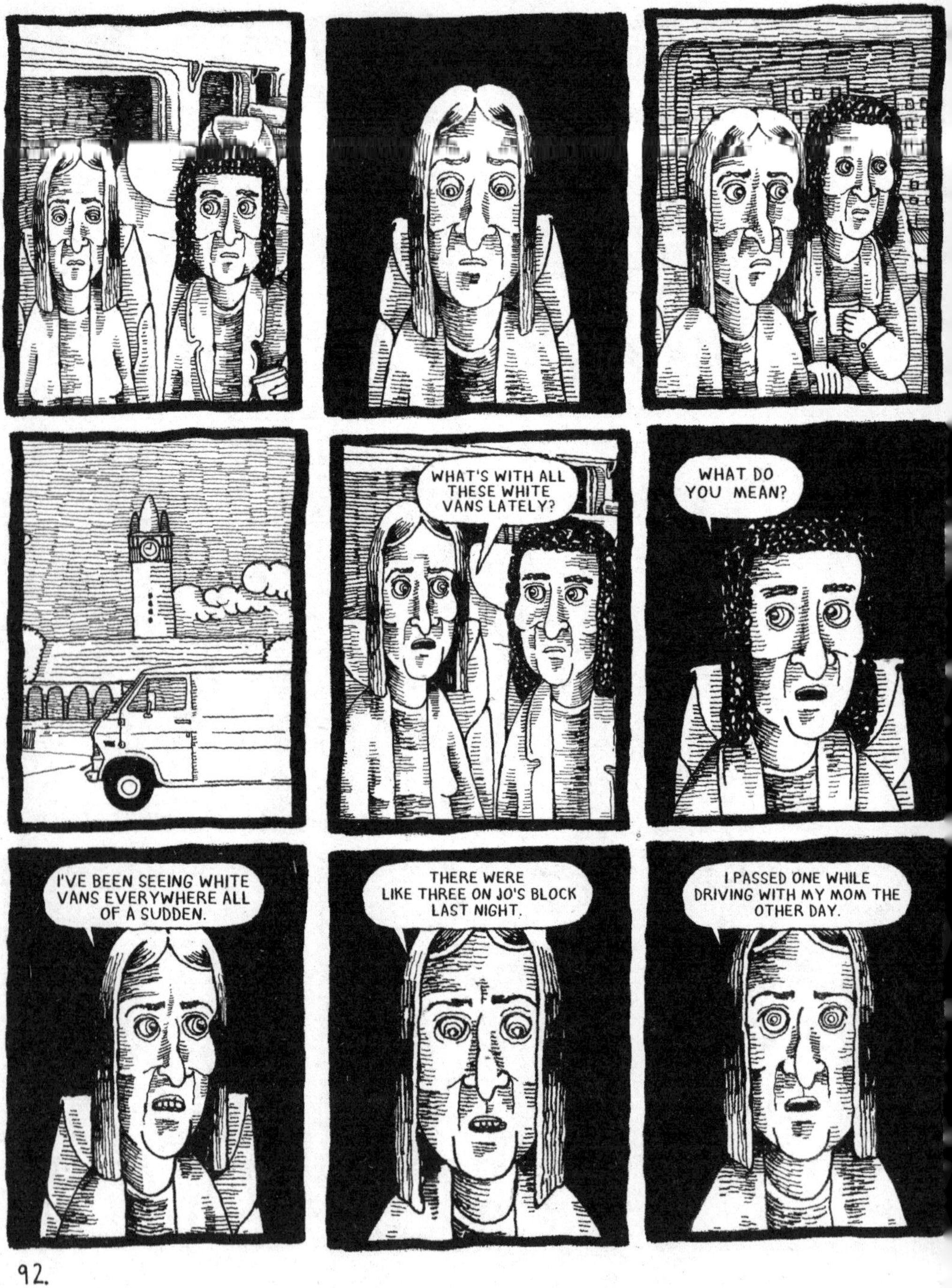
WHAT'S WITH ALL THESE WHITE VANS LATELY?
WHAT DO YOU MEAN?
I'VE BEEN SEEING WHITE VANS EVERYWHERE ALL OF A SUDDEN.
THERE WERE LIKE THREE ON JO'S BLOCK LAST NIGHT.
I PASSED ONE WHILE DRIVING WITH MY MOM THE OTHER DAY.

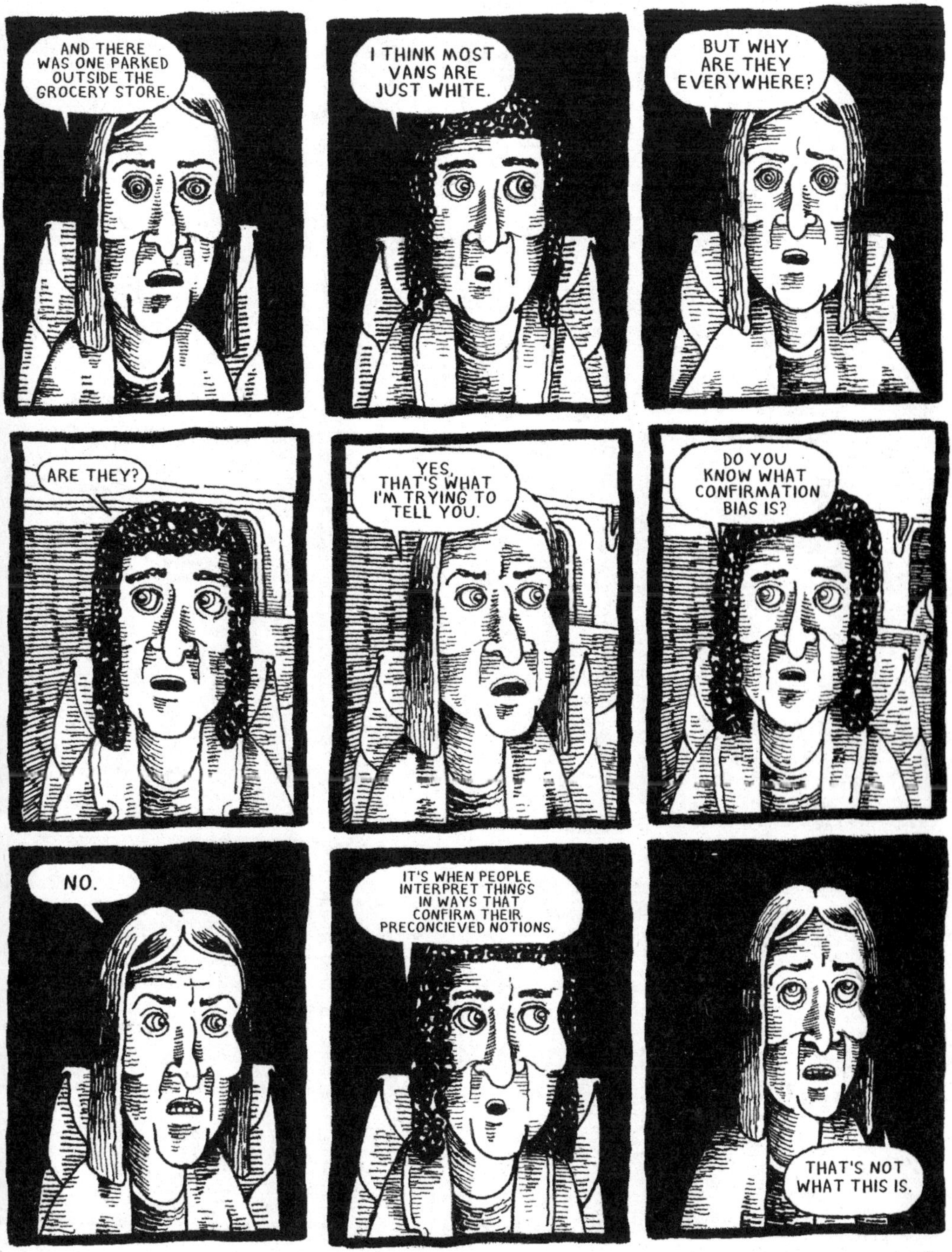
AND THERE WAS ONE PARKED OUTSIDE THE GROCERY STORE.
I THINK MOST VANS ARE JUST WHITE.
BUT WHY ARE THEY EVERYWHERE?
ARE THEY?
YES, THAT'S WHAT I'M TRYING TO TELL YOU.
DO YOU KNOW WHAT CONFIRMATION BIAS IS?
NO.
IT'S WHEN PEOPLE INTERPRET THINGS IN WAYS THAT CONFIRM THEIR PRECONCIEVED NOTIONS.
THAT'S NOT WHAT THIS IS.

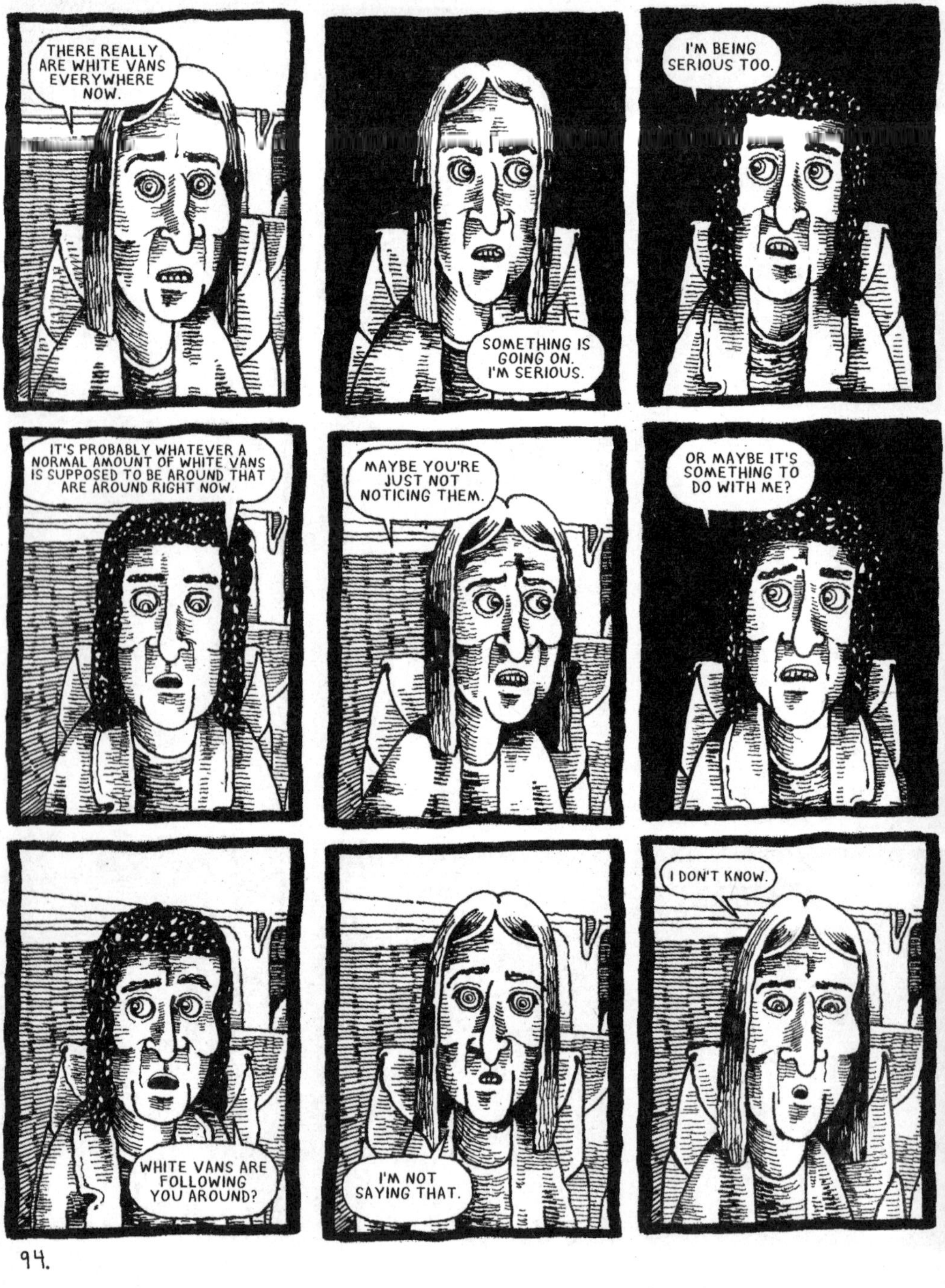
THERE REALLY ARE WHITE VANS EVERYWHERE NOW.
SOMETHING IS GOING ON. I'M SERIOUS.
I'M BEING SERIOUS TOO.
IT'S PROBABLY WHATEVER A NORMAL AMOUNT OF WHITE VANS IS SUPPOSED TO BE AROUND THAT ARE AROUND RIGHT NOW.
MAYBE YOU'RE JUST NOT NOTICING THEM.
OR MAYBE IT'S SOMETHING TO DO WITH ME?
WHITE VANS ARE FOLLOWING YOU AROUND?
I'M NOT SAYING THAT.
I DON'T KNOW.

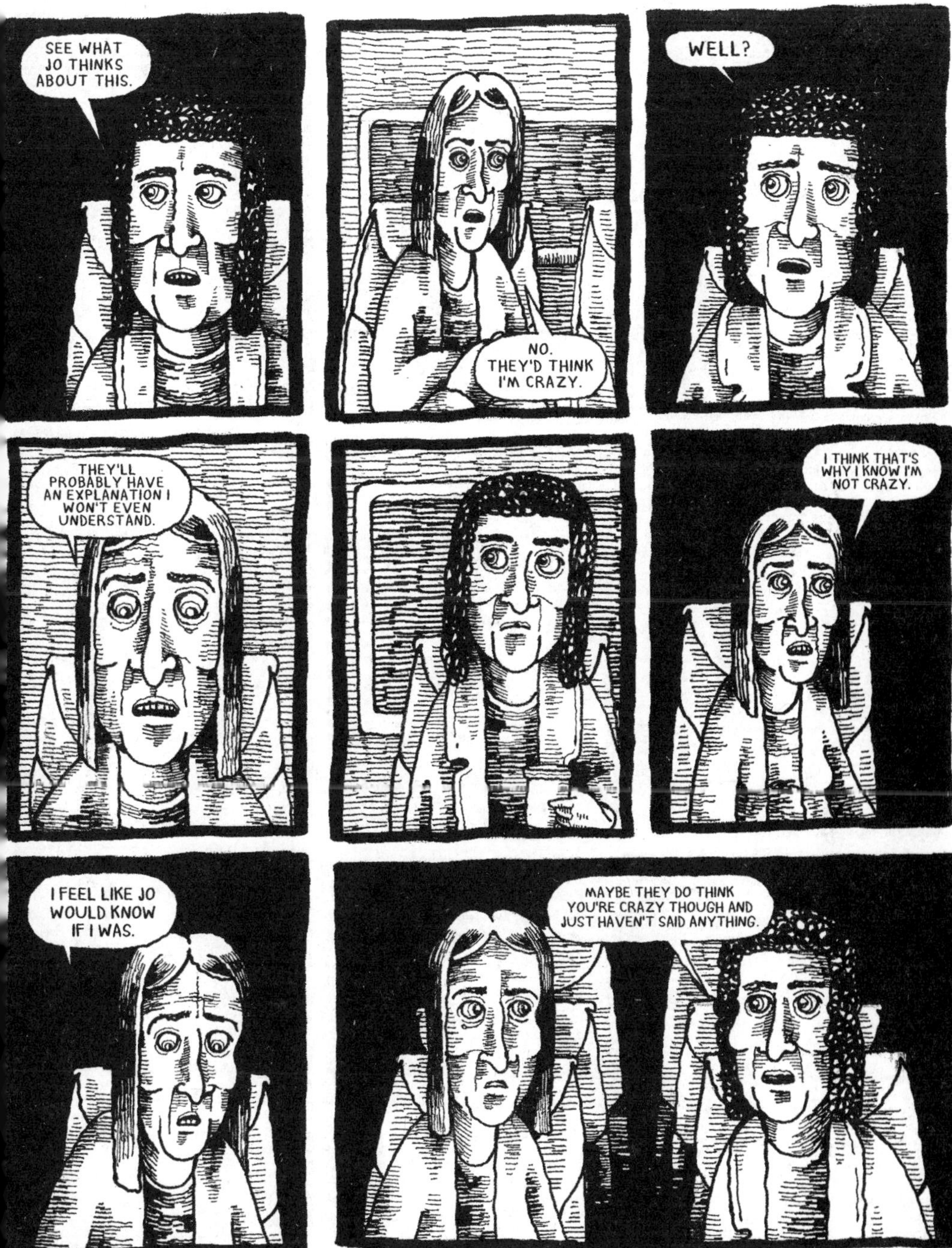
SEE WHAT JO THINKS ABOUT THIS.
NO. THEY'D THINK I'M CRAZY.
WELL?
THEY'LL PROBABLY HAVE AN EXPLANATION I WON'T EVEN UNDERSTAND.
I THINK THAT'S WHY I KNOW I'M NOT CRAZY.
I FEEL LIKE JO WOULD KNOW IF I WAS.
MAYBE THEY DO THINK YOU'RE CRAZY THOUGH AND JUST HAVEN'T SAID ANYTHING.

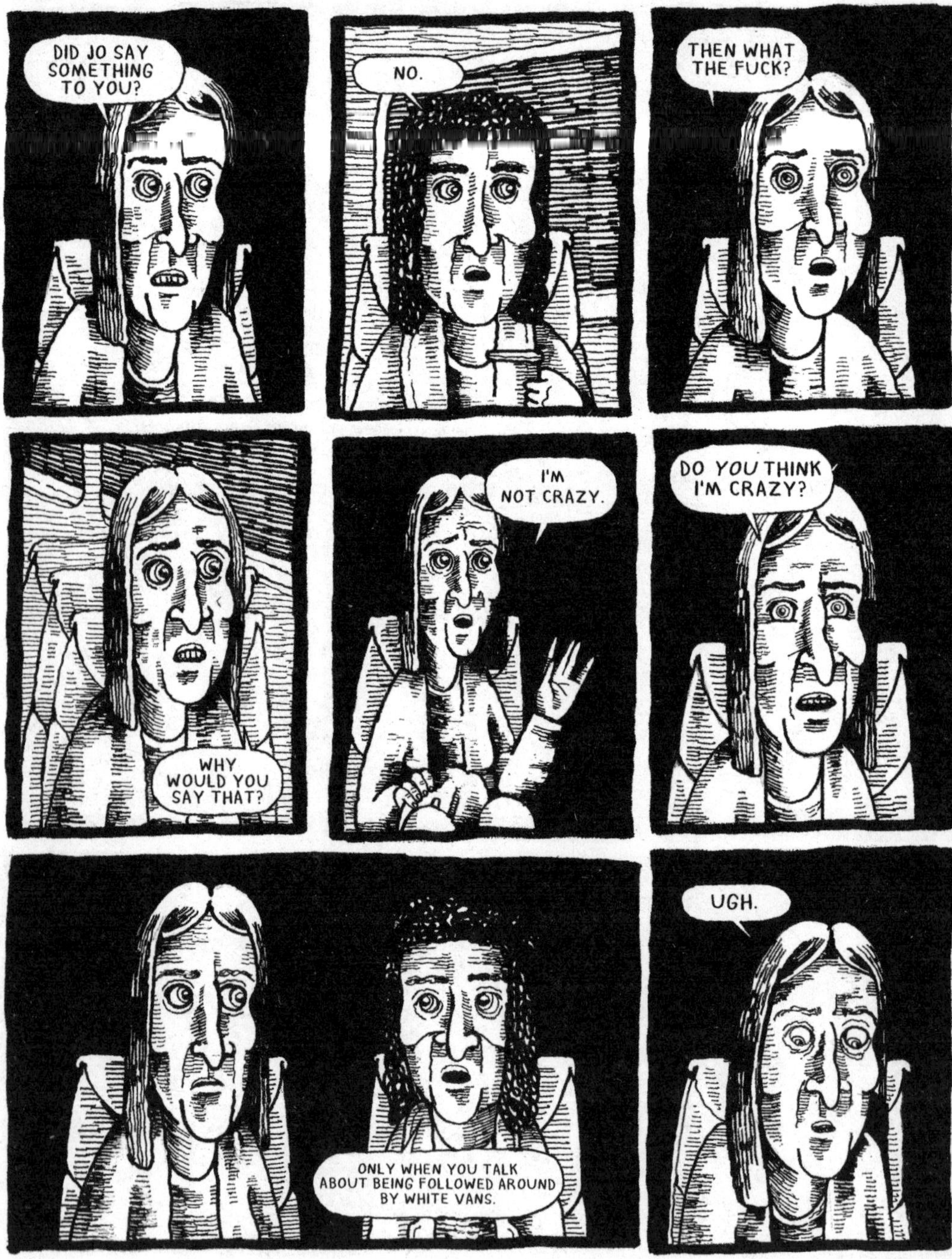
DID JO SAY SOMETHING TO YOU?
NO.
THEN WHAT THE FUCK?
WHY WOULD YOU SAY THAT?
I'M NOT CRAZY.
DO *YOU* THINK I'M CRAZY?
ONLY WHEN YOU TALK ABOUT BEING FOLLOWED AROUND BY WHITE VANS.
UGH.

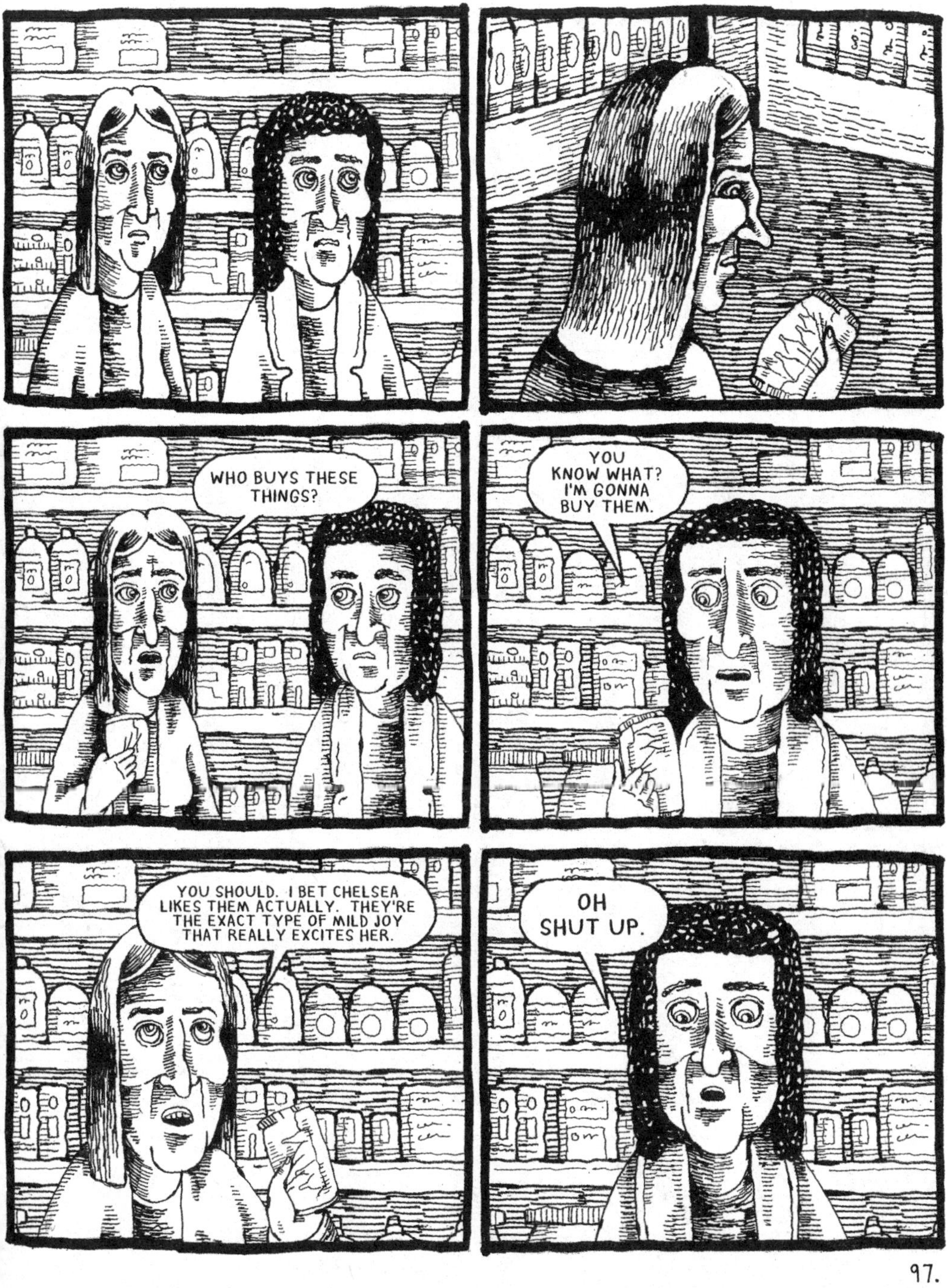
WHO BUYS THESE THINGS?
YOU KNOW WHAT? I'M GONNA BUY THEM.
YOU SHOULD. I BET CHELSEA LIKES THEM ACTUALLY. THEY'RE THE EXACT TYPE OF MILD JOY THAT REALLY EXCITES HER.
OH SHUT UP.

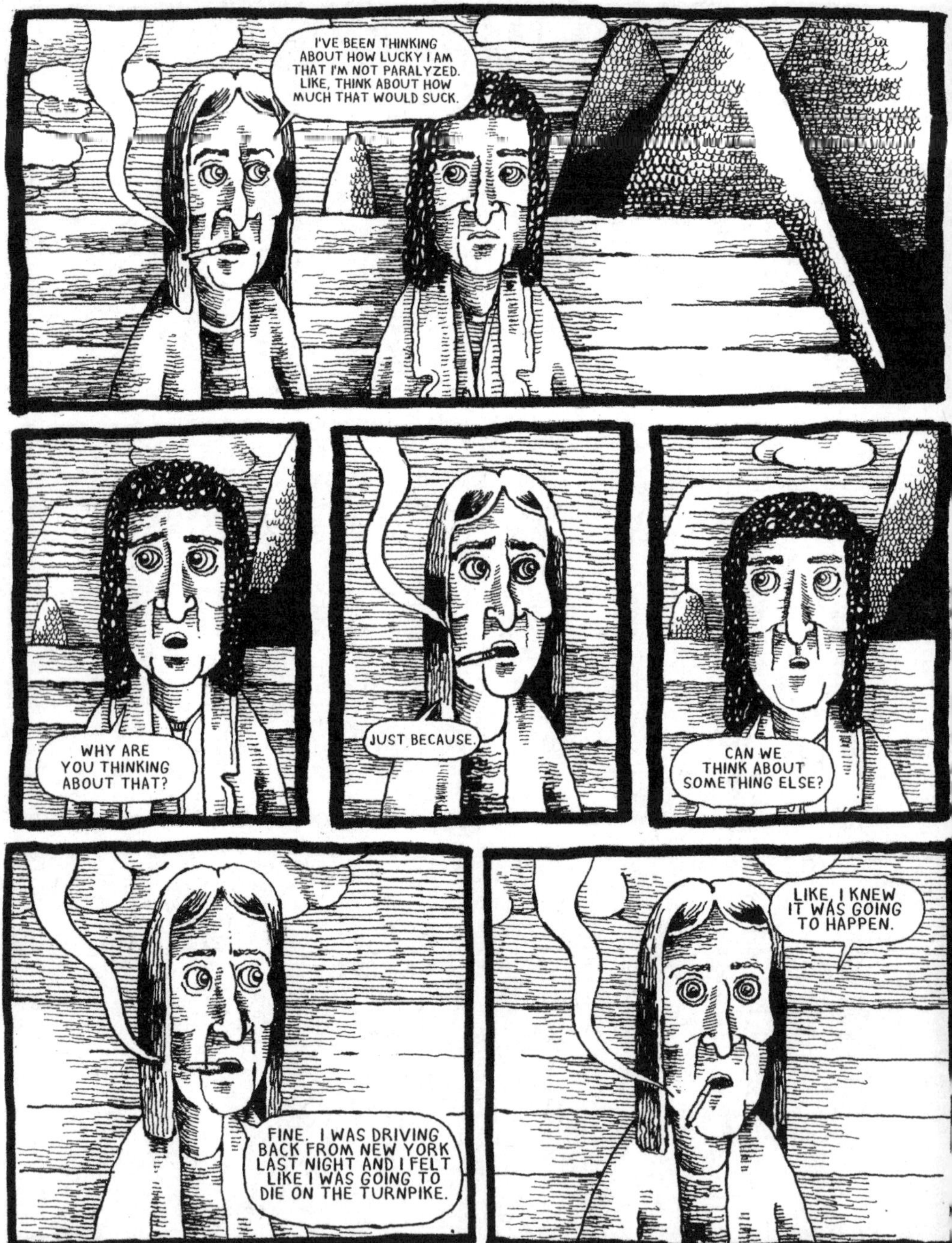
I'VE BEEN THINKING ABOUT HOW LUCKY I AM THAT I'M NOT PARALYZED. LIKE, THINK ABOUT HOW MUCH THAT WOULD SUCK.
WHY ARE YOU THINKING ABOUT THAT?
JUST BECAUSE.
CAN WE THINK ABOUT SOMETHING ELSE?
FINE. I WAS DRIVING BACK FROM NEW YORK LAST NIGHT AND I FELT LIKE I WAS GOING TO DIE ON THE TURNPIKE.
LIKE, I KNEW IT WAS GOING TO HAPPEN.

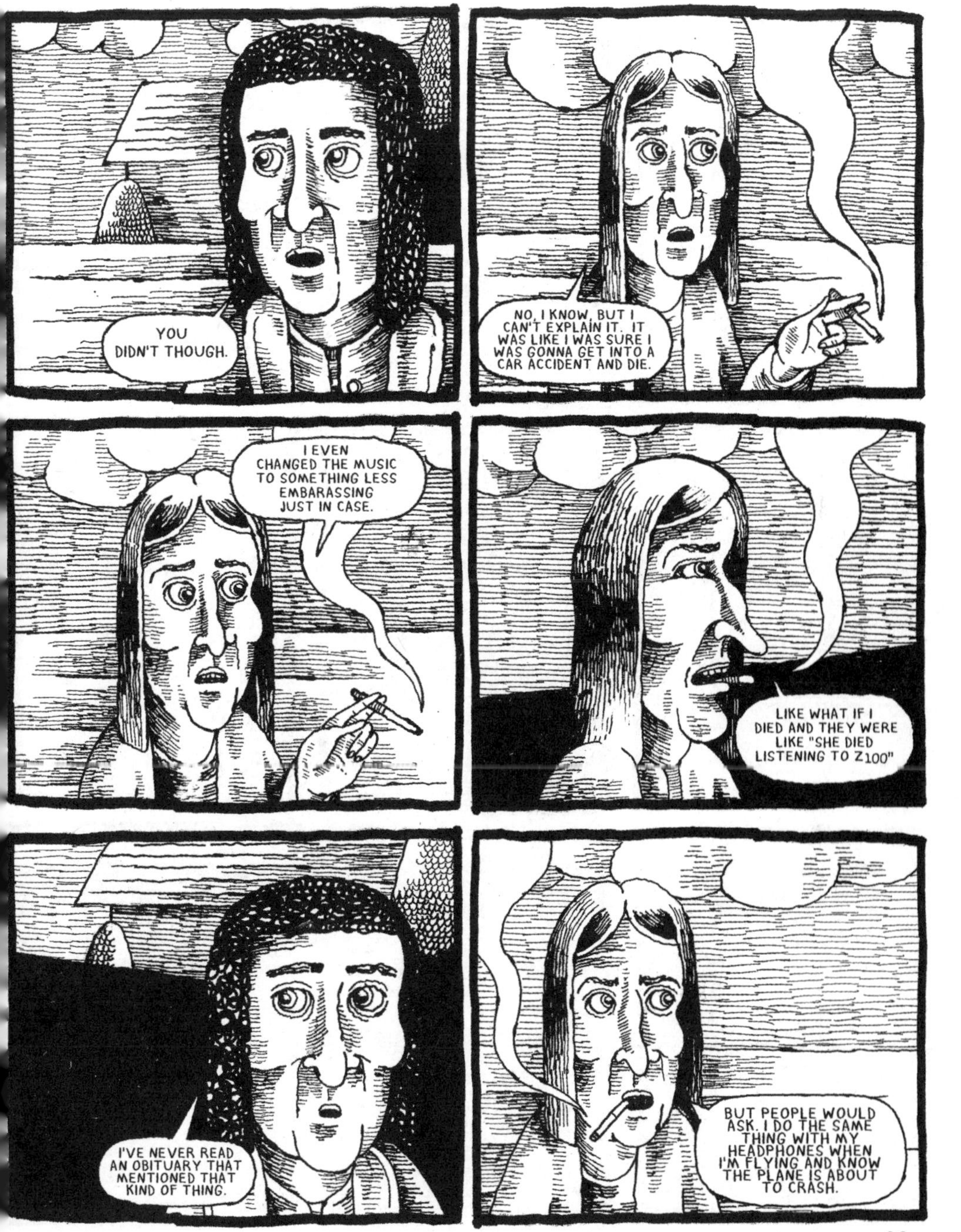
YOU DIDN'T THOUGH.
NO, I KNOW, BUT I CAN'T EXPLAIN IT. IT WAS LIKE I WAS SURE I WAS GONNA GET INTO A CAR ACCIDENT AND DIE.
I EVEN CHANGED THE MUSIC TO SOMETHING LESS EMBARASSING JUST IN CASE.
LIKE WHAT IF I DIED AND THEY WERE LIKE "SHE DIED LISTENING TO Z100"
I'VE NEVER READ AN OBITUARY THAT MENTIONED THAT KIND OF THING.
BUT PEOPLE WOULD ASK. I DO THE SAME THING WITH MY HEADPHONES WHEN I'M FLYING AND KNOW THE PLANE IS ABOUT TO CRASH.

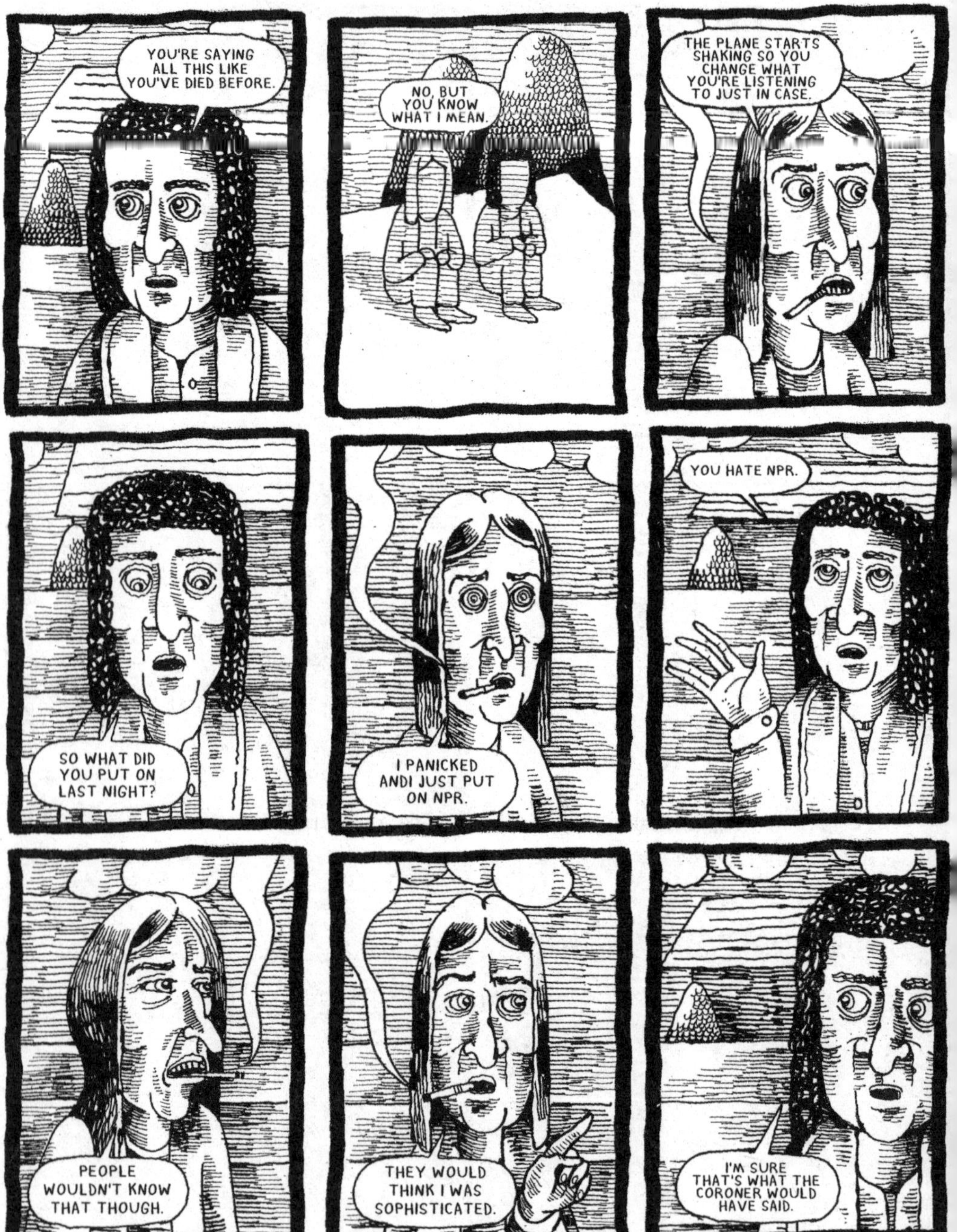
YOU'RE SAYING ALL THIS LIKE YOU'VE DIED BEFORE.
NO, BUT YOU KNOW WHAT I MEAN.
THE PLANE STARTS SHAKING SO YOU CHANGE WHAT YOU'RE LISTENING TO JUST IN CASE.
SO WHAT DID YOU PUT ON LAST NIGHT?
I PANICKED AND I JUST PUT ON NPR.
YOU HATE NPR.
PEOPLE WOULDN'T KNOW THAT THOUGH.
THEY WOULD THINK I WAS SOPHISTICATED.
I'M SURE THAT'S WHAT THE CORONER WOULD HAVE SAID.

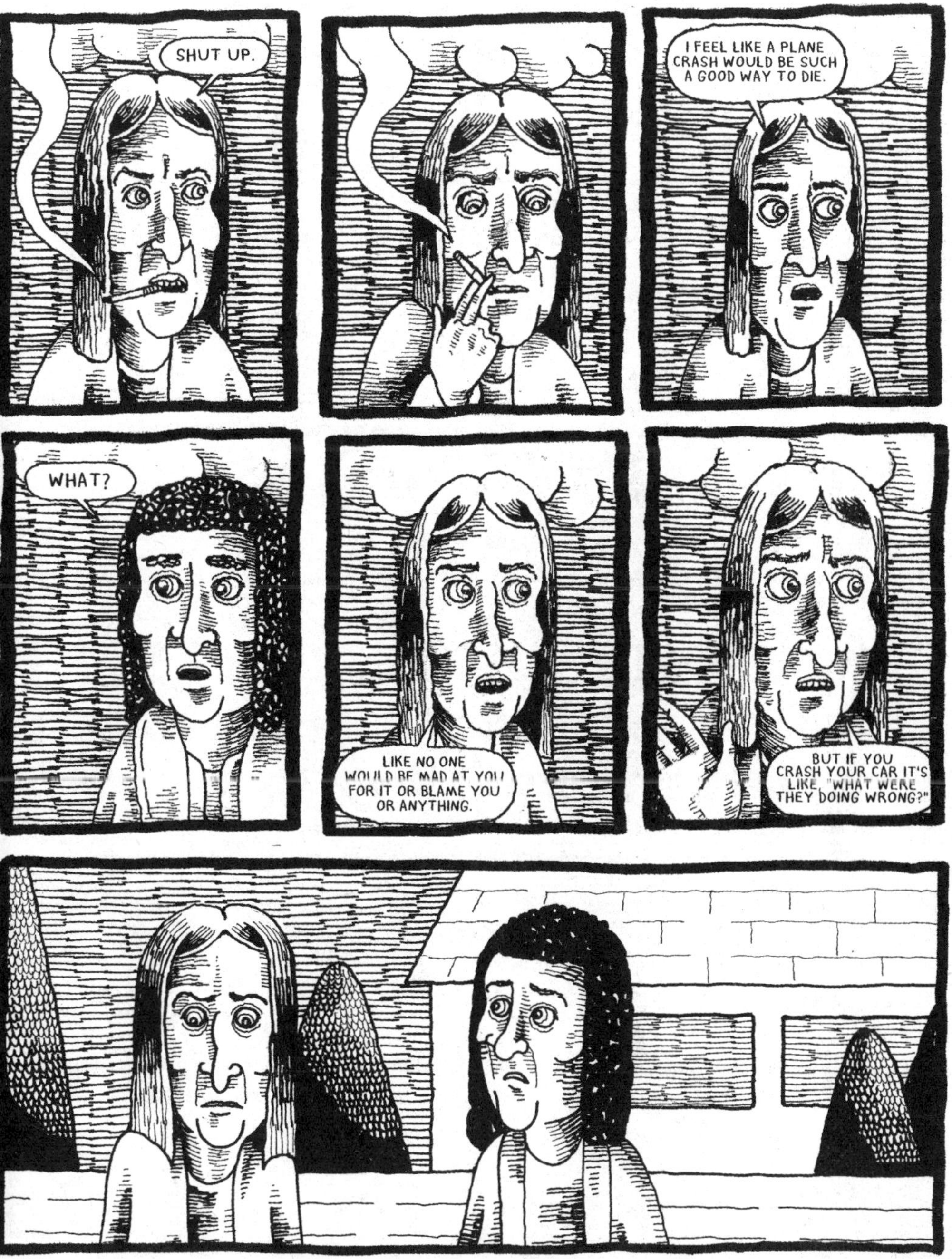
SHUT UP.
I FEEL LIKE A PLANE CRASH WOULD BE SUCH A GOOD WAY TO DIE.
WHAT?
LIKE NO ONE WOULD BE MAD AT YOU FOR IT OR BLAME YOU OR ANYTHING.
BUT IF YOU CRASH YOUR CAR IT'S LIKE, "WHAT WERE THEY DOING WRONG?"

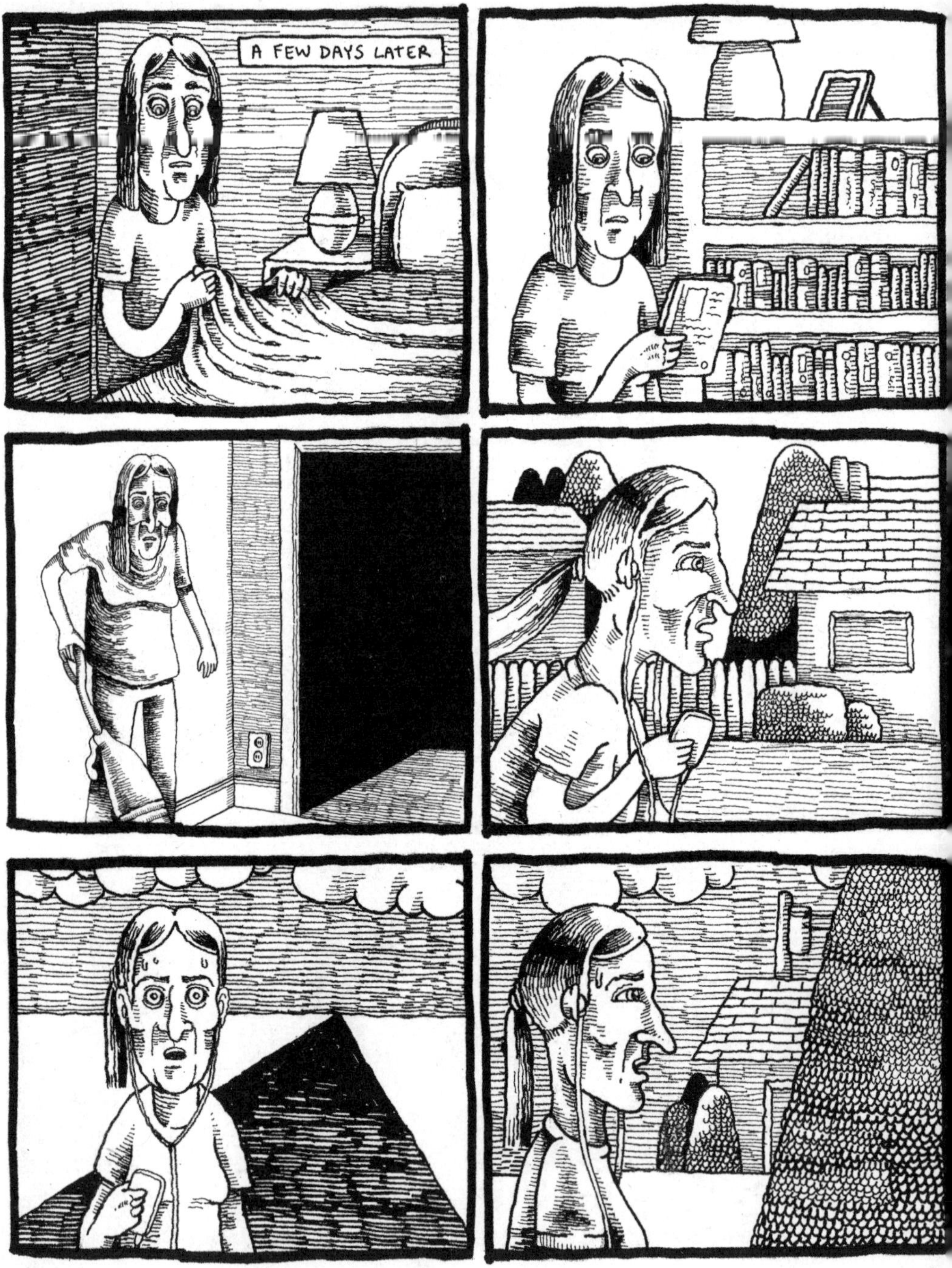
A FEW DAYS LATER

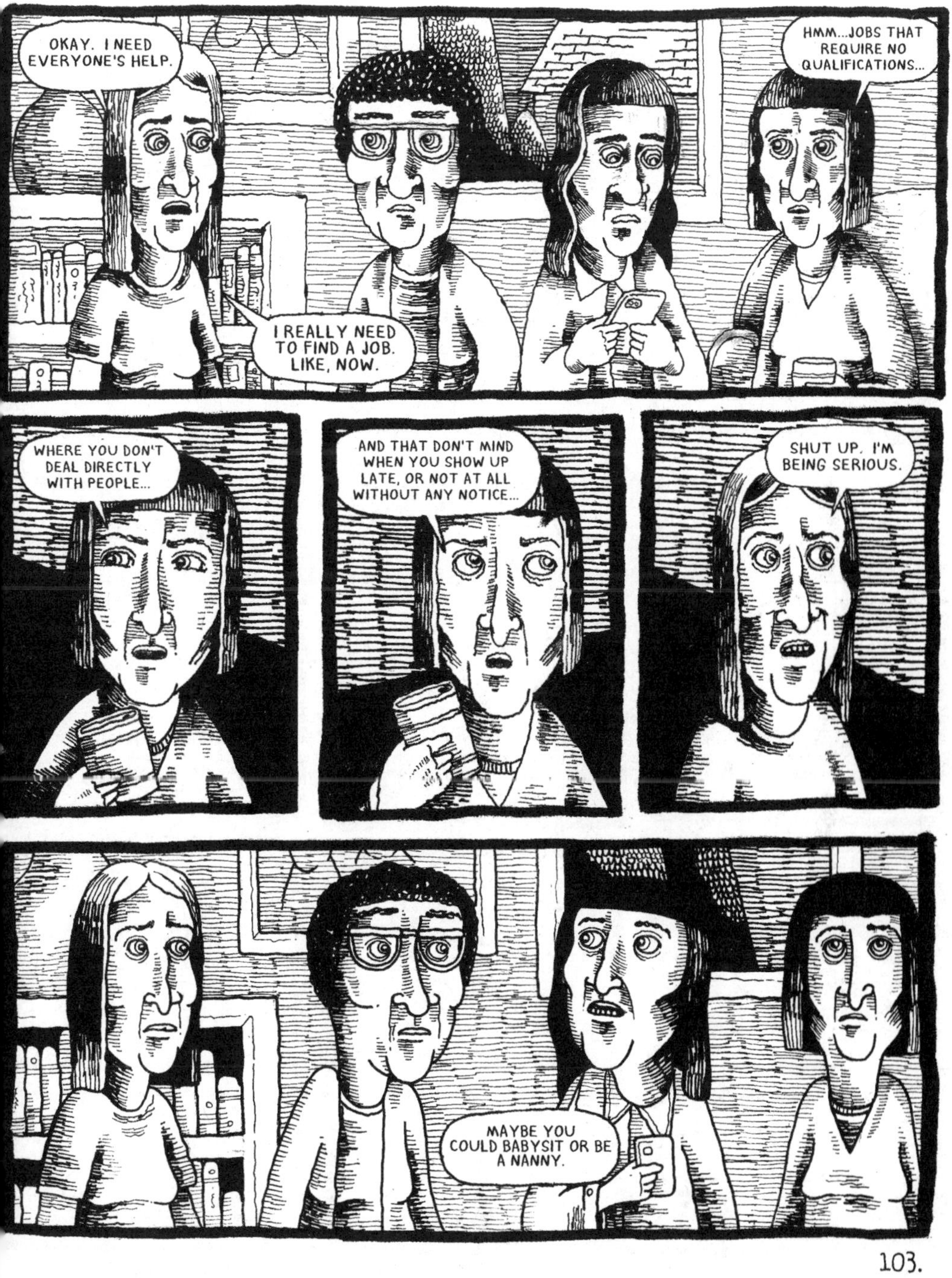

OKAY. I NEED EVERYONE'S HELP.
I REALLY NEED TO FIND A JOB. LIKE, NOW.
HMM...JOBS THAT REQUIRE NO QUALIFICATIONS...
WHERE YOU DON'T DEAL DIRECTLY WITH PEOPLE...
AND THAT DON'T MIND WHEN YOU SHOW UP LATE, OR NOT AT ALL WITHOUT ANY NOTICE...
SHUT UP. I'M BEING SERIOUS.
MAYBE YOU COULD BABYSIT OR BE A NANNY.

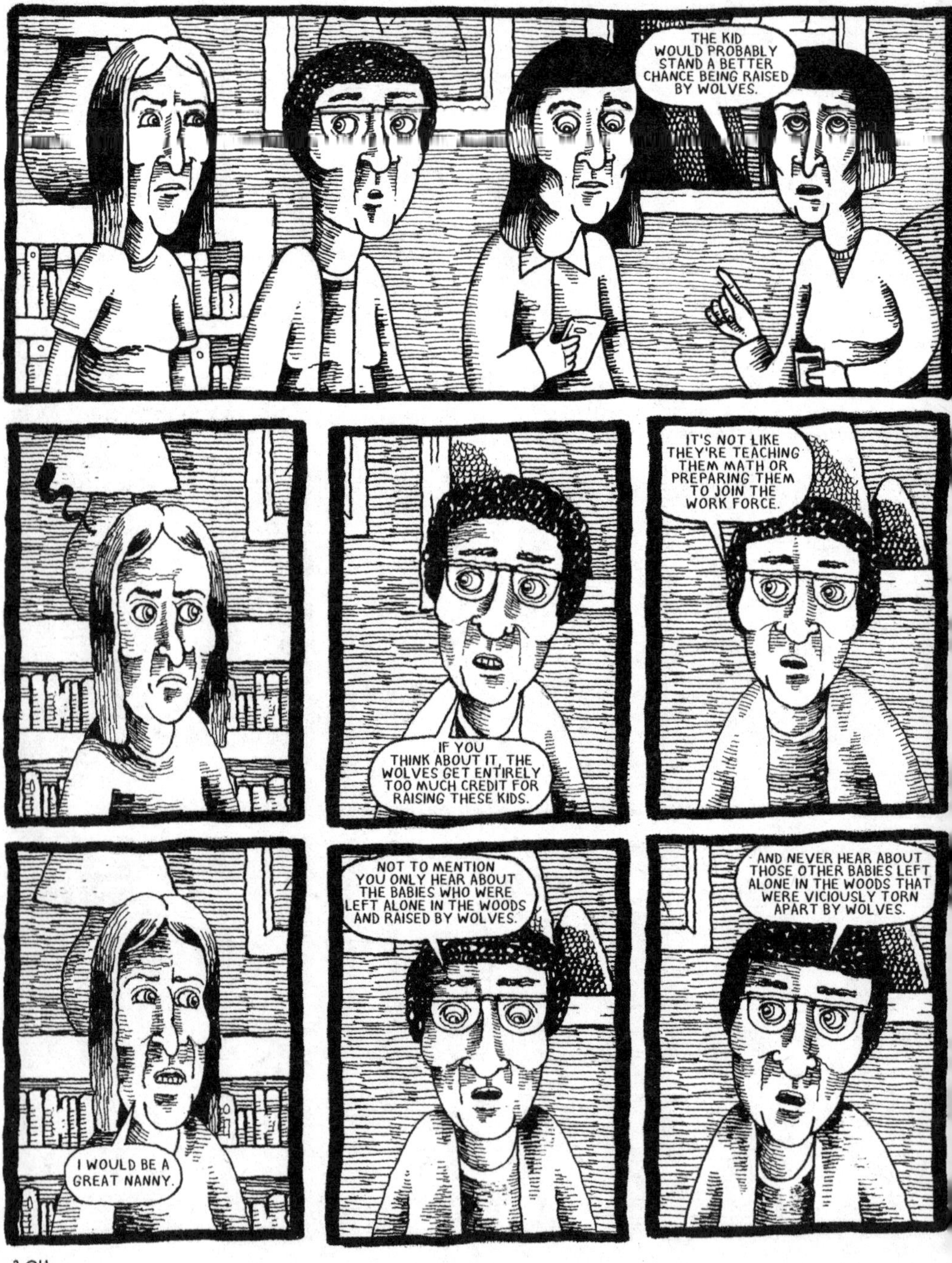
THE KID WOULD PROBABLY STAND A BETTER CHANCE BEING RAISED BY WOLVES.
IF YOU THINK ABOUT IT, THE WOLVES GET ENTIRELY TOO MUCH CREDIT FOR RAISING THESE KIDS.
IT'S NOT LIKE THEY'RE TEACHING THEM MATH OR PREPARING THEM TO JOIN THE WORK FORCE.
I WOULD BE A GREAT NANNY.
NOT TO MENTION YOU ONLY HEAR ABOUT THE BABIES WHO WERE LEFT ALONE IN THE WOODS AND RAISED BY WOLVES.
AND NEVER HEAR ABOUT THOSE OTHER BABIES LEFT ALONE IN THE WOODS THAT WERE VICIOUSLY TORN APART BY WOLVES.

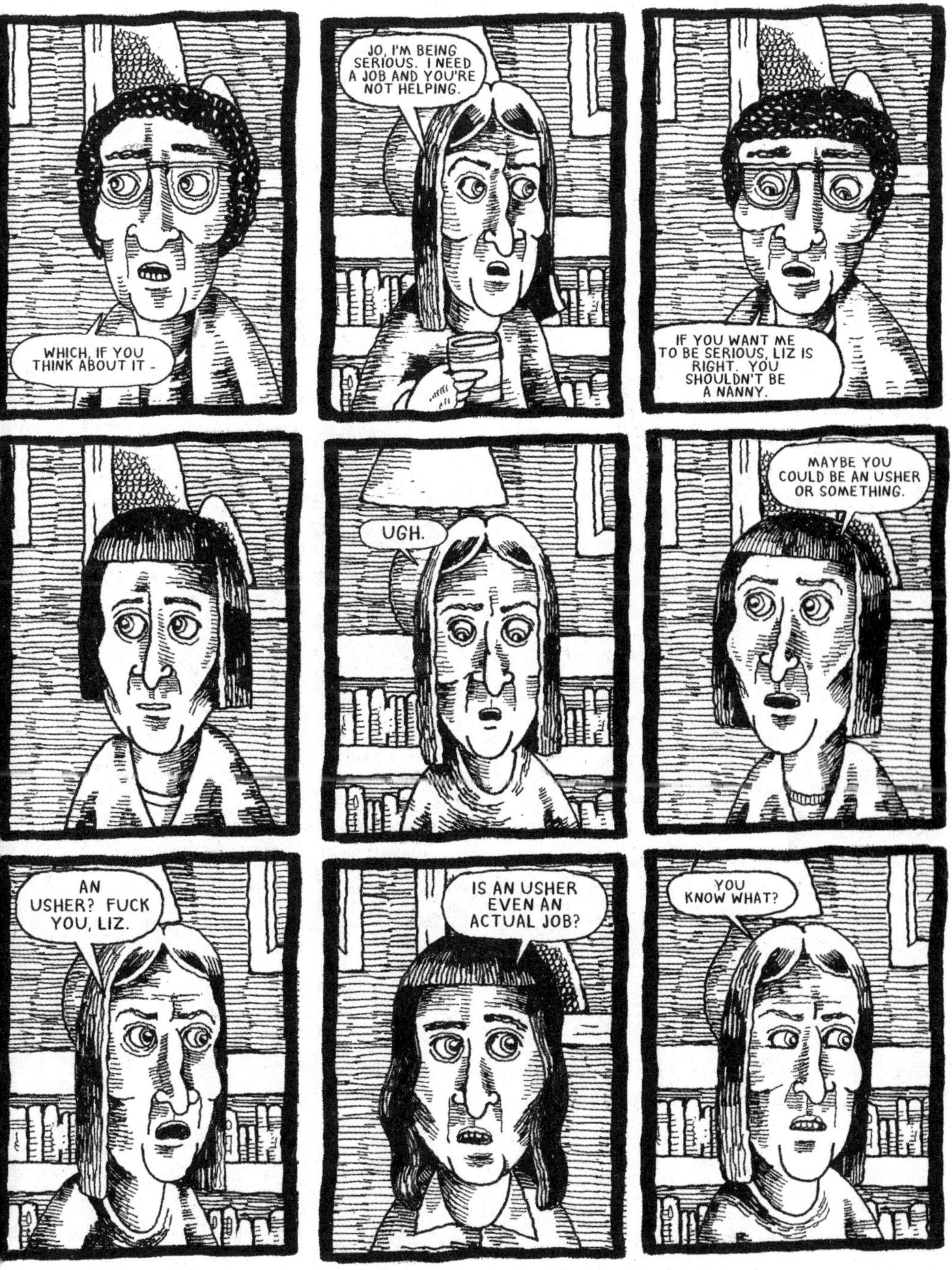
WHICH, IF YOU THINK ABOUT IT -
JO, I'M BEING SERIOUS. I NEED A JOB AND YOU'RE NOT HELPING.
IF YOU WANT ME TO BE SERIOUS, LIZ IS RIGHT. YOU SHOULDN'T BE A NANNY.
UGH.
MAYBE YOU COULD BE AN USHER OR SOMETHING.
AN USHER? FUCK YOU, LIZ.
IS AN USHER EVEN AN ACTUAL JOB?
YOU KNOW WHAT?

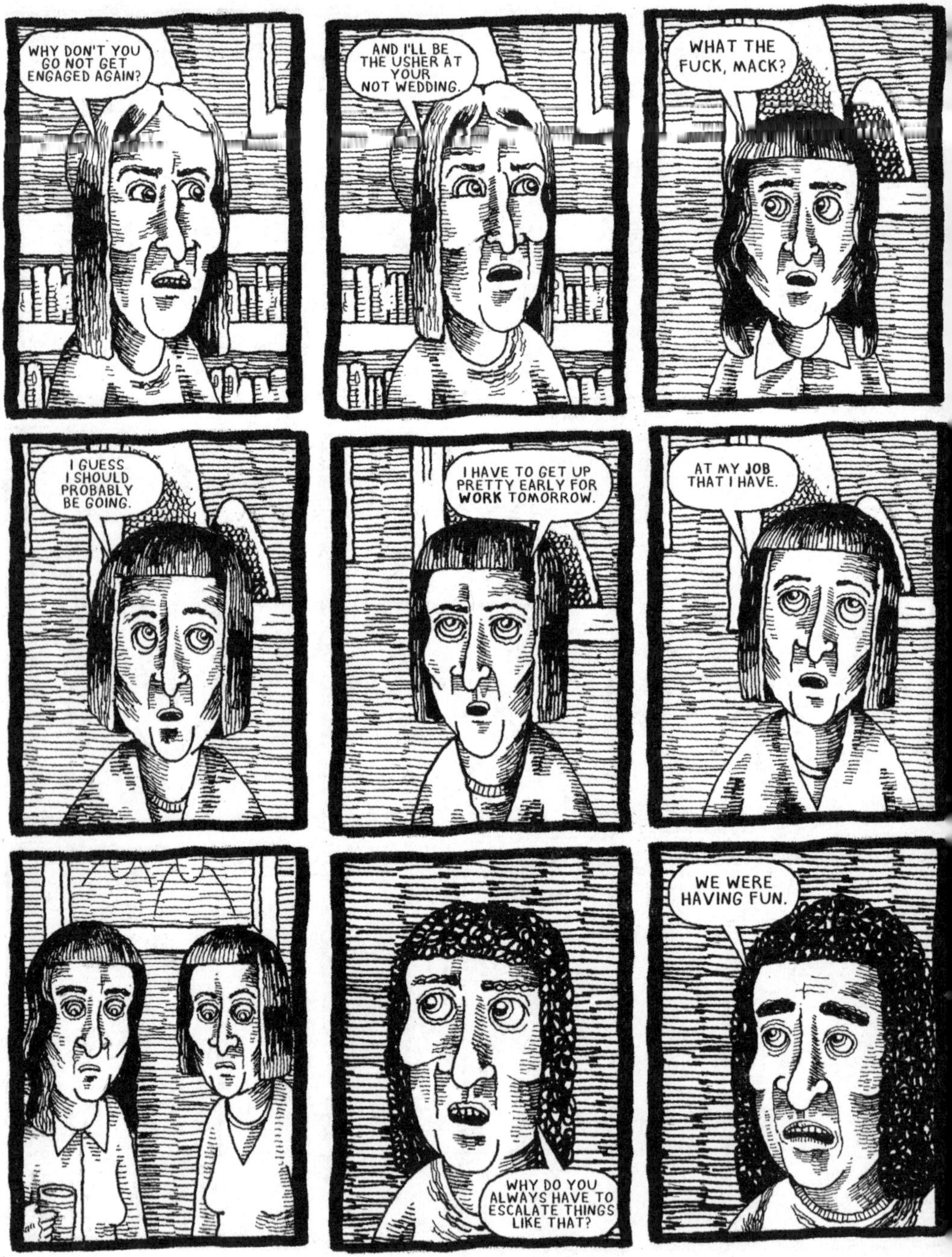
WHY DON'T YOU GO NOT GET ENGAGED AGAIN?
AND I'LL BE THE USHER AT YOUR NOT WEDDING.
WHAT THE FUCK, MACK?
I GUESS I SHOULD PROBABLY BE GOING.
I HAVE TO GET UP PRETTY EARLY FOR **WORK** TOMORROW.
AT MY **JOB** THAT I HAVE.
WHY DO YOU ALWAYS HAVE TO ESCALATE THINGS LIKE THAT?
WE WERE HAVING FUN.

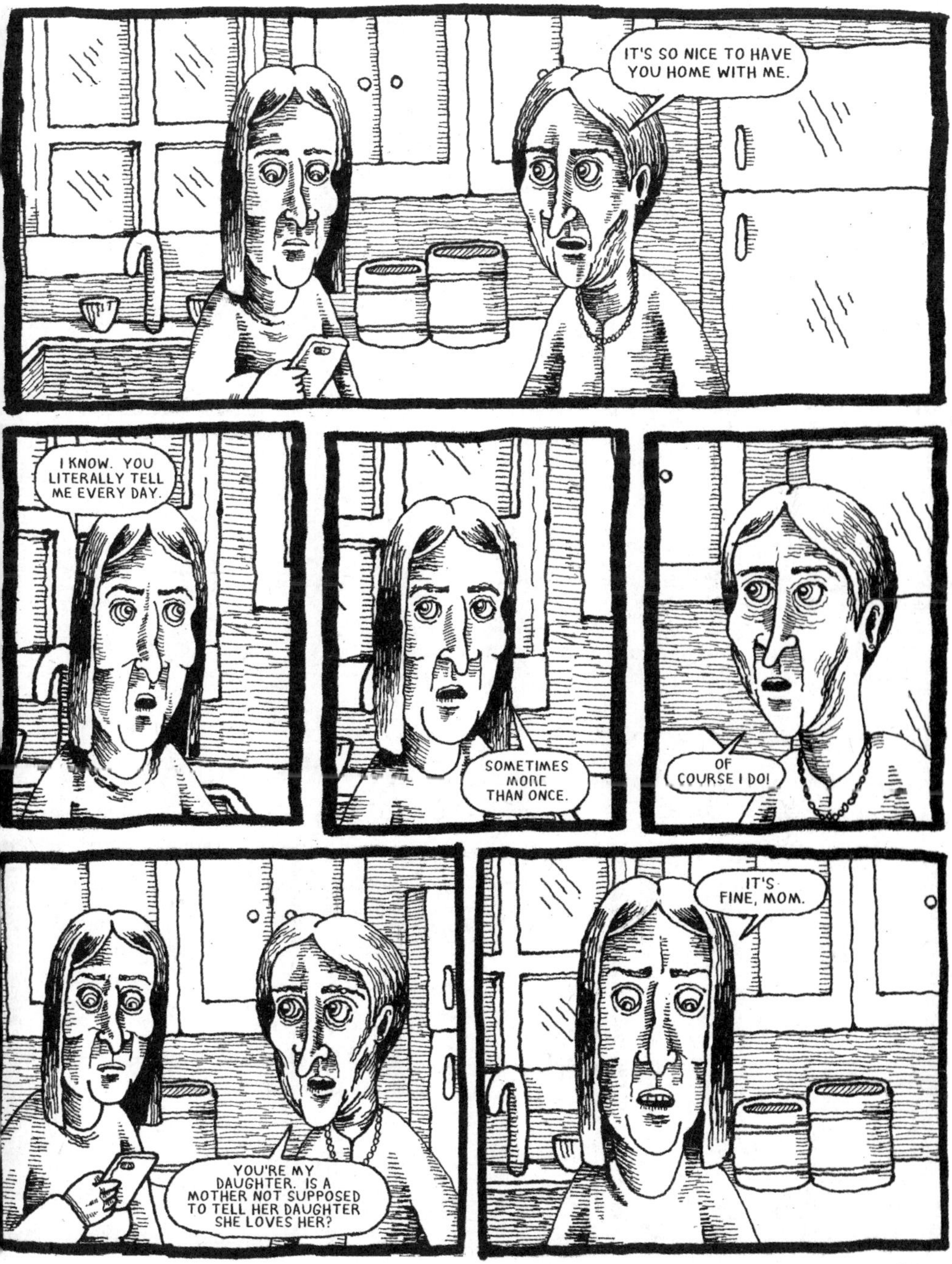
IT'S SO NICE TO HAVE YOU HOME WITH ME.
I KNOW. YOU LITERALLY TELL ME EVERY DAY.
SOMETIMES MORE THAN ONCE.
OF COURSE I DO!
YOU'RE MY DAUGHTER. IS A MOTHER NOT SUPPOSED TO TELL HER DAUGHTER SHE LOVES HER?
IT'S FINE, MOM.

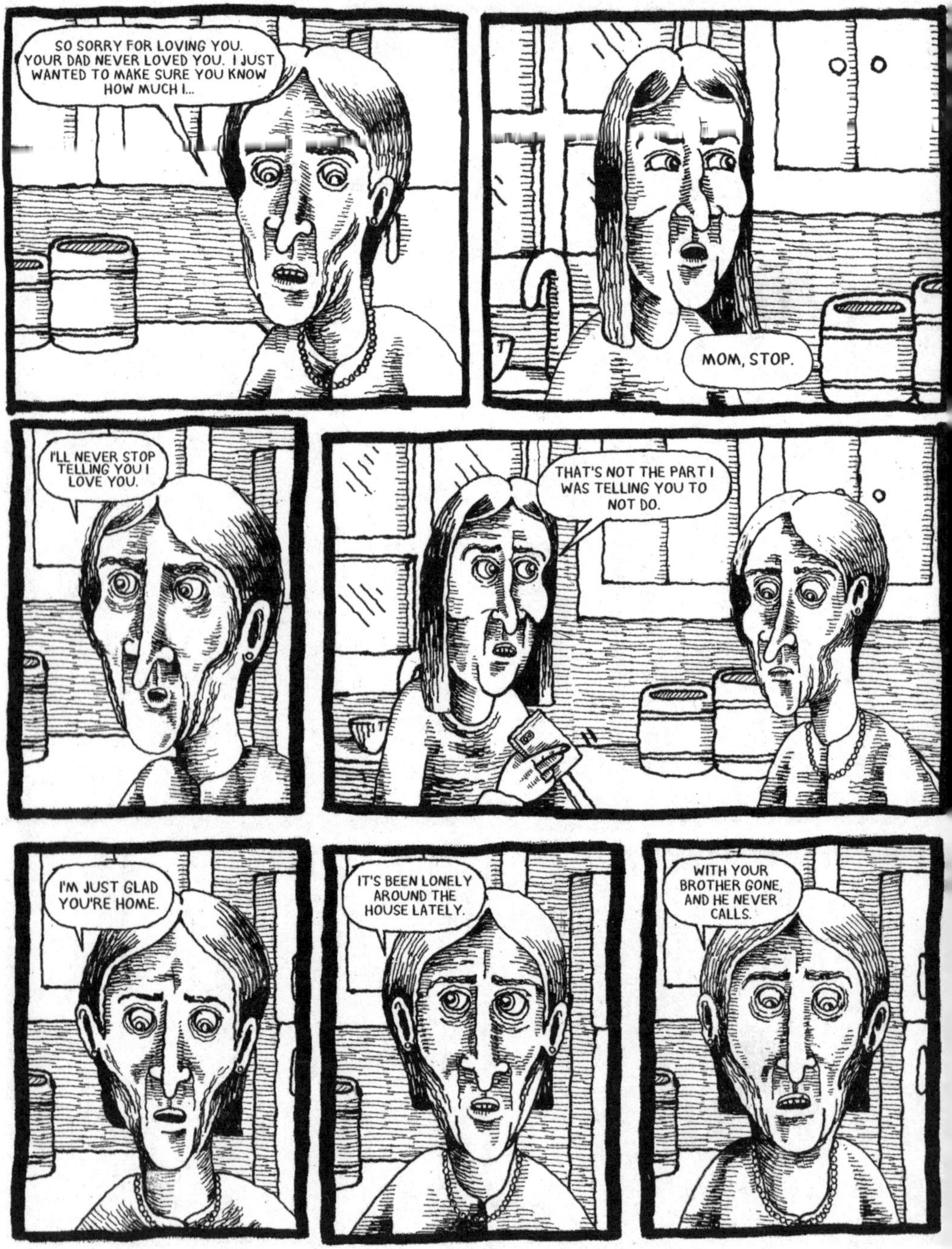
SO SORRY FOR LOVING YOU. YOUR DAD NEVER LOVED YOU. I JUST WANTED TO MAKE SURE YOU KNOW HOW MUCH I...
MOM, STOP.
I'LL NEVER STOP TELLING YOU I LOVE YOU.
THAT'S NOT THE PART I WAS TELLING YOU TO NOT DO.
I'M JUST GLAD YOU'RE HOME.
IT'S BEEN LONELY AROUND THE HOUSE LATELY.
WITH YOUR BROTHER GONE, AND HE NEVER CALLS.

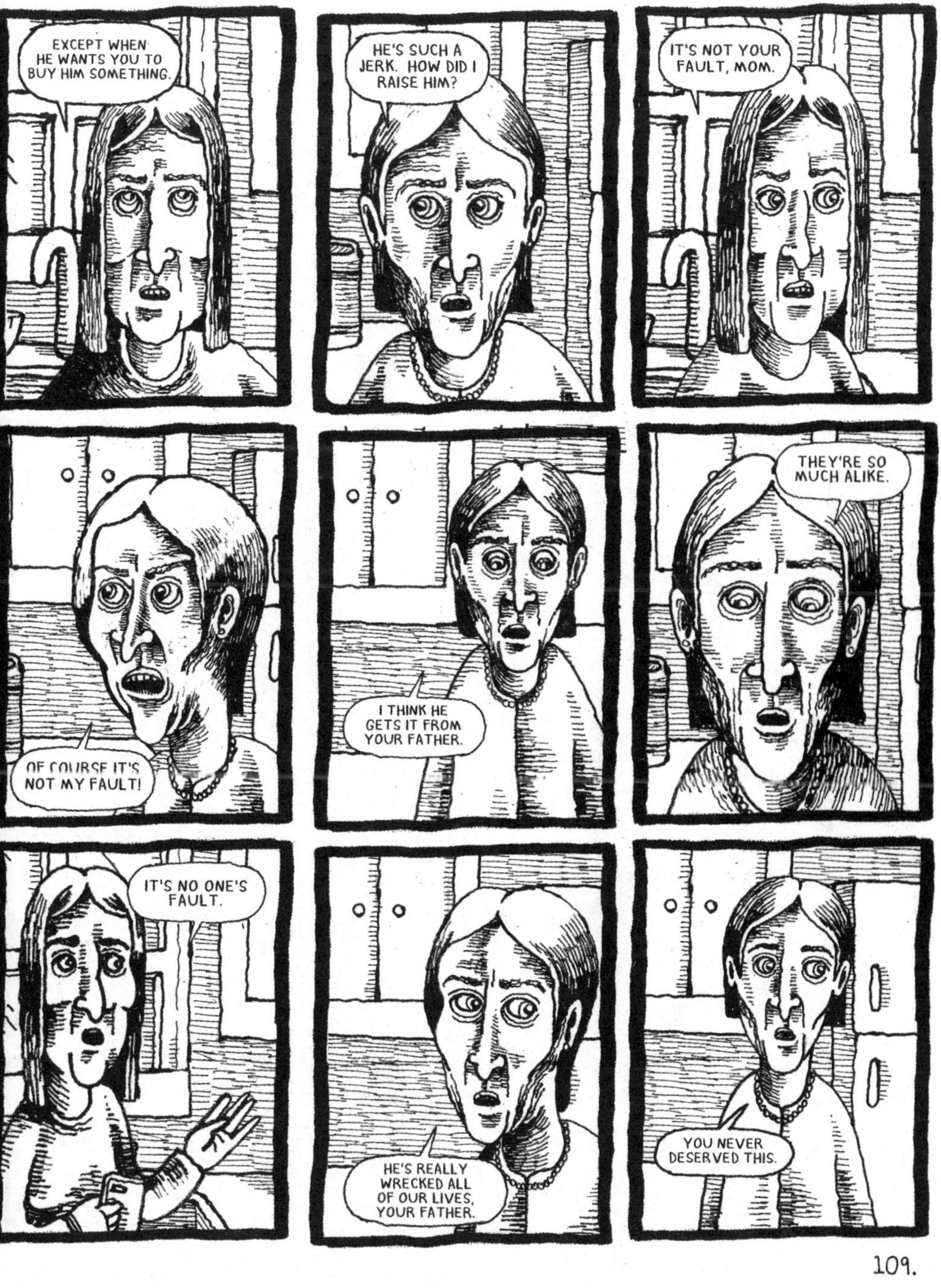
EXCEPT WHEN HE WANTS YOU TO BUY HIM SOMETHING.
HE'S SUCH A JERK. HOW DID I RAISE HIM?
IT'S NOT YOUR FAULT, MOM.
OF COURSE IT'S NOT MY FAULT!
I THINK HE GETS IT FROM YOUR FATHER.
THEY'RE SO MUCH ALIKE.
IT'S NO ONE'S FAULT.
HE'S REALLY WRECKED ALL OF OUR LIVES, YOUR FATHER.
YOU NEVER DESERVED THIS.

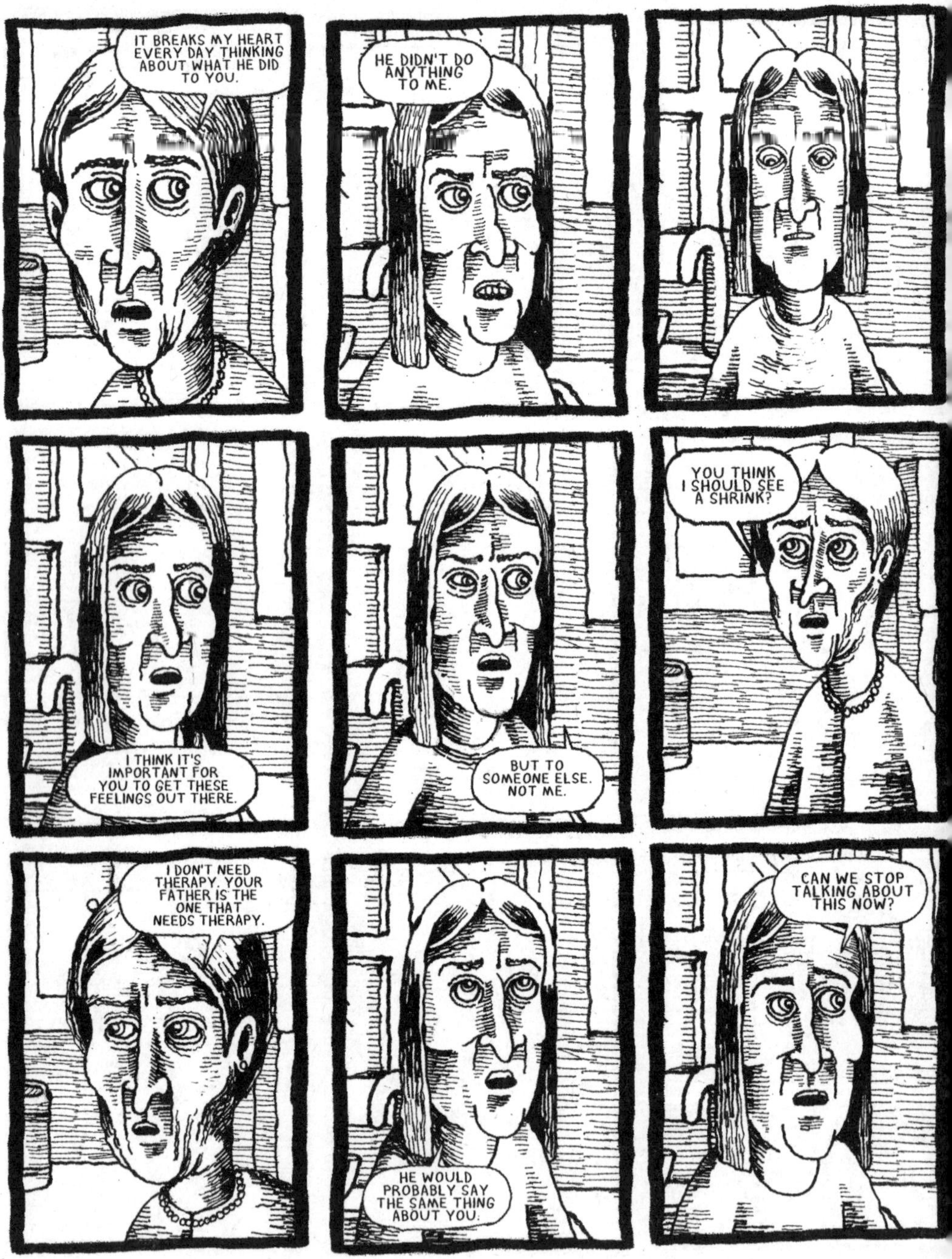
IT BREAKS MY HEART EVERY DAY THINKING ABOUT WHAT HE DID TO YOU.
HE DIDN'T DO ANYTHING TO ME.
I THINK IT'S IMPORTANT FOR YOU TO GET THESE FEELINGS OUT THERE.
BUT TO SOMEONE ELSE. NOT ME.
YOU THINK I SHOULD SEE A SHRINK?
I DON'T NEED THERAPY. YOUR FATHER IS THE ONE THAT NEEDS THERAPY.
HE WOULD PROBABLY SAY THE SAME THING ABOUT YOU.
CAN WE STOP TALKING ABOUT THIS NOW?

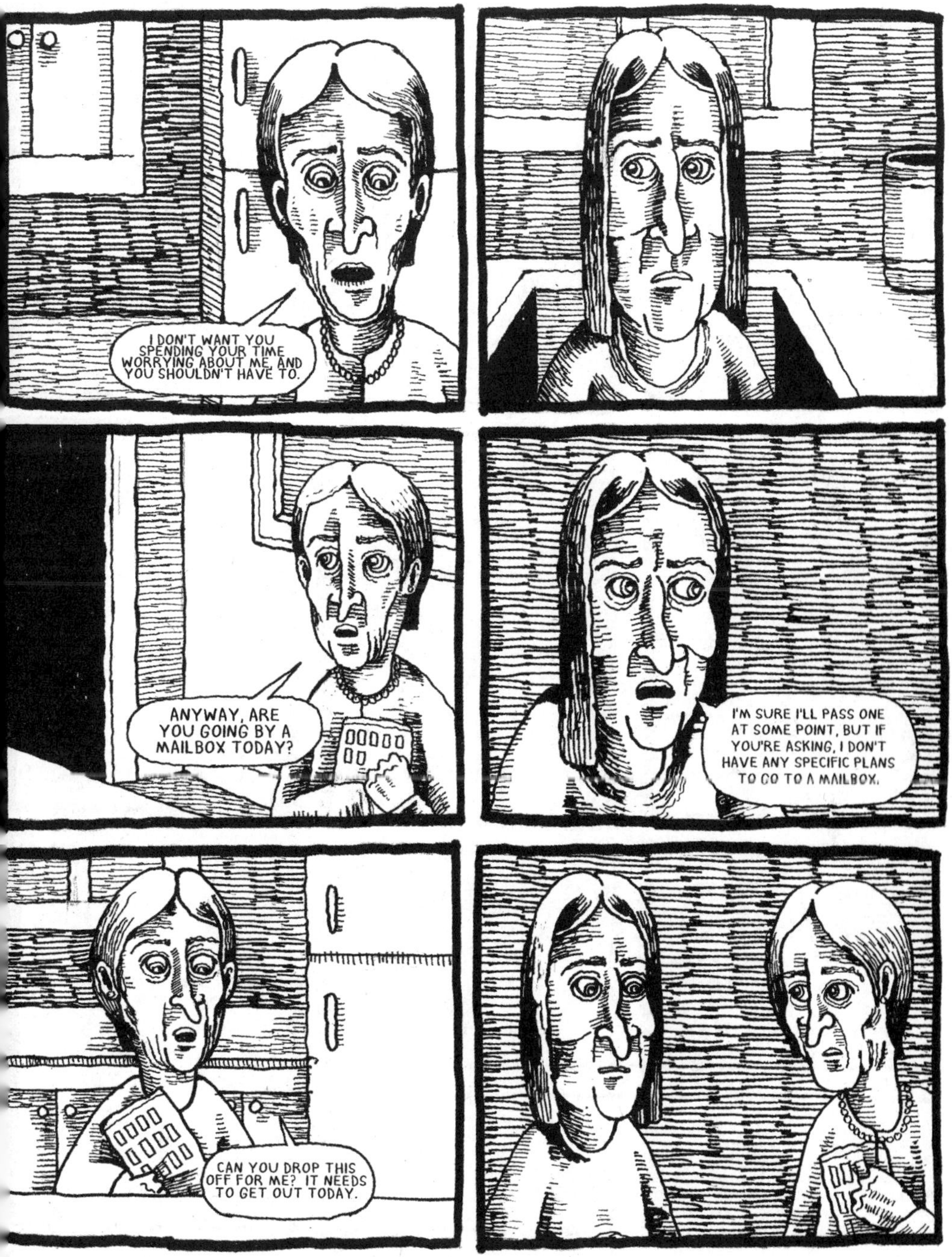
I DON'T WANT YOU SPENDING YOUR TIME WORRYING ABOUT ME, AND YOU SHOULDN'T HAVE TO.
ANYWAY, ARE YOU GOING BY A MAILBOX TODAY?
I'M SURE I'LL PASS ONE AT SOME POINT, BUT IF YOU'RE ASKING, I DON'T HAVE ANY SPECIFIC PLANS TO GO TO A MAILBOX.
CAN YOU DROP THIS OFF FOR ME? IT NEEDS TO GET OUT TODAY.

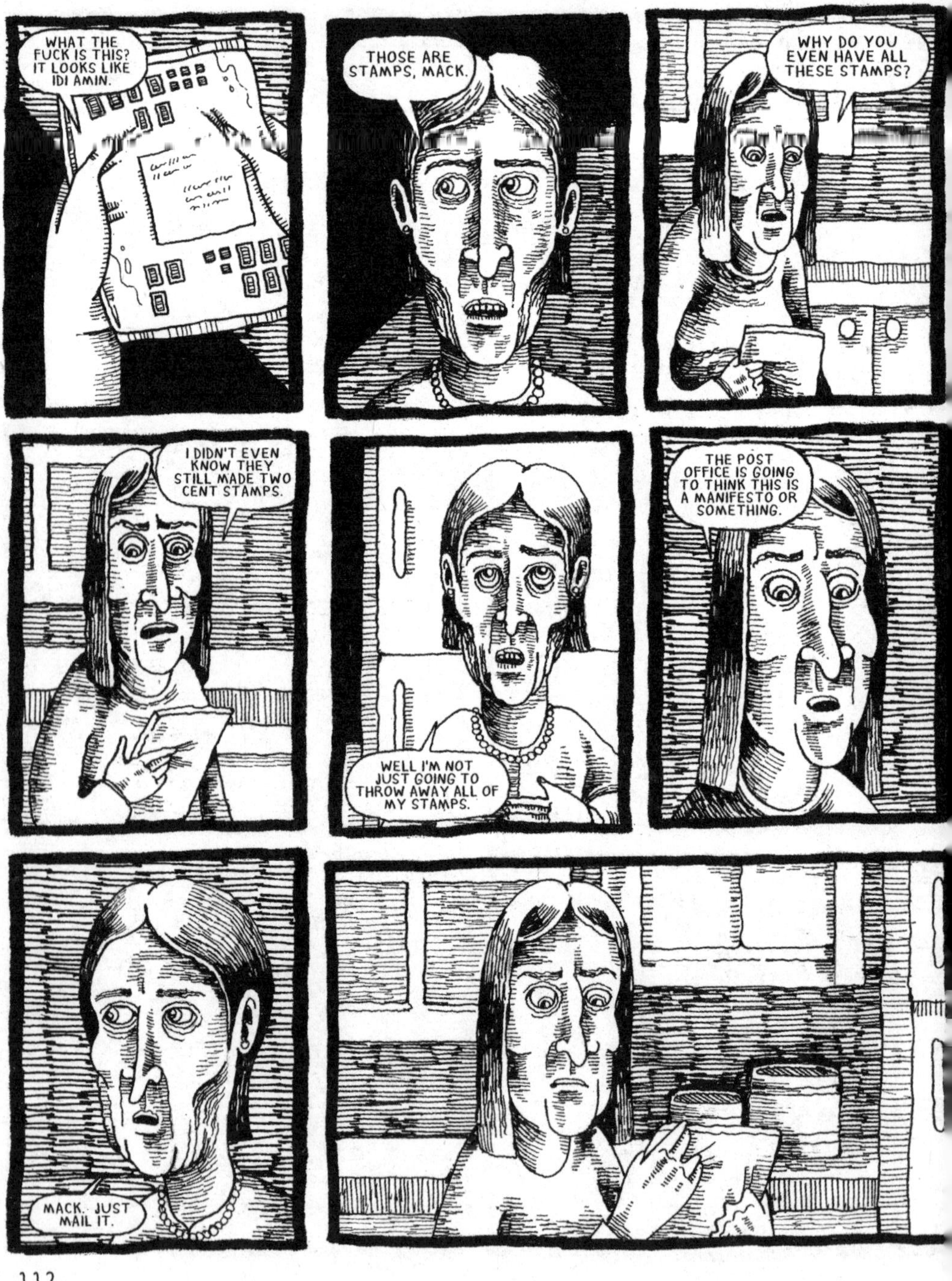
WHAT THE FUCK IS THIS? IT LOOKS LIKE IDI AMIN.
THOSE ARE STAMPS, MACK.
WHY DO YOU EVEN HAVE ALL THESE STAMPS?
I DIDN'T EVEN KNOW THEY STILL MADE TWO CENT STAMPS.
WELL I'M NOT JUST GOING TO THROW AWAY ALL OF MY STAMPS.
THE POST OFFICE IS GOING TO THINK THIS IS A MANIFESTO OR SOMETHING.
MACK. JUST MAIL IT.

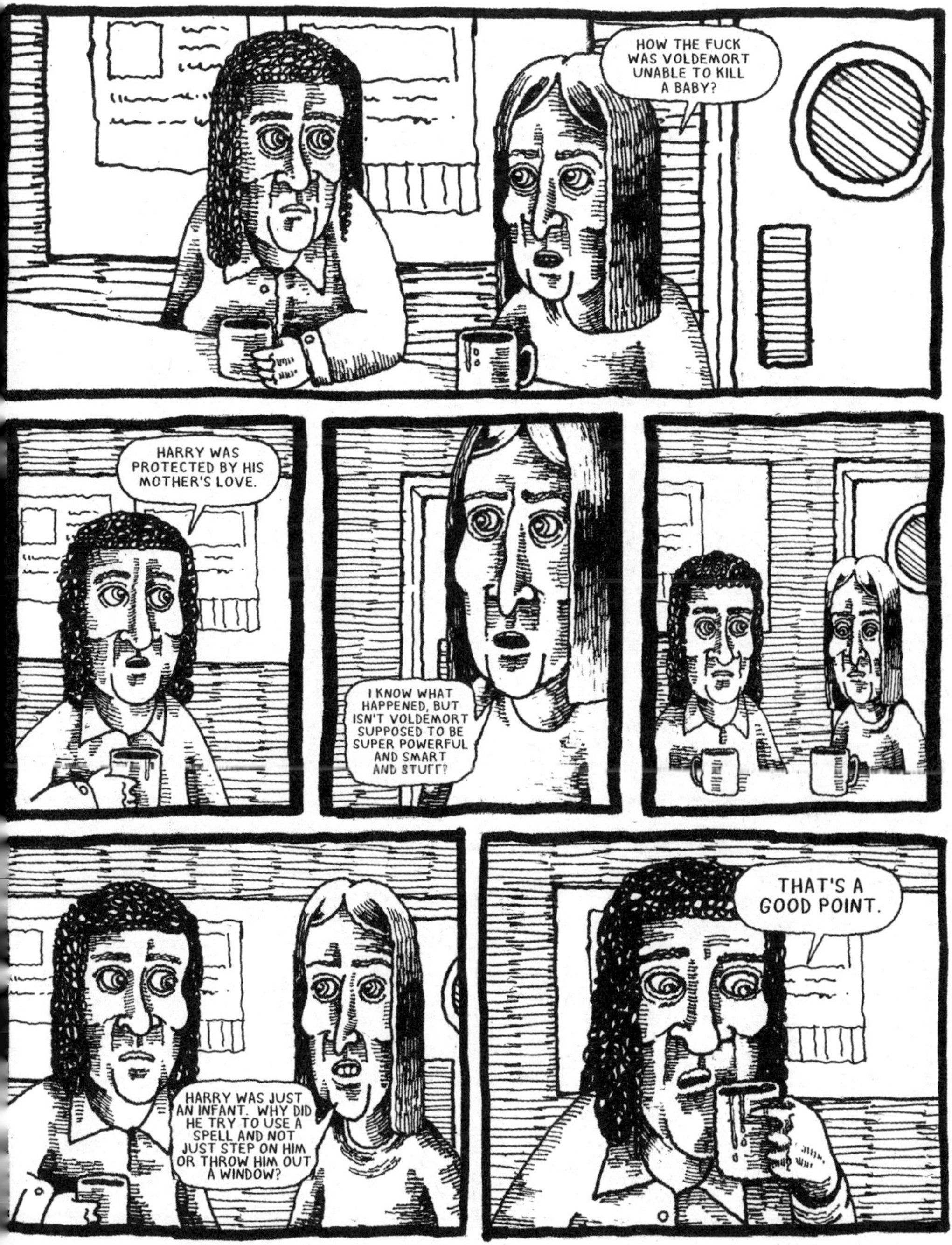
HOW THE FUCK WAS VOLDEMORT UNABLE TO KILL A BABY?
HARRY WAS PROTECTED BY HIS MOTHER'S LOVE.
I KNOW WHAT HAPPENED, BUT ISN'T VOLDEMORT SUPPOSED TO BE SUPER POWERFUL AND SMART AND STUFF?
HARRY WAS JUST AN INFANT. WHY DID HE TRY TO USE A SPELL AND NOT JUST STEP ON HIM OR THROW HIM OUT A WINDOW?
THAT'S A GOOD POINT.

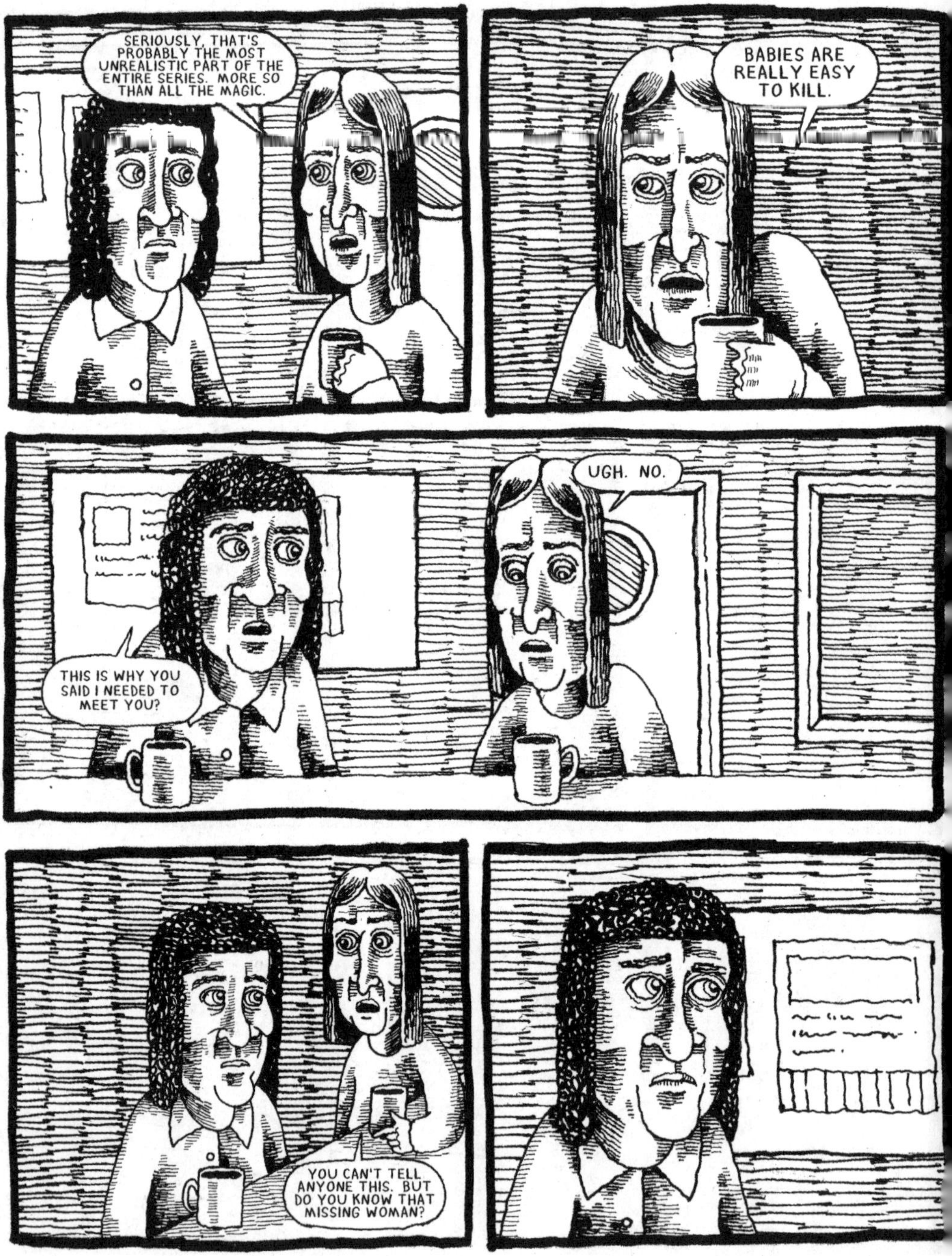
SERIOUSLY, THAT'S PROBABLY THE MOST UNREALISTIC PART OF THE ENTIRE SERIES. MORE SO THAN ALL THE MAGIC.
BABIES ARE REALLY EASY TO KILL.
THIS IS WHY YOU SAID I NEEDED TO MEET YOU?
UGH. NO.
YOU CAN'T TELL ANYONE THIS. BUT DO YOU KNOW THAT MISSING WOMAN?

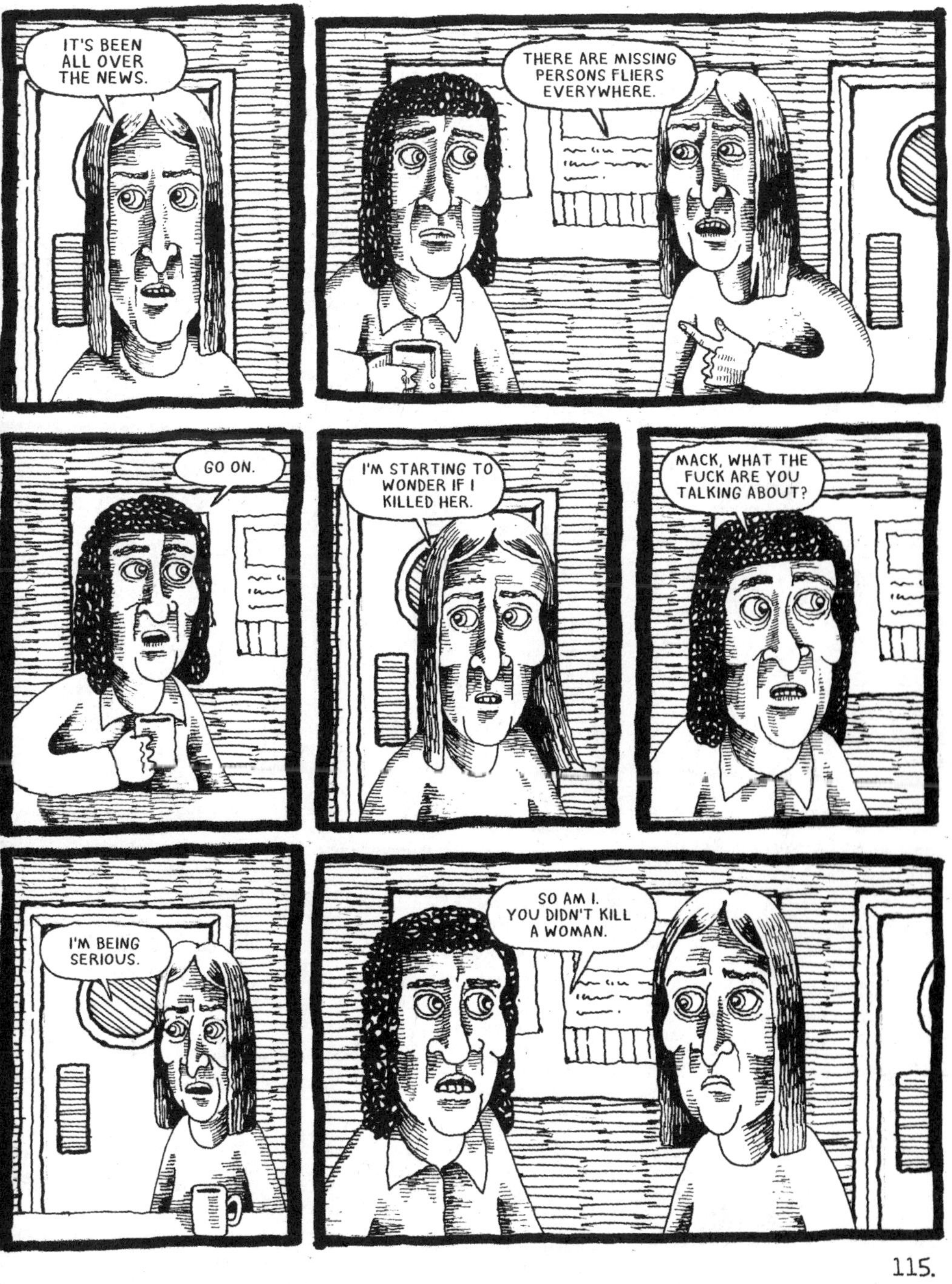
IT'S BEEN ALL OVER THE NEWS.
THERE ARE MISSING PERSONS FLIERS EVERYWHERE.
GO ON.
I'M STARTING TO WONDER IF I KILLED HER.
MACK, WHAT THE FUCK ARE YOU TALKING ABOUT?
I'M BEING SERIOUS.
SO AM I. YOU DIDN'T KILL A WOMAN.

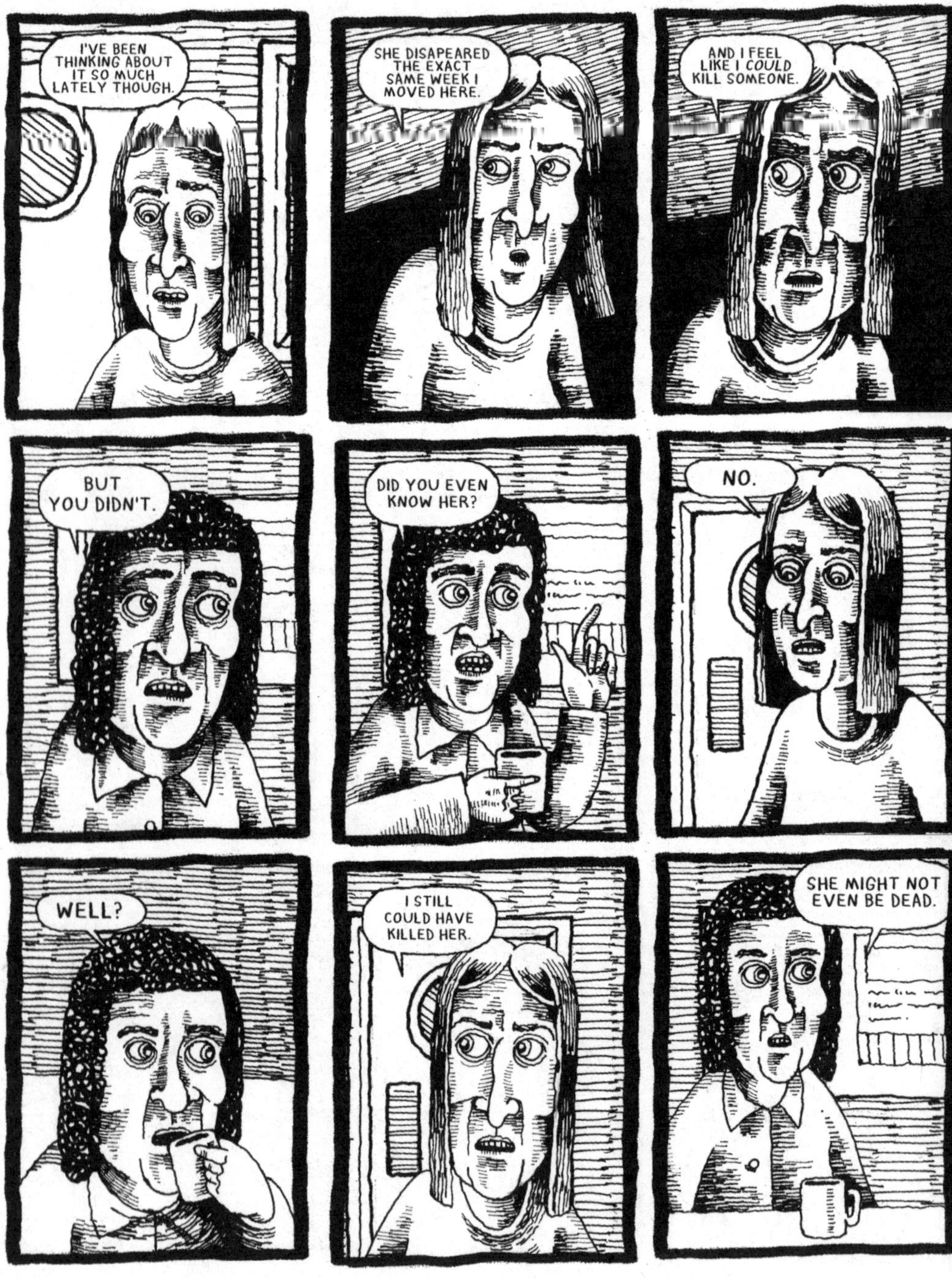
I'VE BEEN THINKING ABOUT IT SO MUCH LATELY THOUGH.
SHE DISAPEARED THE EXACT SAME WEEK I MOVED HERE.
AND I FEEL LIKE I *COULD* KILL SOMEONE.
BUT YOU DIDN'T.
DID YOU EVEN KNOW HER?
NO.
WELL?
I STILL COULD HAVE KILLED HER.
SHE MIGHT NOT EVEN BE DEAD.

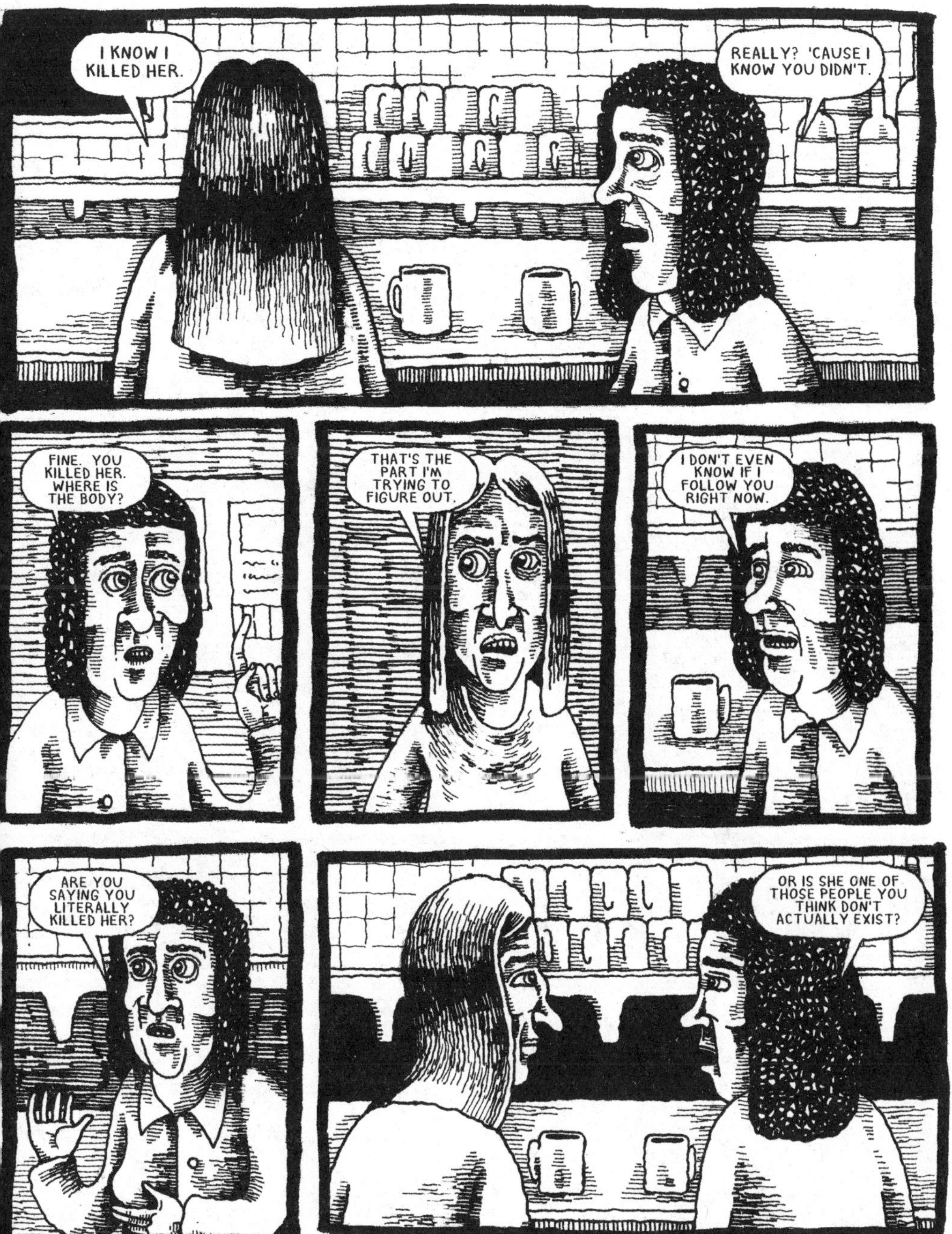
I KNOW I KILLED HER.
REALLY? 'CAUSE I KNOW YOU DIDN'T.
FINE. YOU KILLED HER. WHERE IS THE BODY?
THAT'S THE PART I'M TRYING TO FIGURE OUT.
I DON'T EVEN KNOW IF I FOLLOW YOU RIGHT NOW.
ARE YOU SAYING YOU LITERALLY KILLED HER?
OR IS SHE ONE OF THOSE PEOPLE YOU THINK DON'T ACTUALLY EXIST?

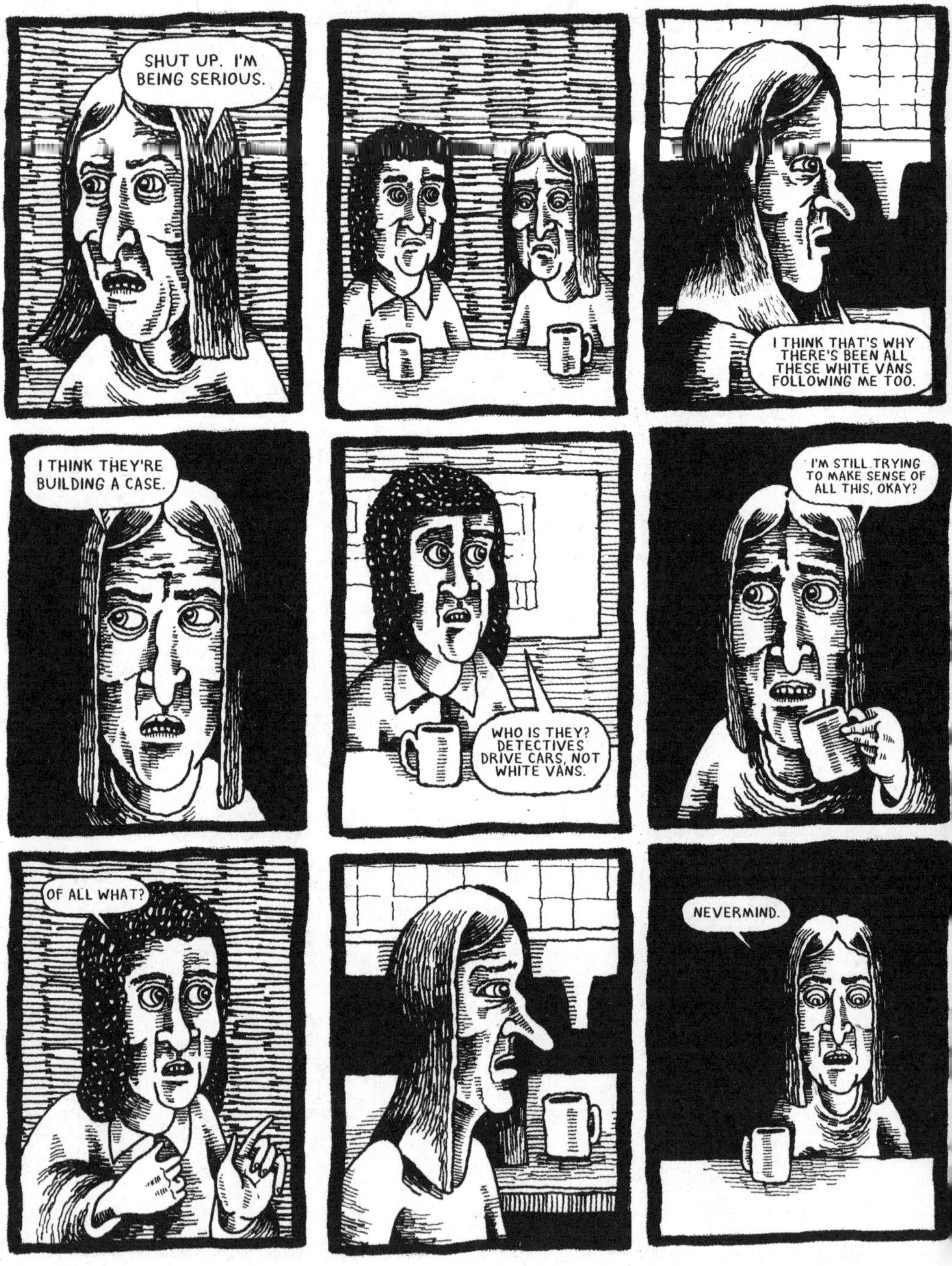
SHUT UP. I'M BEING SERIOUS.
I THINK THAT'S WHY THERE'S BEEN ALL THESE WHITE VANS FOLLOWING ME TOO.
I THINK THEY'RE BUILDING A CASE.
WHO IS THEY? DETECTIVES DRIVE CARS, NOT WHITE VANS.
I'M STILL TRYING TO MAKE SENSE OF ALL THIS, OKAY?
OF ALL WHAT?
NEVERMIND.

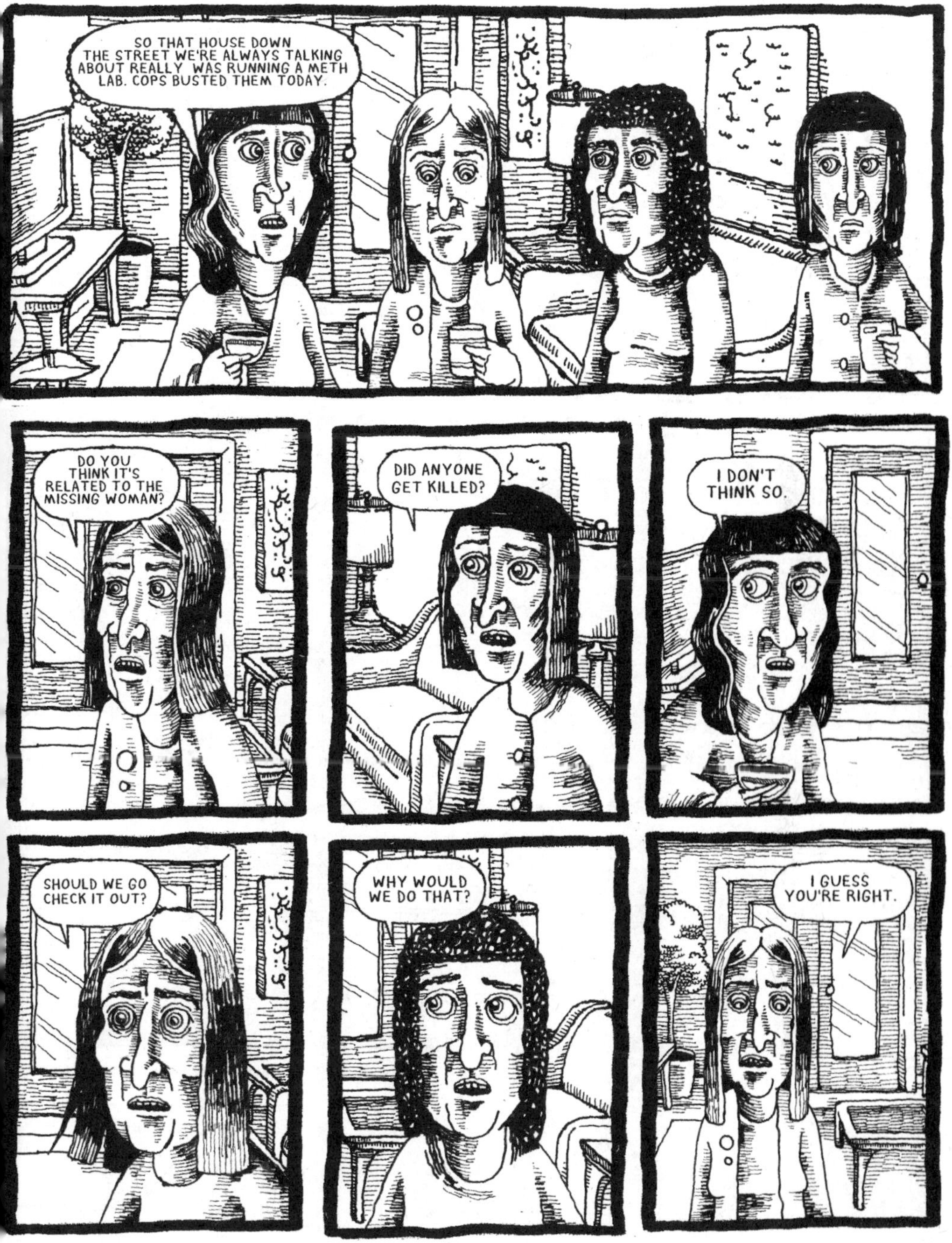
SO THAT HOUSE DOWN THE STREET WE'RE ALWAYS TALKING ABOUT REALLY WAS RUNNING A METH LAB. COPS BUSTED THEM TODAY.
DO YOU THINK IT'S RELATED TO THE MISSING WOMAN?
DID ANYONE GET KILLED?
I DON'T THINK SO.
SHOULD WE GO CHECK IT OUT?
WHY WOULD WE DO THAT?
I GUESS YOU'RE RIGHT.

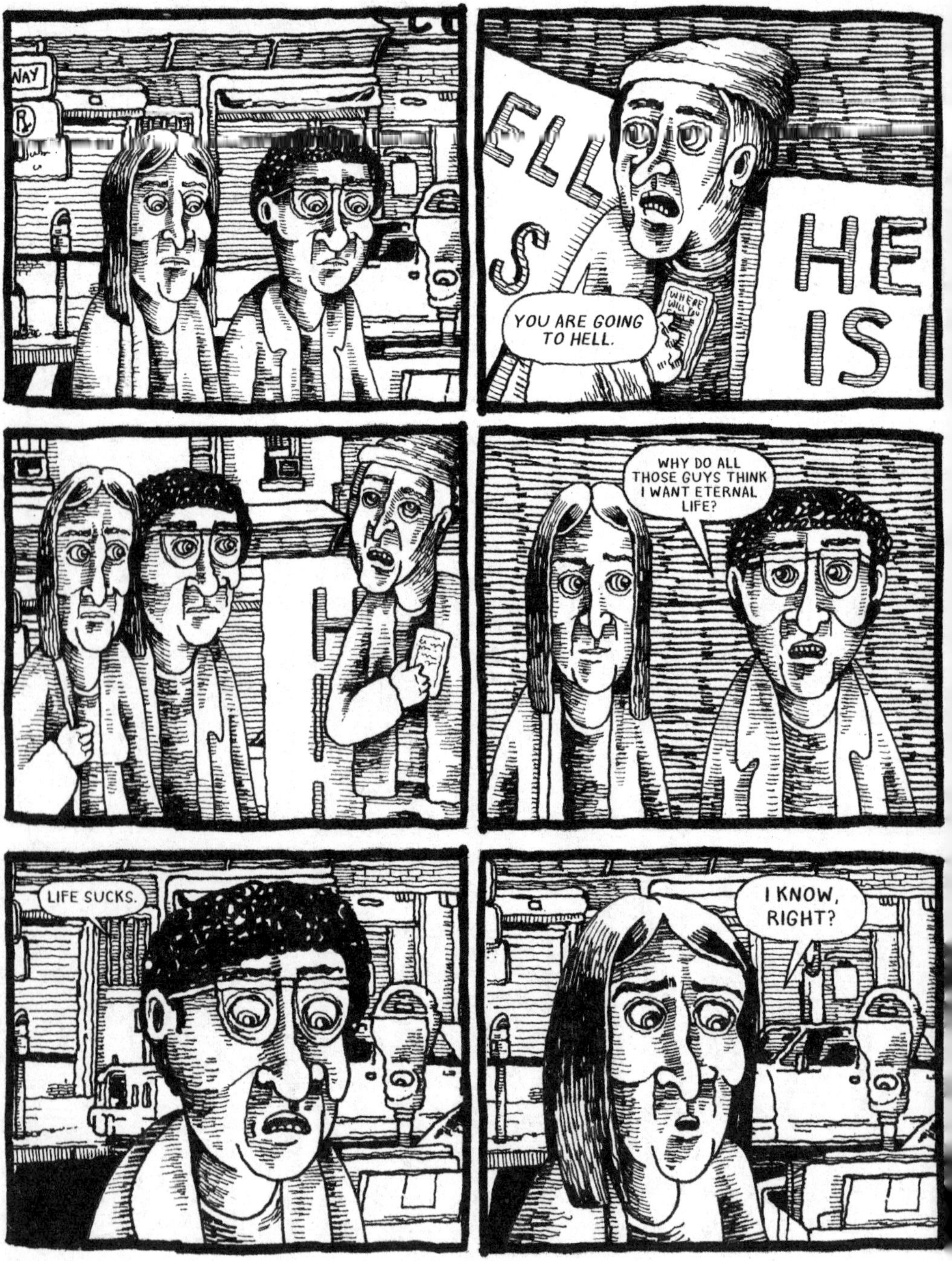
WAY
YOU ARE GOING TO HELL.
WHY DO ALL THOSE GUYS THINK I WANT ETERNAL LIFE?
LIFE SUCKS.
I KNOW, RIGHT?

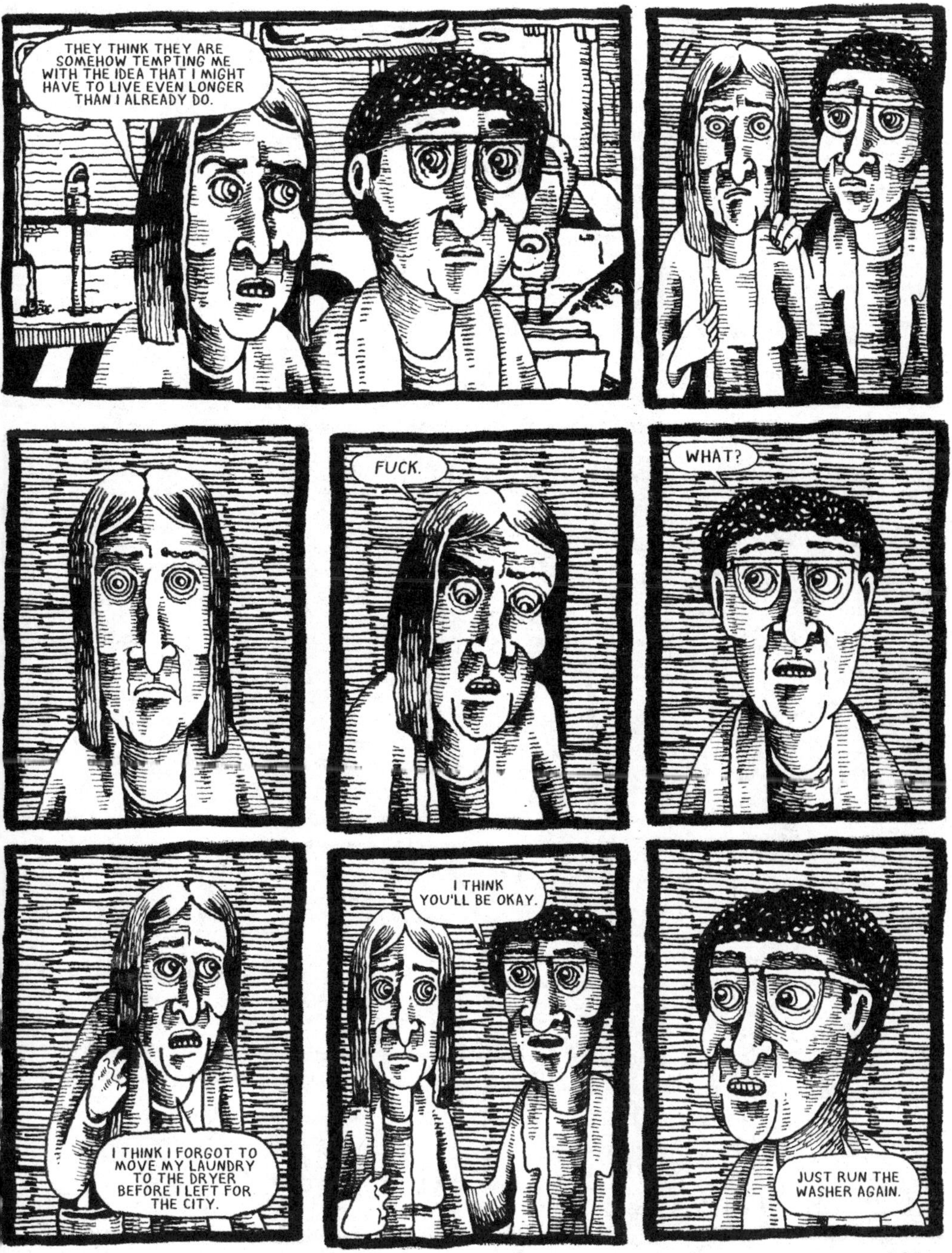
THEY THINK THEY ARE SOMEHOW TEMPTING ME WITH THE IDEA THAT I MIGHT HAVE TO LIVE EVEN LONGER THAN I ALREADY DO.
FUCK.
WHAT?
I THINK I FORGOT TO MOVE MY LAUNDRY TO THE DRYER BEFORE I LEFT FOR THE CITY.
I THINK YOU'LL BE OKAY.
JUST RUN THE WASHER AGAIN.

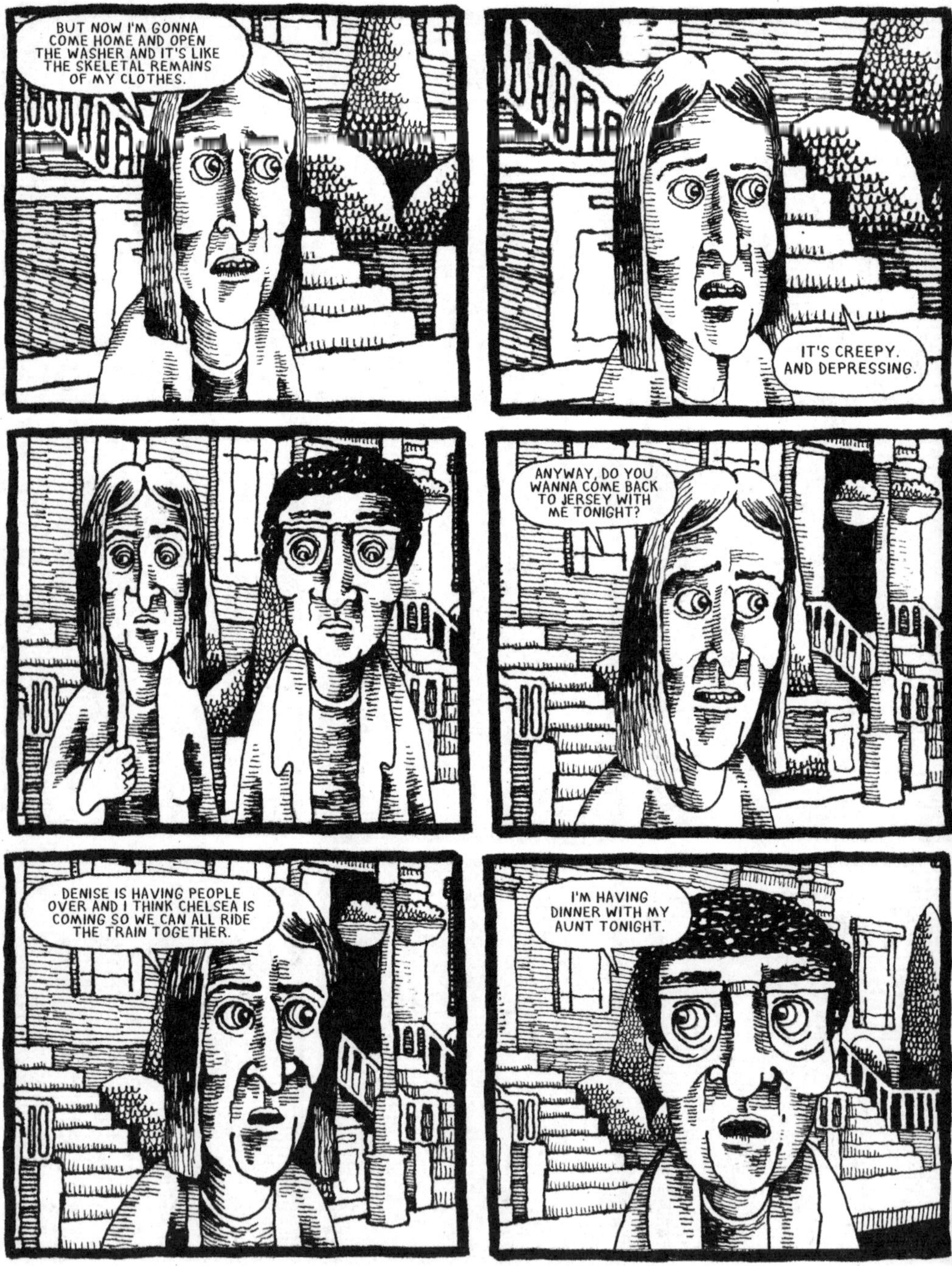
BUT NOW I'M GONNA COME HOME AND OPEN THE WASHER AND IT'S LIKE THE SKELETAL REMAINS OF MY CLOTHES.
IT'S CREEPY. AND DEPRESSING.
ANYWAY, DO YOU WANNA COME BACK TO JERSEY WITH ME TONIGHT?
DENISE IS HAVING PEOPLE OVER AND I THINK CHELSEA IS COMING SO WE CAN ALL RIDE THE TRAIN TOGETHER.
I'M HAVING DINNER WITH MY AUNT TONIGHT.

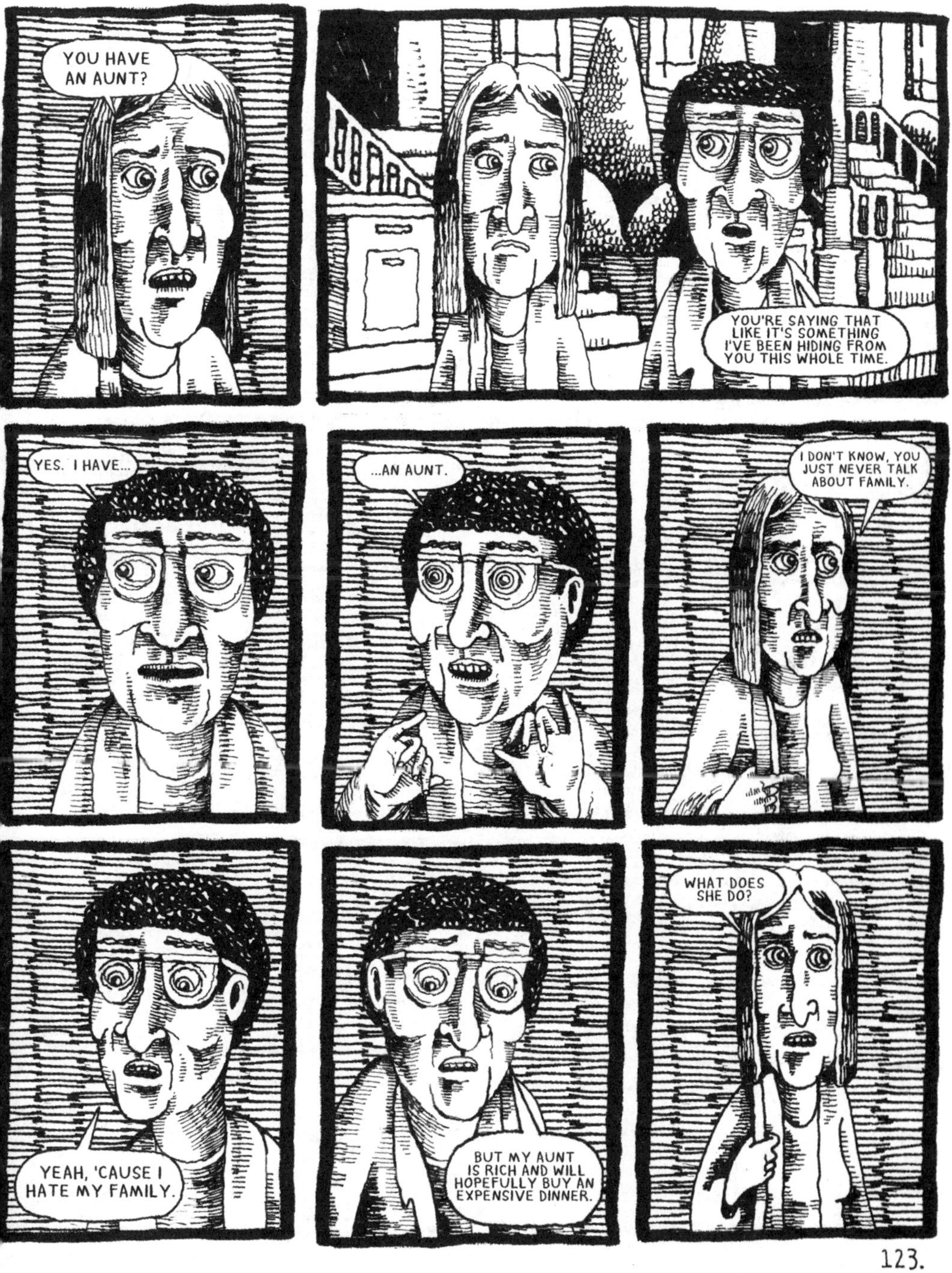
YOU HAVE AN AUNT?
YOU'RE SAYING THAT LIKE IT'S SOMETHING I'VE BEEN HIDING FROM YOU THIS WHOLE TIME.
YES. I HAVE...
...AN AUNT.
I DON'T KNOW, YOU JUST NEVER TALK ABOUT FAMILY.
YEAH, 'CAUSE I HATE MY FAMILY.
BUT MY AUNT IS RICH AND WILL HOPEFULLY BUY AN EXPENSIVE DINNER.
WHAT DOES SHE DO?

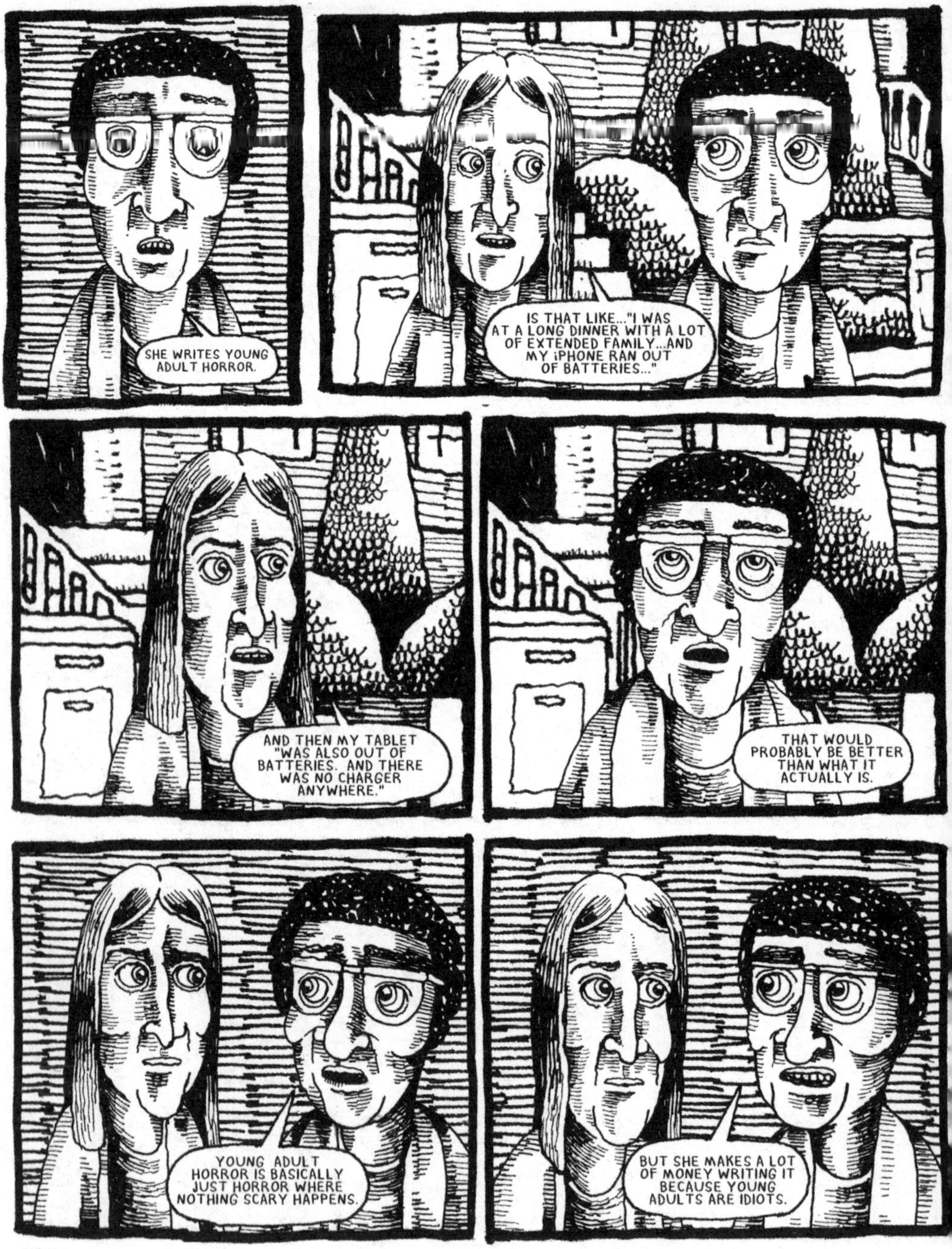
SHE WRITES YOUNG ADULT HORROR.
IS THAT LIKE..."I WAS AT A LONG DINNER WITH A LOT OF EXTENDED FAMILY...AND MY iPHONE RAN OUT OF BATTERIES..."
AND THEN MY TABLET "WAS ALSO OUT OF BATTERIES. AND THERE WAS NO CHARGER ANYWHERE."
THAT WOULD PROBABLY BE BETTER THAN WHAT IT ACTUALLY IS.
YOUNG ADULT HORROR IS BASICALLY JUST HORROR WHERE NOTHING SCARY HAPPENS.
BUT SHE MAKES A LOT OF MONEY WRITING IT BECAUSE YOUNG ADULTS ARE IDIOTS.

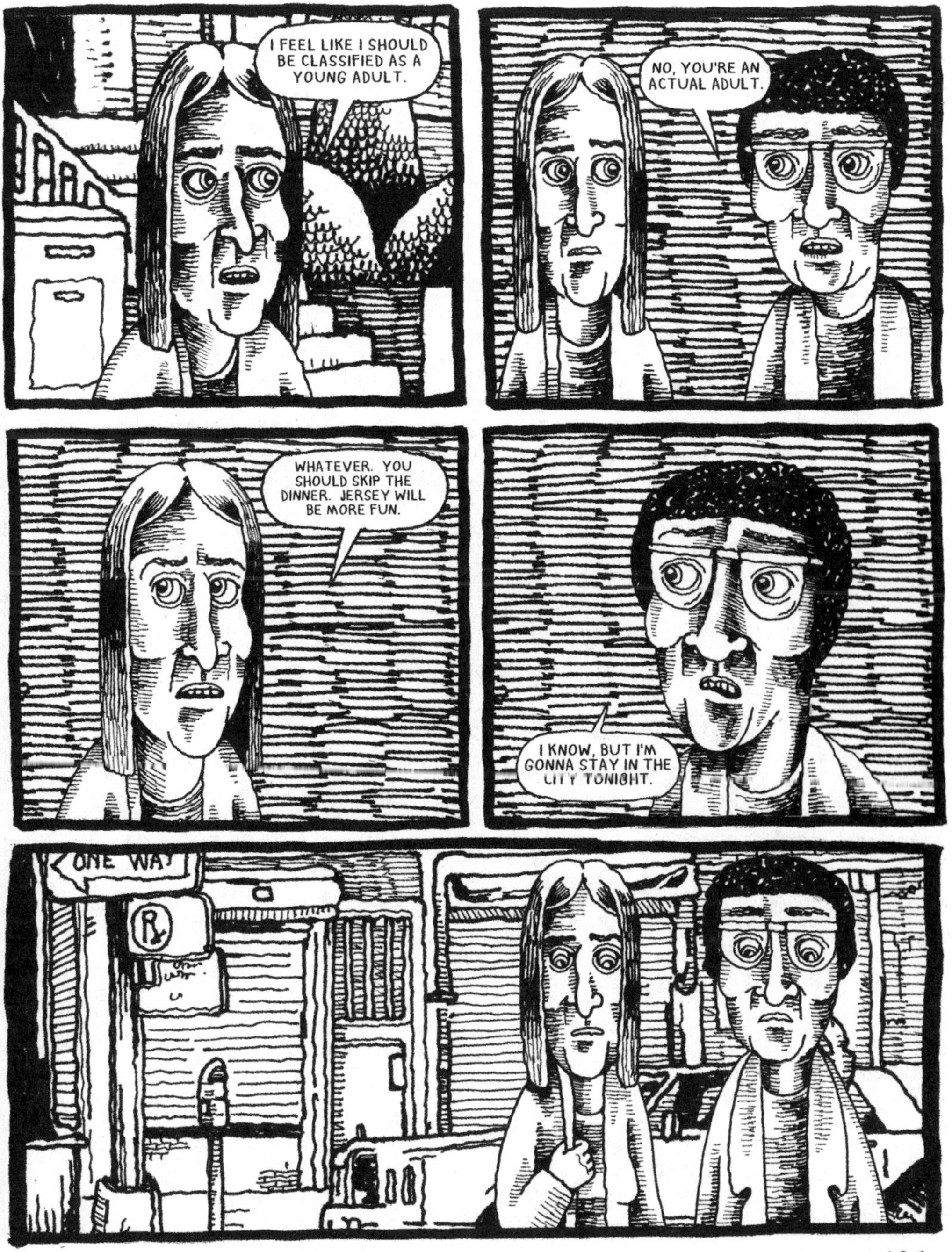
I FEEL LIKE I SHOULD BE CLASSIFIED AS A YOUNG ADULT.
NO, YOU'RE AN ACTUAL ADULT.
WHATEVER. YOU SHOULD SKIP THE DINNER. JERSEY WILL BE MORE FUN.
I KNOW, BUT I'M GONNA STAY IN THE CITY TONIGHT.
ONE WAY

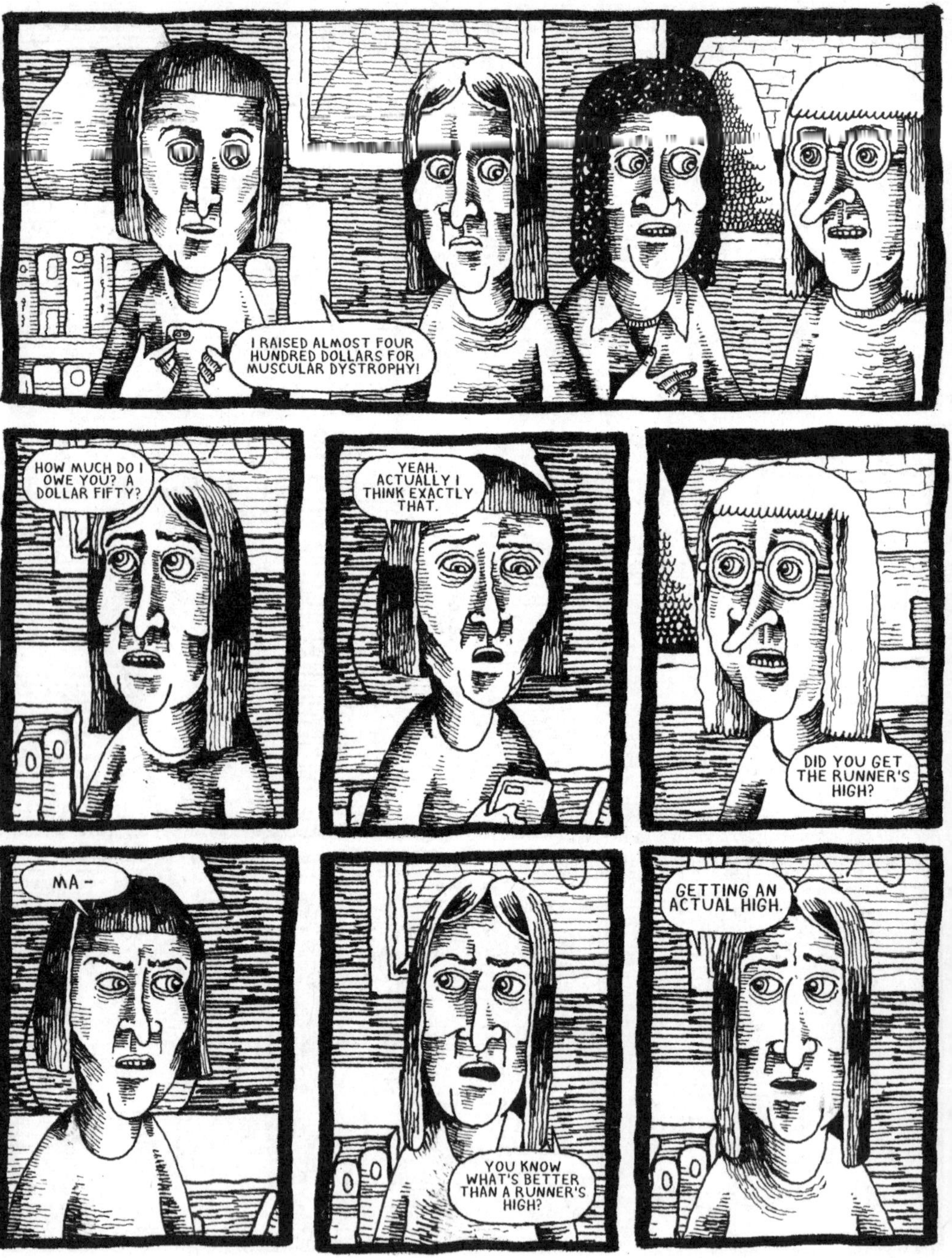
I RAISED ALMOST FOUR HUNDRED DOLLARS FOR MUSCULAR DYSTROPHY!
HOW MUCH DO I OWE YOU? A DOLLAR FIFTY?
YEAH. ACTUALLY I THINK EXACTLY THAT.
DID YOU GET THE RUNNER'S HIGH?
MA-
YOU KNOW WHAT'S BETTER THAN A RUNNER'S HIGH?
GETTING AN ACTUAL HIGH.

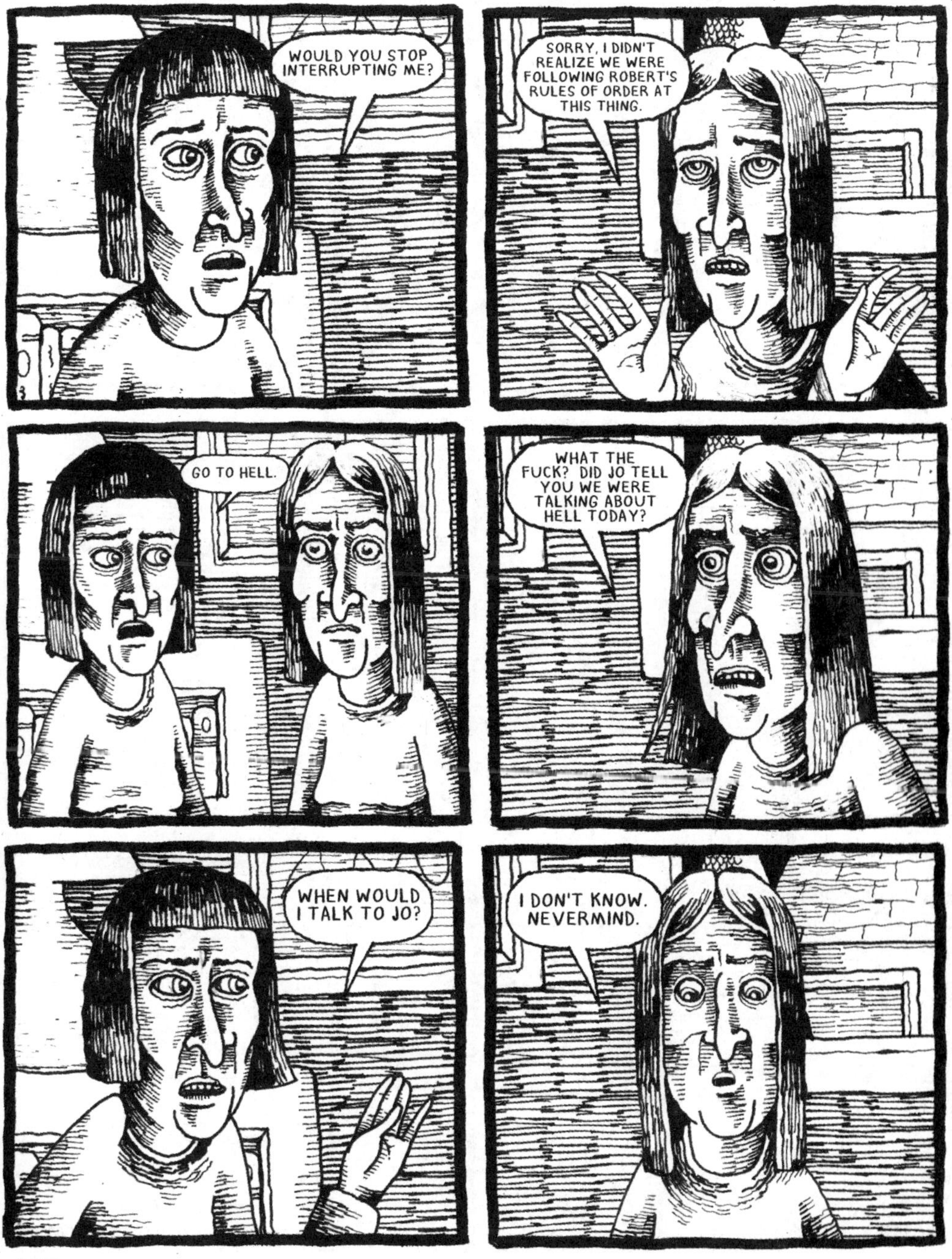
WOULD YOU STOP INTERRUPTING ME?
SORRY, I DIDN'T REALIZE WE WERE FOLLOWING ROBERT'S RULES OF ORDER AT THIS THING.
GO TO HELL.
WHAT THE FUCK? DID JO TELL YOU WE WERE TALKING ABOUT HELL TODAY?
WHEN WOULD I TALK TO JO?
I DON'T KNOW. NEVERMIND.

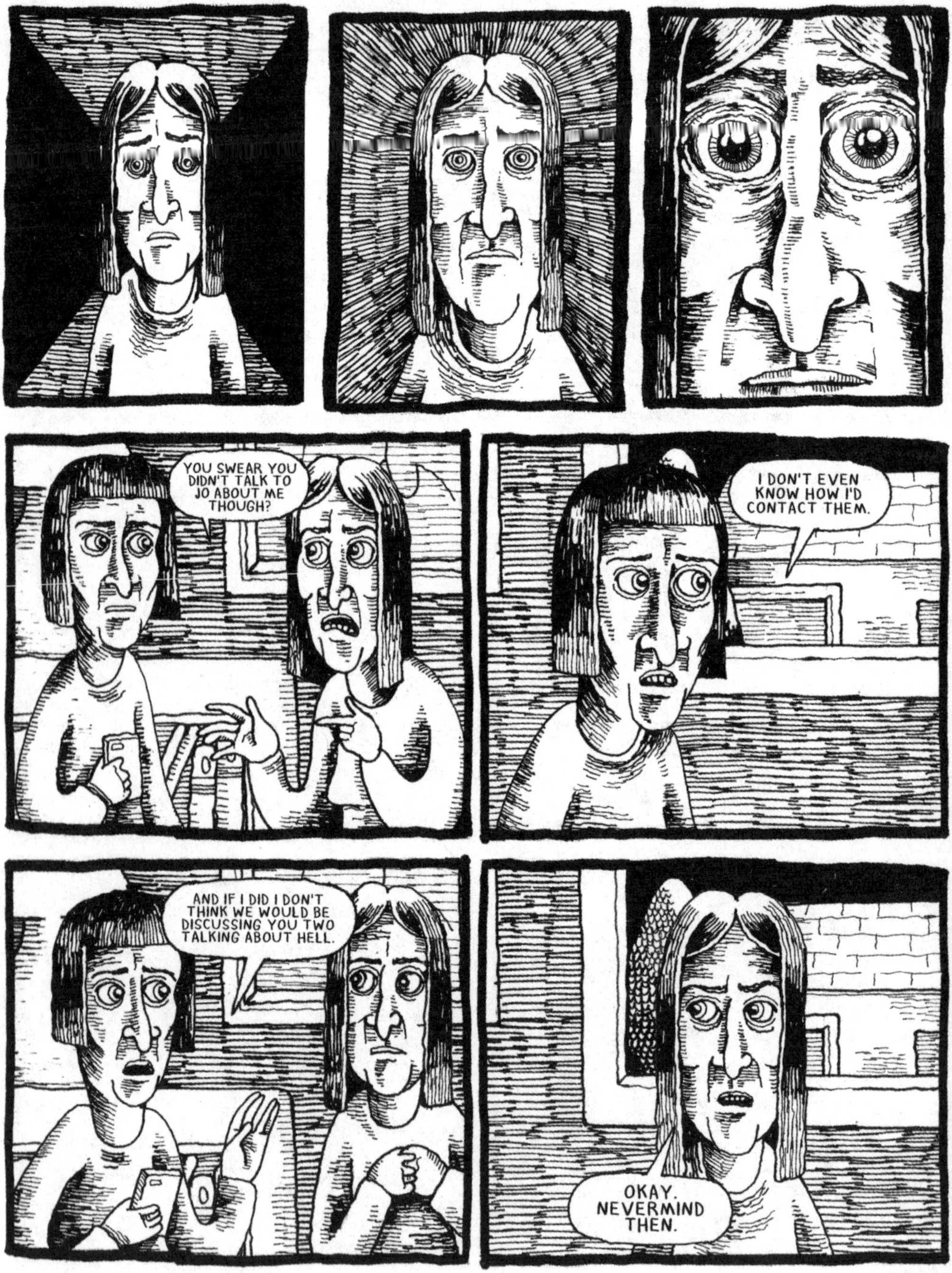
YOU SWEAR YOU DIDN'T TALK TO JO ABOUT ME THOUGH?
I DON'T EVEN KNOW HOW I'D CONTACT THEM.
AND IF I DID I DON'T THINK WE WOULD BE DISCUSSING YOU TWO TALKING ABOUT HELL.
OKAY. NEVERMIND THEN.

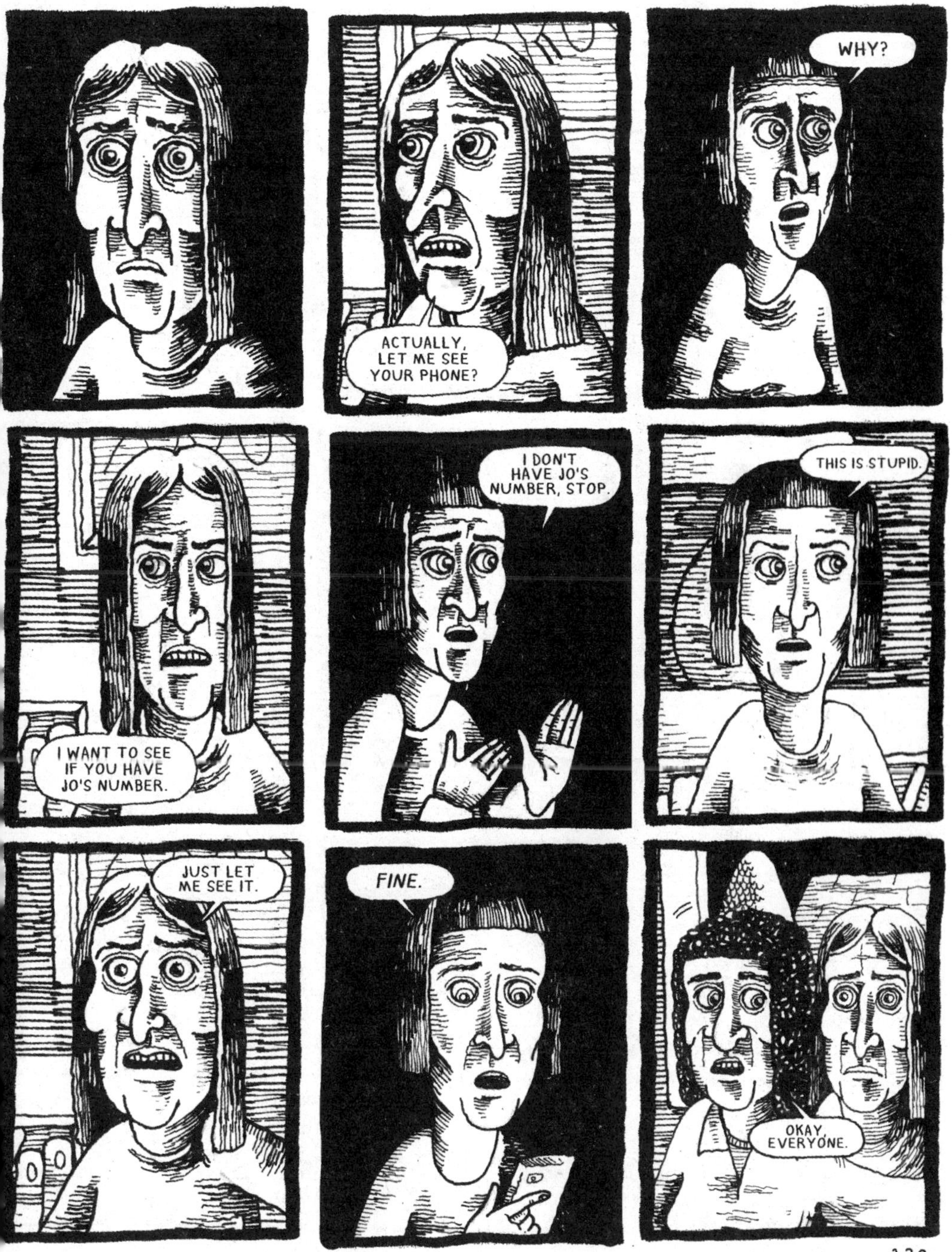
ACTUALLY, LET ME SEE YOUR PHONE?
WHY?
I WANT TO SEE IF YOU HAVE JO'S NUMBER.
I DON'T HAVE JO'S NUMBER, STOP.
THIS IS STUPID.
JUST LET ME SEE IT.
FINE.
OKAY, EVERYONE.

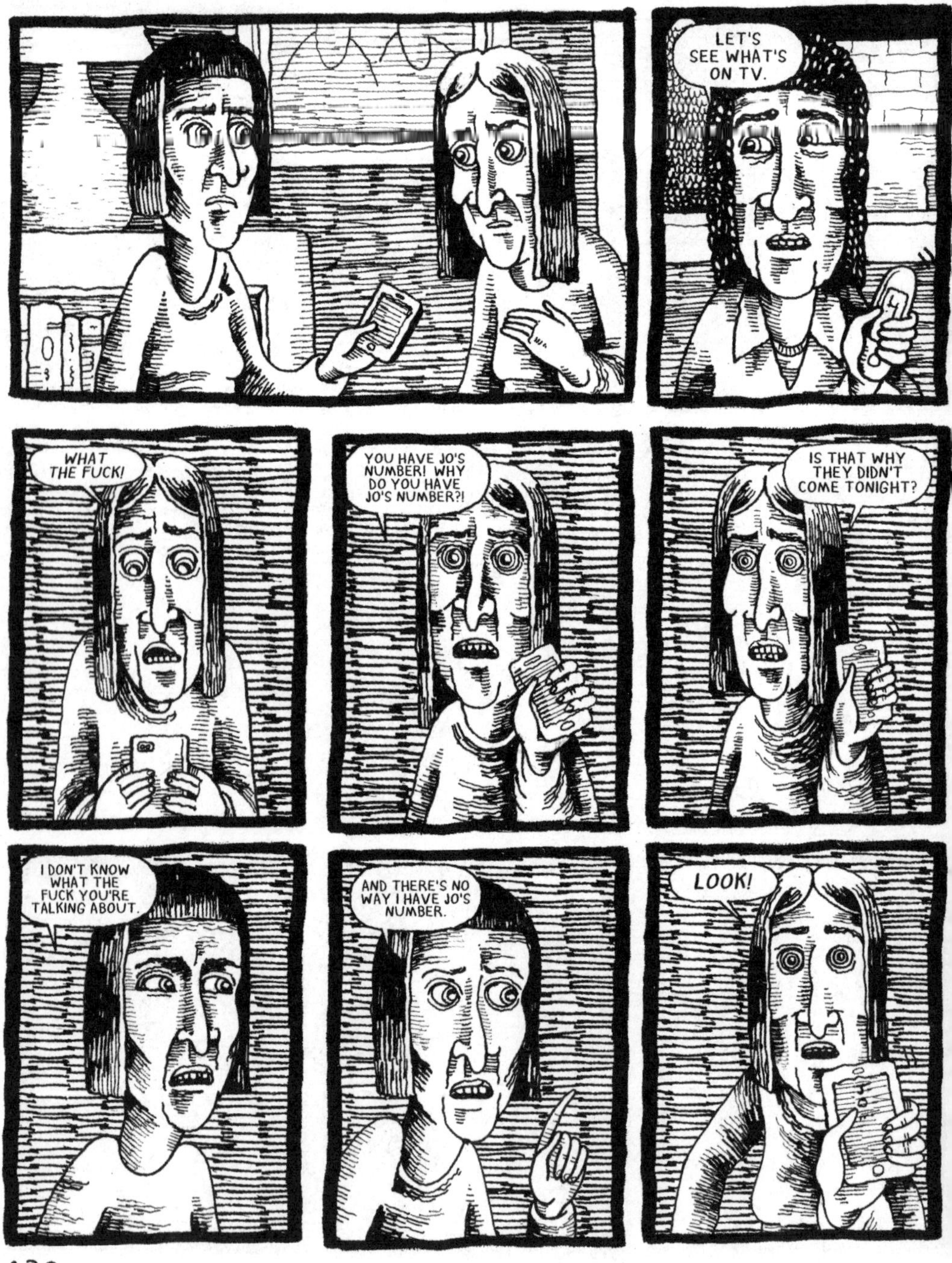
LET'S SEE WHAT'S ON TV.
WHAT THE FUCK!
YOU HAVE JO'S NUMBER! WHY DO YOU HAVE JO'S NUMBER?!
IS THAT WHY THEY DIDN'T COME TONIGHT?
I DON'T KNOW WHAT THE FUCK YOU'RE TALKING ABOUT.
AND THERE'S NO WAY I HAVE JO'S NUMBER.
LOOK!

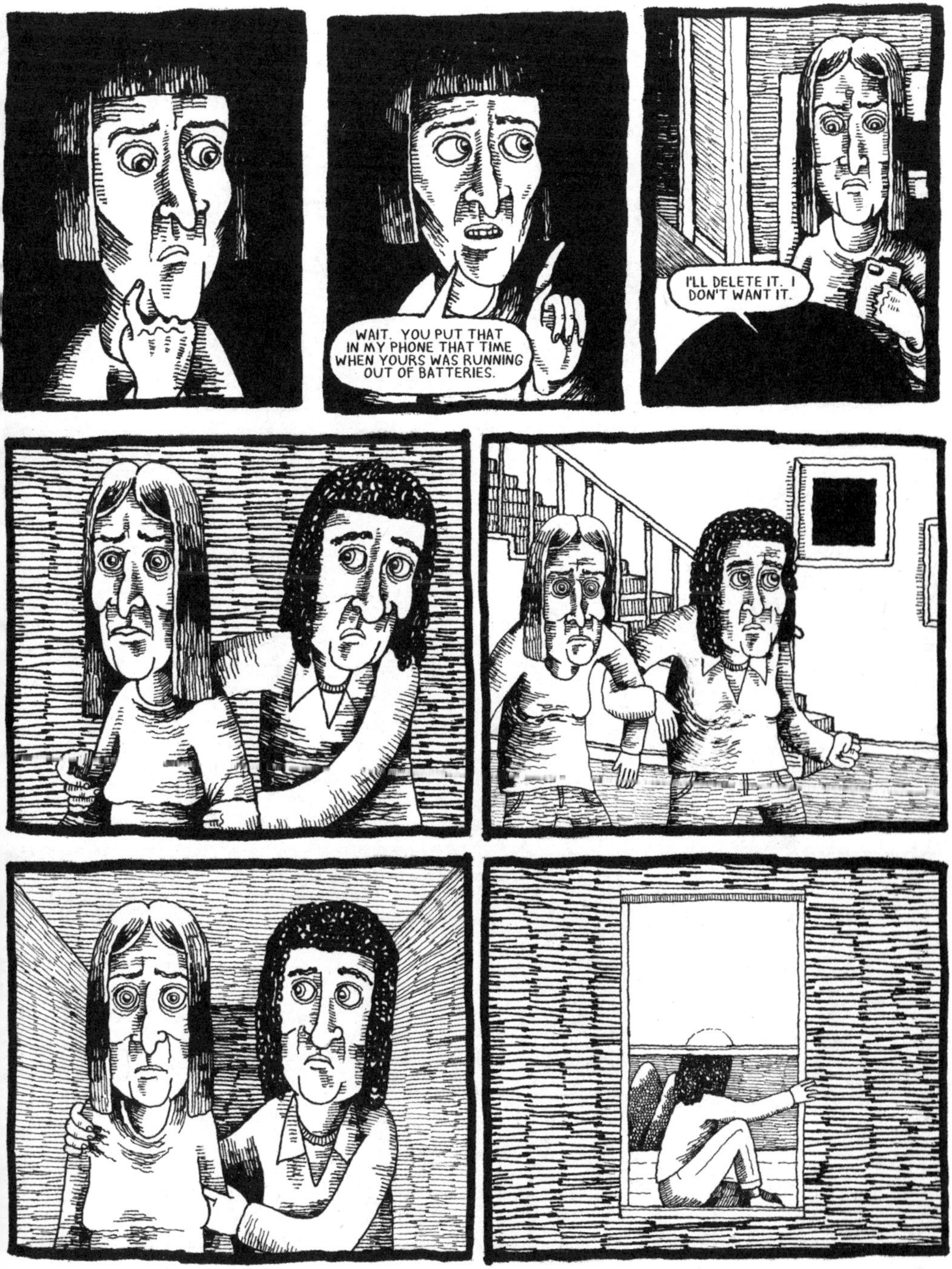
WAIT. YOU PUT THAT IN MY PHONE THAT TIME WHEN YOURS WAS RUNNING OUT OF BATTERIES.
I'LL DELETE IT. I DON'T WANT IT.

MACK, WHAT IS GOING ON?
I DON'T KNOW, JO WAS REALLY WEIRD TODAY AND DIDN'T COME OUT TONIGHT BECAUSE THEY SAID THEY WERE GOING OUT WITH THEIR AUNT.
BUT THEY NEVER MENTIONED HAVING AN AUNT BEFORE.
WE'VE BEEN FRIENDS FOR LIKE TWENTY YEARS AND I'M NOT SURE I'VE EVER MENTIONED MY AUNT BEFORE EITHER. I ACTUALLY HAVE TWO.
HAVING AN AUNT IS ONE OF THE LEAST INTERESTING FACTS A PERSON CAN SHARE.

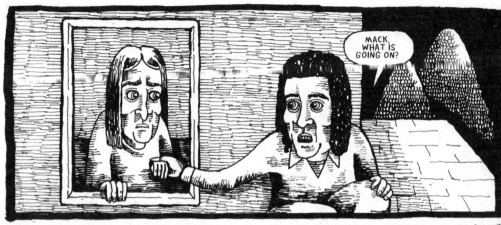

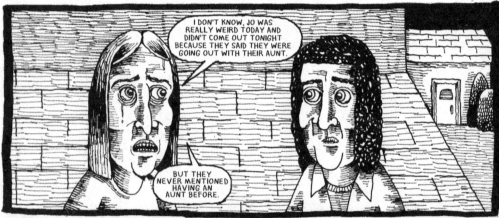

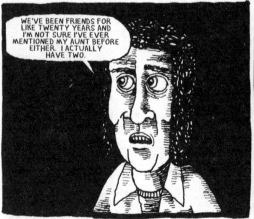

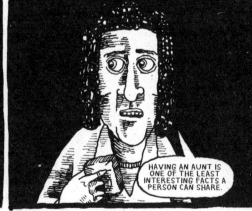

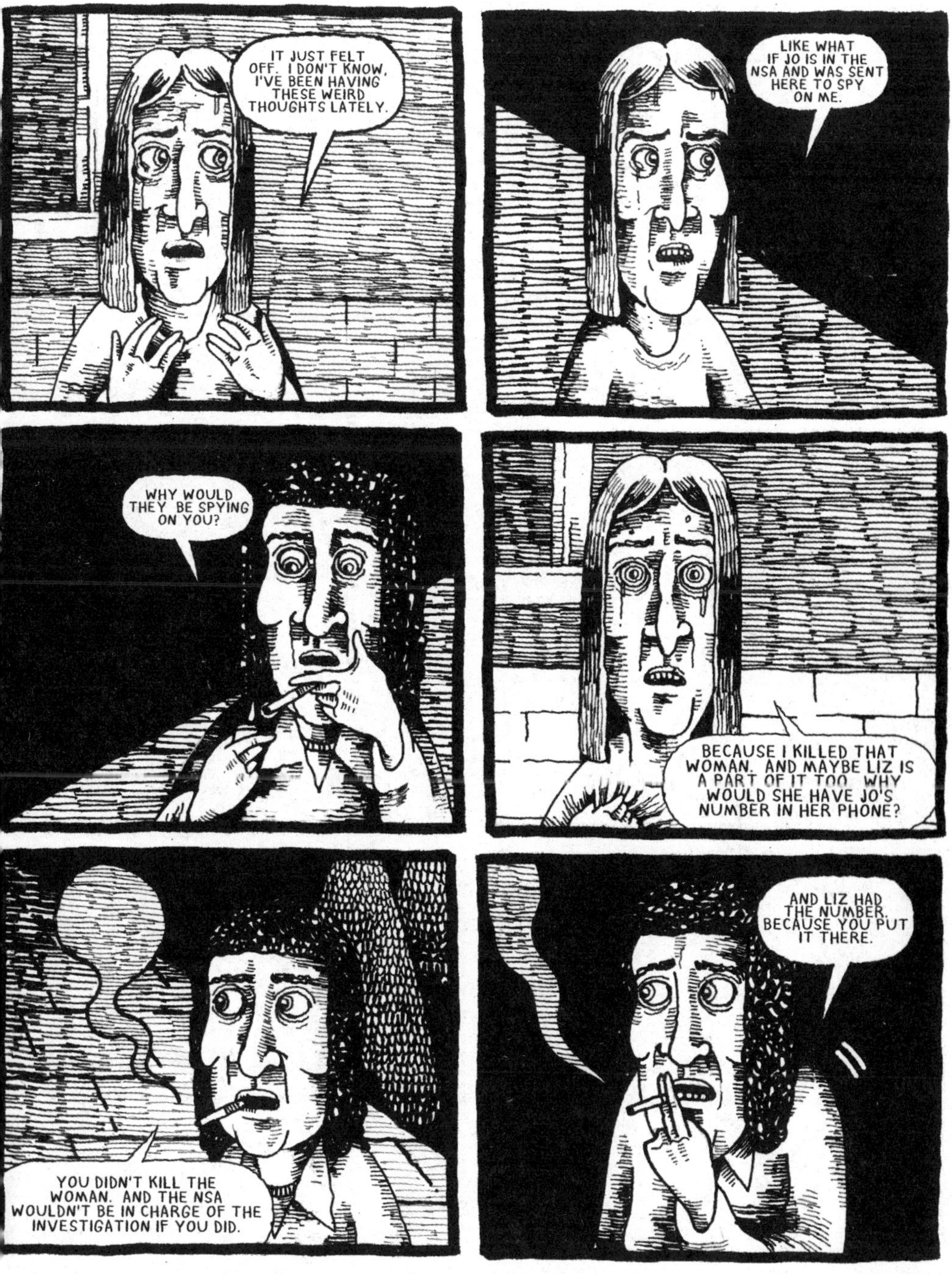
IT JUST FELT OFF. I DON'T KNOW, I'VE BEEN HAVING THESE WEIRD THOUGHTS LATELY.
LIKE WHAT IF JO IS IN THE NSA AND WAS SENT HERE TO SPY ON ME.
WHY WOULD THEY BE SPYING ON YOU?
BECAUSE I KILLED THAT WOMAN. AND MAYBE LIZ IS A PART OF IT TOO. WHY WOULD SHE HAVE JO'S NUMBER IN HER PHONE?
YOU DIDN'T KILL THE WOMAN. AND THE NSA WOULDN'T BE IN CHARGE OF THE INVESTIGATION IF YOU DID.
AND LIZ HAD THE NUMBER. BECAUSE YOU PUT IT THERE.

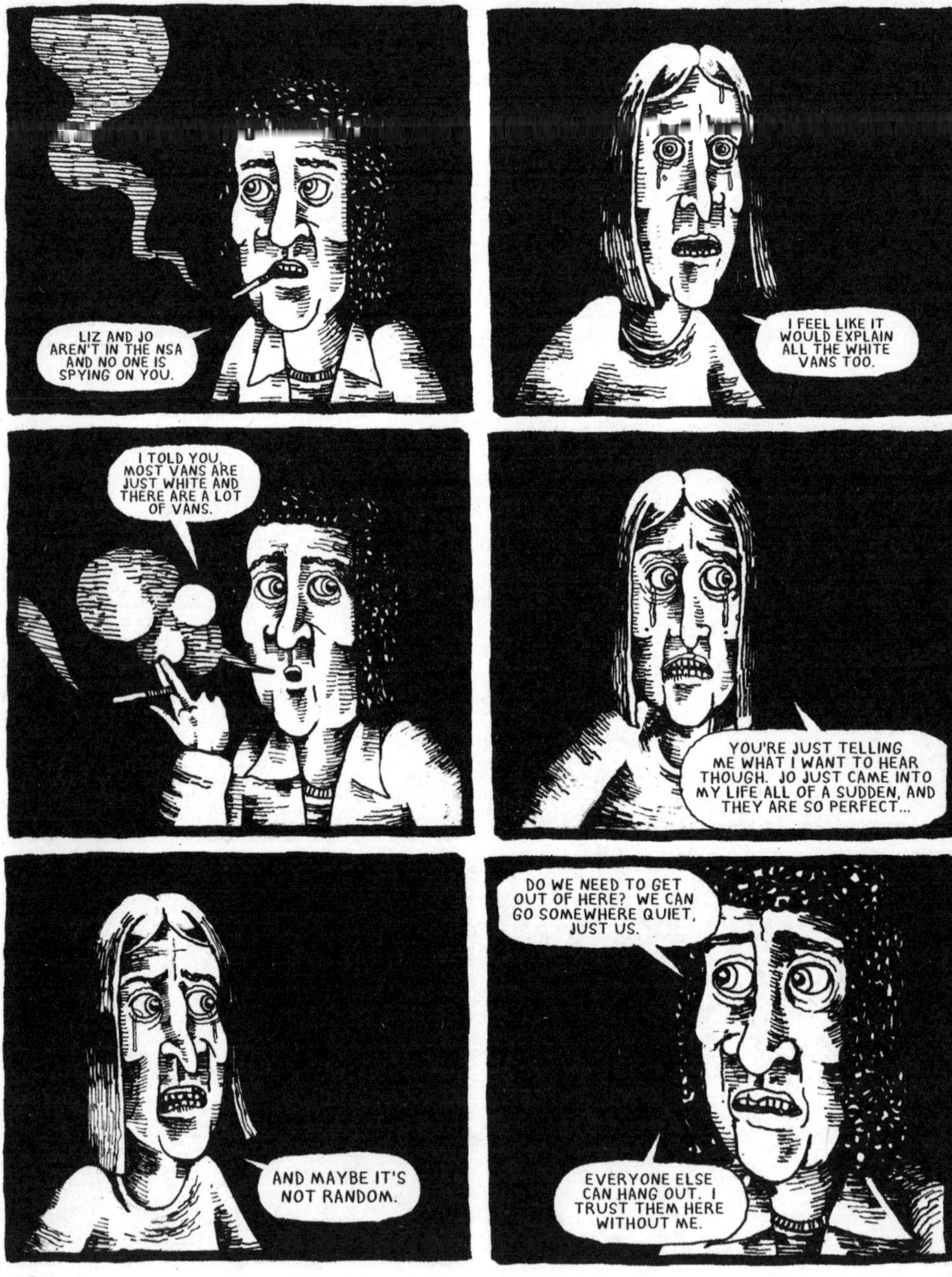
LIZ AND JO AREN'T IN THE NSA AND NO ONE IS SPYING ON YOU.
I FEEL LIKE IT WOULD EXPLAIN ALL THE WHITE VANS TOO.
I TOLD YOU, MOST VANS ARE JUST WHITE AND THERE ARE A LOT OF VANS.
YOU'RE JUST TELLING ME WHAT I WANT TO HEAR THOUGH. JO JUST CAME INTO MY LIFE ALL OF A SUDDEN, AND THEY ARE SO PERFECT...
AND MAYBE IT'S NOT RANDOM.
DO WE NEED TO GET OUT OF HERE? WE CAN GO SOMEWHERE QUIET, JUST US.
EVERYONE ELSE CAN HANG OUT. I TRUST THEM HERE WITHOUT ME.

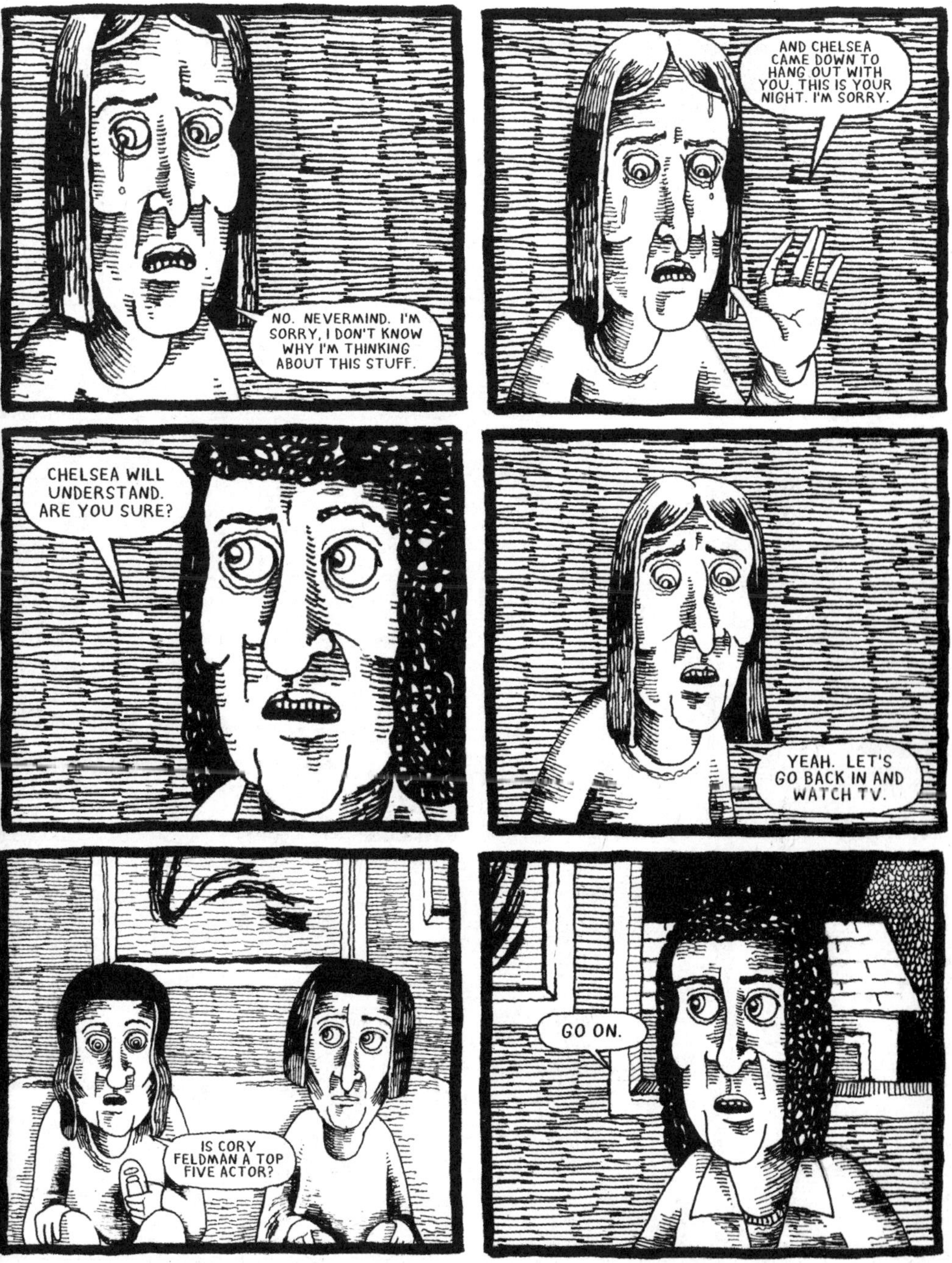
NO. NEVERMIND. I'M SORRY, I DON'T KNOW WHY I'M THINKING ABOUT THIS STUFF.
AND CHELSEA CAME DOWN TO HANG OUT WITH YOU. THIS IS YOUR NIGHT. I'M SORRY.
CHELSEA WILL UNDERSTAND. ARE YOU SURE?
YEAH. LET'S GO BACK IN AND WATCH TV.
IS CORY FELDMAN A TOP FIVE ACTOR?
GO ON.

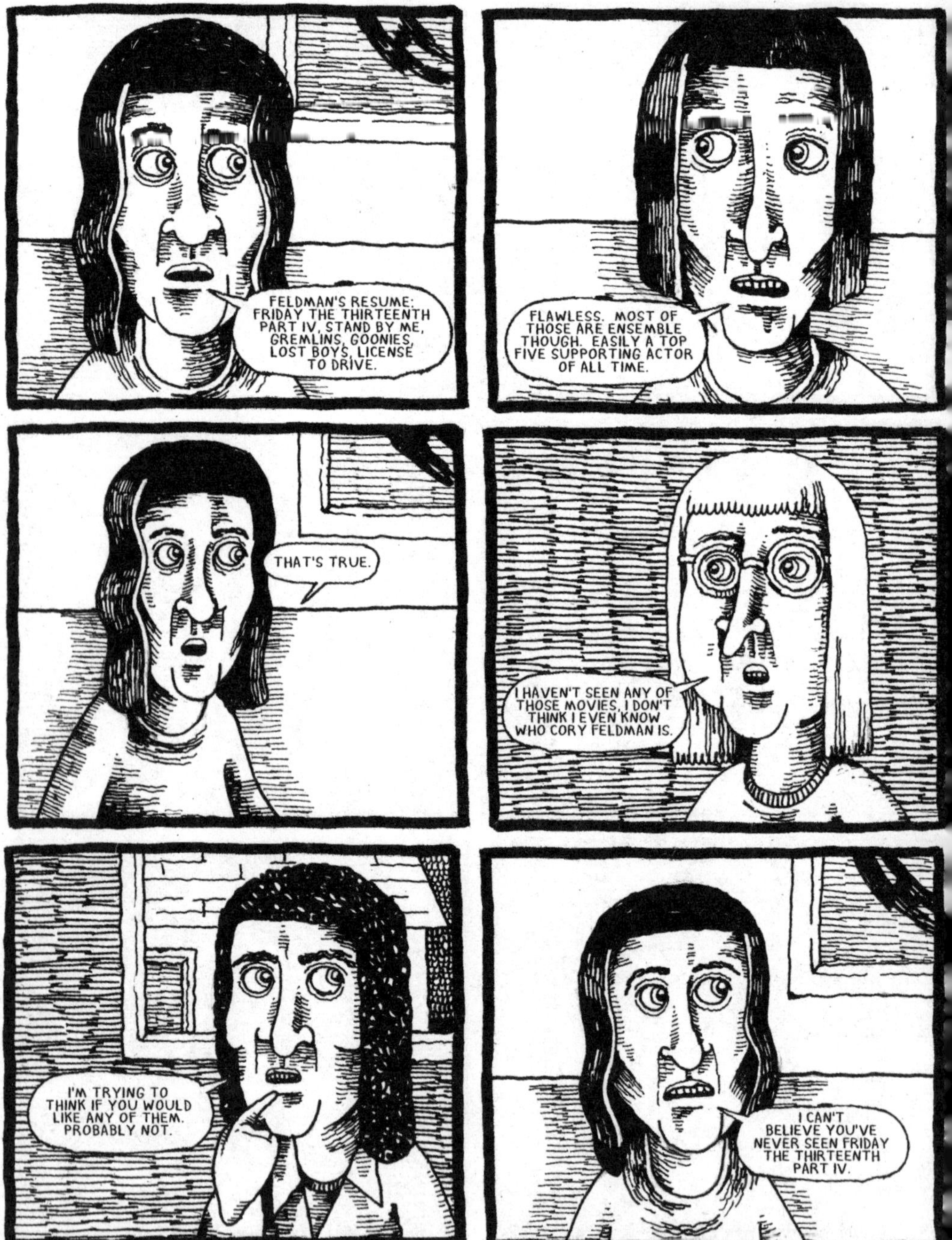
FELDMAN'S RESUME: FRIDAY THE THIRTEENTH PART IV, STAND BY ME, GREMLINS, GOONIES, LOST BOYS, LICENSE TO DRIVE.
FLAWLESS. MOST OF THOSE ARE ENSEMBLE THOUGH. EASILY A TOP FIVE SUPPORTING ACTOR OF ALL TIME.
THAT'S TRUE.
I HAVEN'T SEEN ANY OF THOSE MOVIES. I DON'T THINK I EVEN KNOW WHO CORY FELDMAN IS.
I'M TRYING TO THINK IF YOU WOULD LIKE ANY OF THEM. PROBABLY NOT.
I CAN'T BELIEVE YOU'VE NEVER SEEN FRIDAY THE THIRTEENTH PART IV.

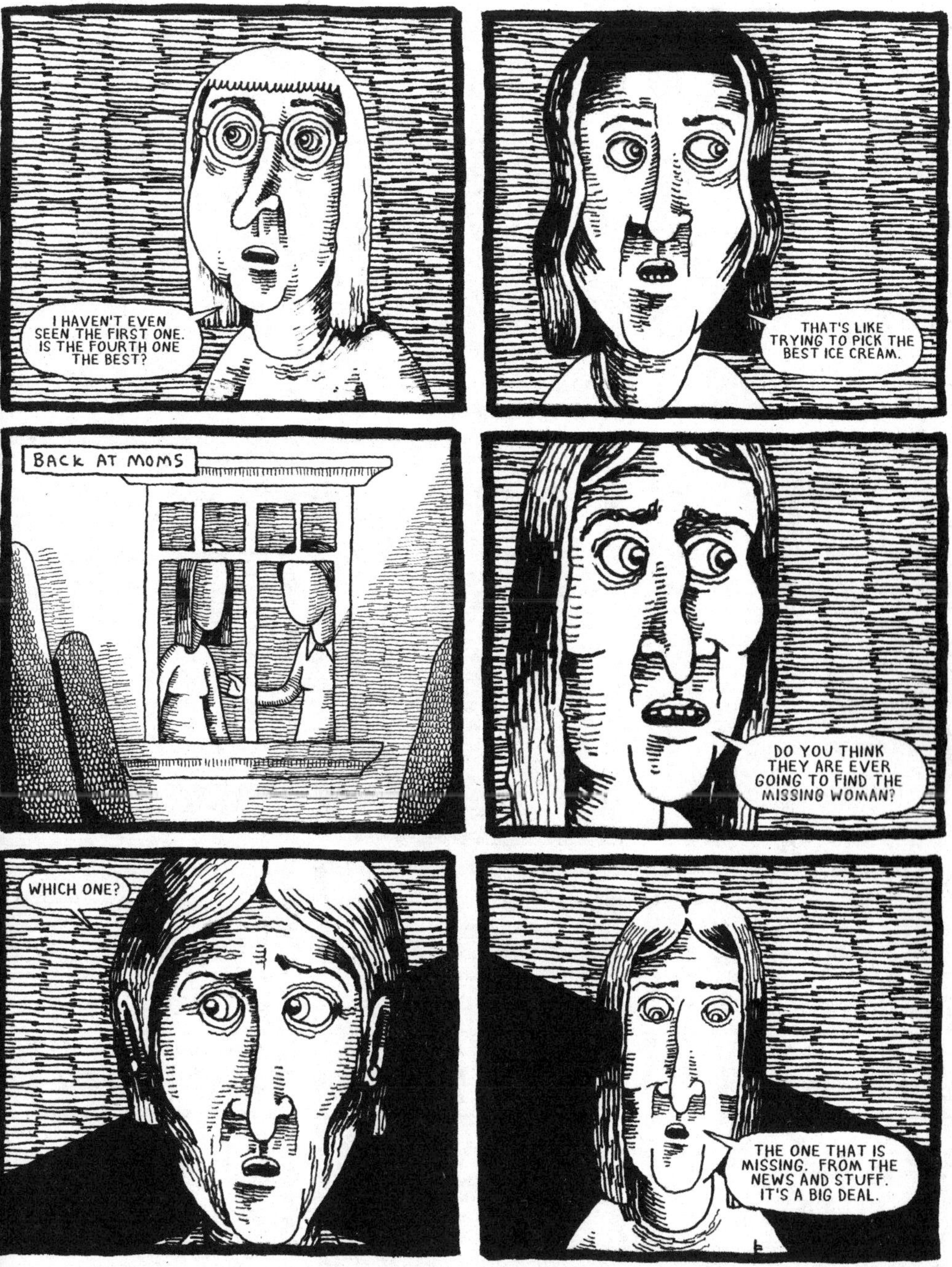
I HAVEN'T EVEN SEEN THE FIRST ONE. IS THE FOURTH ONE THE BEST?
THAT'S LIKE TRYING TO PICK THE BEST ICE CREAM.
BACK AT MOMS
DO YOU THINK THEY ARE EVER GOING TO FIND THE MISSING WOMAN?
WHICH ONE?
THE ONE THAT IS MISSING. FROM THE NEWS AND STUFF. IT'S A BIG DEAL.

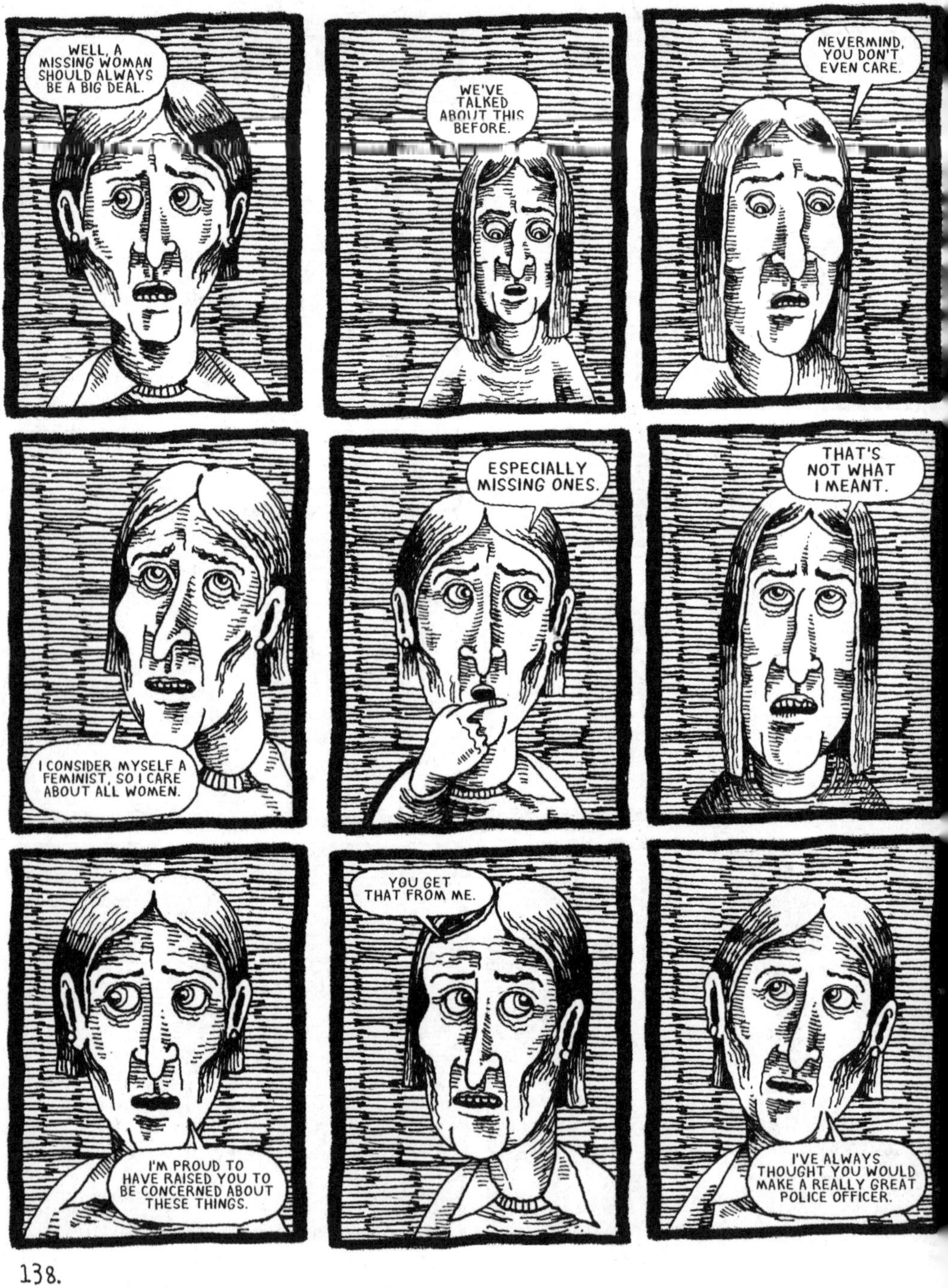
WELL, A MISSING WOMAN SHOULD ALWAYS BE A BIG DEAL.
WE'VE TALKED ABOUT THIS BEFORE.
NEVERMIND, YOU DON'T EVEN CARE.
I CONSIDER MYSELF A FEMINIST, SO I CARE ABOUT ALL WOMEN.
ESPECIALLY MISSING ONES.
THAT'S NOT WHAT I MEANT.
I'M PROUD TO HAVE RAISED YOU TO BE CONCERNED ABOUT THESE THINGS.
YOU GET THAT FROM ME.
I'VE ALWAYS THOUGHT YOU WOULD MAKE A REALLY GREAT POLICE OFFICER.

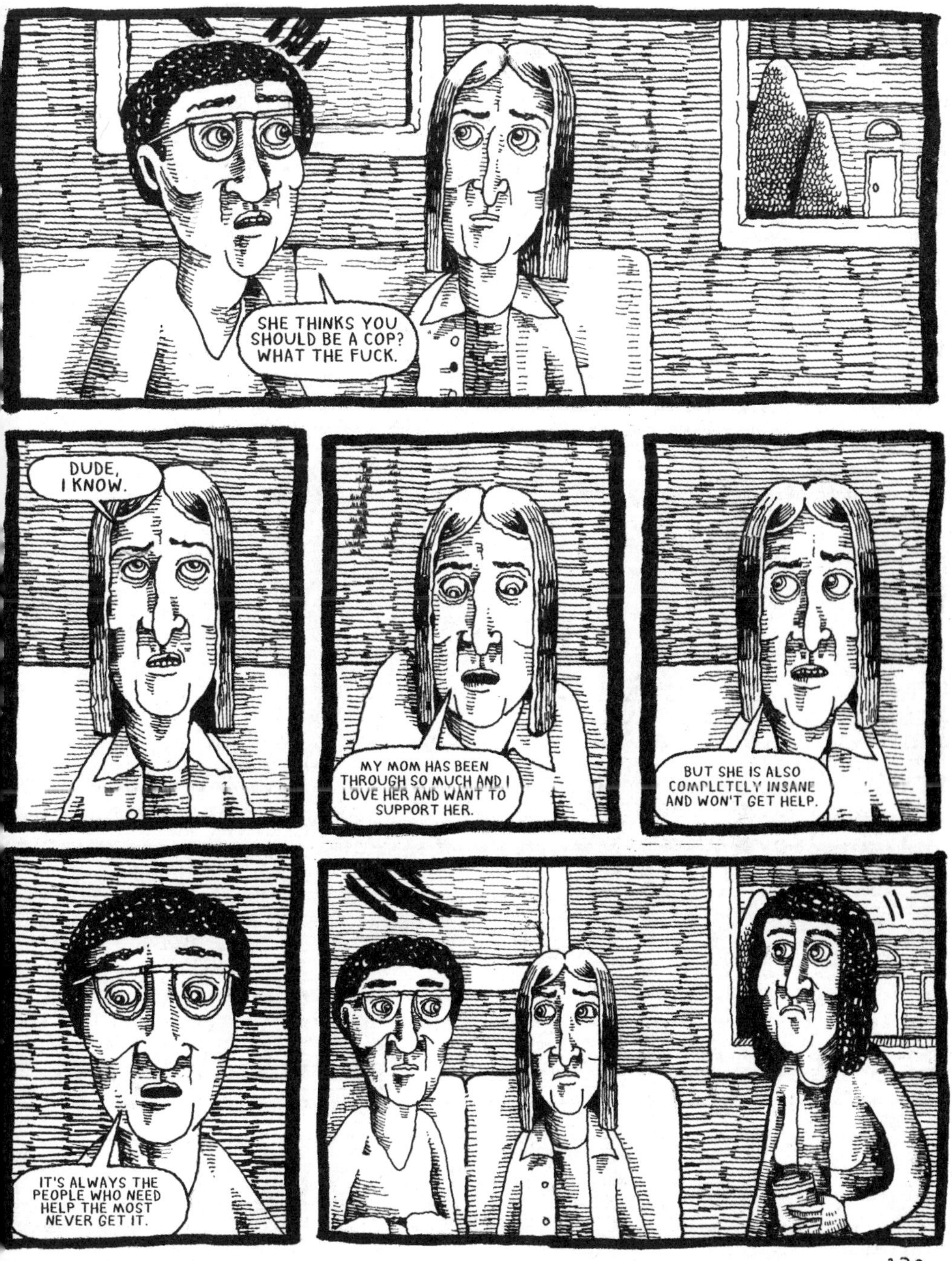
SHE THINKS YOU SHOULD BE A COP? WHAT THE FUCK.
DUDE, I KNOW.
MY MOM HAS BEEN THROUGH SO MUCH AND I LOVE HER AND WANT TO SUPPORT HER.
BUT SHE IS ALSO COMPLETELY INSANE AND WON'T GET HELP.
IT'S ALWAYS THE PEOPLE WHO NEED HELP THE MOST NEVER GET IT.

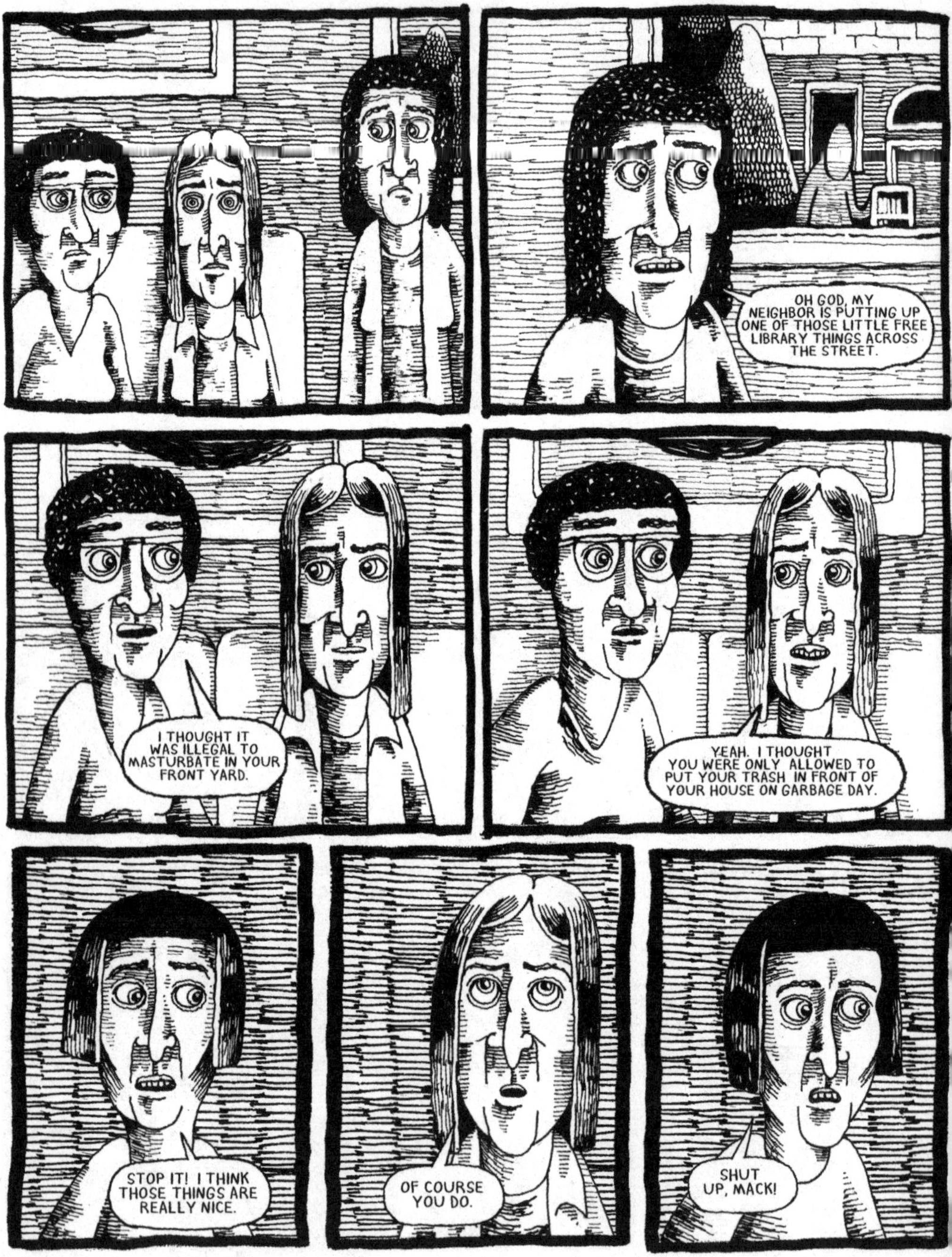
OH GOD, MY NEIGHBOR IS PUTTING UP ONE OF THOSE LITTLE FREE LIBRARY THINGS ACROSS THE STREET.
I THOUGHT IT WAS ILLEGAL TO MASTURBATE IN YOUR FRONT YARD.
YEAH. I THOUGHT YOU WERE ONLY ALLOWED TO PUT YOUR TRASH IN FRONT OF YOUR HOUSE ON GARBAGE DAY.
STOP IT! I THINK THOSE THINGS ARE REALLY NICE.
OF COURSE YOU DO.
SHUT UP, MACK!

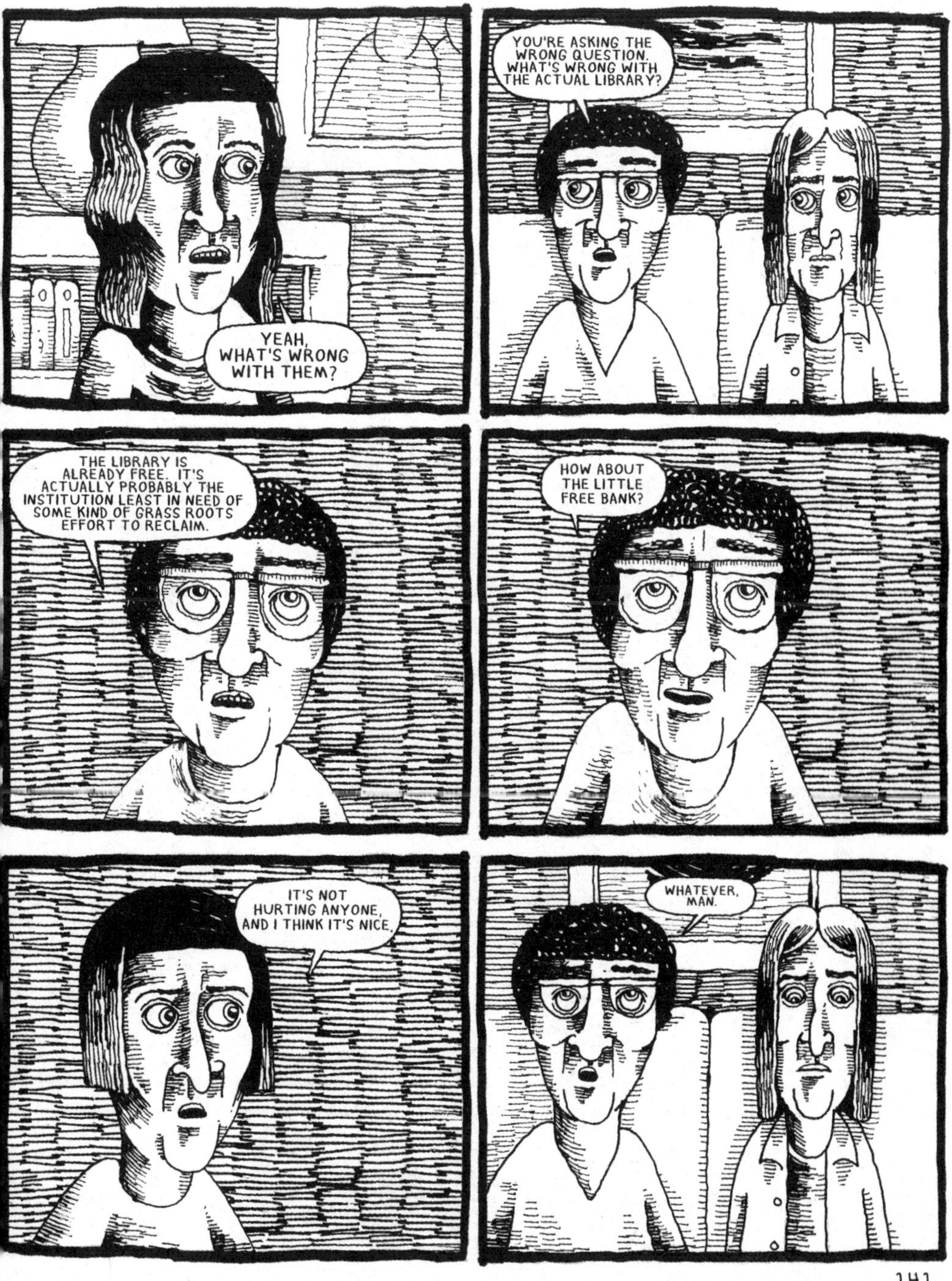
YEAH, WHAT'S WRONG WITH THEM?
YOU'RE ASKING THE WRONG QUESTION. WHAT'S WRONG WITH THE ACTUAL LIBRARY?
THE LIBRARY IS ALREADY FREE. IT'S ACTUALLY PROBABLY THE INSTITUTION LEAST IN NEED OF SOME KIND OF GRASS ROOTS EFFORT TO RECLAIM.
HOW ABOUT THE LITTLE FREE BANK?
IT'S NOT HURTING ANYONE, AND I THINK IT'S NICE.
WHATEVER, MAN.

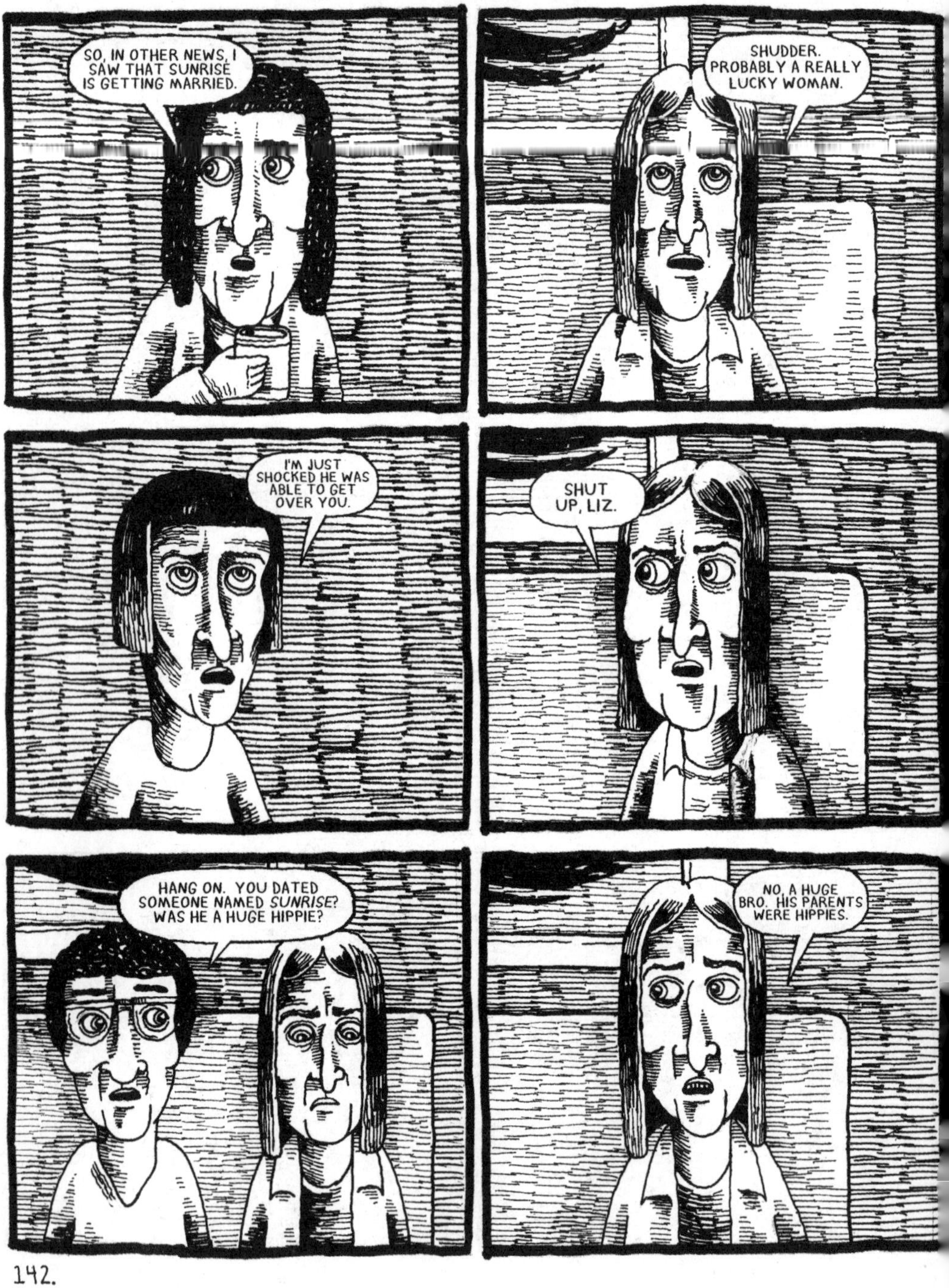
SO, IN OTHER NEWS, I SAW THAT SUNRISE IS GETTING MARRIED.
SHUDDER. PROBABLY A REALLY LUCKY WOMAN.
I'M JUST SHOCKED HE WAS ABLE TO GET OVER YOU.
SHUT UP, LIZ.
HANG ON. YOU DATED SOMEONE NAMED *SUNRISE*? WAS HE A HUGE HIPPIE?
NO, A HUGE BRO. HIS PARENTS WERE HIPPIES.

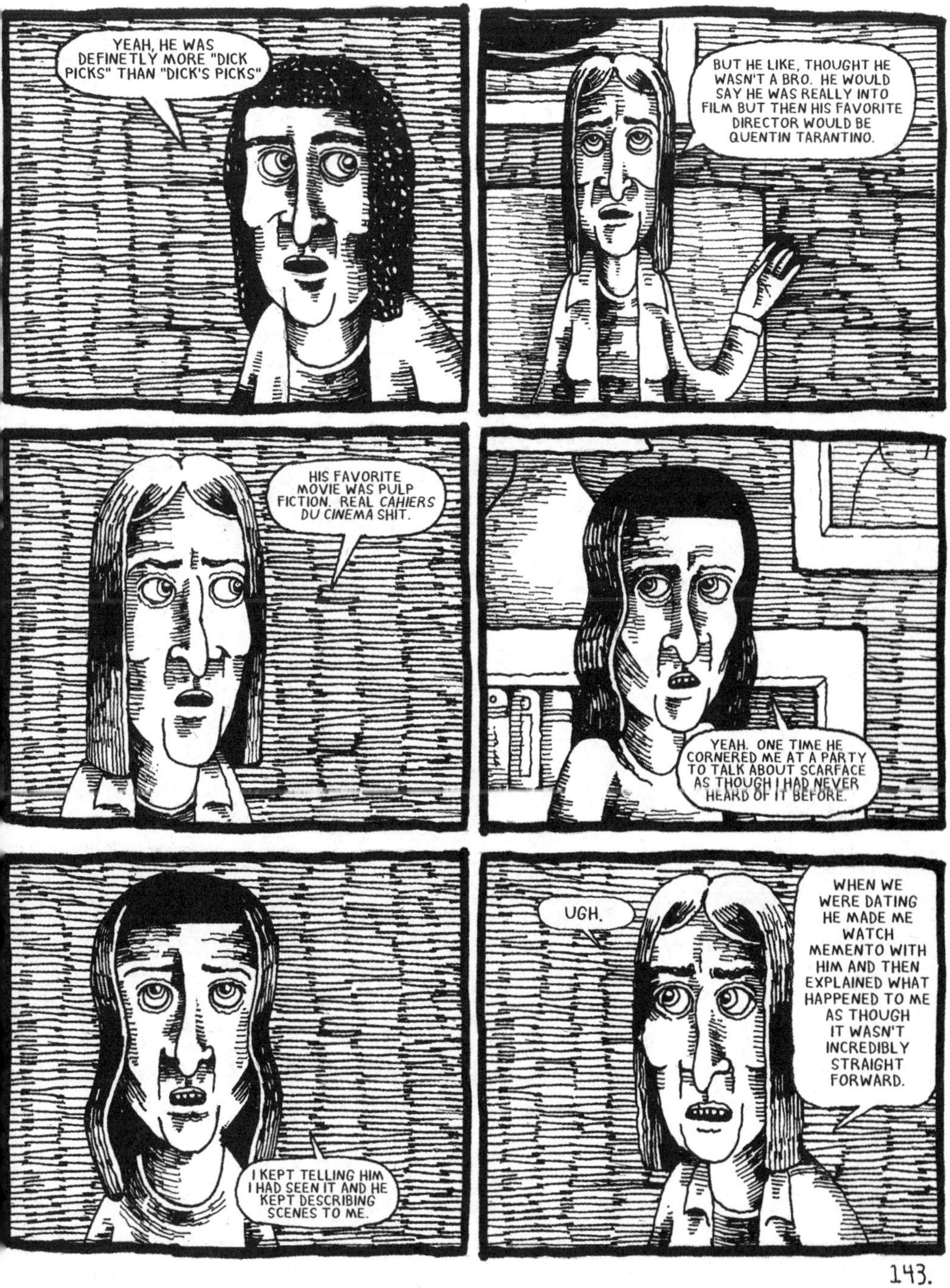
YEAH, HE WAS DEFINETLY MORE "DICK PICKS" THAN "DICK'S PICKS"
BUT HE LIKE, THOUGHT HE WASN'T A BRO. HE WOULD SAY HE WAS REALLY INTO FILM BUT THEN HIS FAVORITE DIRECTOR WOULD BE QUENTIN TARANTINO.
HIS FAVORITE MOVIE WAS PULP FICTION. REAL CAHIERS DU CINEMA SHIT.
YEAH. ONE TIME HE CORNERED ME AT A PARTY TO TALK ABOUT SCARFACE AS THOUGH I HAD NEVER HEARD OF IT BEFORE.
I KEPT TELLING HIM I HAD SEEN IT AND HE KEPT DESCRIBING SCENES TO ME.
UGH.
WHEN WE WERE DATING HE MADE ME WATCH MEMENTO WITH HIM AND THEN EXPLAINED WHAT HAPPENED TO ME AS THOUGH IT WASN'T INCREDIBLY STRAIGHT FORWARD.

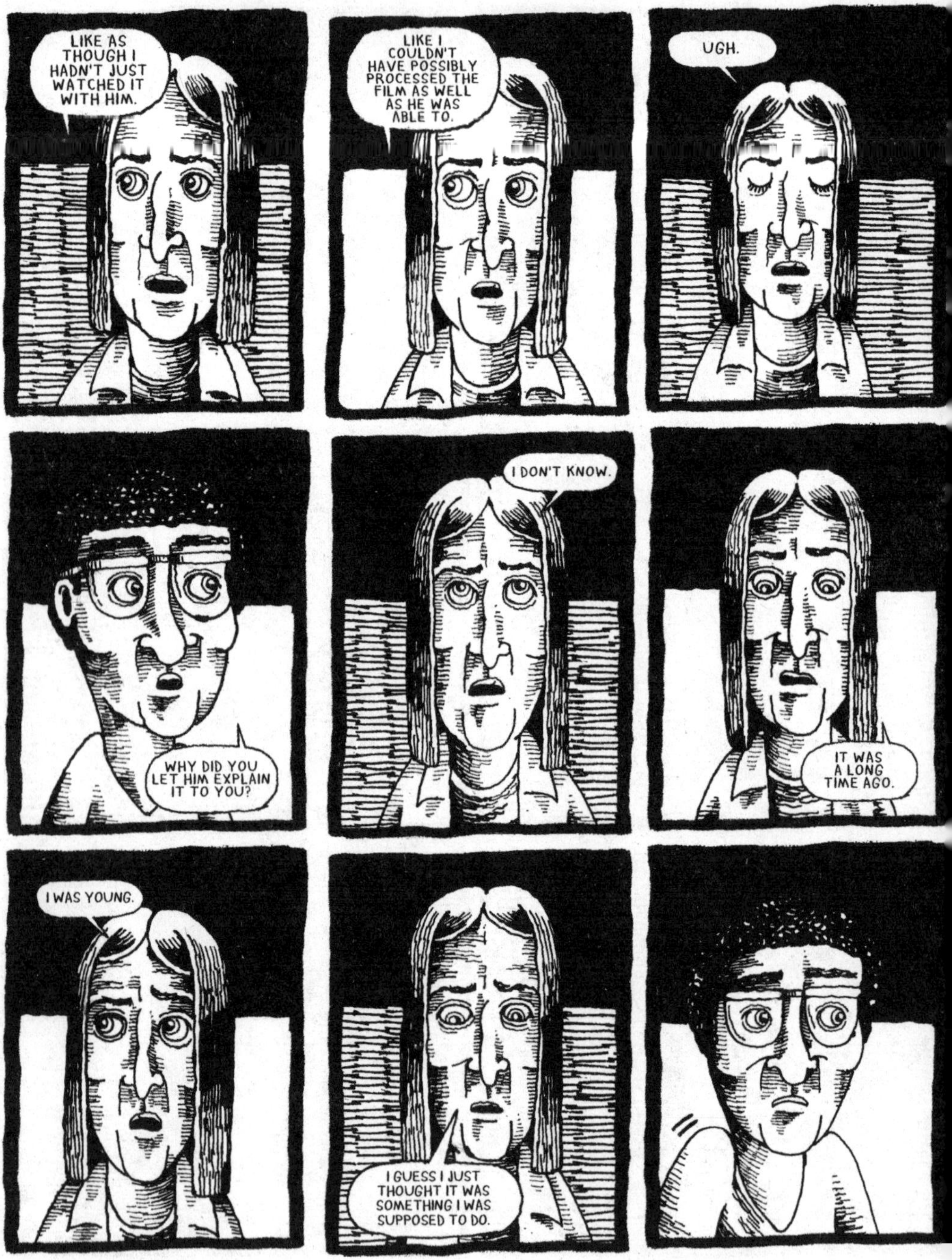
LIKE AS THOUGH I HADN'T JUST WATCHED IT WITH HIM.
LIKE I COULDN'T HAVE POSSIBLY PROCESSED THE FILM AS WELL AS HE WAS ABLE TO.
UGH.
WHY DID YOU LET HIM EXPLAIN IT TO YOU?
I DON'T KNOW.
IT WAS A LONG TIME AGO.
I WAS YOUNG.
I GUESS I JUST THOUGHT IT WAS SOMETHING I WAS SUPPOSED TO DO.

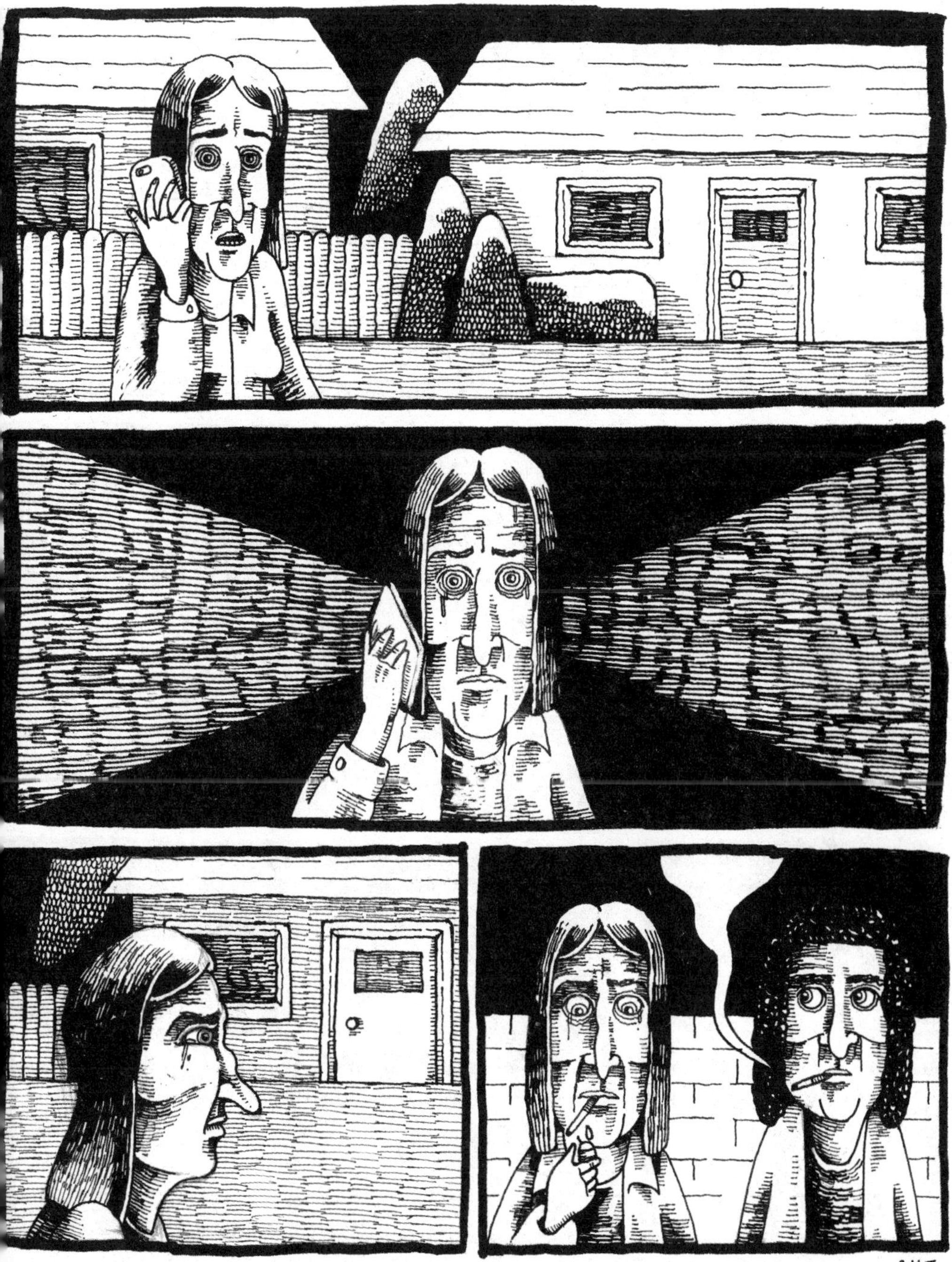

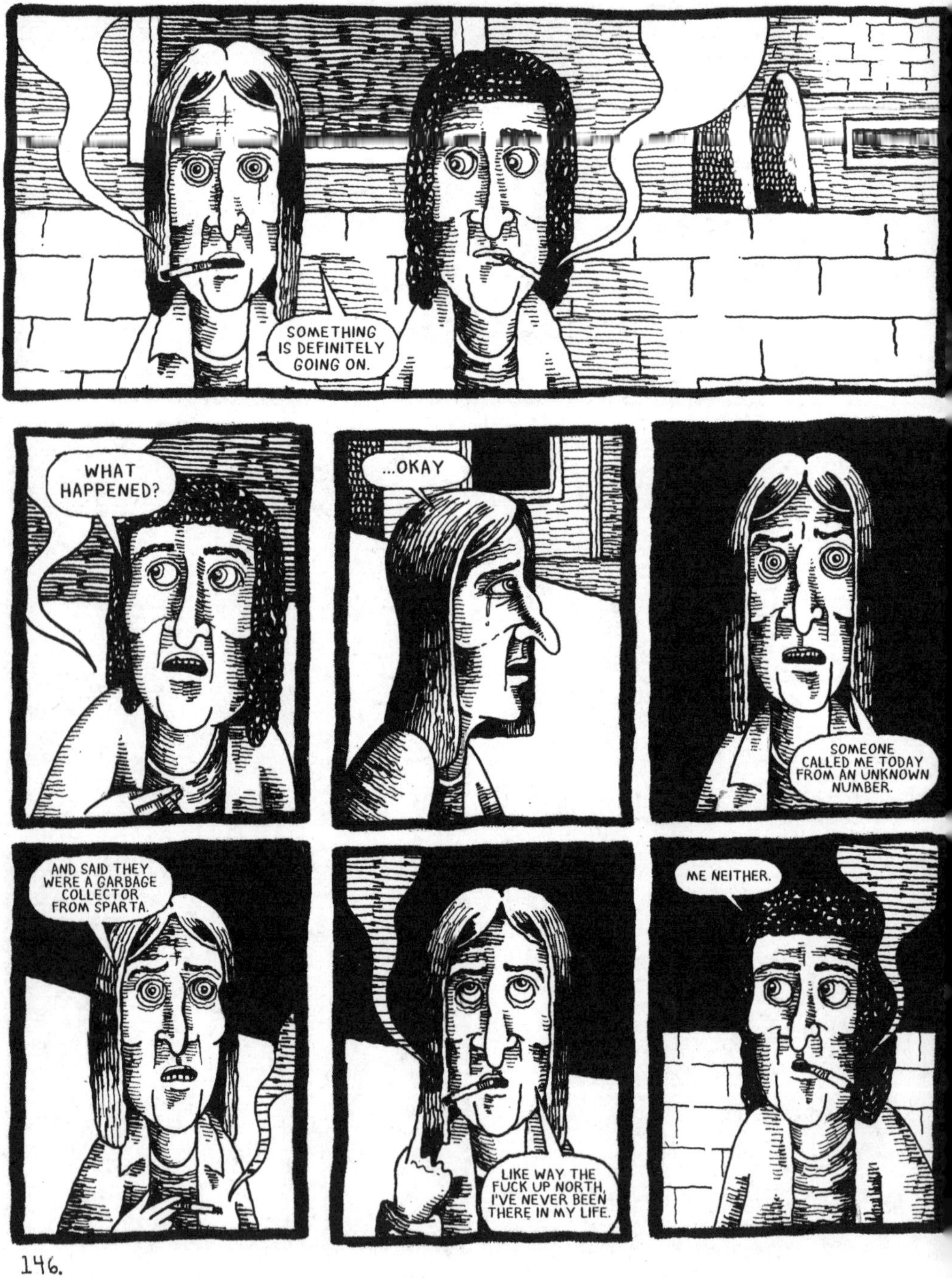
SOMETHING IS DEFINITELY GOING ON.
WHAT HAPPENED?
...OKAY
SOMEONE CALLED ME TODAY FROM AN UNKNOWN NUMBER.
AND SAID THEY WERE A GARBAGE COLLECTOR FROM SPARTA.
LIKE WAY THE FUCK UP NORTH, I'VE NEVER BEEN THERE IN MY LIFE.
ME NEITHER.

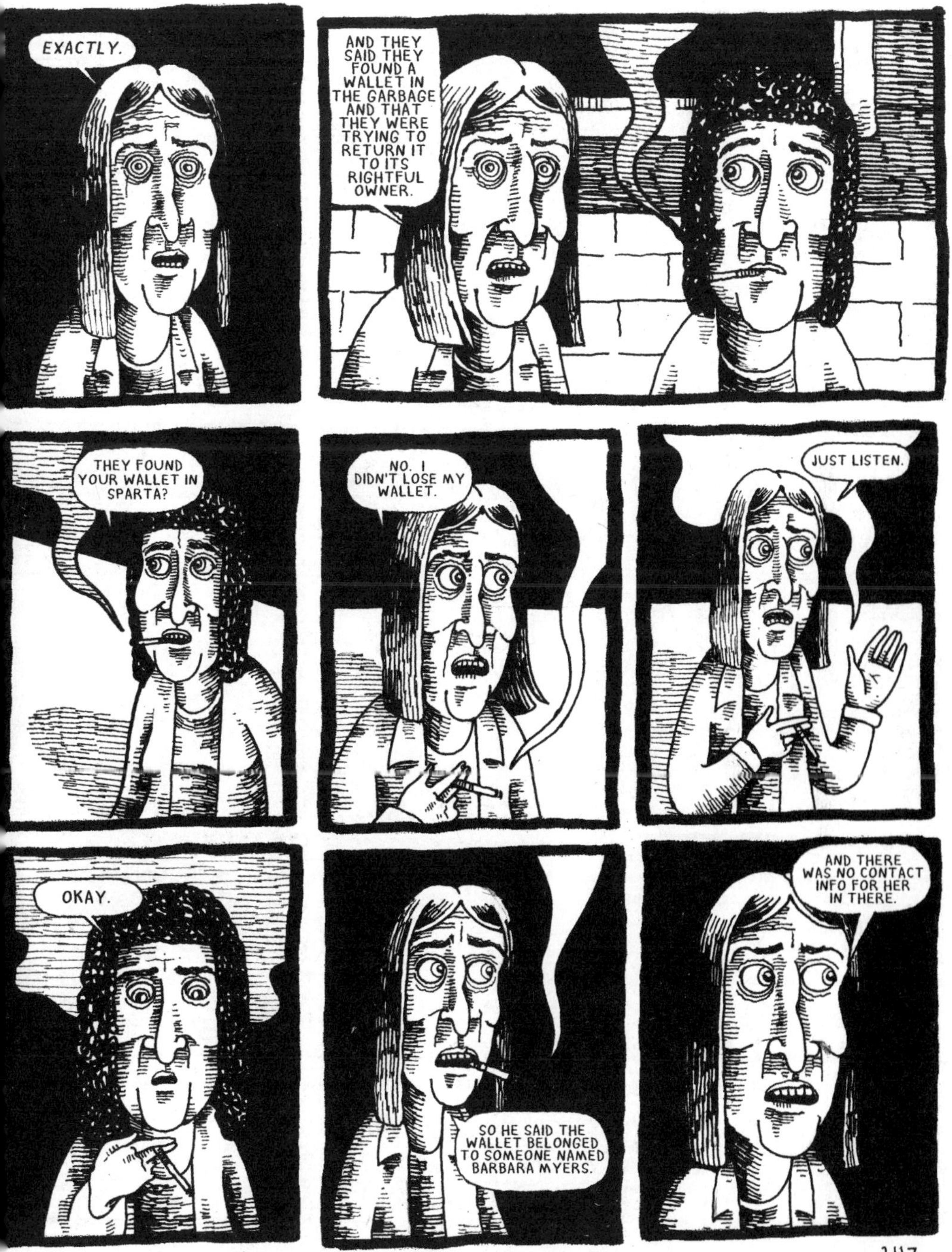
EXACTLY.
AND THEY SAID THEY FOUND A WALLET IN THE GARBAGE AND THAT THEY WERE TRYING TO RETURN IT TO ITS RIGHTFUL OWNER.
THEY FOUND YOUR WALLET IN SPARTA?
NO. I DIDN'T LOSE MY WALLET.
JUST LISTEN.
OKAY.
SO HE SAID THE WALLET BELONGED TO SOMEONE NAMED BARBARA MYERS.
AND THERE WAS NO CONTACT INFO FOR HER IN THERE.

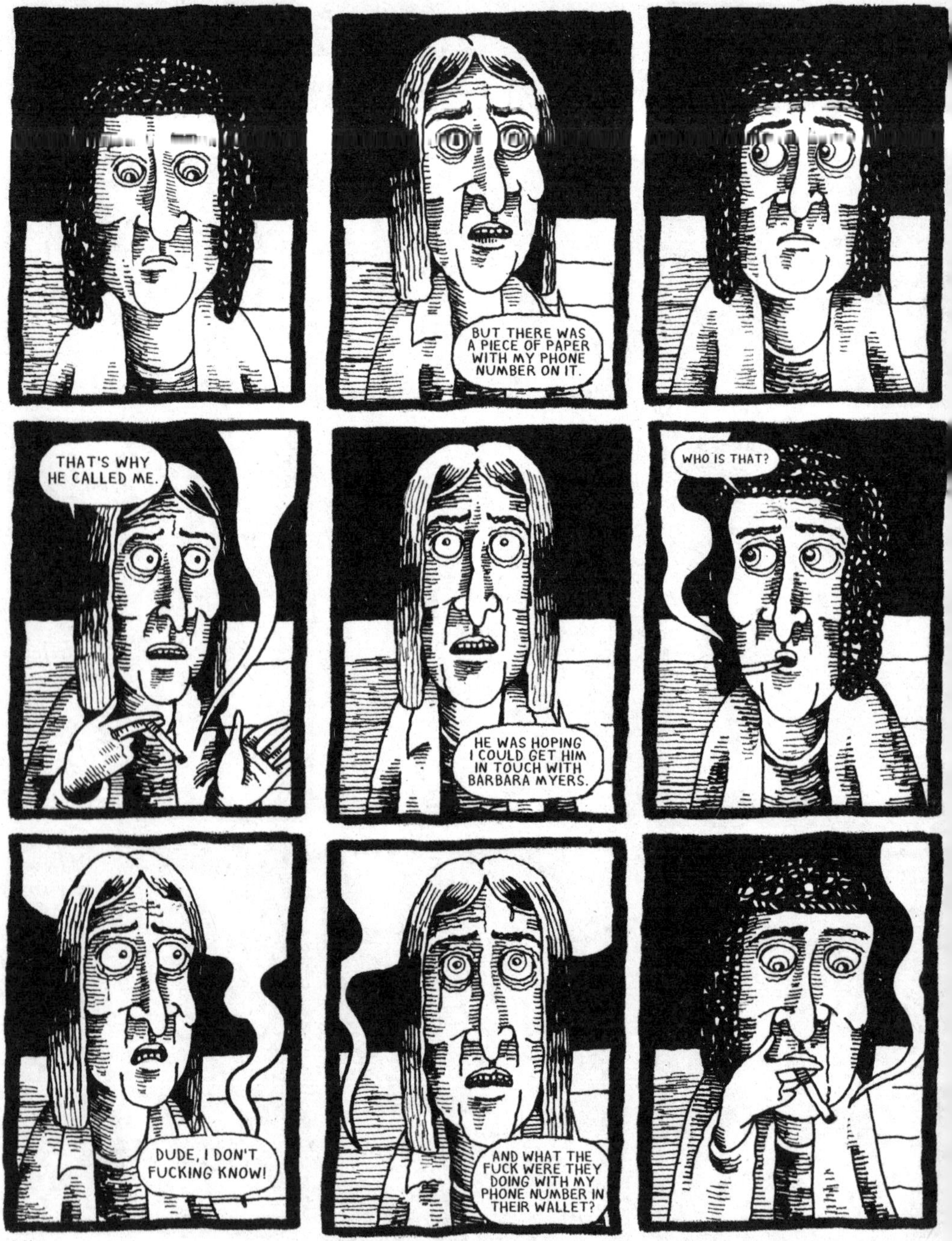
BUT THERE WAS A PIECE OF PAPER WITH MY PHONE NUMBER ON IT.
THAT'S WHY HE CALLED ME.
HE WAS HOPING I COULD GET HIM IN TOUCH WITH BARBARA MYERS.
WHO IS THAT?
DUDE, I DON'T FUCKING KNOW!
AND WHAT THE FUCK WERE THEY DOING WITH MY PHONE NUMBER IN THEIR WALLET?

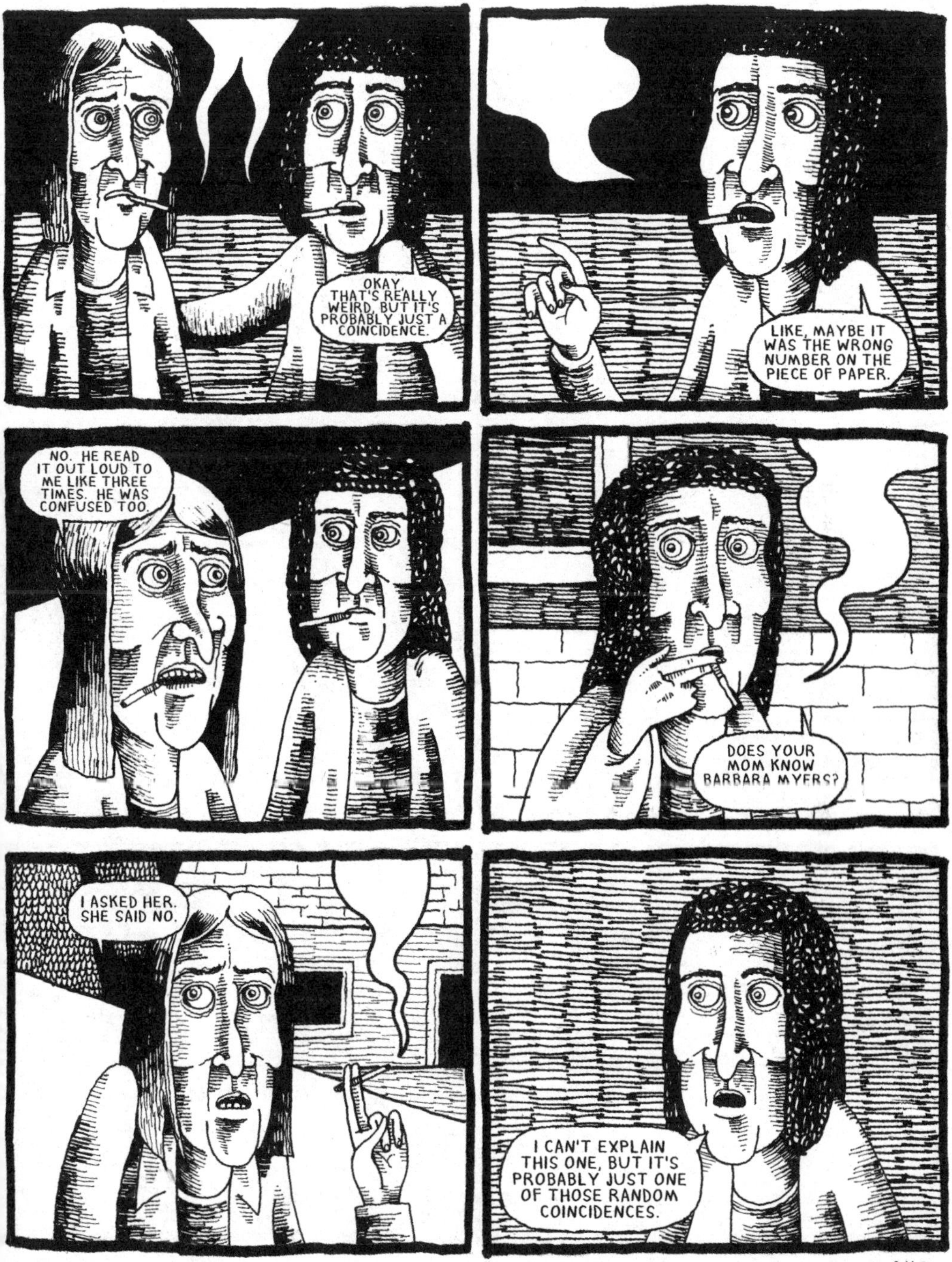
OKAY, THAT'S REALLY WEIRD, BUT IT'S PROBABLY JUST A COINCIDENCE.
LIKE, MAYBE IT WAS THE WRONG NUMBER ON THE PIECE OF PAPER.
NO. HE READ IT OUT LOUD TO ME LIKE THREE TIMES. HE WAS CONFUSED TOO.
DOES YOUR MOM KNOW BARBARA MYERS?
I ASKED HER. SHE SAID NO.
I CAN'T EXPLAIN THIS ONE, BUT IT'S PROBABLY JUST ONE OF THOSE RANDOM COINCIDENCES.

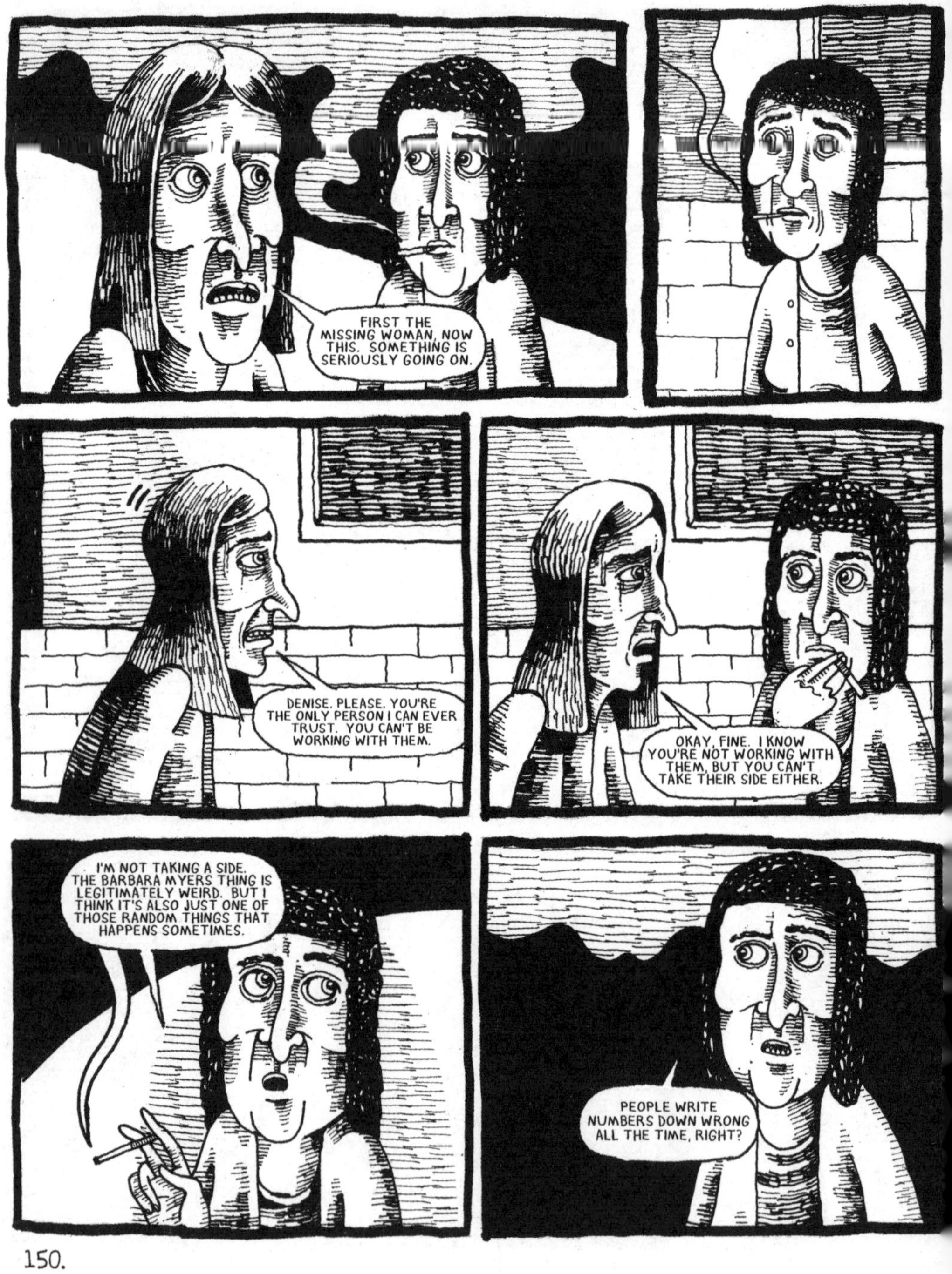
FIRST THE MISSING WOMAN, NOW THIS. SOMETHING IS SERIOUSLY GOING ON.
DENISE. PLEASE. YOU'RE THE ONLY PERSON I CAN EVER TRUST. YOU CAN'T BE WORKING WITH THEM.
OKAY, FINE. I KNOW YOU'RE NOT WORKING WITH THEM, BUT YOU CAN'T TAKE THEIR SIDE EITHER.
I'M NOT TAKING A SIDE. THE BARBARA MYERS THING IS LEGITIMATELY WEIRD. BUT I THINK IT'S ALSO JUST ONE OF THOSE RANDOM THINGS THAT HAPPENS SOMETIMES.
PEOPLE WRITE NUMBERS DOWN WRONG ALL THE TIME, RIGHT?

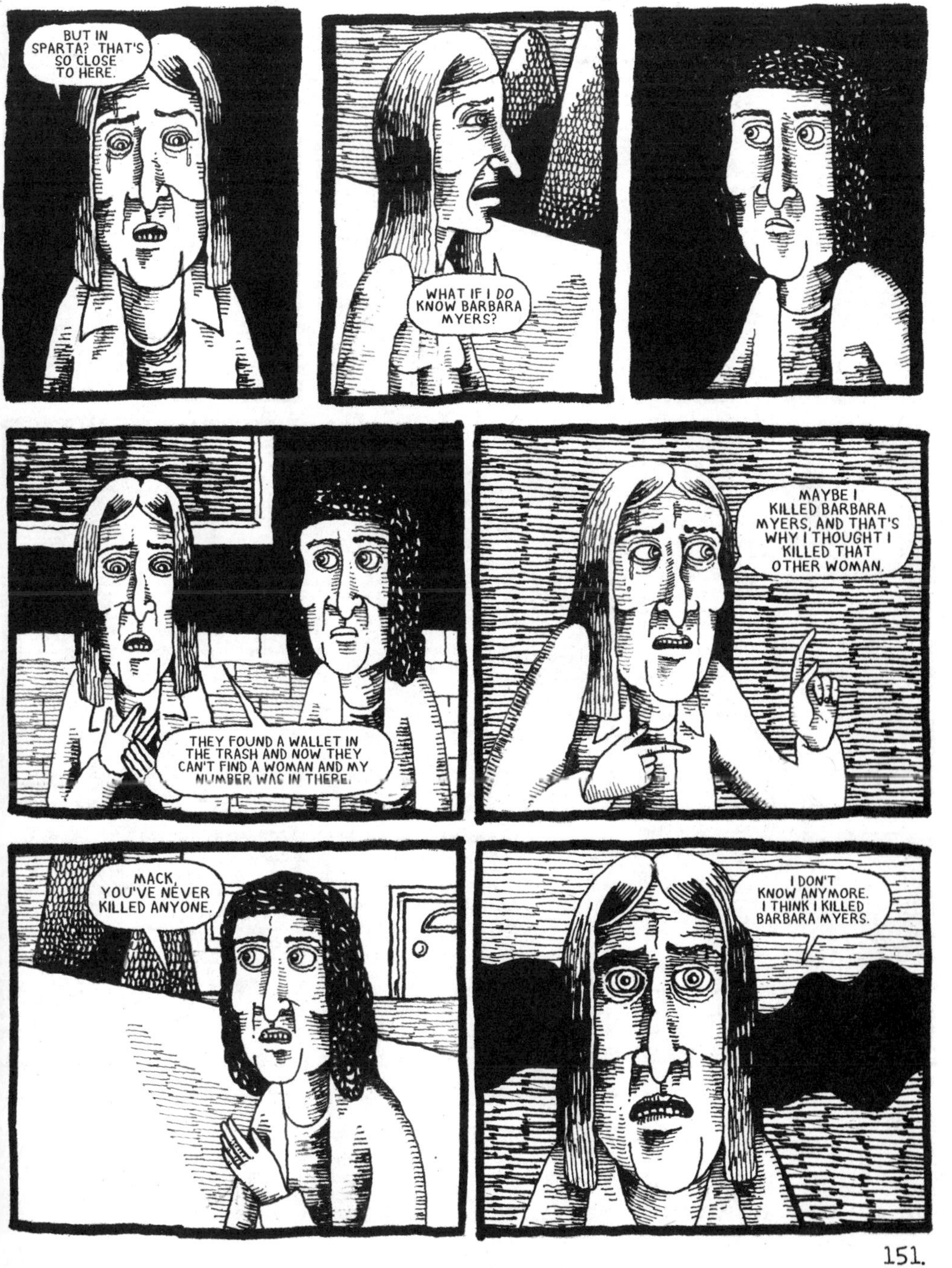

BUT IN SPARTA? THAT'S SO CLOSE TO HERE.
WHAT IF I DO KNOW BARBARA MYERS?
THEY FOUND A WALLET IN THE TRASH AND NOW THEY CAN'T FIND A WOMAN AND MY NUMBER WAS IN THERE.
MAYBE I KILLED BARBARA MYERS, AND THAT'S WHY I THOUGHT I KILLED THAT OTHER WOMAN.
MACK, YOU'VE NEVER KILLED ANYONE.
I DON'T KNOW ANYMORE. I THINK I KILLED BARBARA MYERS.

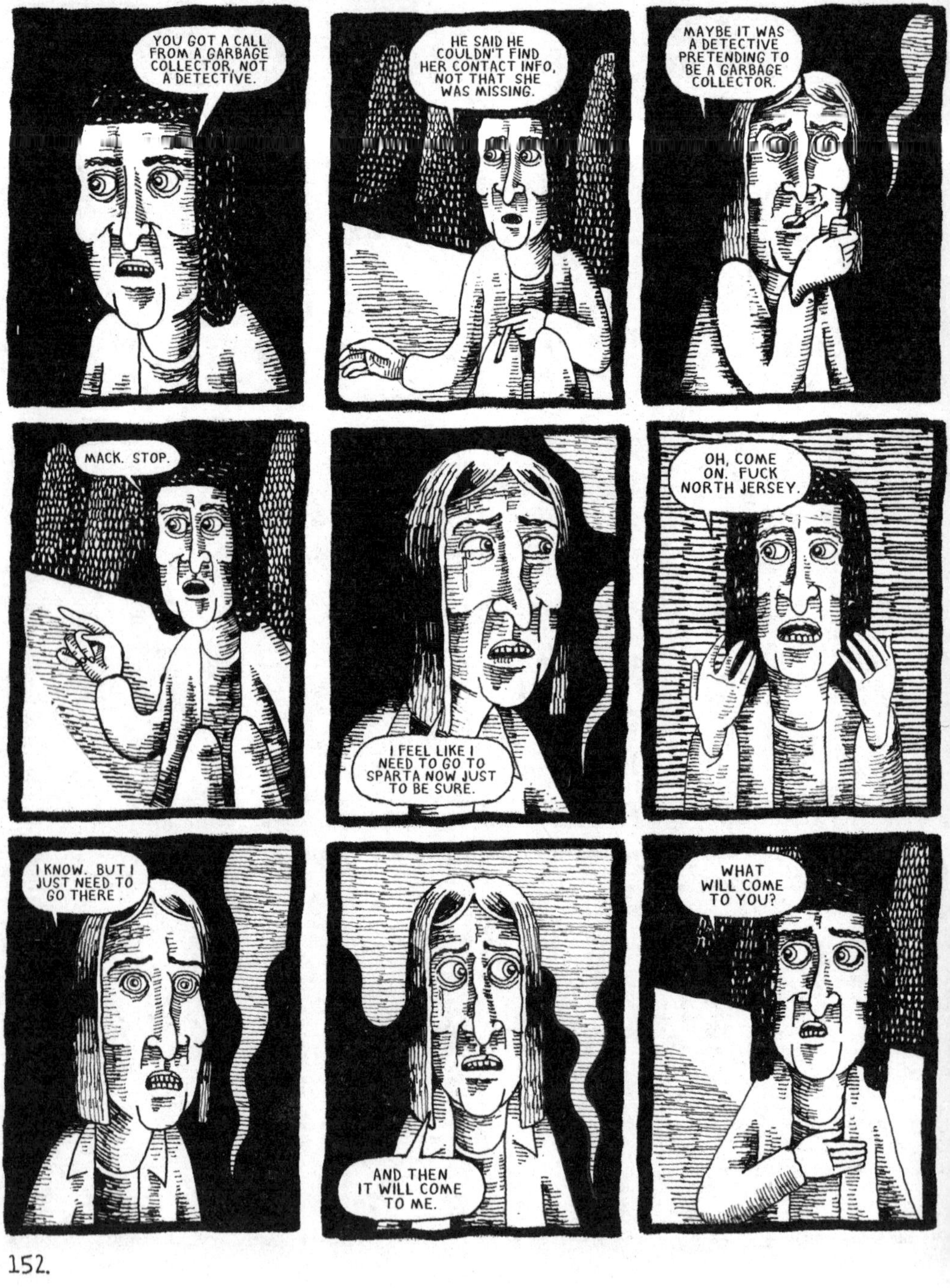
YOU GOT A CALL FROM A GARBAGE COLLECTOR, NOT A DETECTIVE.
HE SAID HE COULDN'T FIND HER CONTACT INFO, NOT THAT SHE WAS MISSING.
MAYBE IT WAS A DETECTIVE PRETENDING TO BE A GARBAGE COLLECTOR.
MACK. STOP.
I FEEL LIKE I NEED TO GO TO SPARTA NOW JUST TO BE SURE.
OH, COME ON. FUCK NORTH JERSEY.
I KNOW. BUT I JUST NEED TO GO THERE.
AND THEN IT WILL COME TO ME.
WHAT WILL COME TO YOU?

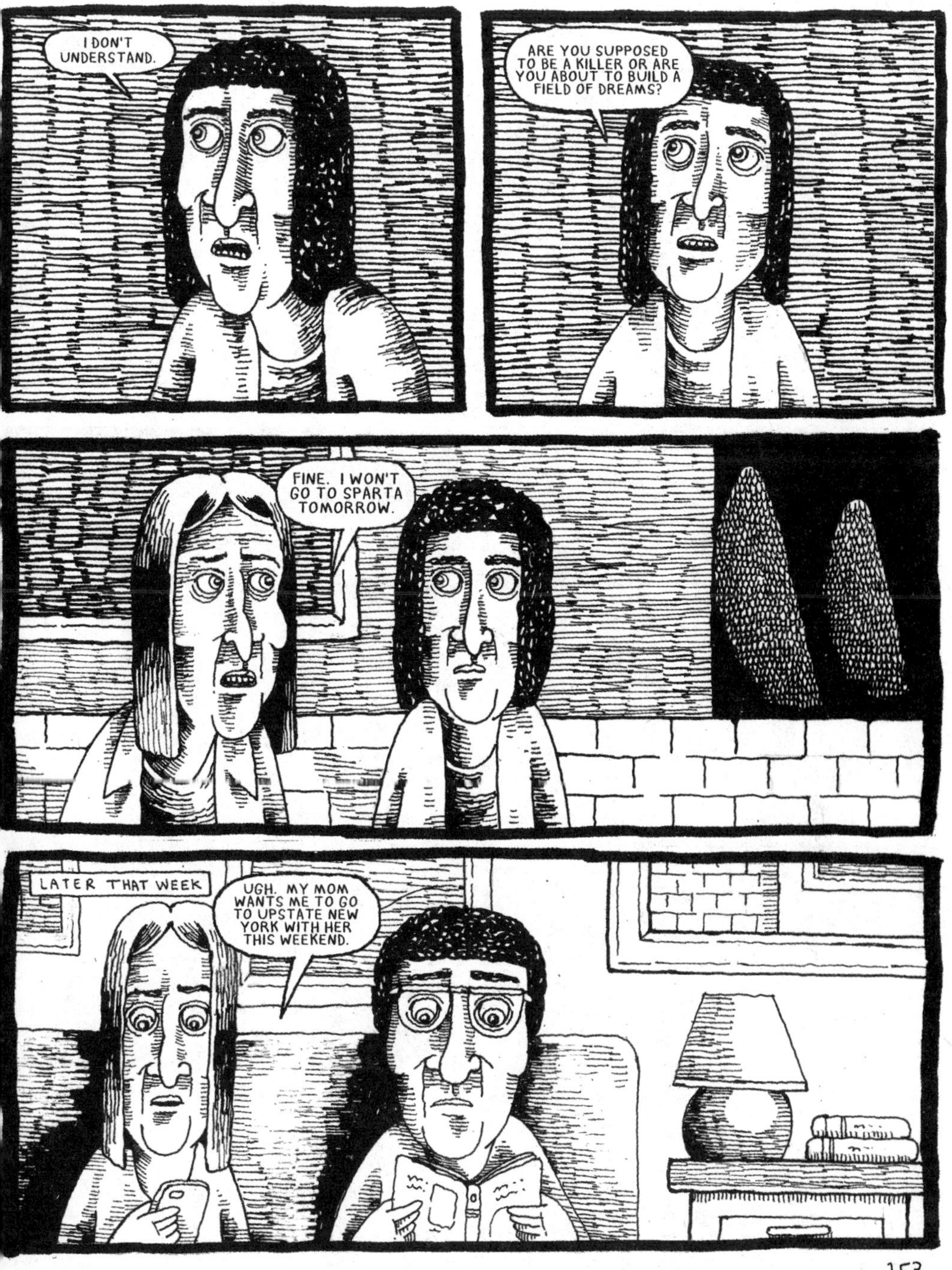
I DON'T UNDERSTAND.
ARE YOU SUPPOSED TO BE A KILLER OR ARE YOU ABOUT TO BUILD A FIELD OF DREAMS?
FINE. I WON'T GO TO SPARTA TOMORROW.
LATER THAT WEEK
UGH. MY MOM WANTS ME TO GO TO UPSTATE NEW YORK WITH HER THIS WEEKEND.

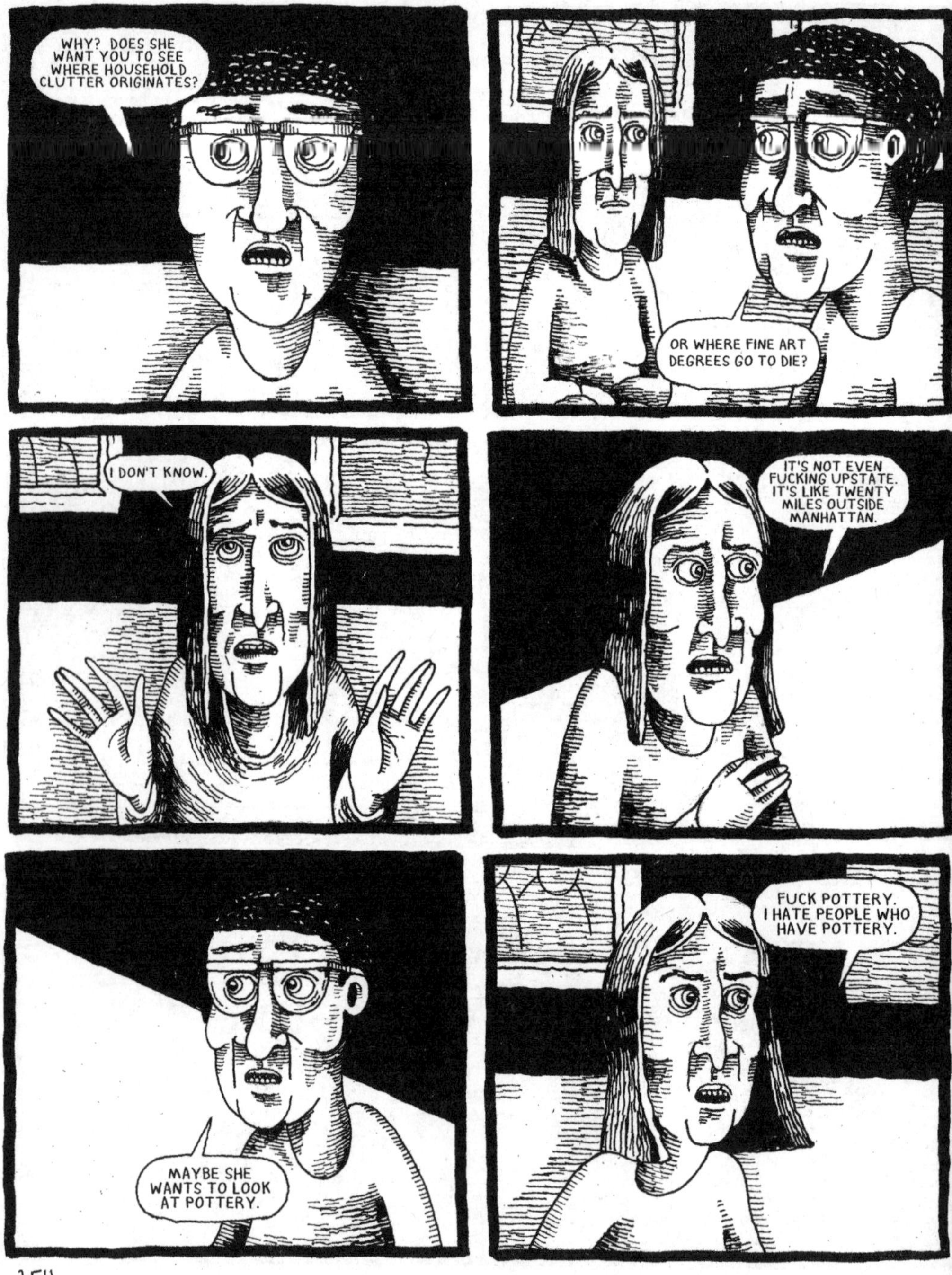
WHY? DOES SHE WANT YOU TO SEE WHERE HOUSEHOLD CLUTTER ORIGINATES?
OR WHERE FINE ART DEGREES GO TO DIE?
I DON'T KNOW.
IT'S NOT EVEN FUCKING UPSTATE. IT'S LIKE TWENTY MILES OUTSIDE MANHATTAN.
MAYBE SHE WANTS TO LOOK AT POTTERY.
FUCK POTTERY. I HATE PEOPLE WHO HAVE POTTERY.

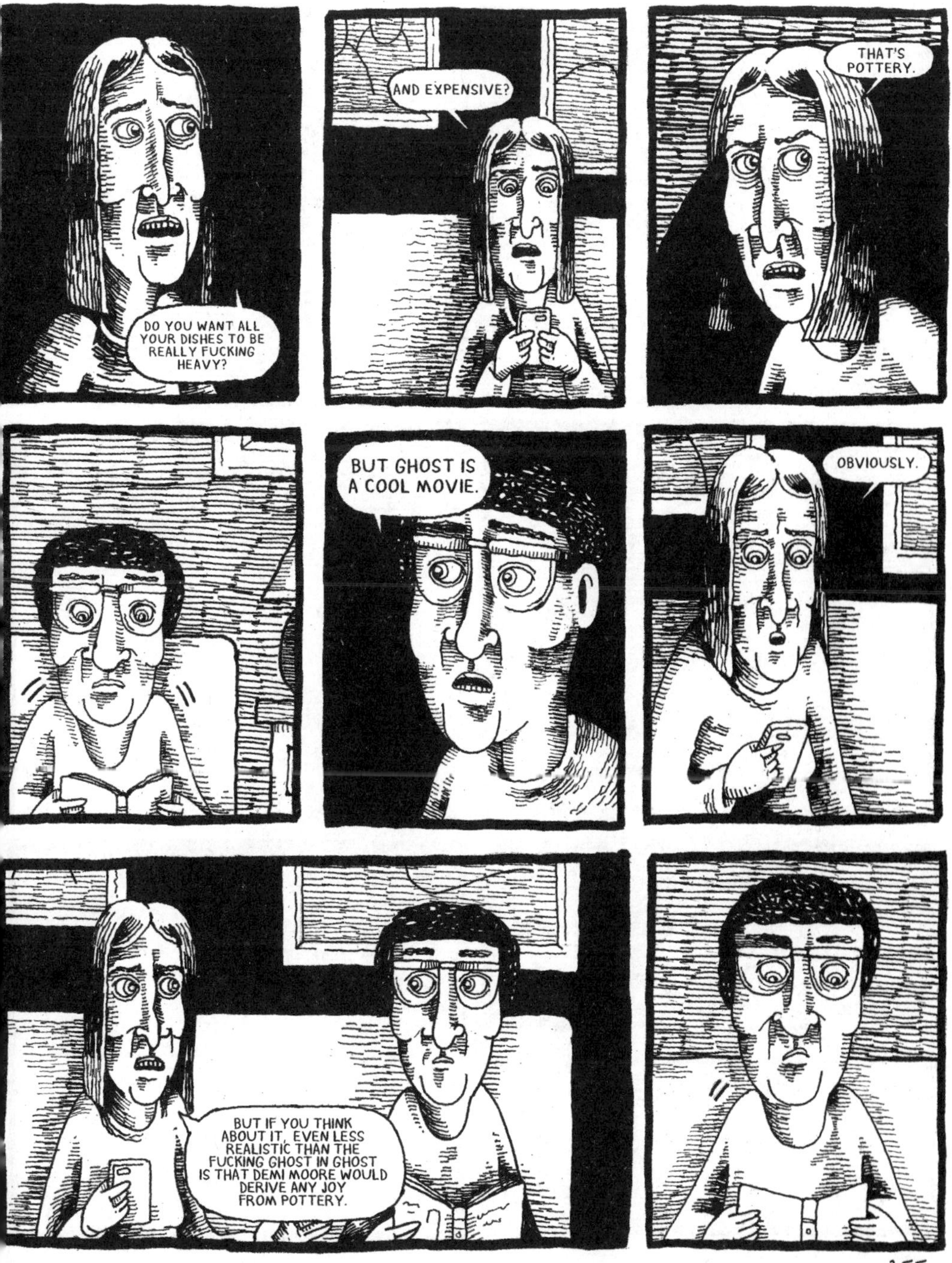
DO YOU WANT ALL YOUR DISHES TO BE REALLY FUCKING HEAVY?
AND EXPENSIVE?
THAT'S POTTERY.
BUT GHOST IS A COOL MOVIE.
OBVIOUSLY.
BUT IF YOU THINK ABOUT IT, EVEN LESS REALISTIC THAN THE FUCKING GHOST IN GHOST IS THAT DEMI MOORE WOULD DERIVE ANY JOY FROM POTTERY.

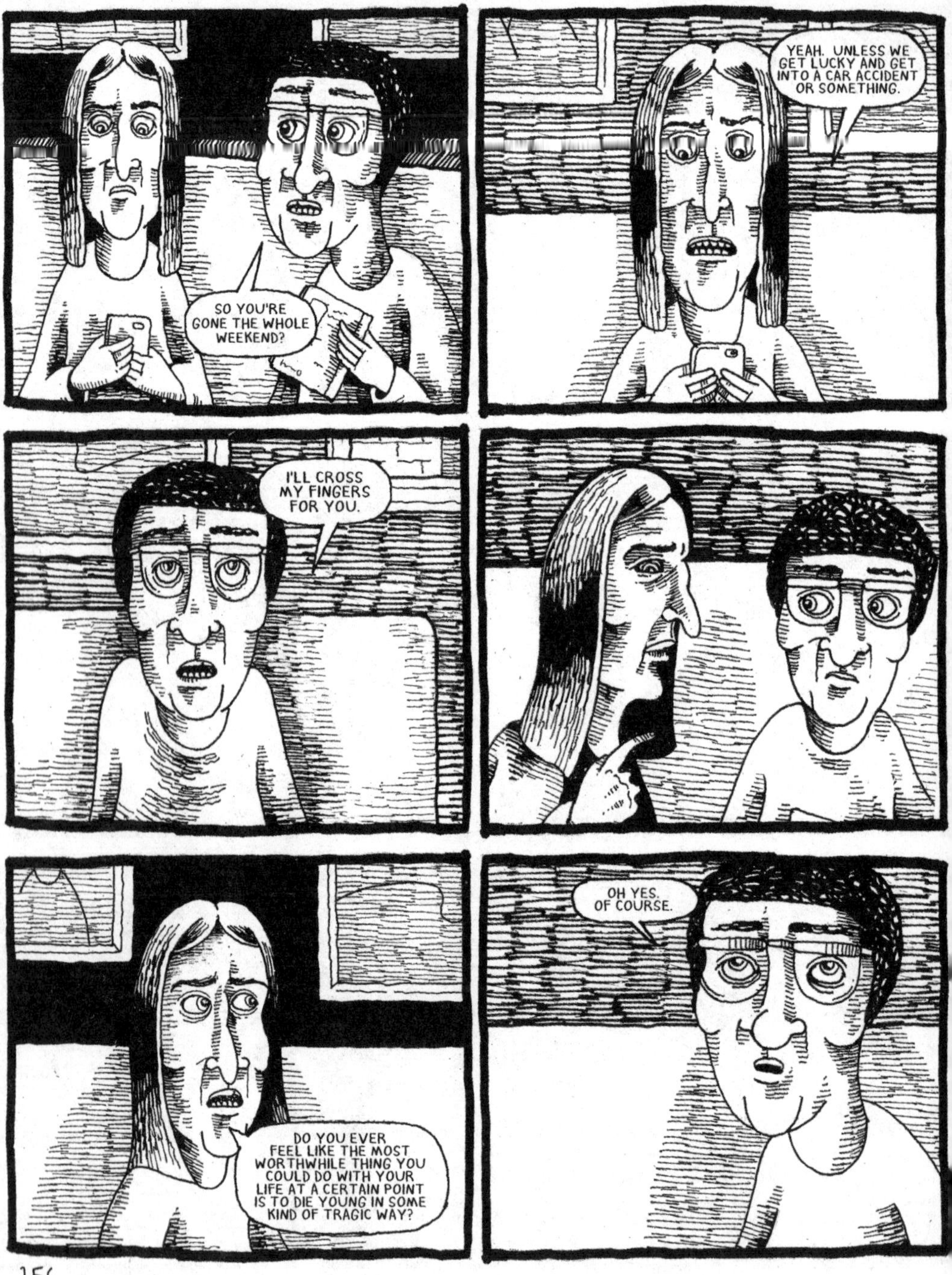
SO YOU'RE GONE THE WHOLE WEEKEND?
YEAH. UNLESS WE GET LUCKY AND GET INTO A CAR ACCIDENT OR SOMETHING.
I'LL CROSS MY FINGERS FOR YOU.
DO YOU EVER FEEL LIKE THE MOST WORTHWHILE THING YOU COULD DO WITH YOUR LIFE AT A CERTAIN POINT IS TO DIE YOUNG IN SOME KIND OF TRAGIC WAY?
OH YES. OF COURSE.

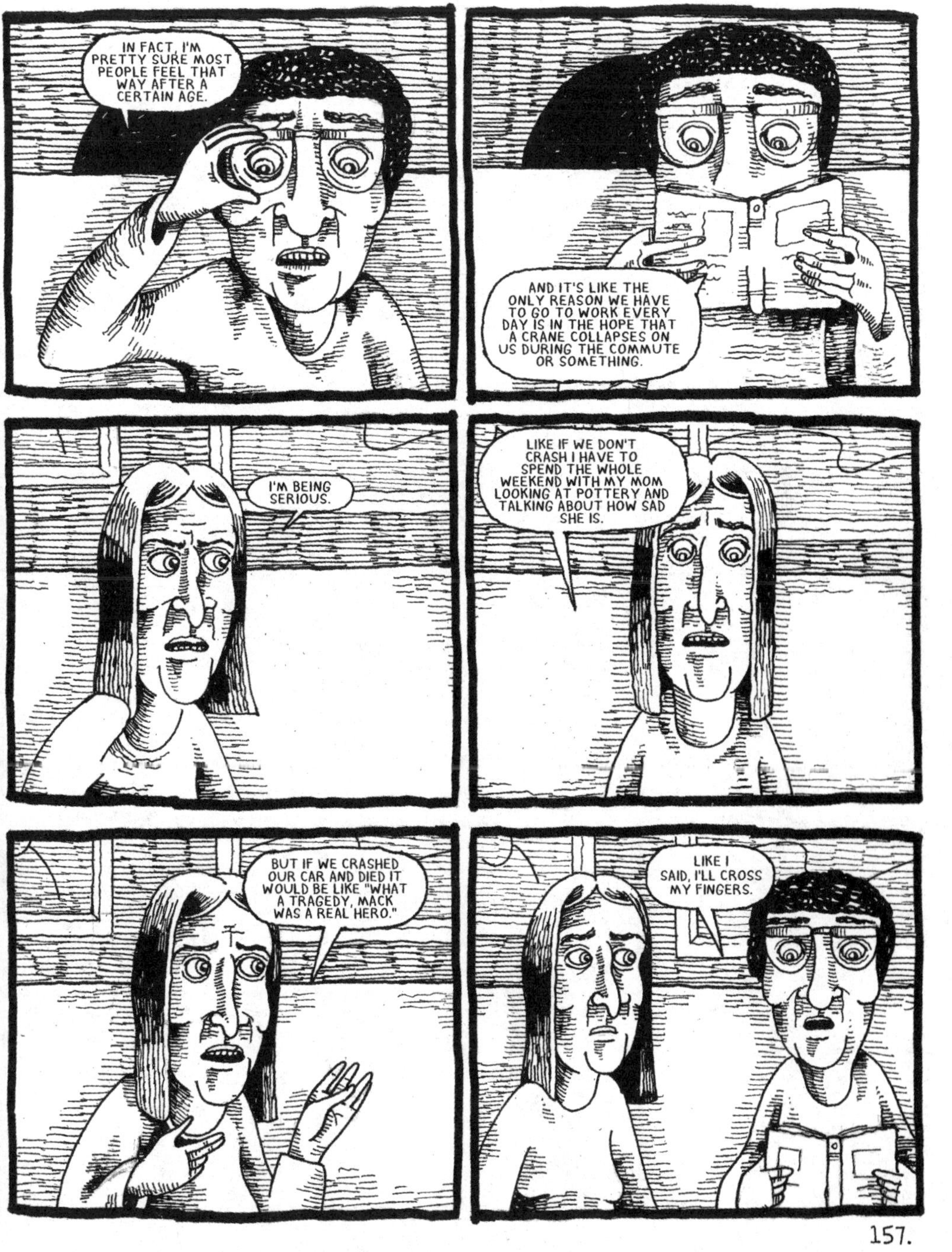
IN FACT, I'M PRETTY SURE MOST PEOPLE FEEL THAT WAY AFTER A CERTAIN AGE.
AND IT'S LIKE THE ONLY REASON WE HAVE TO GO TO WORK EVERY DAY IS IN THE HOPE THAT A CRANE COLLAPSES ON US DURING THE COMMUTE OR SOMETHING.
I'M BEING SERIOUS.
LIKE IF WE DON'T CRASH I HAVE TO SPEND THE WHOLE WEEKEND WITH MY MOM LOOKING AT POTTERY AND TALKING ABOUT HOW SAD SHE IS.
BUT IF WE CRASHED OUR CAR AND DIED IT WOULD BE LIKE "WHAT A TRAGEDY, MACK WAS A REAL HERO."
LIKE I SAID, I'LL CROSS MY FINGERS.

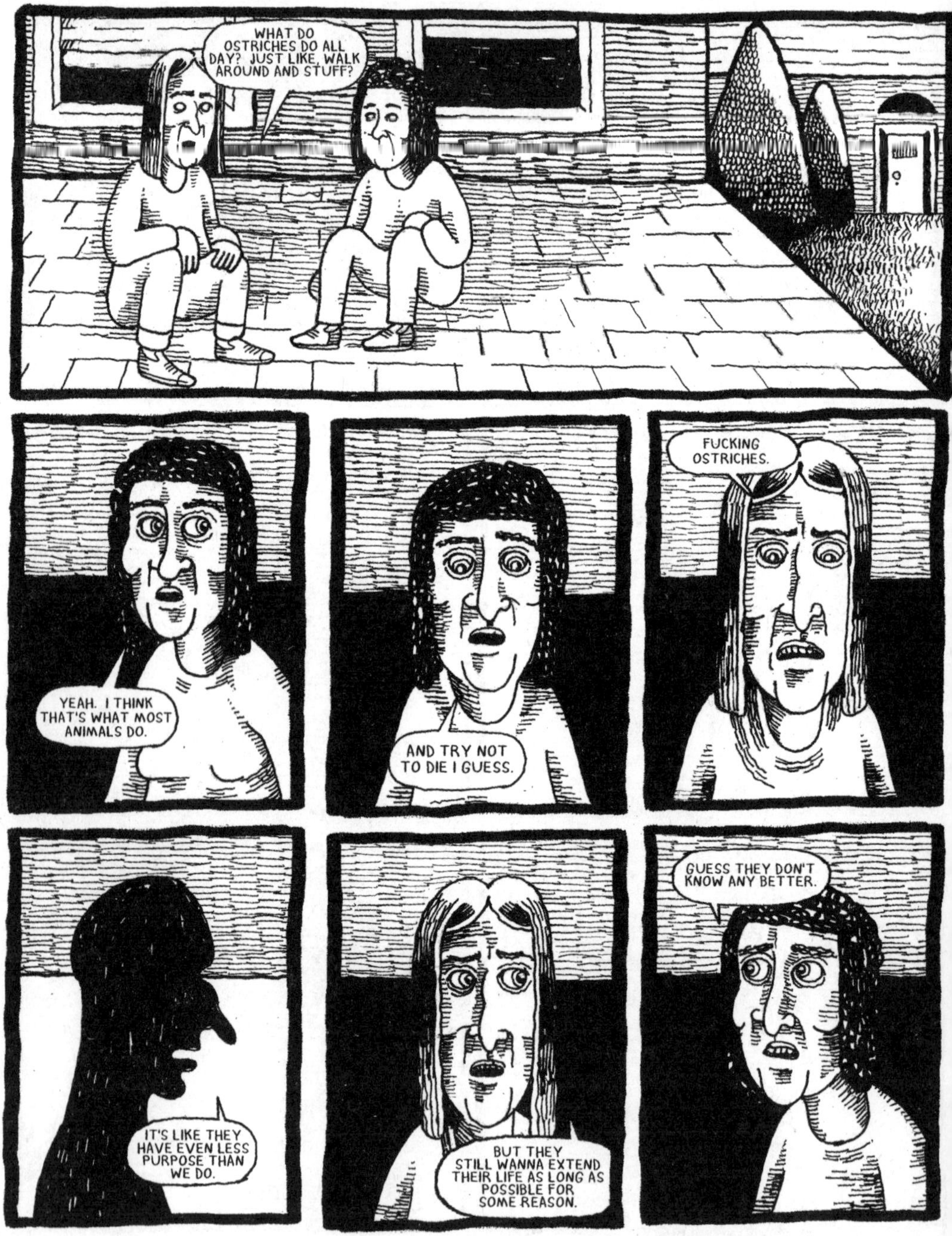
WHAT DO OSTRICHES DO ALL DAY? JUST LIKE, WALK AROUND AND STUFF?
YEAH. I THINK THAT'S WHAT MOST ANIMALS DO.
AND TRY NOT TO DIE I GUESS.
FUCKING OSTRICHES.
IT'S LIKE THEY HAVE EVEN LESS PURPOSE THAN WE DO.
BUT THEY STILL WANNA EXTEND THEIR LIFE AS LONG AS POSSIBLE FOR SOME REASON.
GUESS THEY DON'T KNOW ANY BETTER.

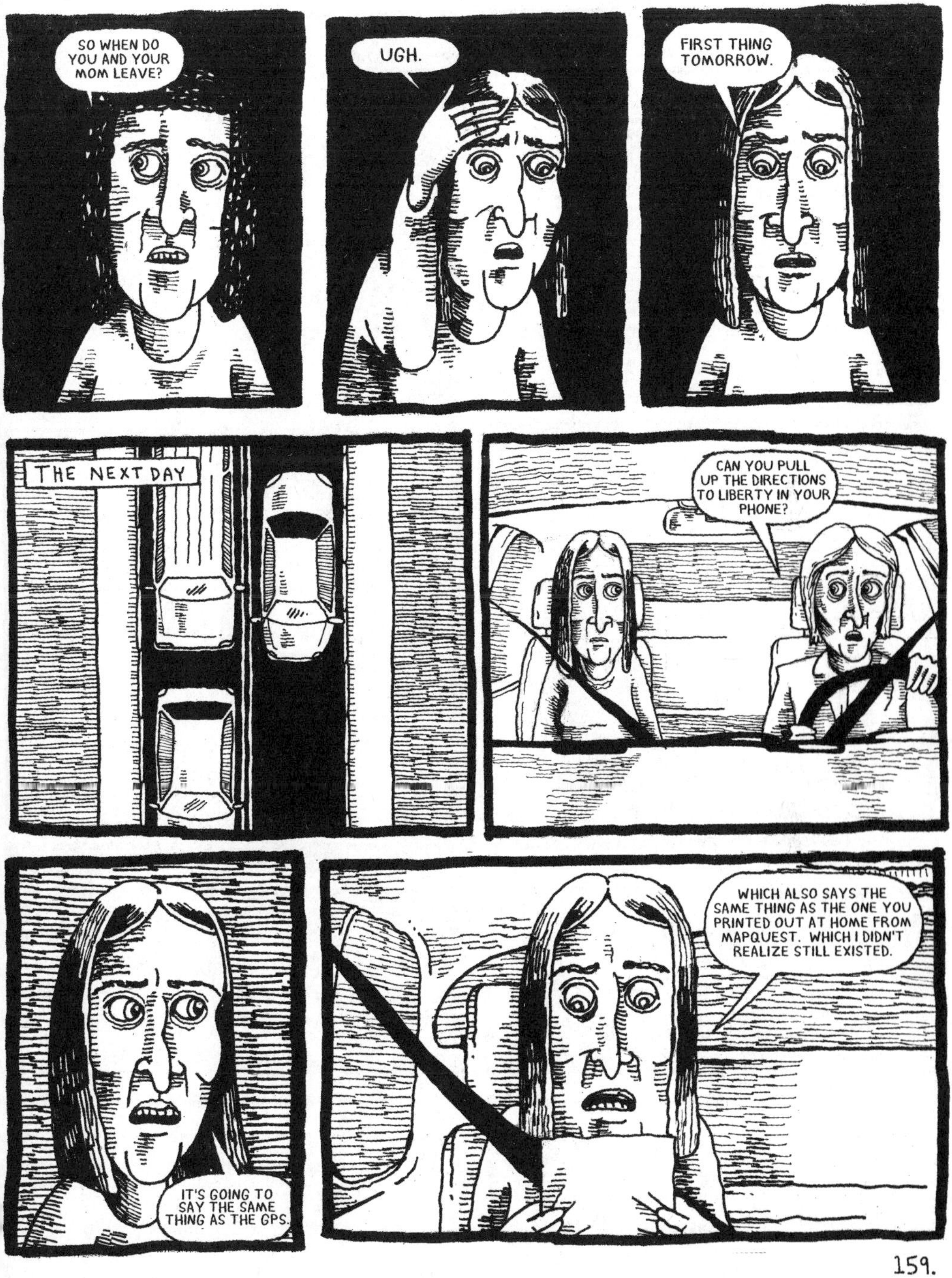
SO WHEN DO YOU AND YOUR MOM LEAVE?
UGH.
FIRST THING TOMORROW.
THE NEXT DAY
CAN YOU PULL UP THE DIRECTIONS TO LIBERTY IN YOUR PHONE?
IT'S GOING TO SAY THE SAME THING AS THE GPS.
WHICH ALSO SAYS THE SAME THING AS THE ONE YOU PRINTED OUT AT HOME FROM MAPQUEST. WHICH I DIDN'T REALIZE STILL EXISTED.

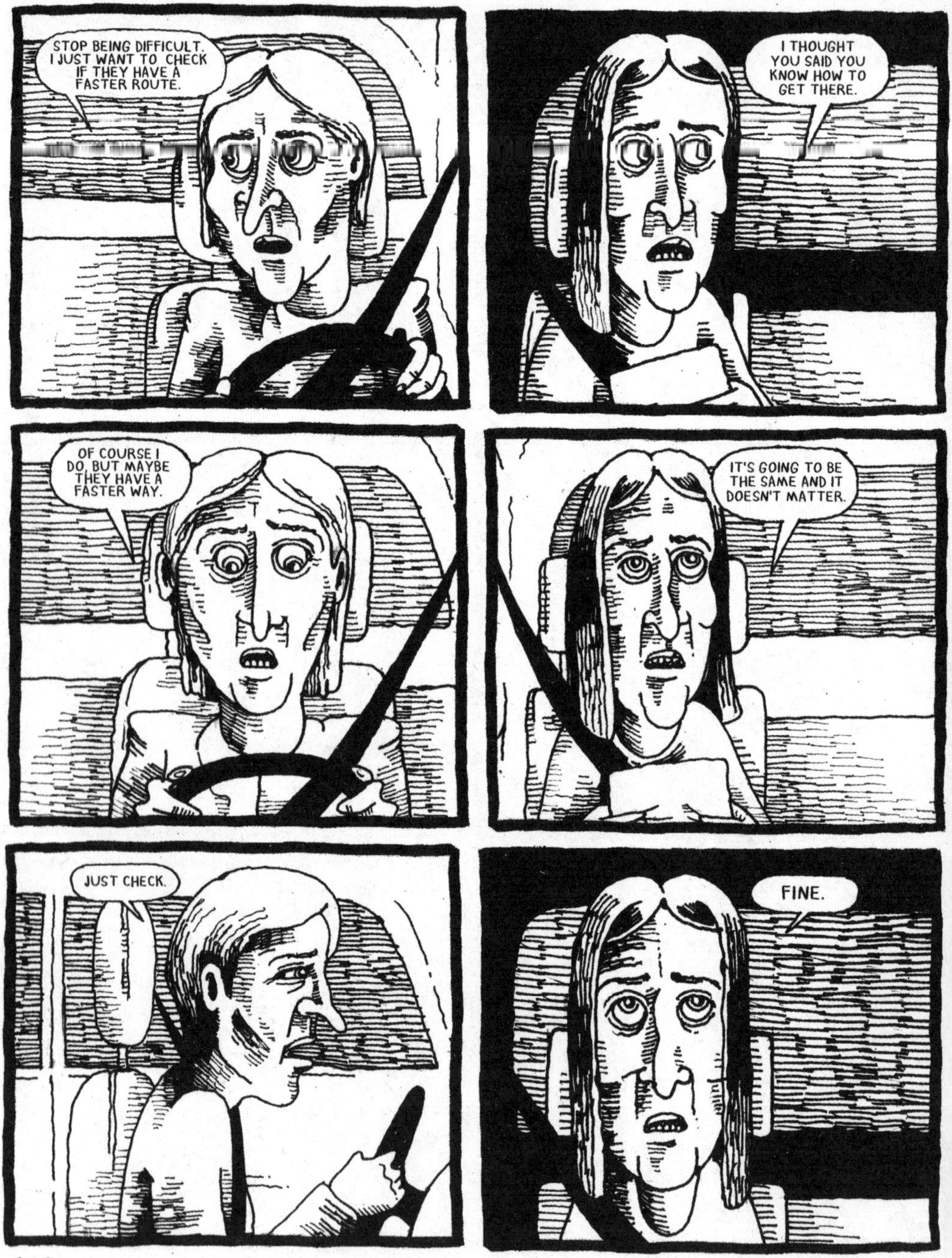
STOP BEING DIFFICULT. I JUST WANT TO CHECK IF THEY HAVE A FASTER ROUTE.
I THOUGHT YOU SAID YOU KNOW HOW TO GET THERE.
OF COURSE I DO, BUT MAYBE THEY HAVE A FASTER WAY.
IT'S GOING TO BE THE SAME AND IT DOESN'T MATTER.
JUST CHECK.
FINE.

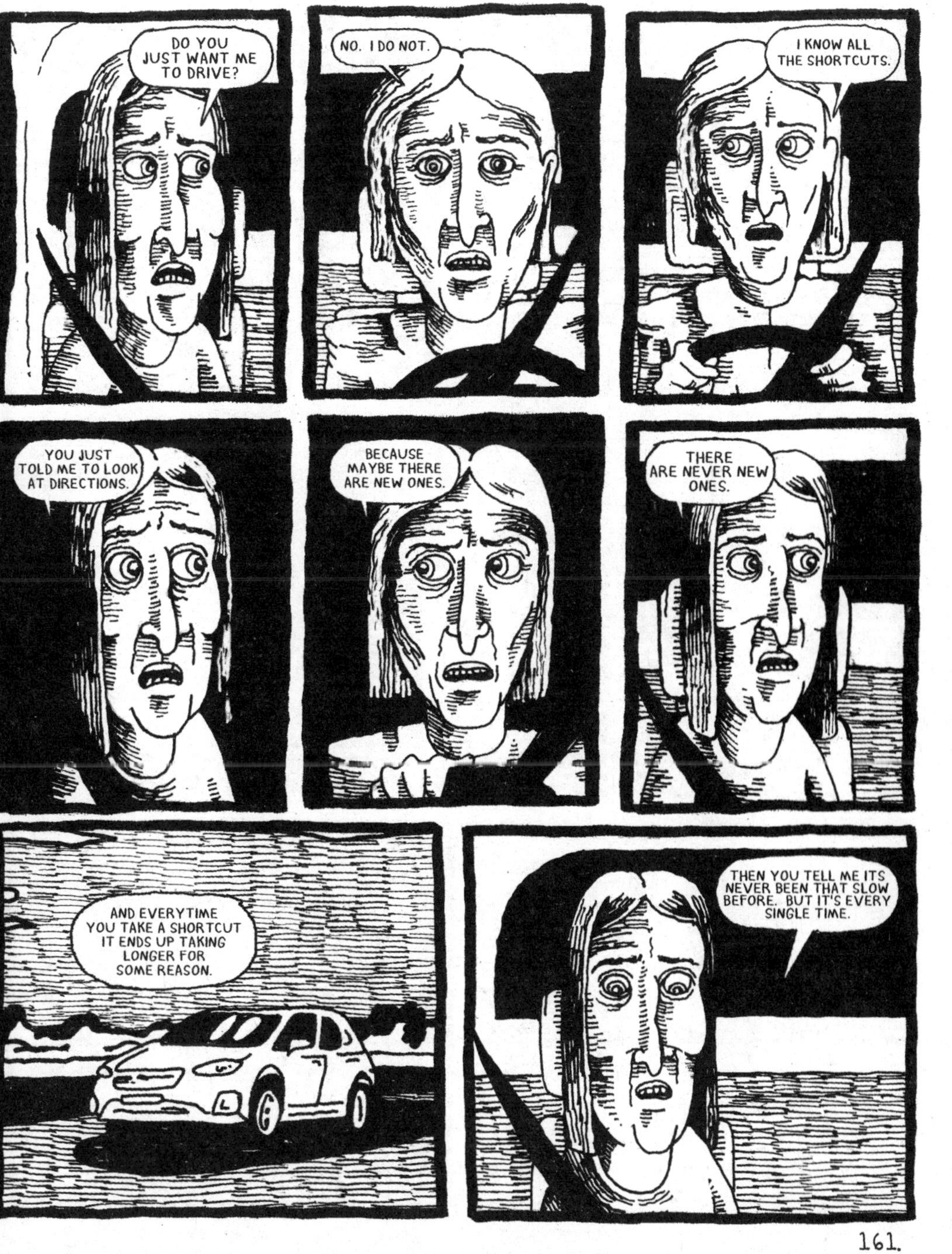
DO YOU JUST WANT ME TO DRIVE?
NO. I DO NOT.
I KNOW ALL THE SHORTCUTS.
YOU JUST TOLD ME TO LOOK AT DIRECTIONS.
BECAUSE MAYBE THERE ARE NEW ONES.
THERE ARE NEVER NEW ONES.
AND EVERYTIME YOU TAKE A SHORTCUT IT ENDS UP TAKING LONGER FOR SOME REASON.
THEN YOU TELL ME ITS NEVER BEEN THAT SLOW BEFORE. BUT IT'S EVERY SINGLE TIME.

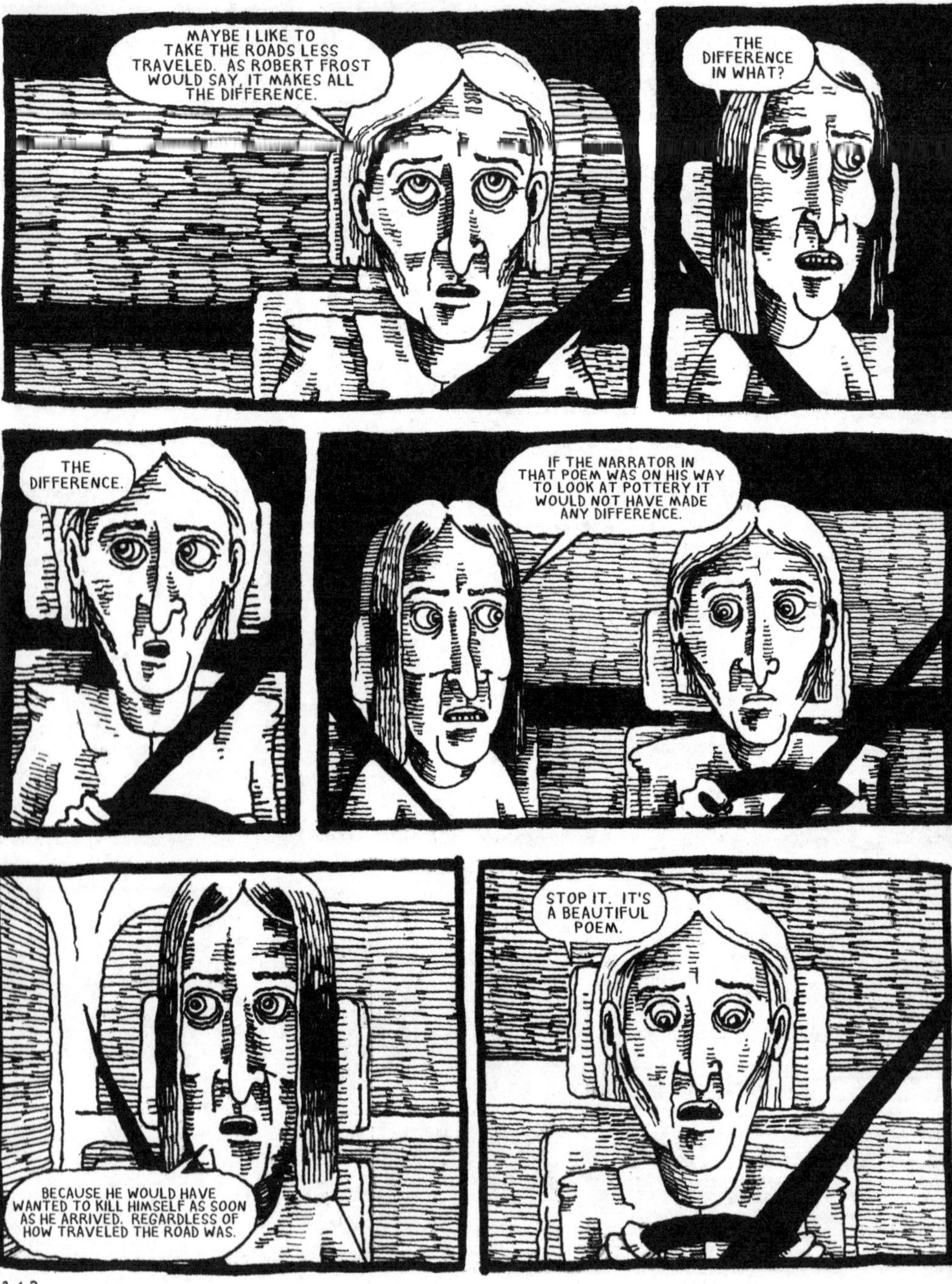
MAYBE I LIKE TO TAKE THE ROADS LESS TRAVELED. AS ROBERT FROST WOULD SAY, IT MAKES ALL THE DIFFERENCE.
THE DIFFERENCE IN WHAT?
THE DIFFERENCE.
IF THE NARRATOR IN THAT POEM WAS ON HIS WAY TO LOOK AT POTTERY IT WOULD NOT HAVE MADE ANY DIFFERENCE.
BECAUSE HE WOULD HAVE WANTED TO KILL HIMSELF AS SOON AS HE ARRIVED. REGARDLESS OF HOW TRAVELED THE ROAD WAS.
STOP IT. IT'S A BEAUTIFUL POEM.

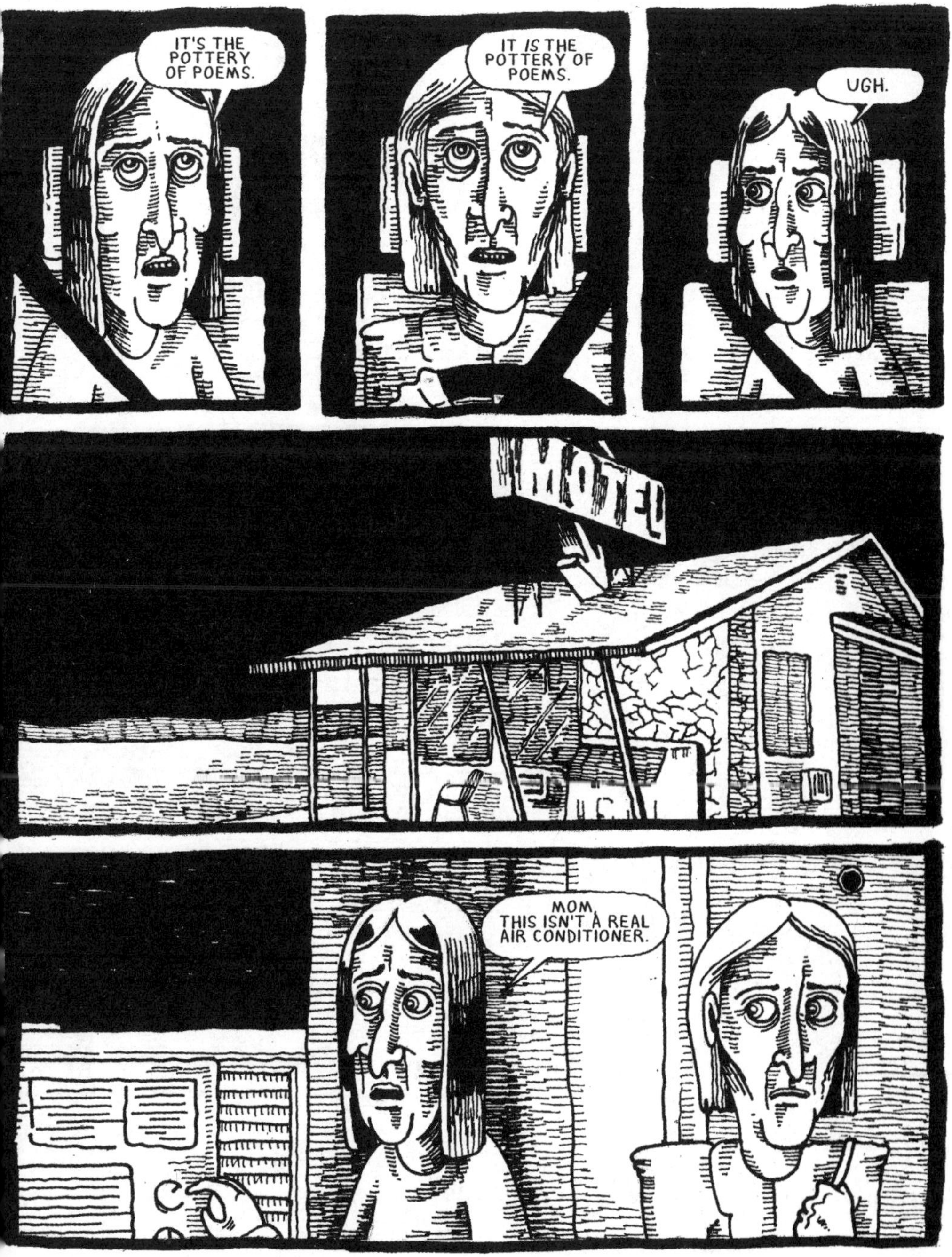
IT'S THE POTTERY OF POEMS.
IT *IS* THE POTTERY OF POEMS.
UGH.
MOTEL
MOM, THIS ISN'T A REAL AIR CONDITIONER.

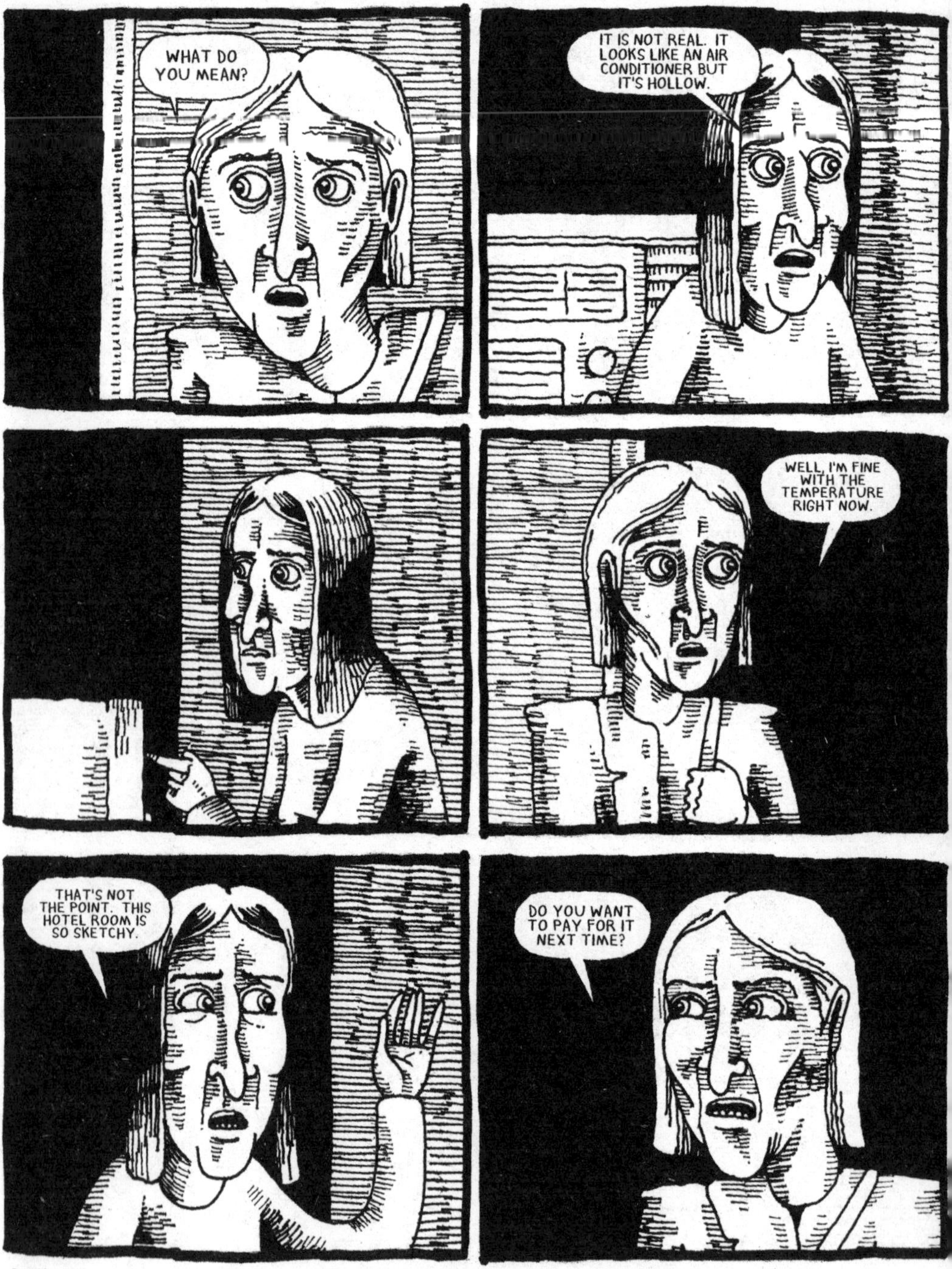
WHAT DO YOU MEAN?
IT IS NOT REAL. IT LOOKS LIKE AN AIR CONDITIONER BUT IT'S HOLLOW.
WELL, I'M FINE WITH THE TEMPERATURE RIGHT NOW.
THAT'S NOT THE POINT. THIS HOTEL ROOM IS SO SKETCHY.
DO YOU WANT TO PAY FOR IT NEXT TIME?

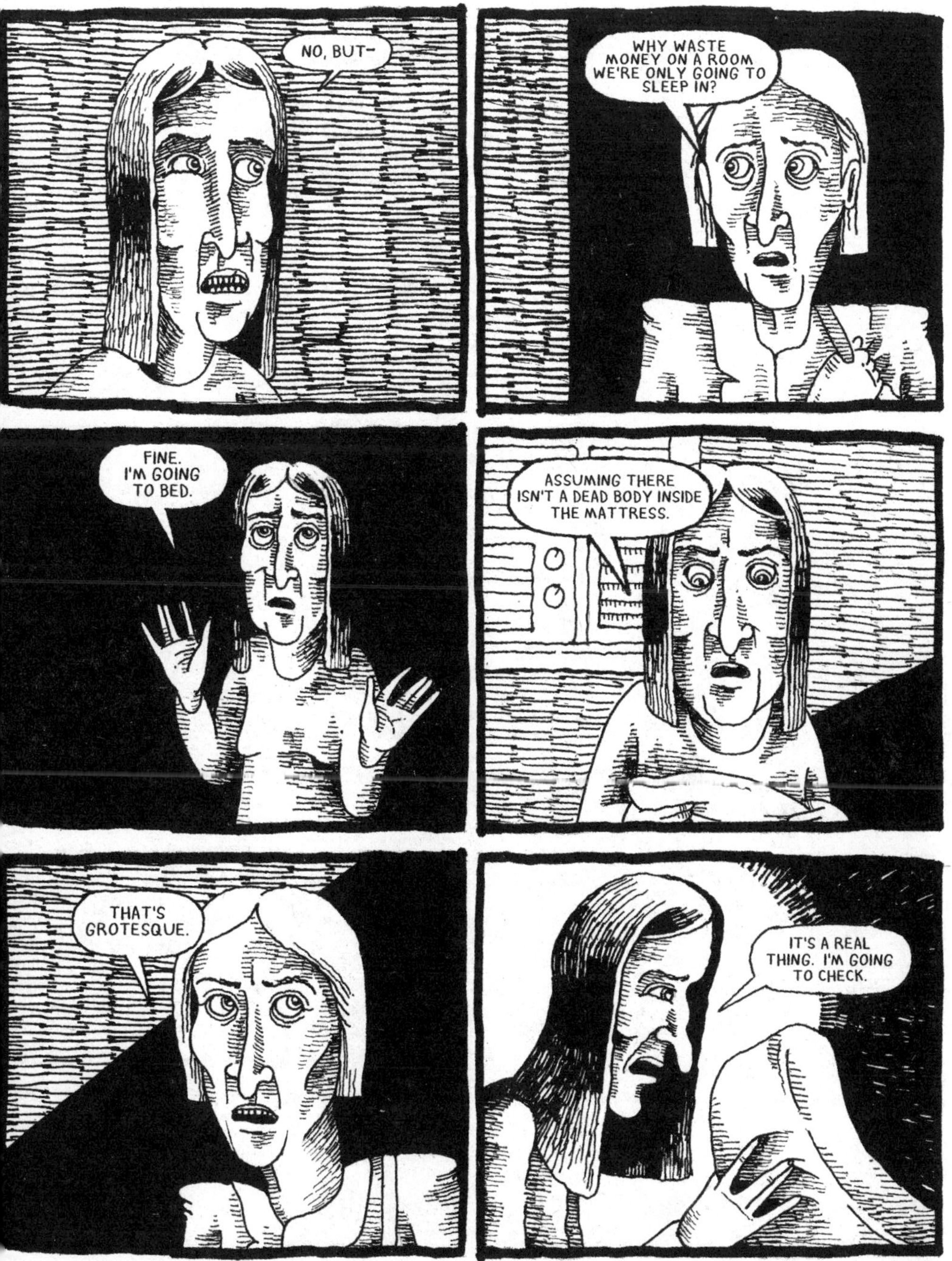
NO, BUT-
WHY WASTE MONEY ON A ROOM WE'RE ONLY GOING TO SLEEP IN?
FINE. I'M GOING TO BED.
ASSUMING THERE ISN'T A DEAD BODY INSIDE THE MATTRESS.
THAT'S GROTESQUE.
IT'S A REAL THING. I'M GOING TO CHECK.

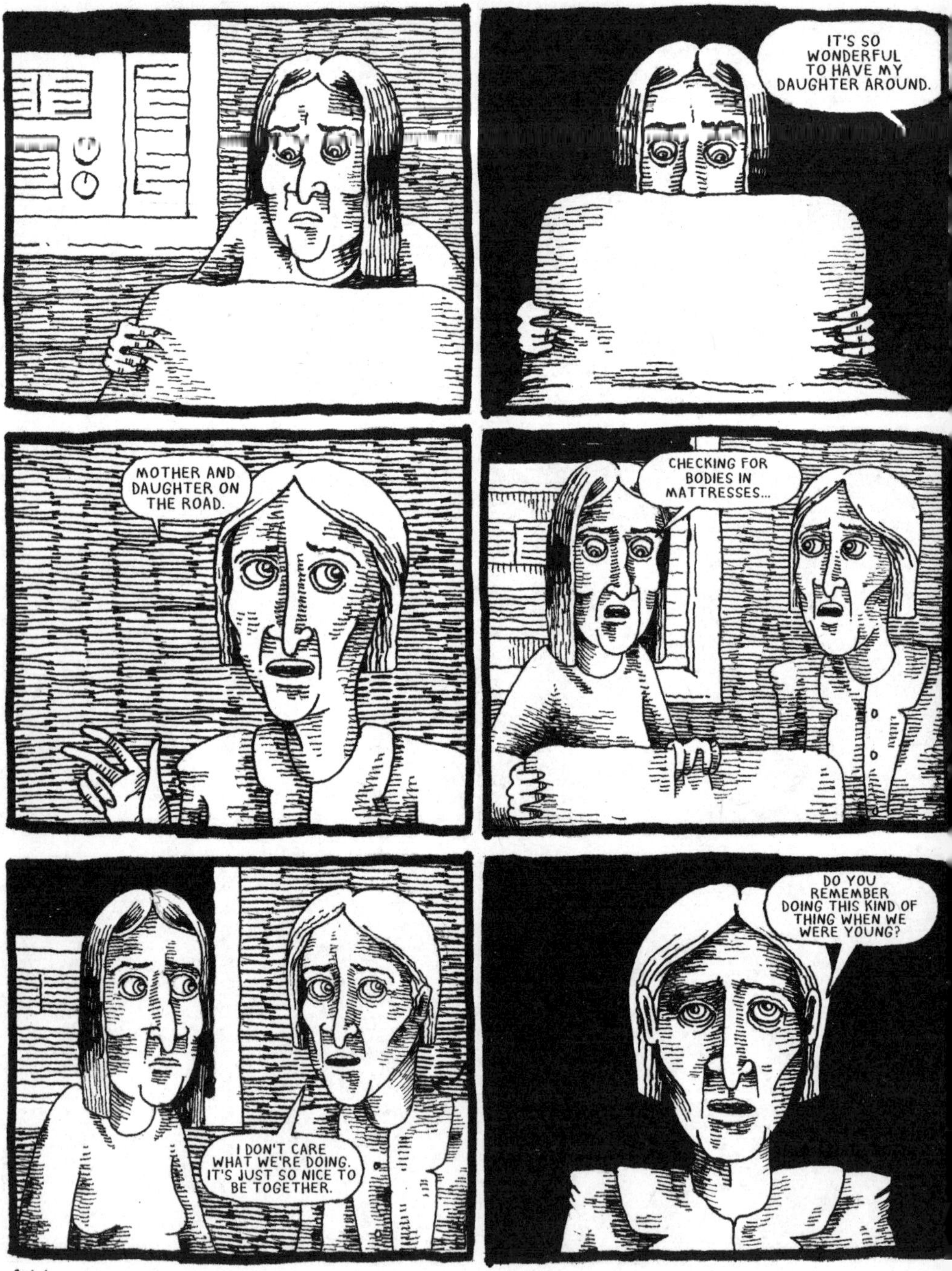
IT'S SO WONDERFUL TO HAVE MY DAUGHTER AROUND.
MOTHER AND DAUGHTER ON THE ROAD.
CHECKING FOR BODIES IN MATTRESSES...
I DON'T CARE WHAT WE'RE DOING. IT'S JUST SO NICE TO BE TOGETHER.
DO YOU REMEMBER DOING THIS KIND OF THING WHEN WE WERE YOUNG?

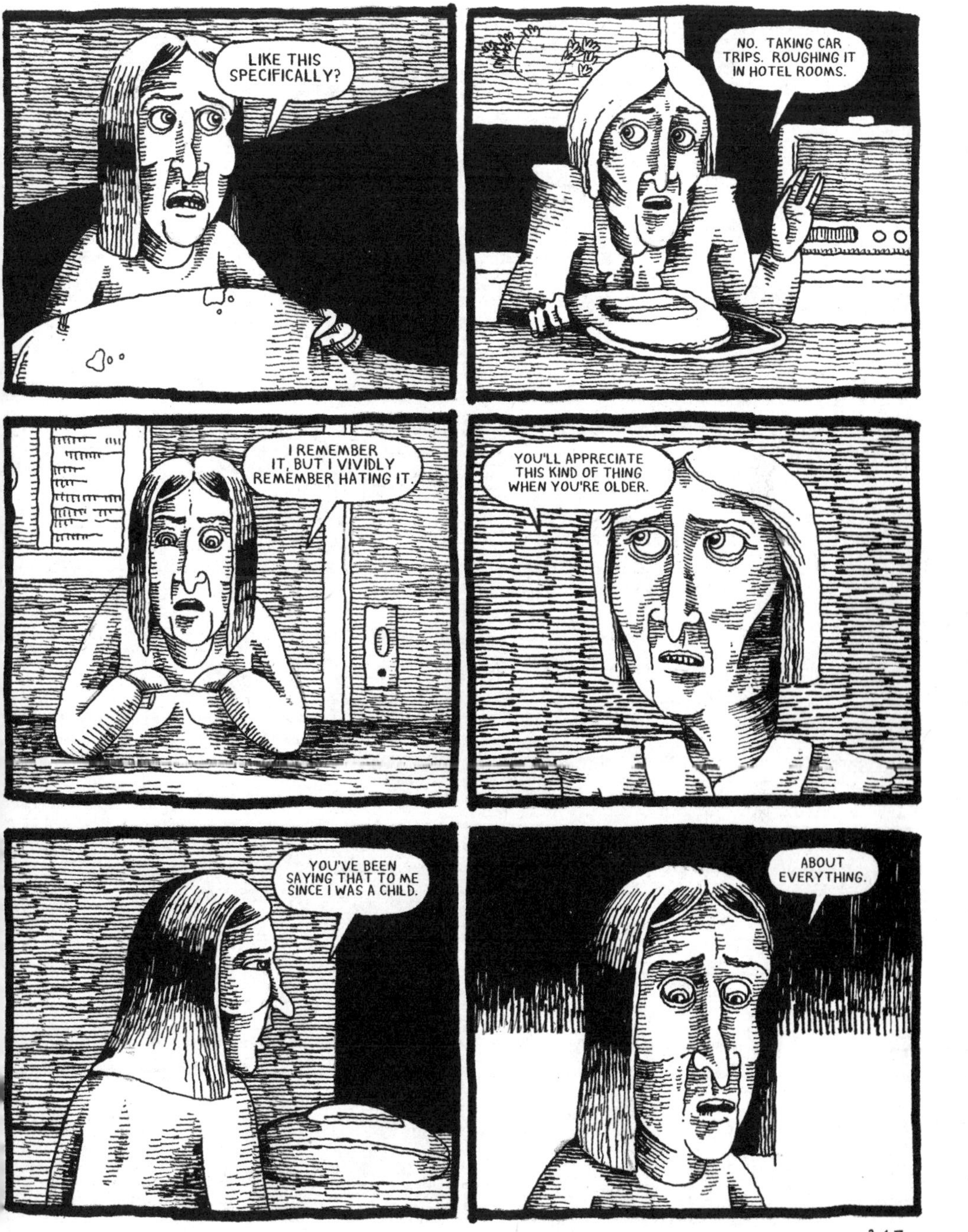
LIKE THIS SPECIFICALLY?
NO. TAKING CAR TRIPS. ROUGHING IT IN HOTEL ROOMS.
I REMEMBER IT, BUT I VIVIDLY REMEMBER HATING IT.
YOU'LL APPRECIATE THIS KIND OF THING WHEN YOU'RE OLDER.
YOU'VE BEEN SAYING THAT TO ME SINCE I WAS A CHILD.
ABOUT EVERYTHING.

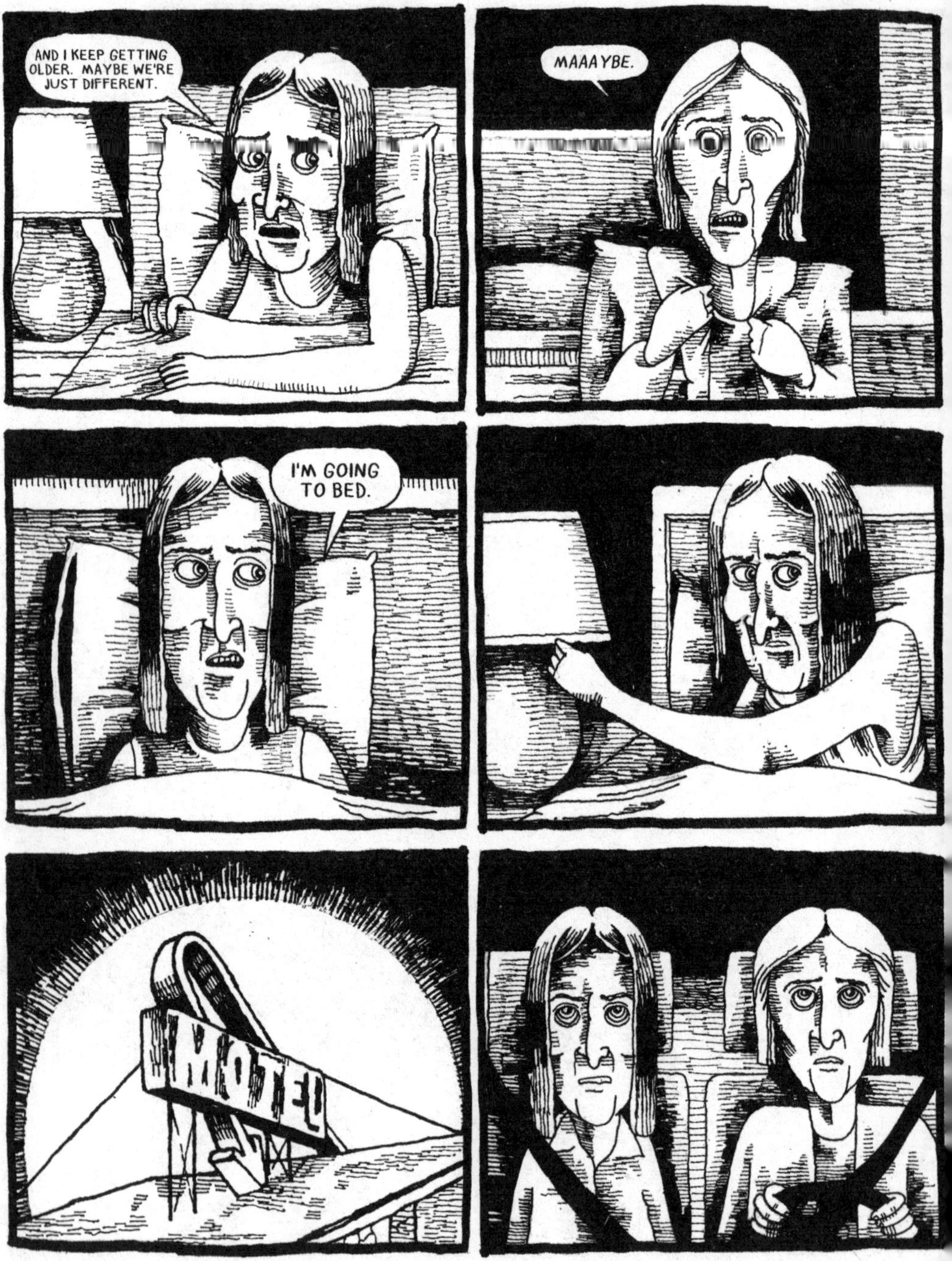
AND I KEEP GETTING OLDER. MAYBE WE'RE JUST DIFFERENT.
MAAAYBE.
I'M GOING TO BED.
MOTEL

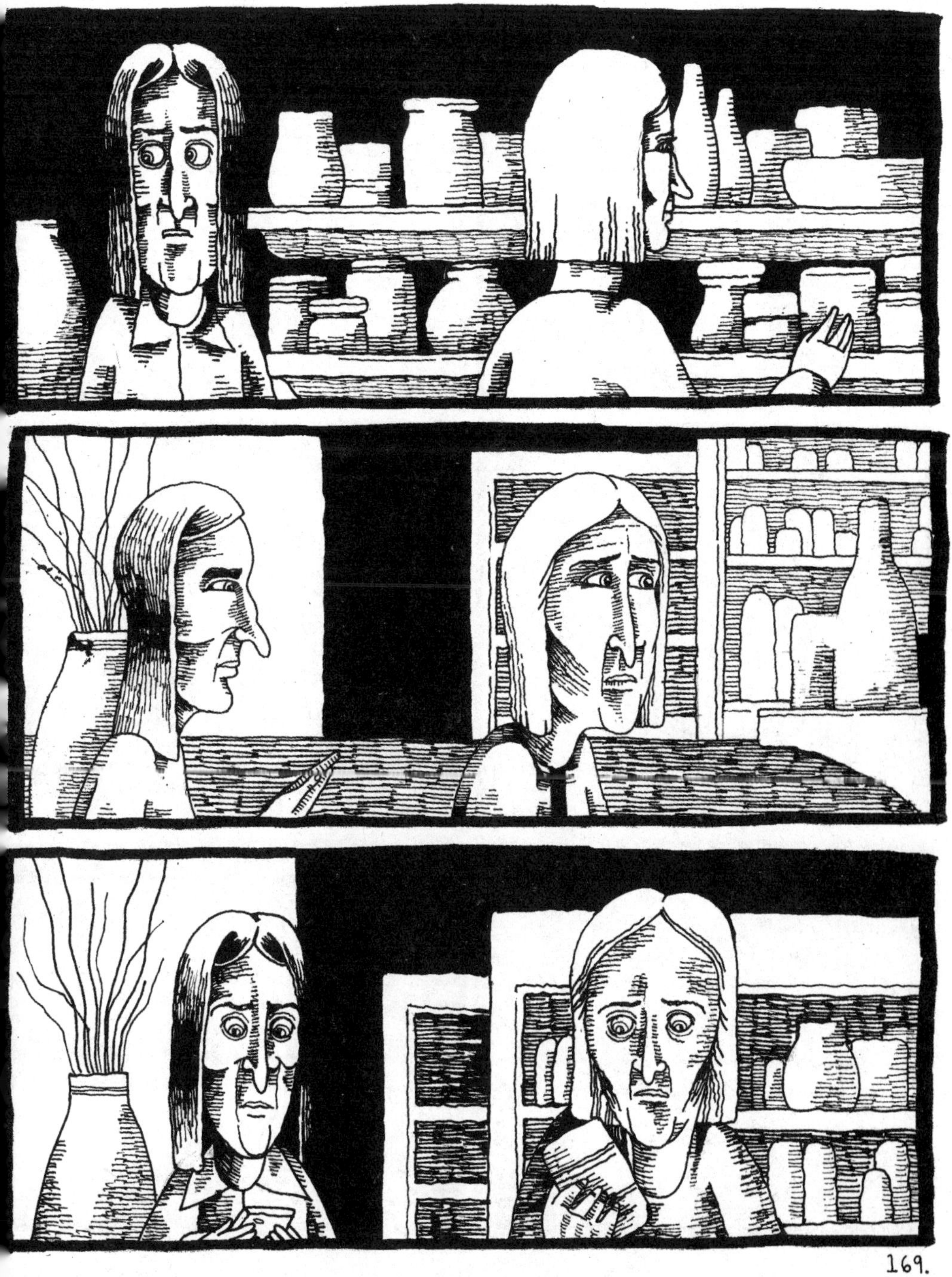

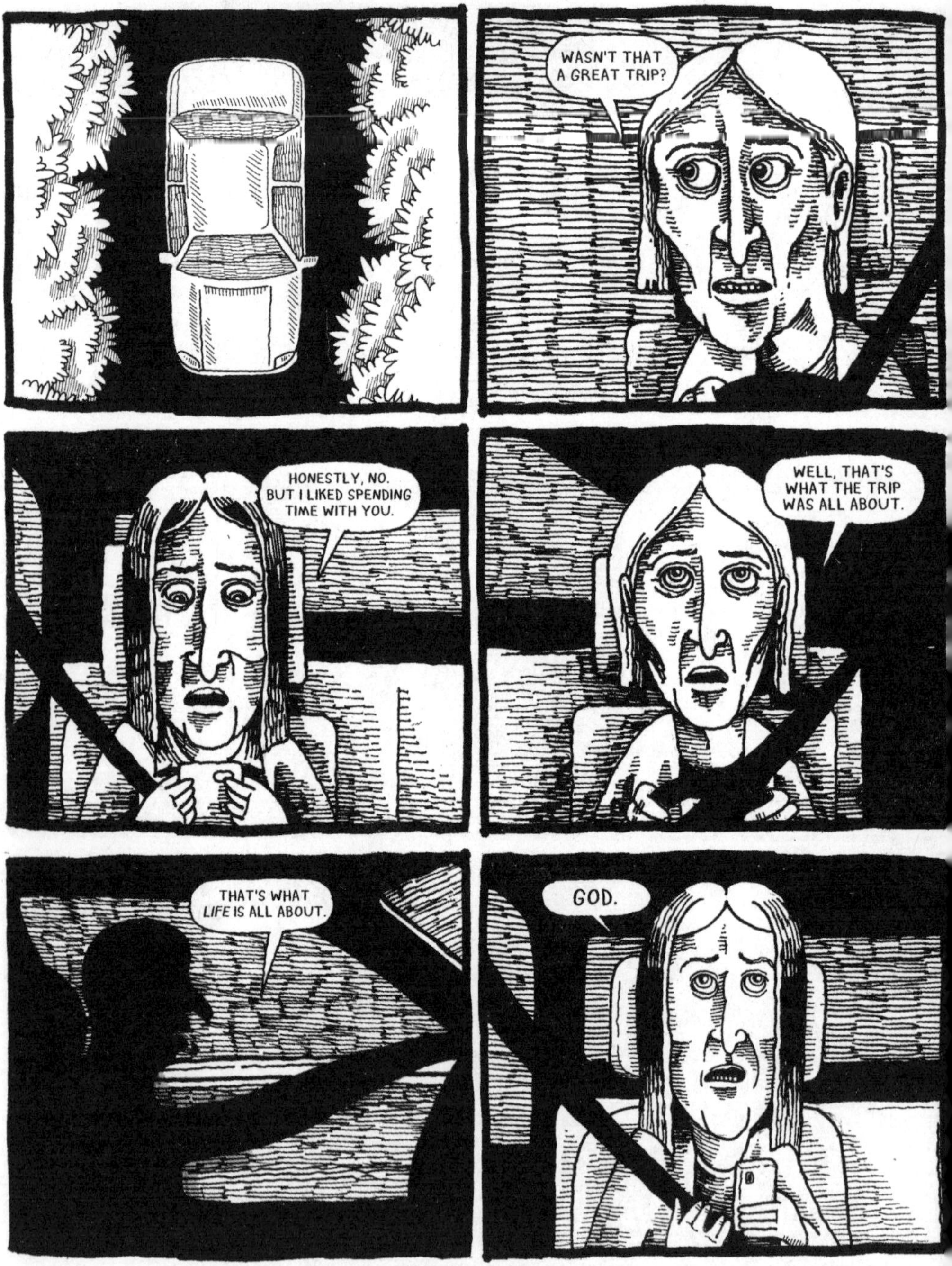
WASN'T THAT A GREAT TRIP?
HONESTLY, NO. BUT I LIKED SPENDING TIME WITH YOU.
WELL, THAT'S WHAT THE TRIP WAS ALL ABOUT.
THAT'S WHAT *LIFE* IS ALL ABOUT.
GOD.

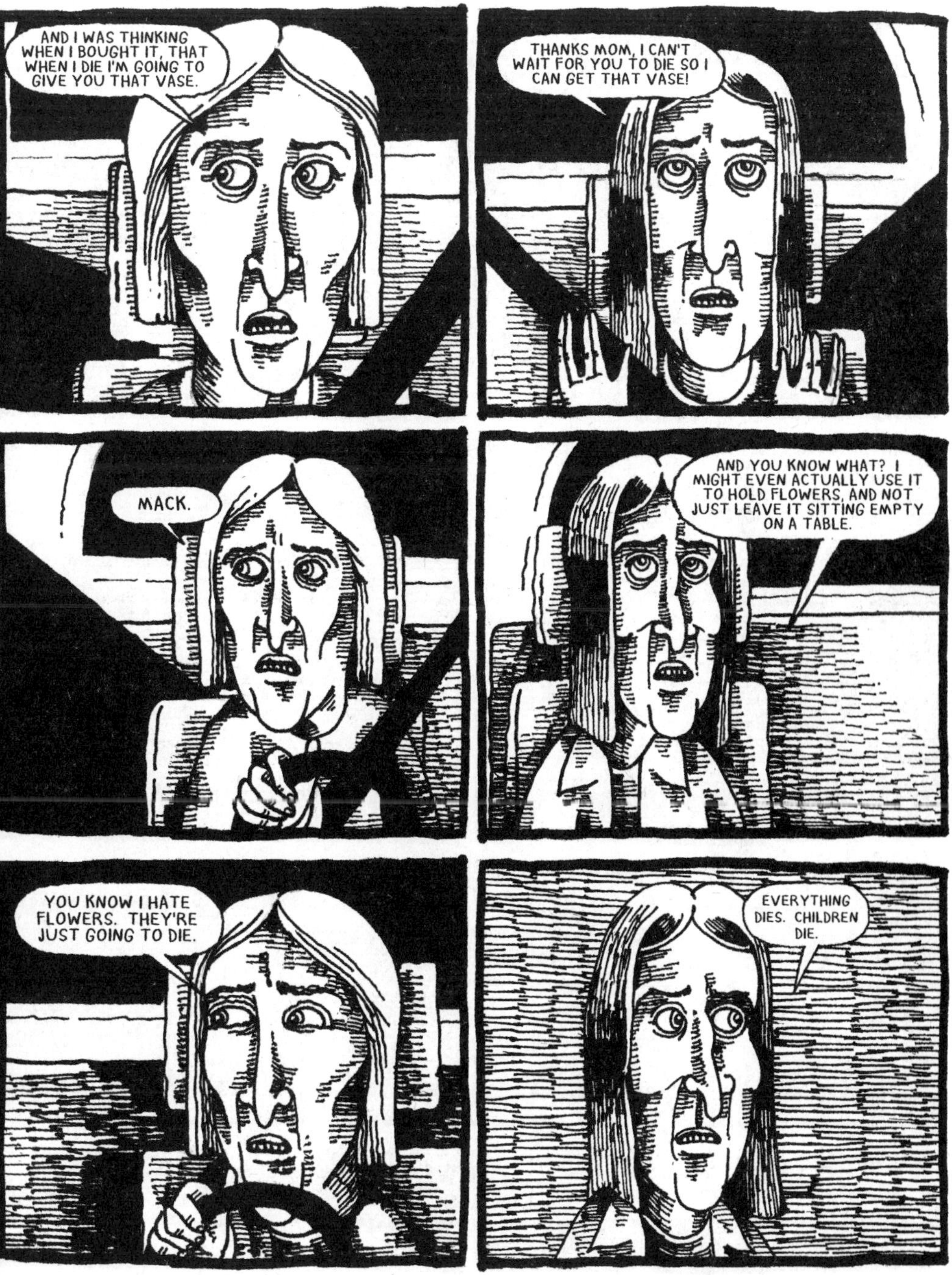
AND I WAS THINKING WHEN I BOUGHT IT, THAT WHEN I DIE I'M GOING TO GIVE YOU THAT VASE.
THANKS MOM, I CAN'T WAIT FOR YOU TO DIE SO I CAN GET THAT VASE!
MACK.
AND YOU KNOW WHAT? I MIGHT EVEN ACTUALLY USE IT TO HOLD FLOWERS, AND NOT JUST LEAVE IT SITTING EMPTY ON A TABLE.
YOU KNOW I HATE FLOWERS. THEY'RE JUST GOING TO DIE.
EVERYTHING DIES. CHILDREN DIE.

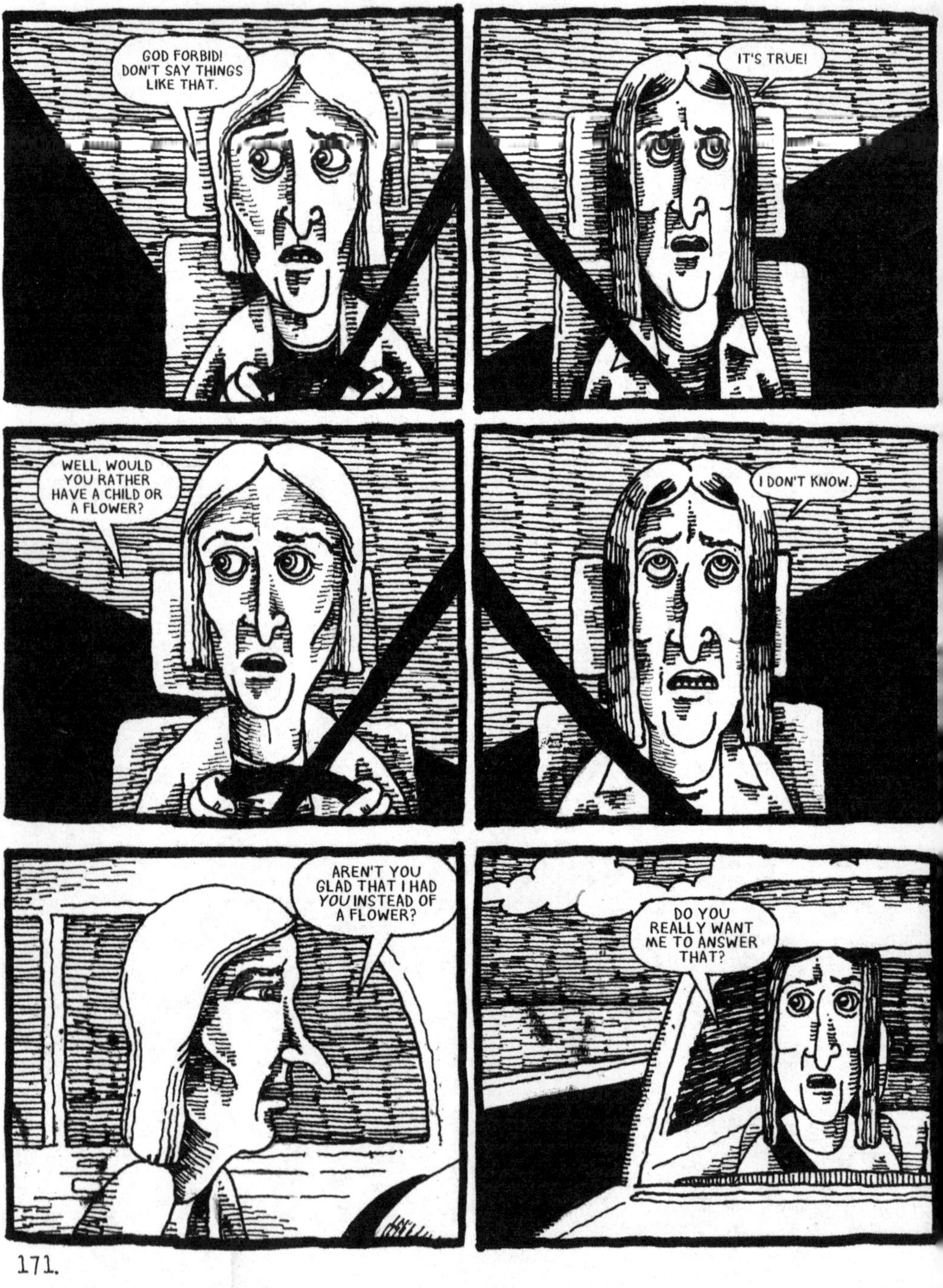
GOD FORBID! DON'T SAY THINGS LIKE THAT.
IT'S TRUE!
WELL, WOULD YOU RATHER HAVE A CHILD OR A FLOWER?
I DON'T KNOW.
AREN'T YOU GLAD THAT I HAD *YOU* INSTEAD OF A FLOWER?
DO YOU REALLY WANT ME TO ANSWER THAT?

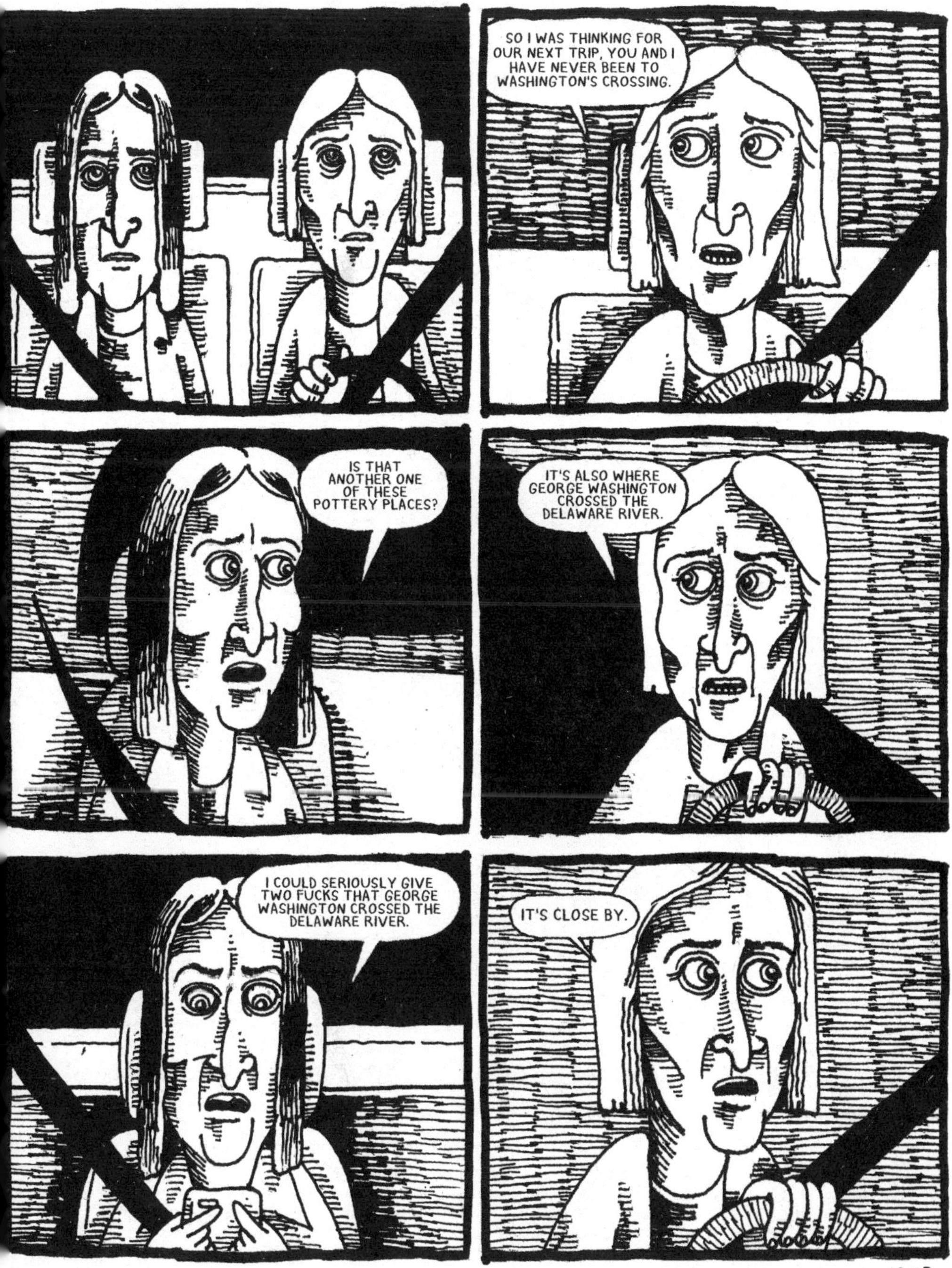
SO I WAS THINKING FOR OUR NEXT TRIP, YOU AND I HAVE NEVER BEEN TO WASHINGTON'S CROSSING.
IS THAT ANOTHER ONE OF THESE POTTERY PLACES?
IT'S ALSO WHERE GEORGE WASHINGTON CROSSED THE DELAWARE RIVER.
I COULD SERIOUSLY GIVE TWO FUCKS THAT GEORGE WASHINGTON CROSSED THE DELAWARE RIVER.
IT'S CLOSE BY.

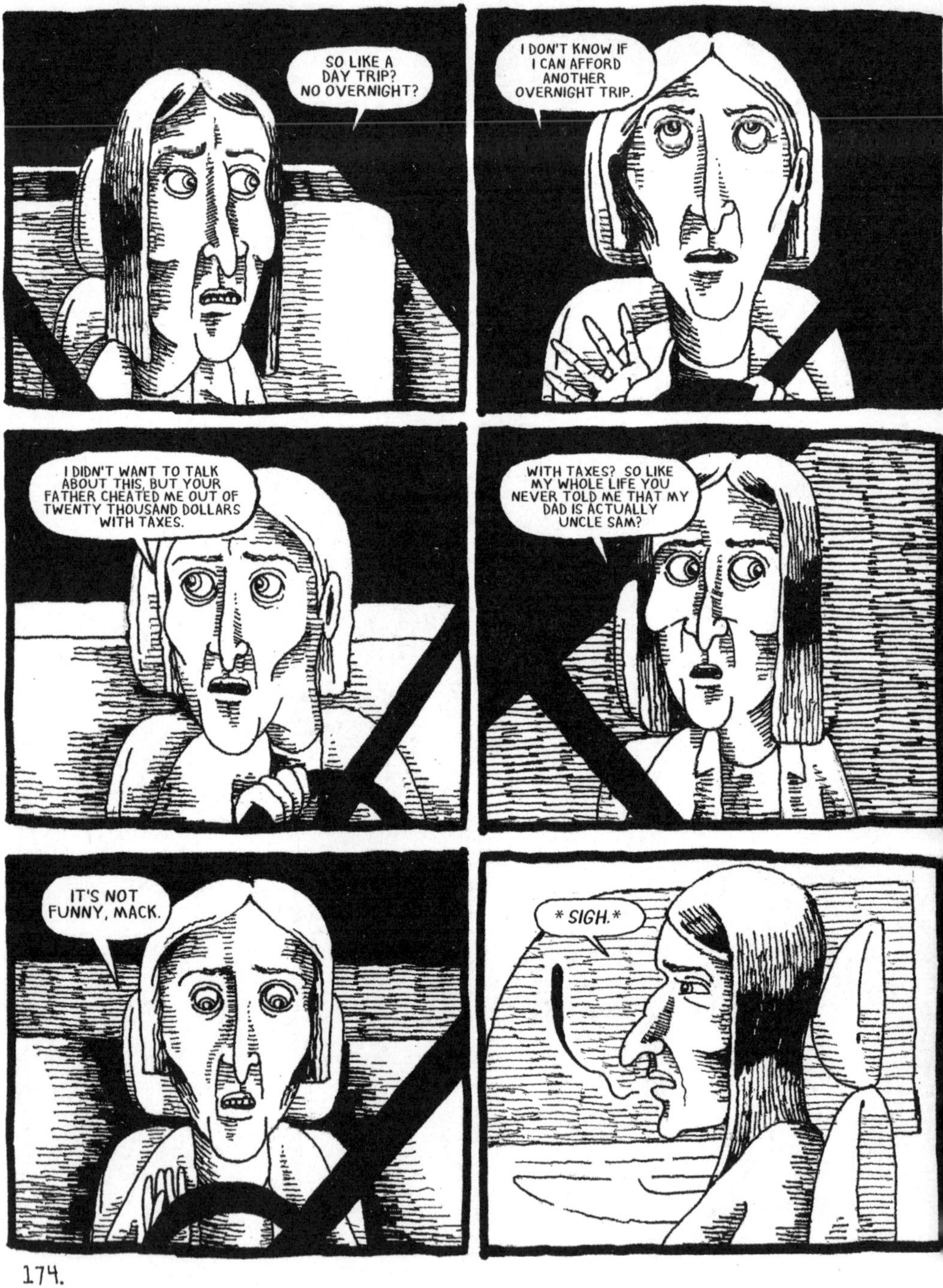
SO LIKE A DAY TRIP? NO OVERNIGHT?
I DON'T KNOW IF I CAN AFFORD ANOTHER OVERNIGHT TRIP.
I DIDN'T WANT TO TALK ABOUT THIS, BUT YOUR FATHER CHEATED ME OUT OF TWENTY THOUSAND DOLLARS WITH TAXES.
WITH TAXES? SO LIKE MY WHOLE LIFE YOU NEVER TOLD ME THAT MY DAD IS ACTUALLY UNCLE SAM?
IT'S NOT FUNNY, MACK.
* SIGH.*

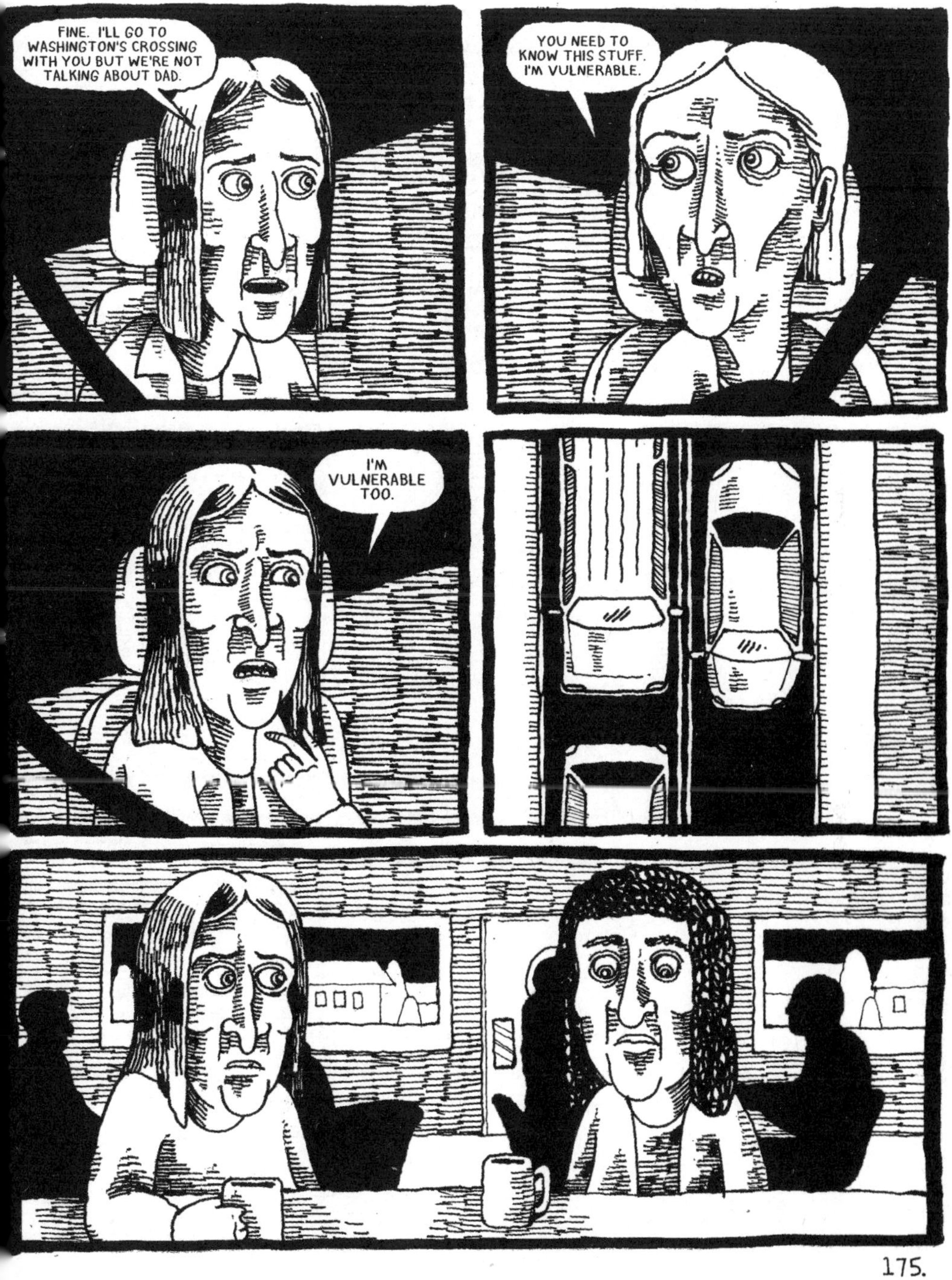
FINE. I'LL GO TO WASHINGTON'S CROSSING WITH YOU BUT WE'RE NOT TALKING ABOUT DAD.
YOU NEED TO KNOW THIS STUFF. I'M VULNERABLE.
I'M VULNERABLE TOO.

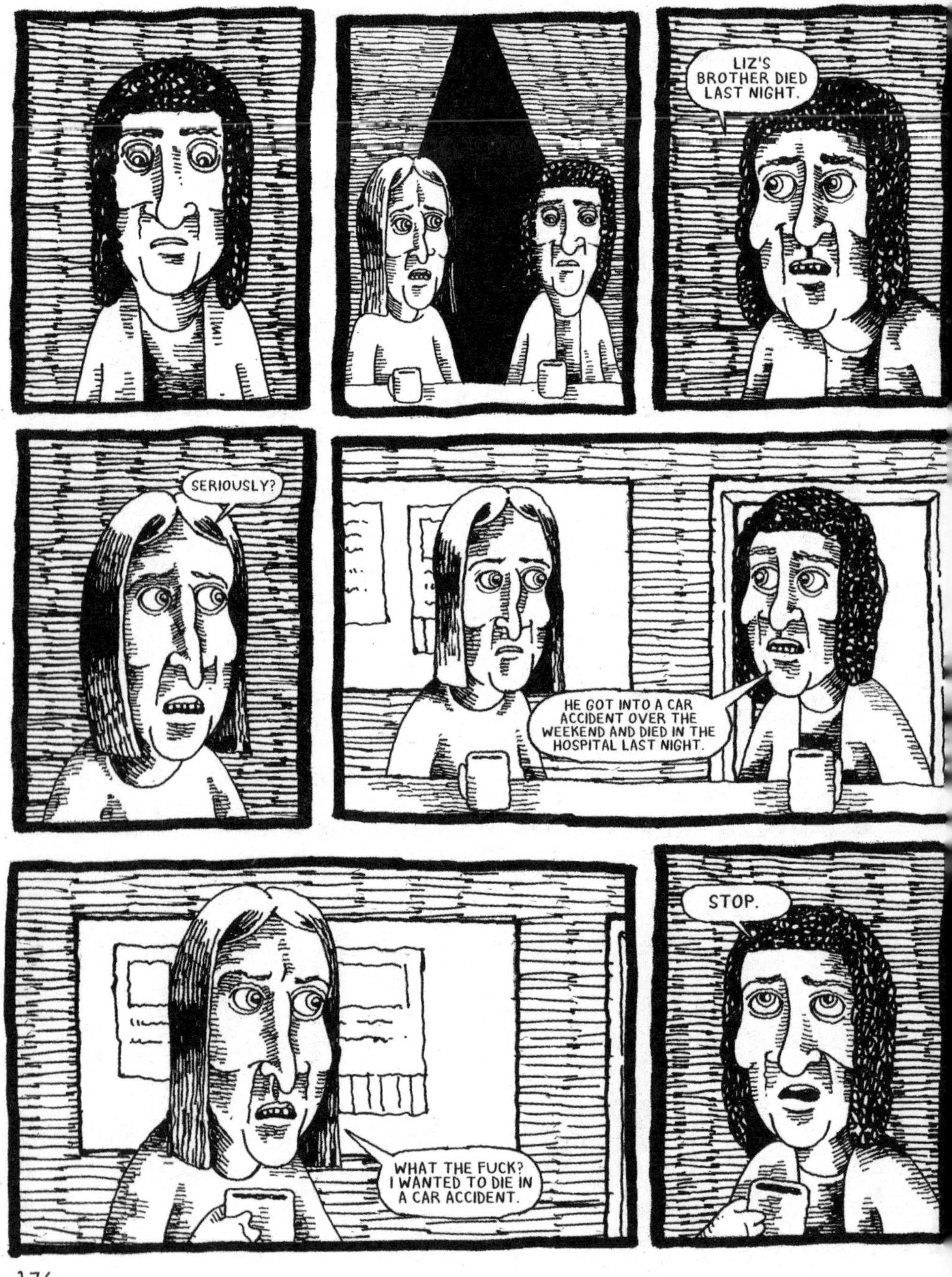
LIZ'S BROTHER DIED LAST NIGHT.
SERIOUSLY?
HE GOT INTO A CAR ACCIDENT OVER THE WEEKEND AND DIED IN THE HOSPITAL LAST NIGHT.
WHAT THE FUCK? I WANTED TO DIE IN A CAR ACCIDENT.
STOP.

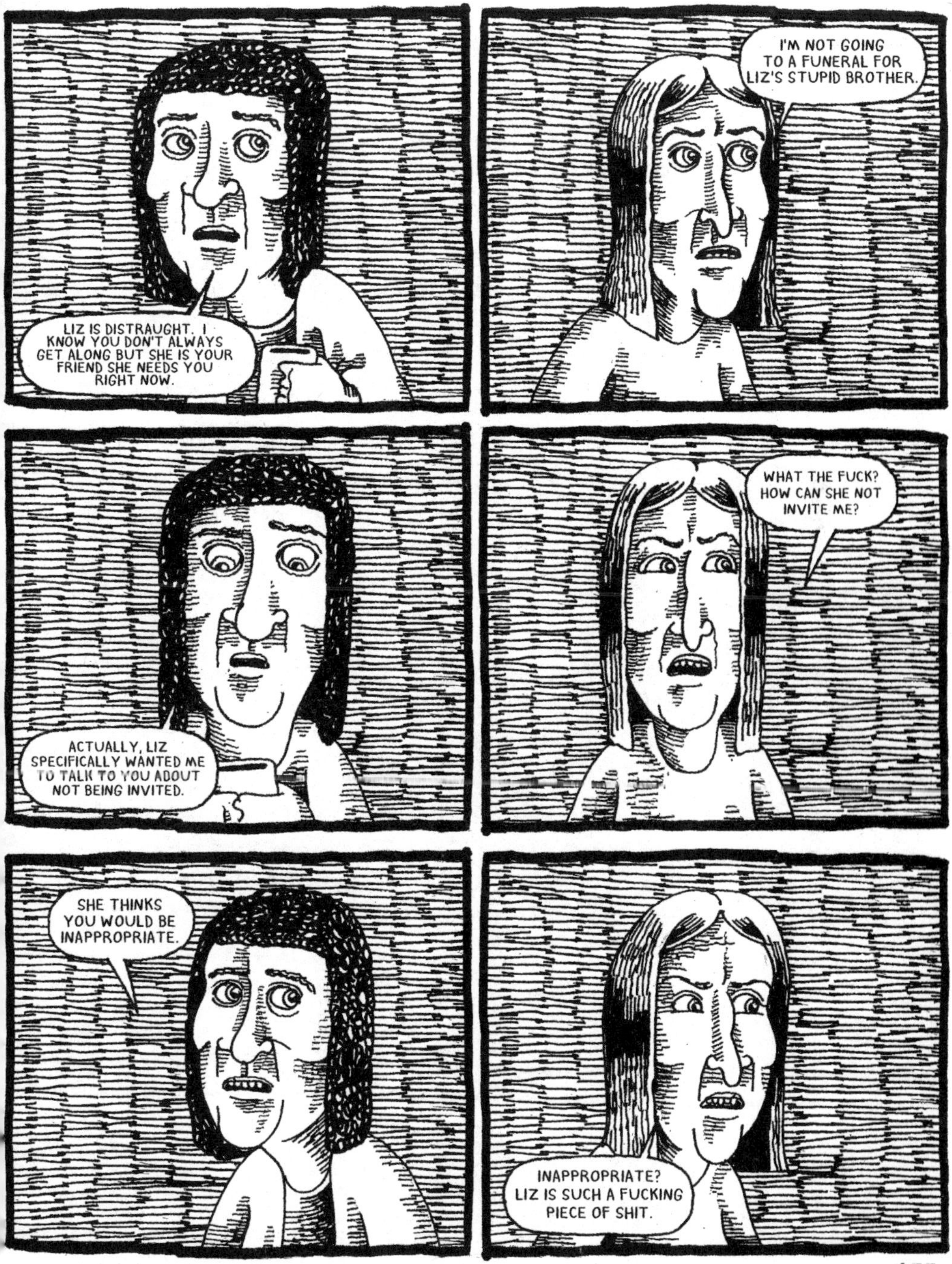
LIZ IS DISTRAUGHT. I KNOW YOU DON'T ALWAYS GET ALONG BUT SHE IS YOUR FRIEND SHE NEEDS YOU RIGHT NOW.
I'M NOT GOING TO A FUNERAL FOR LIZ'S STUPID BROTHER.
ACTUALLY, LIZ SPECIFICALLY WANTED ME TO TALK TO YOU ABOUT NOT BEING INVITED.
WHAT THE FUCK? HOW CAN SHE NOT INVITE ME?
SHE THINKS YOU WOULD BE INAPPROPRIATE.
INAPPROPRIATE? LIZ IS SUCH A FUCKING PIECE OF SHIT.

HER BROTHER JUST DIED.
I'M GOING TO THAT FUNERAL.
YOU JUST SAID YOU WOULDN'T!
THAT'S BEFORE I KNEW I WASN'T INVITED.
IS EVERYONE ELSE GOING?
OF COURSE.

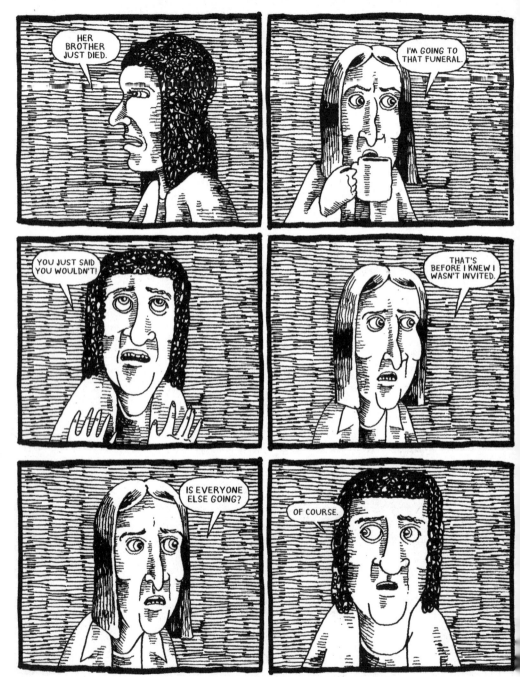

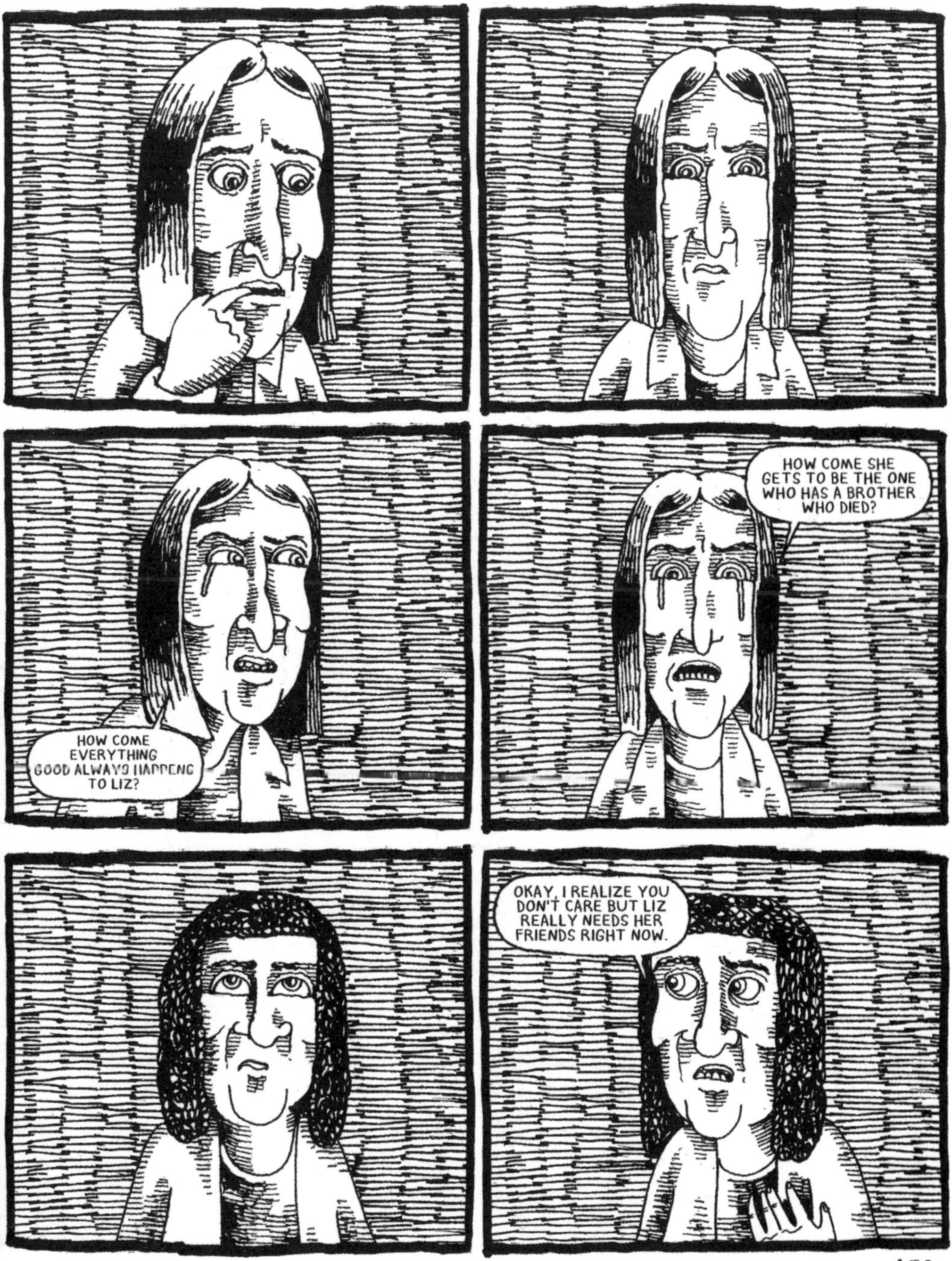
HOW COME EVERYTHING GOOD ALWAYS HAPPENS TO LIZ?
HOW COME SHE GETS TO BE THE ONE WHO HAS A BROTHER WHO DIED?
OKAY, I REALIZE YOU DON'T CARE BUT LIZ REALLY NEEDS HER FRIENDS RIGHT NOW.

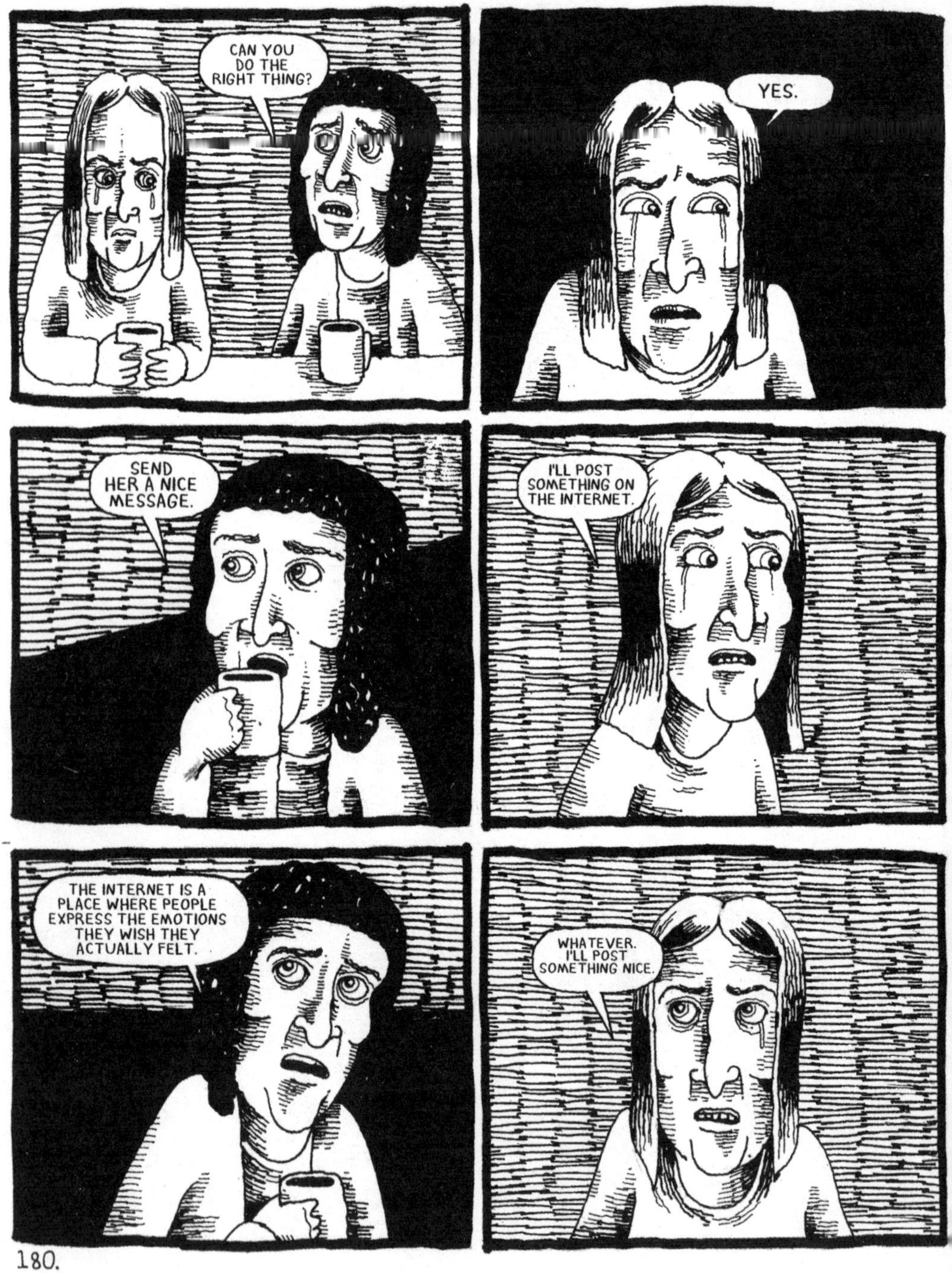
CAN YOU DO THE RIGHT THING?
YES.
SEND HER A NICE MESSAGE.
I'LL POST SOMETHING ON THE INTERNET.
THE INTERNET IS A PLACE WHERE PEOPLE EXPRESS THE EMOTIONS THEY WISH THEY ACTUALLY FELT.
WHATEVER. I'LL POST SOMETHING NICE.

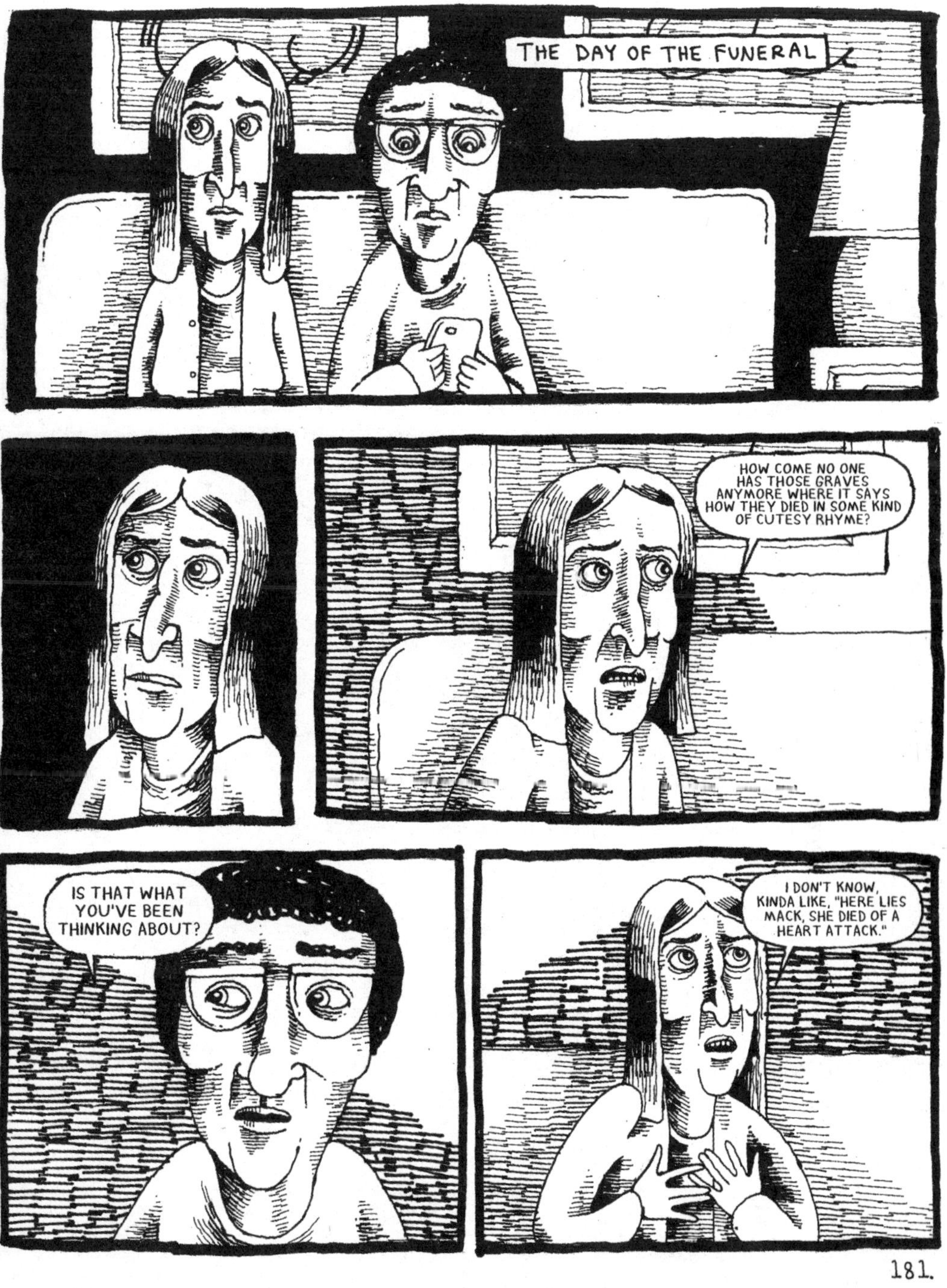
THE DAY OF THE FUNERAL
HOW COME NO ONE HAS THOSE GRAVES ANYMORE WHERE IT SAYS HOW THEY DIED IN SOME KIND OF CUTESY RHYME?
IS THAT WHAT YOU'VE BEEN THINKING ABOUT?
I DON'T KNOW, KINDA LIKE, "HERE LIES MACK, SHE DIED OF A HEART ATTACK."

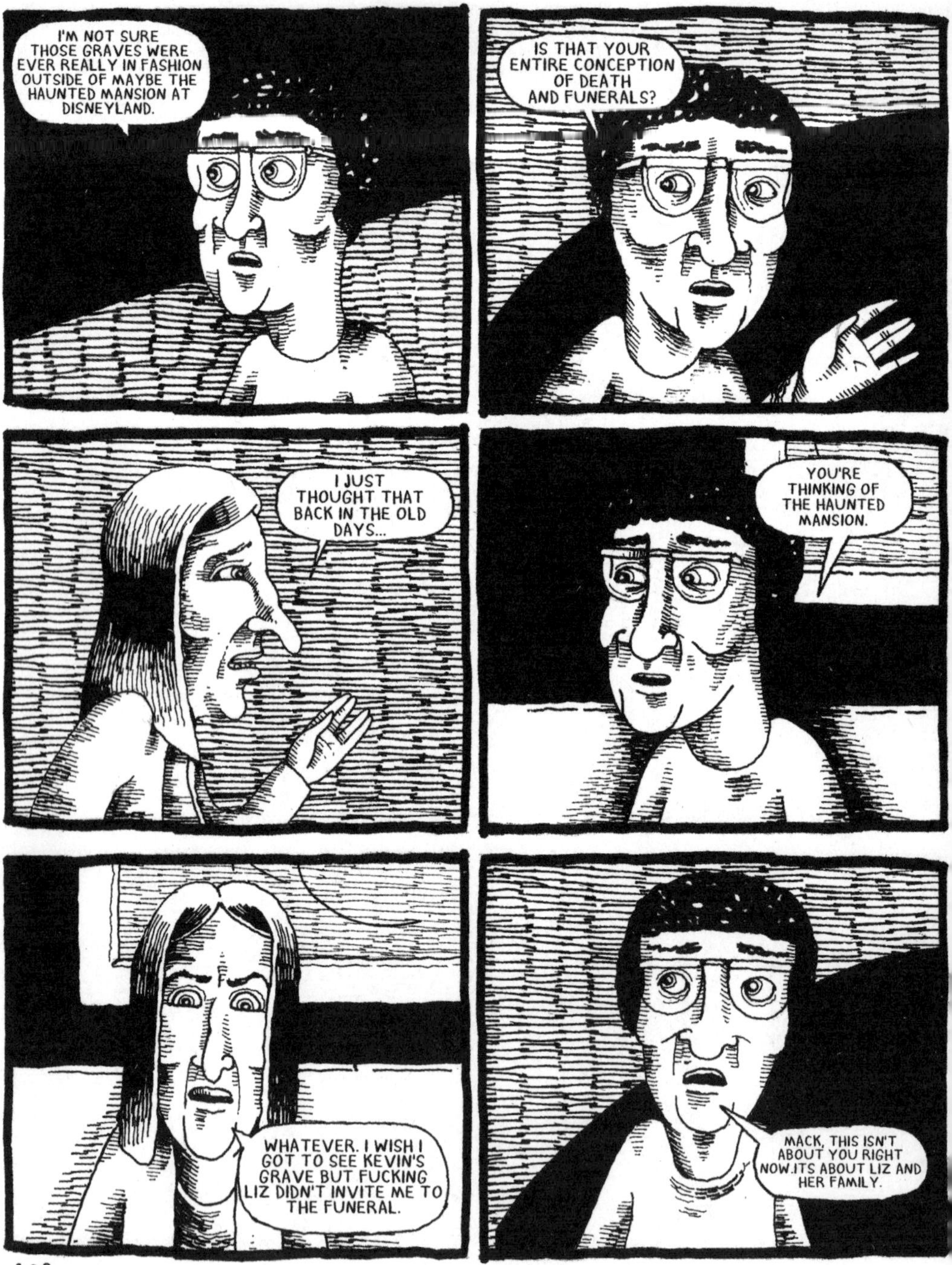
I'M NOT SURE THOSE GRAVES WERE EVER REALLY IN FASHION OUTSIDE OF MAYBE THE HAUNTED MANSION AT DISNEYLAND.
IS THAT YOUR ENTIRE CONCEPTION OF DEATH AND FUNERALS?
I JUST THOUGHT THAT BACK IN THE OLD DAYS...
YOU'RE THINKING OF THE HAUNTED MANSION.
WHATEVER. I WISH I GOT TO SEE KEVIN'S GRAVE BUT FUCKING LIZ DIDN'T INVITE ME TO THE FUNERAL.
MACK, THIS ISN'T ABOUT YOU RIGHT NOW.ITS ABOUT LIZ AND HER FAMILY.

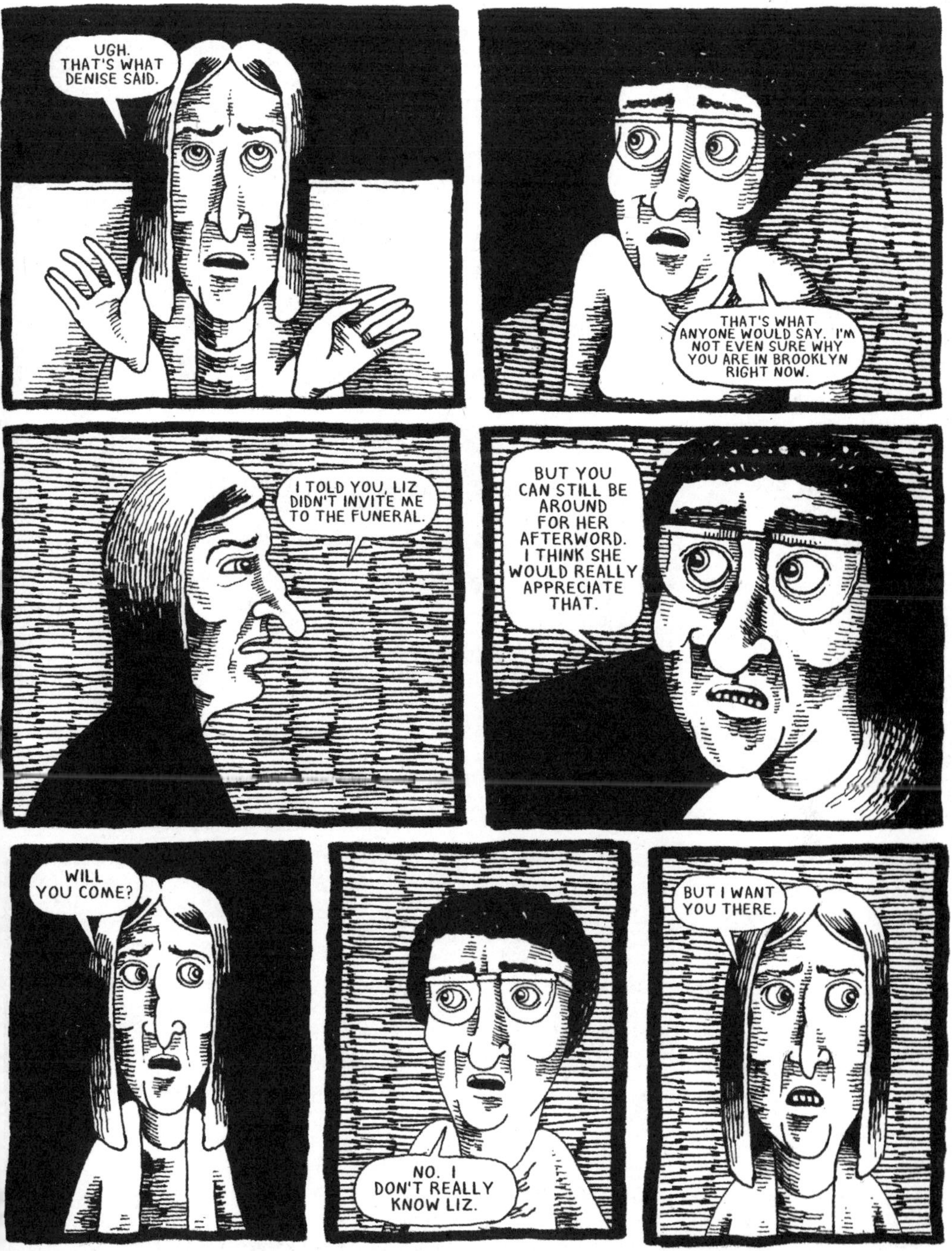
UGH. THAT'S WHAT DENISE SAID.
THAT'S WHAT ANYONE WOULD SAY. I'M NOT EVEN SURE WHY YOU ARE IN BROOKLYN RIGHT NOW.
I TOLD YOU, LIZ DIDN'T INVITE ME TO THE FUNERAL.
BUT YOU CAN STILL BE AROUND FOR HER AFTERWORD. I THINK SHE WOULD REALLY APPRECIATE THAT.
WILL YOU COME?
NO. I DON'T REALLY KNOW LIZ.
BUT I WANT YOU THERE.

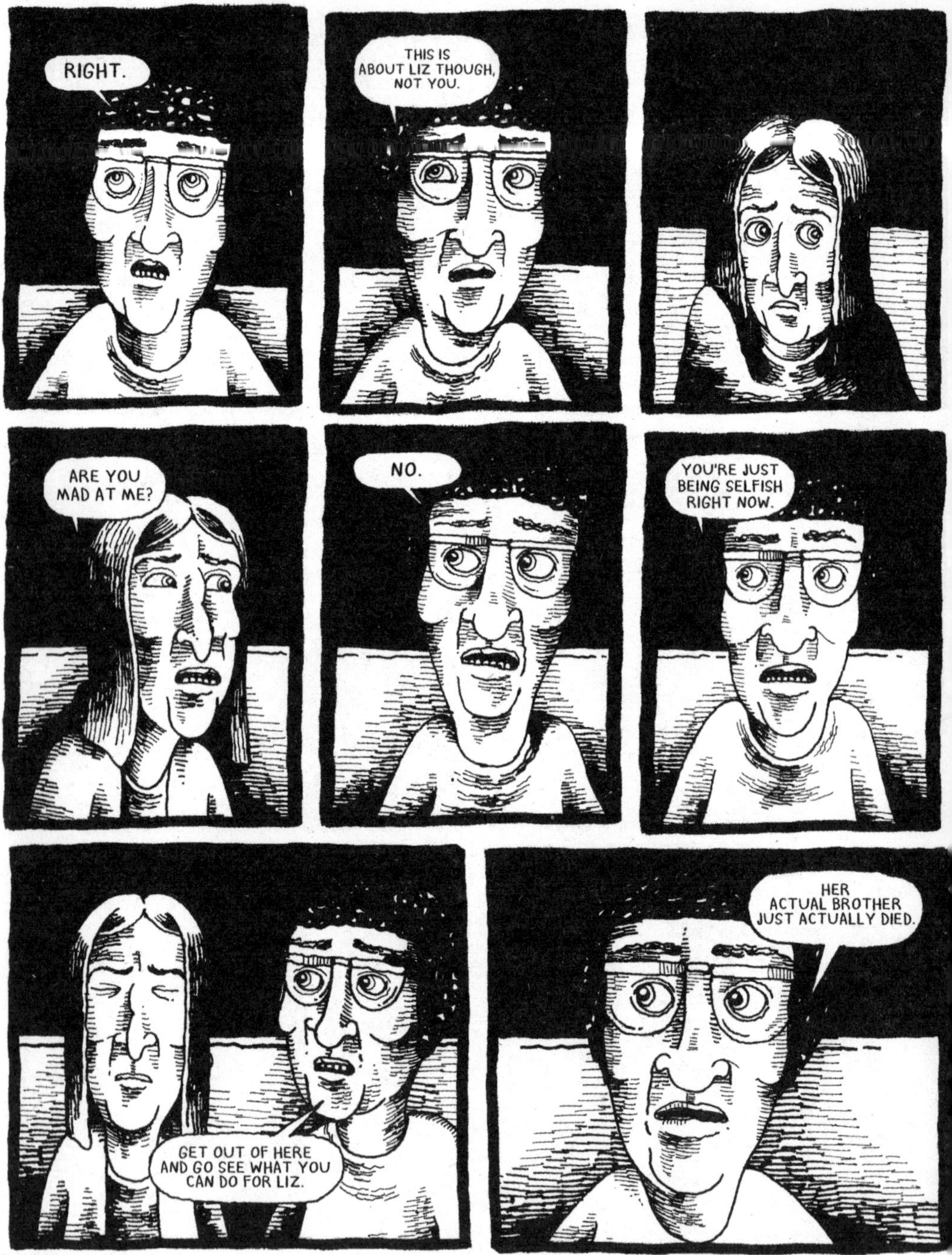
RIGHT.
THIS IS ABOUT LIZ THOUGH, NOT YOU.
ARE YOU MAD AT ME?
NO.
YOU'RE JUST BEING SELFISH RIGHT NOW.
GET OUT OF HERE AND GO SEE WHAT YOU CAN DO FOR LIZ.
HER ACTUAL BROTHER JUST ACTUALLY DIED.

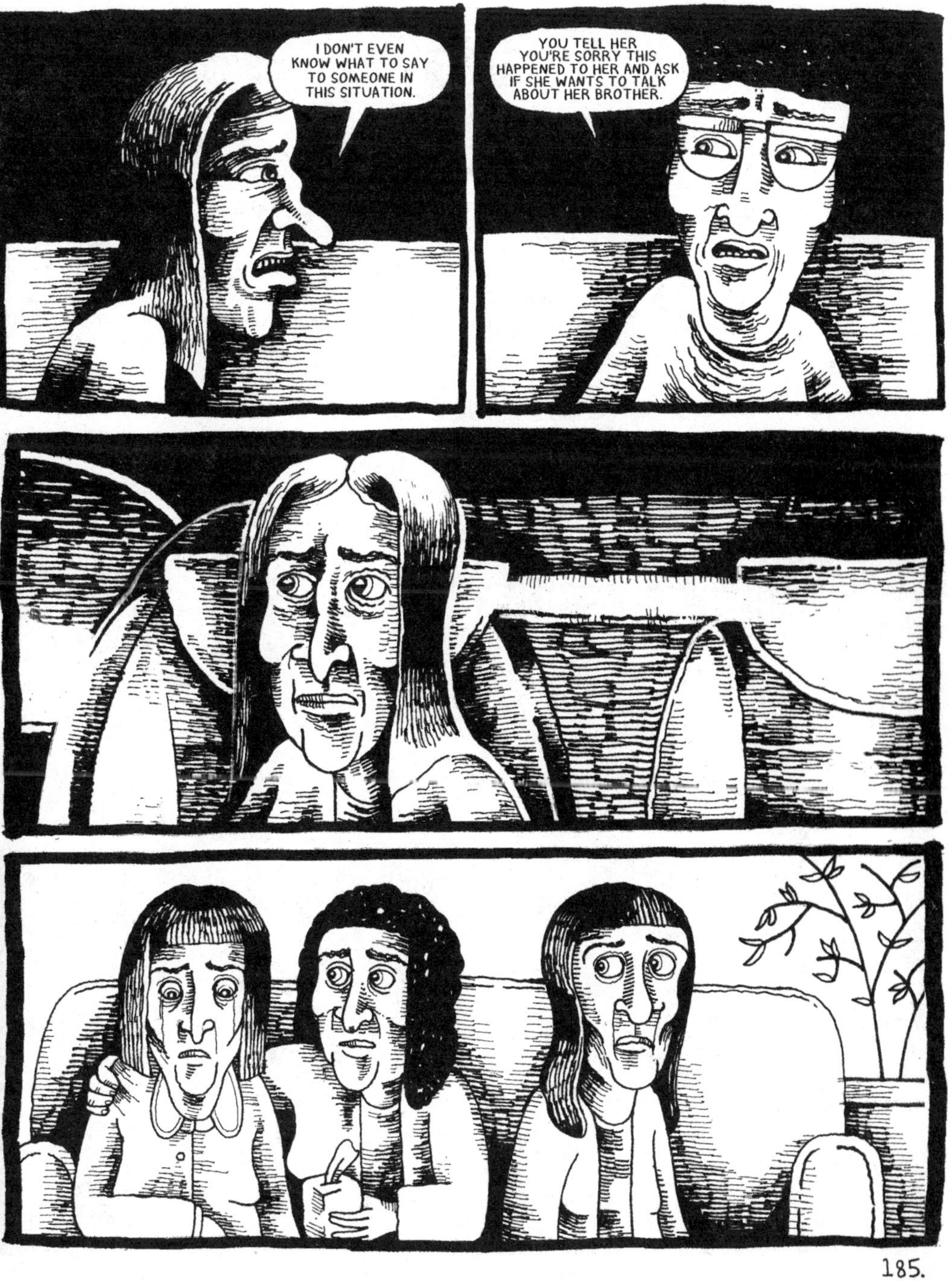
I DON'T EVEN KNOW WHAT TO SAY TO SOMEONE IN THIS SITUATION.
YOU TELL HER YOU'RE SORRY THIS HAPPENED TO HER AND ASK IF SHE WANTS TO TALK ABOUT HER BROTHER.

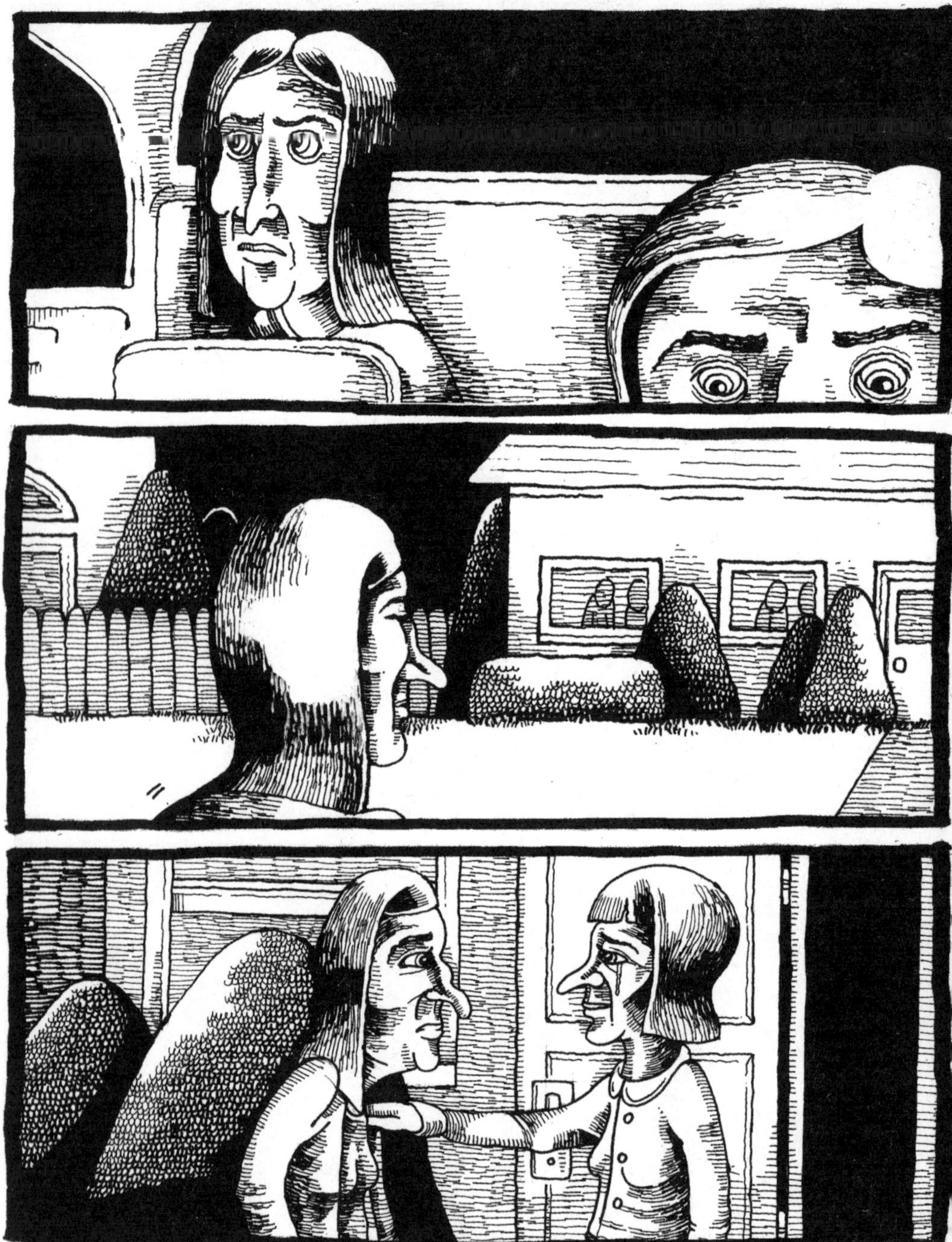

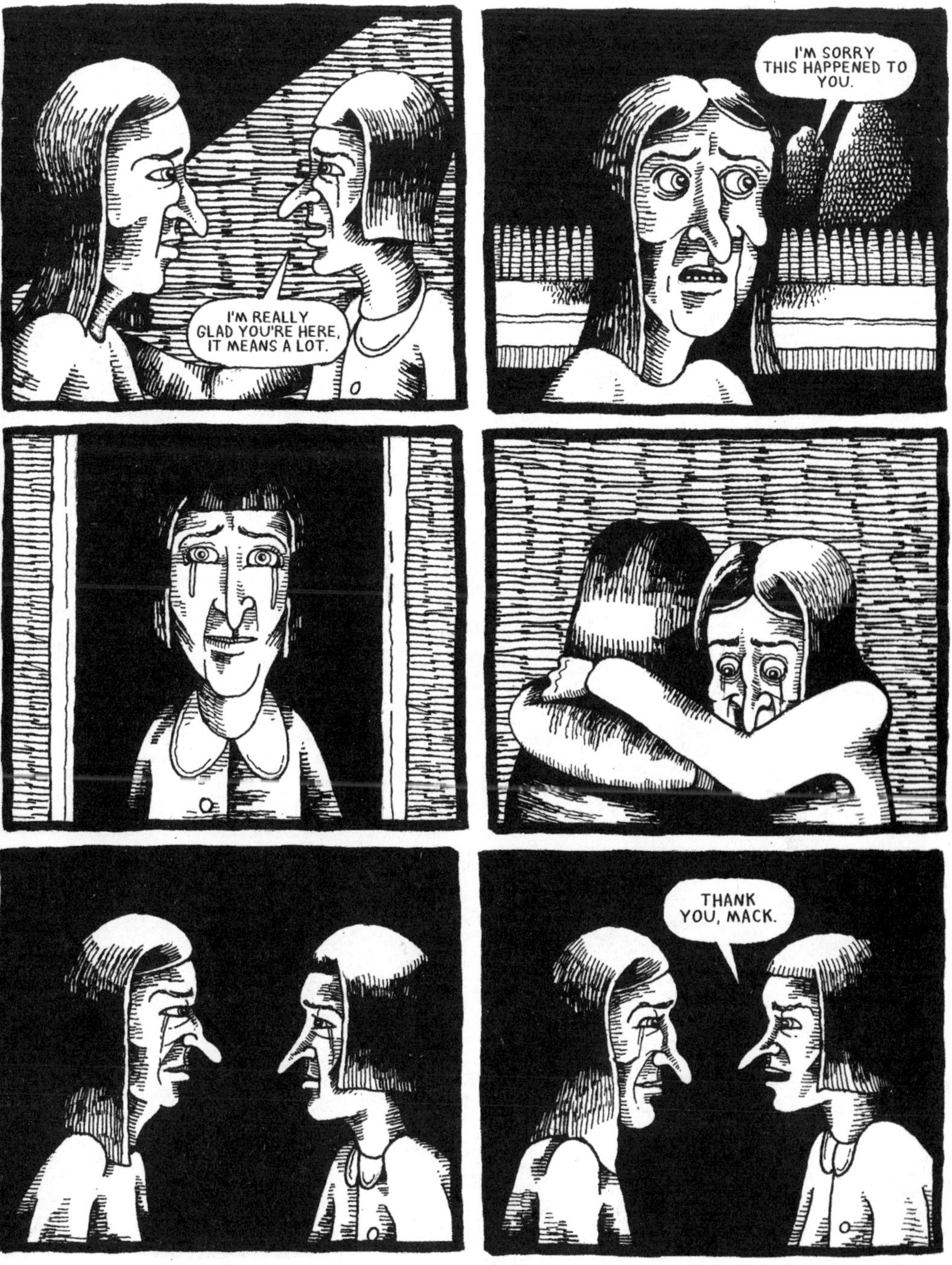
I'M REALLY GLAD YOU'RE HERE, IT MEANS A LOT.
I'M SORRY THIS HAPPENED TO YOU.
THANK YOU, MACK.

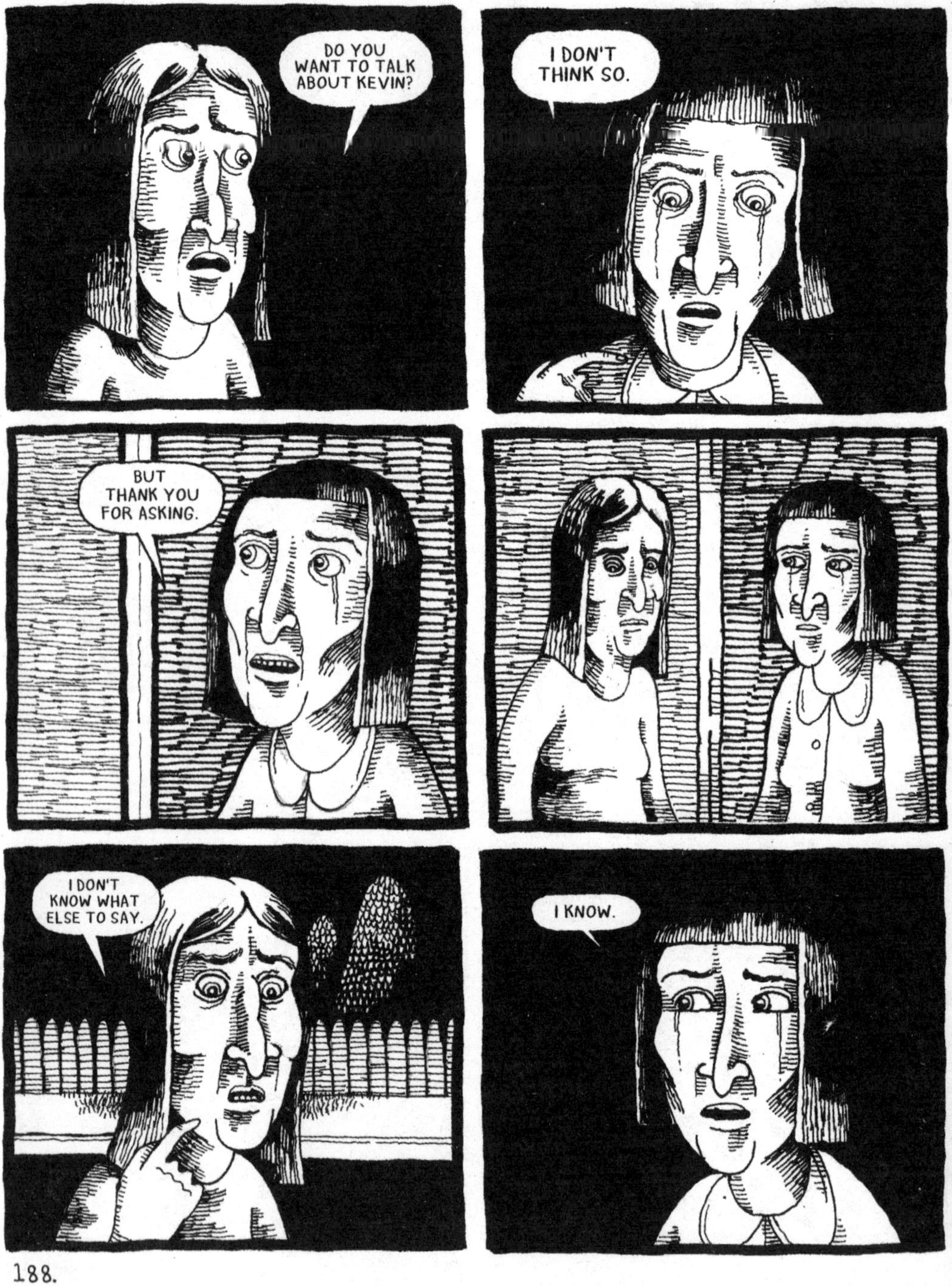
DO YOU WANT TO TALK ABOUT KEVIN?
I DON'T THINK SO.
BUT THANK YOU FOR ASKING.
I DON'T KNOW WHAT ELSE TO SAY.
I KNOW.

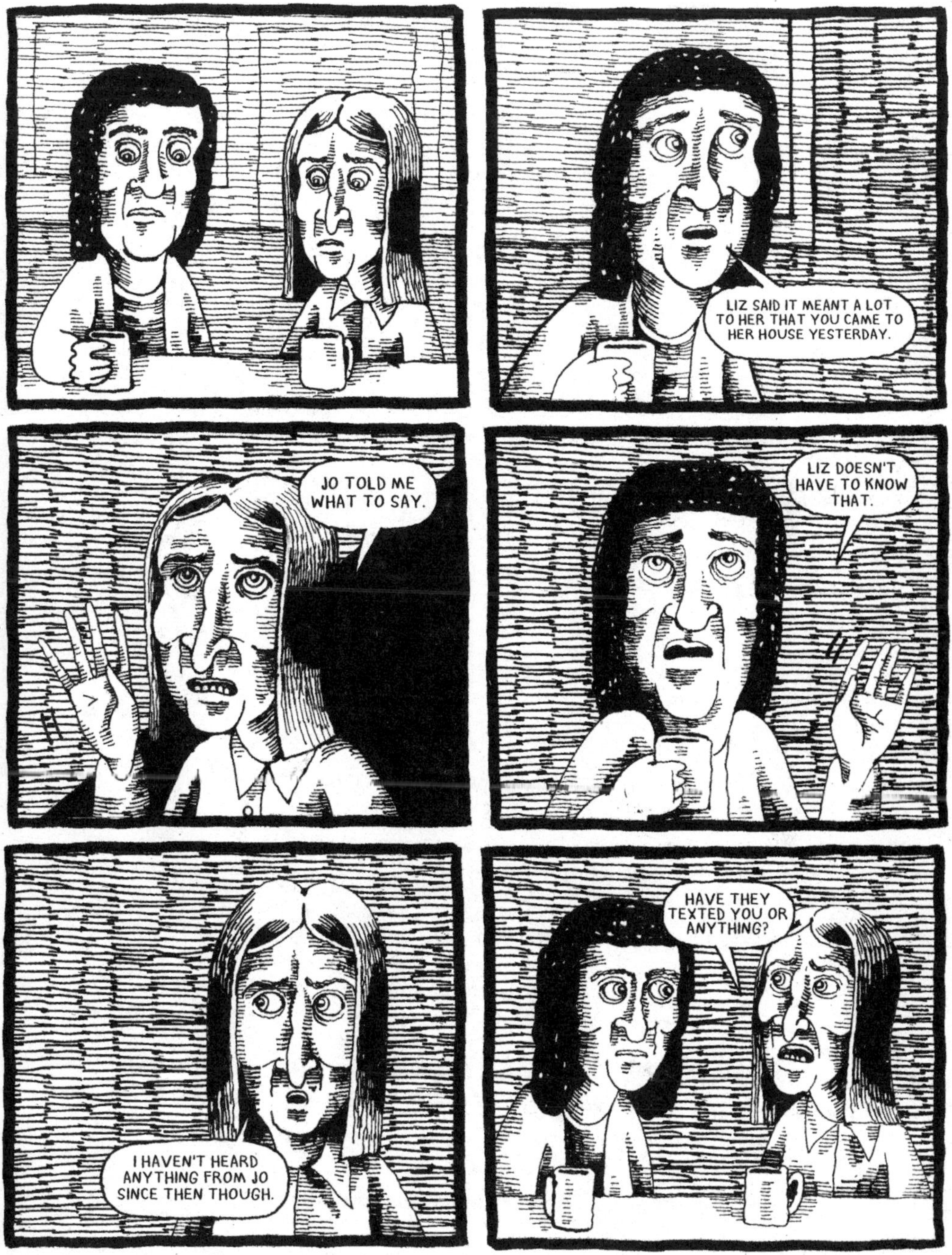
LIZ SAID IT MEANT A LOT TO HER THAT YOU CAME TO HER HOUSE YESTERDAY.
JO TOLD ME WHAT TO SAY.
LIZ DOESN'T HAVE TO KNOW THAT.
I HAVEN'T HEARD ANYTHING FROM JO SINCE THEN THOUGH.
HAVE THEY TEXTED YOU OR ANYTHING?

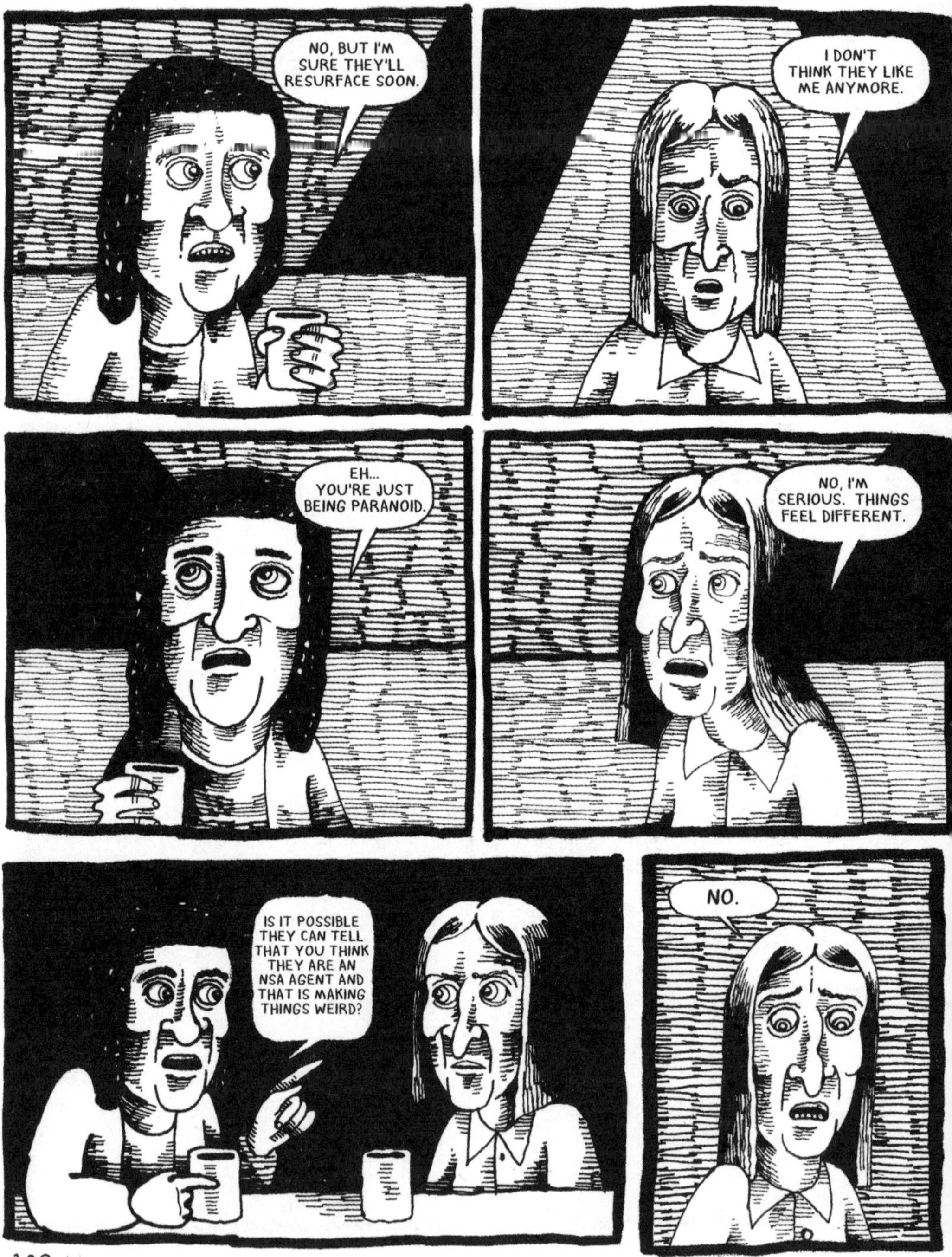
NO, BUT I'M SURE THEY'LL RESURFACE SOON.
I DON'T THINK THEY LIKE ME ANYMORE.
EH... YOU'RE JUST BEING PARANOID.
NO, I'M SERIOUS. THINGS FEEL DIFFERENT.
IS IT POSSIBLE THEY CAN TELL THAT YOU THINK THEY ARE AN NSA AGENT AND THAT IS MAKING THINGS WEIRD?
NO.

hey.
are you mad at me?
are you okay? I really need to talk to you.
is everything ok?

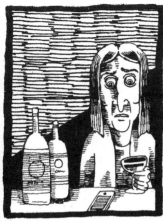

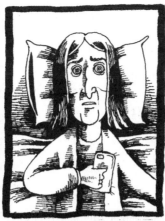

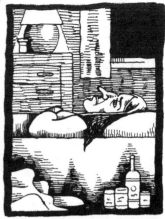

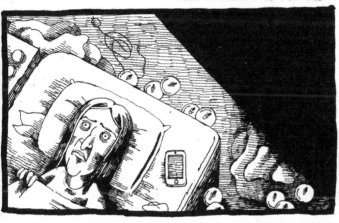

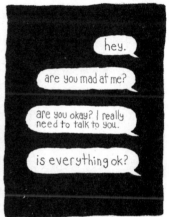

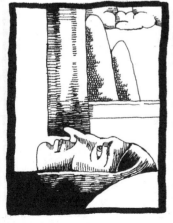

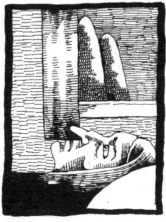

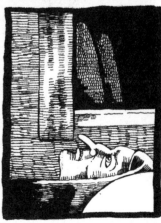

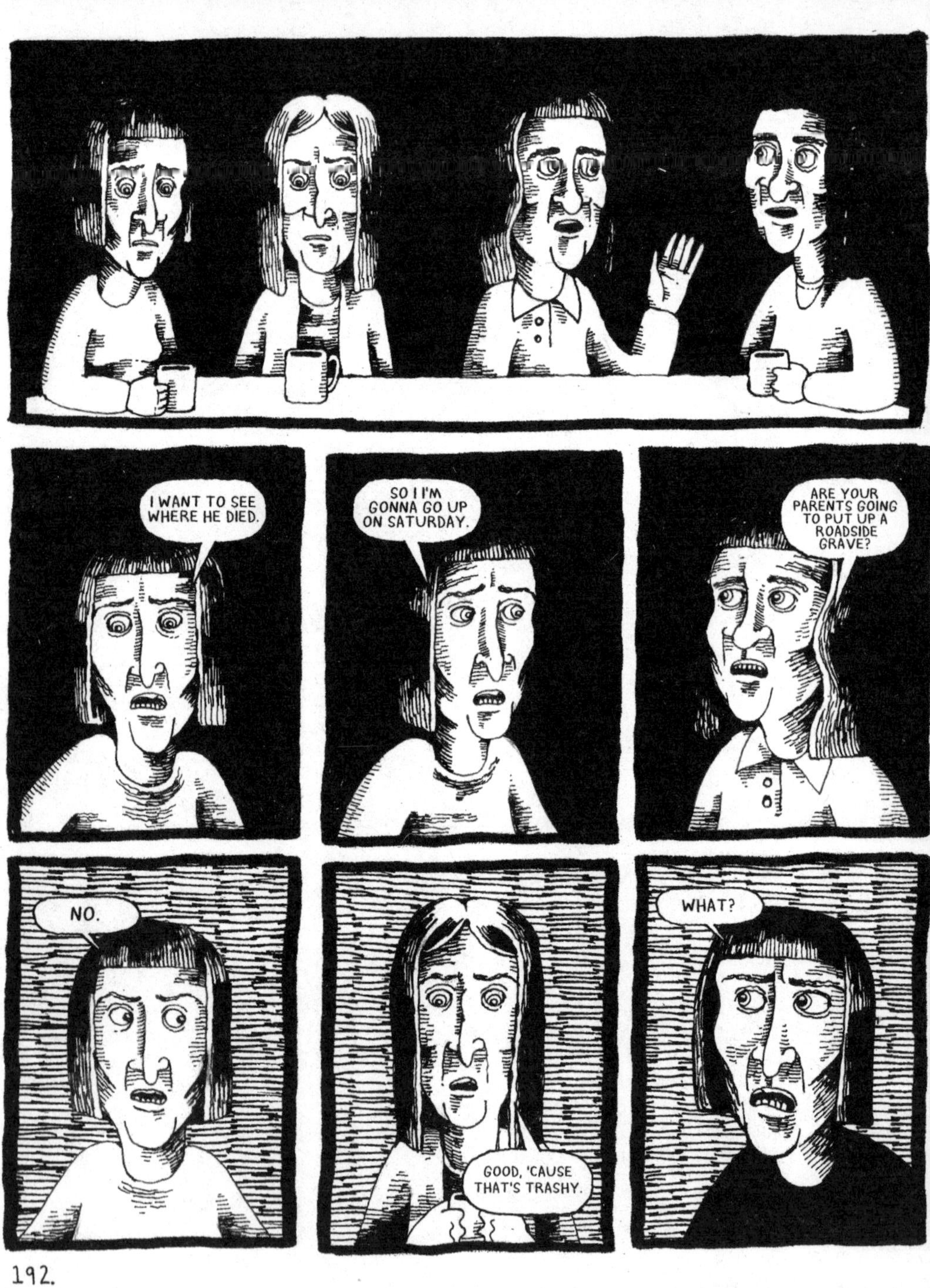
I WANT TO SEE WHERE HE DIED.
SO I I'M GONNA GO UP ON SATURDAY.
ARE YOUR PARENTS GOING TO PUT UP A ROADSIDE GRAVE?
NO.
GOOD, 'CAUSE THAT'S TRASHY.
WHAT?

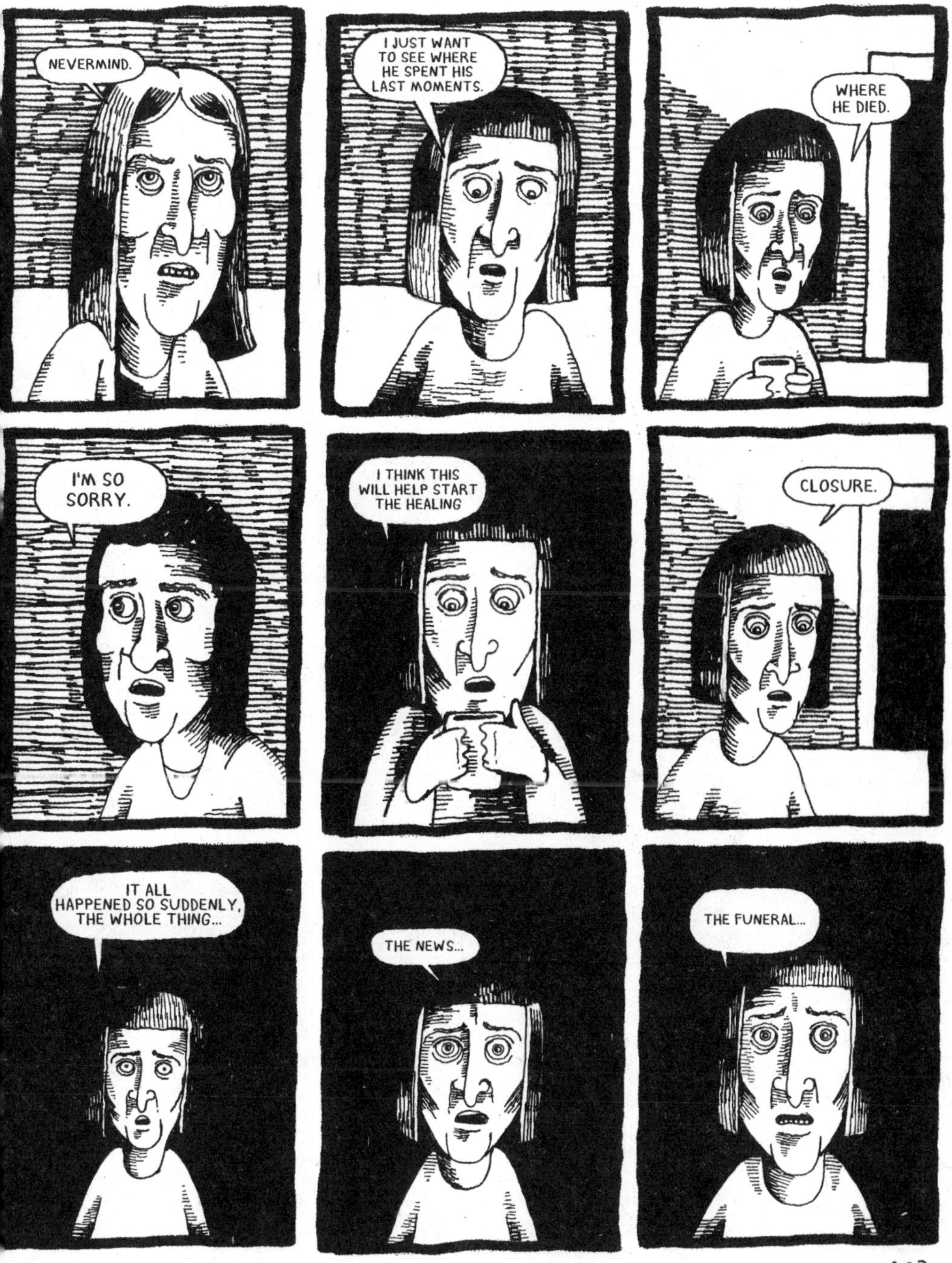
NEVERMIND.
I JUST WANT TO SEE WHERE HE SPENT HIS LAST MOMENTS.
WHERE HE DIED.
I'M SO SORRY.
I THINK THIS WILL HELP START THE HEALING
CLOSURE.
IT ALL HAPPENED SO SUDDENLY, THE WHOLE THING...
THE NEWS...
THE FUNERAL...

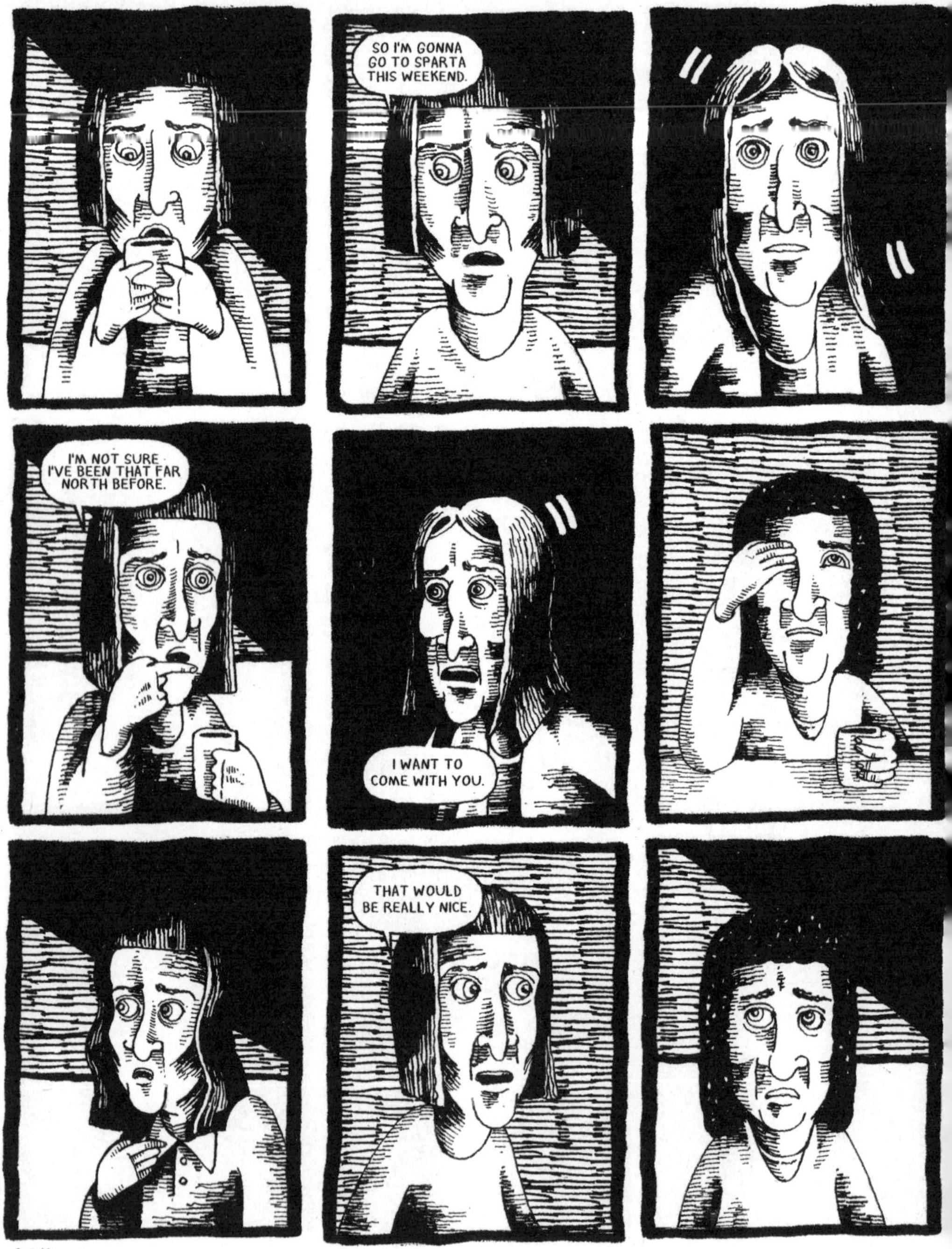
SO I'M GONNA GO TO SPARTA THIS WEEKEND.
I'M NOT SURE I'VE BEEN THAT FAR NORTH BEFORE.
I WANT TO COME WITH YOU.
THAT WOULD BE REALLY NICE.

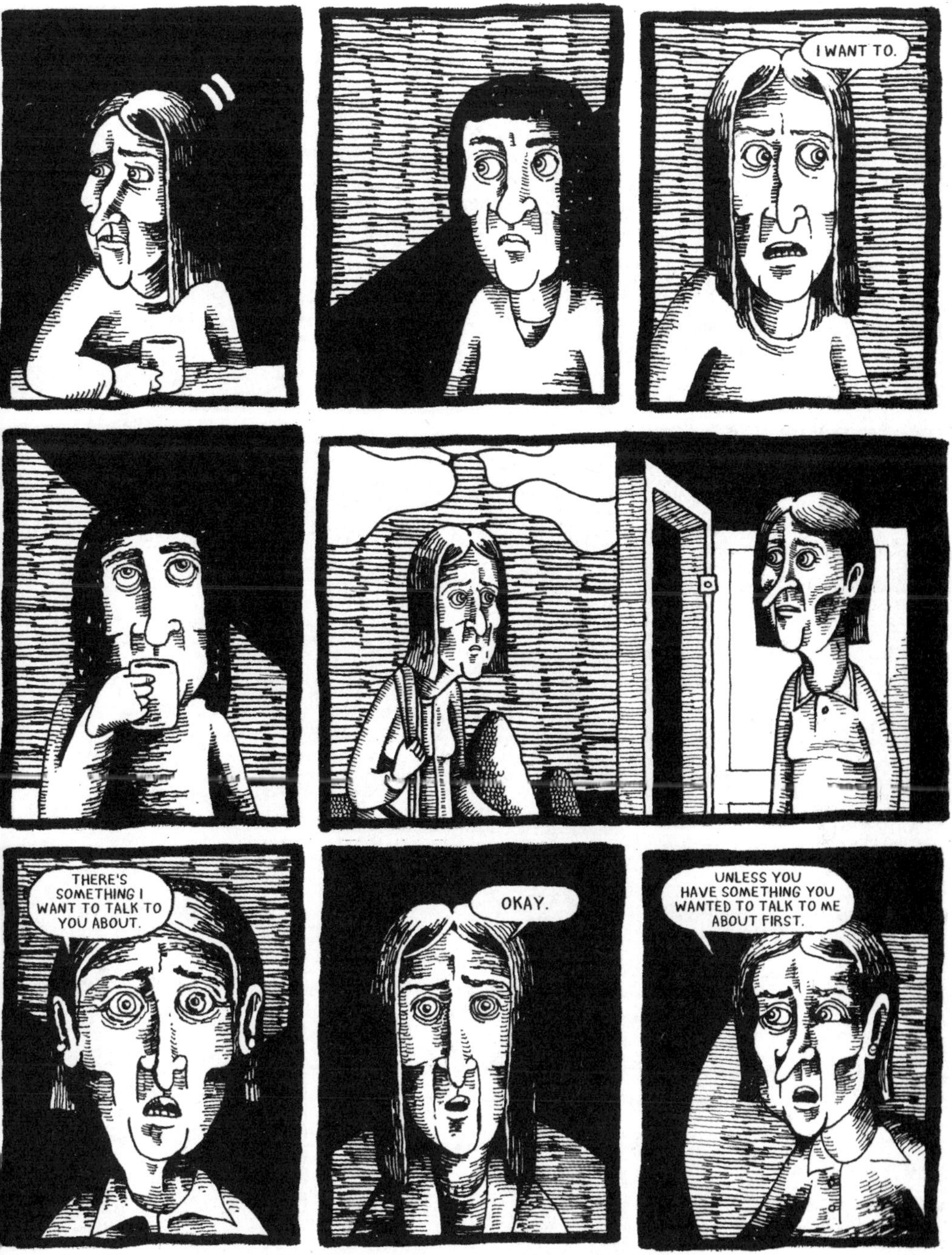
I WANT TO.
THERE'S SOMETHING I WANT TO TALK TO YOU ABOUT.
OKAY.
UNLESS YOU HAVE SOMETHING YOU WANTED TO TALK TO ME ABOUT FIRST.

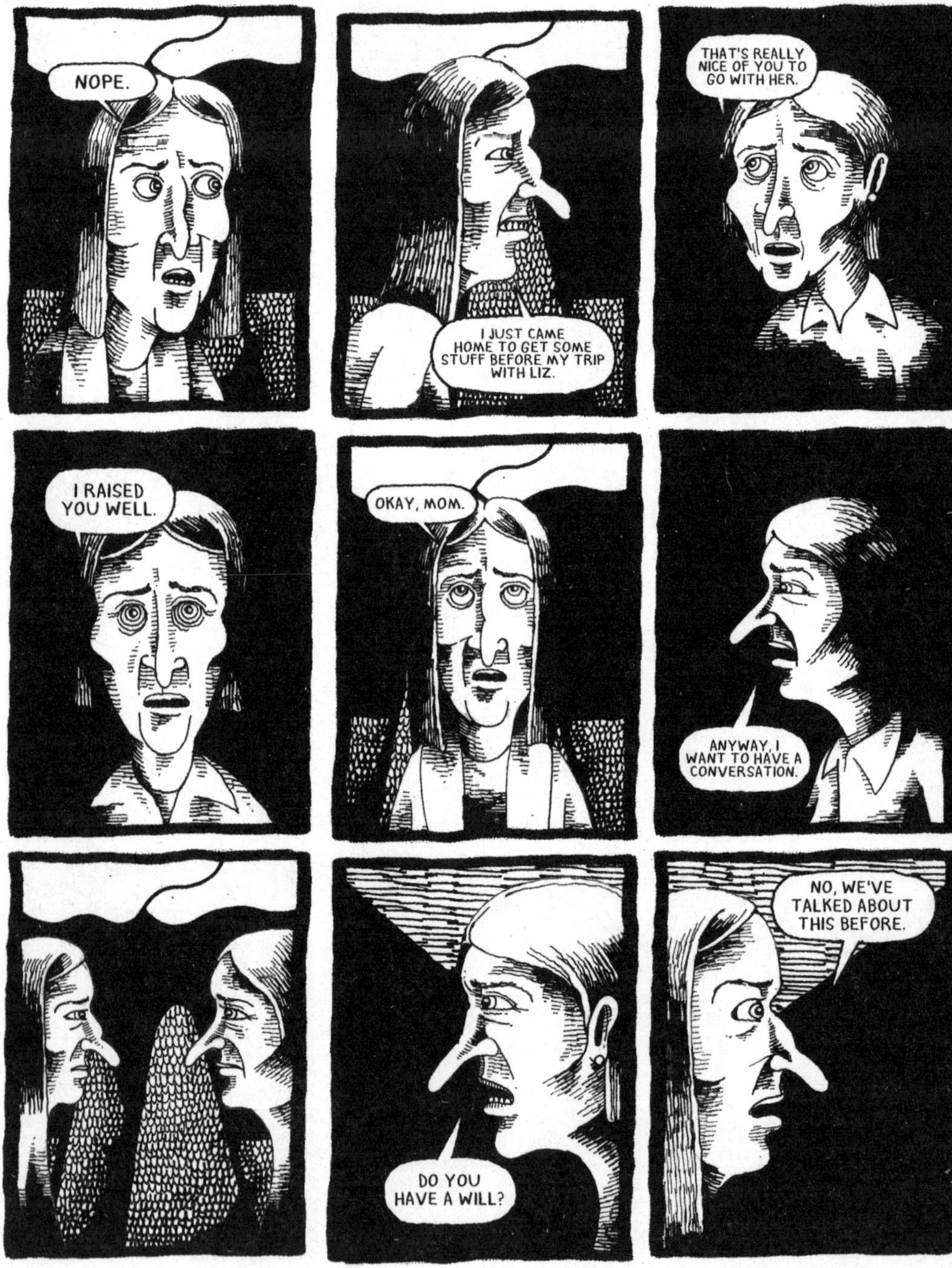
NOPE.
I JUST CAME HOME TO GET SOME STUFF BEFORE MY TRIP WITH LIZ.
THAT'S REALLY NICE OF YOU TO GO WITH HER.
I RAISED YOU WELL.
OKAY, MOM.
ANYWAY, I WANT TO HAVE A CONVERSATION.
DO YOU HAVE A WILL?
NO, WE'VE TALKED ABOUT THIS BEFORE.

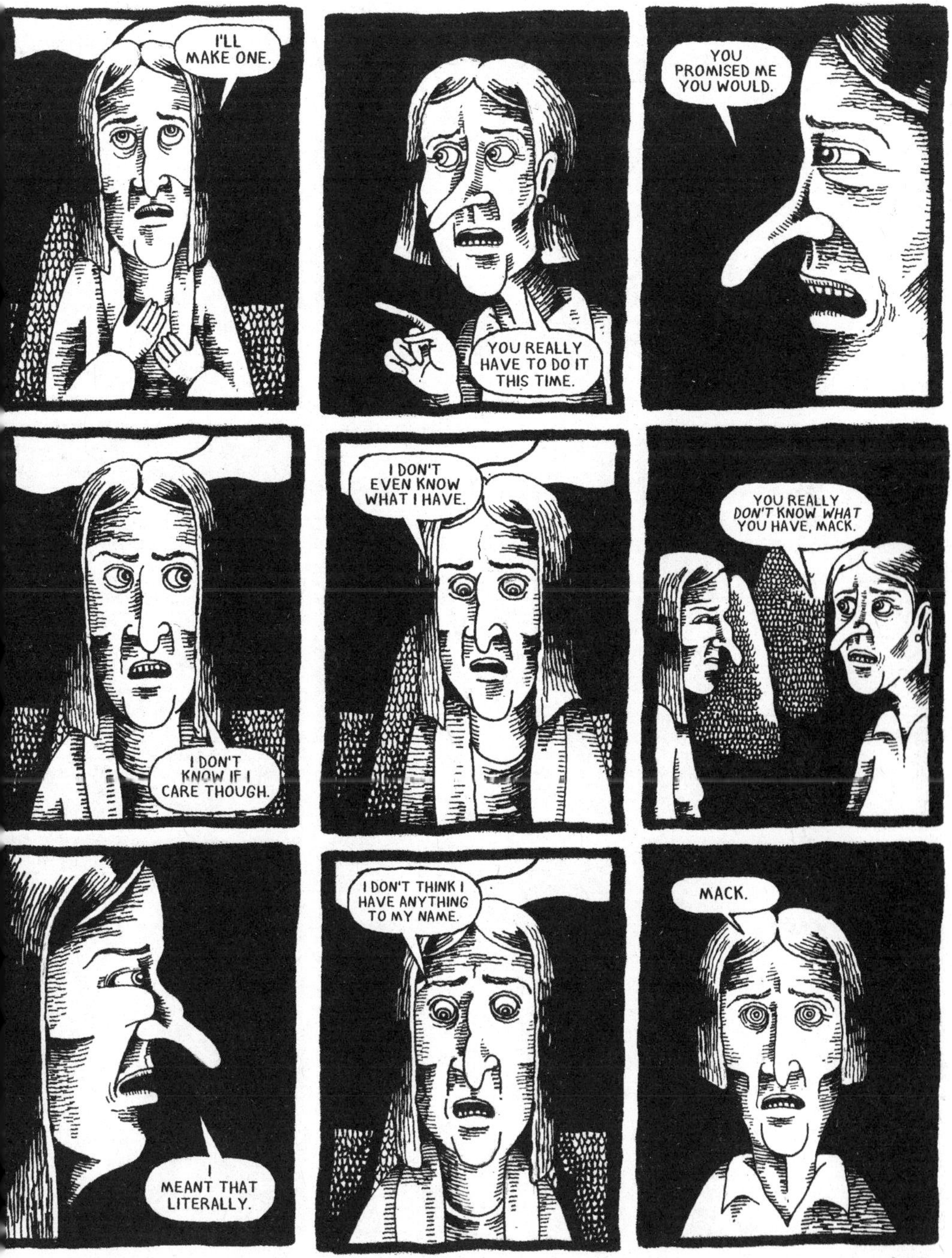
I'LL MAKE ONE.
YOU REALLY HAVE TO DO IT THIS TIME.
YOU PROMISED ME YOU WOULD.
I DON'T KNOW IF I CARE THOUGH.
I DON'T EVEN KNOW WHAT I HAVE.
YOU REALLY DON'T KNOW WHAT YOU HAVE, MACK.
I MEANT THAT LITERALLY.
I DON'T THINK I HAVE ANYTHING TO MY NAME.
MACK.

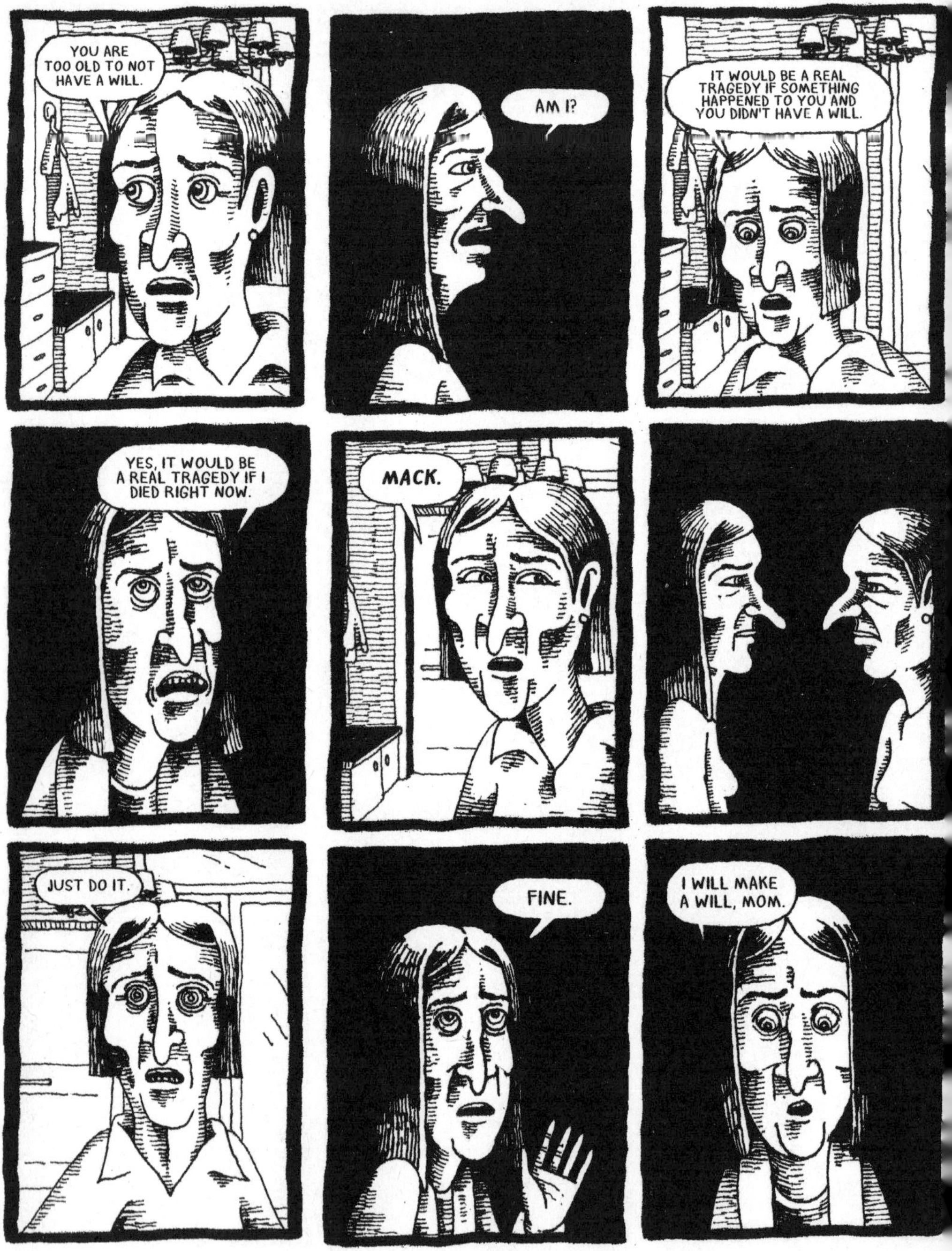
YOU ARE TOO OLD TO NOT HAVE A WILL.
AM I?
IT WOULD BE A REAL TRAGEDY IF SOMETHING HAPPENED TO YOU AND YOU DIDN'T HAVE A WILL.
YES, IT WOULD BE A REAL TRAGEDY IF I DIED RIGHT NOW.
MACK.
JUST DO IT.
FINE.
I WILL MAKE A WILL, MOM.

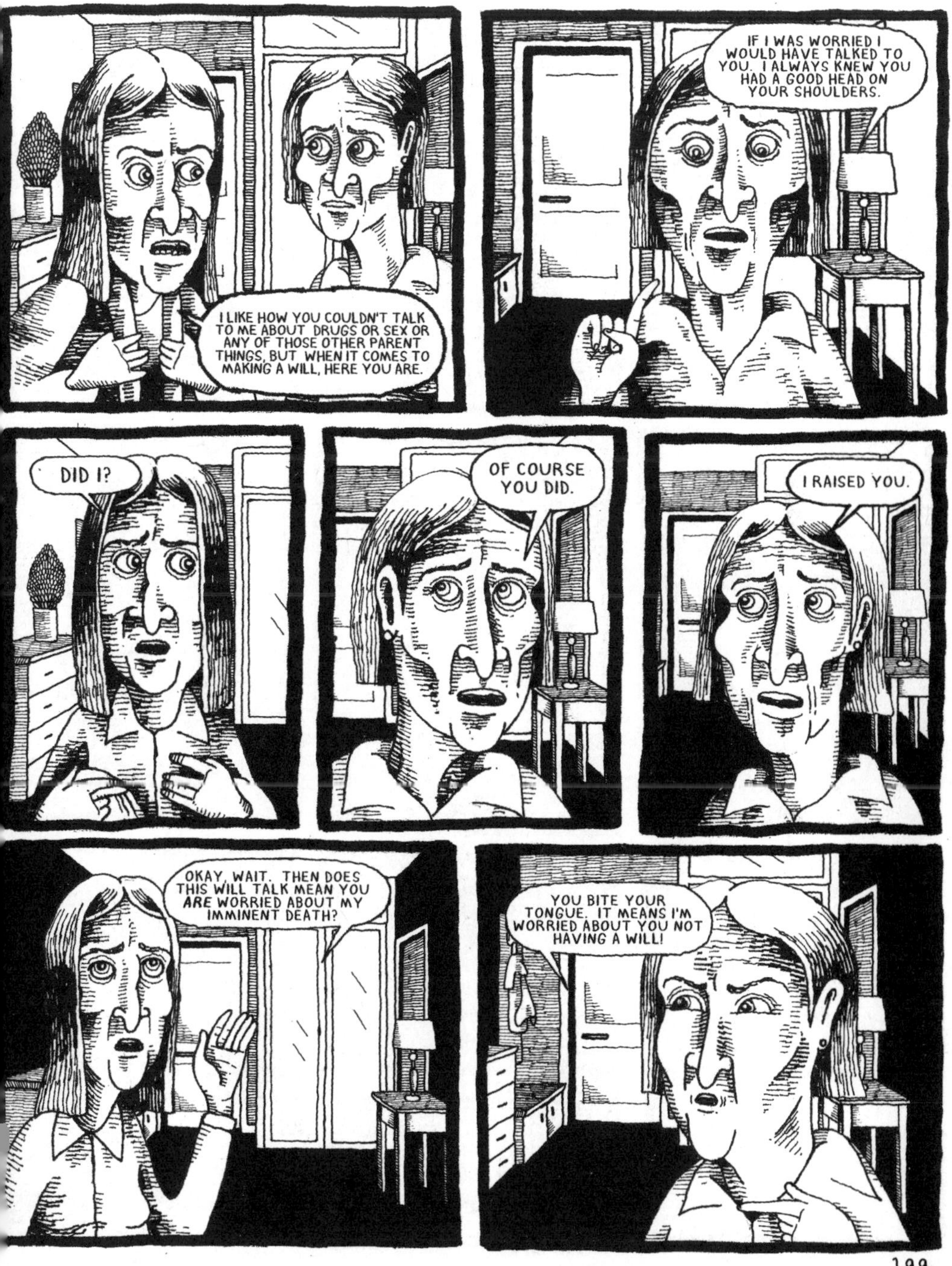
I LIKE HOW YOU COULDN'T TALK TO ME ABOUT DRUGS OR SEX OR ANY OF THOSE OTHER PARENT THINGS, BUT WHEN IT COMES TO MAKING A WILL, HERE YOU ARE.
IF I WAS WORRIED I WOULD HAVE TALKED TO YOU. I ALWAYS KNEW YOU HAD A GOOD HEAD ON YOUR SHOULDERS.
DID I?
OF COURSE YOU DID.
I RAISED YOU.
OKAY, WAIT. THEN DOES THIS WILL TALK MEAN YOU *ARE* WORRIED ABOUT MY IMMINENT DEATH?
YOU BITE YOUR TONGUE. IT MEANS I'M WORRIED ABOUT YOU NOT HAVING A WILL!

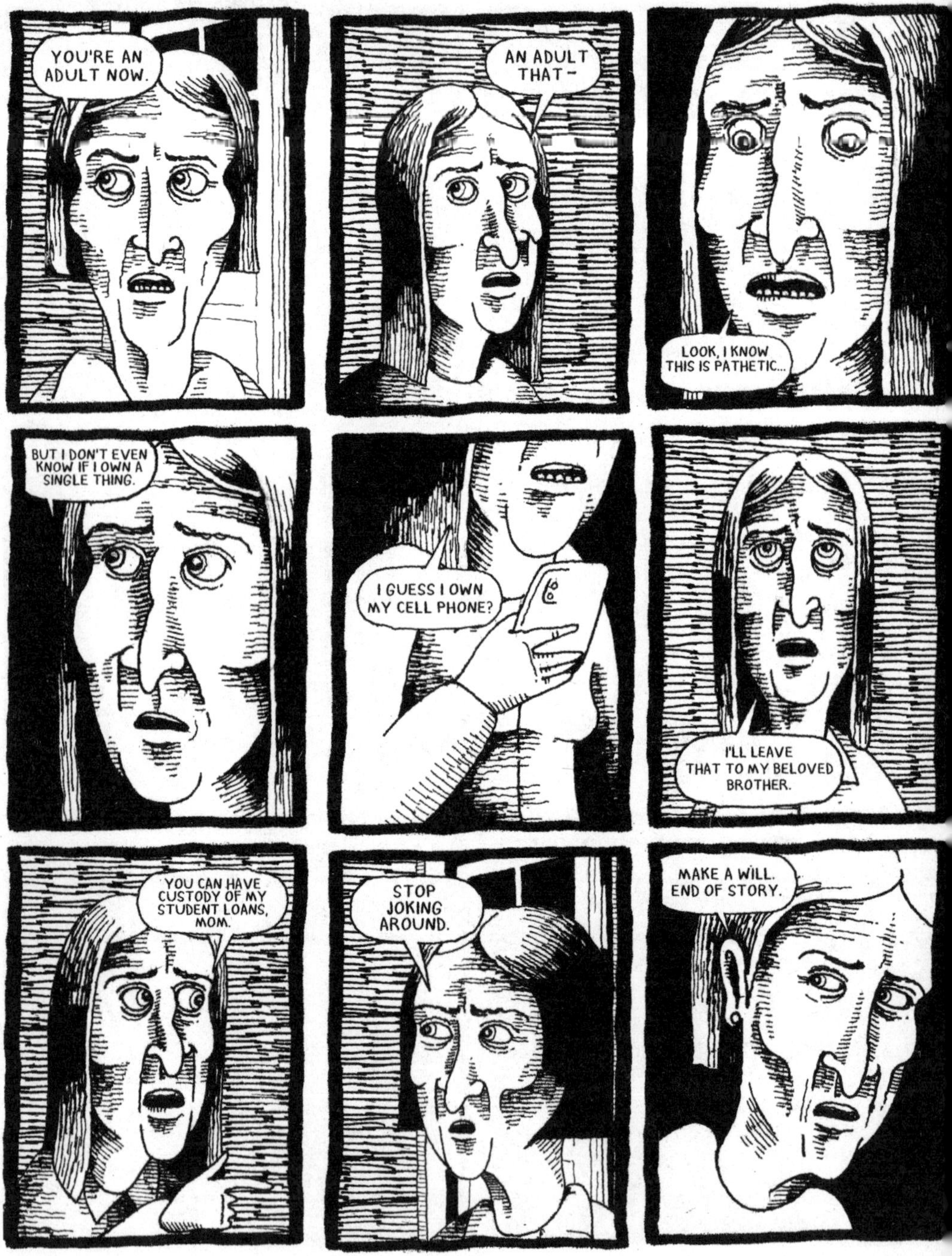
YOU'RE AN ADULT NOW.
AN ADULT THAT–
LOOK, I KNOW THIS IS PATHETIC...
BUT I DON'T EVEN KNOW IF I OWN A SINGLE THING.
I GUESS I OWN MY CELL PHONE?
I'LL LEAVE THAT TO MY BELOVED BROTHER.
YOU CAN HAVE CUSTODY OF MY STUDENT LOANS, MOM.
STOP JOKING AROUND.
MAKE A WILL. END OF STORY.

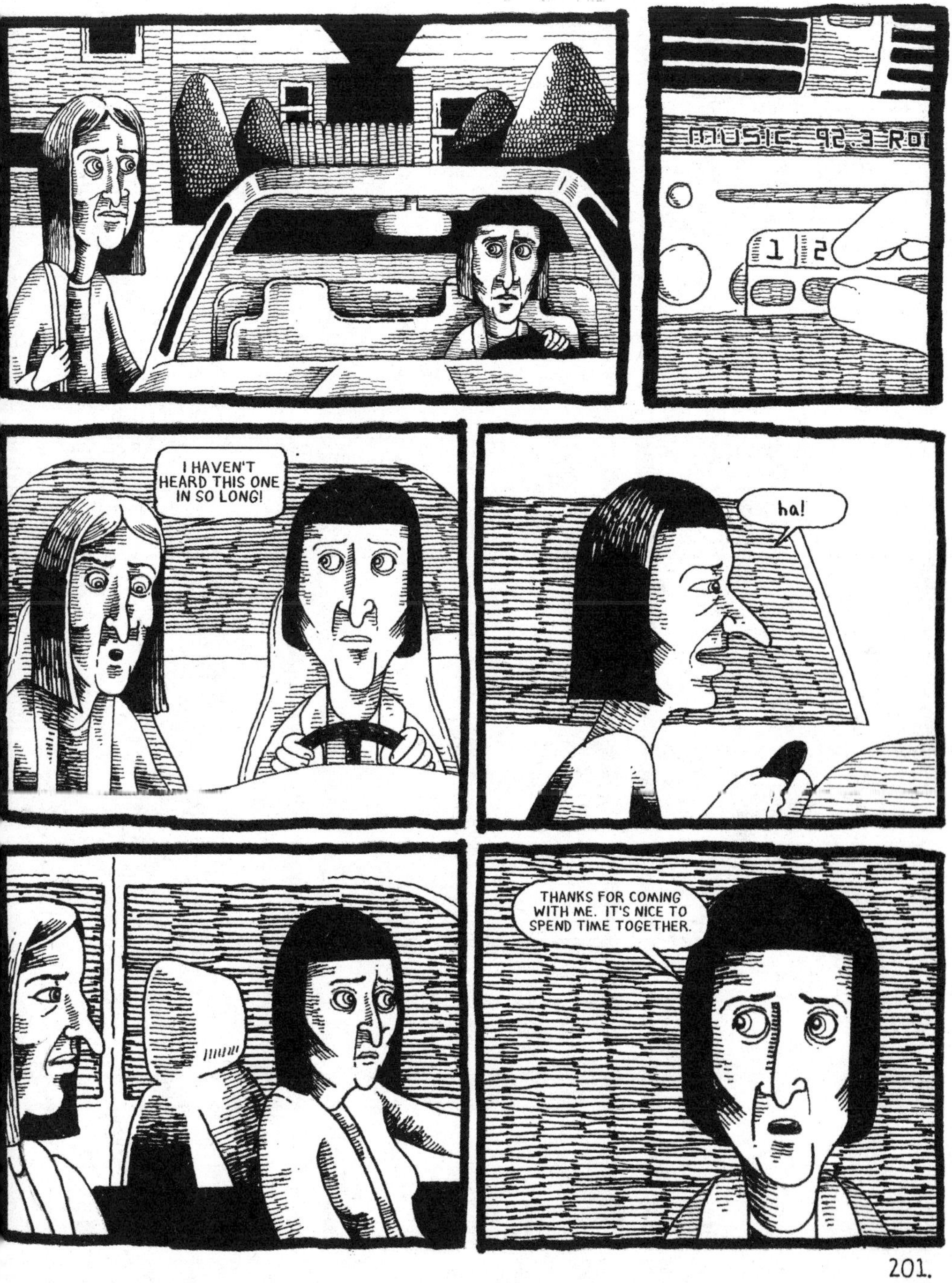
MUSIC 92.3 RO
1 2
I HAVEN'T HEARD THIS ONE IN SO LONG!
ha!
THANKS FOR COMING WITH ME. IT'S NICE TO SPEND TIME TOGETHER.

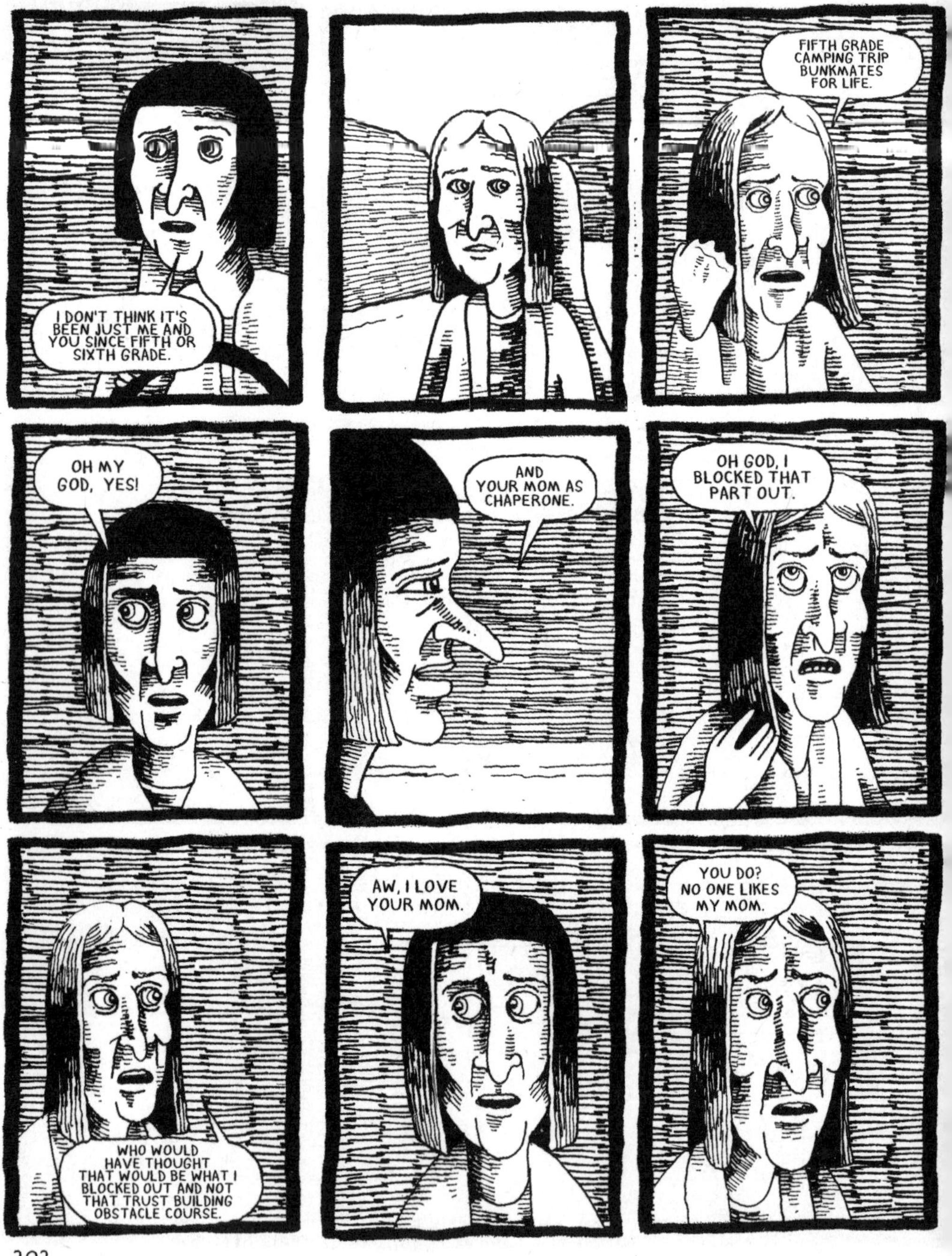
I DON'T THINK IT'S BEEN JUST ME AND YOU SINCE FIFTH OR SIXTH GRADE.
FIFTH GRADE CAMPING TRIP BUNKMATES FOR LIFE.
OH MY GOD, YES!
AND YOUR MOM AS CHAPERONE.
OH GOD, I BLOCKED THAT PART OUT.
WHO WOULD HAVE THOUGHT THAT WOULD BE WHAT I BLOCKED OUT AND NOT THAT TRUST BUILDING OBSTACLE COURSE.
AW, I LOVE YOUR MOM.
YOU DO? NO ONE LIKES MY MOM.

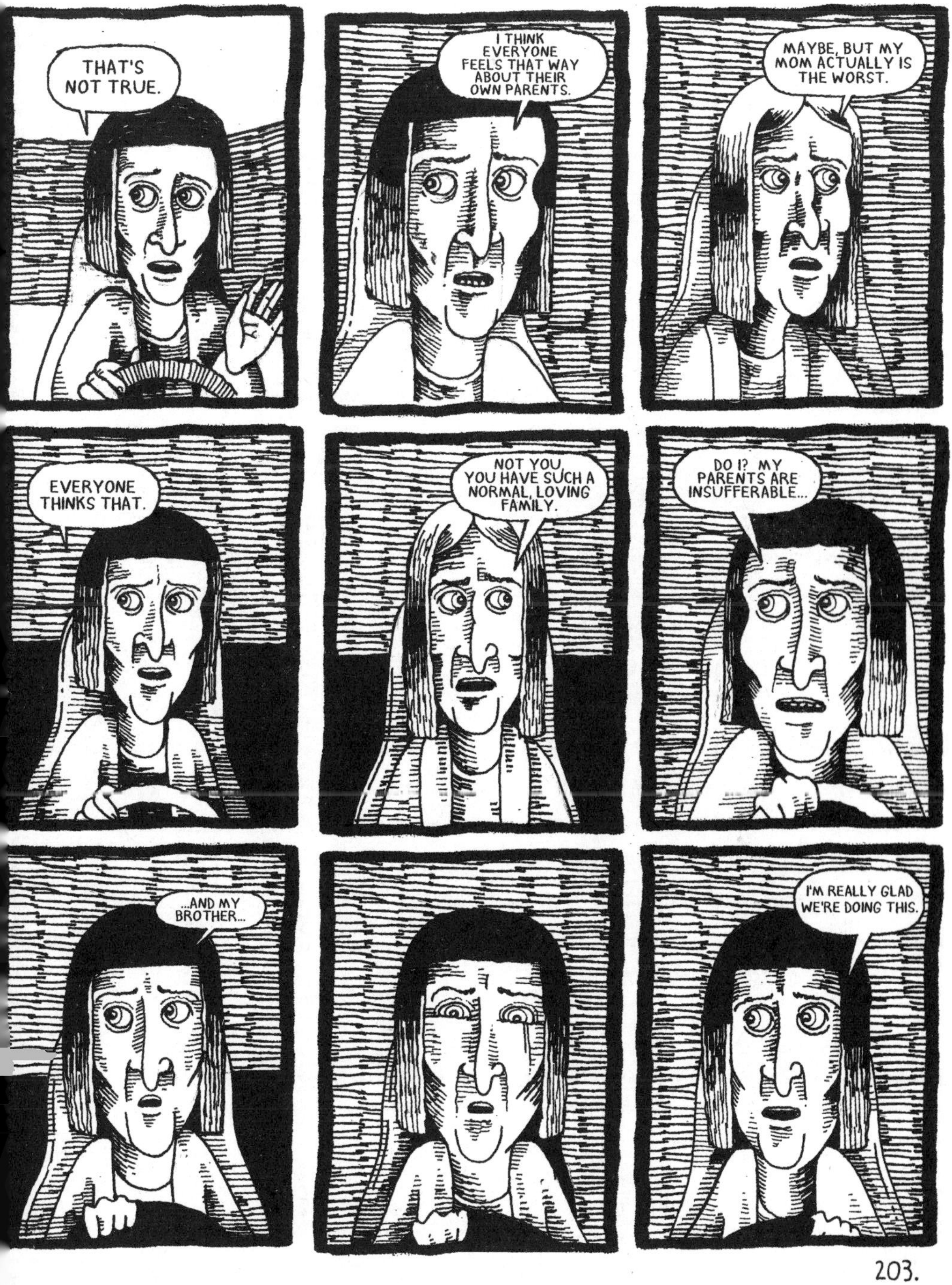
THAT'S NOT TRUE.
I THINK EVERYONE FEELS THAT WAY ABOUT THEIR OWN PARENTS.
MAYBE, BUT MY MOM ACTUALLY IS THE WORST.
EVERYONE THINKS THAT.
NOT YOU. YOU HAVE SUCH A NORMAL, LOVING FAMILY.
DO I? MY PARENTS ARE INSUFFERABLE...
...AND MY BROTHER...
I'M REALLY GLAD WE'RE DOING THIS.

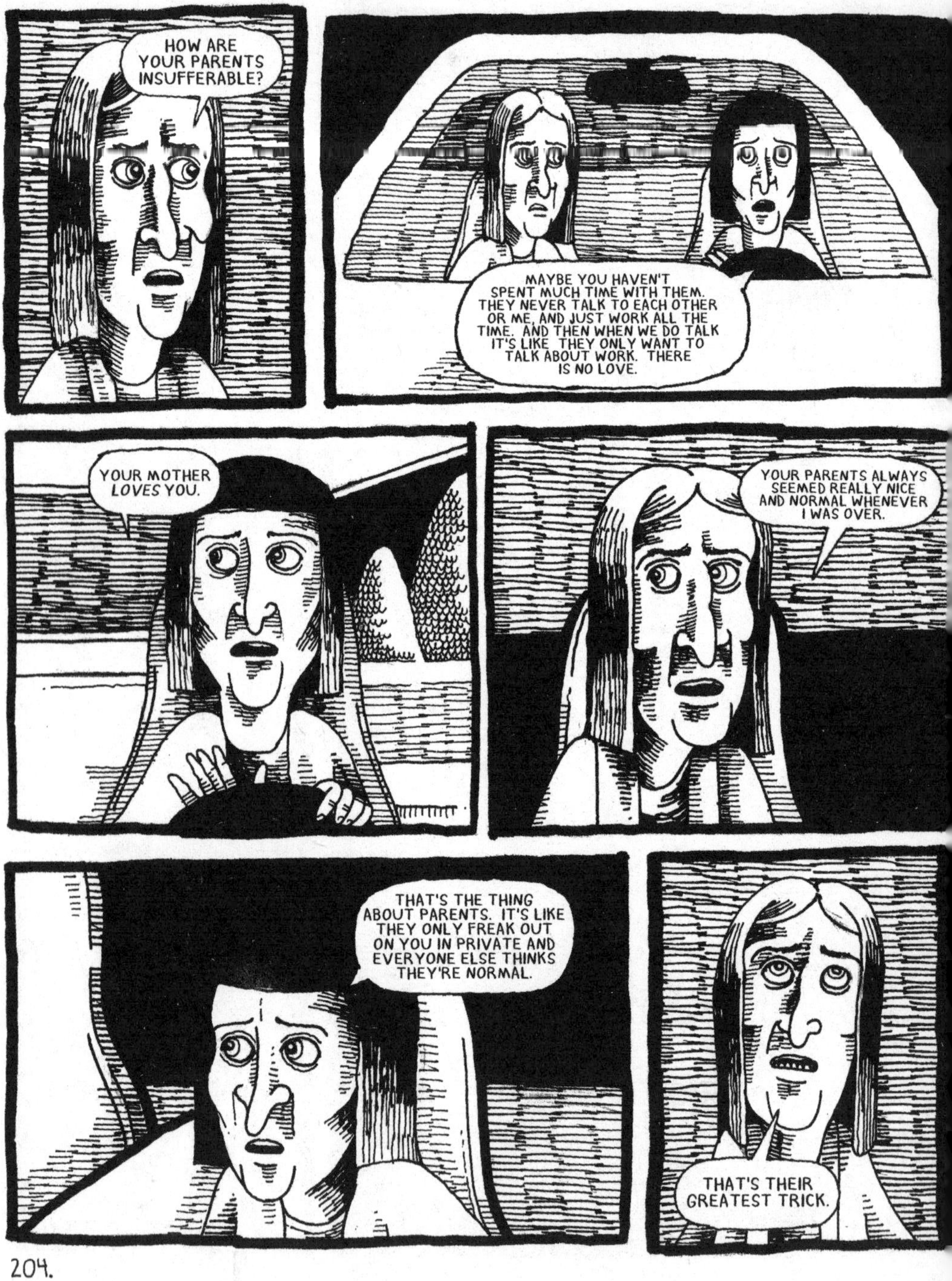
HOW ARE YOUR PARENTS INSUFFERABLE?
MAYBE YOU HAVEN'T SPENT MUCH TIME WITH THEM. THEY NEVER TALK TO EACH OTHER OR ME, AND JUST WORK ALL THE TIME. AND THEN WHEN WE DO TALK IT'S LIKE THEY ONLY WANT TO TALK ABOUT WORK. THERE IS NO LOVE.
YOUR MOTHER *LOVES* YOU.
YOUR PARENTS ALWAYS SEEMED REALLY NICE AND NORMAL WHENEVER I WAS OVER.
THAT'S THE THING ABOUT PARENTS. IT'S LIKE THEY ONLY FREAK OUT ON YOU IN PRIVATE AND EVERYONE ELSE THINKS THEY'RE NORMAL.
THAT'S THEIR GREATEST TRICK.

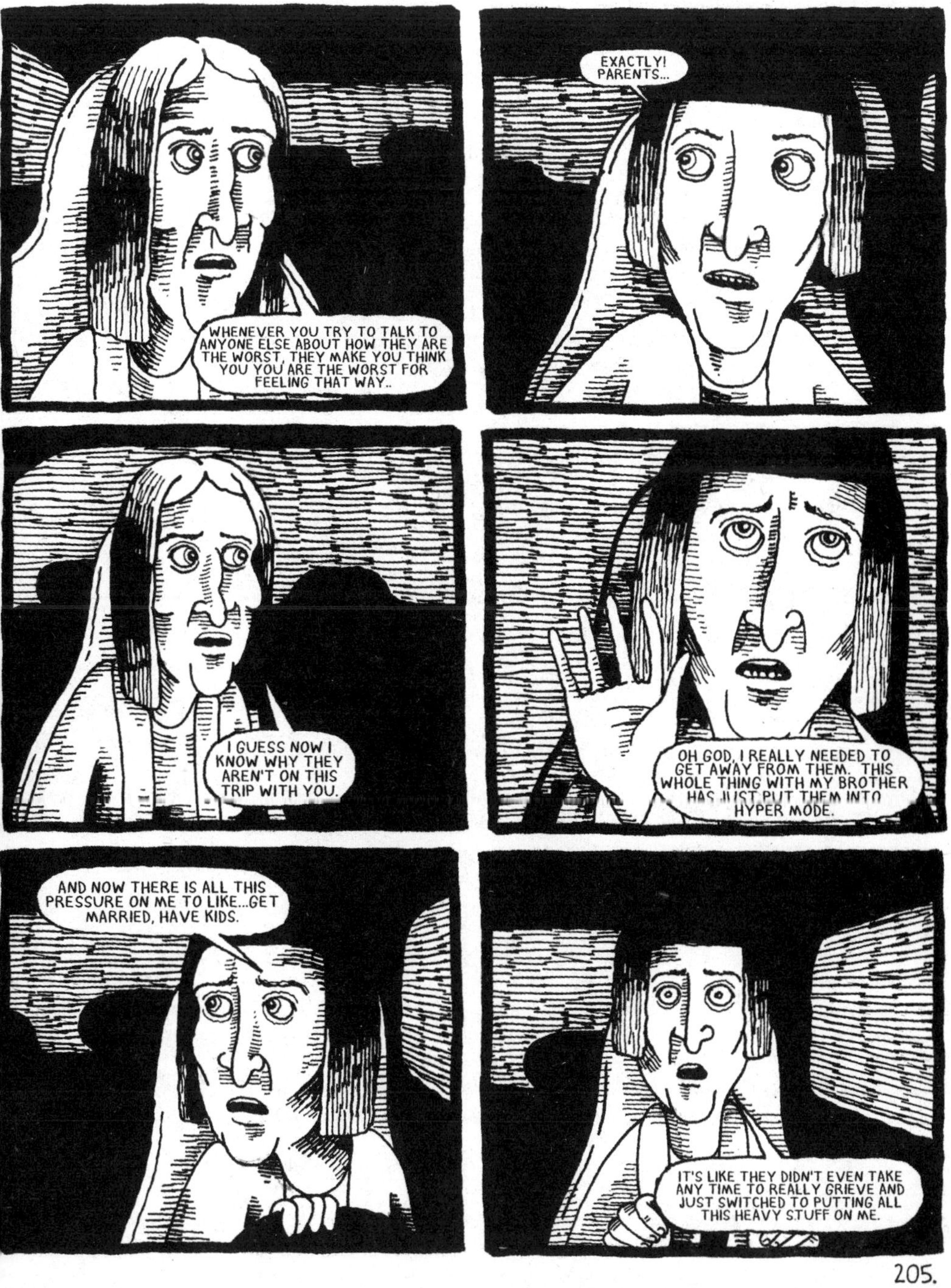
WHENEVER YOU TRY TO TALK TO ANYONE ELSE ABOUT HOW THEY ARE THE WORST, THEY MAKE YOU THINK YOU YOU ARE THE WORST FOR FEELING THAT WAY..
EXACTLY! PARENTS...
I GUESS NOW I KNOW WHY THEY AREN'T ON THIS TRIP WITH YOU.
OH GOD, I REALLY NEEDED TO GET AWAY FROM THEM. THIS WHOLE THING WITH MY BROTHER HAS JUST PUT THEM INTO HYPER MODE.
AND NOW THERE IS ALL THIS PRESSURE ON ME TO LIKE...GET MARRIED, HAVE KIDS.
IT'S LIKE THEY DIDN'T EVEN TAKE ANY TIME TO REALLY GRIEVE AND JUST SWITCHED TO PUTTING ALL THIS HEAVY STUFF ON ME.

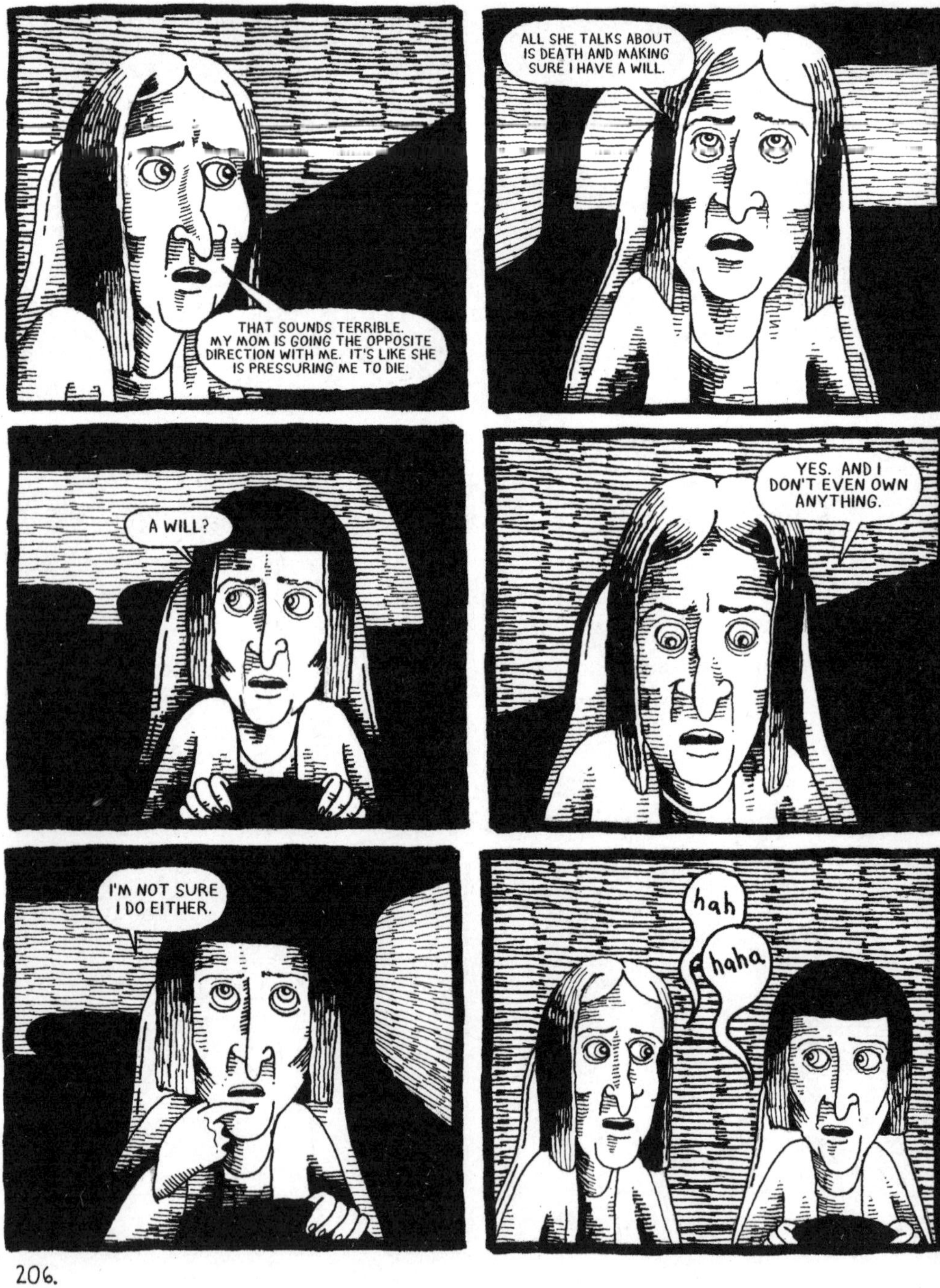
THAT SOUNDS TERRIBLE. MY MOM IS GOING THE OPPOSITE DIRECTION WITH ME. IT'S LIKE SHE IS PRESSURING ME TO DIE.
ALL SHE TALKS ABOUT IS DEATH AND MAKING SURE I HAVE A WILL.
A WILL?
YES. AND I DON'T EVEN OWN ANYTHING.
I'M NOT SURE I DO EITHER.
hah
haha

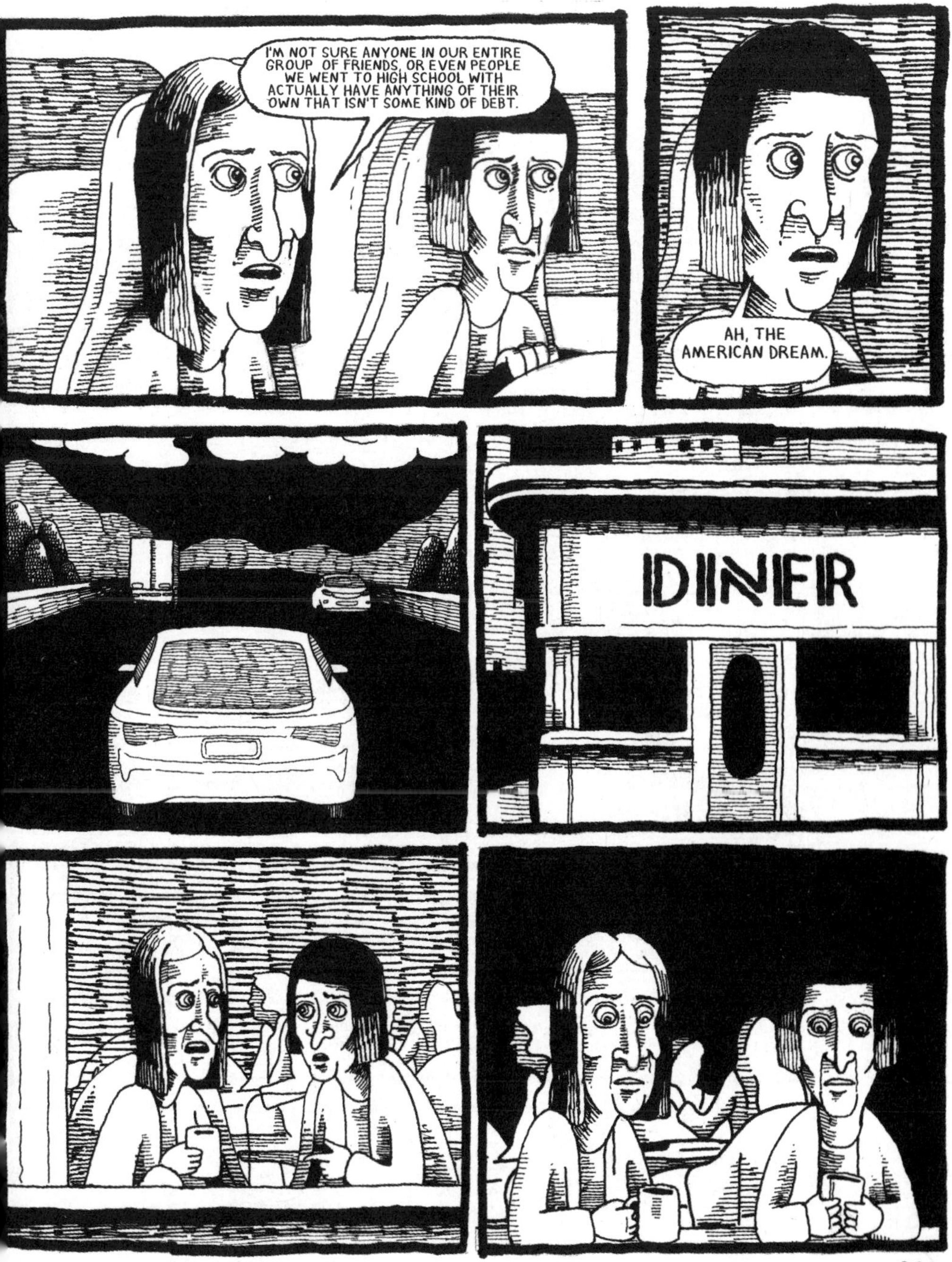
I'M NOT SURE ANYONE IN OUR ENTIRE GROUP OF FRIENDS, OR EVEN PEOPLE WE WENT TO HIGH SCHOOL WITH ACTUALLY HAVE ANYTHING OF THEIR OWN THAT ISN'T SOME KIND OF DEBT.
AH, THE AMERICAN DREAM.
DINER

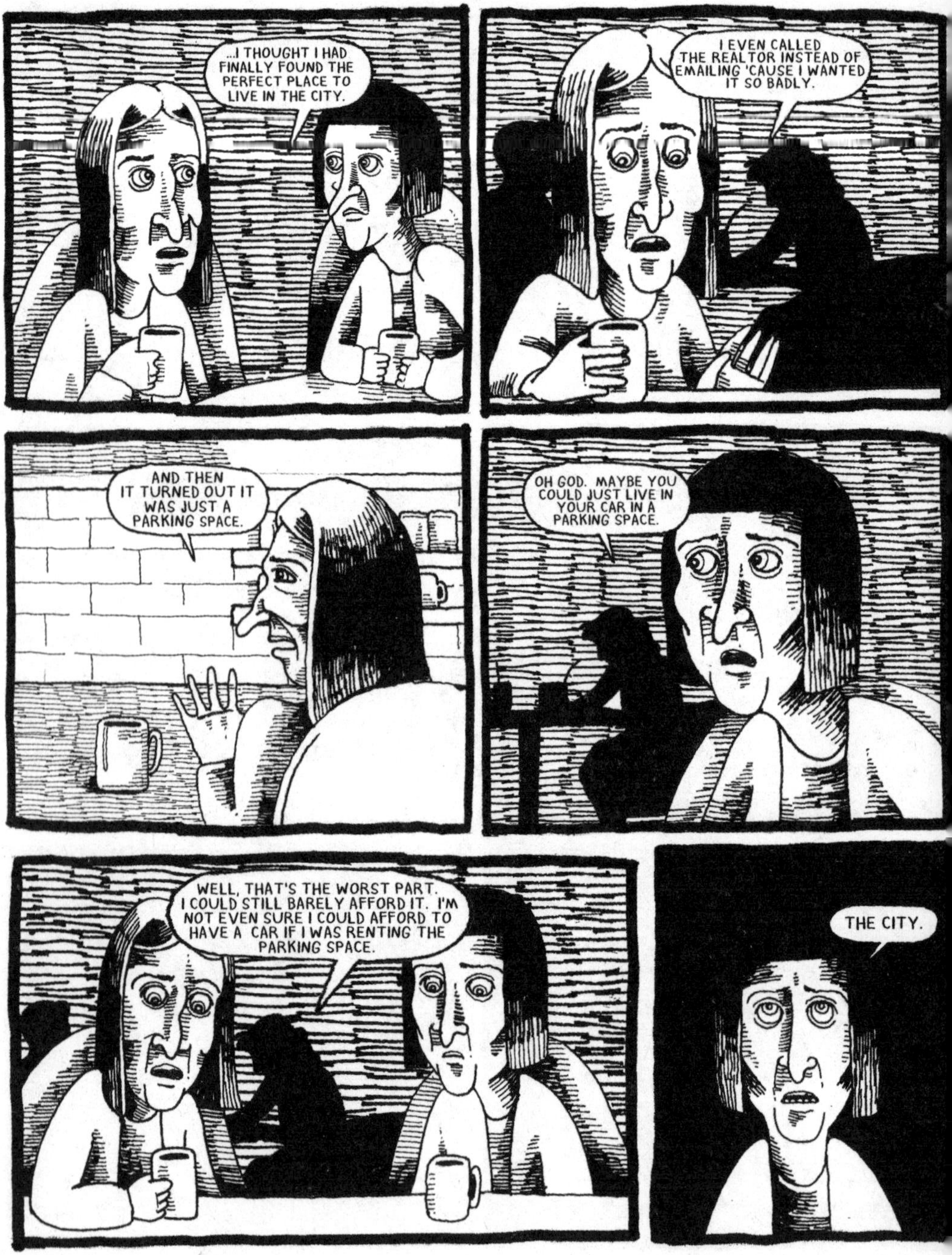
...I THOUGHT I HAD FINALLY FOUND THE PERFECT PLACE TO LIVE IN THE CITY.
I EVEN CALLED THE REALTOR INSTEAD OF EMAILING 'CAUSE I WANTED IT SO BADLY.
AND THEN IT TURNED OUT IT WAS JUST A PARKING SPACE.
OH GOD. MAYBE YOU COULD JUST LIVE IN YOUR CAR IN A PARKING SPACE.
WELL, THAT'S THE WORST PART. I COULD STILL BARELY AFFORD IT. I'M NOT EVEN SURE I COULD AFFORD TO HAVE A CAR IF I WAS RENTING THE PARKING SPACE.
THE CITY.

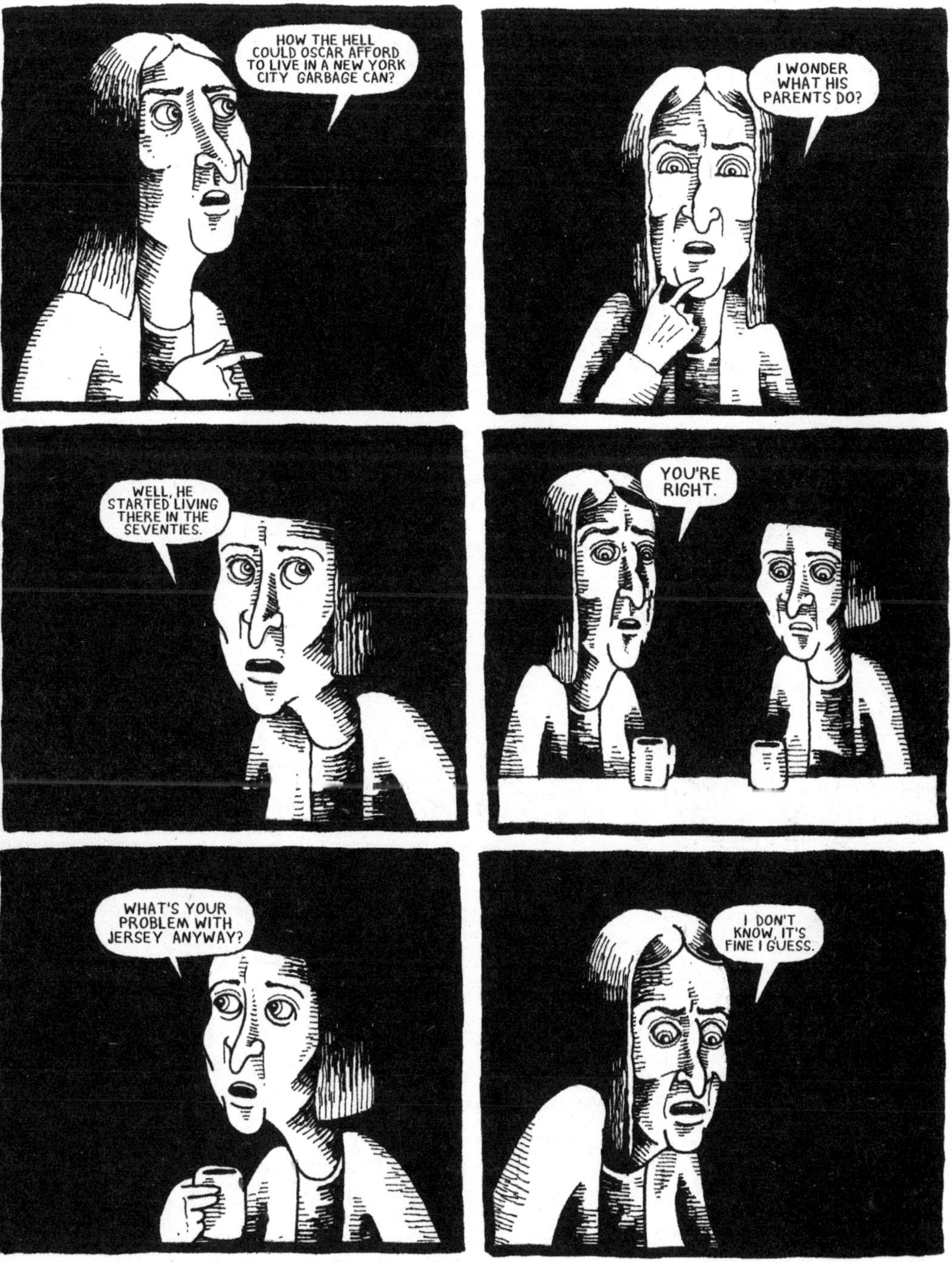
HOW THE HELL COULD OSCAR AFFORD TO LIVE IN A NEW YORK CITY GARBAGE CAN?
I WONDER WHAT HIS PARENTS DO?
WELL, HE STARTED LIVING THERE IN THE SEVENTIES.
YOU'RE RIGHT.
WHAT'S YOUR PROBLEM WITH JERSEY ANYWAY?
I DON'T KNOW, IT'S FINE I GUESS.

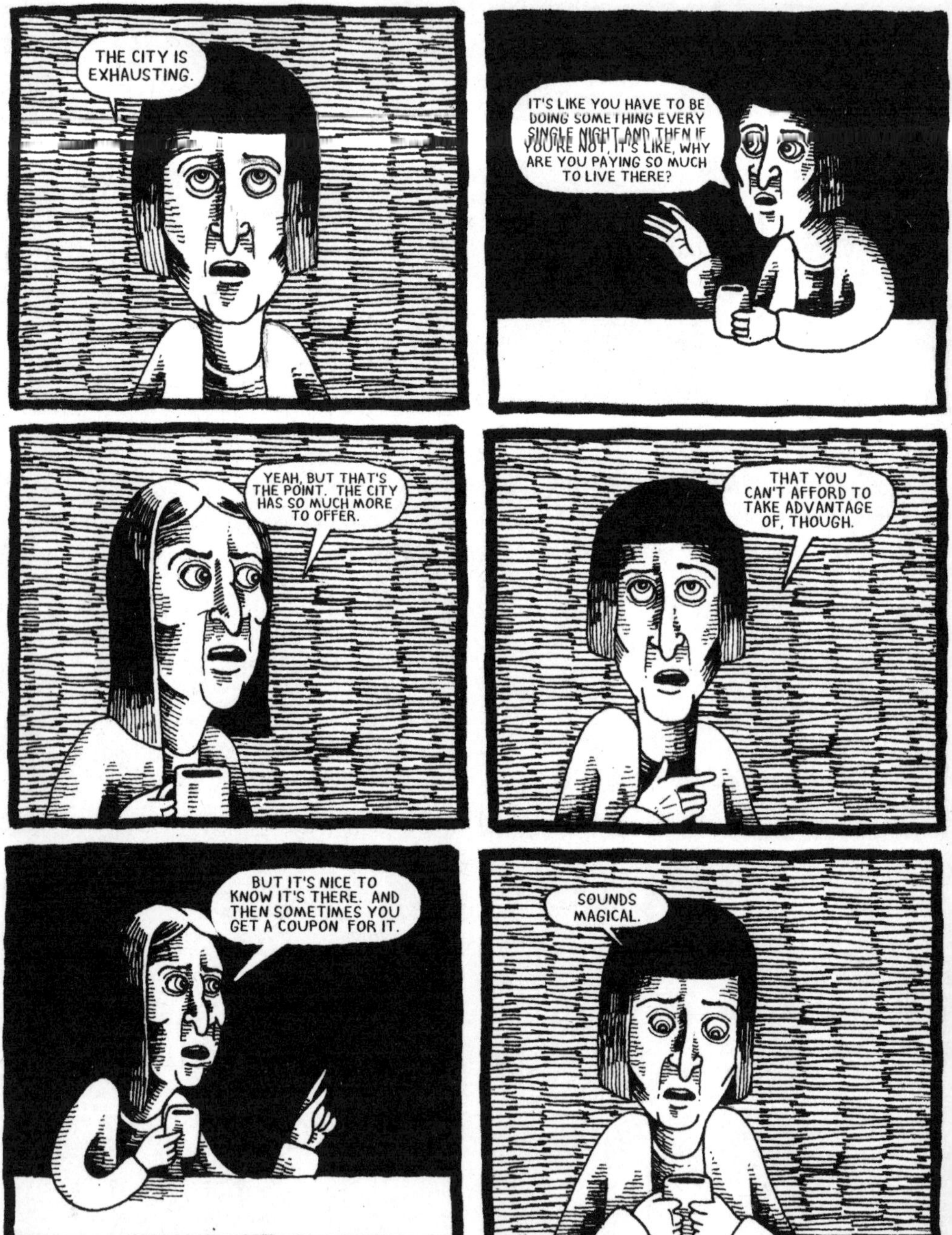
THE CITY IS EXHAUSTING.
IT'S LIKE YOU HAVE TO BE DOING SOMETHING EVERY SINGLE NIGHT AND THEN IF YOU'RE NOT, IT'S LIKE, WHY ARE YOU PAYING SO MUCH TO LIVE THERE?
YEAH, BUT THAT'S THE POINT. THE CITY HAS SO MUCH MORE TO OFFER.
THAT YOU CAN'T AFFORD TO TAKE ADVANTAGE OF, THOUGH.
BUT IT'S NICE TO KNOW IT'S THERE. AND THEN SOMETIMES YOU GET A COUPON FOR IT.
SOUNDS MAGICAL.

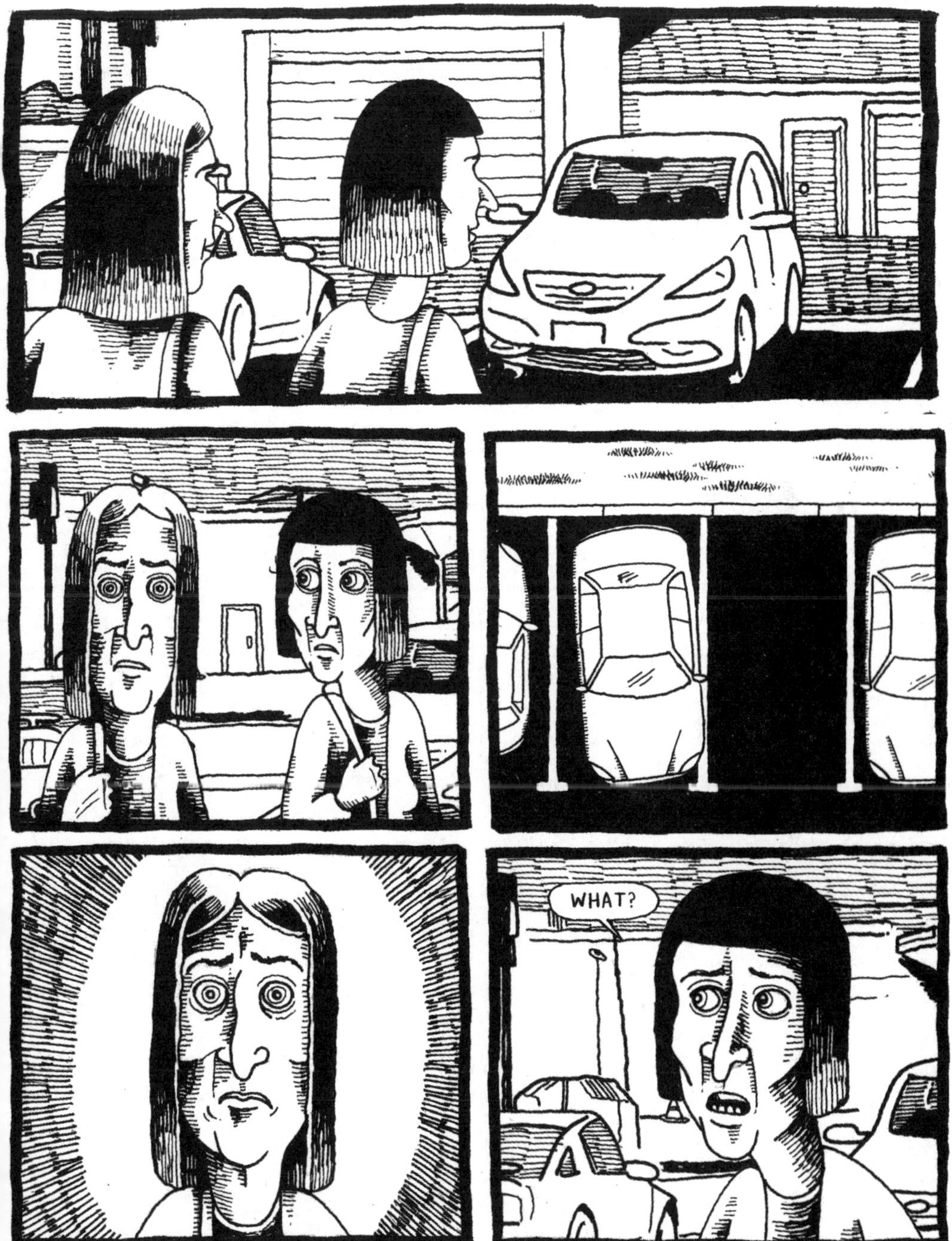
WHAT?

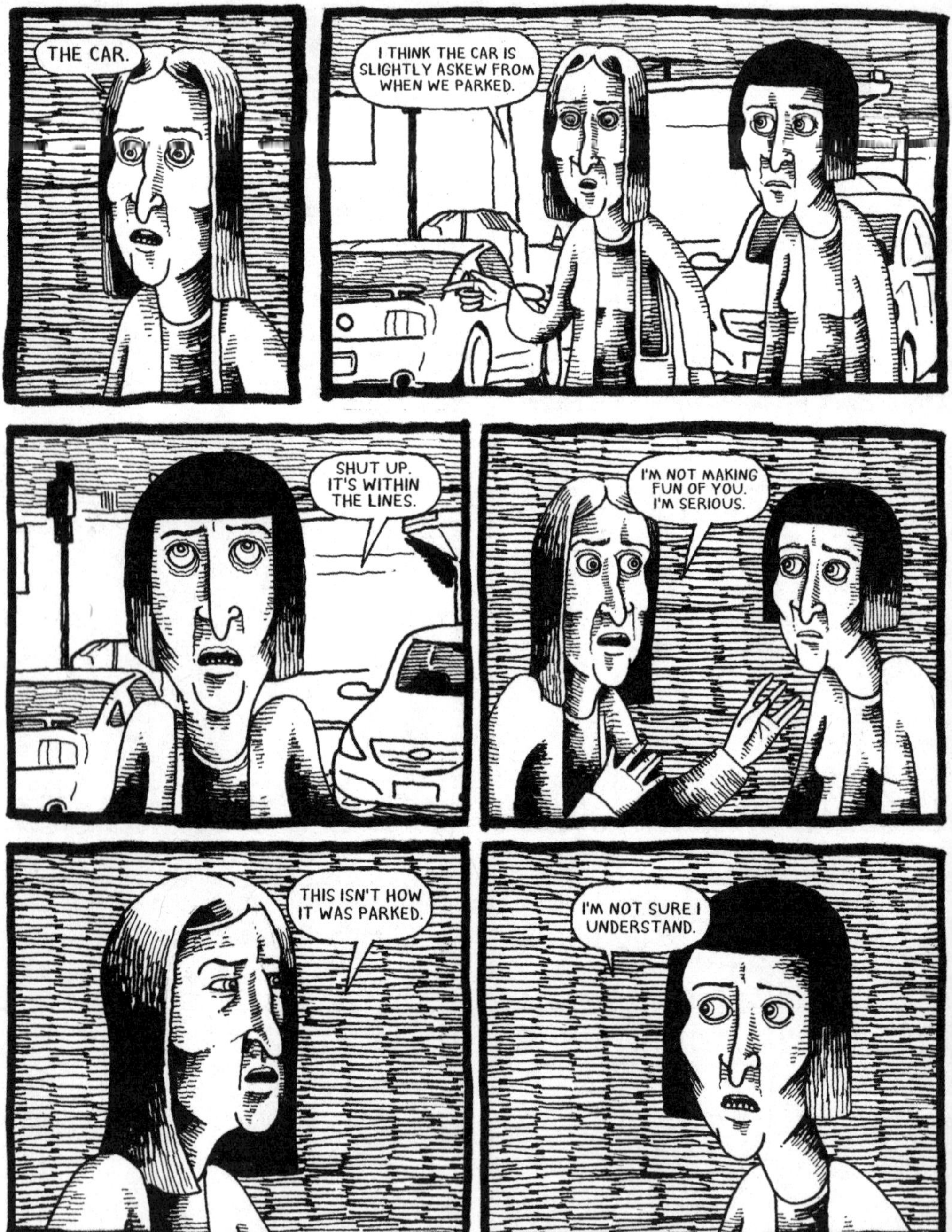
THE CAR.
I THINK THE CAR IS SLIGHTLY ASKEW FROM WHEN WE PARKED.
SHUT UP. IT'S WITHIN THE LINES.
I'M NOT MAKING FUN OF YOU. I'M SERIOUS.
THIS ISN'T HOW IT WAS PARKED.
I'M NOT SURE I UNDERSTAND.

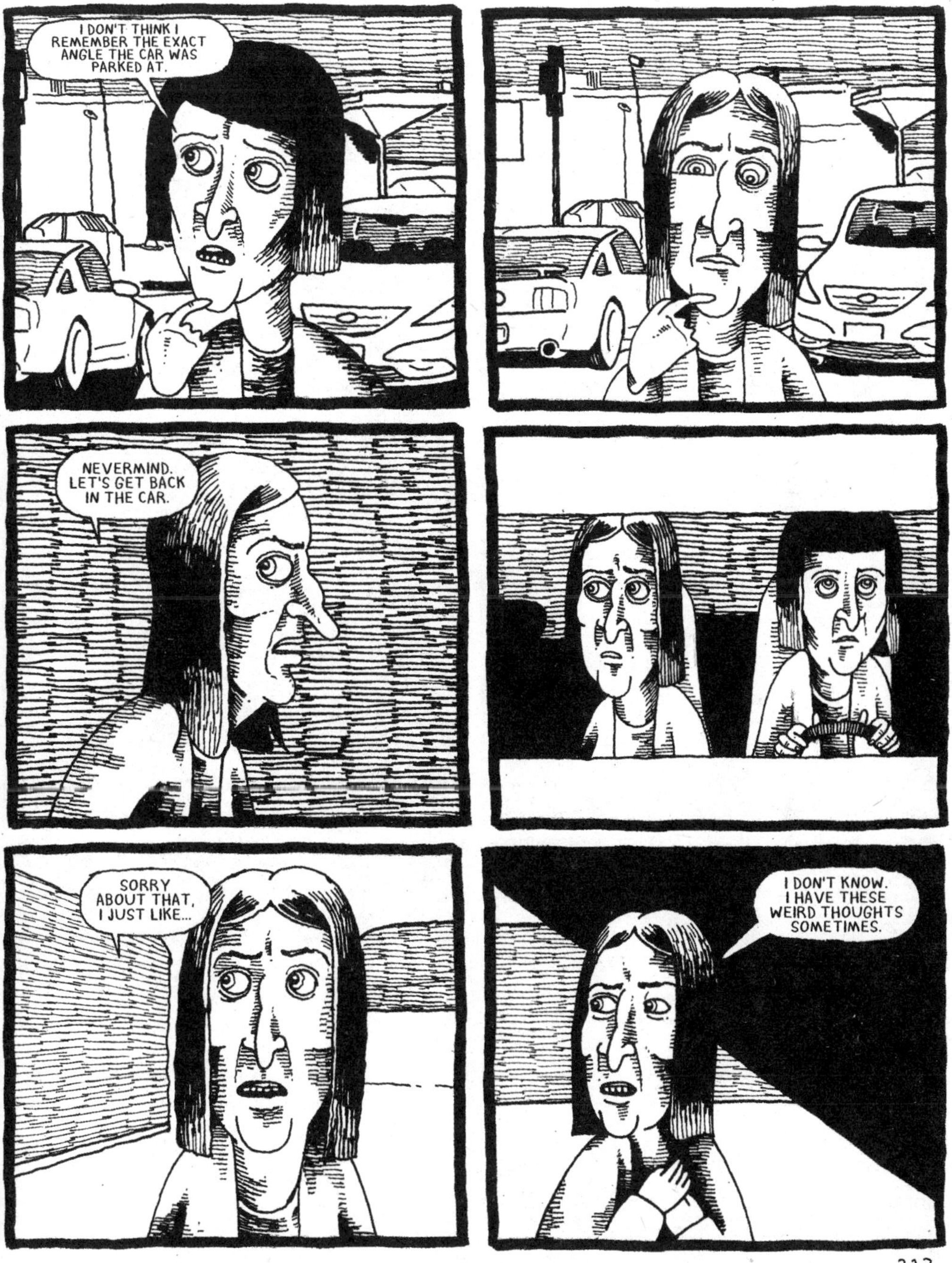
I DON'T THINK I REMEMBER THE EXACT ANGLE THE CAR WAS PARKED AT.
NEVERMIND. LET'S GET BACK IN THE CAR.
SORRY ABOUT THAT, I JUST LIKE...
I DON'T KNOW. I HAVE THESE WEIRD THOUGHTS SOMETIMES.

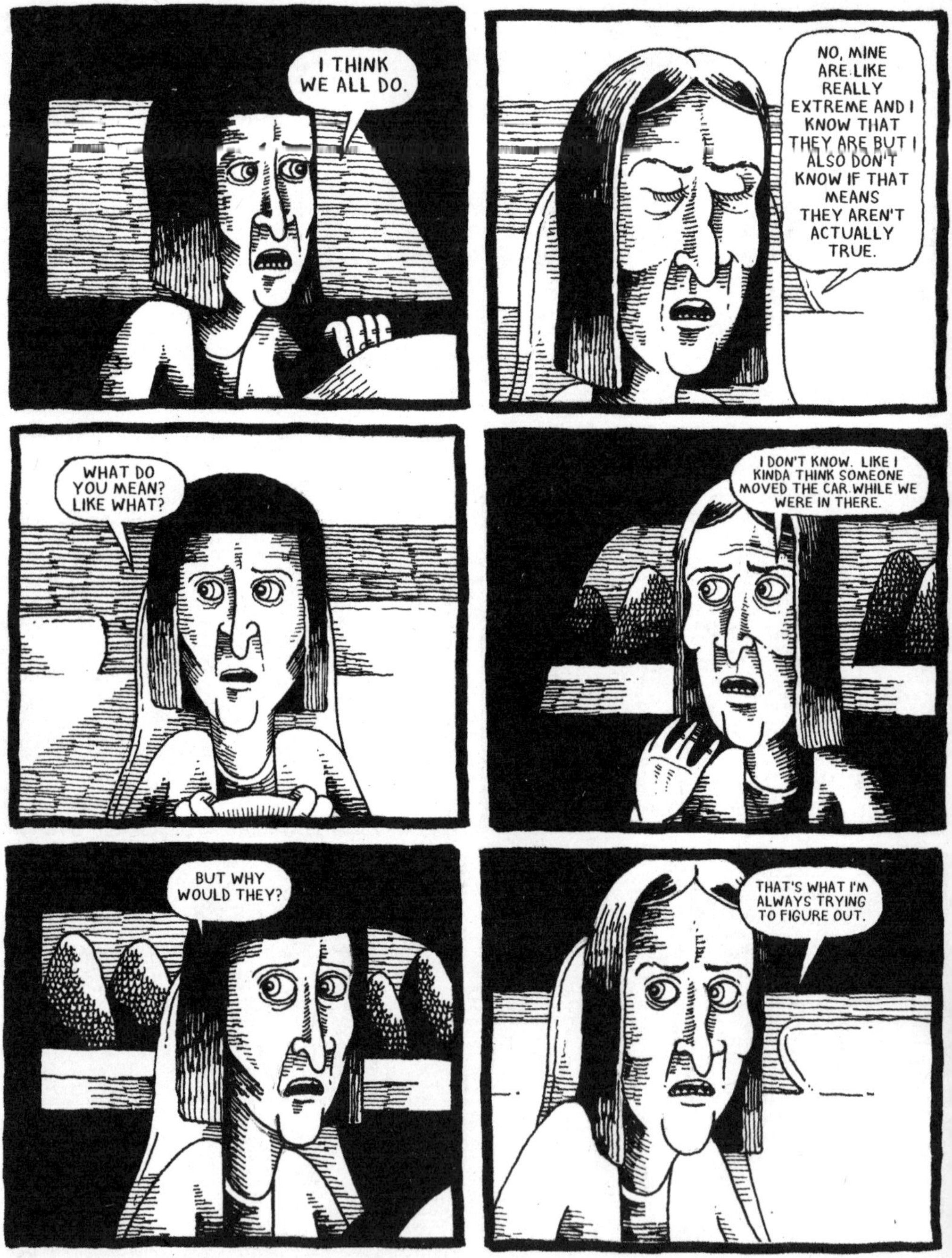
I THINK WE ALL DO.
NO, MINE ARE LIKE REALLY EXTREME AND I KNOW THAT THEY ARE BUT I ALSO DON'T KNOW IF THAT MEANS THEY AREN'T ACTUALLY TRUE.
WHAT DO YOU MEAN? LIKE WHAT?
I DON'T KNOW. LIKE I KINDA THINK SOMEONE MOVED THE CAR WHILE WE WERE IN THERE.
BUT WHY WOULD THEY?
THAT'S WHAT I'M ALWAYS TRYING TO FIGURE OUT.

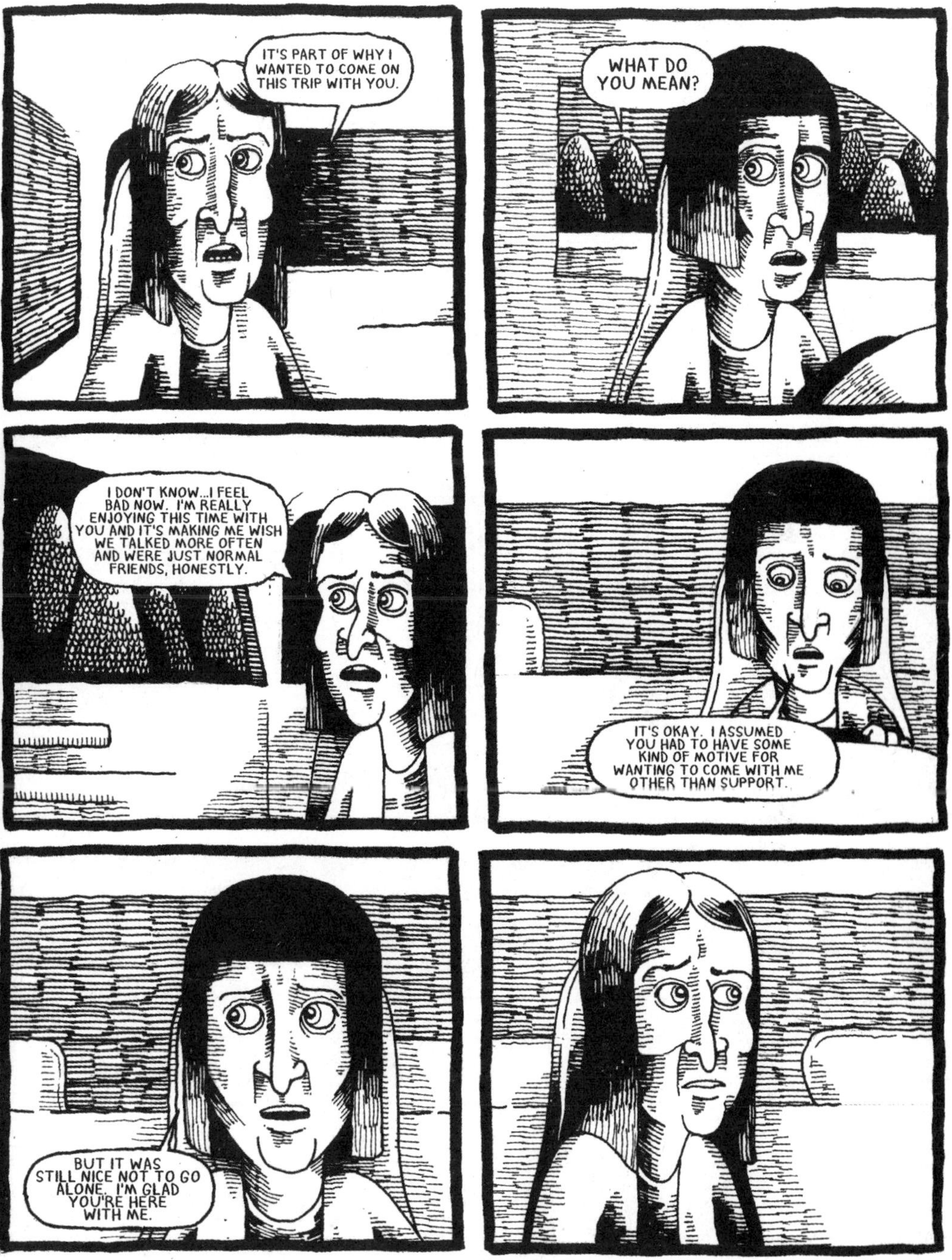
IT'S PART OF WHY I WANTED TO COME ON THIS TRIP WITH YOU.
WHAT DO YOU MEAN?
I DON'T KNOW...I FEEL BAD NOW. I'M REALLY ENJOYING THIS TIME WITH YOU AND IT'S MAKING ME WISH WE TALKED MORE OFTEN AND WERE JUST NORMAL FRIENDS, HONESTLY.
IT'S OKAY. I ASSUMED YOU HAD TO HAVE SOME KIND OF MOTIVE FOR WANTING TO COME WITH ME OTHER THAN SUPPORT.
BUT IT WAS STILL NICE NOT TO GO ALONE. I'M GLAD YOU'RE HERE WITH ME.

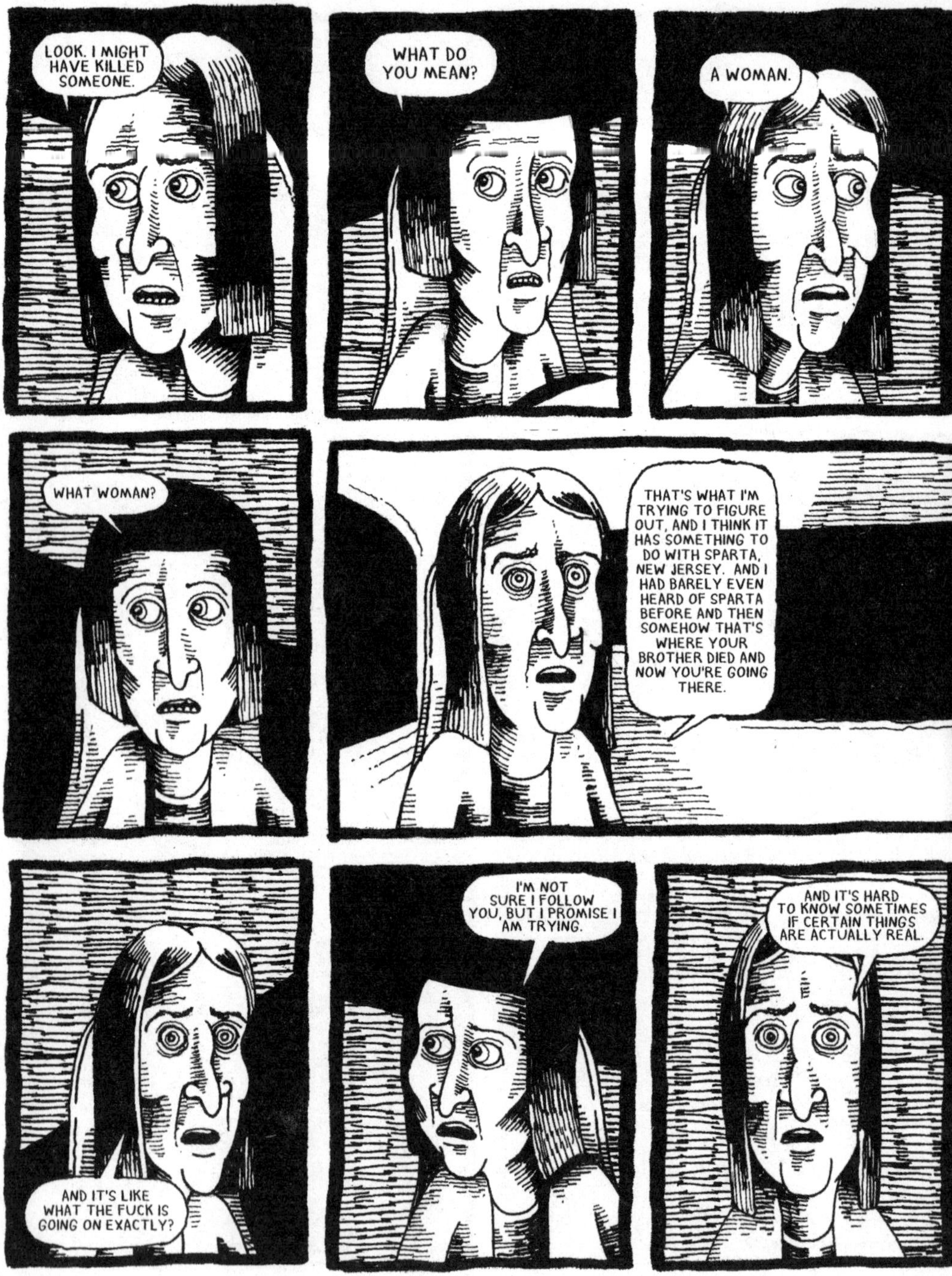
LOOK. I MIGHT HAVE KILLED SOMEONE.
WHAT DO YOU MEAN?
A WOMAN.
WHAT WOMAN?
THAT'S WHAT I'M TRYING TO FIGURE OUT, AND I THINK IT HAS SOMETHING TO DO WITH SPARTA, NEW JERSEY. AND I HAD BARELY EVEN HEARD OF SPARTA BEFORE AND THEN SOMEHOW THAT'S WHERE YOUR BROTHER DIED AND NOW YOU'RE GOING THERE.
AND IT'S LIKE WHAT THE FUCK IS GOING ON EXACTLY?
I'M NOT SURE I FOLLOW YOU, BUT I PROMISE I AM TRYING.
AND IT'S HARD TO KNOW SOMETIMES IF CERTAIN THINGS ARE ACTUALLY REAL.

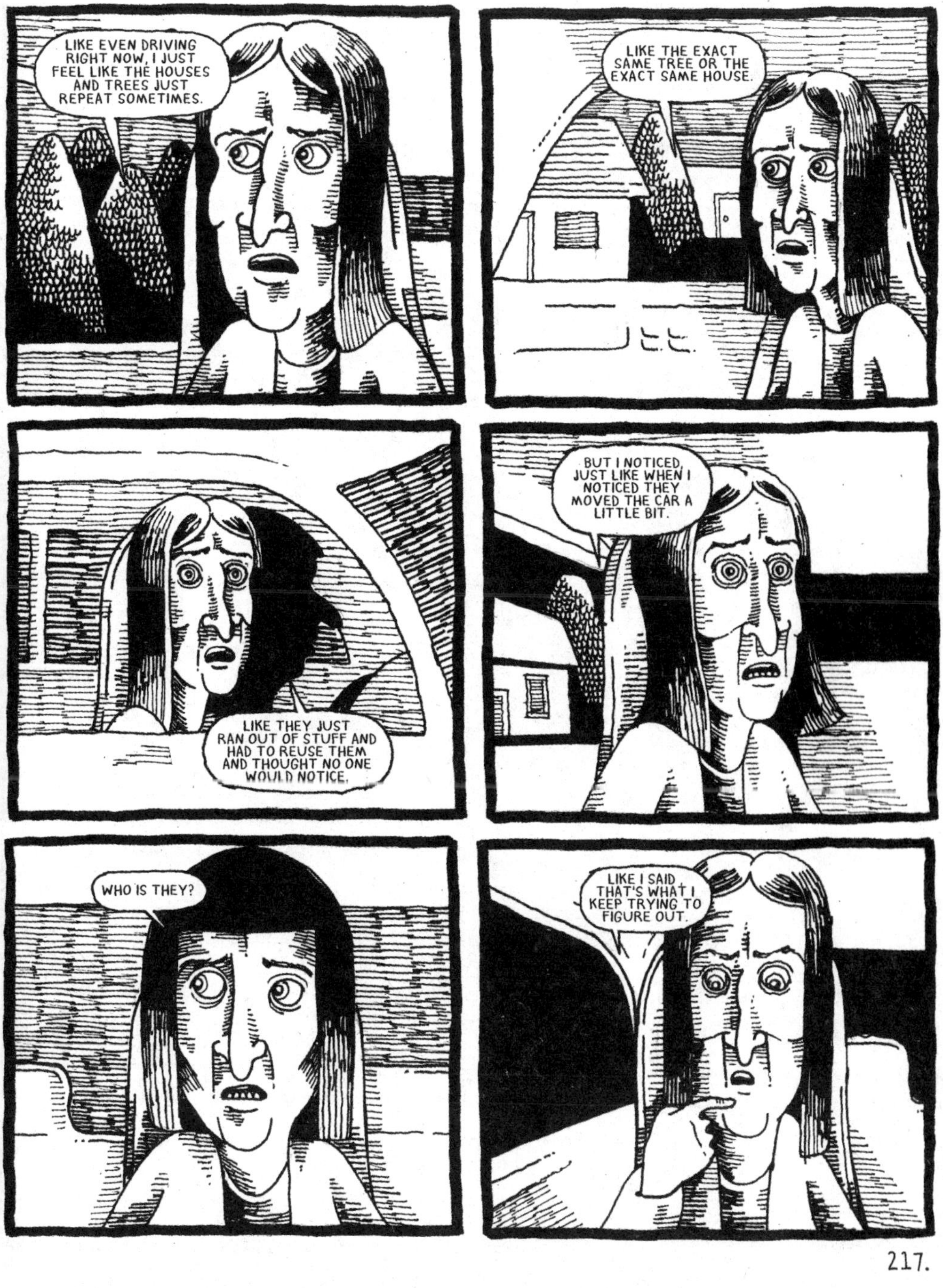
LIKE EVEN DRIVING RIGHT NOW, I JUST FEEL LIKE THE HOUSES AND TREES JUST REPEAT SOMETIMES.
LIKE THE EXACT SAME TREE OR THE EXACT SAME HOUSE.
LIKE THEY JUST RAN OUT OF STUFF AND HAD TO REUSE THEM AND THOUGHT NO ONE WOULD NOTICE.
BUT I NOTICED, JUST LIKE WHEN I NOTICED THEY MOVED THE CAR A LITTLE BIT.
WHO IS THEY?
LIKE I SAID THAT'S WHAT I KEEP TRYING TO FIGURE OUT.

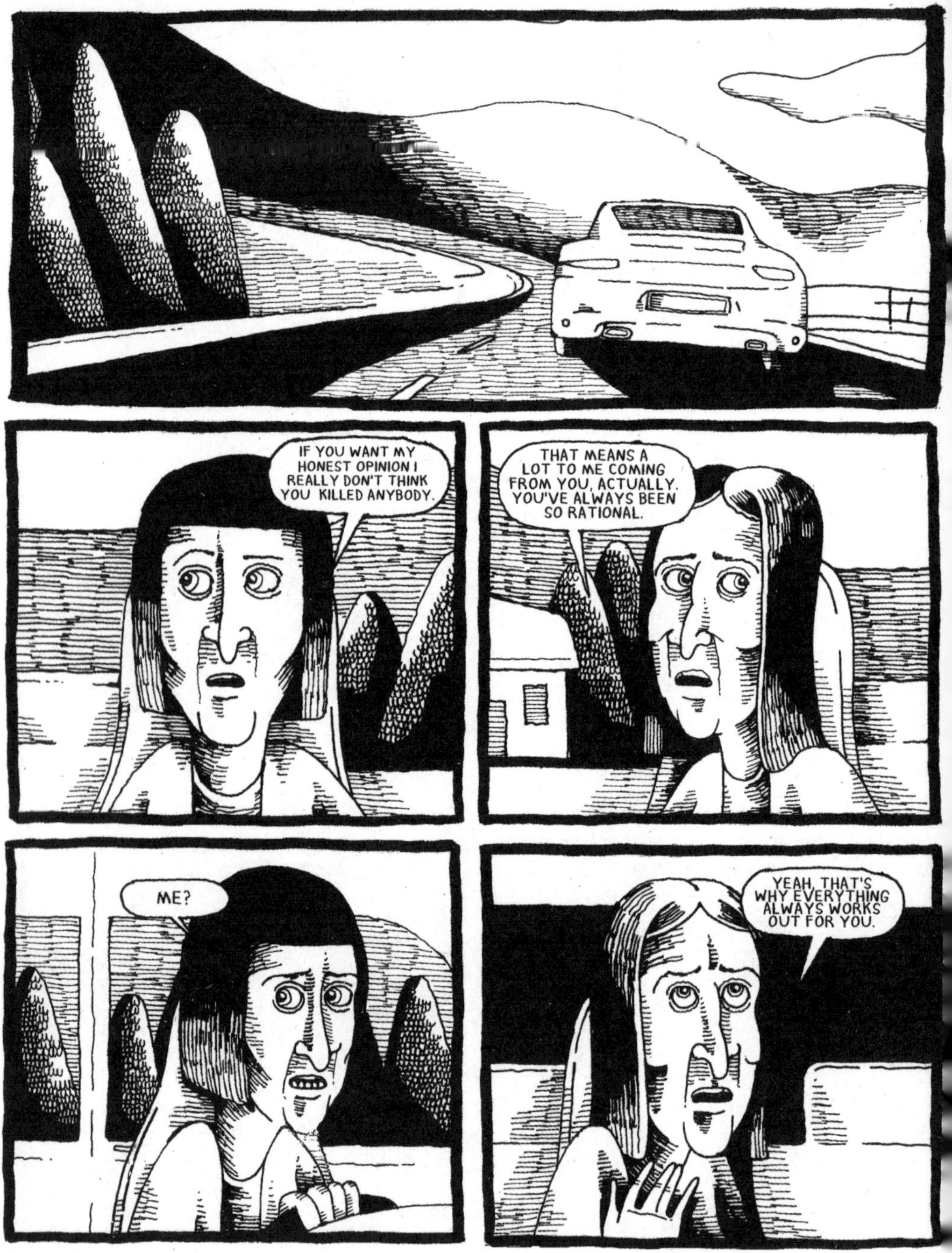
IF YOU WANT MY HONEST OPINION I REALLY DON'T THINK YOU KILLED ANYBODY.
THAT MEANS A LOT TO ME COMING FROM YOU, ACTUALLY. YOU'VE ALWAYS BEEN SO RATIONAL.
ME?
YEAH, THAT'S WHY EVERYTHING ALWAYS WORKS OUT FOR YOU.

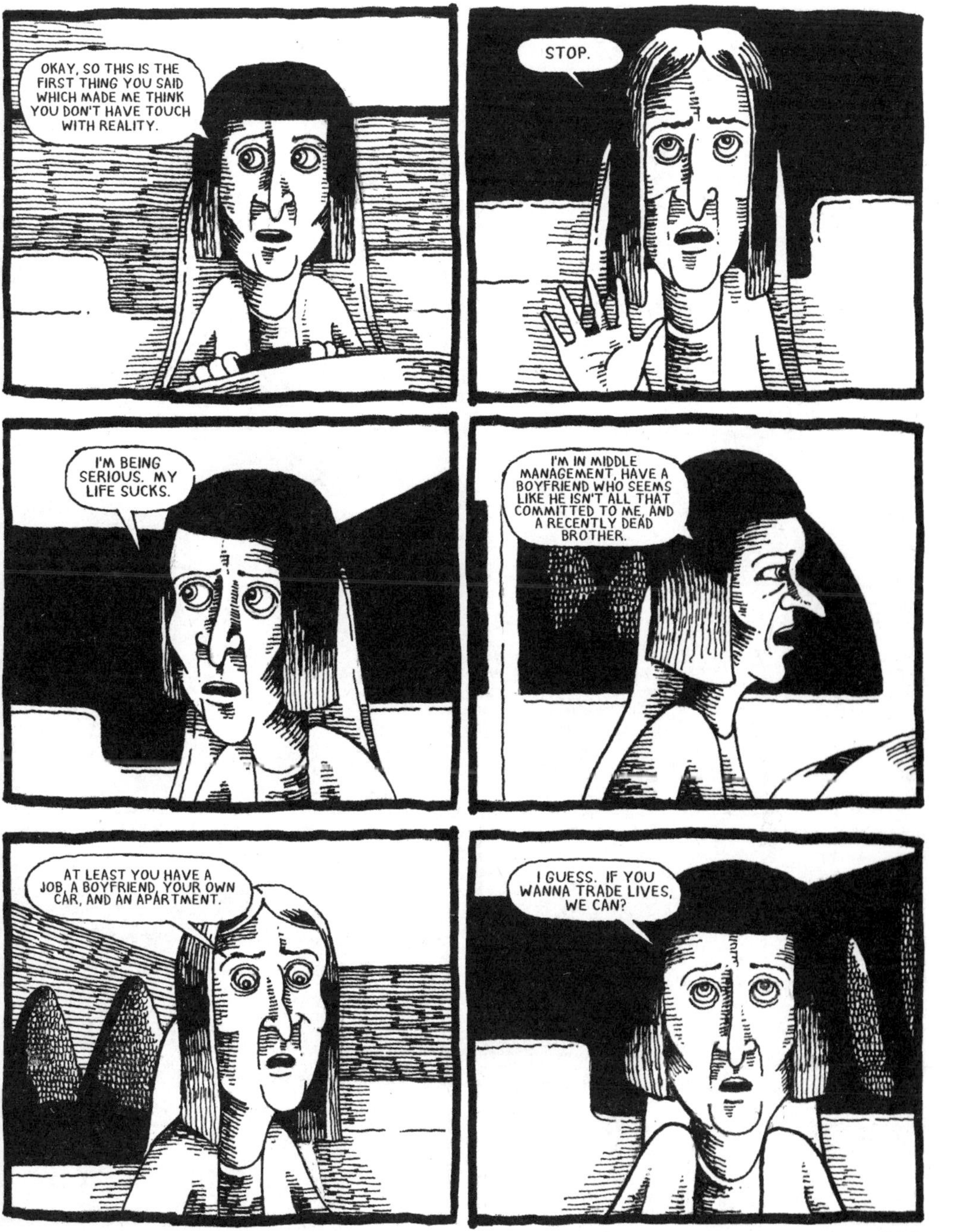
OKAY, SO THIS IS THE FIRST THING YOU SAID WHICH MADE ME THINK YOU DON'T HAVE TOUCH WITH REALITY.
STOP.
I'M BEING SERIOUS. MY LIFE SUCKS.
I'M IN MIDDLE MANAGEMENT, HAVE A BOYFRIEND WHO SEEMS LIKE HE ISN'T ALL THAT COMMITTED TO ME, AND A RECENTLY DEAD BROTHER.
AT LEAST YOU HAVE A JOB, A BOYFRIEND, YOUR OWN CAR, AND AN APARTMENT.
I GUESS. IF YOU WANNA TRADE LIVES, WE CAN?

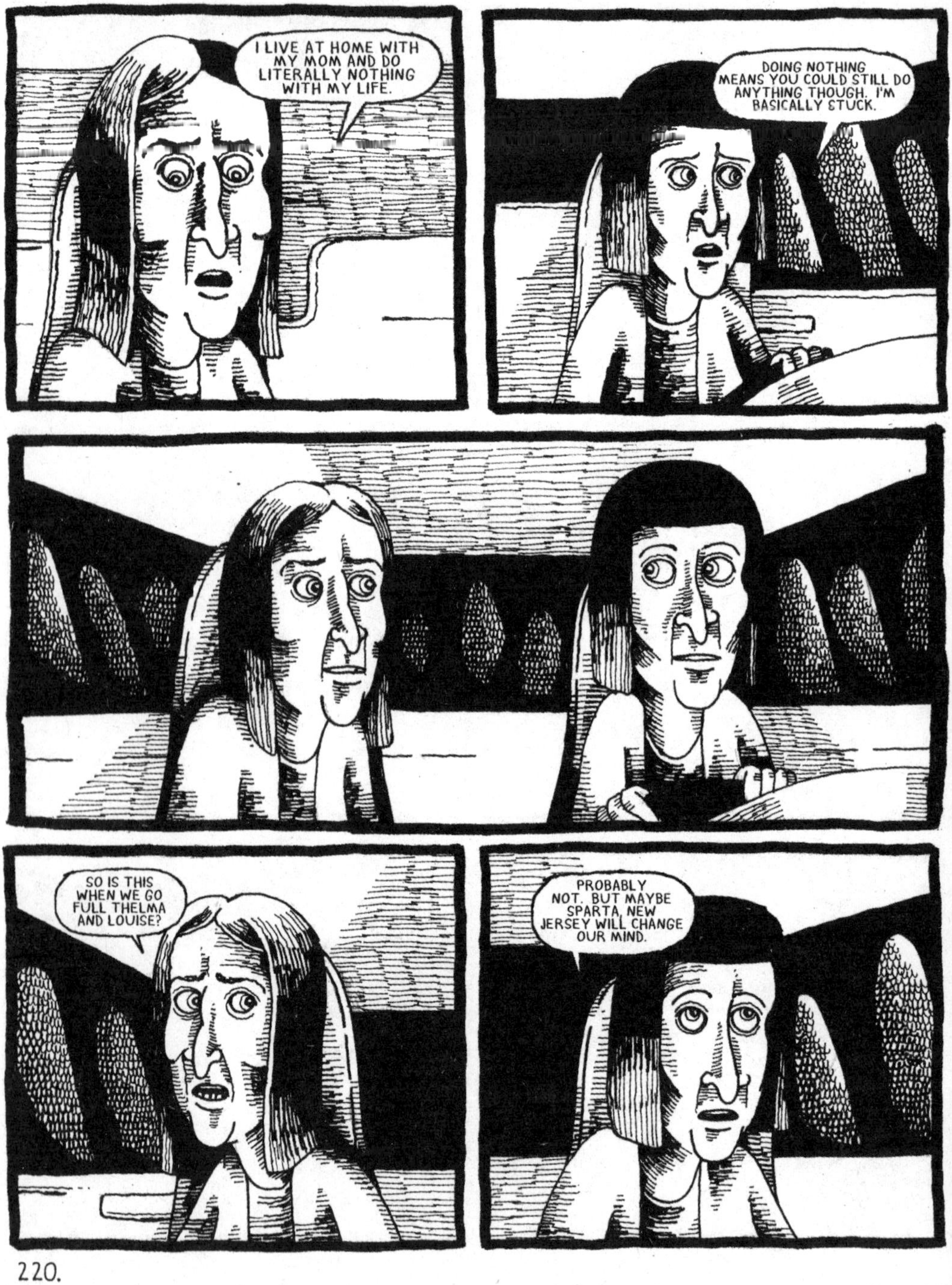
I LIVE AT HOME WITH MY MOM AND DO LITERALLY NOTHING WITH MY LIFE.
DOING NOTHING MEANS YOU COULD STILL DO ANYTHING THOUGH. I'M BASICALLY STUCK.
SO IS THIS WHEN WE GO FULL THELMA AND LOUISE?
PROBABLY NOT. BUT MAYBE SPARTA, NEW JERSEY WILL CHANGE OUR MIND.

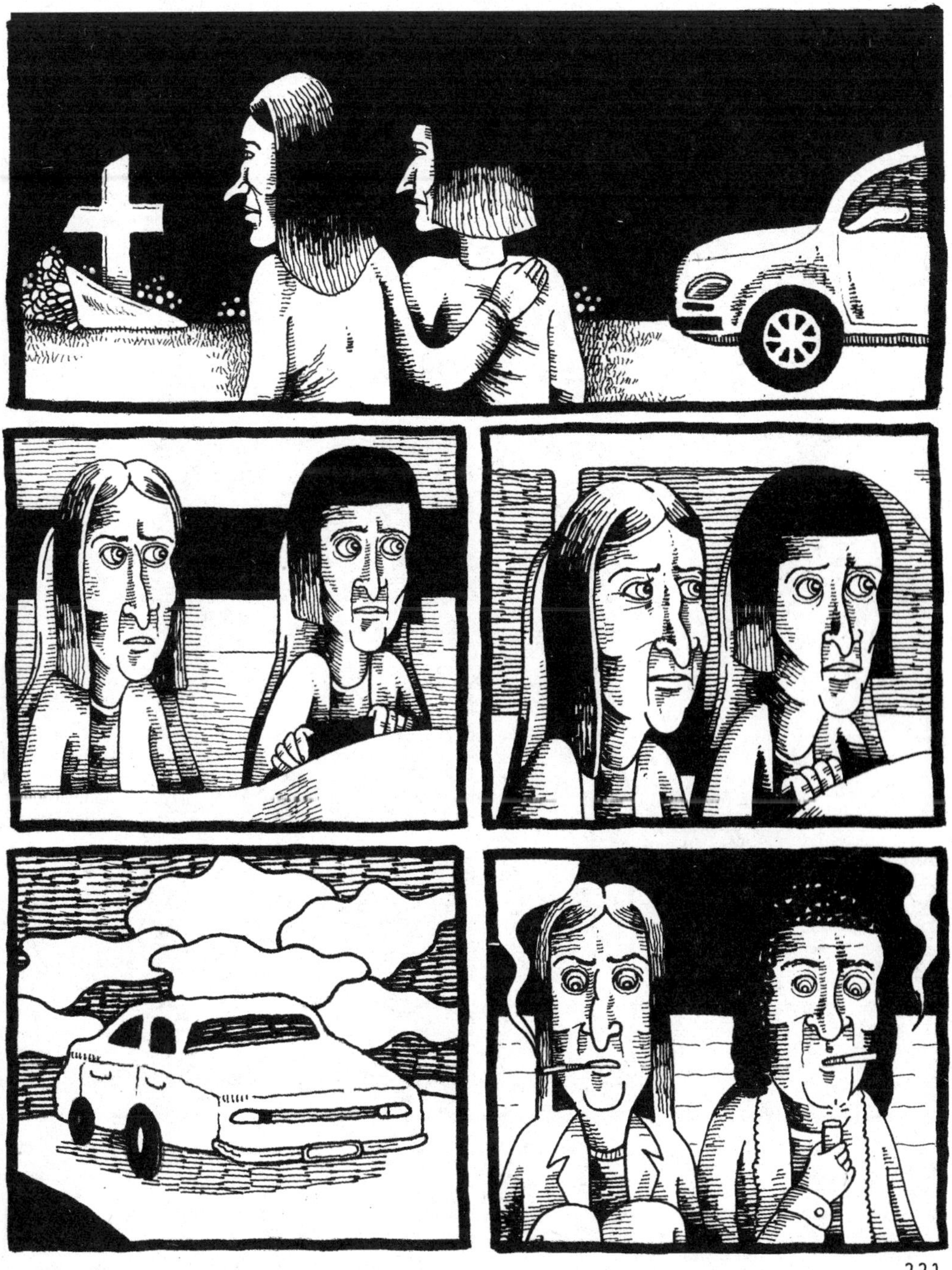

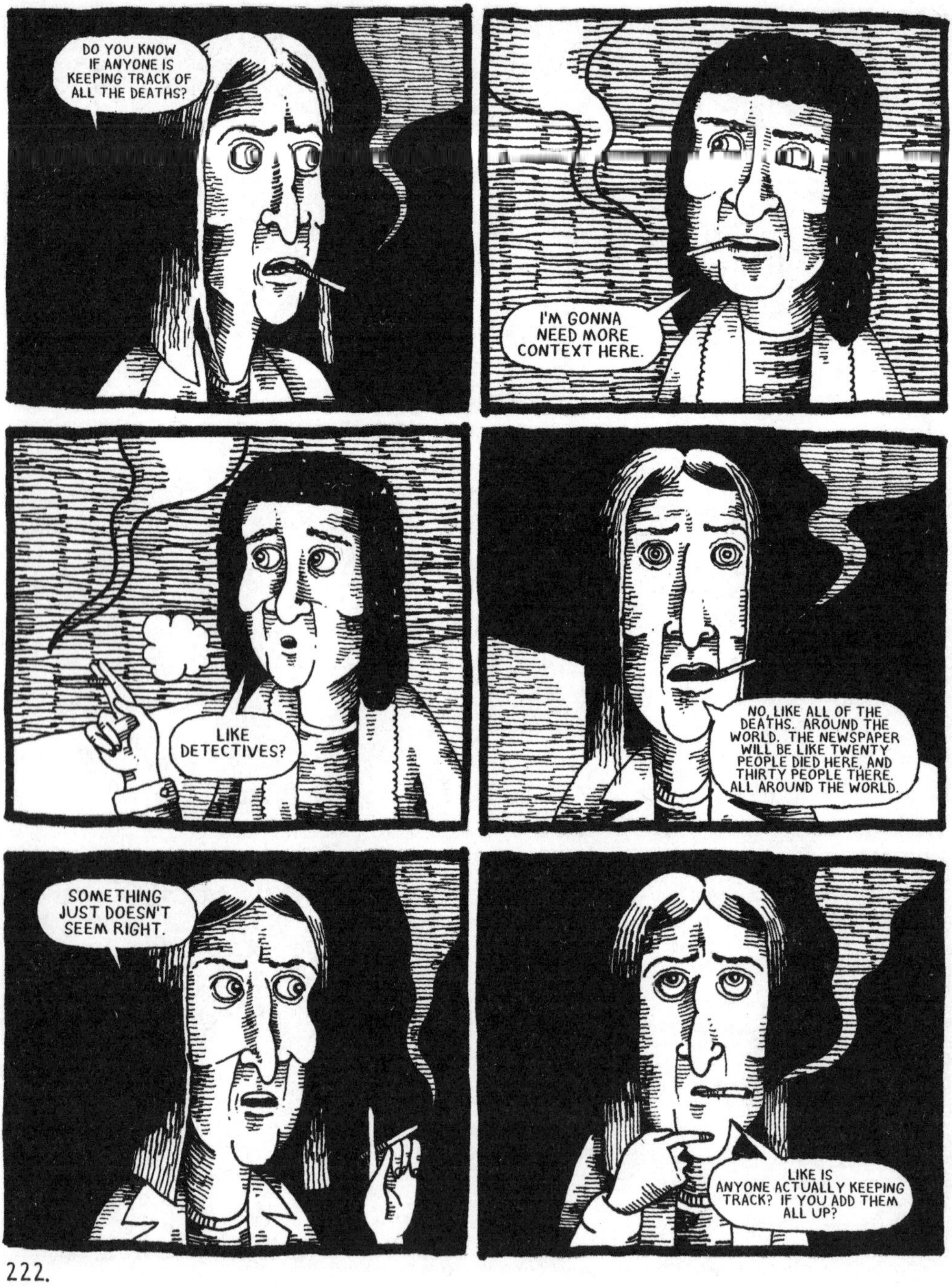
DO YOU KNOW IF ANYONE IS KEEPING TRACK OF ALL THE DEATHS?
I'M GONNA NEED MORE CONTEXT HERE.
LIKE DETECTIVES?
NO, LIKE ALL OF THE DEATHS. AROUND THE WORLD. THE NEWSPAPER WILL BE LIKE TWENTY PEOPLE DIED HERE, AND THIRTY PEOPLE THERE. ALL AROUND THE WORLD.
SOMETHING JUST DOESN'T SEEM RIGHT.
LIKE IS ANYONE ACTUALLY KEEPING TRACK? IF YOU ADD THEM ALL UP?

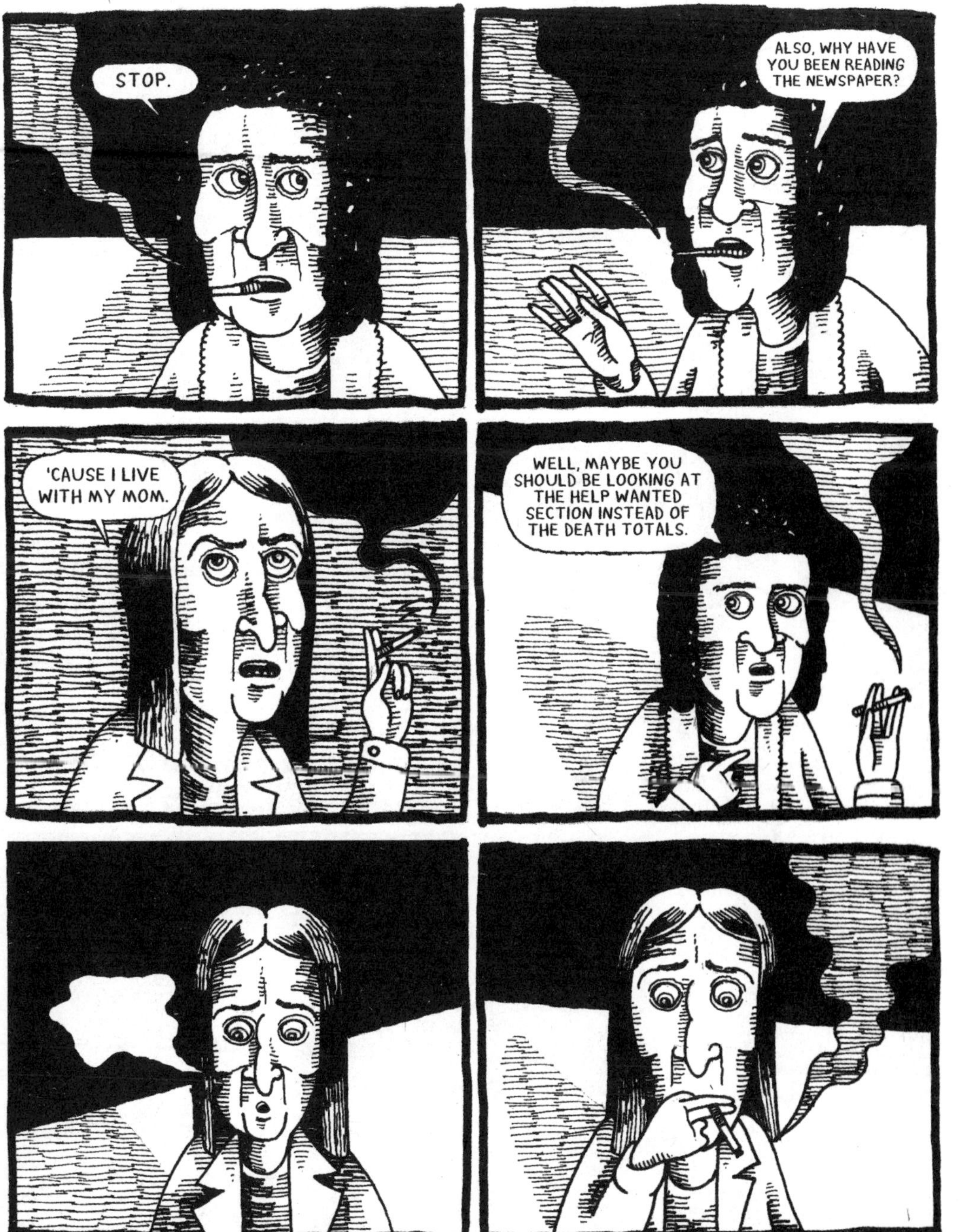
STOP.
ALSO, WHY HAVE YOU BEEN READING THE NEWSPAPER?
'CAUSE I LIVE WITH MY MOM.
WELL, MAYBE YOU SHOULD BE LOOKING AT THE HELP WANTED SECTION INSTEAD OF THE DEATH TOTALS.

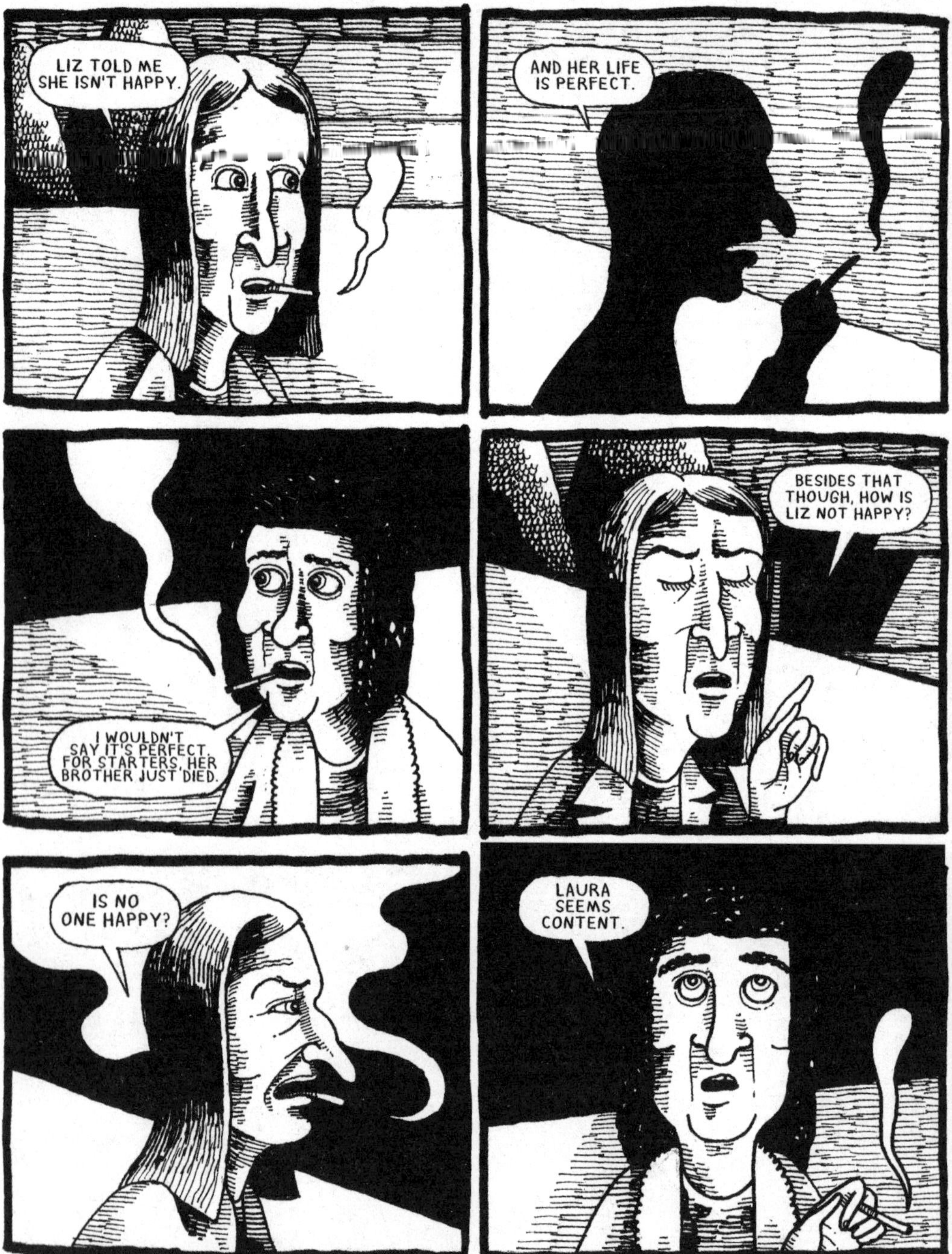
LIZ TOLD ME SHE ISN'T HAPPY.
AND HER LIFE IS PERFECT.
I WOULDN'T SAY IT'S PERFECT. FOR STARTERS, HER BROTHER JUST DIED.
BESIDES THAT THOUGH, HOW IS LIZ NOT HAPPY?
IS NO ONE HAPPY?
LAURA SEEMS CONTENT.

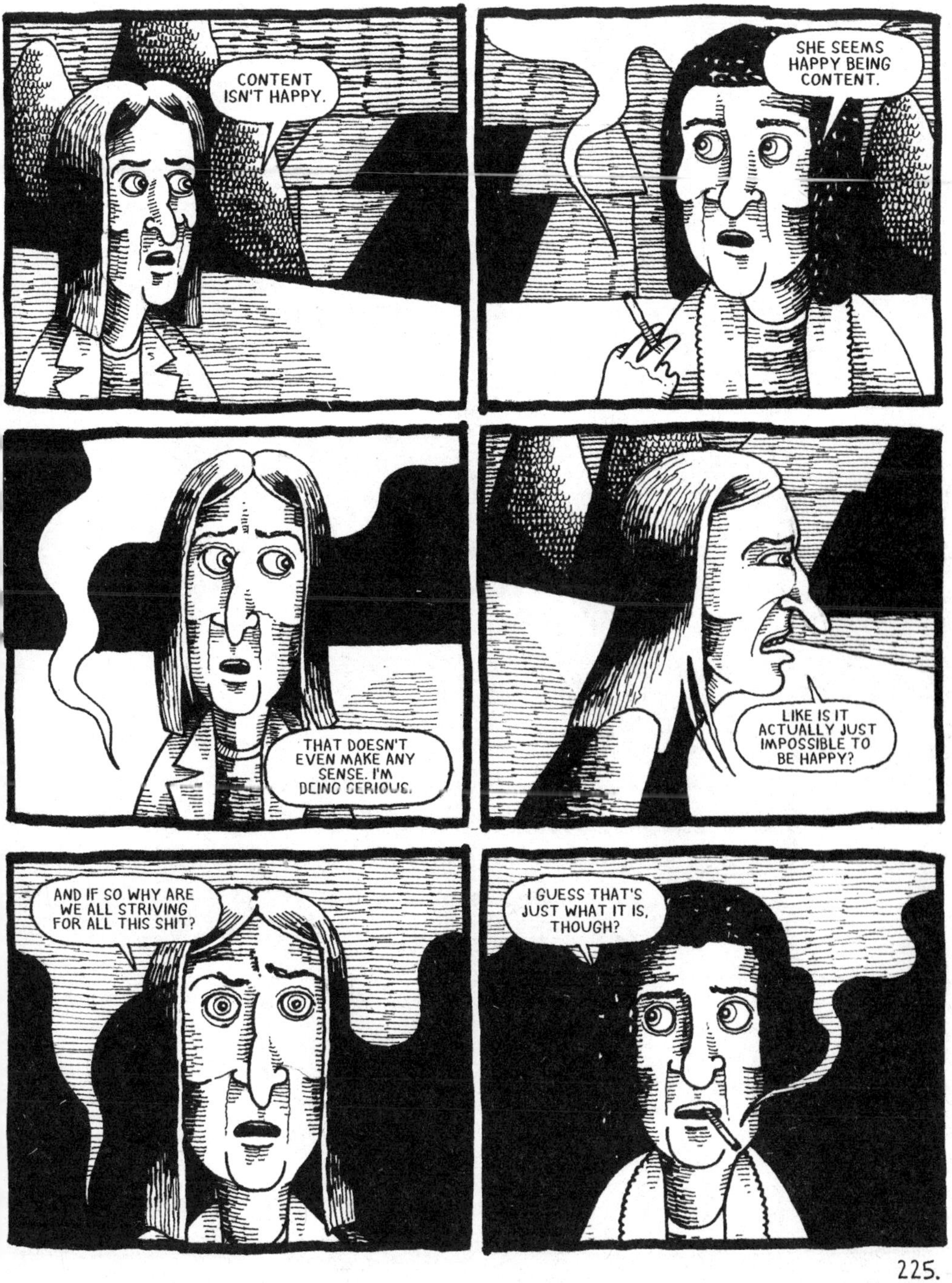
CONTENT ISN'T HAPPY.
SHE SEEMS HAPPY BEING CONTENT.
THAT DOESN'T EVEN MAKE ANY SENSE. I'M BEING SERIOUS.
LIKE IS IT ACTUALLY JUST IMPOSSIBLE TO BE HAPPY?
AND IF SO WHY ARE WE ALL STRIVING FOR ALL THIS SHIT?
I GUESS THAT'S JUST WHAT IT IS, THOUGH?

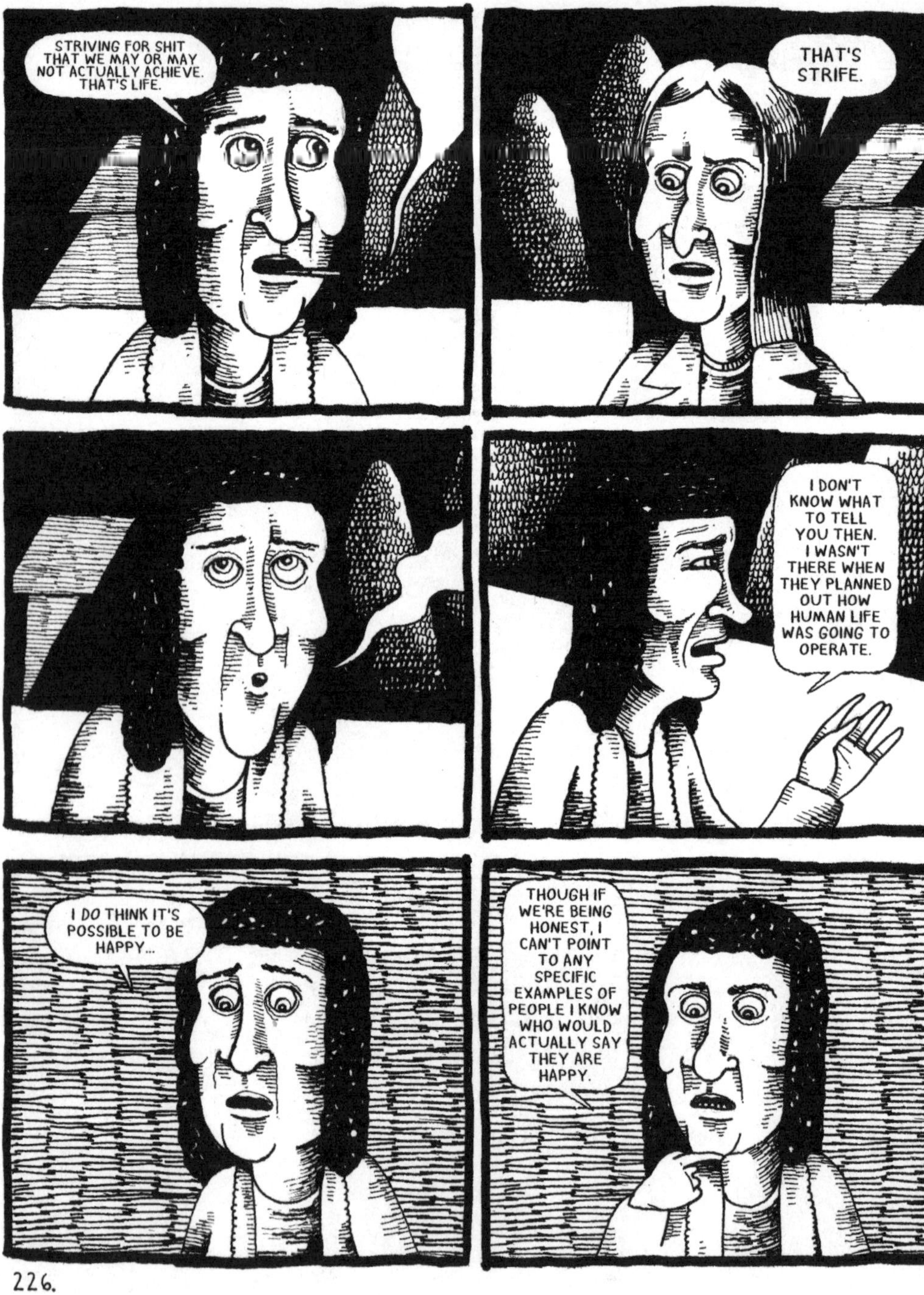
STRIVING FOR SHIT THAT WE MAY OR MAY NOT ACTUALLY ACHIEVE. THAT'S LIFE.
THAT'S STRIFE.
I DON'T KNOW WHAT TO TELL YOU THEN. I WASN'T THERE WHEN THEY PLANNED OUT HOW HUMAN LIFE WAS GOING TO OPERATE.
I DO THINK IT'S POSSIBLE TO BE HAPPY...
THOUGH IF WE'RE BEING HONEST, I CAN'T POINT TO ANY SPECIFIC EXAMPLES OF PEOPLE I KNOW WHO WOULD ACTUALLY SAY THEY ARE HAPPY.

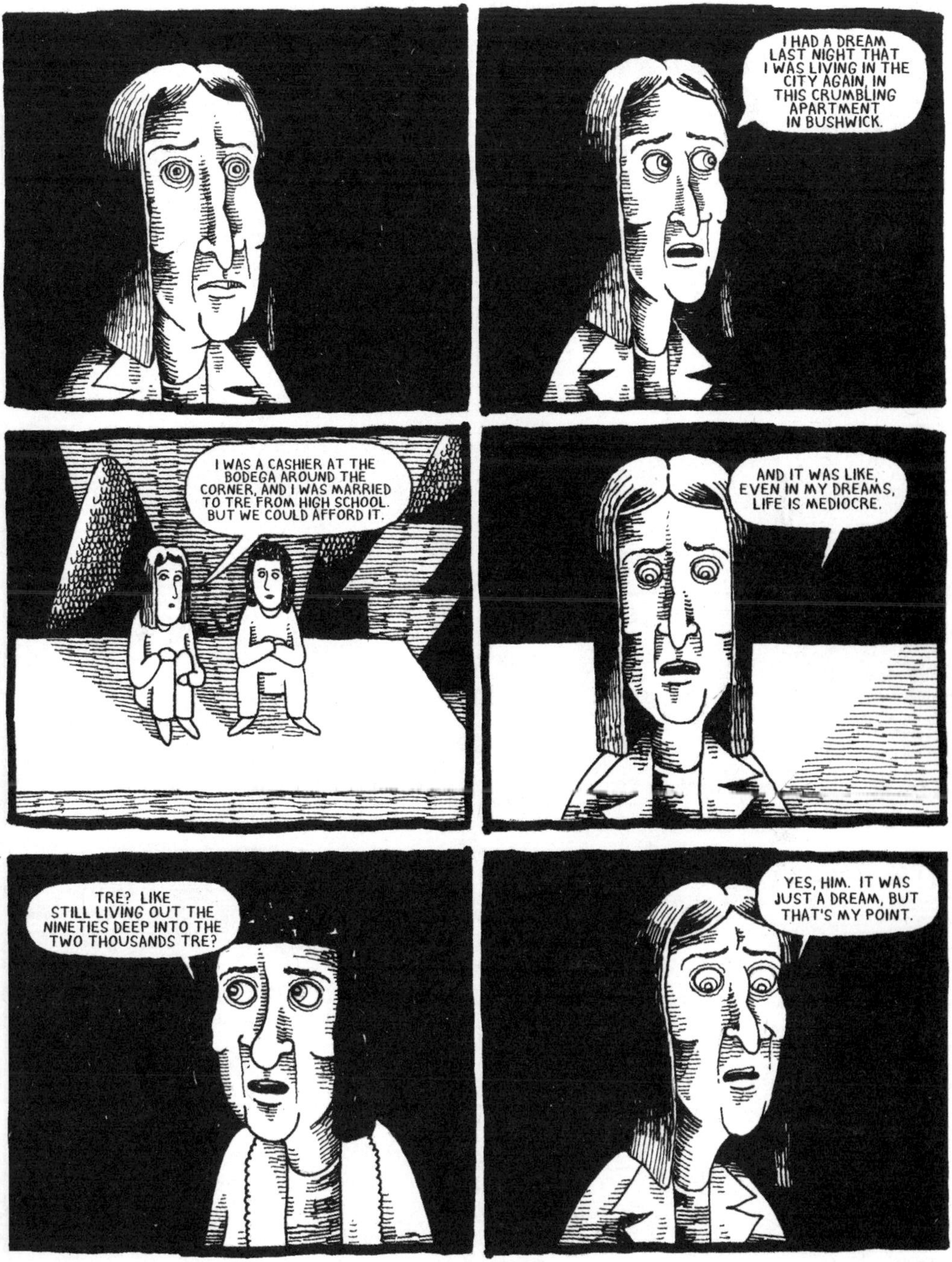
I HAD A DREAM LAST NIGHT THAT I WAS LIVING IN THE CITY AGAIN, IN THIS CRUMBLING APARTMENT IN BUSHWICK.
I WAS A CASHIER AT THE BODEGA AROUND THE CORNER, AND I WAS MARRIED TO TRE FROM HIGH SCHOOL. BUT WE COULD AFFORD IT.
AND IT WAS LIKE, EVEN IN MY DREAMS, LIFE IS MEDIOCRE.
TRE? LIKE STILL LIVING OUT THE NINETIES DEEP INTO THE TWO THOUSANDS TRE?
YES, HIM. IT WAS JUST A DREAM, BUT THAT'S MY POINT.

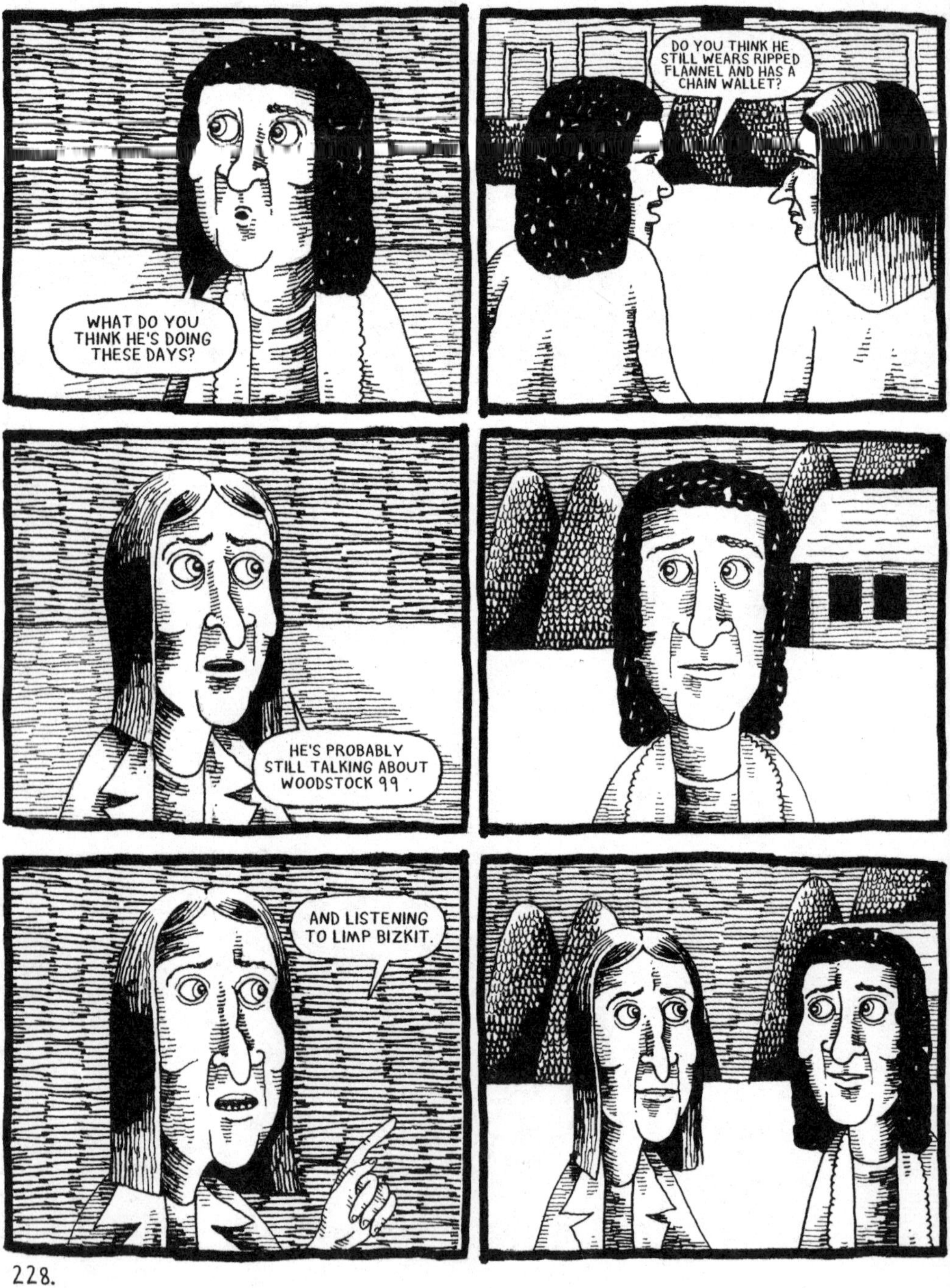
WHAT DO YOU THINK HE'S DOING THESE DAYS?
DO YOU THINK HE STILL WEARS RIPPED FLANNEL AND HAS A CHAIN WALLET?
HE'S PROBABLY STILL TALKING ABOUT WOODSTOCK 99.
AND LISTENING TO LIMP BIZKIT.

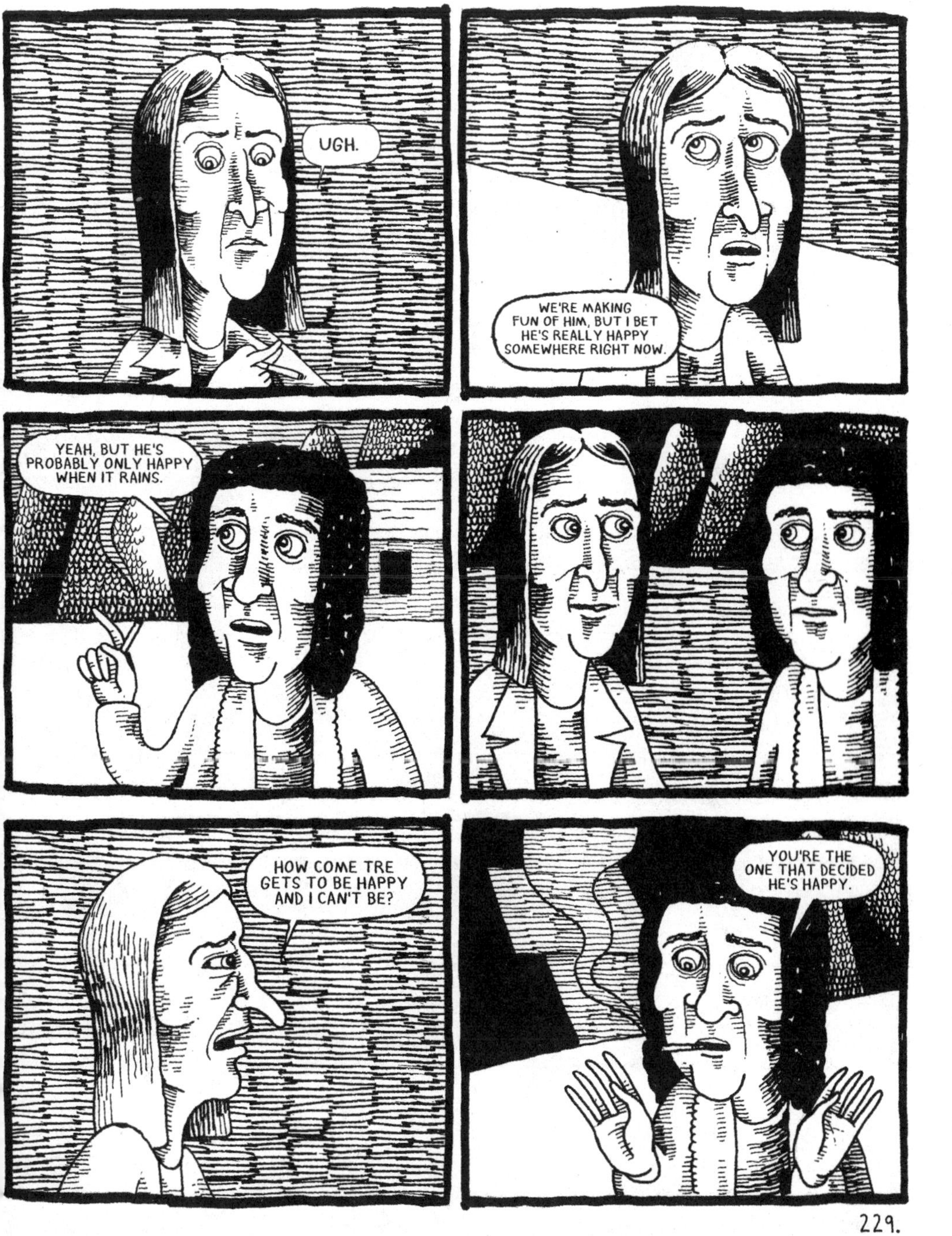
UGH.
WE'RE MAKING FUN OF HIM, BUT I BET HE'S REALLY HAPPY SOMEWHERE RIGHT NOW.
YEAH, BUT HE'S PROBABLY ONLY HAPPY WHEN IT RAINS.
HOW COME TRE GETS TO BE HAPPY AND I CAN'T BE?
YOU'RE THE ONE THAT DECIDED HE'S HAPPY.

HE'S PROBABLY MISERABLE AND IN DEBT JUST LIKE EVERYONE ELSE.
UGH.

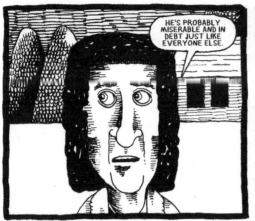

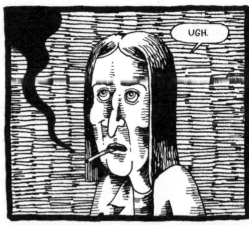

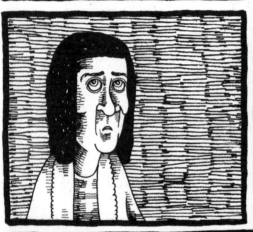

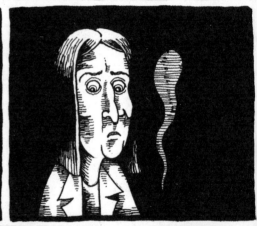

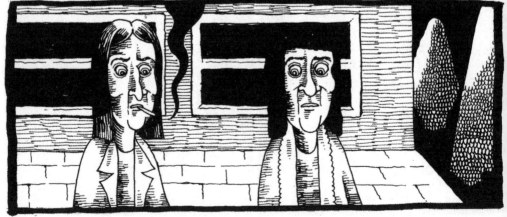

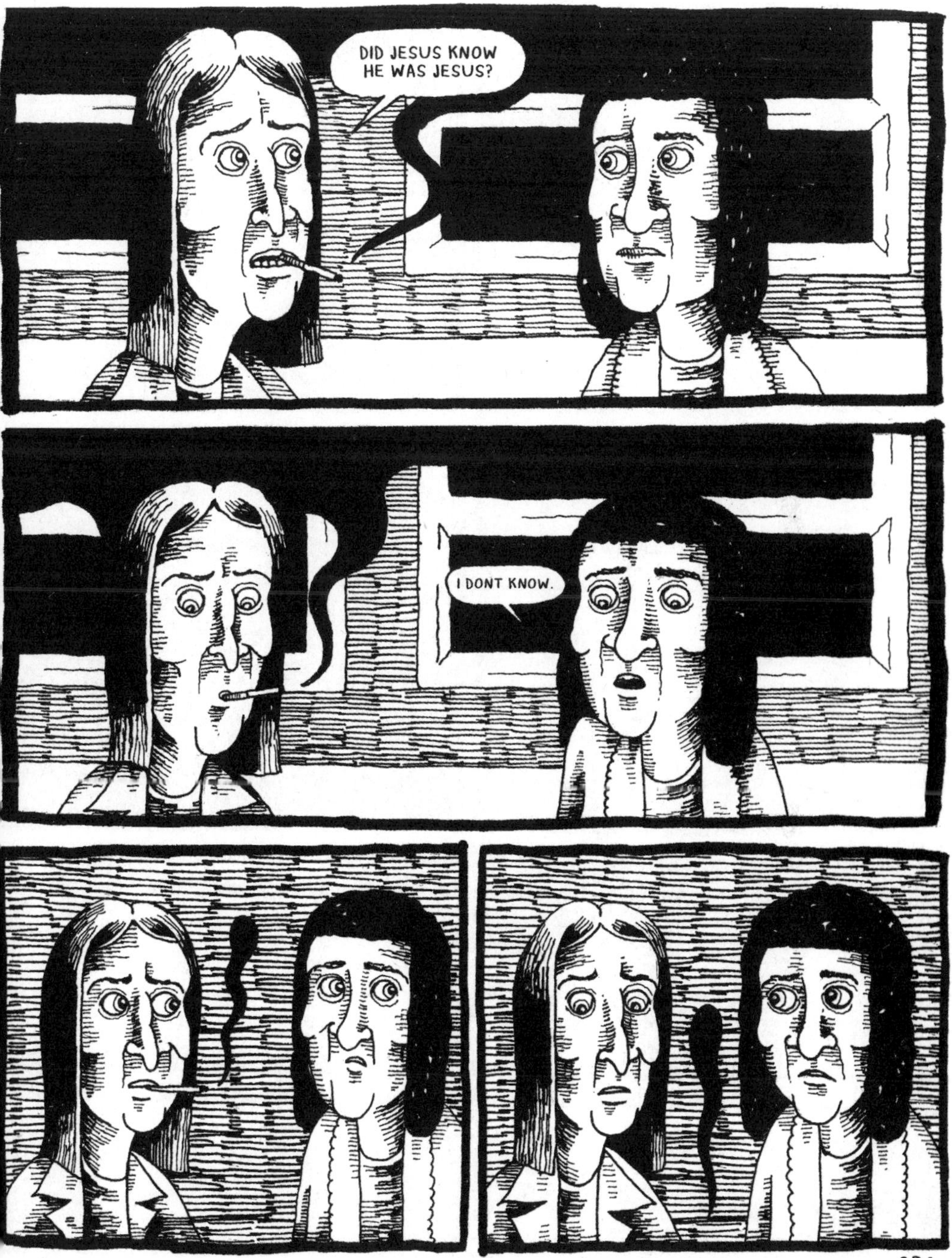
DID JESUS KNOW
HE WAS JESUS?
I DONT KNOW.

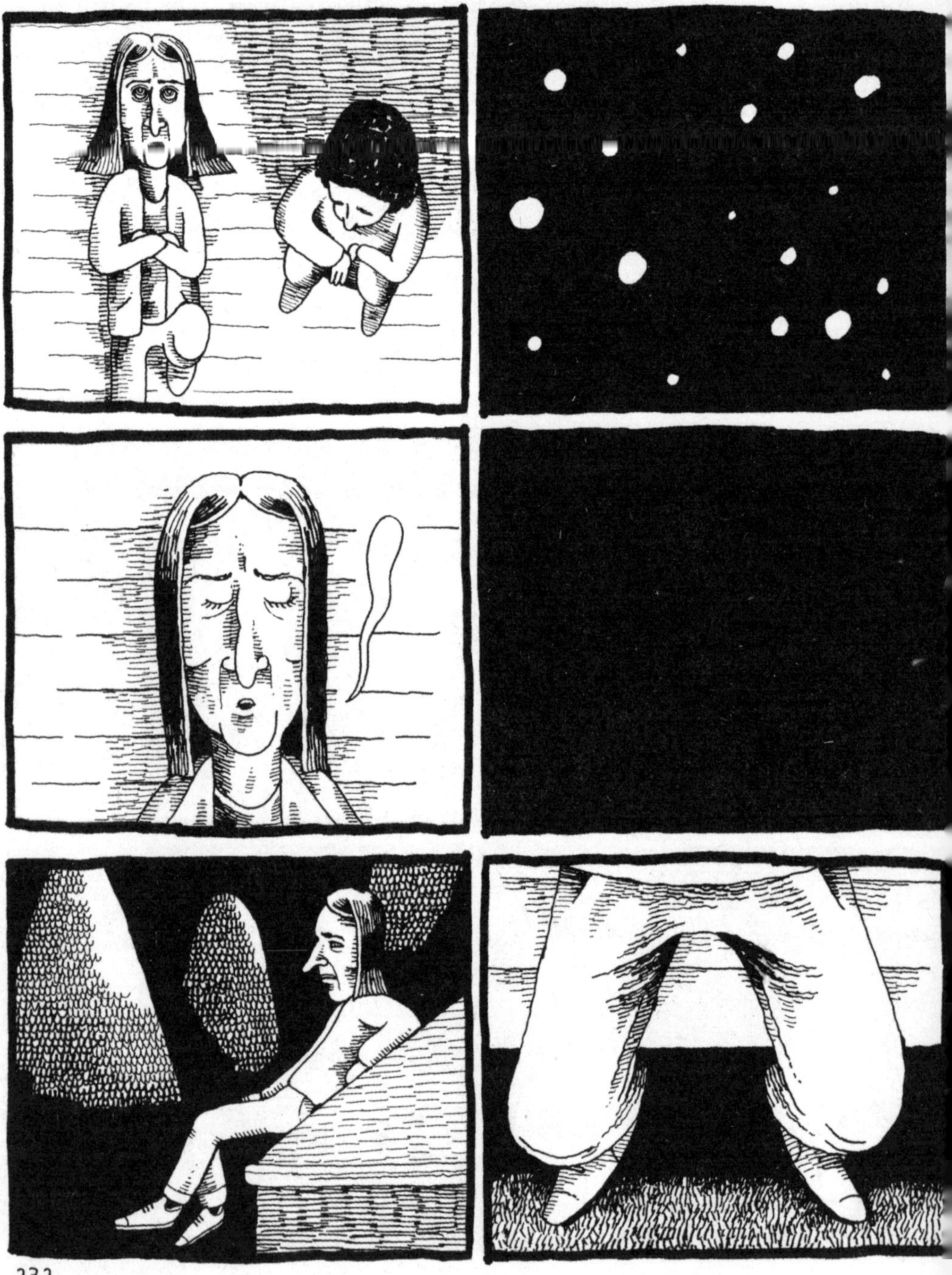

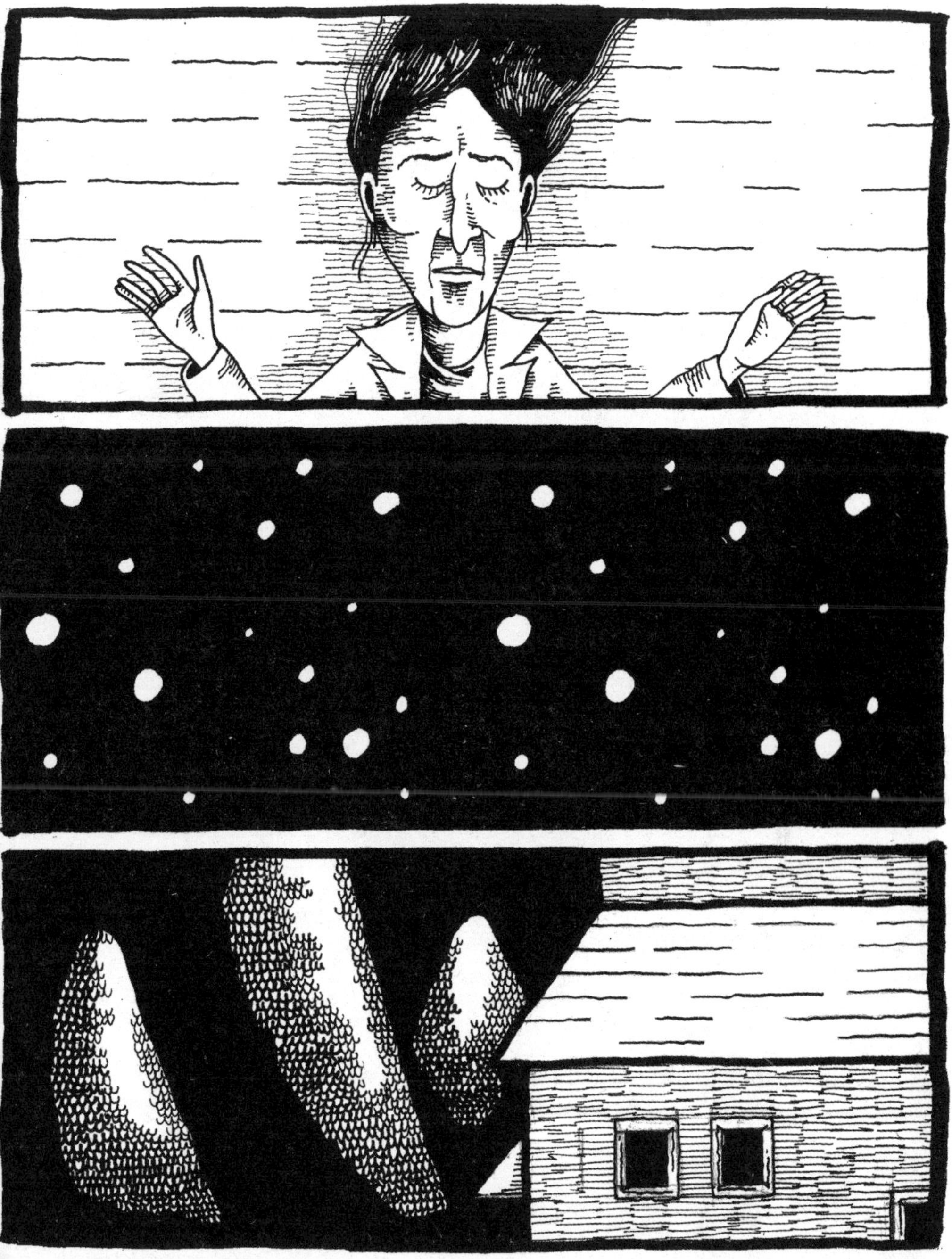

Joe Steinhardt owns and operates Don Giovanni Records, a label which remains committed to furthering alternative culture, independent values, and providing resources for artists who prefer to work outside of the mainstream music industry. He is a published author and an Assistant Professor at Drexel University in their Music Industry Program.

Marissa Paternoster is a visual artist, the lead singer and guitarist for Screaming Females, and was named the 77th best guitar player of all time by SPIN magazine and the 150th best of all time by Rolling Stone. Through her work with Screaming Females and her solo career, Marissa has released 11 studio albums and has been featured on MTV, Late Night TV, and NPR. She has toured extensively, supporting bands like Garbage, Dinosaur Jr., The Dead Weather, Arctic Monkeys, and The Breeders.

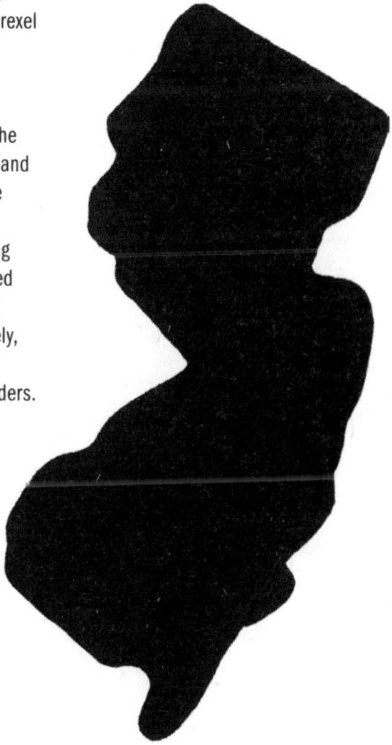

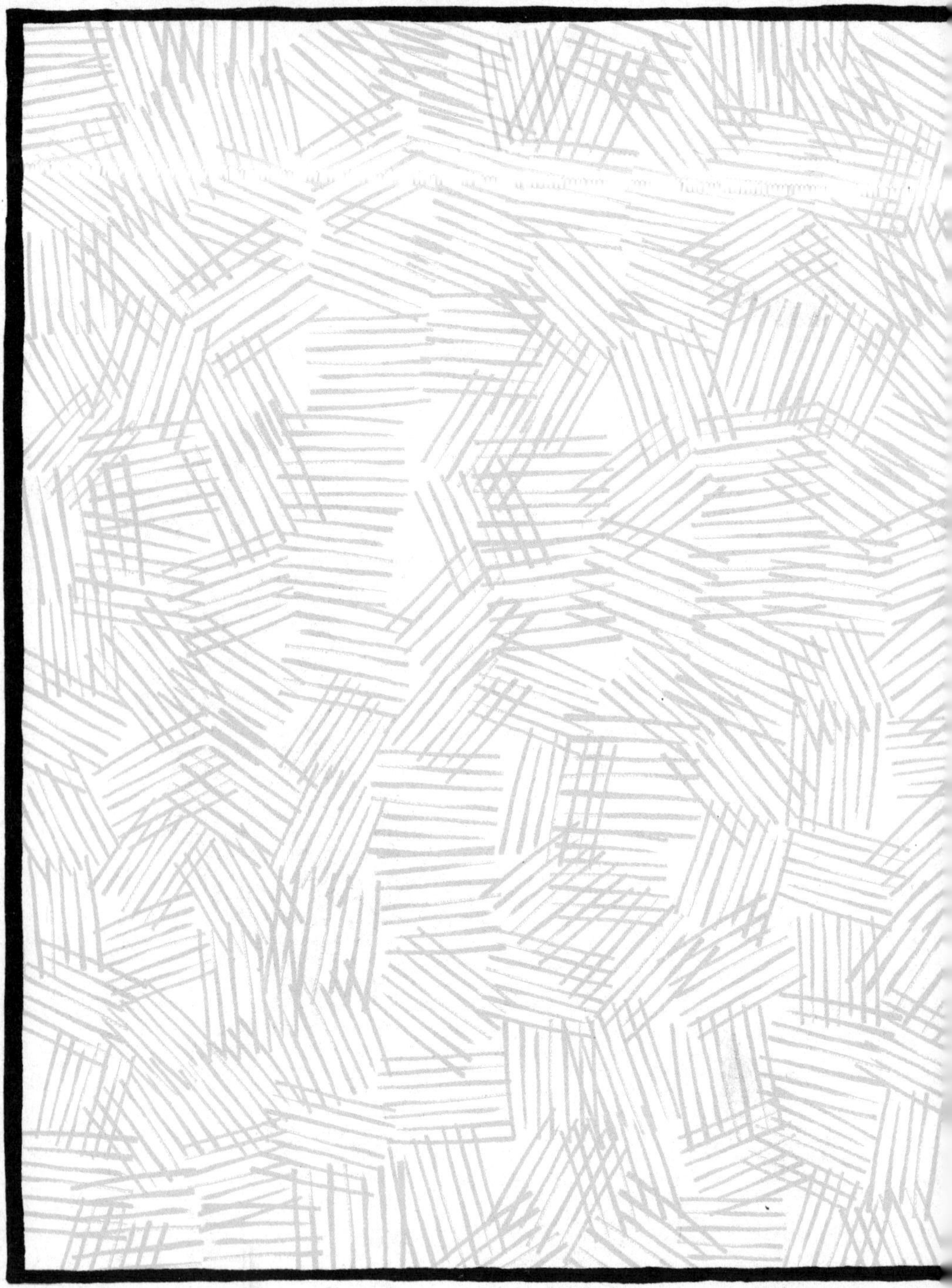